SHATTERED OATHS & MASKS UNDONE

VOIDSCAR CHRONICLES BOOK 2: A TUSK AND TARTS TALE

ETHAN JAKOB

RUNEBEAST PUBLISHING

To my amazing and supportive wife, Denise, who has always had my back and cheered me on in my endeavors. She is my home, my heart and the one that keeps me going. To my sons for helping me strive to be better than I was the day before. To my bestfriend, Shelby, and the other ladies of my beta team (Kristen, Nancy and Sara-tonin) for showing such excitement in reading my books. From the bottom of my Orcish heart, thank you.

OTHER WORKS

BY ETHAN JAKOB, THE BOOK ORC

Voidscar Chronicles Book 1, Lavender & Ginger: A Callus Kordec Tale

The Love We Brew

Please visit my website at
http://www.ethanjakobauthor.com
for more information

FOREWORD

<u>The following novel begins a few months after the final chapter of</u> *<u>Lavender & Ginger, but before the Epilogue of the same title.</u>*

As a refresher for readers of the previous book in the series and new readers alike, I include the following: Welcome to the world of Yonara, a labor of love that started when I was a teen and fully took root when I developed it into a world built for tabletop rpgs for my wife, sons and brother. The world of Yonara is inhabited by humans and other familiar fantasy lineages of people. Magic flows throughout the world but is wielded by few and to varying degrees of power. Minor arcane and magic infused items are more common, with more powerful ones being much more rare. New schools of magic are being discovered as the world ages. The Gods are known and while direct contact is rare it isn't unheard of.

The story takes place in the Scarred Lands. A land that was once covered in rolling plains and forests, both tropical and temperate. Presently, the landscape is harsh desert and rocky crags of desolate wasteland with a few areas only now beginning to make an ecological comeback. All this change took place when nearly three millennia ago the betrayer goddess Zorog used her disciple, Varl, to lead a crusade of corruption across the continents. Their combined efforts were eventually thwarted but the repercussions were vast, and many are still present to this day. The result of their failure brought about an arcane explosion that irreparably changed the realm and the aptly renamed Scarred Lands forever.

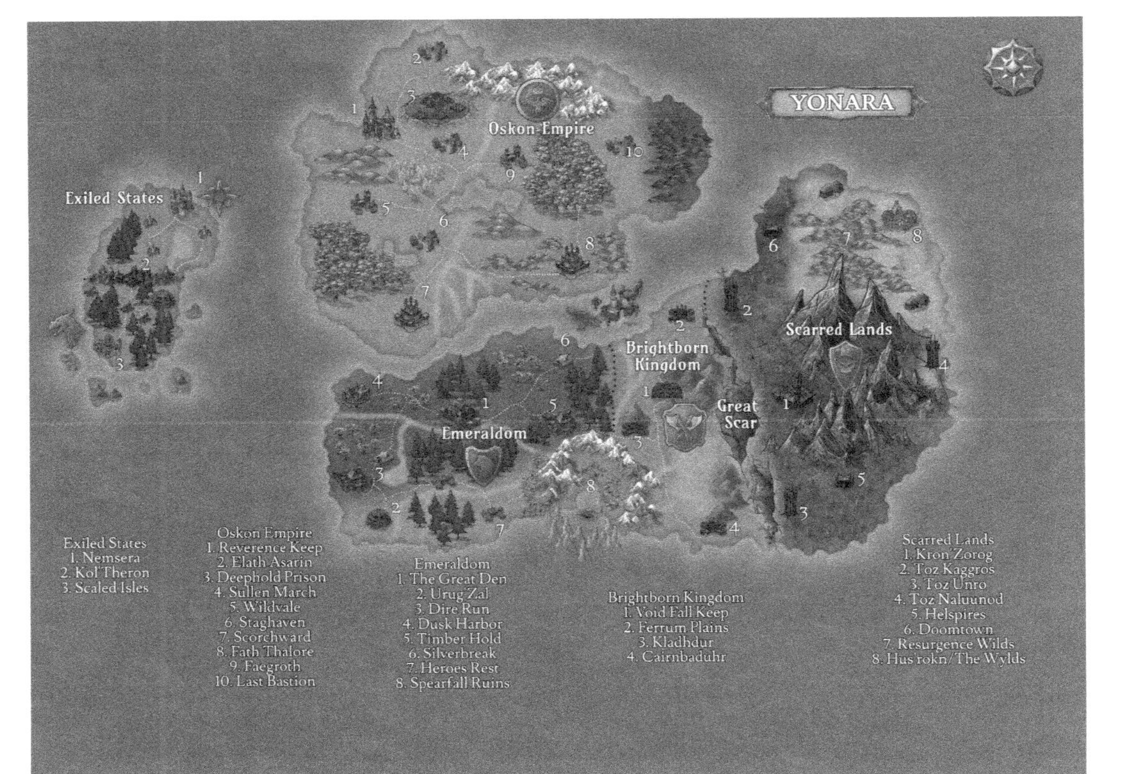

YONARA
Exiled States
Oskon Empire
Oskon-Empire
Brightborn Kingdom
Great Scar
Scarred Lands
Emeraldom

Exiled States
1. Nemsera
2. Kol'Theron
3. Scaled Isles

Oskon Empire
1. Reverence Keep
2. Elath Asarin
3. Deephold Prison
4. Sullen March
5. Wildvale
6. Staghaven
7. Scorchward
8. Fath Thalore
9. Faegroth
10. Last Bastion

Emeraldom
1. The Great Den
2. Urug Zal
3. Dire Run
4. Dusk Harbor
5. Timber Hold
6. Silverbreak
7. Heroes Rest
8. Spearfall Ruins

Brightborn Kingdom
1. Void Fall Keep
2. Ferrum Plains
3. Kladhdur
4. Cairnbaduhr

Scarred Lands
1. Kron Zorog
2. Toz Kaggros
3. Toz Unro
4. Toz Naluunod
5. Helspires
6. Doomtown
7. Resurgence Wilds
8. Hus rokn / The Wylds

CONTENTS

PROLOGUE

THE LUNAR FAE AND THE HALF-BEAST

Many Years From Now

Somewhere in the Emeraldom an old bard and storyteller takes a sip of watered-down ale in a darkened tavern with fewer than ten patrons, half of whom are already face down on their tables asleep. He rubs his aching eyes and begins to recite a tale that he heard whispered somewhere in the Scarred Lands that for the life of him he cannot place. Had he not been so inebriated at the time, perhaps he would have remembered it correctly. Even so, the story has changed and evolved in his mind many times since he first recalled it in a brief moment of sobriety. The current version that his pickled thoughts remember is the one he tells tonight after nearly vomiting from simply clearing his throat.

The origins and reasons for the brief tryst between an Arch Fae of the Lunar Court and a Forgotten Legionnaire are known by few and spoken by none. Perhaps it was love, a brief lapse in judgement or the outcome of charm magic, either way the union resulted in the birth of a female Fae-Forgotten. After the child's birth her mother was cast out from the Lunar Court, for baring her womanhood to a Forgotten and bringing forth an abomination into the Arcane Realms. Under the protection of her mother, the child was well tutored in the inherent arcane knowledge of the Fae and as she grew older, her Forgotten heritage became further apparent when infernal magics began to manifest, usually in uncontrollable ways.

Her father, fearing what would be done to her should his fellow Forgotten learn of her existence, chose to remain in the shadows and untouchable.

The girl and her mother hid on the fringes of the Arcane Realm, an area that danced with the mystical borders of our physical realm. Often, she traveled to the realm of Yonara. There she would watch the mortals and dance under the moonlight. Her favorite thing to do was to hide among the boughs of the tree under which she was conceived and watch the night lanterns of a small town just past the hills move through the streets like fireflies as the people lived their lives of both joy and sorrow. From these very boughs she dreamed of a time when she would not be seen as an abomination, a time when the love, or at least the respect, or her people would be bestowed again upon her mother, and perhaps herself. She yearned for a world where those who were different could still be loved.

The next union is not as mysterious as the first. A human woman and orc man belonged to the same small mercenary band. Over time, they fell in love and had a son. Together they ensured that he had a rowdy, but joyous upbringing filled with adventures and excitement. However, when he was still young, the mercenary band took on an ill-fated contract that ended in a massacre. His father perished and one of his mother's legs was rendered nearly useless. With no future as a fighter any longer, the mother and son were at a loss.

Devoid of coin and a homestead, they wandered. She took work as a barmaid and he as a runner for a tavern. The tavern owner fell in love with the boy's mother and soon they had their own child, a daughter. The boy and his half-sister were quick to bond, and he frequently looked after her when the tavern was busy. She quickly learned she could get away with almost anything with the local kids because they all feared her half orc brother. He loved her more than anything because she never once judged him for his parentage as some in the town did.

As the years went on the boy became a young man and the town grew. Slowly more and more of the populace that moved in as the town expanded looked upon those of the young man's kind with mistrust and sometimes outright distain. Attitudes from across the sea in the Empire to the north toward half breeds and the mongrel races had begun to poison the people of the town. This caused the tavern to fall on hard times. On the best of days, they saw a quarter of the business they were used to and the business they got was often of the kind that resulted in calls to the town guard. The young man felt great guilt and tried to leave many times but to the credit of his stepfather he never got far. His stepfather had always treated him well and never as anything other than his own blood.

Not long after this, an illness came to the town and the young man's stepfather passed away, leaving the tavern to his mother. The tavern saw even harder times and soon the family grew hungry. To further add to their suffering, his sister fell ill with the same illness less than half a year after the death of his stepfather. None who had acquired it had yet lived.

Desperate to make ends meet and unable to get work anywhere in the town, he began to take less than savory jobs. The work rapidly grew in severity from petty theft to assault. The young half orc man began to loath himself but felt he had no alternative. Eventually, he was offered a job that would see his family with enough coin to procure the best healers in the town. All he had to do was make sure a pregnant washerwoman, who had laid with a pious noble, didn't make it home *one night. The young man stilled himself to the task and made iron his resolve. Reluctantly, he agreed. But when it came time to do the deed he could not. He ran from the town and collapsed in the hills under a large oak tree.*

The half Fae-Forgotten girl sat in the branches of the oak tree that rested at the top of a hill and watched the clouds move across the twin silver moons. She sighed and began to toy with a few of the leaves on a nearby branch, causing flowers to bloom. Her silent contemplation was abruptly interrupted by a large and young half orc man yelling in frustration and falling beneath her, against the trunk of her oak tree sobbing. When he touched the tree a bolt of emotion and memories shot through the heart of the tree and into her very soul. She felt entirely overwhelmed with grief and sorrow, pain and anger, ecstasy and joy. The emotions were so powerful that she too began to cry and shake with despair. She could not control her empathy for him, and she floated down off her branch and settled on her knees facing the him.

He felt the slightest gust of wind and slowly looked up from his palms. What he saw sent a jolt of wonder to his heart. Before him knelt a beautiful woman. She was pale, almost glowing, with bright green eyes, blood shot from tears. Her pointed ears could be seen poking out from her wavy reddish-brown hair. She was thin but supple and small in stature compared to the women of the town. There was something otherworldly about her, yet this caused no fear in him.

She, in turn, regarded him in a similar manner. He was light green in skin tone with brown stone-colored eyes. His brow jutted slightly forward, and his lower canine teeth stood out beyond his lips like small tusks. He was well muscled and broad of shoulder, yet stout in the torso. His emotions were still a raw and open wound stinging her mind. She knew that he was kind but quick to anger, jovial but often masqueraded as a stoic, he could smile ear to ear but behind it was always pain. Without a thought she leaped forward and into his arms that now hung by his sides in shock as she began to hug him gently but with a firmness even she couldn't understand.

He fell backwards as she leapt at him. For the briefest of moments, he thought she was perhaps some kind of wraith here to take his soul. As they fell back against the soft grass, the radiance of her emotions intertwined with his and he knew her intention. He had never been touched out of kindness by any female except for his mother and sister. He hesitated for the briefest moment before wrapping his arms around her in return. They looked into each other's eyes and together they both let their roiling emotions lay raw before the other.

For what felt like an eternity but was in reality only the space of several minutes, she laid there against his large chest. As they sobbed into each other she could feel the sadness fading away. The warmth between the two of them grew and she felt oddly whole in that moment. Then a thought came to her. What if she could help both her family and his? What if in doing so she could heal his sister, bring prosperity back to the tavern and at the same time bring some honor back to her family? She pulled her arms off his shoulders and squeezed them beneath his arms that fully encircled her and placed them against his chest. She inclined her head and kissed the tears from his cheeks. Then she gave him her true name.

He felt the thunderstorm of his emotions slowly fade as he held the woman. He felt calm and warm with her small weight on his chest. Through their touch he knew much about her and yet nothing at all. As she stirred against him, he feared she had come to her senses and would flee from him. Instead, she kissed his cheeks and said her name. His heart fluttered and then he spoke his. He briefly hesitated and then slowly brought his lips to hers.

Her body shook slightly as he pressed his lips into hers. She felt little bumps on her skin from head to toe. Goosebumps, she remembered hearing the mortal races call it. Peculiar name that. She too was not *used to being touched in this way so freely. Among her kind she was an abomination, and all gave her a wide birth. She pushed back against his lips, only moderately aware of his tusks. They did not bother her.*

They each began to move their bodies in unison. A melody that soon became a harmony of joy and ecstasy. All manner of moans, squeaks, sighs and laughter escaped them. They danced as if they knew the steps the other would take before they even knew it themselves. Soon they both lay in each other's arms washed in sweat and serenity. Beneath the oak they both gazed upon the full moons in silence.

He was afraid to move. Afraid this was all a dream. Or worse, that he actually had been attacked by a wraith and this was a fever dream before he slid into death. As if she read his mind, she turned to him, "No. I am of the Fae... mostly. I've never even met a wraith."

He smiled and a small laugh escaped his lips. "I always heard the Fae weren't creatures meant to be played with."

This time it was her turn to snicker, "Well, you played with me all the same."

He smiled, "Does this mean I belong to you now?"

She rose from the grass and walked to the oak aware of his eyes upon her the whole way. She placed her hand against that mighty tree, "Come here."

He quickly got to his feet and walked to her, taking her hand. She squeezed his massive hand as best she could, "Put your other hand on the tree."

He thought the request was a little odd and cocked his head to the side. She stretched up on her tiptoes. Not being tall enough, she levitated off the ground to make eye contact with him and kissed him, "Please."

He took in her scent again; she was a spring morning in a fully flowered meadow. He placed his free hand against the oak. They locked eyes with each other and her thoughts surged into him. She told him of her mother's fall from the good graces of the Lunar Court and of her desire to accumulate enough power for them to take notice and admit them back into the Court. She spoke of a pact. She could heal his sister and bring prosperity back to his family's tavern. In return he would accept her as his patron. He would be bound to her, and she would gift him with arcane powers through their pact. The more renown and deeds he achieved, the more power that would come to her familial line. However, with such deals a great sacrifice must be made in equal measure. To receive this boon, he would have to leave his home behind and not return. He would roam the lands of Yonara doing various works in her name and interests.

"You could do this? Save my sister and our tavern?" He asked.

"Only if you agree to the terms of our pact." She gazed into his eyes with hopefulness.

"Will you come with me?" He felt his heart slow at the thought of being separated from her.

"I cannot. Not physically. If you agree we will be able to communicate through our bond. If the moons are not full, I will not always be able to answer, but I will when I can." She tried her best to reassure him. She let go of his hand and placed hers against his cheek. "My family has needs as well. You have been through much. I see the storm of emotions you carry. The love you have for your family. The guilt you feel in your heart for the hatred others have so unrightfully shown you. Together we can both use these experiences to help our families and others like us. But only if you say yes to this pact."

He considered in silence for a long time, gazing up at the moons and then to the town he had lived in nearly his entire life. He leaned into the hand she held to his cheek. He had never felt this for another being before. "I cannot say why but I trust this. I trust you. I feel as though no one has ever been this plainly true to me before. For the sake of my family, yes."

She smiled, laughed and did a quick back flip as she hovered in the air causing him to let loose another smile. It dawned on him that he had not smiled this much in years. This felt right.

She placed her hands on the tree again and nodded for him to do the same. Instead, he came from behind her, his massive form overshadowing hers. His chest rested against her back and his hands laid on top of hers as they both touched the tree. She pushed her head back against his chest and felt his lips nuzzled against her head.

She said, "This pact we make on sturdy oak. Under the twin moons of silver, cloaked. Bound by soul and spirit, this be our yoke."

He felt a wave of coolness run over his skin while another wave of warmth ran through his insides. In his right eye he felt both the coolness and the warmth merge together and he knew at once that his eye had changed. He held his hand up to cup it and saw the faint glow of green light illuminate it.

"To mark our pact." She said, again, knowing his thoughts before he could speak them.

He stepped back and stared at the moons. Their color seemed more vibrant to him now. As he turned to the oak, he could see a light silver aura radiating from it.

She approached him again and he knelt before her. Even kneeling he was almost taller than she was. Both skin clad and starry eyed in the moonlight, she held out two small pieces of bark. Each was no bigger than a coin. She handed him the darker one, "Bury this beneath the threshold of the tavern and your sister will be healed by morning. Those that walk by the tavern will also feel compelled to enter."

His mouth dropped open in awe as he felt the power vibrating from the oak piece. She took the next piece and placed it first against her chest over her heart, then to her lips and then to her womanhood. He knew at once that she was placing the piece to her body in the order in which they met. He watched as in her hand the shape of the oak piece shifted into that of a Willow-wing blossom, slightly oval in shape with petals fanning out at the top. She then placed one of her fingers against her cheek and she pulled from it a tear. She quickly moved it to the top of the blossom where it began to part. There it sat like a small glistening pearl to his eyes.

She placed the trinket against his chest, and he felt warmth surge through him as she pushed it into his skin. His eyes closed as the heat grew almost too much to bear. The pressure from her hand faded and he opened his eyes. Looking down at his chest he saw that the piece was indeed embedded in his flesh. To him it seemed part tattoo and part implanted pendant. Quickly it faded beneath his skin.

She spoke. "This is a symbol of what we share. Every night when the moons are full you are to stand skin clad in the moonlight. Hold your hands to your chest and think of me. I will come to you when I can. Fail to do this and it will mean that either you are in trouble, or you have betrayed our pact." Her eyes took on an ominous mood. "Never, never betray this pact or the Lunar Court will turn a wicked eye to you."

He straightened in his spot, "I will never betray this pact, and I will forever owe you for what you have given me."

Her eyes swelled with tears, and she pulled him up from his kneeling position and levitated again to match his eyes. She kissed him gently.

He felt a lump forming in his throat. "When will we see each other again?" He was baffled by his knowledge of her. He knew she spoke the truth. He knew the nature of their relationship and yet the idea of not seeing her felt like a dagger in his chest.

"My sweet beast. Know that while we cannot be together you have a piece of my heart. Know that when the moons are full, I shall find you and share my heart with you again. The lives of mortals and the Fae are vastly different, and this is the nature of the pacts we make. Now go. Bury the first piece of oak at the threshold and then leave. Your sacrifice must begin immediately after. They can never see you again. I am sorry *for this, but it is a necessary sacrifice." She winced so imperceptivity that the young half orc did not notice. "Then you will set out to bring honor to us both. Remember to always keep a close eye on the twin moons."*

He brought her close and kissed her again. "By your will... thank you." With those words she smiled, a single tear in her left eye, realizing what she had just gained and what she had just done to this sweet man. She turned and she faded away into mist.

The old bard looked up from his empty cup that he had stared into for the last few minutes of the story and sighed. When he finally glanced around, he saw that two more patrons had fallen asleep with their heads on tables. He smirked with a heavy heart but then caught sight of a lithe figure paying for a drink at the bar. He could not make out her face yet, but her feminine form was stunningly clad in leathers of a deep brown and dark shades of red. The tavernkeeper's mouth remained wide open as she served her two small cups of an amber beverage.

A white raven that sat perched on her shoulder, dropped two silver coins, squawked, and then took flight out the open door.

He squinted hard as he looked at her, trying to peer through his drunken haze as if it would give him a better view. She turned to approach him now and he understood exactly why the tavernkeeper remained slack jawed. Orange rust-colored fur sat atop her vulpine ears and tail, swishing behind her, now so plainly visible to him. Her eyes were golden orbs that stared into his as if they were peering into his very soul.

She smiled at him, barely visible wrinkles at the corners of her lips showed her to be in her middle years. He had never seen one of her people in person and she was not what the tales he had heard spoke of. Truth be told he thought her people were gone from this world. Vulpine were said to be innately magical folk that were more beast than humanoid. Other than her ears, tail and the light covering of fur at her forearms she appeared as most human women do. She twirled a small, polished silver knife as she approached. The old man could swear it was a butter knife.

She stopped before him and smiled down as she handed him one of the two cups. With a shaking hand he took the ale offering. Normally he would have downed the liquid immediately but here in front of her, he was dumbstruck.

She snickered and shook her head slightly before downing her own cup. With a smack of her lips and the sigh of someone that has not tasted sour alcohol in a long time she turned her eyes to the fire in the hearth, as though she was running through old memories. The old bard nearly wet himself when she spoke.

"You got most of it right. There was far more to it than that and storytellers nowadays, with the threat of the void everywhere, tend to make tales far happier than they truly were or should be. A small kindness in a world where it is so rarely found." She looked down at her necklace and toyed with it in her fingers.

What he saw was her clenching her jaw tight. What he failed to see was the moisture beginning to glaze over her eyes and the similarities between her necklace and the willow wing blossom in his tale. He swallowed hard and stammered over his words. "Wha...what did I get...wr...wrong?"

She gave him a sad half smile and began to answer when a stout and thick man, larger than a dwarf but shorter than your average human opened the door to the tavern. The old bard leaned around the vulpine woman to set eyes on the man. His skin had a light reddish hue that held a very stark contrast to the shock of purple that ran down the side of his pitch-black hair and wild salt and pepper beard. Most shocking though were his eyes; pure white they were, like the Torvox people of old whose blood began reappearing in people decades ago.

He wore thicker leathers than the woman, and whereas she held no visible weapons, save perhaps the butter knife, he was picking at some sort of toggle or switch on a roughly two-and-a-half foot long metallic device with a slightly bent wooden handle on one end. The contraption had a hole at the opposite end and an eerie radiant purple and silver-like smoke seeped from it. The man looked around quickly and smiled as he saw the woman.

"Saffy, we're out of time. They're coming. I feel it." He twitched his wrist, causing the leather braided bracelet he wore to vanish. Suddenly, a spear taller than the man himself appeared in his hand. He tossed it to the vulpine woman. "We need to go."

She caught the spear as though they had rehearsed the maneuver many times and set the butt of it against the tavern floor. She leaned on it with a sigh, turning her attention back to the old bard, though her eyes fell back to the hearth fire.

"The Fae bitch lied. She never truly loved him. She used the most beautiful and sweet man I have ever known and broke him. Only when she knew she had no other choice did she set him free and give him the life he deserved. If that wasn't enough, all of that out there," She nodded her head toward the front door of the tavern, in refence to the streets, "the void scar reopening. She did that."

"Saffy." The stout man at the door said more urgently.

"Fae be damned Syndrin, I'm coming." She said with exasperation. Her eyes locked with the bard again. "Still, it was nice to hear a sweeter version be told." She set her cup down on a nearby table and walked out past the strange man, stopping and leaning down slightly to kiss him.

The man, Syndrin, smiled at her before turning his pale white eyes to the old storyteller and the few patrons still awake and gawking. His face fell as though he was looking at a room full of corpses. "You all should hide. We'll do what we can but..."

Out in the darkness of the town beyond the tavern door, several bright purple void tears materialized. The guttural and abyssal noises of the void abominations grew louder as they poured forth from the portals.

CHAPTER ONE

NO PLACE FOR INNOCENCE

Many Years Ago

Kasha had been curled up in the corner of the wardrobe for several hours. She had stopped counting the minutes that passed by while her mother was being punished for her own mistake earlier this morning. Kasha had failed to make sure the flower arrangements on the dining room table alternated red to white and red again. For this her mother, Kaitriona, was being punished right now.

Kaitriona had long since stopped crying out, begging her master to stop. She was a human, and human lives were particularly harsh in the Helspires unless they had the power or coin to make their path easier. Something Kaitriona had never had either of.

Kaitriona and Kasha had both been indentured to the troll Zunibar Tolgar, an exotic goods trader, for five years now. Kasha was only a year old when they came to be in his service. Most of her life had been in this terrible mansion in the clutches of the Helspires.

Zunibar bought her mother's debt and with it, Kasha and her mother. The troll treated them both fairly when there were witnesses. All they had to do was clean the mansion and attend to any guests that came by throughout the day, but it all had to be done with perfection. Everything from the way they poured drinks to how pristine they kept their appearance mattered to Zunibar. At night he would punish Kaitriona for anything he felt either had performed with less than faultless precision.

If they had not bowed low enough, left the smallest speck of a water stain on a wine goblet or missed a grain of dirt that a guest had tracked in, Kaitriona would bear the brunt of the pain that night. Worst of all, however, was if Kaitriona dared to try and cover her modesty near him or if Kasha had broken anything around the mansion. These resulted in Kaitriona being forced to spend time alone with Zunibar at night. Anytime this happened Kasha noticed her mother returning to their room with bruises on display, and often walking oddly for a few days after her punishments.

Because of all of this it was ingrained in Kasha to emulate perfection. Nothing, not even a strand of her own hair, must ever be out of place. When she was done with her duties in the rest of the mansion, she would immediately set to making herself and their room as spotless as she could, given the few personal items they were allowed to keep.

The door to their bedroom opened and violently slammed against the wall. The doorknob had long since created a hole in the wall behind it. Being in the corner of the wardrobe, Kasha could not see her mother hit the floor by their bed, but she knew that was what the next loud crashing sound was. Her mother's sobbing almost drowned out Zunibar's words. "Next time you'll show some enthusiasm or perhaps I'll seek my pleasures elsewhere."

Kasha's mother ceased crying almost immediately at those words. "You will not touch my daughter!"

Her words were nearly cut off by the sound of Zunibar's foot colliding with her stomach. Kasha could hear her mother gasping for air. She threw her hands over her ears and pressed them in so hard it hurt. She could not make out his next words, but they were followed with another loud thud and a scream.

There was silence for a time and Kasha pulled her hands away from her ears. She moved as quietly as she could to peek out of the gap in the wardrobe doors. She saw her mother slumped over on the floor. Kaitriona was no longer crying but Kasha could see that she was still breathing. The sound of Zunibar's returning footsteps stopped her from leaving the wardrobe to go to her mother.

The large troll appeared in the doorway and tossed a small leather pouch at her mother's shaking body. His voice was filled with amused disdain. "Here you go, you pathetic heap of flesh. Sleep it off and be up bright and early tomorrow, I am expecting guests, and you will be of top quality. Make sure you cover those bruises."

As the pouch hit the floor blue dust spilled partially from it. Kasha still didn't know exactly what the stuff was, but she knew her mother needed it. Or so she had told her. Her mother had told her that it was medicine that made her pain go away. Kasha hated the stuff but frequently fetched it and a small spoon for her mother on nights like this. She could not stand to see her mother in pain, even though this meant she would not be able to read to her tonight and would most likely not even hold her as they slept.

The door slammed shut. Kasha waited until she could no longer hear the heavy footfalls of Zunibar before she slowly opened the wardrobe and stepped out. She made her way to her mother as quietly as possible. If she had fallen asleep then she did not want to wake her. Once she finally got close enough, she could see the trails of tears that had carved clear rivers on her cheeks through blood from her nose that still trickled to the floor. Zunibar had always been careful to avoid marking her face.

He did not want a misshapen slave to serve his guests. Was her mistake with the flowers really so bad that he went this far? Why wasn't she more careful? This was her fault.

Kasha knelt down to grab the pouch of her mother's 'medicine.' She was going to put it away in the bedside drawer when her mother called out to her in a voice so weak she could hardly hear it. "Sweetling, bring mommy her medicine."

Kasha stopped and her shoulders dropped. "Momma..."

"Please, baby. I need it." Her mother did not even have the strength to reach out to her. She crawled her hand out toward Kasha.

Tears began to well up in Kasha's eyes as her lips quivered. "Yes, momma."

She went to the bedside table and grabbed a small spoon. Kneeling by her mother, she held the spoon and the pouch out to her. Kaitriona tried to grab them with futile effort, which made her tears turn to weak sobbing..

Kaitriona was ashamed. She lacked the strength to do or be anything else. All her past failures surged into her heart like a tidal wave whose only purpose was to drag her under and never let her breathe again. She was not strong enough for this anymore, if she ever was in the first place. She just wanted it to be over.

Kasha's tears were violently falling now. "What do you want me to do momma? Momma?"

A suddenly calmness of acceptance came over Kaitriona. She sniffled and her facial expression became emotionless. "I need you to do it for me."

Kasha drew back slightly. "What momma?" She asked the question from both shock and her mother's voice being so soft she had trouble making out her words.

"Use the spoon, sweetling." Kaitriona managed a small smile at the corner of her mouth.

It took Kasha a moment to gather herself. Nevertheless, she knelt and opened the pouch. With a trembling hand she scooped the blue powder onto it. As she moved it to her mother's nose her hand trembled so much that it all fell from the spoon. She was scared but also felt like she was letting her mother down, and that made it all worse. She did not want her mother to hurt anymore. She hated this place. Her entire life she had never had any sense of peace or safety.

Her mother remained eerily calm at the spilt powder that she always swore to Kasha she desperately needed. "It's okay, sweetling. Try again and I'll read to you in the morning."

Something in her mother's voice betrayed her words, but Kasha could not understand exactly what it was. "Okay, momma."

She sat the pouch on the floor and used her other hand to steady the wrist of the hand that held the spoon. Her hands still shook but she managed to get it to Kaitriona's nose this time. Her mother pitifully snorted several times before she could finish everything on the spoon. "Another."

Kasha sat back on her heels. "But momma-"

"Listen to your mother. I said another." Kaitriona's voice remained emotionless.

Kasha repeated the process and held the spoon to her mother. Within a few sniffs the spoon was empty again. Kasha began to rise to put the pouch and spoon away when her mother reached out and grabbed her ankle feebly. "Again."

The slurring in her mother's voice was unmistakable and something about it drove a terrible despair into Kasha's heart. "Momma..."

"Again. I'm still hurting. Always, hurting."

Kasha returned to her heels and repeated her previous action. The spoon emptied; her mother slurred out again. "Mo...re."

Kasha's shoulders were shaking as she cried now. Her hands trembled as though she were having a fit, and the spoon barely managed to hold any of the powder by the time she made it to her mother's nose.

"Ag...aga...again."

"Momma, please." Kasha's words were dripping with terror.

"H...el...p momma."

Kasha tried to fight it; not to give in to her mother's request. Kaitriona was beginning to look at peace for the first time in her life, but something inside Kasha screamed at her to stop. She did as she was told and gave her mother another wavering spoon.

Her mother only managed to inhale half of the powder before her head slumped fully to the floor. "I'm...sor..."

Kasha saw that her mother was finally sleeping, and she felt relief wash over her. She got up and put the pouch and spoon away by the bed and grabbed the comforter, dragging it over to her mother. She tossed the comforter over her mother and then crawled under it and into her mother's arms. Kasha fell asleep clinging to Kaitriona's arm.

She awoke to the pale light of the sun piercing through the bars of the only window they had in their room. She stretched and moved to sit up, but her movement was halted abruptly by her mother's arm. She felt comforted by the perceived desire of her mother to not let her leave her side yet. That was until she felt the cold stiffness of her skin. "Momma?"

She waited for a response that did not come. She sat up quickly and shook Kaitriona. Her usually warm face was gray and dusky. "Momma?"

Kasha began to sob uncontrollably. The survival instincts that she picked up in all the years of living here went into overdrive and she clamped her hands over her mouth. She grabbed a corner of the comforter and buried her face in it, making her wail as silent as she could.

She was not sure how much time had passed, but she had stopped crying and laid next to her mother's body, holding her cool hand. She felt such guilt. This was her fault, she allowed this to happen. "I'm so sorry, momma."

She did not have much more time to consider what all of this meant for her. From far down the hallway, she heard Zunibar yelling at the top of his lungs. "Didn't I say to be up early! If that pretty face isn't down here immediately, I will be taking it out on her this time!"

Survival instincts again. She had no idea what he meant, but she knew at her core it was bad. She had failed to listen to that feeling last night and now her mother was dead. She would never ignore that feeling again. She moved faster than she ever had in her entire life, grabbing one of her mother's satchels that she used when she had to go to the market with Zunibar. She hastily tossed a pair of trousers and an overshirt into the satchel along with two apples and a small knife. She was still in her night clothes, but she swiftly threw the night gown off and replaced it with a day gown.

Hyperventilating, she rubbed her hands together while wondering how in the hells she was going to get out of here. She was going to have to hide and run past Zunibar when he came in. That would not do, the locks on the front door were higher than she could reach.

A cloud passed by the window, momentarily taking away the little light that was leaking into the room. She had dreamed of squeezing through those bars many times. Now she would find out if she could.

Kasha looked around and grabbed the metal compact that held the concealer her mother used to hide her bruises, and hurled it against the window, shattering it. Down the hall she heard Zunibar's footsteps move at a running pace. She pushed her mother's vanity chair underneath the window and climbed up. She looked down from the third-floor window. Vertigo suddenly overcame her, and she nearly fell right then. Kasha held fast to the bars and steadied herself.

"I'm going to break you for this Kaitriona!" She knew by the volume of his voice that he was nearly at their door.

Her chin trembled. She closed her eyes and pushed through the bars. She fell.

As if one of the Gods watched her and took pity, she fell into the back cart of a linen merchant that had just picked up a shipment of flax. She did not come out of the fall unscathed, however. The sound of her colliding with the cart's contents and the freighted snorts of the ponies that pulled it, drowned out the snap in her forearm. Her holler of pain was matched by the holler of shock from the merchant driving the cart.

She rolled to her back and looked to the driver's seat, meeting the eyes of a goblin man with an oversized hat whose brim would have been huge on a half giant. "What in the bloody hells?"

Her eyes were four shades of red, and her face painted in fear. "Help me, please."

The goblin looked around them, wondering where she came from. His vision rested briefly on the broken glass on the road next to his cart and followed it up to the window. There was then a loud thundering noise of crashing wood and a man's voice yelling from inside the window above. The goblin quickly motioned for her to lay low and brushed loose flax over her with one hand while slapping the reins and urging the ponies forward faster.

CHAPTER TWO

REMEMBERING MOTHER

The three stood a few paces from the splintered doorway, which hung precariously on its hinges, reinforced by hastily affixed boards from the Wyld Trade Authority, cautioning any would-be intruders of dire consequences. Trade Princess Shelani and the Council of Commerce upheld stringent regulations regarding trade and ownership, even in the aftermath of the proprietor's demise. Three weeks had passed since the street outside Mother Maudrid's shop and abode had borne witness to a brutal confrontation between two members of the Talons of Misery and Callus Kordec alongside Arialyn Foghand. The latter pair had dispatched the Talons, but not before Lindri Three Scales had inflicted a slow, torturous fate that would ultimately claim the life of the dearly departed Mother Maudrid.

Callus lingered with a gaze that held the weight of the world, nearly devoid of life. At his side, Arialyn clasped his hand, keeping him from breaking again. While Kasha rested against his other side, though more to keep herself from falling apart. He wrapped an arm around her, drawing her close, his head resting atop hers. "She always spoke highly of your talents, you know?"

Kasha sniffed, a smirk breaking through her sorrow. "She used to insist I leave the Spectacle and pursue a place in the Arcanum Centralis. I told her I wasn't stuffy and pretentious enough for that, and that all the thrill I needed was right here with the Spectacle." She brushed a tear away just as it threatened to fall from her jawline.

Arialyn moved in front of them, grabbing Kasha's hand and looking at each of them in turn. The love of her life and this woman from his past that was quickly becoming her close friend despite her best efforts. She peered over her shoulder at the door and then up to them. "Are you both ready?"

They looked at each other and nodded slowly. Arialyn led the way to the door and produced a small hammer from the pocket of her overalls. She tapped it to a nail holding one of the Council of Commerce boards in place and with a low hum the energy from the arcane infused hammer forced the nail to retract on its own. It was as if the nail no longer desired to be in the wood of its own accord. She repeated the process on each nail and set the boards aside. They filed in one after the other. The environment inside matched the mood, grim.

Kasha, with a flick of her wrist and a snap of her fingers, ignited several candles scattered throughout the room. The flickering flames momentarily brightened the interior, only to plunge Kasha into immediate regret. The remnants of dried blood marred the table and stained patches on the floor, a grim testament to the violence that had transpired. Callus turned away, a grimace of disgust etching across his features.

"Damn it! I'm so sorry," Kasha stammered, her hand forming a fist as the flames extinguished, plunging them back into shadow. Tears welled in her eyes, and she sank into the lone chair that had somehow survived the chaos of three weeks prior. Without hesitation, Arialyn rushed to her side, cradling her head gently as Kasha broke down, her sobs echoing in the heavy silence.

Callus's shoulders heaved with his rising breaths and his vision blurred beneath his own weeping eyes. He raised his fists up together and crashed them through the bloody table with a mournful wail. From there he grabbed both larger pieces and threw them out the front door and into the street, nearly striking a passing man on a horse. That man was about to call out to the source in anger but that thought was immediately halted by the sight of the Hobgoblin Reaver ducking under the doorframe and walking toward the table pieces in the street, lantern in hand.

Callus held the unlit oil lantern out to his side and called out. "Kasha!"

She and Arialyn came to the door with a look of confusion. Callus turned and locked eyes with his childhood sorceress friend. She read the sadness and pleading in his face and looked at the fragments of the table in the street while barring her sharp teeth. She flicked her wrist and snapped her fingers again, lighting the lantern. The table burst forth in flames as Callus flung the lantern onto it with a crash.

Passersby gave the fiery scene a wide birth and a few ran to get the attention of a Wyld Trade Authority agent. Callus stared at the burning wreckage of the table; his heart galloped in his chest and everything around him disappeared. All he could see was the inferno before him. The next several minutes felt like an eternity. He ran back into the house and grabbed anything that looked like it had been broken or damaged in the murder of dear Mother Maudrid. It didn't take long for Kasha's anger to take over as she too began to hurl items into the fire. Arialyn knew they needed this, needed to vent, to mourn in whatever way they could. She stepped out of the way onto the porch and simply watched, her heart breaking for them.

Callus stood just outside the doorway. Finding nothing else he deemed fitting for the fire, he roared in defiance at all the vile events that had transpired after he won that damned Scarred Lands Championship in the arena of the Helspires. That was the cursed event that triggered all this madness. All of this could have been avoided had he just stopped fighting. If he had accepted his body couldn't take it anymore.

A light flashed across his face. He shielded his eyes from the sudden assault to his vision and then he peered to the source. A hanging remnant of mirror glass hung from one of the porch support beams. The wind kicked up and the glass blew to the side, catching Arialyn's reflection. Mother Maudrid's dying words ran through his head. *"It's okay. I got to see my boy smile again.'*

He knew it was her. Mother Maudrid had always had ways to calm him down when he would lose his temper or when he would feel lost inside himself. Now she was showing him the reason *he* was able to smile again. Lavender and ginger. Arialyn. Complete. Home.

He never would have found her had he not won the Scarred Lands Championship. His rage waned and he felt an odd sensation of peace come over him. He smiled at Arialyn in an apologetic manner, and she shook her head in turn. "Don't apologize. I love you."

Callus felt tears of joy form in his eyes as he looked at her. "I love you too. My home."

He knelt as she moved towards him. She grabbed his face in her hands and kissed his tears away. "Kasha needs you, now."

Kasha was standing a few feet away from the fire. Her arms were outstretched, and her head was back as the wind blew her dress wildly, hair curling around her horns. She too felt a sense of peace washing over her. As Callus approached her, he saw a rolled-up bit of parchment in her hand. He came behind her and placed an arm over her chest and the other over her abdomen.

"She's here." He said.

Kasha nodded and placed her hand on his arm. "I know. Look."

She leaned back against Callus and unrolled the parchment. Callus laughed. "Ha! Really?"

Kasha joined in the laughter and nodded. "Really. Watch."

She tapped Callus's arms, and he let her go. Kasha ran inside and came back out a moment later with a few small items. She read the parchment to herself and memorized the phrase written on it. She held out an old raven feather in her hand and then sprinkled dust of dragon's blood onto it. Next, she knelt and took a pinch if dirt and placed in over the feather as well. Finally, she took a small knife that she had expertly hidden between her breasts and made a small cut into the same palm. "Ab aethere clamo ad te. Nomine te Lemmy."

Kasha clenched her fist around the components and then threw the remains of them into the fire of their mourning. For a few seconds nothing happened, then suddenly a white flame burst from the center of the fire and into the sky. The flame sizzled and then all at once took the form of a large white, albino raven. It flew in a wide circle, cawing loudly and then came to rest on Kasha's shoulder.

Lemmy eyed her closely and then nuzzled against her cheek before seeing Callus and flapping over to land on his head. He sighed. "Every damn time."

Lemmy squawked and flapped his wings, tapping Callus harmlessly on the head. "That was from her, wasn't it."

The albino raven flew back to Kasha, but was almost smashed between her and Callus as they embraced. Each felt a sense of strange closure to the terrible events that brought them here, but each knew without those same events they wouldn't be right here, right now. Together again. They felt as if Mother Maudird was telling them to take comfort in that, for whatever it was worth.

They seperated just in time to realize that a crowd had gathered, albeit at a distance. There were now several dozen witnesses to the mania that they had just committed. Callus glanced over to Arialyn who was in the process of showing a Wylds Trade Authortity agent their papers of ownership for Mother Maudrid's hut and reassuring him that they would be taking care of the mess.

Arialyn jogged over to them once she had finished with the agent. "Is that Lemmy?"

Callus nodded. "Yeah, this is Lemmy. In all his white mischevious glory."

Lemmy bobbed his head and fluttered his wings from his perch on Kasha's shoulder.

"The agent said that since Mother Maudrid hadn't put the building in her will that we had three options. Kasha could assume ownership since the will entitled her to all of Mother Maudrid's belongings, we can assign ownership to someone else or we can sell it." Arialyn laid the options out before them.

Callus saw Kasha looking to him for advice. He held his hands up. "This is entirely up to you, Kasha."

Kasha considered and then turned to Arialyn. "It's too small for your arcanomancer work isn't it?

Arialyn nodded reluctantly. "Yeah, by a good margin."

"Well, then I'll sell it and give the coin to you. With that and the half of the coin from the will I'm sure you can buy a nice storefront. Probably one that has a home on the second floor too." Kasha said it with excitement and grasped both of Arialyn's hand while bouncing on her toes.

Arialyn was briefly stunned by the idea. Then, very out of character, jumped up at Kasha and the two hugged exuberantly with deafening squeals of joy as they both hopped around in a circle.

Callus shook his head at the them and then noticed the crowd was still surveying the impromptu bonfire they had made in the center of the street, snapping him back to reality. "I'll get started on putting the fire out." He hollered out to the people. "Sorry, got carried away. No one likes moving!" He rubbed the back of his head sheepishly and set off to get a bucket to draw water from the nearby well.

Off in the distance, behind several curious shopkeepers and citizens that watched the chaotic scene unfold, a large figure groaned in annoyance at the turn of events.

Chapter Three

Make the Lie Become the Truth

Egrim had been searching for Mother Maudrid to help him with a difficult situation. One that needed a solution several months ago. A situation that now had him and Morrigan on the run. It had killed him inside, but he had tried to leave her somewhere safe once. That had not turned out well and led to revelations that now brought him here. The longer Morrigan stayed with him, the more likely she would end up dead or as a bargaining piece for his own life. He was never meant to be a father with the sort of work he did. Yet, all it had taken was a look of pure terror and a breaking heart from her innocent face, and he swore to her he would never do it again. There had been something else there too, something that pulled at his very soul and denied him the ability to let her go even if he had still wanted to.

When he had finally found Mother Maudrid's place of business in the Wylds, all he found was a crazed hobgoblin burning items from her shop in the streets. A red skinned tiefling had helped him and a gnomish woman had stood close by, monitoring the scene. He very briefly considered just going up to them and saying he had been directed to Mother Maudrid for the 'healing' of some sort of ailment and then feeling out the situation and advancing from there. However, the contact that directed him to Mother Maudrid had been very clear that he should use the utmost caution in his approach. The refugee network that the old crone had been connected to had been compromised more than once. Unfortunately, almost always from within by those that were once thought fully trustworthy. The right amount of coin could turn anyone.

After somewhat painfully selling his horse and using some of the coin to grease some palms, he had discovered that Mother Maudrid had died and left her affairs and coin to the tiefling woman he had seen in the street that morning. He had no idea who any of them were. Though after some further palm greasing, and a few empty but intimidating threats, he had been given names. Kasha Volstruk, the tiefling. Arialyn Foghand, the gnome. Callus Kordec, the hobgoblin. That last name had struck him as familiar.

He had watched the hobgoblin and gnome first to gauge the pair. He had learned that they were looking for a place to open a shop called the Amethyst Artificer. Arialyn was known for being something called an arcanomancer. A professional that apparently crafted constructs with more arcane power and less tinkering. The shop was to be their storefront for selling these strange arcane items. Egrim had spotted some of those items as they moved into a new building. They were similar to some of the contraptions he had seen in the Brightborn Kingdom.

Callus, the hobgoblin, was a retired gladiator of great renown. And while he couldn't place his face, he now recognized the name from a time he had passed through the Helspires many years ago. Scarred Lands Champion. Impressive.

Callus and Arialyn weren't just business partners, they were lovers. He was still trying to understand how that relationship functioned... physically.

The information he had obtained told him that Mother Maudrid had been very close to Callus. So, he had watched the pair for a couple of weeks but had finally gotten the feeling they had no idea about Mother Maudrid's 'network' and so he had moved on to the tiefling.

Kasha Volstruk, owner and operator of the Witch's Tits and Tarts Tavern. The tavern was in the neighboring city of Hus'rokn. It was an interesting style of business to say the least. The entire staff was female. Each serving girl remained topless throughout her shift, wearing only a skirt, body oils and various footwear. He had personally taken a particular liking to the long stockings and simple soft footwear, though he couldn't say why. They strictly served tarts and ales. Nothing else. It seemed to be quite popular, and he could see why.

In the process of scouting out Kasha, he learned that this was soon to be the old location. Kasha had apparently won a bidding war for a building in a far better location. The other bidder, a tiefling businessman by the name of Alabaster Jakel, was quit vexed by the whole situation. It was whispered that he had actually outbid Kasha, but she called in a few favors and the paperwork for Alabaster's higher bid had been incidentally misplaced.

Egrim wanted to get a look at the new location before he and Morrigan turned in for the night. He still had no idea where they would find shelter with the little coin he had left. Information gathering in this damn place had a steep price. Which was apparently because the entire city of Hus'rokn was run by a group of gangs known as The Three.

The streets were nearly dead now. The combination of the hour of night and the pouring rain had everyone, even the beggars, seeking somewhere warm and dry to sleep. Which is exactly why Egrim's eyes caught interest in a lone figure that moved smoothly through the streets and in the direction of the soon to be new Witch's Tits and Tarts Tavern. It didn't sway or stumble as the few people who had just left the late-night bars and taverns did. This figure moved silently and with purpose.

Morrigan scratched her right horn and shifted her head against Egrim's chest. He had her concealed under his duster and on his left hip. The cold night's rain caused his skin to shiver. He had been shaving his head every other day for the last month and still the cold on his scalp was a reminder of exactly how fridged it would get in the coming weeks. Morrigan seemed to enjoy his new look and would often absentmindedly pet his head at night. He was worried he would not be able to keep her warm enough. He opened his duster just enough to see that her red skin was still vibrant and not a pale shade of pink he had expected it to be against the chill. He reached inside to feel her arm and thankfully found her to be much warmer than he was.

He whispered into his coat. "Quiet as a meadow mouse now."

Morrigan peeked up at him and nodded with a smile. She knew when he said this he was about to move swiftly and that she needed to hold on tight and remain soundless. Releasing one of the long braids of his beard that she played with when she was bored, she gripped tight and felt her nails dig through his shirt and lightly pierced his flesh.

Egrim restrained a growl. "I know you are doing that on purpose. Is this because I didn't get you the damned candy?"

He could hear her grunt in the affirmative but then a barely audible giggle.

He shook his head and stuck to the shadows within the shadows, focusing intently and spotting even the darkest places in the street. As the figure got closer to the new Tits and Tarts it slowed down and began to skulk. Egrim was better able to discern the mannerisms of the figure and could tell it was male and had honed its skills toward stealth and infiltration. The man was very careful to keep his face hidden.

The man changed his gait and began to stumble around once he was at the neighboring building. *'So now you want people to think you're a drunk.'*

The man stopped and began to act like he was losing his balance and turned. Egrim sensed he was truly attempting to take a look around and make sure there were no witnesses to whatever crime he was clearly about to commit. Egrim ducked into an alley just in time to avoid being in clear view of the man. After a few heartbeats, Egrim peeked around the corner to see the man go into the alley immediately past the Tits and Tarts.

Egrim dashed down his own alley and repeated the same process, looking around the corner carefully. He caught sight of the tail end of the man's cloak as he leapt in through a rear window on the bottom floor of the two-story building. He sprinted soundlessly to the wall, right where the man entered and pressed his back against it. Looking in quickly, he saw what appeared to be a storeroom. There were carts and barrels piled up and several skirts laid out over a small table.

There was no way he was fitting through the same window the burglar had. His shoulders alone were wider that the frame. Thankfully his arm was long enough that he could reach in and unlatch the two security bars on the door. He effortlessly lowered the heavy bars to the floor without making a sound and entered in through the door. Once inside he could hear barely perceptible movement in what he assumed would be the main room. He set Morrigan down behind a crate. "Stay here. Stay small and do not make a sound. Quiet as a meadow mouse. I'll be right back."

Morrigan's face twisted in fear and uncertainty. "Little one, I swore I would never leave you. The lady of this place is in trouble, and we may need her. I need to make sure she is safe."

She almost took longer than Egrim could allow, but she nodded and curled up in the corner. He quickly removed his duster and left it draped over her. Stealthily, he made his way through the open doorway and toward where he heard the sound of spilling liquid.

The man, a dark elf Egrim could now see, was stuffing linen rags into the tops of liquor bottles. He knew exactly what the dark elf's intentions were now. He took a step forward, hoping that the man would be too focused on the task at hand. If he could sneak up behind him, he could easily incapacitate him. Unfortunately, the newly laid wood floor planks had other plans and squeaked beneath his weight. His shoulders slumped and he sighed. "Fuck."

The man dropped one of the bottles to the floor with a shattering crash. Egrim's muscles tensed, and time seemed to slow for him. He saw the dark elf's hands move to his waist. A split second later a dagger whizzed past his ear, and another nicked his left arm as he dodged to the right. "I see we're not going to talk this out."

Morrigan huddled under Egrim's heavy duster. She felt comforted by it, safe. She had never felt safe unless he was near. Only a few moments at most had passed before she heard commotion, and it did not sound good. Egrim had been in several tussles over the last few months, but she had always been there to witness them. Not seeing what was happening was causing her to panic.

She didn't know if he was okay. She had bonded to him ever since the incident. She didn't really understand it, but she needed him. She barely remembered anything from her life before the last few months, and she wished she could forget what little she did. Egrim had an aura about him that she had always felt secure in, and she knew something about that was very important to her.

He was kind. Genuinely kind. Throughout the time she had spent with him she almost always saw a smile set on his square jaw. Sometimes even when she could feel a deep sadness welling up inside him. She still saw it. He was her family now and the only person that had ever truly been there for her. That was a concept that she understood deep in her soul. She had always needed one and was never given the right to have one until the day he found her.

She heard Egrim cry out in a groan of pain. Her breathing grew rapid, and her nerves were on edge in a heartbeat. The fear of the unknown caused dreaded memories to replay in her head. She stood and shook her whole body, doing her best to push them to the back of her mind for now. He needed her. She put Egrim's duster over her like a cloak. If the situation had been different the sight would have been a truly comical one if there had been anyone to witness it. She ran to the door she had seen him disappear through with all the confidence of a kid in her hero's costume on Helsnacht.

She raced to a stop right as she passed the bar counter. There was fire and broken bottles in several areas around the room and Egrim held a dark elf man off the ground by the throat. He was yelling at the man, asking who sent him. She saw the dark elf grab a dagger from his boot. She wanted to scream, to warn Egrim. She even opened her mouth to do just that, but nothing came out. The dagger bit into his chest. Morrigan felt a cold wave of energy wash over her. Egrim immediately dropped the man and fell to his knees. The dark elf kicked him in the jaw, forcing him to fall to his back.

Morrigan was not going to let this stand. She grabbed a lip-stick-stained wine goblet from the bar top and hurled it at the dark elf. It shattered against his ear, and he reeled upon her, holding his bleeding ear. "You little bitch." Then his eyes widened in shock. "It can't be."

Morrigan looked down at her hands. Panic coursed through her. The protection that had been placed on her was gone. She ran behind the bar, passing by a mirror that sat on the floor propped up against the wall. She, indeed, no longer appeared as she should.

The dark elf sprinted toward the bar. "You're going to make me rich."

He had barely finished his last word when Egrim's large boot thrust into the middle of his back. He sprawled forward and bashed his head into the bar top. Egrim caught the man by the neck as he rebounded off the bar. He lifted him up and switched hands midair to chokeslam him into a nearby table.

Morrigan popped back around the bar with a butter knife in hand. Egrim pulled the dagger from his chest. A warm and familiar pulsing emanated from him and Morrigan felt the sensation of protection taking hold again. Egrim held the man by the throat on the floor. "All you had to do was tell me who sent you. But now you've seen too much."

A door above them on the mezzanine burst open. A woman screamed and cursed as she sent waves of arcane frost to consume the flames on the stairs. Egrim looked up at her. The mixture of fire and ice caused the air around the red tiefling woman to shimmer. Her auburn hair waved about in the turmoil and her pink satin nightgown clung to her body in a perfect outline of the beauty beneath it. He shook his head and broke the spell she unknowingly placed on him. Looking back at the dark elf, he sneered. He could not let this man talk, ever. He raised the man's head up and slammed it into the floor with the satisfying crack of his skull in several places. The dark elf gurgled and ceased squirming.

Kasha extinguished the flames quickly and then, and only then, turned her attention to the largest human man she had ever seen and the tiefling girl that remained. She reeled on Egrim, arms and hands extended. "Don't move! What in the hells are you doing to my tavern? Are you one of Alabaster's cronies?"

Morrigan ran in front of Egrim and held the butterknife out toward Kasha in both hands. Egrim rose to his feet. A small trail of blood dripped down his chest, staining his tunic. He placed a hand on Morrigan's head. "Put it down, sweetness."

Morrigan shook her head and waved the butterknife at Kasha. He sighed and pulled it from her hands. Her courage disappeared with her weapon, and she immediately scurried behind his legs. Egrim held his hands up and tossed the butterknife next to the unconscious man. "I have no idea who Alabaster is. We were passing by when I saw this man break in through your rear window. There were no city guard around and I couldn't stand by and let him get away with whatever he was planning. I'm only sorry I couldn't stop him from setting the fires first."

Kasha narrowed her eyes at the man. "You were passing by? In the dead of night? With a young girl? I'm supposed to believe that?"

Egrim shrugged his shoulders. He quickly modified the story he had rehearsed in his head for days. "We arrived in Hus'rokn a few weeks ago. Raiders attacked our caravan, and we were forced to flee with none of our belongings. She is my daughter. I cannot find work, at least none that will allow me to keep her near and I am... devoid of enough coin for a room at the moment. I was trying to find us somewhere safe to bed down in the streets when I saw him." He motioned to the dark elf man.

Morrigan felt a strange stirring inside her at his words. He had never openly called her his daughter before. She peaked around from behind his leg, her golden eyes shimmering with unshed tears. He met her eyes with a smile. He had said the words so easily and she felt the finality in them. She leaned into his leg and squeezed it with a sweet smile.

Egrim followed Kasha's gaze to the body of the dark elf on the floor, blood dripping from his ears. She sighed. "Is he dead?"

He shrugged. "Maybe."

She looked at the body again and scrunched her face up. "No matter."

Egrim lowered one of his hands and placed it calmly on Morrigan's head, smiling down at her. "What happens now? What do you require of me? Sit? Leave?"

Kasha looked from Egrim to Morrigan. The girl looked strangely comfortable for what had just transpired in front of her. Maybe this giant fool was telling the truth. If she had witnessed their caravan being attacked, then perhaps this wouldn't have shaken her as much as it should have.

"She seems oddly calm about all of this." Her eyes bore into Egrim.

He sighed and looked at the ground briefly. "She has unfortunately seen a lot in her short life. After we lost her mother, I had to do a lot of unsavory things to keep food in her belly. A man with my skills and size only gets offered certain kinds of work. One pays far more than the other. I could not always afford to have morals."

Kasha raised an eyebrow at the blatant honesty. "And what kind of skills are those?"

Egrim nodded his head in the direction of the body on the floor. "That and manual labor."

He could see the uneasy feeling in her posture and it was not fading at all. He held his hands out pleadingly. "We'll leave. Do you want me to bring the city guard here?"

Kasha chuckled sarcastically. "They're already on their way. I sent a raven to them after I heard the first bit of chaos down here. You two are staying here until I can get some answers. If you do not agree to that I will shatter whichever appendage I can blast first." Her outstretched hands flared with hoarfrost. Kasha was very talented in the sorcerous arts, but she had never truly used them in any sort of combat situation greater than scaring the occasional ruffian away. However, she wasn't bluffing.

Egrim kept his hands up and slowly backed up until his legs ran into a chair. He sat down into it as the wood groaned under his weight. Morrigan hopped into his lap. "Then we stay. I don't want to cause any further trouble. I'm not sure how long we will be in the city, and I would rather not make enemies right away."

Morrigan tilted her head and studied the floral pattern on Kasha's satin robe. She wanted to go and trace it but knew better than to approach anyone without Egrim telling her it was alright to do so. Instead, she grabbed the edges of Egrim's duster and pulled them tight around her like she had seen the tiefling woman do a little bit earlier with her robe. She then tugged at his tunic, where the blood stain remained. He pulled her hand away. He didn't want any attention brought to the wound.

"What are your names?" Kasha asked as she backed away slowly to the front door and unlatched it. She then kept an eye on Egrim while she removed the steel bar that braced the door shut and set it on its hook.

"I am Egrim, and this is Morrigan." Morrigan anxiously waved her hand for exactly half of a second before trying to make herself small and disappear in Egrim's lap again.

"Where are you from?" She was interrogating them.

Egrim huffed. "A small village outside Kladhdur in the Brightborn Kingdom." He had etched the lie into his brain several times. It already came naturally.

Kasha nodded. She had never been there, but she knew of the place. "Why did you come to the bloody Scarred Lands? Very few leave the civilized nations in the west to come out here."

"In the interest of good faith and so you can begin to trust me, I will tell it to you true. Shortly after I met my wife and her daughter." He looked down at Morrigan. "We decided to start a small business. An inn. We could not afford the licenses required from Kladhdur. That meant we could not get the loans that were necessary to get started. She was working for a rather vile dwarf in his butcher shop, and she stole enough coin from him to get started. He found out and we went with plan B. Come to the Scarred Lands to start our inn here, in the trade hub of the east. We knew they would not pursue us past the border. It would be more costly than the coin she stole." His face was mournful. "She never made it past the border."

Kasha saw the sadness in his face. Morrigan buried herself further into Egrim's chest. Kasha began to wonder if the girl would try to climb inside him if she could. Had she met them under different circumstances she would have allowed her sympathy to pour out. However, she was not sure if she could believe a single word this man was telling her.

"I am Kasha Volstruk. Owner and operator of this establishment. Well, soon to be opened establishment. The Witch's Tits and Tarts will soon relocate here." She looked to the front door and felt severe irritation that Captain Ethan was not already here with his men. She knew Lemmy had to have made it to him by now and the barracks were only six blocks away.

Egrim smirked. "Interesting name for a business." He already knew why it had that name, but he wanted to hear it described by the owner. "Why is it named that?"

Kasha raised an eyebrow. She thought perhaps she should not entertain his question, but she couldn't help talking about her lucrative enterprise. "It's a tavern."

"I gathered that from the name." He smirked even bigger.

Kasha rolled her eyes with a huff. "We sell tarts, and specialty ales. All of the women are topless. Hence the rest of the name."

Egrim smiled. "I'm sure people think it's the tits."

"Clever." It was as if the man was trying to make her roll her eyes at him, or smile. She wasn't sure.

Neither of them had anything else to say. There would have been a roaring bout of awkward silence except that a banging came at the front door. Kasha opened it. Captain Ethan and four other city guards rushed in with their weapons drawn. Only three of them had their full armor on. Those must have been the ones nearby on night patrol.

Captain Ethan and Sergeant Serine, Ethan's second in command and one of the most serious dwarven women Kasha had ever met, must have been roused from their sleep as they were wearing simple linen pants and disheveled shirts with no shoes to speak of. Sergeant Serine had apparently been in such a hurry that she had not bothered with the top few buttons of her shirt and now had to steal a quick moment to stuff her left breast back in after it broke free from their run over.

"Kasha, are you alright?" Captain Ethan surveyed the area and made a note of the scorch marks, overturned table and the unmoving body on the floor. Then his eyes went wide at the giant of a man that sat at a table peacefully holding a small tiefling girl in his lap, both of whom he had never seen before.

The captain had questioned all involved except for the tiefling girl. Had attempted to question her but she refused to talk. Egrim had explained that she had not spoken since her mother died. Ethan sent one of the men to get a litter to carry the dark elf to the holding cells and another to fetch a physician. And the last guardsmen he had sent to verify the information Egrim had given him with the guards at the forward city gate. Everyone that was not a citizen of Hus'rokn or the Wylds was required to check in with the purpose of the visit. He pulled Kasha aside.

"Well, Kasha. I won't know for sure until my man returns but I think he may be telling the truth. There has been a fair number of raider reports coming out of the Scarred Lands lately." He looked back and out the front door where his men had just left with the dark elf. "While I can't guarantee it, Sergeant Serine and I are pretty sure we've seen that dark elf fellow hanging around Alabaster's estate. You know better than I do that he has a vested interest in scaring you off. That 'mishandling' of permits I arranged for you might end up being more trouble for you than it was worth. That kind of financial loss can cripple people. I fear helping you has put you in a rather large amount of danger. I'll make some careful inquiries. I hear he's been sniffing around the Lance for a loan."

"The Lance? Authern is involved in this bullshit now? Gods dammit." Kasha chewed on her lower lip nervously. "No one knows you're behind the permit mishap, do they? I can't live with them coming after you and your wif-" She caught herself too late an shut her eyes and pressed her lips together at the mistake. "Sorry."

Serine sneered at the mention of the captain's wife. Ex-wife. Ethan let out an uneasy chuckle. "Not as far as I know. But don't worry about me. I have ways of staying safe. Besides, Alabaster doesn't have the clout to reach me as Captain of the Guard."

Kasha rubbed her hands together, somewhat nervous. "No, but the Lance certainly does. If Alabaster allies with them they may decide to do some digging."

Ethan shook his head. "We can worry about all of that if it comes to it, Kasha."

He motioned over to Egrim. "What do you want me to do with him. I can take him to the holding cells for the night, but I can't bring the girl. I suppose I can take her to one of the temples."

Kasha watched the pair. Morrigan looked positively frightened now. Egrim rocked her back and forth and ran his hand over her back. She sighed deeply and crossed her arms. She could see herself in Morrigan. Kasha too, had been a terrified little girl on the streets. Only she had not had anyone to protect her until Sylus Mordath's Traveling Spectacles found her.

"No. If your man verifies his story then I'll let them stay in the backroom for tonight. I can't separate her from him, and they won't find a place to stay at this hour of the night. Just look at her."

Captain Ethan did look but it didn't make him feel better about the situation. "I don't know, Kasha. If he does anything to you in the middle of the night, I'll be joining you in the afterlife shortly after Callus hears that I allowed it to happen."

"Luckily Callus is not my keeper then, isn't it." Her face told him her decision was final.

Sergeant Serine stepped up next to Captain Ethan, suddenly looking as stern and stone faced as if she were in full uniform. "Then we remain here until we receive word from the gate, Ms. Volstruk."

Kasha inclined her head down to her. She truly was fond of Serine. She was a serious woman, but honest and genuine. But that didn't stop her from poking at her from time to time to try and get her to smile at anyone other than Ethan. "You know, Sergeant. If you ever grow tired of guard work, I would gladly hire you here. Those would look lovely with a sugar and cinnamon oil rub. You'd make a lot of coin here."

Ethan and Serine followed Kasha's eyes to Serine's left breast that had begun to somehow wiggle its own way out of her shirt again. Ethan bit his lip as to not laugh and Serine turned a brighter shade of red than Kasha's own skin.

Chapter Four

DREAMS REALIZED

He was trying. He really was, but customer service was not his strong suit. Callus flexed his hand into a fist and relaxed it repeatedly behind the shop counter. The customer had already given him the standard confused expression at seeing a large hobgoblin behind the counter of a shop. Hobgoblins weren't known for being the types to take up merchantry as a profession, especially one with as many scars as Callus. "So...interested or still need to browse?" The look on his face was just past the point of concealing his irritation.

In front of the counter, a man in his middle years and dressed far beyond his station turned over one of Arialyn's newest pieces in his hands, considering. "So, this ring can hold a flame within it, and it never extinguishes? Truly?"

Callus reached across the counter, grabbed the man by the back of the head and slammed him into the counter, shattering the man's nose with a satisfying crack. It had been too long since he had felt the blissful rush of a fight.

"Sir? Are you alright? You seemed to stare right through me for a second there."

Callus shook his head, brought back to reality by the man's query. He blinked his eyes several times, disappointed the interaction had only been in his mind. With a sigh he responded. "Aye, as I have said, at length, the flame within will remain for twenty days' time. On the twenty-first day you will need to hold it to another fire source, and it will absorb a portion of the flame which will then be used for another twenty days."

The man nodded his head slowly. He tried on the ring again, placing it on a few different fingers to see which one seemed the best fit. He held his hand at a distance and glanced at it with squinted eyes. "The gold clashes with my skin tone. Does it come in silver?"

Callus' knuckles cracked and he was bringing his hand up when he was very thankfully interrupted by the one thing that could calm him.

"Love!" Arialyn stepped out from the backroom with a large jar of bolts that radiated a faint blue glow. "I can't get this open. Be a doll and give me a hand, would you?" She looked at him with a face that Callus had become quite familiar with lately. It said, *'Get in the fucking back before you break someone.'*

The sight of her sent waves of calm over him. The love of his life stood there in the doorway, her small gnomish form only coming up to half the door height and his fist lowered and he turned to the man. "If you'll excuse me. My lady will be right with you."

As he passed through the doorway he bent down and kissed her head, taking in the scent of lavender and ginger from her amethyst-tinted hair. Arialyn handed him the jar and grasped his forearm with a smile. "Thank you, my love."

She approached the counter swiftly and energetically stepped up onto the wooden ledge that Callus had built for her to be at a more advantageous height to bargain with customers. "Apologies for the interruption, sir. You had a question?"

He looked at her and then back to the ring on his hand, fingers splayed out for a better view. "On second thought I think the gold will make a bigger splash with the fellows at the temple. How much was it?"

Arialyn smiled. "The Ring of Ever Flame is priced at forty gold pieces, my friend."

His eyes widened. "Forty? Hmm, shame. Too much for me." He slid the ring off and set it back on the counter and turned on his heels. "Thank you for your time."

Arialyn spoke up quickly. "That will make Gringar Lightbearer very happy. He was coming in to snatch this piece up tomorrow." She was gambling. She wasn't sure which temple this man attended, but she was betting it was the Progenitor's Sacred Hall in Hus'rokn. Gringar Lightbearer was one of the lesser priests there, but everyone knew him, and most could not stand the orc.

The man suddenly stopped in his tracks and turned back around. "Gringar, you say?"

Arialyn nodded her head and started to put the ring back in the case as nonchalantly as possible.

He took a step forward. "Now, hold on a minute. I'm having seconds thoughts."

She did her absolute best to hide a mischievous smile and pulled the ring back out slowly. "Are you sure? I thought it was too much?"

The man reached for the ring sheepishly and smirked. "Too much to get just for me. However, to be able to throw it in Gringar's face. That is a different story all together." He reached into his coin purse and quickly counted out the necessary pieces and then set down an extra two. "Thank you so much for this. I can't wait to see his irritation." He set the ring on a finger and quickly turned, speeding out the door.

Arialyn collected the coins and placed them inside an arcane lock box in one of the hidden compartments Callus had built into the ledge she had been standing on. "You can come out now, Callus."

Callus hollered back at her from the rear shop door that opened to the alley behind them. She could hear Callus speaking with someone. She glanced around the shop to make sure there were no other customers inside that she was about to leave unattended and moved into the backroom. She spared a glance at a ratty and tattered spell tome she had acquired from an old wizard that smelled like mildew and regret. There were a few minor incantations in it that had nothing to do with arcanomancy, but she had resolved to try her hands and a few other forms of wielding the arcane.

When she got far enough into the backroom, she saw Callus speaking with Guard Captain Ethan just outside the rear entrance to the shop. The captain had changed both in appearance and demeanor since they first met him several months ago when they arrived in the Wylds by way of the Trade Gate from Hus'rokn. Ethan had nearly fallen over his words at meeting his childhood idol from the arenas. She hadn't seen Callus smile so genuinely about anything other than her until that interaction. The captain was in his late twenties to early thirties. He had close kept hair and a neatly trimmed short beard then. Now he wore his reddish hair at shoulder length and sported mutton chops in a similar fashion to Callus. He was close to Callus's height but a little bit broader of shoulder and abdomen. He no longer openly fanboyed over the hobgoblin, perhaps because of their new business arrangements.

Ethan smiled and bowed his head politely toward Arialyn. "I have your parts delivery, Lady Foghand."

Arialyn smiled warmly and moved to a small cart attached to a dappled draft horse. She lifted up the canvas sheeting that covered the 'parts.' Under the canvas was a handful of boxes and chests of various sizes. She looked up and down the alley in a casual fashion as Callus and Ethan unharnessed the horse from the cart and reharnessed it to an empty cart from the previous delivery.

Seeing nobody moving around she opened one of the boxes and revealed gears layered over the top of some straw to protect the items. She moved them aside gently and pushed the straw out of the way to find the secondary canvas layer. Once she lifted that to the side, she was able to see the true order the captain had brought her. Void ore. Everything from rough chunks to dust in small glass vials. She put everything back into place and covered it all back up.

This was the second shipment that Captain Ethan had arranged for her. She, and Callus for that matter, could never have foreseen Ethan being tied to The Three in Hus'rokn. But as it turns out you can't exactly be the City Guard Captain in a place literally run by organized crime and not be a part of it all. Callus had found out about the man's curious connections one night while out at the Tits and Tarts Tavern. Callus said he had been praising Arialyn's work and then accidentally let it slip that she used void ore in many of her creations but was having a very hard time getting it to the Wylds. The use of void ore for any purpose was still extremely new in Hus'rokn and the Wylds and each city had different opinions on the material, neither were favorable. The Wylds strictly outlawed it and Hus'rokn, at present, did not openly allow the buying, selling or trading of the ore. Although, possession of it was allowed. A few days later, Ethan showed up at their shop with an offer to help them get an ample supply chain set up for a modest fee and the required vow to never speak about it to anyone.

She rejoined the pair and noticed them stiffen slightly. With narrow eyes she asked, "What are you two chatting about so quietly."

They didn't even try to look innocent. Captain Ethan brushed the question away by changing the subject. "Nothing, Lady Foghand. Just prattling on about last week's bruise ball game. Oh, by the way, I'd be a fool to forget. Gauntlet Adenus Oteras sends his regards. To you both and a hearty congratulations on the success of your shop. Although, he still wishes you had opened it within the Hus'rokn walls."

Callus absentmindedly looked down at the ring Adenus had given him well over a decade ago when he won the right to fight for the Northern Scarred Lands Championship. He cocked his head to the side. "How is Adenus fairing?"

"Stressed. There have been some rumbles within The Three ever since the former Lance, Wibbrem, decided to take a permanent vacation. Vanishing to the Brightborn Kingdom for some R&R supposedly. The Gauntlet and Shield are not too keen on Authern's succession to Lance in his stead. Authern is a rattling saber waiting to slip from its sheath. But being one of the Three technically makes him one of my bosses, so you won't see me voicing that to anyone but those I hold in confidence. You'll need to thank Adenus, by the by. He is also the reason this shipment got through. I'll just say there was a slight slip up by some of the Wylds Trade Authority men on the Gauntlet payroll and the only thing that got the ore released back into my hands was Adenus applying some...pressure. You know he was always fond of watching you in the arenas in your early days. As well as your recent-" He feigned a coughing fit as he realized he was talking too much. He had a tendency to word vomit around Callus.

Arialyn narrowed her eyes again. "You shouldn't be telling us any of this right?"

The captain chuckled. "Hells, no. But I'm still clinging to hope that I can get your man here to come join me in some excitement in the future. Maybe get some adrenaline pumping into those old gladiator muscles."

He rushed to the end of his words at the sight of Arialyn fiddling with the arcabus at her hip and glaring at him menacingly.

Callus smiled wide and sheepishly.

With a shake of her head Arialyn put the conversation to rest. "Parts look good, captain. Thank you as always."

He bowed again. "Same time in three weeks?"

Arialyn cracked her knuckles. "Yes, but can you see about getting your hands on some void ore from a cinnabar vein? I have some new project ideas I'm itching to work on, and they require that particular type of ore."

The captain placed his hands on his hips and pursed his lips with a whistle. "If I had any idea what the bloody hells that meant, then sure. I'll just relay that request through my contacts. I'm sure they'll know what to look for. Remind me what that one is good for again?"

She looked mildly disappointed at his response but perked up a little when he asked what the void ore that emerged from cinnabar could be used for. She absolutely loved to talk about anything related to arcanomancy. "Void ore that comes from cinnabar is good for increasing arcane potency. I can use the stuff that comes from iron since it is a decent catchall, but it is far less effective and is the only ore that loses its potency over time."

"I'll see what I can do. Well, I best be off. Oh! I can't believe I nearly forgot." He moved to the horse's saddlebag and produced a cloth-covered object before handing it over to Arialyn. "Your copy of The Briar Codex."

She greedily plucked it from the captain's hands and removed the cloth. There in her hands was a rare copy of *The Briar Codex, A Listing of Protective Charms and Plant Based Arcana*. The book was a deep green and bound by vines. It was the one book on nature and primal arcana that she had cared for back home in the Fold of the Silver Cedar all those years ago. It also happened to be the only one she had any luck in understanding and wielding a fraction of what she studied.

"Thank you, captain." She said without taking her eyes off the tome.

Captain Ethan climbed back on to the horse. "See you tonig-later, Callus. See you later." His face fell flat for a moment before he turned and rode off.

"Are you going to tell me what you two were talking about while I was inspecting OUR goods?" Arialyn asked as she opened the large rolling panel door to the shop so Callus could unload the boxes.

"I think it best that I do not." He said with a smile.

She knew what he was up to. He had come home several times now with small bruises and a few cuts and scrapes. The 'squabble at a tavern' excuse no longer worked. He was fighting again. She didn't know where and honestly; she did not care. He needed it. It brought him some happiness and made him feel a bit like the man he was before the Helspires. She didn't need him to tell her that. What she did have a bit of a problem with was the dear captain trying to get Callus to join him in some of his dealings with The Three. They are more cloak and dagger, and politics compared to the Talons of Misery's brutality and violence, but the parallels were there, and she could see that Callus was mildly interested despite him voicing to the contrary.

Callus changed the subject and moved to apologize for the customer interaction earlier. "Sorry about earlier with that asshole, squirt. Sleep has been hard to come by what with helping Kasha with all her renovations." He lifted her up and stood her on the last unloaded box. Even on the box she only stood chest high to him. She slipped her arms under his open green leather vest and got up on her tiptoes to kiss him. "I told you to stop calling me that."

Callus enveloped her around the shoulders and placed his lips on her forehead. "If you don't like the nickname then stop doing the thing that earned it all the ti-AHH!"

She jabbed him in the ribs sternly. "Maybe I take away role play night then?"

"Hey! Let's not get carried away." He looked down at her and saw the look of irritated, albeit playful pleading in her eyes. "Fine. I'll stop."

She pulled away from him. "Good boy." She poked his nose with a 'boop' sound to accent it. "Well, ready to close up shop and head over to her? She said the decorators should be coming tomorrow I think or maybe it was in a few days. Honestly, with all the changes she has made last minute, I have no idea what she said."

Callus sighed. "Why did I agree to payment in tarts again?"

She smacked him on the arm. "Because I told you payment in tits was off the table. Now lock up back here and go get your things. I'll secure the front of the shop."

Callus closed the back panel door and went upstairs to their home. Arialyn slowly made her way to the front of the shop, looking all around her as she did. Her last shop in Toz'Unro had only lasted a few weeks and before that all she ever had was a small cart and portable stall. This one, The Amethyst Artificer, had been open for nearly five months already and she dared to dream that this one would last. The Wylds were peaceful for the most part, nestled between a raging river to the north and south, open sea to the east and access to Hus'rokn in the west via the Trade Gate. There was crime in these parts, to be sure, but it was organized and nothing in comparison to the lawlessness in the west parts of the Scarred Lands that her and Callus had fled from not so long ago.

She smiled wide and allowed a few tears of gratefulness to drop before stowing them away for now. Opening the front door to the shop she looked up and down the streets. It was around midday on Progendra, the last day of the five-day long week, and the day most people rested. So, the streets were thin. She ran her hands over the shop sign Callus had carved. A light, brown-stained wooden sign in the shape of a wrench with the words *The Amethyst Artificer* in a deep purple. She had struggled to name their shop, and he took it upon himself to register this with the Council of Commerce under Trade Princess Shelani. When he unveiled it to her, she had cried at the sweet gesture for nearly ten whole minutes. She turned the open sign around, so it read closed and went back in and locked the front door.

Callus was standing in the backroom doorway with a satchel and a smirk. "Still can't believe it, can you?"

Arialyn shook her head. "No, I don't think I can. What we've built here is... wonderful."

Callus wore a face of mock pain. "You thought I meant the shop? I meant how splendid it must be to have someone as glorious to look upon as myself around all the time. But that's fine...it's fine." He sighed and dropped his shoulders pathetically.

She rolled her eyes with a giggle. "You're a lot. You know that?"

He started slowly backstepping, heading toward the back door. "I know. I know." He stopped in his tracks and that damn mischievous grin of his spread across his face. "Ready squirt?" He bolted out the back.

Arialyn's eyes were fire. "You motherfucker!"

Kasha stood near the center of the large dining area and paced backward until she was leaning against the bar. The front door to the tavern was open and a cool breeze blew in, causing her auburn brown hair to fall away from her horns and into her face. She breathed in the fresh air with a smile and then smoothed out her long white floral sundress. She pushed her hair back over her ears and horns and then flicked her fingers in a smooth practiced motion to each of the sconces in the great room.

All of them, in turn, flared back to full illuminated vitality with a steely blue arcane flame.

This main room alone was nearly three times the size of the original Witch's Tits & Tarts Tavern in its entirety. Mother Maudrid, Bright One rest her soul, had secretly been a bit of a hoarder when it came to her coin. Her will, which she had placed with the Council of Commerce in the Wylds, bequeathed all her wealth to one Kasha Volstruk. Kasha had been floored by not only the amount of coin but that she had left it all to her and not Callus. When she protested that he should be the one to acquire everything he refused and told her there was no reason for Mother Maudrid to have ever expected to see him again and that she had made the right choice. After that she tried to split it with him, and he outright refused. He could not, however, stop her from splitting it with Arialyn.

The new space was going to be everything she had always wanted that the old space had prevented due to its smaller floor plan. Everything was nearly done now. The hard dark wood pillars had been polished and the wooden wall slats properly nailed and seated. All the damage from the fire months ago, fully wiped clean. The decorators would be coming early tomorrow morning to finalize all the final details.

Behind her she heard the back door opening and quickly turned to look into the mirror behind the bar top. The red-skinned tiefling that stared back at her in the mirror was naturally beautiful, although she would never think so. In fact, for most of her life she had done everything she could, short of an aesthetic sawbones, to improve her appearance. She hurriedly made sure her eyebrows weren't flaring, that her wavy auburn hair was falling over her shoulders just right and that her skirt spilled perfectly over her hips. She saw a tarnished spot on the gold seam that held her once broken left horn together and licked her finger to rub away the smudge. No matter what she did, that smudge would not go away, although those she asked about it claimed they could not even see it. She told herself that she obsessed over her appearance because she ran an establishment that benefited from looking your best. There were, however, other reasons that she refused to come to terms with.

Right as she finished, Egrim walked in from the back carrying three crates of wine bottles under his left arm and a pony keg of ale over his right shoulder. She took in his appearance while managing to appear nonchalant in her demeanor. His head was cleanly shaven again, and his black beard neatly kept in three separate foot-long braids that trailed down his lightly tanned chest. He wore dark leather pants and thick black calf high boots. He had been moving boxes, crates and kegs all morning and his naked torso was covered in sweat, several small scrapes and splinters from the wooden crates. Black inked tattoos of various designs and symbols dappled most of his chest, abdomen and arms in a way that could almost make you unaware of the thick hair that was only adding to the heat from outside. He set the wine crates down gently on the bar top and placed the keg in the cabinet under the bar back mirror.

Kasha eyed him with playful haughtiness. "Egrim, you're getting sweat all over my newly stained wood."

He laughed her off and stood straight, cracking his back in the process. "Well, you can either help with the lifting, oil my chest up like you do the serving girls and hope it protects the wood or keep your mouth closed. I suppose you could fire me as well."

She giggled and inclined her head, placing a hand on her cocked hip. "Fine, I'll fetch the oil. We should probably shave all that chest hair off first, though. Best to make the tits pop."

Egrim's mouth dropped open. Kasha always found the way his mouth curled around the scar on his lip amusing in a fiendishly cute way. Which was why she used every chance she could to fluster him. It was like a secret game she played with herself.

He quickly collected himself. "If I see a razor come anywhere near me, I'll carry you to that raging river around the Wylds and throw you in it with all the crates." He sat on one of the stools and wiped his brow.

Kasha grabbed a cloth and a bottle of mead. She brought them over and wiped his brow with a smile before handing the cloth over to him. He grabbed the bottle, about to pull the cork out with his teeth when Kasha smacked his hand. He narrowed his eyes and then pulled it with his hands in an exaggerated bowing gesture for her approval. She placed her hand over the lip of the bottle and frost extended from her finger and down into the now cold liquid.

"Thank you, Madame." His tone was haughty, and he threw back half the bottle right away.

From the opposite side of the bar top, she leaned over on her elbows, holding her chin in her hands. "This is going to be a classy establishment my dear ruffian. Best start acting proper." She smiled at his raised eyebrow.

Egrim glared at her again. "You saying I'm not proper?"

"I would never dare to accuse a beast of a man of being improper...unless of course it is a time where he should be." She caught herself being overly flirtatious and immediately changed the subject. "Are you sure you are okay staying on with me as my muscle? You're okay with Morrigan being in here all the time?"

He shook his head slightly with a smirk. "Why do you keep asking me this? I told you I would."

Kasha shrugged. "Well, there is nothing keeping you here and everything you have told me about your life involves traveling. Just makes sense that you would not stay long."

In truth Kasha was testing the waters. Trying to see if she could allow herself to be attached to someone new, a friend that would not leave when things got rough or when new opportunities presented themselves. Her life was filled with those that left her or quit caring for her enough to stay around. She had found people to love and friendships to hold dear with the Traveling Spectacles, but even that didn't last.

After Sylus took the Traveling Spectacles to the Helspires to follow Callus's gladiatorial career, she parted ways with them all. She had no interest in going back to that wretched cesspool of a city. Since then, she had never had any stable friendships except for the one failed romance that she always tried her best not to think about. But of course, that meant she always thought about it. It was that very relationship she kept secret from everyone. That very relationship that still guided her every move when meeting potential new friends or more.

Callus and Arialyn were here now, and that brought her more joy than she was used to. Yet still, they had each other. She, unfortunately, had become accustomed to hiding her loneliness from everyone.

Egrim paused for a moment, as if he was listening for something, and then looked around the nearly finished tavern. He looked down to his chest for a second, in thoughtful contemplation about something and then looked back into Kasha's shing hazel eyes. "We're good here. For now."

Kasha came around the counter and hugged him from the side. Her arms draped around him the best they could, but his shoulders were far too large for her to accomplish a full embrace. "Thank you, Egrim."

He smiled and leaned his head against her horns. The smile faded away faster than he wanted it to. He wasn't lying to Kasha. He truly was good here, with her. If it were up to him alone, he could see himself staying here permanently. The tavern life would be a much easier life than the one he had signed up for before coming here. But he knew at some point he would have to leave. Sooner or later, they would be found. But for now, he would enjoy the time he had here with Kasha and his daughter.

Had it not been for the raucous cawing of an albino raven emerging from a room upstairs, flying from the mezzanine and down to the bar top they would not have noticed Morrigan's silent descent of the stairs. She rubbed the sleep out of her eyes and scratched behind her horns. Her nightgown was disheveled, and her hair was a rat's nest of tangles. She looked like a thing from the darkest forests.

Egrim threw his arms out and stood in front of Kasha in a protective stance. He turned his eyes to the raven. "Lemmy, fear not. It appears to be a cryptid from the wastes. Perhaps it's just hungry."

Kasha giggled outright and even Lemmy cackled at Egrim's tomfoolery, hoping from one talon to the other. Morrigan was the only one to not be into the joke. Nightmares haunted her most nights. She curled her tail around to the front of her waist, something she had always found comforting and gripped it tight as her lips began to quiver.

Egrim stopped the act immediately and squatted down with his arms outstretched. "Oh, my sweetness. Come here."

Morrigan ran to him and threw her arms around his thick neck. He stood with her cradled in his massive arms. "I'm sorry. I didn't know it happened again. I've got you." He ran his hand over her head between her budding horns, and she rested it against his chest. Something she immediately regretted, since the side of her face was assaulted by sweat. She recoiled off him slightly and wiped her face with her hands. He couldn't help but chuckle a little at the look on her face. Thankfully the act somewhat changed her mood as she smacked his arm playfully and then folded her own arms in a pout.

Kasha stood back a little and smiled at them. A brief mask of sadness crossed her face, and this caught Lemmy's attention. He took flight to her shoulder and perched there with a nuzzle of his beak against her cheek and then bobbed his head toward Morrigan. Kasha looked at the pair with a mixture of sorrow and restrained longing. This time he bit her ear and bobbed his head more forcefully.

She moved behind the bar and opened one of the lower cabinets. She always kept excess and spare beauty items there. Grabbing a stunning silver hairbrush, she moved to the bar top. "Can I give your hair a brushing, Morrigan?"

Morrigan turned to Egrim as if to look for permission. It wasn't permission to go to Kasha, however. It was for permission to trust her. He looked at her with a sincere smile and smoothed her hair back over her horns, whispering to her. "You don't have to look to me for permission, Morrigan. You can always trust Kasha. She's a lovely woman. Go on if you want to."

With that, Morrigan nodded enthusiastically at Kasha and climbed from Egrim's arms to the bar top. She sat down facing away from her and watching the people passing by in the street through the open front door. Kasha slowly and cautiously began brushing her hair and untangling the knots that had formed in the poor girl's sleep.

Egrim leaned back against the counter and cracked his back with a satisfied groan. "Not much more to carry in. I'll be done shortly. What needs doing after that?"

Kasha was lost in the moment of brushing out Morrigan's hair. She remembered Mother Maudrid doing the same for her even when she was a teenager. Her hair used to get dreadfully tangled when she would do her fire dancing for the Traveling Spectacle shows. Egrim was about to tap her on the shoulder and ask her again but then withdrew and softly smiled before heading out to the rest of the work that needed to be done.

Morrigan alternated kicking her legs out and poking Lemmy with her tail. Lemmy hopped excitedly and playfully tried to dodge the improvised weapon. Her hair was nearly knot free when her eyes went wide, and her face perked up. Kasha mimicked the same mood as the low hum of Arialyn's stormer echoed in the street. Morrigan was already halfway to the door, brush stuck in the last of the tangles, when Callus and Arialyn came into view on the contraption.

Stormers were still a relatively new creation in the Scarred Lands. They were arcane mechanical constructs that carried a variety of seating arrangements depending on the owner's needs and preferences. But they all shared the same three points on contact to the ground, a round wheel in the front and two tread belts on either side of the back. Arialyn brought the stormer to a stop in front of the Witch's Tits and Tarts. Callus immediately hopped up and swung his leg over Arialyn to get off the stormer. She scowled at him but couldn't help the small rise of a smile at the corner of her mouth.

Callus squatted down and remained in a neutral position as Morrigan approached him. Morrigan had not only gotten used to seeing them both but was always extremely excited. However, she was still slow to fully trust the situation every time they showed up. She stopped just before him and dropped her eyes to the floor, picking at her nightgown.

Callus held out his hand to her. "Good afternoon, Lady Morrigan. Your hair looks absolutely stunning today."

She looked up and smiled ear to ear. Carefully she placed her hand in his and he slowly wrapped his fingers around hers, squeezing it reassuringly before letting go. "You have a stowaway it seems."

He reached up and with a zephyrlike movement, pulled the brush from her hair. He handed it to her and leaned in a little. "Are you keeping your daddy in line? Making sure he works hard?"

She sheepishly looked away and nodded her head.

Immediately after she began touching the silver metallic brace on his left arm. She always liked to trace the void gems and their sockets. Callus had once removed the brace to show her how little movement he had in his arm when he wasn't wearing it, similar to the one on his right leg. She was baffled by the contraptions that Arialyn had made for him.

Arialyn came up behind him and stopped by his side. She bumped him in the shoulder with her hip, and he plopped over onto his rear. It was his turn to glare playfully at his love. Morrigan found it amusing and snickered with her hand covering her mouth. Lemmy found it to be hilarious and cawed wildly while pouncing on Callus and fluttering his wings about.

Arialyn was of a similar height to Morrigan and this, they had discovered, made her acclimate to her faster than anyone else other than her father. She held her arms wide and Morrigan slowly came to her and hugged her loosely at first, but slowly tightened her arms briefly before letting go. Arialyn gently held her hand and squeezed it softly before Morrigan ran over to a table in the corner with Lemmy who began grabbing and tossing two of the small canvas dolls Egrim had bought Morrigan last week. Arialyn moved over to meet Kasha by the bar top. "She still hasn't said anything?"

Kasha bent low and hugged Arialyn, kissing her cheek. "Not a word. Egrim says she used to talk relentlessly before they lost her mother. Apparently, he used to wish she would be quiet for just a day. Now he wishes that she would say something, anything. He believes it's a coping mechanism. I wish he would tell me more, but he still won't talk about exactly what happened."

"Maybe with a little more time and stability in her environment she'll decide she can." Arialyn said as she looked around the new and nearly finished Tits and Tarts.

Callus approached and Lemmy flew to his shoulder. "Hey buddy. I got you something."

Lemmy squawked with excitement.

"Entrails! Your favorite!" He said mockingly.

Lemmy shook his head in irritation and pecked at Callus's temple. "Calm down. I'm kidding. Here." Callus pulled a linen wrapped bundle from his pocket and unwrapped it. Lemmy hopped up and down on

Callus's shoulder at the sight of a piece of deer liver and then snatched it from his hand before flying up into the rafters to feast.

"Do not get blood stains on the new wood!" Kasha cried out before sighing and looking square at Callus with mock disdain. She welcomed Callus with an embrace and an exchange of kisses on cheeks. She stepped back and looked at him and Arialyn then spun around in a circle with her arms out as if unveiling the new tavern for the first time. "So, what do you both think? Paintings and drapes are being brought in tomorrow as well as a wood carver for a few reliefs I have in mind, but other than that it's all done!"

Callus chuckled at Kasha's excitement. "Dear, you know we were here two days ago. We already told you it looks wonderful."

Arialyn smacked him in the side. "Don't be an ass. She's excited!" She turned to Kasha. "It is a treasure to behold." She turned and looked up at the mezzanine and the four doors that followed one after the other from the top of the stairs. "Are you still thinking of renting those four out to...ladies of the night?"

"Whores. What? I'm not judging." Callus chimed in. He thought to remind them that he had been used in the same fashion for a short time in Toz Unro for higher end women at the Lush Tulips but then thought better of it.

This time they both smacked him.

"Morrigan, did you see that. They assaulted me. Again!" Callus rubbed the ache from his sides.

Morrigan laughed and jumped up onto one of the barstools. She wagged a mockingly disappointed finger at the ladies and then playfully patted the bar top as if to say, *'Barkeep. Another round.'*

Kasha shook her head with a grin and reached under the bar. She grasped a metallic rod that stuck out from the top of a large, insulated box and released arcane frost into it. Arialyn had developed this just for Kasha. All Kasha needed to do was infuse the cooling box with her own arcane frost every few days and anything inside would be nice and chilled. She poured a cold glass of goat's milk and slid it over to Morrigan.

Callus had recovered at this point. "I'm going to go see if Egrim needs some help." He turned and exited to the backroom.

The women giggled after he was out of ear shot. Kasha sighed. "Actually, I already have three of the four rooms spoken for. Two of the women were very amenable to the pricing and terms. I had to negotiate a little harder with the goblin woman, Mufz. A male, human, is coming by later to discuss terms for the fourth room."

"Mufz? Does she?" Arialyn pointed discretely toward her crotch.

Kasha nearly chortled. "It's an absolute forest down there." She shrugged. "To each their own, I suppose."

"What about bouncers? Did Egrim agree?" Arialyn asked.

"Yes, he says they're happy here." The look on her face didn't match her words and Arialyn picked up on it. Kasha could see a question coming, and one Morrigan didn't need to be around for. "Morrigan, sweetness, how about you go ahead and go back upstairs and get changed into some day clothes?"

Morrigan gave a small look of defiance but then immediately gave in and trudged upstairs to her room. Lemmy followed her in and began to roll around on the bed, much to Morrigan's amusement.

Once the door closed Arialyn queued up her question. "What is it?"

Kasha stole a glance at the backroom and then leaned onto the counter. "I don't know. I believe he wants to stay, but it's almost like he doesn't believe it himself. He's still quiet about his past. That could very well just be him trying to avoid dealing with the loss of Morrigan's mother. I clearly trust him enough to let him stay here, and he did stop Alabaster's bloody arsonist from burning the place down before I could even get any organization going on in here."

Arialyn considered for a moment. "You know Callus has been spending a fair amount of time with him. He's been watching him like a hawk, trying to figure him out. He's not going to let just anyone get close to you. He thinks the man is just dealing with some heavy emotions and doesn't feel like he's in a place to process them yet. You know as well as I do that Callus knows a thing or two about that. Hells, we all do. You know, he still breaks down on occasion when something reminds him of Mother Maudrid."

Kasha nodded and chewed her lips nervously.

Arialyn bounced a raised eyebrow at that. "Other than him being an intimidating presence for any patron of the tavern with ill intent, is there perhaps another reason you want him to stay?"

Kasha felt heat rise in her face and was thankful her skin was already red. "What? No. No, I don't want to get attached to anyone. I'm far too busy to be able to give anyone the attention they deserve."

"If you say so." Arialyn wasn't buying Kasha's words and considered pushing her to be honest, but the thought was broken up by Sergeant Serine's stiff footfalls coming in through the front door.

Serine was pristinely dressed in the full uniform of the city guard. Her dress blues were perfectly situated and pleated in the proper Regulations of Hus'rokn City Guard Handbook fashion. Her blonde hair was neatly tied back in a braided bun and her steel shoulder pauldrons, bracers and chest plate were polished so fine that they nearly sparkled even in the low light of the tavern. The only thing about her that did not seem to quite fit with the professional guard motif was the smatter of freckles across the bridge of her nose and cheeks, all of which made her seem younger than she was. She approached the women and stopped a few feet away before bowing lightly.

"Lady Arialyn, a pleasure to see you as always." She said with a straight back.

Arialyn had asked Ethan how the hell he managed to get along with someone so starch assed. He had laughed and said she was actually quite funny behind closed doors but more importantly, she was the most loyal person he had ever known. Arialyn nodded back. "Sergeant Serine."

With that Serine turned her attention to Kasha. "Lady, sorry, Madame Kasha. We have completed the report on the latest threat to you and your establishment."

Kasha sighed at the tone Serine had in her voice and she knew immediately that the news was going to be the same as it always was. Ever damn time. "Inconclusive. Is that what you are going to tell me Sergeant?"

Serine frowned. "Yes. Unfortunately. As far as speculation goes the captain and I are both certain the dead rats were left by Alabaster's men. However, we cannot find anything to trace it back to him. Are you certain there is no one else in the city that would have it out for you for any reason? Any reason at all?"

Kasha had begun to grow accustomed to the runaround with the threats she had been receiving. Every time something happened it was a dead end. The dead rats, the broken windows, graffiti, even the asshole that was stalking her a few weeks back. All of it was investigated and none of it could be linked back to Alabaster Jakel. The only time they had ever actually caught anyone was the dark elf that Egrim had stopped several months back. She could not blame the city guard though. She trusted Captain Ethan and knew he and Serine were doing everything they could to find links to Alabaster. They all knew they were there, but he was, unfortunately, a very careful son of a bitch.

"No, Sergeant Serine. No one that I can possibly think of. At least no one that would go to these lengths to try and scare me." Kasha moved to the bar and poured herself a glass of something amber colored.

Sergeant Serine relaxed her shoulders. "I'm sorry Kasha. We are doing everything we can. He's just too damn careful."

Kasha smiled calmly. "I know. Please let me know if you find anything else out."

Serine nodded to her. "You have my word. I bid you ladies good day." With that, Serine returned to the street, very quickly noting something askew on a merchant's wagon and hollering after him about a safety violation.

Kasha slammed her drink back, poured herself another one and then offered one to Arialyn. They sipped them in the quiet ambiance of the tavern with the noise of the street and Morrigan's laughter upstairs, the only noises heard. Kasha sighed and faced the back wall mirror behind the bar and tightened her face in exasperation. That damned smudge on her horn wouldn't go away. She moved in closer and eyed it while trying to rub it away with her thumb. She felt a swift wave of panic that dispersed quickly thanks to Arialyn's voice.

"Kasha, there is nothing there. Stop fussing over it."

CHAPTER FIVE

BEAUTY IS DEEPER THAN IT SEAMS

*T*he Summer Spark Festival blazed around them in a symphony of colored lanterns and crackling bonfires. Kasha's laughter rang out as she stumbled slightly, leaning into Callus's arm for support. Her hazel eyes caught the firelight as she tilted her head back in mirth.

"I still can't believe you actually threw him out into the crowd." She giggled, her cheeks flushed from excitement and perhaps a bit too much festival wine. "The look on his face when he landed in the dirt!"

Callus grinned, his young face unmarked by the scars that would later define him. At seventeen, he was already broad-shouldered and tall, but there was still a boyish quality to his features that made his smile infectious. "Did you see how he tried to get back up? Like a turtle flipped on its shell."

They were interrupted by a group of children who came running up, their eyes wide with hero worship. "Callus! Callus! Can you sign my program?" A young human boy thrust a crumpled piece of parchment toward him.

"And mine!" A halfling girl bounced on her toes, waving her own program.

Callus's face lit up with genuine pleasure. "Of course! What are your names?"

As he knelt down to their level, carefully signing each program with a charcoal stick, more people began to notice. Adults started gathering, offering congratulations and praise for his fifth consecutive victory in the arena.

"Brilliant footwork tonight, lad!"

"You've got a real future ahead of you!"

"My coin was well placed on you, boy!"

The crowd grew larger, pressing closer, and Kasha found herself pushed to the periphery. She watched Callus handle the attention with grace, but she could feel her chest tightening. The noise seemed to grow louder, the faces more intrusive. Her tail curled around her waist instinctively as she took a step back.

Callus glanced up from signing another autograph and immediately noticed her discomfort. Without hesitation, he stood and raised his hands with a warm smile.

"Thank you all so much for your kind words and support," His voice carrying easily over the crowd. "It means the world to me, truly. But I'm out enjoying the festival with my friend tonight, so we'll be moving along. I hope you all have a wonderful evening and come back to see me next month!"

The crowd began to disperse with good-natured grumbles and final congratulations. As the last of them wandered away, Callus immediately moved to Kasha's side.

"Thank you," The relief was evident in her voice.

He pulled her close, wrapping his arm around her shoulders. "Always."

They wandered deeper into the festival, the tension melting away as they lost themselves in the celebration. Callus proved his skill extended beyond the arena when he won her a stuffed owlbear at a ring toss game, presenting it with an exaggerated bow that made her laugh until her sides ached.

At a jewelry vendor's stall, he insisted on buying her a delicate silver bracelet adorned with tiny bells that chimed softly with her movements. "So I can always find you in a crowd." He said with a grin.

In return, she purchased a crown of summer flowers from an elderly gnome woman, standing on her tiptoes to place it carefully on his head. The yellow and orange blooms looked absurd against his red skin and dark hair, but he wore it with pride.

"How do I look?" He asked as he struck a regal pose.

"Like the most ridiculous gladiator in all the Scarred Lands," Kasha replied, but her eyes were soft with affection.

As the evening deepened, the festival's magic seemed to weave around them like a spell. They found themselves sitting on a low stone wall overlooking the main square, sharing a bag of honey-glazed nuts and watching the dancers spin around the central bonfire. The flower crown had long since fallen from Callus's head, but Kasha's bracelet still chimed softly with every gesture.

"You know," Kasha's voice seemed softer, more intimate in the flickering light. "I used to think the arena was just another show. Just entertainment."

Callus turned to look at her, noting the serious tone. "And now?"

"Now I see how much it means to you. How much you put into it." She shifted closer to him on the wall, their shoulders touching. "You're not just fighting for the crowd. You're fighting for something deeper."

The warmth in her voice made his chest tighten in a way that had nothing to do with combat. "Kasha, I—"

"There's something I've been wanting to tell you." She interrupted, her hazel eyes meeting his. The bells on her bracelet chimed as she reached for his hand. "Something I've fought saying for—"

"Well, well. If it isn't the golden boy himself."

The harsh voice cut through their moment like a blade. Four figures approached from the shadows between the festival stalls—a burly orc with filed teeth, a scarred human with a limp, a wiry halfling whose eyes glittered with malice, and a dark elf whose elegant features were twisted with anger.

Callus was on his feet instantly, placing himself between the group and Kasha. His relaxed festival demeanor vanished, replaced by the coiled readiness the man that would one day be known as the Hobgoblin Reaver. "Gentlemen. Enjoying the festival?"

The orc spat into the dirt. "Not so much, thanks to you, boy. Lost a lot of coin tonight because of your little performance."

"My performance?" Callus's voice remained level, but Kasha could see the tension in his shoulders. "I won. Cleanly. What's your complaint?"

The human stepped forward, his limp more pronounced as he favored his left leg. "Our complaint is that we were told you'd take a dive and yield. Had it on good authority you needed the coin and would play along."

Callus's laugh was sharp and humorless. "Then someone played you for fools. No one approached me about throwing anything, because anyone with half a brain knows I'd never do that. Whoever told you that was clearly trying to swindle you and apparently they were successful."

The dark elf's hand moved to the knife at his belt. "You calling us liars, gladiator?"

"I'm calling you marks." Callus replied, his stance shifting subtly. "Someone saw you coming from a mile away and fed you a story to separate you from your gold. But that's not my problem."

The halfling circled to the side, trying to flank them. "Maybe we make it your problem. Four against one seems like better odds than you're used to."

Kasha felt her hands begin to tremble as arcane frost stirred beneath her skin, her heart hammering against her ribs.

"If you think four is enough then you haven't been watching my fights closely." Callus said flatly. "Walk away now, and we'll pretend this conversation never happened."

The orc cracked his knuckles. "Or what, pretty boy?"

Callus smiled, and it wasn't pleasant. "Or you'll realize you'd have been safer in the arena where we aren't allowed to kill in a normal fight."

The human and halfling rushed Callus simultaneously, clearly expecting their numbers to overwhelm him. They were wrong.

Callus sidestepped the human's clumsy charge and drove his elbow into the man's temple, dropping him instantly. The halfling tried to tackle his legs, but Callus caught him mid-leap and hurled him into a nearby stack of crates. The crash of splintering wood and scattered trinkets echoed between the buildings as the halfling crumpled among the debris.

In the chaos, Kasha raised her hands as frost began to coalesce around her fingers. She aimed at the dark elf, but the orc was faster than his bulk suggested. His massive arm wrapped around her throat just as she released the bolt, sending the shard of ice wide into the darkness.

"Stop!" The orc's voice boomed as cold steel pressed against Kasha's neck. "One more move and I open her throat!"

Callus froze, his hands raised. The dark elf smiled viciously as he drew his blade, while the human struggled to his feet, blood streaming from his nose. Even the halfling was stirring among the wreckage.

"That's better," the orc growled. "Now you're going to learn some respect."

Callus met Kasha's terrified eyes and slowly lowered his hands. "You fucking cowards. Let her go."

The three conscious attackers converged on him. Fists and boots rained down as Callus curled into a defensive position, taking the beating to keep Kasha safe. Blood flowed from his split lip and a gash above his eye.

"I want my pound of flesh." The orc snarled, eager to join the violence.

With casual brutality, he hurled Kasha against the stone wall. The sickening crack of her horn breaking was followed immediately by her agonized scream that cut through the Callus like a blade.

Something primal and terrible awakened in Callus. The beating stopped mattering. The pain disappeared. There was only rage—pure, incandescent fury that showed signs of the man that would one day become the ruthless Hobgoblin Reaver.

He erupted from the ground like a force of nature. His knee caved in the halfling's skull before the small man could react. The human tried to run, but Callus caught him, snapping his arm in three places before driving one of the protruding bones up into the man's own throat. The dark elf managed to thrust forward with his knife but Callus batted it away and shattered his knee with a roundhouse kick just before grabbing the dark elf in a guillotine headlock and twisting it with a snap that sounded like kindling.

The orc backed away, suddenly understanding how seriously he and his friends had fucked up. "Now wait just a—"

A shard of ice punched through his back with enough force to emerge from his chest. The orc's eyes went wide with shock as he looked down at the crystalline spike protruding from his heart. He toppled forward, dead before he hit the ground.

Callus spun to see Kasha standing behind the orc, tears streaming down her face as she cradled the broken piece of her horn in her other hand. Blood trickled from where it had snapped, staining her festival dress.

"Don't look at me," she whispered, her voice breaking. "I'm hideous now. Please don't look."

The sound of approaching boots and shouted orders echoed from the main square. The city guard was coming.

Without hesitation, Callus scooped up both Kasha and the broken horn fragment, cradling her against his chest as he ran into the maze of festival stalls and shadows, heading for the safety of the Traveling Spectacles' camp.

The dice clattered across the small wooden table as Mother Maudrid scooped up her winnings with a satisfied grunt. "That's another three silvers you owe me, you pointy eared peacock."

Sylus adjusted his ornate sleeves and reached for his coin purse. "Your luck tonight is positively supernatural, Maudrid. Are you certain you're not cheating? Should I check you for gambling charms?"

"The only thing I'm cheating is death by boredom listening to that damn mercenary prattle on about proper ale brewing techniques and blasted goat husbandry." Mother Maudrid rolled the dice again, her weathered hands surprisingly deft. "Do you know what that horse's ass told me today? That I was storing my medicinal herbs wrong because they weren't in alphabetical order. Alphabetical! As if the healing properties of moonwort give a damn about coming after lavender in some scholar's dusty tome."

"Carl is purposefully trying to get a rise out of you. Or perhaps he is flirting with you?"

"I'd rather have one of his goats between these old legs. What he is trying to do is drive me to an early grave." She spat out while counting the pips on her dice.

"Firstly Maudrid, an early grave?" Sylus smiled wickedly.

"You little... you know what? The next time you have tea I'm going to make sure that it has something in it to keep that little worm of yours from growing ever again."

Sylus held up a placating hand. "Carl is an old friend. He's been with the Bloody Ale Company for a long time. You don't have to worry about him trying to take up a stable residence here. He's a company man. Besides he brought Callus to me. He saved the boy. Perhaps you could—"

"Perhaps I could what? Smile and bat my lashes at the bastard and giggle like the rest of the girls around here?" She huffed and crossed her arms. "Next you'll be telling me to let him alphabetize my ritual components. 'Excuse me, Mother Maudrid, but shouldn't the salamander scales come before the troll bile?' Bah!"

Sylus was about to respond when shouting erupted outside the caravan. Both of them froze as the commotion grew louder, multiple voices calling out in alarm and concern.

"What in the seven hells—" Sylus rose quickly and moved to the door.

He yanked it open just as Callus appeared at the bottom of the steps, Kasha cradled in his arms. Blood stained her festival dress, and she was clutching something against her chest while tears streamed down her face. Behind them, several members of the Traveling Spectacles had gathered—Balon the fire mage wringing his hands nervously, Xessia the acrobat with her face pale with worry, and old Henrik the animal trainer holding back his trained bears who were agitated by the scent of blood.

"Bright One preserve us!" Mother Maudrid nearly shrieked as she pushed past Sylus. "Callus, bring her in here immediately!"

Callus didn't need to be told twice. He carried Kasha up the steps and into the caravan, gently setting her down on Sylus's plush bed. The elderly healer immediately began fussing over Kasha like a motherly hen, her hands moving with swiftly to assess every part of her.

"Shh, child. Let me see. Let me see what's happened." Mother Maudrid's voice had transformed from its usual gruffness to something much more gentle. It was the only tone she ever used with Kasha. "You're safe now. You're with us."

Sylus closed the door behind them and turned to Callus, his face grave with concern. "What happened, son?"

Callus wiped blood from his split lip with the back of his hand. "Four men. They were angry about losing money on bets. Said someone told them I'd throw the fight." His voice was tight with worry for Kasha. "They tried to jump me at the festival. When I fought back, one of them grabbed Kasha and..." He gestured helplessly at her broken horn.

"They're all dead." The words came out flat and emotionless.

An hour had passed since Callus had carried Kasha into the caravan, but her tears still came in waves. She sat propped against the pillows, clutching the broken piece of her horn like a precious relic while Mother Maudrid gently examined a growing bump on the back of her head where she'd struck the wall.

"Easy, child," Mother Maudrid murmured, her weathered fingers probing the injury with practiced care. "You've got a good knot back here, but nothing that won't heal properly with time."

Kasha's free hand kept drifting up to touch the jagged break where her left horn had snapped, fresh tears spilling down her cheeks each time her fingers found the rough edge. "It's ruined," she whispered for what felt like the hundredth time. "I'm ruined."

Sylus paced near the small window, his ornate robes swishing with each agitated step. His face was etched with worry that went deeper than the immediate injury. He and Mother Maudrid were the only ones who knew the full truth of Kasha's childhood, the cruelty she'd endured, the way Zunibar had used her appearance as another tool of control and humiliation. A broken horn wasn't just a physical wound for her; it was a return to feeling powerless and damaged.

Suddenly, Sylus stopped pacing and snapped his fingers. "Ibrahim! Of course!" He turned to Callus with renewed energy. "Son, I need you to fetch Ibrahim the jeweler from the southern district. Tell him Sylus Mordath requires his immediate assistance for a delicate repair. He's worked with horn and bone before. I'm certain he can reattach it with a gold seam."

Callus started to rise from his chair beside the bed, but Kasha's hand shot out and grasped his wrist with surprising strength. "No," she said, panic creeping into her voice. "Don't leave me. Please don't leave."

"I'll go myself then," Sylus said without hesitation, already reaching for his cloak. "Ibrahim owes me. I'll bring him back here." He paused at the door, his expression softening as he looked at the pair. "Take care of her, Callus."

After Sylus departed, Callus moved from the chair to sit on the edge of the bed. Kasha immediately shifted closer, laying her head in his lap while still cradling the broken horn fragment. His hands found her auburn hair, fingers moving through the silky strands with infinite gentleness.

"I'm hideous now," she whispered against his leg, her voice muffled and broken. "No one will ever want to look at me again."

Callus's hands stilled for a moment before resuming their soothing motion. When he spoke, his voice was soft but certain. "Kasha, you could lose both horns, every tooth in your head, and gain a hundred scars, and you'd still be the most beautiful girl I've ever seen." His voice grew quieter, more intimate. "You're beautiful because you're you, and nothing—nothing—could ever change that."

From her position near the washbasin, Mother Maudrid glanced over at the pair and felt her weathered heart soften. She'd seen many things in her long years, but the tender way Callus held Kasha, the absolute devotion in his voice, she wondered if their friendship would ever transform into something more.

CHAPTER SIX

BOUND

The twin moons were at their respective peaks in the night sky. They played a game of hide and seek among the gray clouds that slowly wandered across the sea of stars. They were like a pair of eyes looking down on Yonara. A pair of eyes that would have witnessed a tall hulking figure wrapped in a pitch-black hooded cloak creeping up to the wrought iron fencing of a majestic mansion that was a gorgeous union between human and elven architecture. Something the figure found odd considering the attitude of the Oskon Empire toward half breeds.

The figure squatted down at the base of the fence and spied around for guards and arcane wards. One of his eyes flared a dull green, granting him vision that would better receive a glimpse of arcane workings and sigils. Reaching up, the figure scratched at his thick beard, and within his mind he reached out. *"Are we sure this is the one?"*

"Have I ever been wrong before, my sweet beast?" The words filled his mind in a voice that reminded him of the gentle thrum of a lyre. Although, they no longer set his stomach to a flutter as they once had.

"No, but I've never done anything like this in Kath Thalore. I'm in the bloody Empire, Oakira. A week hiding aboard a ship from the Emeraldom and four days scouting through the wilderness to find this damned place. I'm exhausted. If we're wrong and they catch me..."

"So, don't get caught. You've done far worse than this. You are more capable than you give yourself credit for, Kovag'Dresh."

He sighed. She only called him by his full orcish name when she was becoming impatient with him.

"I'm going. Calm your tits." With one last look around, he found a space between two windows on the bottom floor and in the blink of an eye he was there. He pressed himself against the wall and peered around again for any change in the status of the guards, traps or sigils. With none in view he set off to find a way in.

Crying. Pitiful crying. They all cried. Every single one of them. Tsarra found it both erotic and nauseating at the same time. She had never understood why. Then again, she had never cared to find out. She stood at the edge of her altar of worship. Spread out in front of her were some of the cruelest and most sadistic implements she owned. A few of which she had special ordered from a revered blacksmith all the way in the Empire's capital of Reverence Keep. Each was pristine and cleaned to perfection. On the back wall of her altar hung the organs of her sacrifices, each one in a different stage of preservation. At the center was her masterpiece, a statue replica of the Forgotten Lord Ulrannoth. She had pieced it together in painstaking detail from the carved knuckle bones of those whose souls she offered up to him.

Her hands moved slowly across her naked form, leaving a trail of blood across it, forming intricate sigils of devotion to her Lord of Torture. She followed the warped lines of her unnatural body that was not quite Elven and not quite Forgotten. She traced the path of her hips up to her breasts before bringing her bloodied finger down her tongue. Her eyes rolled back within her head and a second set of lids rapidly fluttered in ecstasy. She found the flavor exquisite. The more fear and torment in the sacrifice the sweeter the taste.

She moved to a table in the center of the room. Upon it lay the indistinguishable remains of her latest victim. She unceremoniously swiped her arm across the table, the gore splashing and thudding against the floor with sounds that would make most lose the contents of their stomachs. Tsaraa, however, doubled over in raptured euphoria at the sound. "My Lord, you honor me with this pleasure. I will give unto you another blessed life. This one will be of the sweetest and rarest nectar I've ever brough before you. Great lengths were gone to in procuring her for your feasting."

Her eyes moved over the plethora of cages that lined the dark stone room's walls. The cages were of varying sizes, but her eyes shifted to one of the smallest. When her vision locked onto the bars of the cage it shifted backward, as if whatever or whoever was in there was recoiling from the sight of Tsarra. She heard sniffling and a whimper. She lowered her gaze at the cage with a wicked smile. "Yes, it is your turn little one. Come praise Lord Ulrannoth with me and take an exalted place in his hall of the macabre. You are so very lucky to be chosen."

With supernatural speed, she was at the door to the cage. Her smile bent up and touched the corner of each eye, long needle-like teeth dripping with saliva. With a wave of her fingers the lock unlatched, and the door swung open. She squatted down and peered into the darkened space. Barely visible in the dark were two golden eyes, staring back at her with a shimmering wetness from its fear.

"Do not be afraid. Come." She held a hand outstretched toward the figure. Blood splashed across her face as claws swiped out at her delicate hand of tortured artistry. Tsarra brought her hand back slowly and inspected the wounds. She trailed her tongue over the deep gouges. "You dare to desecrate this sacred ritual with your senseless mewling and now you bring your own claws to bare on the artist."

The cage shook again, but this time it was from Tsarra grabbing the figure and throttling it against the side of the cage by the neck. The thing inside yelped and screamed before being dragged out and held up off the floor in front of Tsarra. She held high in front of her a young girl in brown linen rags, Vulpine ears pinned back at the top of her head and her bushy orange tail flared out from the rush of pain that racked her body. The fox beastkin girl's eyes were glazed over, and blood trickled from her nose. There were caked spots of old blood that weren't as easy to spot within the fur at the back of her arms, legs and cheeks. Tsarra licked her lips and sniffed at the scent of dread wafting from the child like perfume.

The girl came back to consciousness at a time when most would have preferred to remain unaware of their surroundings. Her eyes fluttered and strained to focus on the ceiling from the table she had previously seen covered in gore. For the last few weeks, she had the unfortunate honor of witnessing the carnage that this table was used for. The full realization of her fate rested in her head, and she let go what was left in her bladder. Her mouth opened in a soundless cry as she fought against leather straps that held her tight at the wrists, ankles and waist.

"Yes, child. Sing your wordless song. Give me more! My Lord loves the taste of the innocent when they lose all hope." Tsarra spoke facing the altar with her back to the girl. She trailed her fingers over her instruments of worship, considering which would make the vulpine girl's agony bring about the most delightful music. The girl had made no sound other than the occasional whimper since she arrived, but

Tsarra was certain she could make the little birdie sing before the life left her beautiful eyes. This time as she smiled from eye to eye, her cheeks separated and her mouth grew wider. She had found just the tool she desired. She grasped the handle of the implement and turned to face her new canvas.

The girl's head moved in the direction of Tsarra, and she squirmed even harder when her eyes locked on the item in the monster's hand. It looked to be of pure silver and split into three heads at the tip. One resembled a hooked skinning blade, another serrated in a backward facing fashion and the third glowed with arcane heat.

Tsarra strode to the table slowly, reveling in the moment. She wanted to draw this out as long as possible, to savor the taste. Finally reaching the table, she set the burning head of the tool against the table top a mere inch from the girl's ankle. Her face took on a further sinister look as horns began to protrude from her temples. She dragged the tool up the table, ensuring she kept it within an inch of the girl's skin. The smell of burning flesh and fur wafted throughout the room as the girl fought feebly against her leather bonds.

Tsarra was at her head now and held the tool to the girl's ear, slowly dipping it closer, her eyes dilating with orgasmic delight. A delight that was cut violently short when the door to the room exploded and sent wooden shrapnel scattering across the open space. Tsarra reeled to the ground as a jagged plank sank into her side.

The girl turned her head away from the exploding door and winced. When she realized Tsarra was no longer beside her she looked directly at the now open doorway. A large and bloody masculine shaped figure dropped a limp body to the ground, his unbelievably broad shoulders heaving from exertion. The man pulled back a cloaked hood, revealing the face of a half orc with long black hair and a close kept beard. He took in the sight of the room and his stomach lurched. There were body parts everywhere. In many cases they were pieced back together in horrendous visages and bastardized mockery of living creatures that the pieces did not belong to. His eyes moved over to the child's pleading eyes and then to Tsarra, who was slowly getting back to her feet. His face twitched and his tusks tipped in a snarl of fury. Wordlessly he charged her, slamming into her before she could stand fully erect.

He drove her back into one of the cages, snapping her back on the top edge of the blood-stained iron. He raised his hand high and slammed his fist down across her grotesque face with a violent crunch, green arcane light exploding from his hand as he struck. As he brought his fist up again, he felt a force of arcane energy repel him away. He tumbled backward, rolling and going with the motion to arrive on his feet near the sacrificial table. He stood between the vulpine girl and Tsarra, watching in surprised horror as she pushed her broken body off of the cage and contorted herself backward as if doing an upside-down bear crawl. Her head twisted around at the neck with several snaps and now faced him. With a hiss she launched herself into a skitter directly at his core.

He moved his fingers in a deft and subtle motion and his body phased into a blur of three. Tsarra misjudged her trajectory. She latched onto his body, but her teeth closed around the head of one of his mirages. He used the diversion to pound the sharp piece of the broken door that was still embedded in her side. She arched back in a shriek and opened her maw, ready to retaliate with finality. He reeled back against the table and reached up, grasping her at the upper and lower portions of her mouth.

"GRRAAWWW!" He bellowed and pulled with all his strength, even as her fangs pierced his palms. The top of Tsarra's head came clean off, without even a chance to acknowledge that she had lost. He flung the ragged piece to the floor and let the rest of her body fall. His body heaved with adrenaline, and he forced himself to take slow deep breaths to clear his head, focusing on what needed to come next. He moved to the altar and sneered at the blasphemy before him. A symbol at his chest pulsed with deep silver light, pulling something unseen from the bone visage of Forgotten Lord Ulrannoth. The sculpture turned to dust.

He could hear alarm bells in the distance. Someone must have escaped his notice upstairs.

"You were sloppy up above my dear." Oakira whispered into his head.

He sighed in irritation. *"Nothing to be done about it now, is there? Any chance you actually have something helpful to offer?"*

A goading, yet nervous laugh came from her somewhere in the Lunar realm. *"Run?"*

"Right, thanks." He shook his head and ran to the center table. The vulpine girl was terrified, but she didn't pull away from him. His face was strangely kind to her eyes. "My name is Kovag." He began to unbuckle the leather straps that held her in place as fast as he could. "I'm going to take you somewhere safe, but you need to come with me and not make a sound. Okay?"

Her face was raw with tears, and she began to sob in front of him while nodding her head.

'So very young to have seen things that no one should ever have to endure. She is...special.' Oakira said with an immense sadness.

Kovag picked the girl up. She clung to him as if she would fall into an endless abyss if she lost her grip. Hells, he didn't even need to hold onto her if he didn't have to. However, he held her fast to him, hoping that it would give her some semblance of safety.

"Wait! Don't leave us, please!" The words shocked Kovag, and he turned with a raised fist, crackling with the same green energy from earlier. He lowered it quickly when he saw an elderly orc female with a young male bugbear. The woman was rail thin and showed signs of prolonged captivity by Kovag's estimation. The bugbear boy seemed to still be reasonably healthy, as his fur looked vibrant and his sclera white.

"Can you run?" He hurriedly asked them both while ripping the lock off of the cage with an ease the orc woman would have inquired about had she not seen what he had just done to Tsarra.

"He can, most definitely. I'll do my best to keep up, if I fall behind just leave me." She said it with the barest bit of hope.

"Well, that won't due. Can you hold on to my back?" He turned and hoped she would be able.

She didn't respond but he felt her frail weight immediately on him and he looked to the bugbear boy. "Ready?"

"Yes, sir." The boy puffed out his chest with bravado that was thinly veiled over severe uncertainty.

Together they moved to the doorway that Kovag had rent asunder. He turned and grabbed a torch that sat in a sconce right inside the hallway, tossing it onto a collection of bloody clothes that were piled in a corner. The flame took quickly. As they sprinted out of the mansion he tossed every torch, candle and arcane flame he saw on the way out at something flammable. They paused briefly inside the tree line and watched the night sky light up in an orange hue as the fire began to burst windows. Shouting could be heard toward the front of the mansion, and they turned, sprinting off into the night.

Kovag stood at the edge of a small dock with his hood up again, pacing around impatiently and with his eyes scanning the area. The orcish woman and bugbear waited in the shadows of an old boathouse. He had tried to get the vulpine girl to unlatch herself from him for a moment. If he was caught, he wanted them to be unseen and able to run. She had refused and started to scream when he tried to force her off of himself. Luckily his cloak was large enough to completely cover her, and she was small enough to make his shape seem as though perhaps he just enjoyed his meals a little bit more than he actually did.

In the distance a hooded lantern gave off a dull light. It was then hidden three times in slow succession followed by two times that were fast. Kovag held his hands to his mouth and gave a crows caw in the same fashion. The boat changed course from mid river to the dock.

When it arrived at the dock the pilot spoke, "Wrong day to fish for trout in these parts."

Kovag responded. "Perhaps, but it's a good time for dappled moon gar."

They both pulled back their hoods, having responded to the code phrases appropriately. The man was in his sixties by Kovag's estimation. His gray hair was slicked back, and his face held a few days of beard growth to it. Deep lines etched his face. Kovag knew that some were scars from the Mongrel War, but most were just the telltale signs of aging. Kovag extended his hand. "Erland, good to see you're still in the game." He palmed the older human man a small coin purse as they shook hands.

"I'm not stopping this until I die of old age, or the bastards hang me. I've got too much to atone for."

Kovag whistled over his shoulder. The orc woman and the bugbear boy came quickly from the shadows and stepped into the boat as he had previously instructed them. Erland motioned for them to get to the aft and lay down. He grabbed a large, oiled cloth and tossed it over them as they dropped into the back of the boat and curled up.

Kovag pulled back his cloak and looked down at the girl that clung to him like a second skin. "Time to go, little one."

She didn't budge. He moved his hands to pry her off and she started to cry again. "You have to go with them. This man will get you to a ship that will take you to the western edge of the Emeraldom, very far from here. You'll be safe there." She shook her head rapidly. With a sigh he unlatched one of her hands from his leather jerkin. She screamed. Immediately he stopped. He and Erland dropped low on the dock.

They listened for a full minute before Erland looked at Kovag with a concerned but sympathetic face. "She can't do that again."

"I fucking know that." Kovag looked down at her again. "Please, girl. You will be safe. I promise. Erland is a healer. One of the best. He has vowed to help get as many of us 'dirty mongrels' out of the Empire as he can and he's really good at it." She shook her head again and looked up at him with despair in her golden eyes. His heart broke. He sighed heavily and he looked at Erland. "Go. I've got her."

Erland's eyes were as wide and round as the moons above as the clouds parted just enough for him to get a good look at the girl grasping onto Kovag. "A vulpine?"

Kovag shrugged his shoulders. "I have never seen her kind, so I will take your word for it?"

Erland shook his head. "Do you know how rare her people are and why the Empire covets them? Look friend, I know you're a capable man, the big fucker you are, but they are enforcing the Decree of Purity around here to a degree just shy of its severity during the Mongrel War. Publicly those of your kind are just exiled, but in reality…Kovag, you're dead if they find you. She will wish she was dead. I don't know how many vulpine are left in the Empire, but the nobles here used to treat them like currency of the most high value. They *will* come looking for her. At the very least they'll put a bounty out, and bounties don't have borders. I've been getting a lot of noses poking around lately as it is. I'm going to have to drop off the map for a little while now that I know she is involved. The network is already falling apart. Many have been caught, and others are quitting for fear of the same. You won't get far carrying a frightened child, especially that one."

The old man's eyes lingered on the girl for a moment as if he was recalling some old memories that haunted him.

"So, what? Am I supposed to leave her in the Empire?" As he said the words, she gripped him even tighter.

"Hells no. I just want to make clear to you the situation you are in." Erland's look of sincerity both disturbed and heartened Kovag.

He nodded with a heavy sigh. "They won't catch us."

"Kovag... do everything you can to get her out of here." The old man's eyes shimmered in the moonlight.

"Erland?" Kovag's head tilted questioningly.

"I just knew one of her people long ago. I thought she was the last of the vulpine, and I wasn't able to get her out." Erland cleared his throat and held his hands on his hips, suddenly taking an interest in the dock. "You don't just need to get out of the Empire. They've been slowly poisoning the border towns of the Emeraldom and the Brightborn Kingdom with their hate. You'll need to be very careful about who sees her. If you can get to the Brightborn Kingdom, there are a few temples to Thromgrid in the Ferrum Plains. There is a priestess at one of them that is part of the network. She can direct you to my sister, Maudrid. I'd tell you where she is myself, but we keep information like that secret from each other for a reason. The priestess's name is Matron Vadrida. Bornar should know how to contact her."

Kovag nodded sullenly. "Thank you, Erland. It's been too long since I have seen the crotchety half-breed anyway. I will keep her safe. I swear."

Hearing the resolute tone in Kovag's voice Erland nodded, regretfully. "Bright One be with you."

"Ehrmus with you." Kovag and Erland shook hands again and Erland got back in the boat, pushing it away from the dock.

Kovag watched the boat leave. Once it was safely in the middle of the river he flexed his shoulders. "Hold tight."

She somehow, beyond his understanding, gripped him tighter than she already had. Despite the situation, he found himself smiling at the girl's resolve as he darted off down the riverbank.

CHAPTER SEVEN

LUNAR ABOMINATION

The silence of eternal night was broken by a light ripple of bubbles as they crested the top of the Lunar Pool, living their short lives of contained air before bursting. Willow trees swayed to a wind that was always blowing serenely under the twin moons that were ever present in the sky. There were many pools throughout the Lunar Court's territory, every one secret and secure, nestled away in the highest portion of the arcane realm that the Fae had laid claim to near the dawn of Yonara's creation by her namesake and the Progenitor. They were used strictly for ritualistic bathing. This particular ritual was the most strict in terms of its requirements and esoteric law. It was not often that one was summoned to the keep of one of the Arch Fae.

The bubbling ceased when two bodies emerged from the Lunar waters, bursting forth from its depths and throwing their heads back. The motion made twin arcs of mane and lunar rain. The twin moons of Yonara shined eternally in the sky of the Lunar Realm and shone down on the bodies of the pair with such radiance that most mortals would have fallen from pure shock at the beauty of the scene before them.

First to emerge from the waters was Isque, a tall and lithe Fae man with blonde hair that hung at the back of his knees. The waters dripped down his flesh, using his musculature like rivers. He glanced up at the moons and smiled. "Have you heard any court whispers on what Arch Fae Thruva could want that carries so much import that it requires two Seekers?"

Amjani floated peacefully on the waters, her amber hair was equal in length and in her floating state nearly appeared as a bed that she floated upon. Isque's interest changed from his question to the dappled drops of water that traced down her round, heavy breasts and back to their home in the Lunar Pool. Her body turned in the water and he glimpsed his deepest desire. Her legs were slightly agape and there was more glistening there than just moonlight and water on porcelain skin. Amjani could sense his eyes on her. "You are staring darling. Stop."

Isque scoffed. "I will look where it pleases me, thank you."

Amjani sighed with slight annoyance. "How many times must I tell you that we must not focus on desires that cannot be fulfilled? The Seeker oath forbids it."

"It doesn't forbid what I do up here." Isque said while pointing to his temple. "Up here, you are quite the naughty one."

Amjani climbed out of the pool, both satisfied that the ritual cleansing was appeased and irritated that Isque had to ruin the serene calm that she had been in with his damned lust for her. She dried herself off and found herself drawn to look in his direction. She was perfectly happy to lie to everyone else, including Isque, about what she desired. But she wouldn't lie to herself. She peered down at him as she dried off her legs. She felt a heat rise in her loins as she traced him from his calves to his toned hips and buttocks. His manhood was always pleasing to her eyes. He started to turn to face her squarely and so she quickly averted her gaze before standing upright. "As far as our Lord requesting two Seekers? I have as little information as you. However, to require both of us, it must be of the utmost importance. Now come, I don't want to be punished for being late."

As she passed by him, she quickly reached down and grasped him tightly. He squealed in a mixture of pain and pleasure, something he immensely enjoyed. "Stop. Staring. At. Me or I'll remove it from the root."

"The trauma might be worth it." Isque teased.

Amjani yanked hard and walked away briskly. She wouldn't let him see how much she didn't want to let go; how much she truly wanted it to be possible.

Isque shivered. "Come back. Two more yanks might just do it!"

One profession that was never pursued in the Fae portions of the arcane realm was that of an architect. There was no need for one. Every room in the realm of the Fae Courts held the same walls and ceiling as the other. The only difference being what portion of the night sky those walls and ceilings shown upon themselves. Here in the Lunar Court the floors covered an expansive square or ovular area and then appeared to drop off into nothingness, while the walls were a living night sky with the twin moons stood vigil high above.

Sitting upon a stone throne atop a dais in the Lunar Citadel was the Arch Fae of the Lunar Court. He had a physique that rivaled the Stormsmith himself. He was draped in fine silk robes with white gold highlights, and silver rings on each finger that held a gemstone. Each gemstone signified the total mastery of a particular school of magic and arcane power. He fiddled with the one he had most recently acquired, rotating it around his finger. Behind him at each side of the Lunar Throne one of his brides, wearing matching robes with only a few of the mastery rings, brushed out his sleek silver hair and massaged the long-pointed ears that curled back from his head like scythes of flesh. All the Fae of the Lunar realm held long pointed ears, but the ears of Thruva, ArchFae of the Lunar Court, were by far the longest. They were a true sign of just how old he was.

At the base of the dais that held the Lunar Throne of Lord Thruva stood Battle Master Argus Thilandri. The color scheme of his gear was the same but that was where the similarities ceased. Argus's armor appeared to be plate to the uninitiated eye. But it was in fact a very light lunar weave, constructed with the silk of the Lunar Spiders of the court. It was woven so tight that the threads could not be seen with the naked eye. He also wore no rings. Battlemasters pledged to forsake the arcane for pure martial prowess. They were gifted linked bracelets by their ArchFae to symbolize their own mastery of each weapon and style of martial combat. Argus had them all. He was beginning to grow impatient as he waited for his master to give him leave to speak. Finally, ArchFae Thruva waved his hand to bid him start.

"My Lord Thruva, the Seekers you requested have arrived. They anxiously await your orders." Argus bowed low.

"Send them in." Thruva said.

The night sky near the southern wall parted like a curtain as Isque and Amjani entered into the chamber. They were donned in their Seeker armor now. The Seekers were specially trained hunters sent to hunt the enemies and traitors of the Fae Courts. They had the authority granted to them by not just their Court but by the Council of Courts made up of all of the Fae. They were granted the right to use any and all means necessary to achieve their goal.

Their rank was not shown with badges or shoulder patches, but by phases of the moon. A master Seeker was permitted to wear a suit of full silver lunar weave, symbolizing the full moons. Whereas a novice was given black lunar weave to show new moons status. Amjani wore the full silver weave of a master, while Isque wore a suit of three-quarter silver, leaving this left arm, leg and a small section of his torso black. Isque had not yet achieved the master rank he so desired, but he was rapidly closing in on the honor. They knelt before the dais and kept their eyes on the smooth marbled floor until they were given permission to speak and look upon their Lord.

"Master Seeker Amjani. Seeker Isque. It is a pleasure to have you both in my citadel again. You may rise." ArchFae Thruva's voice was quite literally a symphony. Its tone and pitch wavered in ways that reminded them of the epic story songs sung by the Flame Singers of the Solar Court.

"Thank you, Lord Thruva. We are eager to hear what deed requires the talents of two Seekers and we are honored to be the chosen." Amjani bowed lower before raising her head to meet the gaze of the ArchFae.

Lord Thruva smiled genially and circled his new ring around his finger with his other hand. "I will get right to the matter at hand. Are the two of you familiar with the dalliance of the former Lady Elirel from our very own court?"

Amjani scowled. It was an extremely rare thing for her to be unaware of the comings and goings of anyone in the Lunar Court. It was then unheard of for her to have never even heard the name of one of their own people. "No, my Lord. I am afraid I am not."

Lord Thruva raised his eyebrow with curiosity. "I must admit it vexes me that you have not done your due diligence in your spycraft, and yet at the same time, it pleases me. We did our best to wipe her deed from the murmurings of the few Fae that could recall who she was."

Isque knew what he was about to do broke the etiquette of the citadel, but in truth he didn't care. As Master Seeker, it was Amjani's place to speak. Not his. This was a chance to show Lord Thruva he deserved his full silver lunar weave. "My Lord."

Amjani turned to face Isque with a stare that sent daggers to his heart. "Do not speak to our Lord without permission, Seeker Isque."

Isque rolled his eyes and leaned on one hip. "Our Lord asked a question that I happen to know the answer to. Am I to just sit here like a rock in a stream as everything transpires around me, Master Seeker Amjani?"

Lord Thruva circled the ring around his finger again. "Now, now Master Seeker. Let us not be so harsh. If Seeker Isque is making the decision to break protocol, let us first see if it was worth the risk to his life. Please, you may speak."

Isque's gaze moved slowly up from the feet of Lord Thruva. They paused on the new ring momentarily before meeting the eyes of his Lord. "My Lord. I have heard of this name...and the tale that I believe you are speaking of. Though, the rarity of its speaking made it... problematic in seeking out the whispers."

The ArchFae raised his eyebrows and smirked, leaning back in his throne. "Is that so? Then please, illuminate Master Amjani to the tale."

Amjani was livid but hiding it as well as she could. She turned herself entirely toward Isque and prayed what he had to say would be enlightening or she knew Lord Thruva would have her execute him on the spot. Had she been of a clearer mind at that moment she would have let her duty see that as a blessing. It would eliminate the distraction he presented her with so often.

Isque cleared his throat. "It is said that Lady, excuse me, former Lady Elirel of the Lunar Court committed the perverse act of laying with a member of the Forgotten Legions. Speculation as to why has varied from love to lust and charm to rape. In any case this union bore an abomination to both the Courts and the Legion. It also presented a potentially devastating threat with the birth of her half breed child. Elirel was said to be a powerful member of the court and as such was given the right to plead her case. She instead chose to flee and no one was ever able to locate her and the offspring. The Council of Courts came together and placed the blame on the Lunar Court and instructed your predecessor, Lady Valene, to correct the stain on our people. Lady Valene chose instead to cleanse the memory of Elirel from the minds and records of all the Fae by using one of the Forbidden Vitae spells." A long silence stretched within the chamber before he added, "...as I understand it, my Lord."

Amjani was so stunned by the news that she had not realized her mouth had fallen open in shock. Another deafening silence hung in the air. Even Lord Thruva's two brides were dumbstruck. The symphonic laugh of the ArchFae broke the tension.

"Very good, Seeker Isque. My predecessor tried her damnedest to eliminate all knowledge of this from the Courts but, it would seem, that what life force she had left in her was not sufficient enough to complete the spell in its entirety. Some birds still know the tale, and those little birdies like to whisper to each other in the eternal night. Master Seeker Amjani, it appears even as a master you could learn a few things from those beneath you about the gathering of intel. That is one of your chief duties. Always listen. Is it not?" Lord Thruva chided.

Amjani was still reeling so wildly from the influx of information that she could not decide if she should be more concerned that Isque made her look bad or thankful that she was not going to have to execute him after all.

Isque bowed low again, catching Lord Thruva's constant turning of his newest ring. He kept his head low enough that even with his eyes peering out below his own brow Lord Thruva was not able to see where his eyes were set.

The ring circled again and again as the ArchFae considered his next words carefully. He waved off his two wives and they moved to the back of the room, behind the throne. With a wave of Thruva's hand a doorway appeared and they both stepped through before it vanished. "This next course of information I am about to bestow upon you requires that you each swear to me that it will never reach the ears of anyone else within the Lunar Court. Step forward if you are amicable to this arrangement."

Amjani did not hesitate, ever the loyal servant. Isque waited a few heartbeats after Amjani, but he knew that it did not matter at this point if he was amicable to the agreement or not. If he refused, he would not be allowed to leave this room alive and that would ruin everything he had secretly been working on these last several decades.

Lord Thruva held out his hands. Amjani knelt and kissed each one. "I swear." Her armor hummed with an arcane seal of compulsion. Should she violate her vow while Lord Thruva drew breath, she would forfeit her life.

Isque knelt next to Amjani. He kissed one hand and then moved to the other. This hand wore the ring that Lord Thruva had been incessantly playing since their arrival. Isque may not have been a Master Seeker yet, but that did not mean he hadn't mastered many of the talents that were necessary to achieve the rank. Observation and insight were his strongest gifts and in truth he far surpassed every Master Seeker that currently drew breath. Though none would know this because he made sure he never let anyone ascertain how much he could learn just from the way someone moved about a room. There was power in the ignorance of others. This talent was how he knew that Amjani had a cluster of five freckles the size of a grain of sand high up on her inner right thigh without ever being close enough to enjoy the folds that neighbored those very freckles.

He studied the ring in his rapidly chaotic mind, and felt a cold dread wash over his heart at the realization of exactly what that ring was. He did not pause in his action, however, and kissed the ring. The same arcane hum pulsed over his armor, and he too rose. They stepped back down to the bottom of the dais and awaited their Lord's words.

"Your tale was true Seeker Isque. But allow me to fill in some gaps that are imperative to the task I am sending the two of you to deal with. Elirel was allowed to give birth to her little half breed within the Court. Since she was a Lady in very high standing at the time, she and her offspring were ostracized but received no further punishments. Lady Valene wanted to keep them close. The Lunar Court tolerated their presence until Elirel began to feel immensely slighted by her treatment and whispers emerged that she bade her child to begin seeking out a pact with a mortal. The abomination was already an unstable threat but with a pact mortal she could then begin to syphon power so that she and Elirel could be a true threat to the sanctity of the throne." He stopped to scoff at the arrogance.

"A mutt using our laws for a pact and with only the barest understanding of what she was doing. You can imagine the scandal. When this came to the Court's attention, Lady Valene had no choice but to sign over a death warrant for them both. This is when Elirel and her spawn vanished, and my predecessor chose to wipe them from memory instead of pursuing them. You may wonder why Lady Valene chose to enact one of the three Forbidden Vitae spells, magic so powerful that it demands your life in exchange?" He paused for dramatic effect.

Isque had to restrain himself from rolling his eyes. *"Why do all of the Fae insist on such useless theatrical suspense?"*

"Elirel was Lady Valene's daughter." Thruva spoke the words with disdain. He would have spit if it wasn't beneath him to do so.

The two Seekers took a step back in shock. Amjani looked at Isque as if for confirmation on the claim. He shook his head. Even he had not heard anything that could have led him to such a conclusion.

Amjani's eyes widened even further at a new realization. "If Elirel was Lady Valen's daughter, that means..."

Lord Thruva nodded his head. "Yes. Elirel is my sister, and her abomination my niece."

Isque felt a further dread grip him. *"Hells, this complicates everything."* He thought.

The ArchFae allowed that to sink in for a minute before he continued. "My mother could not bring herself to kill her own daughter and instead chose to potentially damn the courts and leave her a threat to my reign and the peace of our court. Unfortunately, my sister is nothing if not clever, and I have been unable to find her. However, much to my surprise my niece has somewhat recently been successful and acquired a pact mortal, and they have been quite busy. The mortal recently managed to siphon a large fount of power from one of Forgotten Lord Ulrannoth's followers. This little surge also revealed just how much power the mortal has accumulated for her and my treacherous sister, and it is...worrisome. I will not have it. There is a reason the union of Fae and Forgotten is forbidden and we cannot have her anywhere near this Court, especially with that much power at her disposal. I need you two to locate her and my sister and see to it that they are eradicated from the realms of the living by any and all means necessary. I am granting you the rite of The Reaping. Understood?"

The Seekers faces failed to hide their shock. The Rite of the Reaping was almost never used. Isque could only recall it being used five times throughout history in all of his studies. The Rite of Reaping granted the Seekers full power to exterminate the very soul of their quarry, any who get in the way and even those that might have knowledge that could aid them in their hunt. They recovered quickly and placed their right arms across their chests in salute and bowed in unison. "Understood."

Lord Thruva gave the most miniscule bow possible and flicked his fingers from the throne to send a small parchment to Amjani. She caught it deftly and placed it within her belt pouch. "With the notice of the power surge we managed to backtrack it to several places we noted similar arcane signatures. I'm sure the two of you will be able to get a rough idea, at least, of where they could be going next. Within the parchment is their location when the power surge was noted as well as a few places that the pact mortal appears to have stayed in long enough to leave an arcane signature. My niece has been wise to have him keep on the move, though one of the spots in the Emeraldom must mean something to the mortal because he has returned there often."

Amjani turned to walk away but Isque stayed. "My Lord, may I inquire something about our quarry?"

"If you believe that it will aid in their demise, you may." Lord Thruva returned to his throne.

"Do we know who from the Forgotten Legions sired the abomination? In case we run into any of the Legions servants I'd like to know who we are dealing with." Isque dared to hold eyes with the ArchFae.

"As much as I hate to admit it, no. Even I do not have that information. My mother saw fit to strike that from my own mind as well. Now go. Time is of the essence."

Isque knew he was lying. He saw it in the millisecond twitch at the corner of Lord Thruva's left eye. Potentially more troublesome, while he could not be entirely sure, was the small speck of purple that he felt he saw in the corner of that same twitching eye. He bowed before the ArchFae and turned to follow Amjani.

The two Seekers exited the citadel throne room through another of the vanishing arcane doors. They were shunted into a space between the realms of the arcane and the material, surrounded by dense trees with the sun peaking in between holes in the canopy. It took several seconds for their eyes to adjust.

Amjani reeled on Isque. "Don't ever embarrass me like that again!" She wanted to strike him, make him bleed for the insolence he committed before their Lord. She found herself, however, shaking. She was still processing that she thought she was going to have to execute what she felt was the only true friend she ever had.

"I'm sorry Master Seeker." He considered for a moment. "Something about our Lord caught my eye and I was duty bound to see it through. Did you notice the new ring he wore?"

She glared at him now. She could not believe how nonchalant he was being about what he had just done. "Everything that I just learned-that we just learned, and you ask me if I noticed a fucking ring?"

He ignored her raving at him. "It was raw void, my sweet Amjani."

She huffed. "Stop talking to me like that." She took a deep breath. "What do you mean raw void?"

"He was toying with a ring around the middle finger of his left hand. It wasn't there when he sent me on my last mission. That was only two mortal months ago." He rubbed at his smooth chin.

"Raw void ore. So what? Even some of the mortals have learned how to harness its power properly." She shrugged, finally coming down from the anger of her outburst.

"No." Isque shook his head. "I didn't say raw void ore. I said raw void. Unpurified arcane void energy."

Amjani threw her hands up in frustration. "And if it was? Lord Thruva has mastered all forms of the arcane. I'm sure he can handle the damned void. We've got work to do, Isque. On the way to the site of the initial disturbance, you will tell me what makes this abomination such a threat and what Lord Thruva meant when he said she was unstable." She grabbed Isque and kicked him hard in the ass to spur him forward.

Her sudden touch snapped him out of his worry. He hoped she was right, but in his experience with these things, she was not. "If you're going to touch my ass, could you do it with your hands?"

She shrugged. "If you insist." Amjani reared back and punched her fist into his buttocks, causing him to yelp.

"You enjoyed the touch, didn't you?" He smirked over his shoulder at her.

She shook her head. "Never."

"You're lying." He whispered.

They had not walked far when Isque excused himself to find a tree off in the distance. "Drank a fair bit of wine this morning, my dearest Amjani. Solar vintage. Say what you will about the brighties, but they make a wine that is almost impossible to put down."

Amjani rolled her eyes and groaned. "Hurry. Try not to play with it too long."

"Trust me, if you had it in your hands, you would have a hard time not letting it go either." Isque winked over his shoulder.

He found a large tree that was a good thirty yards away and would shield him from Amjani's view. He did pull himself out and relieve the urge, but he had other reasons to go off for a moment of privacy. He pulled a small golden coin from his pocket. It looked like your average mortal currency to the undiscerning eye. A closer inspection, however, would reveal the tiniest imprint of the Forgotten Duke Dalmoth the Sundered's crest; a broken horn with a chain holding the pieces together.

Isque rubbed the coin thrice clockwise, once counterclockwise and then tapped it with his thumb twice. The crest glowed dully. "My Liege. It is as you feared. Lord Thruva plays with the void."

A voice came from the coin, quiet as the near silent flapping of a bat's wings, but with a deepness that always made Isque think of a large boulder sliding down a mountain surface. "Is there any sign they suspect your true allegiance?"

Isque's eyes darkened as he felt the weight of his betrayal. "No, my Liege. The thought that one of their own Seekers would betray them is so far beyond the realm of possibility in their minds that they have not wavered for a second."

The voice hummed again. "Excellent. You are performing magnificently. Proceed as planned. Assure no lasting harm comes to the half breed." Isque had lied about where he heard of the tale of the Fae and Forgotten abomination. Duke Dalmoth had warned him that Lord Thruva would be looking for the girl soon.

"If she perishes or is imprisoned, then my plans will be ruined...and so will the dream of your prize."

Isque winced at the harshness of Duke Dalmoth's words. He had seen him render a legionnaire's insides into a puddle and make his flesh into a fancy cloak just because he vomited in his presence. Failure at this stage of his liege's plan... he did not want to know what would be done to him. "My Liege, the half breed is his niece. Were you aware?"

"Of course I was aware. Some things I need you to find out on your own. If I tell you every detail, then your usefulness will wane as your skills go as limp as a mortal's cock after a measly three hours of fucking." Duke Dalmoth's tone was sharp but with a hint of amusement.

Amjani called out to Isque. "Hurry the fuck up! If you are not careful you are going to yank it off!"

He rolled his eyes and continued to whisper to the coin. "My Liege, I still have your assurances that she will be free? Free to be mine?"

"Once Thruva is dealt with she will have no one left to remain dutiful to. So, unless she discovers that you were responsible all you will have to do is charm yourself between those moonlit thighs. Now go. Before she becomes suspect."

Isque stowed both himself and the coin away and jogged back to Amjani. "As I said, it is so hard to let go of it sometimes."

CHAPTER EIGHT

A RUSH REDISCOVERED

Callus had retreated to the backrooms of the new Witch's Tit and Tarts Tavern. The ladies had not enjoyed his jest with the 'whores' comment. He, on the other hand, thought he was the only one in the room that could have called them that. In Toz Unro he had been coinless for a time and many still knew the glorious battle tales of the Towering Tactician and Hobgoblin Reaver, Callus Kordec. He had racked up a generously large tab at the Lush Tulips, the most prestigious brothel in Toz'Unro.

Madame Elora had been very kind to him in his early days slumming it throughout the city. Callus had made several waves when he arrived. He started a plethora of brawls and caused a lot of property damage to several taverns and bars. She had pitied him and had given him a place to stay. That particular night ended in an arrangement that he had somewhat reluctantly agreed to. He would have an open and never-ending tab with a place to stay on occasion as long as when an upper-class female came in requesting a male of exotic rarity he would step in to, quite literally, fill that hole or holes. They weren't his proudest moments, but he'd be lying if he said he didn't enjoy it, most of the time. If for no other reason than it numbed the pain he was going through after his fall from grace in the arena and the massacre of everyone in Sylus's Traveling Spectacles.

Callus found Egrim stacking ale barrels on top of one another, sorting them all by style it seemed. He noticed Egrim had placed all the dark ales toward the front and the imperial pale ales at the back. When they first met, Callus was very wary of him, and he felt the same energy coming at him from the large man. Their shared taste in ale was the first item toward a very slowly growing trust between the two. "Hiding the bitter shit behind the good stuff? I take it she still refuses to get rid of it?"

Egrim turned and dusted off his hands while shaking his head. "Stubborn as a draft goat. She says, and I quote, '*The hippogryph riders thrive on the stuff and they have plenty of coin to spend.*' Fucking hippsters. I'll never understand the desire to drink something that makes you squint your face up like a damned cat's asshole. Dwarven whisky does the same thing, but at least with that, after three shots you stop noticing it."

He moved over to Callus and the two clasped each other's right forearm in greeting. The first time the two had met Egrim's size gave Callus flashbacks to his fight with Umrun'kra for the Scarred Lands Championship. The only difference was Egrim was bigger still.

"I personally think the small drop in profits would be worth the loss of the smell of unwashed bodies and patchouli. I can handle one or the other, but together it's like having a troll rub its taint across your face." Callus smirked. "Would be a shame if you just happened to drop a barrel and get that piss water all over the floor."

Egrim chuckled. "You'd be digging me an early grave if I messed up the new floors already. But more importantly, how in the Hells do you know what troll taint smells like?"

Callus huffed. "You ever get roped into a grappling match with two of the nasty bastards at a bar and you'll find out."

Egrim moved to the door and peaked down the hallway quickly, making sure Kasha wasn't coming. "Have you been able to get any more information on that Alabaster jackass?"

Callus shook his head regrettably. "No. Nothing more than Ethan knows. This asshole is good at hiding his tracks, appearance, true intentions, fuck, everything. This city reminds me more and more of Toz'Unro every day."

They both sighed in irritation at the lack of results they had been able to achieve for months.

Egrim changed the subject. "Still clear to go back to the Shale Grounds tonight?"

Callus's eye lit up. "Hells yes. Do you have any idea how many customers I've broken in half in my mind over the last few weeks? I saw Ethan earlier, he still has us slated for the two-on-two tournament."

Egrim grabbed a sleeveless drab linen duster he had laid over one of the extra barstools in the backroom and put it on. He noticed it still had a few small drops of blood on it from their last trip to the Shale Grounds. "Shit. Do you think she noticed?"

Callus laughed with a shrug of his shoulders. "Kasha? Probably not. She's been so focused on the impending opening I don't think she has paid attention to much else. Arialyn, on the other hand. I have a feeling she knows but doesn't want to spoil it for me. I think she knows I would feel guilty. What with everything fighting in the arena got me in the first place." He looked mildly bereft at the thought.

Egrim raised an eyebrow. "Well, these are semi-regulated brawls, and no one is dying. Nothing like before is happening here." He quickly moved on. "Kasha wanted me to make one more trip with the cart to the old place to pick up a few more things and check in on Lorisse. The stress of running the old spot while Kasha deals with getting this place ready is beginning to show. You coming?"

Callus smirked. "Of course. Lorisse always makes sure they have the lemon tarts hot and ready and the ladies up front won't be there to smack me if I my eyes wander. I swear that woman has a charm spell tattooed on her somewhere."

Egrim raised his eyebrow. "She is...pleasant to look upon." He moved into the hallway and called out, "Kasha! I'm making the run to the old Tits. Morrigan okay here with you?"

"She's up in your room. If she starts to have an issue, I'll send Lemmy for you. And tell Lorisse it's just a few more days. Then she can take a few off while we deal with the grand opening here." Kasha yelled back.

Egrim shook his head and turned to Callus. "You think Lorisse would stay away from the tips of an opening night?"

"Not a chance. She'll make sure she's so damn oiled up and shiny it blinds people right out of their coin."

The old Tits, as they had come to call it, wasn't terribly far from the new Tits. But they had to go through the main thoroughfare to get there. Kasha had told Egrim to rent a draft horse from one of the grooms at the stables, but he had refused and told her to save the coin. Instead, he attached a thick leather strap to the cart and threw it over his shoulder. As he and Callus made their way through the streets there were almost as many people pointing and marveling at the size of Egrim as there were recognizing Callus from his beginning days in the gladiatorial arenas.

Before he had been crowned the Scarred Lands Championship in the Helspires, in the first ever unified Scarred Lands bout of the north and south, he had been the Northern Scarred Lands Champion, and all those bouts had been fought in either The Wylds or here in Hus'rokn. Those were the days before everything went tits up for him in the arenas.

People waved and gawked, depending on which one of them caught their attention first. Callus was enjoying it. Egrim was not. "If we keep slowing down for you to greet your adoring fans my work is going to run late and that means we get to the Shale Grounds late."

"You make an excellent point, my friend. One I will choose to ignore for just a bit longer." Callus smiled and shook hands with an elderly man who was beaming ear to ear and saying something about witnessing him defending the Northern Scarred Lands Championship for the first time.

Egrim groaned and continued being a voluntary beast of burden. He did, after all, bring this upon himself. A few moments later they were out of the hustle and bustle of Hus'rokn.

Callus dipped under the leather strap and shared the weight of the cart now. "How is Kasha doing?"

"She's your best friend. Shouldn't you know that answer?" Egrim kept his eyes forward.

"True enough, but you're around her much more than I am. When I see her, she's all smiles, but there's a sadness there that she won't open up to me about. She's always been good at hiding how she really feels from everyone. Even when we were little, she was one of the only people that I sometimes couldn't feel out. A lot has changed while I was... gone. Maybe it's just the stress from the purchase and remodel."

Egrim grew thoughtful for a moment. "No...there is something bothering her. But I don't know what it is. I see her staring off into nothing at times. When she does that there is this aura of...sorrow around her. Not very heavy but noticeable."

What he didn't tell Callus was that those same blank stare moments occurred when she was watching him and Arialyn together and she thought no one was watching her. He hadn't been told directly but he had managed to suss out that Kasha and Callus had some kind of history. He figured maybe they used to be lovers but never dared to ask.

An emptiness opened in Callus when he heard the way Egrim described it. He hated that she wouldn't tell him what was going on. She may have always tried to hide her emotions in the past, but he had always managed to get her to open up to him sooner or later. Now though, anytime he had broached the subject with her she deflected to the remodel or said she was fine. He wanted to do something, anything to help her but he had no idea where to start if she wouldn't open up. He had asked Arialyn to try and feel it out, maybe see if she would speak to another woman about what was going on. All that had gotten him was Arialyn telling him that if Kasha wanted to talk about it then she would, and he should just be there for her in case she decided to unburden herself to him about whatever it was. "Egrim, if you stay, I'd appreciate it if you would look out for her when I'm not around."

Egrim stopped in his tracks, the sudden shift in weight of the leather strap going tight against Callus, and he turned to Egrim. "What?"

"Callus, this is none of my business. Kasha is an amazingly beautiful woman in every way, and I enjoy whatever friendship it is she is willing to offer me, but my daughter and I are going to have to leave at some point. The thought of getting too close to her, only to end up leaving and her having another friend abandon her so close to what happened to Mother Maudrid. I don't want to do that to her. I think it's best if I keep some distance." Egrim felt terrible saying it. He felt even more terrible that he didn't mean it. He wanted nothing more than to promise that he would stay, but he couldn't. Something always came along and forced him to grab Morrigan and move somewhere else or run.

Callus snapped his head, a sneer upon his face. "Abandon her? Don't you fucking dare insinuate that I abandoned her. She is the one that decided to stay behind when everyone else moved on from here."

The change in Callus's tone raised Egrim's hackles. "From my understanding, no one was given a choice. You and that Sylus fellow decided for everyone and if they wanted to keep making a living, they had no choice but to follow you."

Callus turned to face Egrim fully, looking up at the larger man. "You're dancing on a dangerous subject, Egrim. I think you should hold your fucking tongue before I rip it out."

"If you think you're fast enough old man, go for it." Egrim leaned in, brow furrowed.

A crowd was beginning to take notice of their raised voices and gathered around the two. Most of those in the crowd managed to have good enough sense to keep a safe distance from the two large men if it turned violent. Among them, however, a lanky man saw an opportunity and began to cut purses with practiced ease.

Callus took another step forward, putting himself within a foot of Egrim and planted a finger into his chest. "You show up out of nowhere and put out a fire at the new Tits just days after Kasha bought the damned place. The only witness to the arson is the supposed arsonist, so you claim, who you conveniently bludgeoned so badly he's still drooling on himself in his cell four months later! You tell us the bare minimum of your fucking past. It's clear to me that you're running from something or someone. So, who did you abandon, Egrim? Who did you leave to fend for themselves? How are they doing? Probably not as good as the woman running her own tavern!"

Egrim smacked Callus's hand away. His massive knuckles cracked loudly as he clenched both fists. "I don't care what your reputation is, Callus. You put another damned finger on me, and I'll shatter your good arm."

"Boy, you have no idea what I'm capable of. I can gut you before your hands move." Callus flicked his right hand. The leather noose bracelet, given to him by The Hanged One himself, pulsed and the ornate mithril tipped Hangman's Spear appeared in his hand.

A shout came from the crowd behind Callus. "Hey! That bastard stole my coin purse!"

The scrawny cutpurse burst from the crowd, attempting to dart past Callus and Egrim to get to the other side of the crowd in the street. Without looking Callus turned the shaft of the spear toward the man's ankles. The poor fool tripped directly into Egrim's outstretch and waiting hand. He caught the man by the throat and raised him off the ground a few feet. Callus and Egrim stared daggers at each other, neither of them moving.

After an uncomfortable amount of time, particularly for the man whose face was beginning to turn blue, an elderly woman slowly stepped out of the crowd and approached three men. She hesitantly reached into the man's pockets. "If you don't mind, I'll just grab..." She fiddled around in the man's clothes until she found her own coin purse. "...got it. Thank you."

She slowly backed away with a very awkward bow of thanks to the two large men. A moment later another came to grab their missing coin and then another and another. The man's face was turning purple now and he had entirely ceased to squirm. Still Callus and Egrim just stared at each other.

"You're going to kill him."

"And?"

Callus tilted his head just a tad.

Egrim breathed out with a huff and dropped the man to the ground with a thud.

Another voiced called out from behind the crowd. "Alright everyone! What's with the crowd! Back up, City Guard coming through."

Callus and Egrim both recognized the voice of Guard Captain Ethan. By the sound of the footsteps approaching, either the commotion or a citizen had fetched the captain and at least four other guardsmen. They would have been able to accurately count them had each of them not been so stubborn about not wanting to be the first to break eye contact. Their eyes had been open so long without blinking that they were beginning to water.

Captain Ethan stopped short at the sight of Callus. When the Towering Tactician returned to the area several months ago, Captain Ethan had been starstruck. He had grown up watching Callus's gladiatorial bouts, even witnessing his debut fight. Even now, with their new business dealings he still had to fight the urge to fanboy at the living legend. Had it not been for the shock of seeing Callus here in this moment he would, certainly, have seen Egrim first. The size of the man was astonishing no matter how many times you saw him. Callus was a large man to be sure, but Egrim forced the hobgoblin to look up when they spoke to one another, and his shoulders were nearly as wide as the cart they stood in front of.

Ethan wouldn't say the two were friends necessarily, but they had been seen out in the city running errands together for Kasha several times over the last couple of months, speaking and laughing over ale bottles and they were currently the favorites to win the two-on-two tourney that he was running in the Shale Ground later tonight. If these two were going to come to blows in the middle of the street, the loss of coin from the bets tonight would be the least of his headaches. He didn't want to have to attempt to break up the fight, arrest them either or think of the cost in damages they would tally up together.

The sound of the choking thief shook Captain Ethan from his stupor. He straightened himself up and tried to act as official as possible, he was the Guard Captain after all. Ethan looked down at the gasping man and then up at the pair locked in a match of wills. "Either of you want to tell me exactly what in the Hells happened here?"

"Cutpurse." They said in unison.

The captain put his hands on his hips. "That explains the half dead man on the ground. Now, what about the two of you? Do I need to fetch an entire squad to handle a scuffle?" The captain honestly didn't think an entire squad would be enough to subdue Callus alone, let alone adding the giant into the mix. The two of them said nothing and continued to keep their eyes locked on the other.

Captain Ethan moved in closer and out of ear shot of the crowd as the rest of the guard with him began to disperse the throng. He was about to speak when he saw faint tears trailing from the dry and red eyes of the pair. He tried not to chuckle from the sight and failed. "You two look...well, fucking ridiculous right now."

They growled. He wasn't sure if they were growling at each other or him; he prayed it wasn't at him.

"Gentlemen, if I may? Could we refrain from bloodshed in the streets? Or at least do me the curtesy of waiting until after the tournament tonight. Perhaps as a favor to me." As Guard Captain he was used to ordering people around. Yet still, he had to summon up courage for his next words. He leaned in and whispered to them. "Callus, please don't make me remind you of our partnership for your lady. And Egrim, I stopped more than a few city officials from digging into the arsonist you brained. For the record, I believe your story and I think the bastard got what was coming to him, but some would say you went too far in your sense of justice. You both owe me."

For a brief moment he worried he had gone too far. But then they both nodded with echoing groans. However, they still wouldn't look away from each other. The captain sighed and pinched the bridge of his nose. "For fuck's sake. Will you agree to both look away if I count to three?"

They narrowed their eyes at each other, both dangerously close to blinking. "Yes." They said again in unison."

"You're both children. One, two-"

"Wait." Callus said. "Are we looking away on three or is it technically on four. Like one, two, three, pause and then look away?"

"Does it fucking matter?" Ethan's voice was passing from strangely amused to irritated. Before him stood, arguably, the two best fighters in the entire city and they were behaving pettier than children who couldn't share a toy.

"Yes, it matters. I'll not look away first. Which is it?" Egrim spoke up this time. His eyes were burning red with dryness.

"Fine! Look away on three. One, two, three."

Egrim blinked several times to clear his blurring vision while Callus kept his stare long enough for Egrim to notice that he had indeed looked away first. "You asshole!"

The Shale Grounds, aptly named for the shale that surrounded the open area of the mine deep beneath the city of Hus'rokn, had been the spot Guard Captain Ethan had chosen as the best place to set up his underground fighting scene several years ago. He had been inspired to set up this place because he remembered tales of many gladiators getting their start in places like it and he wanted to be a part of that. The final bout of the tournament was well on its way.

Egrim grabbed a tiefling man by the neck, lifted him up off the ground and spun around before slamming him into the shale floor by the throat. His body twitched for a brief second before it became limp. Egrim roared with his arms wide to the crowd and then turned to see how Callus was fairing. He crossed his arms and waited with a somewhat smug look on his face. "What's taking you so long, cripple?"

"Fuck off, pink skin!" Callus was grappling with another hobgoblin. The other hobgoblin had been pretty cocksure coming into this fight tonight. He was a little more than half Callus's age, younger, more hungry and felt that he would roll through the retiree. Much to his surprise, his reasoning had been severely flawed. He may have been half The Ruiner's age but that also meant he had half the life and combat experience. Callus wrenched down on his opponent's arm and held tight as he flung his legs up and over the younger man's shoulder and chest. They fell to the ground and Callus pulled back swiftly to hyperextend the other hobgoblin's arm in a perfect armbar. He stopped just short of breaking it. "Give up?"

The hobgoblin was continuing to fight against the pressure, but Callus had the armbar locked in solidly. If he didn't give up, then Callus would be forced to snap it at the elbow. Callus respected the younger man's grit, but he was about to put him out of the fighting game for several months if he didn't relent. "Don't make me break it, kid."

The bastard kept squirming, fighting through the building pain of the inevitable. "Fuck your mother, you old prick."

Callus sighed. "Kids these days." He pulled back hard with a loud snap.

"Ahhh fuck!"

Callus stood up quickly. "I said I was going to break it. Did you need me to explain how that worked first, you Gods damn child?"

The patrons that filled the small wooden and raised circular stands cheered at the result. Callus and Egrim had teamed up four times now and they had been a major draw every time. Tell people that The Hobgoblin Reaver is making a sort of comeback and then throw in a man of sideshow attraction size, and you have a guaranteed recipe for successfully attracting a crowd that was ready to throw coin around.

Medics carried off the tiefling and helped the still cursing hobgoblin through the crowd. Captain Ethan came to the center and grabbed both the winners by the wrists. He held them high, well, as high as he could considering the height difference. "Your two-on-two tournament winners, The Hobgoblin Reaver, Callus Kordec and The Behemoth of Brutality, Egrim!"

He slowly turned them around the fighting circle so every section of the crowd could see their winners and cheer or boo their excitement and sorrow at the outcome of their bets to their faces.

They were both still fuming from earlier and the adrenaline from the three rounds of the tournament wasn't helping. Ethan felt like a conduit for their rage as he held their arms up for the fans. He had hoped the tension between them would be quelled after getting some of their aggression out in the pit. He was ready to bolt the minute either of the two made a move at the other.

Callus spit at the ground. "You ask me what was taking so long? You jackass. Finesse. Fighting is an art, boy, and you treat it like a child with fingerpaints."

Ethan immediately released their wrists and backed away. "And that's my queue."

Egrim rounded on Callus. "If you'd like I could paint the shale with your blood, you has-been."

Callus's eyes narrowed. "I guess art class is in session today." He shifted and threw a leg kick directly into the side of Egrim's calf. The strike was fast and given with the precision of the artist of combat Callus truly was. Egrim was forced off his feet and to his back.

Captain Ethan turned to the criers immediately. "Don't just stand there! Start taking bets! If they're doing this, we might as well profit off of it."

Egrim growled and moved faster than Callus had ever seen him before. He grabbed Callus's ankle and wrenched it out from under him, forcing him down as well. Callus landed in a push up position with his face mere inches from the shale floor. Egrim scrambled off the floor and onto his feet in a movement no one of his size had a right to perform.

Callus had pushed himself to his feet at the same moment and the two now stood ready for more.

Egrim moved first with a combination of jabs and crosses that Callus blocked and dodged with relative ease. He countered with his own in return. Most managed to hit their marks but Egrim didn't show the pain they were pushing through his body. Callus was pushed head over heels as Egrim placed his massive foot into his chest with one of the strongest push kicks Callus had ever been given. The breath was knocked out of him with a huff of air.

Egrim was already charging forward for a follow up but caught an upper cut from Callus when he righted himself and sprung up into the strike with full force. Egrim stumbled back, seeing flashing lights dance in his vision. Callus continued the assault and began hammering strikes into Egrim's ribs. Egrim raised his fists together and aimed them at Callus's head, but he saw it coming and managed to take the blow on his shoulder instead which didn't make it much better. The pounding of his fists sounded like they were striking against stone.

Bets were surging back and forth as the fight continued to tilt one way and then the other. Callus was far more seasoned and placed every strike with grace and eloquence, but Egrim was stronger and when he managed to connect it forced Callus back and dazed him for several moments.

The fight had been going for a solid three minutes and Ethan got the sense that Callus was holding back. Callus had been picked up and slammed against the ground twice and Egrim had been drilled in the back with knees enough times that no one was sure how he was still standing.

Callus was evaluating everything about Egrim's movements. How he shifted his weight, where his eyes darted when Callus moved, and how his speed increased at just the right time. The senses of the Towering Tactician knew there was something Egrim wasn't showing or using that he had in his arsenal. Had this been a true gladiatorial bout like the old days, Callus knew he could have ended Egrim on three separate occasions already. However, He just wanted to teach the man a lesson, not maim him for life.

Callus saw an opportunity to finish this farce in Egrim's attack. As Egrim moved in close, Callus grabbed him by the back of the neck and drove his knee squarely into his jaw. What he didn't see, being at such close range and missing his left eye, was the colossal overhand right Egrim barreled into his skull at the same time. Both men dropped to the floor, unmoving.

Everyone went quiet except for the Guard Captain who just realized all the bets on the impromptu fight were now forfeit. "Well, fuck!"

CHAPTER NINE

BACK ON SOLID GROUND

Kovag had thankfully been able to make it to his rendezvous with the vessel scheduled to return him to the Emeraldom, despite the extra weight he now carried. The vulpine girl was quite light, if he was honest, but he had still been worried that the incessant need for bathroom stops would make him late. Then there had been the need to bribe the captain of the damn ship to keep his mouth shut about his new passenger. For all the talk of despising the Mongrel races the Empire certainly had a fancy for keeping certain ones as slaves. Vulpine females in particular, it was said, were sought after for the sex trade.

Had the captain actually seen the child, Kovag was sure he would have refused and probably turned them in for whatever reward had been declared. But Kovag had kept the child hidden underneath his cloak. Still, it had taken nearly all his coin, but the captain finally relented and accepted the unexpected addition.

During the seven day voyage, in their secluded quarter of the ship, the girl hadn't allowed Kovag to get more than ten paces from her before she would start to weep, scream or run after him. He had felt great pity for her each time, but his life was no way for a young girl to live and what kind of guardian could he be? A half orcish man in his late twenties that travels from place-to-place picking fights with the most monstrous of people. Bornar, his old mentor, was the best option. Get to him, get the location of this Matron Vadrida and then on to Erland's sister Maudrid. However, first he would need to collect more coin for the journey.

The pact with Oakira forbade him from seeing his family but that didn't mean he couldn't get close and check on them. He kept a hidden cache of coins buried in the roots of the oak whose branches he and Oakira had sworn their oath to each other. This was the perfect excuse to see how his mother and sister were fairing and it had been several years by his reckoning since he had set eyes on them from afar.

The poor child hadn't been able to tell him her name. Hells, she hadn't told him anything. She was afraid to sleep because, as far as Kovag could tell, she had nightmares. Which he found fully understandable. She wouldn't eat unless he damn near forced her to and the moment he sat down she would jump into his lap and eventually grow so exhausted her mind would shut off and she gave into the need for rest. About the only thing she had done the first time he told her to was when he bartered some cheap clothing away from one of the swab boys and asked her to change into it.

Most bothersome to him, however, was that the more time she spent latched onto him the more he began to feel a deep emotion pulling at him. He knew what it was and was trying desperately to ignore it. He had held her and rocked her, singing old orcish lullabies his mother had told him his father had sung to him when he was a babe. The battle between what he wanted and what he could not have was wearing his nerves thin.

He had reached out to Oakira for guidance, but the moons had already begun to wane and that meant their communication was very difficult for her to achieve. Over the years they had long periods of silence but those always transitioned to periods of abundance, save for the last couple of years when she only reached out if she had a new target for him. Prior to that, she had come to him on a few occasions and shared herself with him again as she did under the tree when they first met. Each of those times had ended the same, with her lying in his arms but reminding him that Fae and mortals could not be more than they were now and him feeling a growing emptiness swell inside him. For a while he had told himself that this suited him just fine. He understood the reasons and was content to have someone he could be with when the moons allowed it. However, he found that as he had gotten older the desire for a deeper connection was echoing in his soul. A family, he wanted a family. He was just beginning to come to terms with not allowing himself to hope for a future that held that kind of life when this girl fell into his lap and now that she was here, he desperately wanted her gone for her own safety and to stop his foolish dreaming.

Now that they were back in the Emeraldom, a new idea had come to his mind. If he could get her back to his family in Silverbreak then she would be cared for and loved. More importantly, she would be safe.

The pact prevented him from seeing his family ever again, but he could work around that. He considered paying one of the kids in town to go and inform his mother and sister that he was outside the city and needed them. Then he would leave the girl with a message explaining as much as he safely could. He knew they would take care of her far better than he could. She would grow up with the best older sister she could hope for and a doting mother. It took a few minutes after he had come up with that flawed plan to realize that he hadn't spoken to his mother or sister in twelve years now, was it? Fourteen? He had only witnessed them from the hill outside the city where the oak tree stood. Had it not been for the gift of enhanced vision that Oakira had given him, he would not have seen them in twelve or fourteen years either. Even still, it had been many years since he had stood there and caught glimpses of them in the streets of Silverbreak.

His sister would most likely be married by now. Perhaps she could raise her as her own daughter. None of that mattered, however. The girl barely gave him enough time to relieve himself, let alone enough for him to tell her to stay in a single spot and wait for someone to come for her any time throughout the day. He would have to somehow sedate her. Maybe he could acquire a sleeping potion from the edge of town.

He shook his head at his foolish thoughts and glanced about the coast. There had once been ports on the northern border of the Emeraldom. Those were long gone after the Mongrel War. The Oskon Empire's navy had outmatched the Emeraldom's in nearly every way. Those ports had been decimated and were now either vacant mounds of rubble and rotted wood or had been converted into battlements to watch for incoming vessels and determine if they were threats.

They walked along the beach, the girl inspecting objects near their feet. A few more miles and they would turn inland. There had long been a blacksmith with stables roughly ten miles south of the turn ahead. He'd see about acquiring a horse to get them to Silverbreak. Unfortunately, by acquiring, he meant steal. For now, he pointed out hermit crabs and shells that he thought she might like, as well as washed up trinkets.

He squatted down when he came upon a hermit crab that had made its home inside of an old ring box. The girl refused to get too far from him, but at the moment she was about fifteen feet away and looking at the vast mountain range far to the south. Those mountains held the secrets of Spearfall behind them, the fabled pre-Voidscar Meritocracy that the current Wolf Lords of the Emeraldom claim to be descended form. Kovag figured she had never seen mountains like those before and allowed her a moment to take in the sight before he called out to her. "Psst, girl. Come see."

She turned quickly, her tail swishing back and forth in a constant state of curiosity. She jogged over and squatted down to take in the funny sight of the hermit crab and its improvised home. She poked at it, causing it to jump comically, before retreating back inside its home. She looked up at Kovag and smiled for a second before her face darkened again. She moved to him quickly, curled her arms in front of herself, and pressed into his chest. He exhaled heavily and put his arms around her to try and bring her some comfort. "You're safe."

He felt her body relax a little. His eyes became wet as he fought off tears that came. He wondered about the horrors she had to have seen within that damn dungeon, not to mention anything that may have happened to her before. For all he knew she had never seen any place other than that Hells forsaken place. "Are you ever going to tell me your name, little one?"

The girl did not respond to his question for a time but then finally gave him the most responsive communication she had ever given when he asked her a direct question. She lightly shrugged her shoulders, and he felt her grip on him tighten further.

Kovag rested his chin on her head and held her firmly. "Well, I'll need to call you something. I can't keep calling you girl. People will start to ask questions. The people that hurt you can't reach you here, but if old Erland is right then they may send people here to find you. So, we want the fewest discerning eyes on us as possible. Which means we need to keep you hidden from prying eyes and when that is not possible, I need to be able to call you something other than 'girl.' Do you understand?"

She pulled back from him and looked up with a nod. Behind her, however, waves crashed onto the shore and seagulls called out to one another. Her attention was now gone and fully on the seagulls as she turned around in Kovag's arms and watched the scene of an airborne fight over a fish playing out.

Kovag ran through a list of names in his head. "Talia?"

She shook her head furiously. The hair of her vulpine ears hit his nostrils. He brought his hand up and rubbed it against the tip of his nose, fighting off a sneeze.

"Zora?" He inquired again.

She again shook her head and caused her fur to tickle at Kovag's nostrils. This time he wasn't fast enough to stifle the sneeze. He turned his head to the side quickly and let it out. The girl giggled.

Kovag looked down at her head and chuckled. "I believe you're doing that on purpose."

She seemed to consider if she was, indeed, doing it on purpose and then nodded her head and continued giggling.

"How about this? I keep my nose well away from you ears and go through several names. You nod when you hear one that you like?"

She watched one of the seagulls divebomb the other and make it drop the fish before folding its wings and plummeting to catch it's stolen meal. Once it had achieved its goal, she appeared to weigh his question and then nodded again.

Kovag stood and held out his hand. Instead of grabbing it with her own, she gripped it firmly between both of her hands and held them close to her chest. Kovag had to lean heavily to his right side to adjust for the height difference. They returned to walking down the coast to the road that would take them south to the stables.

"Lora. Iris. Temperance. Alba." He continued through a list of nearly every girls name he had ever heard. He only omitted the ones that also belonged to anyone that had ever wronged, irritated, betrayed or insulted him. If he was honest, that took several dozen names off of the potential list. Having reached the end of names he could think of at this exact moment and not having a current copy of 'Popular Baby Names of the Emeraldom' on hand, he stopped in his tracks. She looked up at him inquisitively with those golden eyes.

He was reminded of the sweet rolls his mother would make for him once a year on his birthday. She used a very expensive spice that gave the rolls an earthy sweetness that he could never get enough of. His mother had said it was also the reason that the rolls had a bright red hue to them when they were fully baked.

"Saffron?"

She tilted her head to the side and bunched up her lips, considering the name. She raised herself up on her toes and then rocked back on her heels. Kovag noticed her tail swishing back and forth. He could tell she was on the fence about it. He had no more names in the banks of his memory and hurriedly tried a tactic to push her verdict in favor of Saffron so that he didn't have to start naming random items he saw lying around on the beach.

He held his hand up to get her to pause in her judgement. Her ears perked up and twitched. He cleared his throat and spoke with the tone of a herald. "Saffron, High Lady of the Forests."

She bunched up her face with distaste and shook her head in definite disagreement. He was losing her. Time to go in the opposite direction. "Saffron, The Unyielding Doomicorn of Yonara."

Her eyes went wide enough to rival the size of the rare platinum pieces of the Brightborn Kingdom. She jumped up and down and bobbed her head in zealous agreement.

"Excellent, Saffron the Unyielding Doomicorn of Yonara. Let us proceed on our way."

They stopped about a mile or so down the road when the stables began to come into view. Kovag squinted and allowed his Fae touched green eye to peer at the blacksmith's forge and stables as though he were a hawk tracking a field mouse from the sky. He could see the movement of a few people and smoke coming from both the house and the large lean-to shed that the forge was built under.

Saffron saw Kovag peer in the direction of the buildings and squinted. She imitated him and squeezed her eyes nearly shut as she tried to see what he seemed to. She could not see any better and thought perhaps she was not trying hard enough. She squinted even harder, as veins began to pop up out of her forehead. She surmised that only made it worse and wondered why she could not make out any difference.

Kovag felt her tiny hands strengthen their grip, and her nails push into his forearm. He briefly wondered what kind of strength Saffron would have when she reached adulthood. He looked down at her to see her face all pinched up and her leaning forward on her toes, dangerously close to falling forward off balance. He could not control his amusement and laughed almost loud enough that he feared it would be heard down the road.

Saffron stared at him and noted his laughter. Her face changed from stern concentration to embarrassed irritation. She pulled her hands away from him and crossed her arms, screwing her face up into a pout this time and turned around to face away from him.

His amusement was palpable, and she was making it worse with her overexaggerated sulking. He knelt down beside her, still towering over her small form. Still trying to do everything he could to make her feel safe, he sat down and crossed his legs and tapped on her shoulder. She harrumphed and pulled her shoulder away. He knew this should not be as funny to him as it was, but he could not help himself.

He now crossed his arms in a mock pout. "Do you want to keep pouting, or do you want me to help you?"

She slowly turned to him with a sneer on her face. She was trying to convey that she was not pouting but was of course, doing a very poor job of convincing even the squirrels in the nearby trees. She relented and moved to him. He shifted his rear so that he was facing the blacksmith and stables down the road again and gently pulled her in front of him and facing her in the same direction.

Oakira had taught him many tricks and arcane enhancement spells over the years. Most were not the kind that could be briefly bestowed upon others and those that could he had only done a handful of times and always out of absolute necessity. This would be a first. He placed his finger to her temple and his eye flashed a deeper green.

Saffron felt a buzzing behind her eyes and shook her head. She turned and looked at Kovag, eyes wide in shock. He smiled and pointed down the road. "Try again."

She did as he said and slowly returned her vision to the buildings. Her sight zoomed forward, and she felt nausea come to her stomach. She pushed back against him to steady herself and closed her eyes.

He placed his hand lightly over her forehead. "It'll pass. Just give it a second."

Saffron breathed through the nausea, something she had unfortunately grown used to over the years. The feeling left faster than she had expected, and she opened her eyes again, slowly. Her eyes focused on everything in such rapid succession that she felt the nausea returning. An elderly halfling man in a leather apron walked out of the front door and turned back just enough to receive a kiss from a halfling woman of a similar age, before returning on his course to the forge. At the same time a middle-aged human woman rode up from the opposite direction on a swift brindle horse and into the log-built stables. Two hounds lounged in the middle of the rocky road, sunning themselves and stretching.

Just as quickly as her eyes had focused, they blurred. She blinked several times, and her vision returned to normal. Saffron turned to

Kovag with those wide golden eyes again. She jumped up and down with sheer joy and a beaming smile. She turned to look back to the stables. She grabbed Kovag's index finger and placed it at her temple again, pressing it against herself several times.

He snickered under his breath. "Sorry, Saffron. I can't do that again for a while. Magic takes a bit of energy from the caster and some spells, just by their nature, can't be used often."

Saffron nodded at his explanation but looked at the tip of his finger with a small amount of disappointment all the same. She released his hand and pointed down the road, ready to move on. She had internally decided she wanted to see the brindle horse up close.

Kovag shifted his mouth into a sign of regret and scratched at the back of his neck. "About that, Saffron. I'm out of coin."

Saffron shrugged and pointed at the stables again, insistently. She tugged at his cloak and made the slightest grunting sound of effort.

He wondered if she was even aware of the concept of coin and commerce. "I have nothing to trade them in order for them to give us a horse. They will not give us one for free."

She tilted her head to the side and bit her lip, thinking. She threw her hands up in frustration, failing to understand what the problem was.

Kovag looked down at the ground around them. He needed a demonstration. He found a polished stone of red and handed it to her. "This is yours."

She accepted it and turned it over in her hands, studying its shape.

Kovag then picked up three smaller stones that were not as polished. He held them out in his hand. "I will give you these three stones if you give me your one prettier stone."

Saffron looked at him curiously. She wondered if this was some kind of trick. She grabbed the three stones from his hand quickly and held on to all four.

Kovag smirked. "Now, you have to give me your bigger stone because I gave you the three smaller ones for it." He extended his hand out toward her expectantly.

She shook her head and put them all in her pocket. He chuckled at the sight. "Well, at least you have a grasp on theft. Which is exactly what we're going to have to do tonight."

They had moved back down the road and away from the blacksmith and stables before moving into the tree line and slowly flanking the buildings. Kovag was not sure what kind of dogs the family had, but he did not want to get too close and find out they were hunting dogs or worse, guard dogs. So, they stayed back about one hundred yards into the trees. Saffron had curled up against him and fallen asleep. For Kovag, however, it was imperative that he remained awake and watchful. He needed to see the comings and goings of everyone to gain insight into any patterns they had or quirks that might ruin the horse theft to come.

So far everything seemed standard. There were three people living there from what he could tell. The elderly halfling couple and the female human that, from what he could tell, worked for them. She carried herself like someone who had served in the military, probably during the Mongrel War. He paid particular interest in her movements. She walked with a bent back for the first few steps when she arose from a seated or squatting position and there was a limp in her gait due to something afflicting her right leg. He hoped everything would go smoothly and he would not have to exploit that weakness.

He had waited as long as he felt necessary. There was no light coming from the home of the halflings and only a dim candlelight coming through a small window in the shack that the human used as her quarters. He very gently brought Saffron awake by patting her back. She stirred and looked up at him with sleepy eyes. He held his finger up over her mouth. "We must be very quiet. No talking."

He thought that perhaps she would find that amusing. She did not. In fact, she did not even acknowledge the jest. She simply climbed out of his lap and waited for Kovag to begin moving toward the stables.

Kovag picked Saffron up and his pact eye flared dully. He made sure that his sight would allow them to avoid every fallen branch and collection of leaves. He scanned back and forth over the property, checking for the hounds. They were either simply pets or were old enough that they had lost their touch and could not smell them coming, something he was sure they would be able to do since neither of them had bathed since boarding the ship from the Empire.

He stopped in his tracks when he noticed a shadow pass in front of the candlelight from the window of the shack briefly. Listening so intently he could hear Saffron's rapidly beating heart, he paused, waiting to hear the door open. It did not.

Continuing to move forward, they pushed past the edge of the stable wall that was set furthest from the rest of the buildings. He peeked around it and saw no signs of movement. He set Saffron down and held her hand. She followed him so closely that he couldn't take full steps. As they entered the stables a few of the horses stomped their feet in annoyance. He held his hand up quickly and mumbled an incantation under his breath. The spooked horses immediately calmed. He was thankful he had not gotten rusty with that spell. The last time he had used it was on a few worgs in the Helspires and it had quite literally saved his life at the time.

They moved to the biggest horse in the stable. It was a sable Timber Shire horse. The Emeraldom had long ago bred these horses to be large enough and fast enough to run alongside the now extinct dire wolves of the old Emeraldom military. He feared no other horse in the stable would be able to sit him for long. It eyed him warily but coolly as his spell kept it from balking at his approach.

He turned to Saffron. "I have to let go of your hand for just a moment. I need to put a saddle on this horse." He whispered.

Saffron nodded and reluctantly let go of his hand. She wrapped her tail around her waist and fidgeted with it while biting her lip nervously. When she was not holding on to Kovag she felt alone. She did not like feeling alone. He was nearly done with the last buckle when she could not take the fear of loneliness anymore. She rushed to close the short distance between them and in doing so caught a hanging bridle on to the cuff of her tunic, pulling it off its hook. It clambered onto a set of leatherworking tools that were hanging beneath it before crashing into a watering bucket on the floor.

Kovag whirled at the noise right as Saffron slammed into his leg. Unsure of exactly what happened he picked her up against him with one hand and threw out his other in a fist that shined dully with green light. He peered around and pieced the puzzle together quickly. "Shit."

Saffron squirmed against him, burying her head into his chest. Kovag huffed. "No time for the bridle now." He hoped the horse was tame enough to cooperate with a stranger without one.

In one fluid motion he grabbed her by the waist and leapt up onto the Timber Shire, throwing his cloak around her. He grabbed a handful of the horse's mane, kicking the stirrups to urge it forward. The horse burst through the open stall and made its way to the large half-open double doors of the stable. Kovag had dared to hope they would get out of here unnoticed. A hope that was dashed when lantern light briefly blinded his improved night sight. He dispelled his enhanced vision and pulled up on the horse's mane, causing the goliath to rear up and Saffron to shriek. He wanted to get them out of here, but he was not willing to mow one of these innocent people down to achieve that goal. At least, not yet.

Standing defiantly in the doorway was the human woman. She held a lantern high above her head and a hand crossbow aimed right at his chest in the other. Kovag had seen hand crossbows like it before and he now knew for sure that she had not only served in the Emeraldom military, but she had also been in the Grayback Rangers during the Mongrel War. They were a special unit that had been detached into the Oskon Empire to find internment camps and free their occupants. She was still in her night clothes but was wide awake. "Get down horse thief or I'll release a bolt into your neck and your cock to follow!"

Kovag looked the woman over quickly. She definitely looked capable of such violence, but there was no way she could outmatch him. However, the crossbow was aimed far too close to Saffron for his comfort. "I can't do that. I need to borrow this horse. I'll leave it with the stablemaster outside Silverbreak and coin to make up for the trouble."

She smirked. "No, you won't. Silverbreak is three days ride and if you were going to do that then you would have come to us and simply asked. We take coin up front, but it's too late for that now. You have three seconds to get off my gods damned horse before this bolt goes through you and into the wall behind you."

Kovag sighed. "You served in the Grayback Rangers, correct?"

Her eyes narrowed and she held the hand crossbow out further. "You're too young to have served in the Mongrel War. How do you know of the Graybacks?"

He pointed at her hand crossbow. "I've had an exciting enough life to know my history well. Only the Grayback Rangers carry those dual shot hand crossbows." He decided it best to leave out the part where he first learned about the Grayback Rangers hand crossbows when he killed a former member that was making the wrong kinds of deals with a Forgotten legionnaire.

The woman did not care where he was going with his inquiries and placed her finger on the trigger. "One, two-"

"Wait!" Kovag threw open his heavy cloak to reveal Saffron cowering against him beneath it. "Please. I rescued her from torture in the Empire. The Grayback Rangers helped the mongrel prisoners and refugees during the war. She is a refugee. I just need to get her as far inland as I can. Her people are prized there, and I cannot guarantee that they won't come looking for her."

The woman slowly lowered the hand crossbow. She squinted to get a better view of the girl. "Vulpine? Can't be. Her people are all but gone from this world. I know very well what her kind meant to those fanatics. I heard tale of a group of them that took their own lives, rather than serve the Empire's perverse desires. I was led to believe they were the last of her people." She looked at Saffron. "Girl, is he telling the truth? Is he hurting you, if he is I'll see to his end. You can be sure of that."

Saffron slowly turned her head and eyed the woman and then looked up at Kovag before burying her face back into his chest and whimpering lightly. Kovag pleaded one last time. "Please."

The woman growled to herself. "I'm afraid I can't let you go. Not with the horse. This horse is very expensive, and I will certainly lose this job. I can, however, give that child a warm place to sleep for the night and a hot meal." She slowly moved to the side of the horse and held a hand up to help Saffron down.

Kovag wanted to oblige. A night under a roof that did not have rocking waves beneath it would be a welcome luxury. As well as a warm meal. He had no reason to not trust this woman, but he also had no reason to believe her. Something in his gut told him to run and fast. That's when he saw the woman stealthily flip the safety catch off on the hand crossbow. He looked down at Saffron and whispered. "Hold tight."

The woman tilted her head. "Sorry, I didn't hear tha-uff"

Her words were cut short as Kovag slammed his boot into her chest and spurred the horse forward again. The Timber Shire was out of the stables and several yards down the road before he heard the woman hollering at him. He hoped now that she was not a good shot. Saffron was so incredibly small that he knew there was no way a crossbow bolt would miss him from behind and hit her, but his instincts told him to ball up around her as much as he could anyway. His breath momentarily left him when the first bolt punched into his left shoulder. The second bolt of the dual shot crossbow whistled past his ear. By the time she had loaded more bolts they were too far down the road for her to make them out.

Well, he had no choice in the matter now. He was going to have to go into town once they got to Silverbreak. Unless things had changed much since the last time he walked those streets, the few sawboneses in Silverbreak were toward the city center. That meant a highly increased risk of seeing his mother or sister and breaking the pact. He would still have to stop by the oak first and collect the cache to pay the damn healers. Oakira reaching out to him with increasing infrequency, picking up a stray child, a bolt in his damn shoulder and risking breaking the pact. Nothing was going right.

CHAPTER TEN

PEACE ACCORD

E grim sat on the barstool moving his jaw back and forth while holding a frosted rag to it. It had thankfully been reset while he was out cold. Guard Captain Ethan had brought his fight medics to treat them both in the Shale Grounds, separately of course and then released them back out into the city with a plea to each one to not let this spill over into the city proper, warning that then he would have to arrest them.

Kasha had been pacing back and forth in front of him for several minutes. Thankfully Morrigan was sleeping through the tirade. He had stopped listening to her after the third minute of the lecture about how stupid both he and Callus had been. The iced cloth was helping his jaw but the morning sunlight coming through the windows was rapidly elevating the throbbing in his head.

The only thing that eased the pain to any degree now was when he allowed himself to become distracted by the silhouette that swam in Kasha's light pink sundress. How many times had he fallen under this spell that she was unconsciously casting on him. Or was it on purpose? Subliminal on her part perhaps? Her breasts were of medium size and still high set despite being a few years shy of her forties, though she had never had children. He judged they would fit well in the palms of his large hands. They matched well with her waist, which was somehow both slim and full-bodied. His eyes traveled down to her rounded hips. As she turned in her ranting, throwing her hand up in exasperation, he saw how the sundress hugged her backside. Had it not been for her protruding tail, which was also swaying with her irritation like a cat ready to pounce on its prey, he imagined the dress would be devoured by her.

"Are you even listening to me?!" Kasha turned on him. She set her hands on her hips and leaned to one side.

That stance did not help his distraction in the least. "I stopped listening after 'you men are impossibly stubborn and ungentlemanly' and then something about needing a vacation. I am betting the next several minutes were just rephrasing the same thing over and over again." He gave her the widest sarcastic smile he could muster.

Her eyes narrowed and she was about to start yelling again, but he just held that damn smile. Kasha's shoulders relaxed and her tail flitted with exasperation. She moved over to him and took the rag, setting it down on the bar top. Even with him sitting on the barstool she still had to look up at him slightly. She grabbed both of his hands and washed her eyes quickly over the scar on his lip again. Something about it always drew her attention. "Egrim, opening day is just around the corner. It's going to be big. I'm counting on you to keep the peace here."

He nodded. "I know. I'm sorry."

She looked down at her hands, they seemed so small in his. "What got into the two of you? You've both been friendly with one another. Why now?"

Egrim looked ashamed and turned his face away with a sigh. "He's just doing his job and being protective of a friend. He doesn't fully trust me, and I don't blame him. I may have goaded him a little too. Perhaps unfairly. I wish I could give you all more." He looked up at Kasha's eyes for a moment and then looked away again. "I would if I could, but I have to keep Morrigan safe."

Kasha saw a hint of moisture forming at the corner of his eyes. Running the tavern for so many years, she had certainly seen her fair share of men trying so very hard to not be vulnerable, but this was striking her deeper and she didn't want to admit why. Her right hand moved to his arm, and she caressed it softly before giving it a gentle squeeze. "How bad is this trouble you two are in?"

He shook his head. "Kasha, please."

She relented and placed her hand against his cheek with care, moving his face back to hers. "Am I in danger if you stay here?"

Egrim's shoulders slumped. "I don't know, maybe. We should leave." He began to stand up.

"No, sir!" She was yelling again. She pushed her palm against his chest, and he felt a pulse of arcane energy push him back onto the stool. "I hired you to do a job and you are going to do that job until I tell you that you are relieved from it."

Egrim shook his head. "Kasha, we shouldn't stay. I've been selfish to stay here."

She could see it in his eyes now; he really did want to stay but was clearly fighting with the feeling that he shouldn't. *'For me? No, surely not...'* She thought to herself, daring to hope. "Selfish?"

Egrim looked at her and then looked away, wincing slightly as his jaw tightened. "I-we like it here. The tavern, the work... you."

Kasha stepped closer and again lifted his face by the chin. "You listen here, young man. I decide who I associate with and what risks I will take. Not you. Not Callus, who everyone seems to think is my keeper. Not even the Gods themselves decide for me. You and Morrigan are staying right here. Is that understood?"

Egrim's lips curled in a small smile around his scar again. "Yes, Madame."

Kasha straightened herself before him and smoothed out her sundress. "Now, about tomorrow. I need you focused and healed up, as much as possible. Callus and Arialyn will be attending as well. So, you need to go over to the Amethyst Artificer and make up right now. He's my best friend and you're…"

Egrim tilted his head, unsure what she was about to say.

She hastily continued. "I can't have the two of you at odds or making things awkward tomorrow. I need to be able to focus, and I need Arialyn to help keep me calm. Which means neither of us has the time to make sure the two of you play nice. Take a bottle of the Mommy Milkers Breakfast Stout. It's his favorite."

She turned to make her way back upstairs when he called out to her. "Kasha."

"Yes?" She had made it up the first few steps and turned around. Seeing him there, his hulking mass barely fitting on the barstool and wearing that blessed smile caused her to miss her next step and stumble slightly. The slip made the sundress to wrap around her hips even tighter.

Egrim was flustered and forgot exactly what he was about to say. So, he just said what had been going through his head nearly every day he had been here. "I'm sorry."

She tried to speak but her eyes moved from his face to his shoulders and down to his arms. She realized too late that she was staring and just nodded at Egrim before hurriedly going up the stairs and closing the door to her master suite behind her. She leaned against the door. *What the Hells was that?*

He watched her rush off with a slight blush. He listened intently for several moments, waiting to see if he could hear Morrigan moving around. He didn't want her to wake up from another nightmare and find him gone. She tended to wake up right at dawn or nearly midday and never in between the two. He heard no stirring coming from their room and went to the back stock room to grab a bottle of the breakfast stout that Kasha had ordered him to take.

He got to the front door and tugged on the collar of his linen shirt. Kasha had gotten it for him. She was attempting to get him used to wearing slightly more formal attire for when they opened. *'Your civil training shirt.'* She called it. The only problem was there was a reason he wore the open dusters and cardigan style attire. Shirts did not fit and tailors always either laughed and shooed him away or asked for four times the cost of a regular shirt. Even though Kasha had commissioned this one it was still a little too tight around the neck. Taking a big breath and bracing for the blinding sunlight that was sure to set his head to spinning as he opened the door.

He was instead greeted by a hobgoblin with a massive black eye, well there was no eye in that particular socket though, so was it still considered a black eye he wondered. "Pfff." Egrim could not fully restrain his laugh.

Callus raised an eyebrow. "Strange reaction from someone with a reset jaw that's swollen to the size of a blitz ball."

Arialyn pushed past Callus and Egrim. "You're both fucking ridiculous. Is she upstairs?"

Egrim managed to regain himself. "Yes. She's in the master."

She moved up the stairs calling back to them both with jabs of mockery, before knocking on Kasha's door and entering.

Callus and Egrim stood there for a minute, each one waiting for the other to break the silence first. Neither did, but Egrim held out the bottle to Callus. He looked down at it and back up at Egrim before grabbing it and motioning for him to follow him.

They walked wordlessly for a good while. They passed through the Trade Gate together, much to Captain Ethan's surprise. He watched them with wide eyes, waiting for some interaction of any kind. All he got was two brief nods that he felt implied a thank you for the patch up job last night and possibly a wordless apology for their behavior.

Once in the Wylds, Egrim continued to follow Callus to the city's edge where the rivers that bordered on every side were kept torrential by the Wyld Mages. The security measure was enacted several decades ago by the former Trade Prince at the time. The only time the waters were calmed was when trade vessels needed to get into the docks and on extremely rare occasion when someone of high status passed away. Currently the river was a chaotic combat zone of wave-on-wave violence.

Callus climbed a high stack of boulders that rested at the edge of the riverbank. Egrim followed suit and they both sat at the top. Callus uncorked the bottle and took a long drink from it. His lips smacked at the familiar and favored taste of citrus. He handed it over to Egrim who looked at him for a moment before taking a drink and returning the bottle.

Egrim cleared his throat. "She said we weren't to be at odds for the grand opening."

Callus smiled. "I win."

"You're a right cunt. You know that?" Egrim growled after realizing he was the first to break the silence and began to stand up.

"Sit the fuck down. I'm yanking your chain, kid." Callus held the bottle out again.

"Knock it off with the boy and kid shit and I will, for Kasha." Egrim took the bottle and waited.

"Fine. Fine. You need a thicker hide Egrim. Which is saying something. Hitting you is like hitting a damn tree." Callus grabbed the bottle back.

Egrim sat again and looked out at the river. "Why did you bring me here?"

Callus closed his eye and listened to the waves in their constant battle with each other. "I don't fully trust you. I've trusted three men in my life. One was like a father to me and is dead, another killed my family when I was an infant, and the last used me and tried to kill both me and Arialyn."

He took a swig off the bottle and looked out at the waves, considering his next words. "Kasha trusts you, however. She is a good judge of character. So, if you're going to be around her, I'd rather try and help you in whatever way I can. She's my dearest friend and we've been through a lot together. I want to see her happy and safe. This place always quiets the chaos in my head." He motioned out to the river with the bottle in his hand. "The noise of the waves drowns out everything else. Whatever it is you have going on that you refuse to talk about, I thought this might help."

Egrim considered Callus's words, searching for any deception in them. He reached out with an unseen force and found none. The hobgoblin just sat there with elbows resting on his bent knees, his eye closed and letting the wind wash over him.

He too looked out over the waves in silence. In time the worry and doubt in his head began to quiet and then vanished. He found himself smiling without knowing it. "It's not that I don't want to talk about the past. I can't. It would put my life in potential jeopardy, but more importantly the life of my daughter. I can't have that. I'm sure you've kept secrets for less."

Callus opened his eye but continued looking forward at the water and nodded. "Sure, I have. Never turned out well for me though. You certainly don't have to tell me. You should consider telling her at some point in the future though. Don't wait too long. Kasha can forgive a lot. Probably more than she should, but she has her limits. Finding your home, whatever it is, is the most rewarding thing in this life."

Egrim looked away thoughtfully before reaching for the bottle and throwing it back, only to find it was empty. "You limp cock."

"She shouldn't have told you to bring my favorite one." Callus said with a grin.

Egrim looked back out over the river and then turned to look at the Wylds behind them. It was just far enough away to offer them peace but close enough they could see the outskirts of the buildings. Thankfully, for the nature loving in the Wylds, Trade Princess Shelani had written into law that there must always be at least a mile and a half between the edge of the city's buildings and the river. This was both for security purposes as well as peace. She reasoned it was good for the owners of the businesses within the Wylds to have an easily accessible place to clear their heads and release their stress.

"You and Kasha..." Egrim let the words slip out without thinking.

Callus knew what he was getting at. "No. There was a time when we were teenagers. Looking back, it was obvious we both had feelings for the other, but it never lined up and when it could have, I was in no place to mentally accept it and give her what she needed. You two on the other hand."

Egrim balked slightly. "I..."

"Look, if she wants you to stay and you make her happy, then whatever you're running from we can all handle. It's been kind of boring around here lately anyway."

Egrim appreciated the gesture but knew if Callus knew the full truth he would change his tune real fast.

"Do you ever miss the merc life? Any part of it? Although, the way Kasha talks about it, it seems like the Talons of Misery were more of a gang." Egrim knew it was a loaded question but if Callus was going to be able to put him on the spot as he just had, then he could do the same.

Callus opened his eye with a heaviness that spoke of regret but something more. "We called ourselves a mercenary band but we were definitely more of a gang. We had connections and a web around Toz'Unro but nothing like the organization of the Lance, Shield or Gauntlet here. I miss parts of it." He picked up the empty bottle and toyed with it, turning it over in his hands. "There were...we did terrible things. I did terrible things. Arialyn and Kasha have only heard the worst parts. I've never talked about the good things because that feels wrong after everything that happened. To be clear, I don't mean that we did good things. I'm talking about the laughing, drinks, and camaraderie. I've never told either of them about those times because I don't think they could understand what I mean. How can you explain to the people that love you the most that you sometimes miss the worst parts of yourself. There was a sense of unity there, as twisted as it was, I found it somewhat comforting"

He trailed off in his thought, deciding he didn't want to go back to that dark place. "I miss the controlled chaos. The intrigue. I miss using my tactical mind. Setting up plans and executing them. I miss my racing heart, and it's beat resounding in my head to deafening levels. I miss riding side by side on wargs with brothers and sisters that had my back."

He scoffed at himself and shrugged his shoulders. "When my gladiator days fell apart in the Helspires in that last bout...I grieved for those that were lost, and I hated myself. I hated that I wasn't strong enough to win and that I wasn't strong enough to cut my losses and leave before it happened. Too blinded by pride and the need to be worth something. When they killed the entirety of the Sylus's Traveling Spectacles, they killed my friends and some I called family. I grieved them, but you know what I hated myself the most for? A larger part of me grieved the loss of who I was. No longer was I the Towering Tactician, The Hobgoblin Reaver or the Bloody Ruiner...I was just a man. A crippled and worthless man. People stopped looking at me with awe. Their gazes changed to pity and spite. The Talons of Misery, as misguided and foolish as I was in my despair to join, gave me a place to use my anger and change the way people looked at me again. I preferred looks of fear to pity and if they looked at me with spite it was because they were angry about what I could do to them and not because they lost money betting on me in the arena. But then my home found me. Arialyn found me. She resurrected the man that I thought fully died in the Helspires. I am full now, Egrim. I don't miss those days, but I do miss feeling like I had brothers and sisters to run wild with."

Callus tossed the bottle hard out into the river. The waves drowned out the sound of it crashing into the surface. "I like what Arialyn and I do. It fills me with great warmth, but I still find myself staring off and getting lost in the thoughts of riding wargs and feeling completely free. The customers, for fuck's sake the customers! I don't know how she puts up with them. For every rational person there are ten irritating and mind grating twats that need to have reality beat them in the face. I could never seek something like that out again though. I don't want to hurt her or see worry in her eyes."

Egrim nodded along with Callus's reasoning. They were at odds only moments ago but now they were just two men sharing, as much as they were willing to, thoughts of past lives that no longer belonged to them.

"I knew this blacksmith when I was a kid. He was an older man in his twilight years. He used to sit outside of one of the taverns and watch the younger blacksmiths work the forge every day. His back was hunched over and his right arm withered to the bone. He was a pleasant enough fellow. He always smiled when my mother and I walked by, but I always saw something missing in him, like a rotted-out tree trunk. I asked my mother once why he sat there every day and why he seemed so sad. She told me he had been one of the best blacksmiths in the area for decades. As he got older his craft started to decline, so he worked harder and longer hours to make up for it. He suffered a stroke. That's what took his smithing arm from him. He fell to drink and his wife left him. She tried her best to explain to me how it must be to lose the ability to do the very thing that made you who you are. I think you just made me understand that."

Callus eyed Egrim. "You prick, did you just call me old?"

The hour was late, but the streets were still a swarm of activity. Callus and Egrim made their way back to the Witch's Tits and Tarts Tavern. After their time at the riverbank, they had meandered around the streets of the Wylds and grabbed some food from the street vendors. Callus found a tabby patterned grimalkin woman selling candied scornfruit, on a stick of course. He had given Egrim one and had been pleased to learn that Egrim found it repulsive. That meant more for him.

They passed by what used to be Mother Maudrid's abode and occult shop. The man who bought the property from Kasha was a cobbler. He had done the place up in bright colors of yellow and orange. Something Mother Maudrid would have been mortified to see. Egrim nearly let it slip that he had seen what her shop looked like before. It put him in an even more somber mood. He was already tired of keeping his past hidden. He knew it needed to be this way but that didn't make it any easier.

The rest of the way to the Tits and Tarts was spent mostly in silence. They spoke no words that weren't absolutely necessary. They found the front door closed when they arrived. Kasha had closed it to hide the final touches of the remodel from the crowd of people that past by in the streets. She wanted opening day to feel as special as possible.

Across the street and down a block, a figure watched the pair. He saw the hobgoblin extend his hand to the larger man. After a brief moment of consideration, the man clasped the other's forearm. The figure saw them exchange words, but in his current position he couldn't read their lips and by the time he got to a better vantage point they were inside and closed the door behind them.

The figure scratched as a pustule on his cheek and gave into a coughing fit. An elderly human couple past by with a look of disgust. The figure eyed them with a cold stare and purposely coughed in their direction, sending phlegm to land on the woman's shawl. The elderly man briefly made to advance on the repugnant individual, but the quick flash of a rusty dagger sent them both running.

With a swift movement the figure opened a pocket on his dark wool coat and chittered. A large locust crawled out and into the figure's mangy beard. He spoke to it in a broken tongue. "Inform Master after being back in Hus'rokn for merely a day I uncover dreadful news that small one, Marvin, failed in surveillance. Tell Master Jakel hobgoblin thorn is here. Is with Ms. Tits."

The locust fluttered its wings and shifted back and forth before flying off into the night.

OILS, TITS AND WINE OH MY!

Kasha stood nude in front of her full mirror and held skirts of various lengths for tomorrow against herself. She was going back and forth between a harlequin pattern of gold and onyx or one of alternating light green and purple chevrons. She couldn't decide which colors went best with her overall skin tone and that of her darker areolas. The harlequin one was shorter but now that she was a Madame she thought that perhaps she should wear the longer and more formal chevrons. "What do you think, doll?"

Arialyn was sitting at the main table in Kasha's bedroom with an array of scented oils in front of her. She was trying to help Kasha decide which she should wear and which she should anoint the waitresses with on opening day. Arialyn had a fondness for lists and as such, she had a small sheet of parchment for each bottle with notes of the initial scent of the oil, followed by the lingering scent and lastly how they felt on her skin. Kasha was obsessed with making sure everyone's first impression of the new Witch's Tits and Tarts Tavern was flawless. The scents were all lovely when they were separated. The combined smell of them all on the same table was a little much for Arialyn and she was starting to feel a little lightheaded. It was a moment before she registered that Kasha was talking to her. "Sorry, what?"

Kasha huffed. "I said, which of these do you think would be best for tomorrow? I'm stuck."

Arialyn watched her hold one skirt in front of herself and then switch it out with the other and then back again. "The harlequin colors bring out the color of your nipples, but the chevrons are longer and now that you are a Madame I think they will do a better job of setting you apart from the girls that work for you." She stated it all very matter of fact.

Kasha took her advice in mind and then turned back to the mirror, trying on the light green and purple chevrons. She placed her tail through the hole in the back and then turned to see herself from all possible angles she could in the full mirror. "You are right as always, Arialyn. Wouldn't be a bad thing for you to take some of your own fashion advice and wear something flashy from time to time."

Arialyn shook her head. "No, thanks. Overalls are efficient and don't wear out quickly."

Kasha threw her hands up and sat down across from Arialyn. "You're impossible. Do you have any idea how quickly Callus would faint if he saw you in a dress? Hells, just a skirt?"

Arialyn stopped her oil note taking and looked at Kasha thoughtfully. "He quite readily jumps me every chance he gets as is. I'll pass."

With a sigh, Kasha moved the conversation along. "What about the oils?"

Arialyn grabbed two of the parchment pieces and moved them over in front of Kasha. She pointed at each one in turn. "This one would be good for your girls. Cinnamon and vanilla with a hint or cedar, and it gets shinier as it dries. Brings more attention to the tits but won't get everything all greasy. For you, I'd recommend this one. Clove and rosemary with a splash of gold dust in the mix. Your scent will be more robust, and the glittering of the gold will set you apart as someone of higher station."

Kasha smiled wide and squealed as she shook her hands in excitement. "Arialyn, you're the best." She leapt over the table and hugged Arialyn tight, unfortunately for Arialyn, this positioning pressed her face directly into Kasha's breasts. Thankfully they were not currently oiled. She gave her a big kiss on the cheek and then went to grab herself a top. "Now, come with me. We need to see my seamstress about your dress for tomorrow."

She grabbed Arialyn by the hand and pulled her without giving her a chance to properly protest. "If I see a tape measure I will cut you."

The possible need to cut her friend was taken away with a gentle knock at Kasha's door. The unmistakable knock of Morrigan soon followed by the rapid beat and much louder knocking of Lemmy's beak. Arialyn readily pulled her hand from Kasha's and practically ran to the door. "Looks like Morrigan needs something!"

Morrigan smiled wide when she saw that Arialyn was still here, and Lemmy flew to perch on top of Kasha's bed canopy. Morrigan looked over to Kasha with the faintest tears in her eyes. She held a small book under her arm and extended a candle holder with one of Kasha's arcane candles. The normally bright blue flame had dwindled down to the point it was about to extinguish itself.

Kasha smiled sadly. "I'm sorry sweetness. I can't light it again until tomorrow. My magic is all tapped out for the day. We'll have to use a regular candle for you to read tonight." She took the candle holder from Morrigan and extended her other hand to take Morrigan's in hers. "Come on. We'll get a regular candle lit and I'll explain why I can't light this one until I've had some rest."

Twenty-three years earlier...

Kasha fidgeted in the wooden chair, her tail curled nervously around her leg as it shook up and down. She stared at the collection of tomes and spell books scattered across Mother Maudrid's table. The apothecary tent smelled of dried herbs and something vaguely medicinal that made her nose wrinkle. Her polished horns caught the candlelight as she shifted uncomfortably.

Mother Maudrid approached with two steaming cups, her purple robes rustling softly. "Here, child. Chamomile tea. It'll settle your nerves." She set one cup in front of Kasha and took the seat across from her.

Lemmy hopped from the back of Kasha's chair to perch on her shoulder. He nuzzled against her left horn with gentle affection, and despite her anxiety, Kasha couldn't help but giggle at the tickling sensation.

"That's better," Mother Maudrid said with a warm smile. "Now then, tell me again exactly what happened tonight. And don't you dare give me that look. You're not in trouble, girl."

Kasha's shoulders relaxed slightly, though her hands remained wrapped tightly around the warm cup. "Well... Callus and I, we thought it would be fun to..." She trailed off, glancing up at Mother Maudrid's expectant face. "We wanted to watch the bards perform from the rooftops, you know? Get a good view without all the crowds."

"Aye, and?"

"And we thought... well, we thought it might be more fun with some wine." Kasha's cheeks flushed red against her crimson skin. "So, we snuck into Sylus's caravan through the window. We were just going to borrow one bottle, honest! We were already climbing back out when..."

She paused, her brow furrowing as she tried to make sense of what had happened.

"When Sylus coughed," Mother Maudrid prompted gently.

"Yes! It scared me something fierce. I don't know how it happened, but suddenly my hands got so cold, colder than I've ever felt them. I panicked and just... dropped the bottle." Kasha's voice grew smaller. "It shattered when it hit the ground, but not like normal glass. It was like it froze solid first, then exploded into a thousand pieces."

Lemmy cawed softly and preened at her hair, offering what comfort he could.

"Callus tried to take the blame for it," Kasha continued, a fond smile crossing her face. "He always tries to cover for me. But Sylus just laughed at him and sent him off to bed. Then he brought me here." She looked up at Mother Maudrid with confusion. "He didn't seem angry at all. I thought for sure we'd be some kind of trouble."

Mother Maudrid chuckled, her eyes twinkling with mischief. "Oh, he wasn't mad, child. Hard to be upset about losing a bottle of goblin swill he had no intention of drinking anyway. Probably did him a favor, really."

"Goblin swill?"

"Terrible vintage. Sylus only keeps it around for emergencies or to trade with folks who don't know any better." Mother Maudrid leaned forward, her expression growing more serious. "Sylus brought you to me because out of everyone in the Spectacles, I know the most about what you're about to start going through and can help you."

Kasha's brow furrowed as she processed Mother Maudrid's words. "What do you mean, what I'm about to go through?" She set down her teacup with a soft clink, her tail unwinding from around her leg to twitch nervously behind her chair.

Mother Maudrid settled back in her seat, studying the young tiefling's face carefully. "Child, what happened tonight with that bottle, the freezing, the way it shattered, those are signs that you're beginning to manifest arcane abilities."

"Arcane abilities?" Kasha's voice pitched higher with surprise. "But... but if that's true, why didn't Sylus take me to Balon? He's the one who does all the magic tricks for the shows."

Mother Maudrid let out a sharp bark of laughter that made Lemmy ruffle his feathers. "Balon? That fool barely knows which end of a wand to hold, let alone how to teach someone proper arcane control. He's more likely to set himself on fire than help you understand what's happening to you."

She leaned forward, her weathered hands clasped together on the table. "There are different ways people come to wield the arcane, Kasha. It's important you understand this."

Kasha nodded eagerly, her earlier nervousness giving way to curiosity.

"First, there are the wizards of the Arcanum Centralis, that floating city between here and the Oskon Empire, you've probably heard tales of. They study the arcane like scholars study books, spending years learning formulas and incantations through trial and error. Every day they must practice and memorize, slowly building their understanding of how to harness spells."

Mother Maudrid paused to sip her tea before continuing. "Then there are warlocks, those who make pacts with arcane beings. The Fae, the Forgotten, even lesser demigods sometimes grant mortals arcane power in exchange for services or deeds. These people become imbued with magic as a gift, but always at a price."

Lemmy hopped down to the table and began preening his wing feathers, as if settling in for a long explanation.

"Divine magic is different still," Mother Maudrid continued. "Clerics, priests, and paladins receive their power directly from the Gods and Goddesses themselves. Their magic flows from faith and devotion even if it gets a little... twisted."

She straightened in her chair with a certain amount of pride. "There are those like me who work with the natural flow of the world itself. We don't bend the arcane to our will like wizards or receive it as a gift like warlocks and clerics."

She gestured toward the bundles of dried herbs hanging from the tent's ceiling, their earthy scents mingling in the warm air. "We learn to speak with the essence of life and death, to understand the spirits that dwell in plants and stones. We use charms, rituals, and the natural properties of things that grow from Yonara herself."

Kasha's eyes widened as she followed Mother Maudrid's gaze around the tent, seeing the collection of bottles, bones, and preserved specimens in a new light.

"Instead of commanding power, we ask for assistance. We form partnerships with the forces around us." Mother Maudrid smiled warmly. "The cold that touched your hands tonight. That wasn't you forcing magic to obey. That was something responding to your emotional state, offering to help when you were frightened."

"So, I'm like you?"

"No, my dear." She fixed Kasha with an intense stare. "I believe you are what we call a sorceress. Most arcane users think of sorcerers as the lucky ones. Their power manifests naturally, usually around the teenage years. They don't need to study or make pacts or pray for their abilities. They simply have an innate connection to the Arcane Web that flows throughout Yonara and binds all the realms together."

Mother Maudrid reached across the table and gently touched Kasha's hand. "All signs point to you being a sorceress, girl."

Kasha's mouth fell open, her hazel eyes wide with a mixture of excitement and heavy uncertainty. The implications crashed over her like waves, power she never knew she possessed, abilities that could change everything about her life with the Traveling Spectacles. Her hands trembled slightly as she stared at Mother Maudrid, searching the older woman's face for any sign this might be some elaborate jest.

"A sorceress," she whispered, the word feeling foreign on her tongue. "What kinds of things will I be able to do? What kinds of arcane powers can I use? I don't want to hurt people. Can I heal people? Can I use it whenever I want? Is there a limit?"

Mother Maudrid began laughing and nearly spit out her tea. Lemmy joined in on the laughter and began squawking, although he honestly didn't know what was so funny. "Take a breath, Kasha. Let an old woman gather her thoughts for Bright One's sake."

She took another sip of her tea as she shook her head. "We will have to learn what you can do, but we will do that together. Every sorcerer is able to wield a few different elements but none, that I know of at least, can wield them all. Whether or not you hurt people is more or less up to you. Unfortunately, sorcerers are not usually able to wield arcane medicae spells. Yes, there is a limit. Just like, say with Callus, he must train daily to keep up his combat prowess and get better at what he does. But there will always be a limit before he is too exhausted and needs to rest. All arcane users function the same way. Imagine you have a well inside of you that holds arcane power and every time you draw from it for a spell you use a portion of it. Eventually, without rest, you will not be able to pull anymore from it. Understand?"

Mother Maudrid realized Kasha was no longer listening and was instead intently staring at the teacup while touching it with her finger.

"Kasha, if you break one of my favorite teacups, I will make sure that you are scrubbing every damn pot in the kitchens for a month."

Kasha jerked her hand back from the cup as if it had burned her, though frost crystals sparkled briefly where her fingertip had touched the ceramic. "I wasn't—I mean, I didn't... " Her tail whipped back and forth behind the chair. "I was just... examining the pattern on the cup!"

Mother Maudrid raised an eyebrow, her weathered face creasing into an amused smirk. "Uh-huh. And I suppose those ice crystals we were just talking about came from Lemmy?"

"Maybe?"

"Don't get smart with me, girl." Mother Maudrid waved a dismissive hand. "Come back tomorrow evening after the shows. We'll try a few controlled exercises, see what you're actually capable of without you accidentally turning my tea service into frozen shards."

Kasha nodded eagerly, already anticipating the lessons ahead.

"And next time you want to impress my Callus," Mother Maudrid continued with a wicked grin, "at least steal the good wine from Sylus's personal collection. The dwarven vintage he keeps hidden behind his ledgers. If you're going to get into trouble, might as well make it worthwhile."

Kasha's cheeks flamed crimson. "It's not about Callus! We're just friends!"

"Sure, you are, dear. Sure, you are."

CHAPTER TWELVE

FRAGMENTS OF THE TRUTH

At the center of a large circle of pulsing arcane glyphs Elirel sat on her knees, hands resting in her lap in a state of constant meditation. The discomfort was beginning to become unbearable again. She had to go through this meditating spell ritual more and more frequently ever since they fled the Lunar Court. She had performed the casting circle every week since, but now she needed to perform the ritual more often as Oakira's pact mortal bought more power for them.

With the blunder of the mass power influx from his most recent slaying, however, she had been forced to do this every day. Elirel had told Oakira to make sure she chose low to mid-level targets. This, Tsarra, was neither. In truth, Elirel was surprised Oakira's pact mortal had survived the encounter, let alone slayed the Forgotten pact wretch. She was once able to rest for several days and regain her full strength but was now only able to rest for hours at a time.

Her gown clung to her skin, and she could feel sweat dripping down her hair and long, currently drooping, ears as it pooled around her. She was going to need a break soon. The concentration required to obscure their revolving location was immense and nearly more than she could bear. At the end of every casting, they would be pushed to another random location within the Fae portions of the arcane realm. They were never given a chance to be truly at ease.

The last several mortal years had been the most painful of Elirel's long life, more so than having to flee from her own family. She had been well aware of the taboo nature of the relationship she had with her Forgotten fling. A fitting name for their tryst since the spell her mother had cast upon the Courts struck the name of Oakira's sire from even her own mind.

There were a few things she could remember still. She could recall his silhouette when she thought of their times together, but other than that and a few jumbled recollections of his voice, she had nothing in her mind that could identify him. She remembered he was charming. So charming that she had given in to his advances, despite the risks. However, for all of the things she wished she could remember there was one she wished she could forget. There was this feeling that she was never able to quite shake. A feeling that he had lied to her about something, a falsehood that had broken her heart into a million pieces. A betrayal of the gravest kind. What that was specifically she wasn't sure. However, when she looked upon their daughter, she always did her best to focus on the positives that she still had stored in her mind.

Oakira had been the biggest blessing in her life. She knew the threat that her daughter posed to the courts, but the court did not know that or understand how sweet of a child Oakira was. All they could see her as was a great peril and treated both of them as such. The irony was that in doing so, they created a greater threat that had not existed to the court prior.

When the circle casting became too hard Elirel would focus on Oakira's firsts. The first time she walked, her first spell and first time flying beside her were of her most treasured memories. Oakira's laugh had been the sweetest notes of music she had ever heard and still were. Although her bouts of laughter were sparse as of late.

Elirel named her after the oak tree under whose branches she was conceived. When she saw that tree in her memories it always brought the most genuine smile to her face. She had taken Oakira there when she was little, just so she could watch her play in the roots and surrounding hills. It was the only way she would ever know anything about her father, and she figured she owed her that. All of these were the places that she tried to contain in her mind while she sat in her circle of torment.

Elirel walked slowly and soundlessly under the twin moons toward a large oak tree that sat upon a hill. Off in the distance the sound of revelry rang out from a town that was normally sleeping at this hour. But today was different. Today was one of the mortal holidays and the people were celebrating with raucous joy. Elirel could not have said what the holiday was, but she had never cared for such things. She didn't look down on the mortals of Yonara like many of her people in the High Courts, but she didn't place much stock in them either. She saw them as an accessory, a power source to be treated like pets.

It didn't matter whether a Fae made a deal with a mortal out of compassion, lust or greed. In the end the true reason was because their deeds gave the Fae more power. Her own mother, Lady Valene, had grown to her immense power partially from her pact with Faowric Terestaisson, one of the heroes that ended the onslaught of High Sorcerer Varl Marzadal and the Cult of the Void Heart all those thousands of years ago. You became an ArchFae by nature of accumulating enough power, and the deeds of pact mortals for supplemental arcane presence was paramount. At least until you acquired enough. Elirel had a few pact mortals herself until the Lunar Court required her to excise those attachments upon discovering she was carrying a half-Forgotten child.

This was the only time Elirel had ever wept for mortals. Fae pacts operated differently from those of their Forgotten cousins. The Forgotten were experts at finding ways to turn pacts to their benefit and the detriment of the mortal. They left loopholes for themselves to leave a pact and curse the mortal that was witless enough to enter into it in the first place. Fae pacts were honored at their intent, not their wording and as such the pact was binding unless one of the pact members died or both consented to its end. Seekers had been sent to kill the few pact mortals Elirel had to her name. She had a love for those mortals. However, losing a mortal pet was only a passing distress to her.

She came up to the trunk of the tree and placed her hand upon it. Above her she could hear her young daughter crying, and when she made contact with the tree, she could feel the crippling sorrow she held in her heart pulse through it. "Oakira, my little acorn, I know you are upset but you cannot run away from me like this. I fear what might happen to you if I am not by your side to protect you."

In the branches above, Oakira shifted, pulling her knees up to her chest and resting her head on them. She had been crying for so long that her tears had gone dry, yet still she convulsed with sadness. "I do not want to do what you ask mother. Why do they all hate me? I have not done anything. If they did not hate me, would you still make me do this?"

Elirel floated up and sat gently beside Oakira, placing an arm around her shoulder. She pushed Oakira's long hair over her shorter ears and wondered if her Forgotten heritage would prevent them from growing long like all Fae. "They fear what they do not understand. They fear what you mean and what you could become. If they would just open their eyes, they would see that you are not someone to be feared. They would see how gentle of a soul you truly are. We are past any chance of that, my little acorn. That is why you need to do what I asked of you."

"I do not see the mortals as you do mother. It feels wrong to use one." Oakira shifted, resting her head against her mother.

"Oakira, you still have forty-two years before you reach adulthood. When your three hundred and fiftieth cycle comes, you will believe differently. The mortals are precious, but they are still just blips in time compared to us. The lives of the canines the mortals hold dear are the same in comparison to them. They care for them, but in the end, they are forgotten when they are gone." Elirel kissed the top of Oakira's head, smelling the hint of heat that emanated from her mixed heritage.

"If I could just get the chance to change the court's mind about me then I could fix it. I cannot do that if no one gives me a chance. All the kids run away from me any time I get close and if I chase them to try and play, they scream in horror. The adults look at me with scorn and malice. I don't understand what they are so afraid of." Her neck was weak from sobbing for so long, she tried to pick her head up but failed and remained leaning against her mother.

Elirel took a deep breath. She thought it was still too early, but she couldn't take seeing her little one like this anymore. She hoped she would be able to comprehend what she was about to try and explain to her. She leaned her daughter away from her just enough to see her face. She ran her hand through Oakira's hair and then raised her eyes to the night sky. "My little acorn, I am going to tell you a story and I need you to pay very close attention to it okay?"

Oakira straightened up and peered into the same sky, closing her eyes. She always found it easier to listen if she kept her eyes closed. Once she was settled, she nodded. "Yes, mother."

"Long ago, when our people were brand new to this world we lived in the physical plane, right here on the world we sit right now. We helped bring life to it. Flora and fauna of all kinds. We were here when the Goddess Yonara herself began making the mortal races. Did you know that?" Elirel asked.

Oakira shook her head and managed to smile. She loved it when her mother told her old stories like this.

"You know that we were created by the spilled pleasure of Yonara and the Progenitor, but do you remember how the Forgotten were created?"

Oakira shook her head, no. She did know, however, all Fae knew. She just enjoyed anytime her mother took the time to tell her stories and enjoyed dragging them out as long as she could.

Elirel smirked, knowing what Oakira was up to. "The twin Gods that we know now as The Bright One and The Hanged One were betrayed by their own sister, Zorog. From their spilled blood Zorog manifested the Forgotten, Archdevils, demons and the like. We had never seen anything like them before and our people attempted to nurture them, for their birth into our world was a truly traumatic one. However, being born of betrayal, selfishness and jealousy made them prone to the very same. It was not long until we were at war with one another. Only two, one from each side of the conflict, refused to partake. They had fallen in love and desired to see an end to the war, hoping that the offspring of our two peoples could bridge the gaps and bring peace."

Oakira looked up at her mother with new enthusiasm. "Someone like me?"

Elirel smiled down at her daughter with barely restrained sorrow. "Yes, my little acorn, someone like you." She leaned her head down and kissed Oakira's forehead before continuing. "They hid their child until he was near adulthood. Together the three of them managed to summon a council to bring the leaders of both sides together and sue for peace. The only peace they managed was to have both sides agree to a temporary hold on the war to deal with what they all saw as a threat to both the Fae and the Forgotten, a child of mixed blood. The Fae feared they would not be able to bring themselves to harm one of their own and so they agreed to stand by as the Forgotten slew the parents. Then together they would slay the child. The Forgotten set upon and slew the child's parents at the meeting and as agreed the Fae stood and watched, doing nothing. The child was so stricken by anger and grief. It knew that the Forgotten were likely to turn on them but had never dreamed the Fae would stand by while such a violent act occurred to one of their own. The child stood defiant and renounced her Fae heritage and burned it out of her very soul. We, the Fae and Forgotten, are beings filled with the arcane. What came to be known too late was that a soul mixed of Fae and Forgotten blood was highly volatile. When one side is vanquished the other erupts in an uncontrollable burst of arcane energy as the remaining side tries to fill the void. It is much like lightning in a storm. There is a buildup of energy that becomes so charged so quickly that it becomes a destructive force. The child's soul engulfed all present in an arcane inferno whose ripples echoed so violently throughout Yonara that Fae and Forgotten were shunted into their own planes of existence. The Fae were forced into the arcane realm and the Forgotten into the Hells."

Elirel took a long breath and closed her teary eyes. They sat in silence for several minutes and continued to watch the stars in the night sky.

"That is why they hate me? They are afraid I might become that very force and bring about destruction again?" Oakira questioned.

"That tale is kept very quiet and known only to the ArchFae of the Courts. That is why the elders fear you. Everyone else just hates the part of you that is not like them." Elirel spoke the truth, the tale had been a closely kept secret among the ArchFae from the beginning. No one wanted such knowledge to get out. They feared that their enemies might essentially forge someone of mixed heritage and use them as a weapon.

Oakira shifted again and crossed her arms with a sneer. "Then maybe they should be nicer to me, so I do not destroy them all." She giggled.

Elirel looked at her daughter in shock. "Oakira!"

"I am just teasing mother! I swear. I do not want anything to happen to you., at least" She threw her arms around her mother and held on tight. The embrace lasted until the small town finally seemed to quiet down just before dawn. They both turned and watched as the sun crested over the horizon and the color spectrum danced between the buildings.

Elirel saw the awe in her daughter's eyes. "Why do you like watching them so much? The mortals?"

"Many of them are like me. They are different from each other and just want to be loved."

Elirel's heart broke. She looked upon her daughter and wanted nothing more than to tell her that everything would change one day. She knew that would be a grievous lie. The time for that kind of peace was long gone. Her brother would never allow them back into the good graces of the Lunar Court.

Oakira suddenly pointed into the city, her keen eyes zooming in on a being that she had not seen before. "Mother? What is he?"

Elirel followed her finger and eyes to a young man with sharp features and light blue skin. On the lowest portion of his back was a thin and pointed tail and on his head were horns that resembled that of the mortal ram. "He is what the mortals call a tiefling."

Oakira looked at her mother with great interest. "I have not seen his kind before. Where do they come from?" she asked.

Elirel ran her hand through Oakira's hair and watched the young man move through the streets. "They come from the very story I told you moments ago. When the child of Fae and Forgotten allowed himself *to be that conduit of arcane destruction that forced Fae and Forgotten into other realms, it covered Yonara in the combined arcane life force of the Courts and the Legions that perished that day. That life bled into the mortal races. Occasionally it manifests in their bloodline and their offspring are born like that young man there. These mortals are the closest to us that any mortal could ever be. They carry the barest sliver of our arcane power. A very special few of them can bend the arcane web to their will without needing to study. There are even a few tall tales that some of them have become so powerful that they too can create pacts like the Fae and Forgotten."*

Oakira's eyes were beaming with all the knowledge her mother had gifted her with tonight. She wanted to know more about how their home and the home of the mortals intertwined together. She leaned back against Elirel. "Tell me more mother. Please."

Elirel was more than a little worried about Oakira's infatuation with the mortals races, but her enthusiasm still brought a smile to her lips. Nevertheless, she changed the subject. "Let's move on from the tales of mortals, Oakira. How about I tell you of spells so secret that many of the ArchFae and Forgotten Lords do not even know them? The three Forbidden Vitae spells that come at the cost of the life of the caster? There is no telling what the future holds for us and if you ever hear me begin to use one of these spells I want you to flee from me and whatever threats are upon as fast as you can. Do you understand?"

Oakira came upon her mother, nearly slumped over in the casting circle and ran to her. "Mother!"

Elirel straightened just enough to come off her hands that had caught her from falling forward. She threw her hand up. "No! You'll disrupt the circle." She was panting heavily with exertion. "I'm almost done for the day."

Oakira stopped mere inches away from the circle's edge. She began to pace around the casting, ringing her hands together with worry. *"This is all my fault. Why did I not listen to her?"* she thought.

After another half hour the arcane circle dimmed and faded. Elirel fell to her side, nearly fully asleep right then and there. Oakira ran to her and dropped onto her knees. She scooped Elirel up and was horrified at how frail her body felt. This was killing her. Guilt rushed over her again. Oakira had felt a lot of that as of late and it was wearing her thin. She placed Elirel down on a bedroll near the faded casting circle and held a cup of cool water to her lips. "You cannot keep doing this mother. It's killing you."

Despite her drained energy Elirel managed to snap at Oakira. "You should have thought of that before you sent that mortal of yours after one of Forgotten Lord Ulrannoth's prime pact mortals. That was too much power at one time. That creature was more Forgotten than mortal. Foolish girl!"

Oakira recoiled from the sudden rebuke. "I just thought tha-"

"Thought that you knew better? Thought your millennium-old mother didn't know what she was talking about? To top it off, he is now carrying around a vulpine child. You might as well have told him to throw a flare into the arcane realm for the Lunar Court to follow. Your lack of clear judgement with this mortal is palpable. You have grown far too attached to him. Were I not as wise as I am I would begin to wonder if you were actually developing true feelings for your pet." Elirel saw the look of culpability on her daughter's face and sighed with a guilt of her own.

Oakira's own stress was high as well. This whole ordeal had been Elirel's plan to begin with. The lies and tension she had created with Kovag in order to get him to follow their plans weighed heavily on her, but she had never considered turning that frustration on her mother. Not until now. "A millennium old ArchFae that knew the consequences of laying with someone from the Forgotten Legions and did so anyway? A millennium old ArchFae that gave birth to the most dangerous of abominations? Is that who I am to compare my carelessness to, mother?"

Elirel gave in and fully collapsed into the bedroll. They sat in silence, both hating themselves for their own words to each other. Elirel finally reached out and placed her shaking hand over Oakira's. "I am sorry, little acorn. I am just tired. So very tired."

Oakira relented and held her mother's hand tight, lying down next to her and looking into her eyes as they slowly closed. "I love you mother. I am sorry too."

"No child, you only did as I instructed. It was too much power to collect all at once, but it places us very near where we need to be to challenge your uncle. Just a few more stolen threads of power and then we will be ready." She was starting to fall asleep.

Oakira moved closer to her mother and held her now shivering body against hers. She pulled the blankets over them and readied herself to feel the shifting of the planes around them. "The plane shift should be coming soon, mother. I will keep watch while you sleep when we get to wherever it is we are arriving."

The area began to hum with arcane energy. Around them everything became a blur as the shifting magic of the teleportation spell took root.

"There they are! Quick throw up the dome!" The voice of an unfamiliar female rang out, barely audible over the arcane hum of the circle.

Oakira looked up and over her mother's sleeping body. The spell had just enough time left for her to see two figures clad in the lunar weave of Seekers sprinting toward them before everything went momentarily black.

Her eyes looked about in the darkness of the in-between. Then blindness struck her as sunlight assaulted her eyes. The teleportation was complete. Wherever they were, it was a beautiful solar-filled morning and there were no Seekers in sight.

Chapter Thirteen

DEBT AND BEWILDERMENT

Alabaster Jakel rubbed his temples in an attempt to comprehend the rapid stream of stupidity he was dealing with. Mounting debt, a failed property grab that has now resulted in him seeking a loan from the Lance, whom he had previously helped finance on occasion, and the sudden reappearance of one of the biggest thorns in his ass. To top it all off, this particular thorn had been living just a few miles away for the last seven months or so and no one had bothered to mention it to him. He began to hum a soothing tune to himself in a vain attempt to reach some sort of calm.

The humming made Marvin, a strangely rail thin halfling, even more anxious. Alabaster had called him in after receiving the news that Callus Kordec was alive and not only living in the Wylds but was also, it seemed, very close with the woman that stole his property project out from under his nose. The very property that had Alabaster in an incredible amount of debt. He knew that Mr. Jakel would be furious that he had not found this information out several months ago.

He scanned the area around Alabaster swiftly to see what was within the onyx tiefling's reach that could quickly become a projectile aimed at his head. He noted that Alabaster's favorite letter opener was the only thing he felt would do any lasting damage and prayed it would not be the first thing Alabaster grabbed.

Marvin rubbed his hands together nervously. Not being able to take the silence anymore, he made the rash decision to speak up. "Mr Jakel, I'm sorry. I did not know that he was of any importance to you. I was not aware of your histo-"

He was cut short. Thankfully just from Alabaster's raised finger and not the letter opener. "Shhh." Alabaster took a deep breath and placed his hands flat on his desk. It was a specially commissioned solid wood desk made from preserved and bleached oak driftwood pieces. He felt the contrast of the stark white wood to his dark skin made him look bigger and '*the center of the room*' as he told the carpenter.

"Marvin. My dear sweet Marvin. Out of my men, I have always considered you to be the wisest. Now, I must come to terms with either being incorrect in that assessment or being dreadfully sorrowful that you are indeed the wisest of my men. Did it not occur to you that even without the history between Callus and MYSELF that I should probably be informed that one of the closest confidants of Ms. Kasha Volstruk, the bane of my financial existence, is the former Scarred Lands Champion? The Towering fucking Tactician? A man that once killed and entire room of men with his fists and a quill? A BLOODY QUILL, MARVIN!"

Marvin shrank back against the wall, his eyes darting back and forth from Alabaster to the letter opener just inches away from his boss's hand.

Alabaster stood so suddenly that his chair fell over behind him. He held his hands out and pinched his thumbs and forefingers together and closed his eyes. "Pick up the chair."

Marvin slowly stepped forward until Alabaster opened one eye and glared at him through it. After which he rushed behind him and stood it up. Alabaster resumed his humming for a longer period than before. This time Marvin kept his mouth shut.

"Marvin, I have decided to take the meeting with the Lance. Please take this correspondence down." Alabaster said through slowly un-clenching teeth. He was desperately wishing Callus, the Talons and other gangs had not been so thorough in wiping out all of his men in Toz'Unro. They never would have let something like this escape their attention.

Marvin scrambled with parchment and quill. In his rush he hit the ink well with a corner of the parchment causing a drop of black ink to splatter on the pure white desk. Alabaster's eye began to twitch. Marvin froze; certain the letter opener would be finding a new home somewhere in his body. Instead, Alabaster cleared his throat and spoke.

"My dear Lance Authern, I would be pleased to meet you to discuss our new business partner, Mr. Zunibar Tolgar, at the proposed time and place. I understand that his travel time from the Helspires will place him here in a few weeks. I am most grateful for your assistance and look forward to a profitable partnership for all of us moving forward. As requested, until the meeting's outcome has arrived, the frequent 'visits' to the Witch's Tits and Tarts will cease.

Yours sincerely, Alabaster Jakel."

Marvin finished, dusted the parchment, rolled it up ad sealed it with the wax seal of Mr. Jakel. "I will deliver it at once Mr. Jakel."

Alabaster shook his head. "No, Marvin. Have one of the city couriers deliver it. I will not have it delivered by one of my own men. If they think I am so scarce of coin that I must send one of my own men, then they will know exactly how badly I need this partnership and I will get the shortest end of the shortest stick. Inform Beetle of the time and place and instruct him to be outside the casino and ready at a moment's notice should events go awry."

Marvin shivered at the name. He would never get used to that orc. He smelled of mold and death. Not to mention the bugs that crawled all over the man. "Yes, Mr. Jakel." Marvin turned to head out the door.

"Marvin."

"Yes, Mr. Jakel?"

"If my desk is not restored to the condition in which it was before you found it necessary to mar it, I will decorate it with your bleached skull."

Marvin choked back a squeal and bowed low before rapidly fleeing Alabaster's office.

Alabaster Jakel stood there staring at the new ink spot and took several slow and deep breaths before looking around at all of the items, artefacts and trinkets he had acquired since his arrival in Hus'rokn a few years ago. He grabbed his bone white leather coat that hung from the back of a soft cashmere lined chair in the corner and threw it on.

His peripheral vision caught sight of himself in the large oval standing mirror he had purchased from a merchant in the Wylds. It had been the very mirror a notorious serial killer from Toz'Naluunod had used as a means to admire his work. The edges of it were beautifully worked dark brown wood from some exotic tree he could not remember the name of. It grew near the ruins of Spearfall, or so he was told. That knowledge alone made it special but add the bloody history of the item and he had to have it for the story it provided.

He meandered over to the mirror and admired his own sharp features. Alabaster scoffed and recoiled a fraction from the mirror at the sight of a newly noticed wrinkle near the edge of skin where his left horn bud would have grown, if his horns had ever come in. He rubbed at the imperfection. "Crone's crusty nethers."

He thought of Callus and all of the rumors the ill-mannered hob-goblin cur had spread as to why he was and remained hornless. All of them had been base and deplorable accusations. While one of them had been an act he had indeed participated in, it was certainly not the reason he was the only hornless tiefling in known memory. The truth was he had simply been born with some disorder that caused his horns not to grow and his tail to split from tip to midway up the appendage. Very few knew about his tail, however. He had learned at a very young age to curl the ends around each other in a spiral and then conceal them further when he could.

So far in his time in Hus'rokn he had reinvented himself. New name, new businessman and a polish on his old personality. He had only been willing to give up so much of the man he was before. Reinventing himself and rarely making appearances in public had helped him remain hidden from those he figured might go the extra mile to find him and remove him from this world.

He set his hands on his hips and squared up in the mirror, puffed out his chest and raised an eyebrow. "Callus shit-heel Kordec. This nightmare just won't end. How your presence here escaped my knowledge is baffling. I suppose I'll have to bring the old Alejak out to find a proper way to put you in the ground. Permanently."

* Three Years Ago *

Callus laid in his bunk in the Talons of Misery Barracks, sharpening one of his scimitars. He was still nursing a hangover from the night before. Every pass with the whetstone made his head throb painfully, but it needed to be done after the attack on the Brightborn recon team that had managed to work its way into Toz'Unro. Their mission didn't have anything in particular to do with the gangs of Toz'Unro, but the Talons were not going to let them get their coin into the hands of anyone that might upset the careful balance that was held within the city.

They celebrated at the Lush Tulips. Madame Elora had finally broken her rule and taken him to bed. Callus had always had a nearly irresistible attraction to the dark elf proprietor. He surmised long ago it was because of the strong yet elegant grip of authority she held over the Lush Tulips. They had a passionate night of releasing four years of built-up tension. She had even brought the elvish twins, Geniveve and Roxy, to their private party.

He should have known something was up when she did that, but all he saw in the moment was six legs, three sets of gyrating hips with smooth lips peaking at him and six gorgeous tits. They had loved him up good and waited for the afterglow to set in before trying to talk him into leaving the Talons. Madame Elora had never supported his decision to join them. He didn't blame her for that either, but he was getting tired of her trying to ply him into leaving the only outlet of belonging he had. Then she used sex to try and convince him to change his mind. He would never admit it to them, but that had genuinely hurt him all the way to what was left of his heart.

The perceived betrayal had him in a melancholy mood. So much so that when he arrived at the barracks in the morning, he immediately went to Blims's bunk and relieved himself on it. He had hoped the little goblin bastard would make a move against him and give him a reason to put him down, but Blims had been pulled away by the hulking and laughing minotaur, Qurezen.

After that, everyone had vacated the barracks, feeling it was best to avoid Callus until he was in a more agreeable mood. He sat up in his bunk and looked over the edge of the scimitar blade. *The only thing left to do was to check how sharp it was. He dropped off the top bunk and walked nonchalantly over to Blim's trunk at the end of his bed. He kicked off the lock and opened it.*

When he spotted the goblin's favorite red bedtime robe, he knew exactly what he should test the blade on. He held it up and smiled as the blade carved through the linen like butter. He waded the shreds up and tossed them back int Blims's trunk. He was getting ready to close it when he spotted something lacy. He feared touching it, unsure where Blims would have gotten it from. He used the tip of his scimitar to pick up the lingerie garment. It was too small to belong to any of the women in the Talons. That's when he noticed the light brown staining at the rear end of the garment. He abruptly laughed out loud and then flung it into the middle of the barracks floor. "I wonder if he wore these when we were butchering the recon team?"

The barracks door creaked open as Raseg stepped in. "My dear, hobgoblin, have I got some good news f-what the fuck are those?"

Callus welcomed the sight of his half orc friend and smirked. "I found them in Blims's trunk."

Raseg's smile was far wider than should have been possible. "You're joking."

Callus shook his head and chuckled. "Thankfully, I am not."

Raseg began laughing so hard that he doubled over. Once they had both recovered from their bout of hysterics and collected themselves Raseg said. "I wonder if they are comfortable?"

Callus raised an eyebrow to which Raseg replied. "Don't be such a prude. Have you never noticed how soft the lingerie of the women at the brothels is when they rub up against you? I don't care that one of the men here is wearing women's undergarments. What I do care about is humiliating Blims. We have to do something special with this information."

Callus chose to drop the topic of who wears what undergarments and focus, like Raseg, on how to use this against Blims. "We could write his name on the waistband and then find a way to leave them in Lindri's desk drawer?"

Raseg's eyes became as wide as an owl's. "Callus, I am certain that this is the best plan you have ever come up with."

Callus was nearly drooling over the what the aftermath would be. "Then we sneak into her office tonight."

The half orc shook his head. "No, as good as this is, it'll have to wait. As I said when I entered, I have some good news for you."

"Well, spit it out then." Callus urged him on with the wave of his hand.

"Alejak finally fucked up. He's been greenlit by the gang bosses. The son of a whore was giving intel to the Brightborn spy detachment we killed. I convinced Lindri and the other bosses that we would be the best men for the job. We are to kill him and seize his assets. Unless, of course, you have better things to do. Perhaps trying on lingerie?"

Callus couldn't remember a day in recent years that had brought him this much happiness. Alejak was the hornless, onyx tiefling that ran the Hornless Devil, a bar that served as a neutral ground for all the gangs of Toz'Unro to meet. That tiefling was filled with so much false bravado that it drove Callus mad. He was a street slag playing at being a debutante. He had never liked Alejak and would have killed him already had the agreed upon accords of the gangs not prohibited any violence from being brought against him. However, if he had turned rat, then he was no longer protected. His desire to drive a blade through the tiefling's belly was possibly the strongest it had ever been for anyone since the arenas. "Does he know we're coming?"

The smile on Raseg's face grew wicked. "Callus, my lingerie kink friend, he doesn't even know that the gangs are aware of his activities."

Callus's smile now matched Raseg's. "If I wasn't so thrilled, I would shove these disgusting panties down your throat. Let's go get the detail from Lindri."

Callus had managed to distract Lindri Three Scales long enough for Raseg to deftly use his arcane hand spell to float Blims's undergarment of shame into one of the drawers of her desk. They had spoken with their dragonscale leader to hammer out the full details on how they were allowed to proceed. She had agreed to give them free rein to do as they willed as long as it did not get in the way of any of the activities of the other gangs' business within the Hornless Devil. Moments after leaving Lindri's office, they were more than a little pleased to hear a guttural roar of anger from inside. A roar that very plainly summoned Blims.

Raseg sat at the usual table on the second floor of the Hornless Devil. It was situated in a corner that overlooked the entirety of the bar, so Alejak could manage everything at will.

The hornless tiefling reclined on a bench across the table from Raseg. "So, Raseg, what business do the Talons of Misery need from me and where is your oh so charming hobgoblin friend?"

Raseg took a sip of the wine that Alejak always had brought to the table when he had business guests. "Callus is on his way. He apologies for his tardiness."

Alejak smirked mid drink. "We both know that is not true." He finished his wine in one go and set the goblet down.

Raseg couldn't help himself. "I have never known you to not savor every drop of wine slowly. Everything alright, friend?"

Alejak shifted in his seat and Raseg noted his eyes shift for just the fraction of a moment to the two guards he had stationed just outside the booth. "Of course, dear Raseg. Of course. It has just been one of the longest days in recent memory. If we could just get down to business, I would greatly appreciate it. I have other items of the utmost importance to attend to."

Raseg could hear Callus approaching and he saw the two guards shift to block his entrance. Callus stopped in front of them with his usual appearance of high irritation anytime he had to be in the presence of Alejak. He stared at the guards with murder in his eyes; incidentally, also his usual mood for being here. Then he said the go words. *"Rusty Trombone."*

The guards looked at each other, confused. Raseg snapped his fingers, and a fire blade extended from his fingertip to Alejak's nose. He then flicked his other hand in a swirling motion that sent a gust of wind into the back of one of the guards. He tumbled forward and burst through the railing, falling to the first floor and landing on a roulette table. The turret of the roulette wheel pierced through the back of his neck and out of his mouth.

Callus grabbed the other guard by his sword arm and coat. He dropped to the ground, pulling the guard to him and then used his leg to lift and kick the man over the railing to join his friend on the first floor.

Callus immediately recovered his feet and in one swift motion unsheathed his scimitar and rested the tip against Alejak's neck. Alejak squealed and managed to squirm a few inches away from the blade.

Downstairs there was yelling and fighting breaking out as the remaining bodyguards and workers that were loyal to Alejak went to war against members of the Talons and some of the other gangs that were privy to the plan.

Alejak cleared his throat and raised his voice to be heard over the commotion. *"Gentlemen, there seems to be a misunderstanding of epic proportions. Let us talk as civil men."*

Raseg chuckled at his feeble attempt to gain some manner of control over the situation. Callus spat at Alejak. *"Any civility I had to aim in your direction long since faded into whatever hole you weaseled out of, you rat."*

Alejak clutched his hand to his chest. "Me? How dare you accuse me of violating the most sacred tenets of my own establishment?"

Raseg pushed the fire blade a little closer toward Alejak's face. "We know about the Brightborn recon team. One of your little birdies saw the opportunity to take you out. Seems he was tired of playing the role of your little...piggy."

Alejak's look of shock changed almost immediately to one of disinterest. He sighed. "I had such a good thing going here. I've always loathed the two of you. A puffed up self-flattering sorcerer and a has been that cannot see his time in the spotlight has long since collapsed into obscurity, just like his imploding life."

Callus had enough. "Bleed." he said, thrusting the scimitar forward and through Alejak's throat. The blade passed through harmlessly and the tip sank into the wall behind Alejak.

Raseg sneered. "You crafty son of a bitch."

The false image of Alejak looked down at the scimitar blade that would have killed him had he actually been sitting there. "You fools. I am more than a little hurt that you believe me so daft. You really thought that I would not see this charade coming?"

Callus was enraged. He grabbed the table that was between Raseg and the image of Alejak and threw it over the balcony. A few of the people below cried out as it slammed into them.

Alejak groaned. "That was a very expensive table."

"We'll find you." Raseg said with an eerie calm.

"No, my dear bitter friends, you will not. I told no one where I was going, and I have not truly been in Toz'Unro for several weeks. I took the coin the Brightborn jackoffs gave me, as well as most of my own and have moved on to greener pastures. If you do manage to find me, I

can assure you I will make your lives and the lives of anyone that cares for you extremely painful. Tata."

With that the false Alejak faded and vanished. The two Talons stared at the now empty space with the utmost hatred. Callus couldn't even speak. Raseg finally broke the silence between the two of them. "Try not to hurt anyone important."

Callus hurled the two nearest stools off the balcony and began to move to the stairs. He was going to find any of Alejak's people that were left alive and correct that status. He stumbled before the first stair down and barely caught himself on the railing as lightning shot down his right leg for the fourth time today.

He could hear Raseg's slow footsteps behind him and he growled even deeper as he felt the half orc's hand on his shoulder. "You picked a fine time to lay down on the job."

"Get fucked." Callus spit toward him.

"Good idea. Maybe we hit the Lush Tulips after the dust settles?" Raseg smiled coolly. "Fret not, however, take the next few minutes off. I've got this part." He opened his palm and aimed it down the stairway at three of Alejak's workers that were already fleeing and unleashed a wave of fire upon them.

CHAPTER FOURTEEN

YOU WEREN'T THERE

It was within sight now, though only because of the enhanced vision of his Fae touched eye, as blurry as it was at the moment. The moons were high but no longer full and clouds covered the sky completely. The oak he and Oakira had sworn on still stood boldly on the forested hill overlooking Silverbreak. The trees around it spaced back several yards and bent toward it as if they were bowing to the sacred tree in reverence.

Kovag had made great time getting here. He and Saffron had only stopped for the necessary breaks that she required to relieve herself as they had before. She slept in the saddle, leaning against him and he harvested leaves from the native thrivenstalk plants on the road. The Emeraldom soldiers had made good use of the plant during the Mongrel War. When chewed it gave the imbiber a sense of euphoria and a burst of energy.

He had managed to break the wooden shaft of the crossbow bolt in his shoulder so that it did not catch on to anything. He had originally planned on leaving it as it was until he was able to get to a sawbones.

However, after the third time it thrummed against a branch he reached back and broke it in half. He had nearly bitten his tongue in half from the pain.

Saffron had remained quiet for the most part. She had excitedly pointed at different animals she had never seen as they rode and Kovag smiled through the radiating pain in his shoulder, telling her what each of them were and everything he knew about them.

Thankfully they passed very few people on the road to Silverbreak. He had heard most coming, but Saffron's vulpine ears had caught a loan rider earlier than he had once. They would turn off the road and hide when they were able. When they were not, he was forced to throw his cloak back over the two of them and hide her and the visible part of the bolt in his shoulder.

Kovag's enhanced eyes were only able to see in shades of gray, so it wasn't until they got closer, and he blinked the vision away that he saw the state of the oak and the trees around it. His shoulders slumped and the breath was driven out of him. Many branches littered the ground and those that were still secure on the tree were sickly looking. The grasses around the base were mostly grayish and brown. He pulled the horse's mane gently once they were securely under the canopy of the tree and hoped off. He still could not breathe. He stumbled to the oak and felt the willow wing blossom in his chest pulse dully. Touching the trunk with his hand he searched for the lively energy that had always flowed through its core. It was there but so very weak.

He pressed his forehead to it with grief and dropped to his knees, looking at the ground where he had buried the cache. The dirt showed signs of disturbance, several months ago by the looks of it. He frantically dug with his fingers. It was gone. He dug deeper and wider in a futile attempt to will it into existence. Maybe he had buried it farther down or more to the left. Finally, he took a deep breath in, and his body shuddered.

All the manufactured energy of the thrivenstalk plant left him. His shoulder throbbed hard enough for him to fall to his side. He had felt the warmth of infection spreading from the bolt since the day after he had been struck, but he had forced it out of his mind. He just needed to make it to the cache and then he could get it remedied. He had made himself believe it. The terrible condition of the tree and the loss of the cache took that determination away from him and his mind suddenly registered just how dire his situation was.

Saffron had watched him with confusion. As soon as he fell, she panicked and slid off the horse. Her foot caught on the stirrup and jerked hard on the side as she fell to her back. Even laying on his side and feeling suddenly overwhelmed by a fever Kovag could tell the horse was spooked and it's hoof was about to trample down on Saffron. He pulled at the arcane reservoir within his chest and threw himself, nearly instantly, over Saffron in a protective shell..

Saffron's eyes were closed but she still heard the hard and hollow sound of the hoof bearing down on Kovag's back and skipping up to clip the back of his skull. She barely heard the grunt that left his lips before unconsciousness found him. She was so terrified at what had just happened that she didn't even notice the sounds of the horse galloping deep into the woods and far away from the two of them.

The assault by the horse had moved Kovag enough that her upper torso and arms were no longer underneath him, coming out just under his extended arm. Saffron wiggled and shimmied to try and get out from under him while shaking him gently at first and then frantically as she realized she was stuck.

With his massive weight upon her she could barely breathe and her inability to stop hyperventilating was making it worse. She was restrained again, just like in the box and the table and the crates with a hole in the floor before that. Her memory was flooded with the torments of the dungeon. His massive weight began to feel more and more oppressive over her. She remembered the sounds of other people crying and screaming. Sounds of chopping and of knives being sharpened. The smell of burning flesh rushed into her nostrils. She lost control of herself and began to beat her arms against Kovag's lifeless body relentlessly. Tears streamed down her face to mix with the dirt that had been kicked up onto her cheeks from the fall. Her mouth opened in a soundless scream. Inch by inch she squirmed free, but the torture still went on for several minutes before she managed to get out from under him.

Frantically she pushed herself away from him, scooting backward on her hands and feet until she had her back against the tree. She brought her knees up to her chest and buried her head in her arms. Her eyes stayed wide open. She couldn't have closed them if she wanted to. Fear that she would see the dungeon again gripped her entirely. Her tail came up and around her in the comforting way that it had always seemed to do on its own.

It took some time, more time in her mind than in truth. Every minute seemed like it stretched out for hours. Kovag groaned, still on the ground facedown several feet away. Saffron moved her head up just enough for her eyes to glance at him over her folded arms. There was a small trail of blood from the back of his head and down his neck. His face lay in the dirt, half visible. She was struck then by the same overwhelming feeling of connection she had when he stood over her as she lay strapped to the table in the dungeon of that monstrous woman.

She sniffled and wiped her nose and eyes on her tail before crawling over to him. She sat on her knees next to his head and gently petted his cheek. *'He has a kind face. Always kind to me,'* she thought. She pushed at his shoulder in a vain attempt to rouse him. She slapped his back, poked his ribs and even tried pitching him on the back of the arm. Nothing worked. Her tears were falling freely, and she realized that for the first time she was not crying for herself. She was not crying out of fear of pain being brought to bear against herself. She wept at the thought of Kovag being gone from her life, gone from this world. It was a foreign feeling that she didn't know how to fully process.

She gave into being unable to wake him and instead pushed herself under his arm and curled up against him. His body moved slightly against her as he breathed, and she felt a little comfort as she recognized that the rhythm was the same as when he slept. She burrowed her head under his chin and closed her aching wet eyes.

Roughly two years ago. Southern Brightborn Kingdom

The stars were more visible to him now than they had ever seemed before and in her presence, they were always more splendid in their sparkling color palettes. She had come to him for the first time in five months. The time she allotted for him had dwindled over the years. But every time she came back, she apologized and explained to him again how their relationship could never be more than it was, and every time he forgave it and felt foolish for wanting more than what was agreed in their pact.

For at least a decade now he had been out in the world slaying Forgotten, renegade Fae and their followers to help siphon power for Oakira's aims. Much had changed since the first days. He remembered all the targets she had given him. The first had been dreadfully sloppy and he nearly got himself killed. The last one, a few nights ago, had been flawless. While he got better at siphoning power for her; better at killing, other aspects of their pact had started to dwindle away.

When this all started, she would not go a day without speaking to him through their connection or sending a vibration into the willow wing blossom to let him know she was watching. She would never go more than two months without embracing him under the full moons, that sliver of time when she could physically visit him. He had told her once that he feared she was becoming bored with him. She floated in front of him and cradled his face in her small hands and explained to him that they were gaining power quicker than she imagined, but she needed to make absolutely sure they were powerful enough to withstand any opposition to their reconciliation with or ruination of the Lunar Court before they could be found out. Every time she came to him it sent a ripple of energy through Yonara's arcane web. The more powerful they became, the more noticeable that ripple was.

What she did not tell him was that her mother had been able to sense their small surges of power in the web and feared that if she could feel them while being so far removed from the Court, then surely the Lunar Court itself had noticed. Without more power the Court would quell their meager resistance and snuff them all out permanently.

It had been a couple of days since he set up camp in a meadow several miles south of the last river crossing before Cairnbaduhr. While his last target had been handled with relative ease, thanks to a well-timed spell to mute the corrupt Fae of the Umbra Court, it was still a Fae that he had gone head-to-head with and that always meant several severe contusions at least. His ribs had stopped breaking over the last few years, finally growing accustomed to the punishment they were being repeatedly given. He had developed an unfortunate habit of allowing blunt weapons, kicks and fists to impact with his core so he could lock his own arm over the blow and trap whatever was used against him with his, typically, greater strength.

Oakira was not too far off in the distance, staring at something or someone on the horizon. Kovag had seen her go through this little ritual time and again. After they lay together, she would grow quiet and walk away, using her Fae sight to watch people go about their business. This ritual always preceded informing him that she needed to leave.

He rose to a sitting position and stared after her forlornly. He began to reminisce about their first years. They used to laugh and tease each other before she left. They would share long moments just staring at each other with the sort of smiles that would have made people sick. He allowed himself to truly believe that she was in love with him then. Now he knew he was just being young and foolish. He shook his head to cut the thread in his mind that attempted to remember those simpler days. He clutched his ribs and stood before bending down to grab a cloth and walk to a nearby stream. The water flowed all the way from the mountains over Void Fall Keep. No matter what time of year it was nearly as cold as ice. He squatted down with a groan and submerged the cloth in the cool water. He pressed it to his throbbing ribs. Slowly, he rocked backward onto his rear and closed his eyes as he sensed Oakira hovering over the ground toward him. She felt suddenly aloof. He knew what was coming and he found that he didn't want her to speak.

"Do you remember the Helspires?" He quickly spat out.

Oakira stopped a few feet behind him. She tilted her head to the side. "With utmost clarity."

"What was the bastard's name? The voidsmith that was making those void tainted weapons for the gladiator bouts. Hells, I can't-Balcazar. That's what it was, Balcazar." He threw one of his hands up and snapped his fingers as he suddenly remembered the name.

Oakira straightened and floated next to him now. She moved into a sitting position, with her chin on her knees next to him, still hovering a few inches off the ground. "Half Forgotten slave of Kathal Mortis. He was making blades for a real sinister halfling, Xapos, if memory serves. The crimes that little man committed before he was enslaved for the arenas were...atrocious. Why do you bring that up. That was what eight years ago?"

Kovag continued on as if she had not said anything. "I snuck in there real quiet. Right into the bowels of that damned citadel. I had never been so scared in my life then, or since. Had I been just half a second slower that dagger he was working on would have taken my throat out." He looked down at his forearm and stared at a small scar of a healed burn. "Glad it was just the tongs in his hand at that point. Had it not been I'd probably be dead from void poisoning, just like whoever those blades had been meant for, poor fool."

He chuckled lightly. "I remember hiding just long enough to hear that eerily monotone voice show more concern that the blades had not been full void charged, before telling someone I couldn't see to track me down. Had you not cast that concealment spell, I am sure I'd be dead. That whole mess was sloppy."

"Kovag." She turned her head to him.

He wanted to say he remembered that being the last time he felt she truly showed any worry about what might happen to him if things went wrong, but then he thought better of it and held back. He kept his gaze forward. "How are my mother and sister?"

Oakira felt a deep sorrow in him. It was the same one she had felt growing slowly over the last few years. For a moment her heart almost overrode her senses. She had to mentally force herself not to reach for him. She and her mother had a plan, and she had already gotten far closer to this pact mortal than she ever should have. At the mention of his family, she tensed. Had Kovag not had his eyes closed, he would have seen the change in her posture. A telltale sign that she had momentarily grown uncomfortable.

"They are well. The tavern is running optimally, and you sister is being courted by a baker's youngest son." The words felt like a dagger dragging down her spine as she spoke them.

He relaxed his shoulders and moved to wet the cloth for his ribs again. Muscles in his lower back spasmed briefly and he fell forward onto his hands and knees.

Oakira lurched forward and caught him. "Why will you not let me heal any of this anymore? Do you have to be so stubborn all the time?"

The tone of her voice changed and Kovag could almost feel the same emotion in her voice that she used to show him every day and his own response, while factual, had a playful edge to it. "I told you. It is a reminder that even with the power you give me, I can still die. I don't want to get too cocky. I'd like to see what life has in store for me once we finish with the Lunar Court and if I allow myself to think that you'll swoop in and save me from this pain every time... I'll get careless."

He cleared his throat and attempted a deep breath. "If I am ever bleeding out though, by all means, override that concern."

She felt her softer side pushing out from the veil she had erected to try and keep a barrier between her and her deceit. "You are incapable of not being too 'cocky.' You cannot help what you are born with." She said with a smile while pushing a warm healing sensation through him and soothing the muscle spasm and bruising away from his ribs.

Kovag allowed his pride to take a break and did not fight the spell. After a few deep breaths all of the pain was gone, and he sat back on his haunches. "Are Fae men not so gifted in that area?" He pushed his head against hers and allowed himself to fall back into the banter they had shared so rarely these days.

She kissed his temple. "I would not know. But my mother always said that no Fae could stand up to a passionate mortal, no matter how they are equipped. Something about mortality filling Yonarans with far more lust and zeal in the act. She may have just used it as an excuse to live with lust though. She was not always as rigid as she is now."

They shared a chuckle between them. Kovag moved his eyes to hers. "I miss this."

Oakira's smile faded. "I have to go. I can feel the pull from the moon cycles too keenly. It is weakening me and making me dizzy. I'll try my best to get back to you next cycle."

As she softly kissed him, he felt the usual mix of emotions course through him. There was the encompassing sadness that he had grown used to at this point, but then there came a wave of comfort. A wave that vanished as soon as she faded away. It made the sadness turn to despair, but not because she was gone. It faded because he knew the comfort was something she willed into him, and that felt like betrayal.

The dreams came to her like clouded memories seen with eyes open under murky waters. It was chaos, there was darkness followed by blinding light and the cries of a woman. Soon there was humming and a soothing hand brushing over her hair and ears as she began to feel full and sated. That memory, the only kind one she could recall, never lasted long. Soon the humming turned to shrieks and sobbing. There was a hard thud and a wailing followed by deafening silence, only broken by her own outcry and confusion. After that there were various memories of houses that came and went. Sometimes she would see a regal study filled with books, and a fireplace with a human, dwarf and elf conversing while puffing smoke into the air.

In this memory there was always an orcish woman in the corner, wearing fine clothing that her masters did not take the time to have tailored for her. The woman would spare quick smiles in her direction and contort her face in amusing ways that she first found odd but then amusing. She would sneak into that room at night when no one else was around and give her scraps of food from somewhere else in the home until the day the elfish man caught her and beat her to death right in front of the cage.

After that, all she remembered before Tsarra's dungeon cellar was pain and rebukes of the pull of a leash and toe of a boot anytime she showed the slightest bit of happiness or curiosity. She was not allowed these simple dignities. She lashed out once and only once, and that bite found her relocated to the worst conditions she had ever been forced to live in. Here, any attempt to move or make noise was always met with a the whack of a stick or the shaking of her cage accompanied by harsh words that she did not understand. Once she grew old enough to comprehend the speech of those around her, she began to cover her ears. While she could understand the words, she couldn't comprehend them and something deep within her made her feel that it was best she could not.

"We should steal her. She'll be of an age to take to bed not too long from now. Think of the coin we can get from selling her offspring. The mistress keeping her alive just to sacrifice is a bloody damn waste. Her kind have so many more uses."

"You want to double cross Tsarra? Are you mad? That woman will flay you alive and then try and breed you. All while laughing and whipping you with that thorny lash she loves so fucking much."

"A fella can dream, can't he?"

"Hold the Hells on. Are you dreaming about the lashing or the vulpine girl?"

"Do I have to choose?"

"You need serious help, Lars. Serious bloody help."

"Is it true they can heal people too? Wasn't that what Mistress Tsarra was trying to do with her originally? Get her to heal these poor sods between torture sessions, drag out the pain?"

"Yeah but, supposedly they can only do it if they bond with the person they are healing. At least that is what I overheard Mistress Tsarra raving about when that dark wizard brought her that tome. Most nobles are too obsessed with using them as sex slaves to try and find out, I think. I'd imagine forcing them or grooming them into being a cock warmer and pussy licker might cause them to not be too agreeable to bond with someone. Let's be honest with ourselves, it is a pretty nasty practice, sex slavery."

"Pays good though and not like the beast folk or the Mongrels are actually people in any case. Speaking of, we still celebrating Mishika's birthing day at the Velvet Grimalkin? Gods, I love that place."

"Aye, Mishika said she wants to taste that goblin bitch again."

"Good, I'm almost done cleaning the hooks and blades. She really got them gummed up this time. Tsarra said she wants each quarter of the body placed at the corners of the mansion's borders. You get the wheelbarrow, and I'll meet you out back."

After the men left, she dared to open her eyes again. She always tried her best to pretend to be sleeping the majority of the time she was in the cage. She crawled to the bars and peered out into the cellar. The only light came from the tiny rectangular windows that were placed near the ceiling. She never dared to think about escaping. The fear of what would be done if she failed was far too great and it gripped her chest tightly. It was a good thing it did. Even if she managed to get out of her cage the windows were too small even for her to fit through. It would not be long before more people were brought here for the mistress to play with.

That's what Tsarra told her when she was first brought here, and the sights and sounds scared her more than she thought possible.

'Do not be afraid my child. I am just playing with them. They like the games I play.'

She may have been naïve, but she knew the pleading and the screams people made were not the noises people made when they were playing.

A few weeks passed with a handful of play sessions with others before Tsarra had decided it was time for her to be on the table. She was so filled with panic that she would have gnawed her own arm off if she could have. Her bestial instincts were in overdrive. Her pupils were dilated nearly to the edges of her eyelids and her heart and lungs burned with overexertion. The pain that followed was made worse because it brought what was left of her rational mind to the forefront and she was able to feel the fear of death, but then he came.

When she saw him burst through the door. Her spirit lurched in his direction. Something happened to her that she was simultaneously clueless of and yet fully understanding at the same time. She could see what looked like mists of strange energy around the half orc that she would come to know as Kovag, silver swirls with green hues. Her eyes moved to Tsarra when she noticed that she was not by the table anymore. When she found the monster getting up from the ground, she could see mist of dark blood red glittered with a black so deep that she had to pull her eyes away for fear that it would draw her in. Even with her eyes closed she could make out her own mist. Shades of gold and yellow moved in patterns that made no sense. She didn't understand then that she was seeing traces of the arcane.

It seemed an eternity before Kovag made it over to her and unbound her from the table.

The warmth of the sun coupled with a lightly cool breeze of the morning and the smell of wildflowers greeted Kovag as he stirred awake. He yawned and began to stretch, immediately stopping when he awoke enough to feel Saffron curled against his chest and under his arm. A smile broke upon his face and then vanished with the flooded memory of the bolt lodged in his shoulder blade.

He didn't feel the fever upon himself anymore and there was no pain. He slowly peeled himself away from Saffron and sat up, using the opposite arm to reach around and feel for the wound. He felt nothing. His flesh held no sign that the bolt had been there to begin with.

He turned to look for a blood pool and did indeed see one where his shoulder would have been resting for most of the night. He also saw the bolt laying there, as if it had been expelled from his body.

'How?'

He looked at the oak tree he and Oakira had sworn their pact on and reached out, trying to feel the tether to it. He wondered if perhaps Oakira had visited him in the night and healed him, but the moons had not even been full last night. There was no lingering tingle of her magic.

It was only when he placed his hands down on the ground to stand up that he felt the wildflowers he had smelled just seconds ago. The flowers had bloomed around him and Saffron during the night. Even in his muddled state last night he was absolutely certain there were no flowers here before.

Kovag gazed upon Saffron. She slept peacefully and squarely in the middle of the flower patch.

'Did she?'

Saffron wiggled and reached out into the space Kovag had been in when he woke up. Her wiggle turned into a shake and her face contorted into something that danced on whatever one might suggest comes after terror. Her hands searched again for him, but more frantically. Not feeling him, she shot up and looked around, tears beginning to fill her eyes. In the back of her mind, she saw it again, the dark and warped figure of black and deep purple void. She attempted to push it from her mind but before she could, she already forgot why she was frightened. Almost every time she awoke, she had the sense she was forgetting something terrifying. Her eyes were set on Kovag, and she ran to him quickly.

He dropped to a knee and opened his arms, folding them around her as she barreled into him. Her heart was thundering so heavily he felt it in his own chest. He held her for a moment until he felt her heart no longer pounding. He unfurled his arms and set his hands about her shoulders, pushing her back slightly.

"Are you alright?"

Saffron nodded and wiped a single tear from her cheek.

"Did you do this? Did you heal me?" He pointed first at the patch of flowers and then inclined his head to motion at his shoulder.

Saffron looked at the flowers puzzled, and then at Kovag's shoulder. She walked behind him and lifted his cloak and tunic to see the bolt no longer there. Her head tilted to the side in further confusion before moving in front of him again.

She motioned with a big shrug and rounded innocent eyes before walking over to the flowers, bending down and picking the ones that were orange, blue and pink.

Kovag remained motionless, unable to fathom what exactly had happened. If Saffron had done this, what other magics did her people possess? Or was this a talent specific to her?

She skipped back over to him and began weaving several of the flowers into his beard with a ridiculously large smile on her face.

A new feeling hit him harder in the chest than the bolt had four days ago. Kovag stared at Saffron in wonder. *Is this what it would have been like? Is this what I allowed to be taken from me?'*

A sudden pull came from the oak, nearly making Kovag lurch forward toward the tree. Saffron too felt it. However, where Kovag felt a sense of relief, albeit a fading one, Saffron jumped behind him at the feeling of the unfamiliar arcane jolt.

Oakira's voice came in a broken whisper. "We pulled too much at once. I'm sorry Kovag, they are coming. Leave the girl somewhere safe and do not use the arcane, the Seekers will track it. I am... sorry."

Her voice echoed in his head in a way it never had before, as if she were trying to subvert the usual method of contacting him through their pact.

"Oakira, are you in trouble?" Before he finished reaching for her the arcane pull of the oak was gone.

Chapter Fifteen
RENEWED FEAR

A full week had passed since Callus and Egrim had made up over a bottle of Mommy Milkers Breakfast Stout. To both Kasha and Arialyn's astonishment the pair had not just returned to normal with each other but were palling around in their off hours half the time as well. They had both come home late two nights ago with more fresh bruises and a tale of a bar scuffle the women actually believed may have been true this time.

It had also been a full two weeks since anyone or anything had shown up in or around the Tits to harass Kasha. On the one hand she was thankful for the interlude and hoped Alabaster had grown bored of the childish bullying. On the other hand, she feared the break was because something more sinister was being brewed and he was attempting to distance himself from the situation for better deniability.

Nearly every table within the Tits main room had cloth of some kind upon it. Kasha was currently directing Callus, who stood on a tall ladder to fold an amber colored drape of long decorative lacy silk cloth over a woodworked gargoyle between the first and second floors. This particular gargoyle, while grotesque and dog-like in the face, had breasts that were two sizes too big by Callus's estimation. Three if you asked Egrim. The amber color was meant to catch the arcane firelight from the sconces nearby and make the breasted dog look like it had a sheer gown that was caught in the sunlight.

Egrim was holding the base of the ladder even though Arialyn had installed two stabilizing feet on it. When weight was applied to the bottom rung of the ladder three spikes from each foot would pierce whatever surface the ladder stood on, stabilizing it. When the weight was removed, the arcanomancy enchantment she placed on it would mend the holes made by the spikes no matter what the surface had been. Unless the holes had been placed in organic material. Which is why, even though she didn't need to, she told them both to make sure they did not get their feet stuck under it.

"You know Kasha, the way these nipples stick out, you could hang the damned drape from them. These are ridiculous." Callus chuckled.

"Don't gawk too closely, Callus. You'll lose the only eye you have left." Egrim called up to him.

Kasha rolled her eyes with a heavy glare of silent annoyance. "It's art you uncultured asses. Besides, Sylus had one just like it on the outside of his caravan."

Callus leaned back on the ladder and inspected it further with discerning eyes.

Not too far away at a mostly clear table Arialyn showed Morrigan the mending spell she had learned a few months back. She was currently piecing a few broken mugs back together. When she was done with each one you couldn't even tell they had been used before, let alone see that they had been damaged. She looked up at Callus and then smiled at Morrigan. "Two cinnamon candies says he falls."

Morrigan looked up to see Callus leaning back and even she shook her head at how far back he was leaning. Egrim looked like he was ready to let go of the ladder he was uselessly holding and catch him.

Callus's eyes went wide with recognition, and he smiled wide. "Ah-ha. I remember that now! I knew I had seen nipples like that somewhere!" He lowered his voice then but only barely. "Hells, I jacked off to that thing when I was a kid."

Arialyn laughed out loud. Egrim groaned and hoped Morrigan was not paying attention and Kasha stood there with her mouth open before crying out, "Bright One's heart, Callus. Really?! That is disgusting."

"Interesting, I thought you just said it was art."

Arialyn piped in. "Art should be appreciated, Kasha."

Kasha turned her head to Arialyn, a little shocked that she had taken his side on the matter. "Well, there's a child here."

Callus scrunched up his lips. "Yeah, a child in a brothel pub. Might be she hears a lot worse very soon."

Kasha raised her finger and tried to think of something to retort with and could find nothing to counter the validity of what he had just stated.

Callus looked down at Egrim and gave him a shrug of apology. Egrim shook his head and snorted, albeit with a smile on his face.

A moment later, a knock came from the door and Captain Ethan called out from the other side. "Open up! Hus'rokn Guard."

Kasha was thankful for the interruption because for the life of her she could still not think of a retort to Callus's comment. "Coming!"

She opened the door and gave a false look of concern. They had recently agreed to stop making it appear that they were all on very friendly terms with one another just in case Alabaster and his men were watching. Something they wished they had done previously.

"May I speak with you inside Madame Volstruk?"

She nodded tentatively. "Yes, of course. Please come in."

Once inside and with the door closed, Ethan relaxed his posture. "Good morning, everyone."

Morrigan waved at the captain and then put her hand out to Arialyn expectantly. She looked over to see Callus step off the ladder and narrowed her eyes at Morrigan playfully before reaching into her pocket and pulling out four pieces of cinnamon candy instead of two. Morrigan's eyes glowed at that. She whistled up at Lemmy in the rafters and shared a piece with him when he landed on the table.

Callus approached Ethan and clasped his forearm in greeting. "How goes the day?"

Ethan smirked. "Not so great actually and that's why I'm here. I stopped by the Amethyst Artificer and when I saw you weren't home, I figured the two of you would be here. I may need to hire you to protect me from your lady I'm afraid."

Arialyn realized what day it was. Precisely three weeks had passed since the last shipment of void ore. She had been so caught up in helping Kasha that she had somehow let it slip her mind that she needed to be home today. She couldn't believe she had been so careless, and with her precious shipment to boot. "Hells, it's Bridra. Sorry, Captain. I completely let it slip my mind. Kasha, we'll have to come back. Callus and I need to unload-"

The captain coughed hard and looked equal parts embarrassed and angered. "Actually, that won't be necessary, Arialyn."

She and Callus both looked at him slightly perplexed. The captain's tone remained apologetic, but he was clearly frustrated. "Both the shipment and my men have not returned through the gates."

"You think they got delayed out in the Scarred Lands?" Arialyn said as she fell in line next to Callus.

"I am doubting they were simply delayed."

Callus noted that the more Ethan talked about the matter the more irritated he got. "Raiders?"

"I don't know who else it could be. I'm sorry for my current state. I've never had shipment issues before. Your last shipment got held up at the Trade Gate and now this. It is highly unprofessional and not the reflection I want when I do business. I want you to know I'll have it handled. I am taking Sergeant Serine and a few of those I trust into the Scarred Lands to see if we can figure out what happened. Most things I would just write off as a loss and make a deal with the client for discounted goods next time around, but your particular items are far too valuable and dangerous not to go after." Ethan shook his head in disappointment. "I'm sorry about this mess."

Arialyn shook her head and waved off his apology. She was very upset about the matter, but she knew there was nothing he could do about it now. She was definitely planning on having a conversation with him about increasing the number of men that guard the shipment next time but now was not the time and knowing how the captain was, he was going to make sure he did that anyway. Regardless, she was hoping her face wasn't as red as she felt it was. "I know you will do what you can. Do you need Callus to go with you?"

"Sweetheart, are you asking our dear captain if he wants my assistance or am I being voluntold to go?" He looked down at her with a quizzical glare.

The Captain held his hand up. "Normally I would jump at the chance to tempt your man into my line of work, but this is my mess, and I will be the one to get it cleaned up."

"If you change your mind, I would be agreeable to getting out of the city for a little while. So would Egrim." Callus waited for the large man's reaction.

"Fuck you." Egrim spoke the words without even looking up from his current task or relocating the ladder.

"There it is." Callus said.

The Guard Captain shook his head. "Again, my friends, I appreciate the willingness to aid me in this, but my people and I need to take care of it. I just wanted to make you aware of the situation. With that, I must be going. We need to use as much of the daylight as we can before nightfall."

Captain Ethan made a hasty exit to avoid further offers of assistance. It was definitely not that he didn't want the help. However, he truly felt an obligation for he and his men to rectify the situation themselves. He also didn't want anyone to see him and Callus leaving the city together and possibly coming back with a cart full of goods. The less attention paid to his operations the better. The city might be run by organized crime, but that didn't mean there weren't other people ready to pounce on his operation and potentially take it over. No one's business in Hus'rokn was safe unless they could keep it that way.

Not to mention the anonymity of his clients was often a larger portion of the coin he collected than the coin for the actual goods. A client would pay him extra for added reassurance that their items were kept beyond secret. He had even recently had a very shady gnomish gentleman from the Emeraldom attempt to schedule an import several months back. The added security request for this little importation was to kill the men the gnome sent to deliver the goods to Hus'rokn. Dead men tell no tales and all that. The good Captain was not squeaky clean, but cold-blooded murder, that was something he would never abide. So, he declined the offer and told the gnome to go fuck himself.

Arialyn watched the captain rush off toward the main guard posting and sighed in frustration. "Callus, that much void ore missing...this is dangerous."

He placed a hand on her shoulder to attempt to reassure her. "I know, love. If he isn't back in three days, I'll head out to look for him."

"WE will head out to look for him." She said looking up at him with a stare that dared him to argue.

"We." He agreed.

They shut the door to the Tits and moved to continue getting the tavern ready. There had been several minutes of silence before Kasha asked Arialyn how much of a setback that amount of lost void ore would put on her work. Before Arialyn could answer a pounding knock came at the door rapidly followed by a single louder thud.

Egrim groaned. "I've got it."

As he approached the door he called out. "You had damned well better have a groveling apology for the aggressiveness of that fucking knock."

As soon as he unlatched the door an eruption of smoke and flames blew the door off its hinges and sent Egrim, in flames, several feet away onto his back.

Kasha's instincts were thankfully quicker than her shock could register and was on Egrim almost right as he hit the floor; her hands spread out as a burst of frosty wind blew the flames out.

Arialyn pushed Morrigan behind her and drew her arcabus at the door while Callus was already out in the street with the Hangman's Spear, surveying the street to look for the culprit of the attack. His eyes scanned in both directions but found nothing and no one he could pinpoint. Nothing seemed out of the ordinary, other than those in the street fleeing the explosion and an intensely angry hobgoblin wielding a spear in the street.

Kasha ripped open Egrim's shirt and inspected him for wounds as he lay there groaning. There were a few abrasions from the splintered wood of the door but other than that there was no damage to him except the smell of burning hair and most likely a headache from hitting the floor. Her eyes seemed to lose focus for a moment, and she saw a faint glow on his chest. When she looked directly at the spot it was gone. She blinked her eyes several times and wondered if there was an arcane charge to the explosive that left a rapidly fading residue there.

"Egrim! Are you okay?" She placed her hand on his cheek and leaned over him.

His senses came back to him, and he grasped her hand in his. "I'm fine. How's the beard?"

She saw Callus come back in through the front door with a shrug and knew that they were safe for now, she breathed a sigh of relief. "Completely burned away I'm afraid."

He sat up in a panic and grasped at the braids of his beard, finding them mostly intact. He glared at her. "Evil."

"Do you think I would be this calm if your beard was gone?" She thumbed at the scar on his lower lip. "If you didn't have the beard no soul alive would find you intimidating and you would be of no use to me." She blushed lightly. Truly she would have probably been more outraged than he if the beard had been taken. She loved the look of it on him.

Egrim didn't have time to retort before Morrigan slammed into his chest sobbing. He wrapped his arms around her and held her tight. "Shh, I'm fine sweetness." He kissed the top of her head and stood up slowly.

Despite the circumstances Kasha smiled at the way Morrigan looked nearly like a baby in Egrim's massive arms. "Arialyn could you?"

Arialyn motioned for Egrim to sit down. "Over here big man. I'll get those cuts sealed." She was already pulling her gloves off and the warm blue light of arcane medicae dully glowed around them.

Callus moved over to Kasha while keeping an eye on the door. "I saw no one of note, but this was nailed to the outer wall by the door."

He handed her a folded piece of parchment with a wax seal that was unfamiliar to him.

Kasha took it from his hands and tore her eyes away from Egrim and Morrigan. She looked down at the parchment in her hands and turned it over to see the red wax seal. Her blood ran cold. The impression in the wax was a familiarly stylized 'Z'. Her hands began to shake, and the color drained from her face. Unconsciously she could hear Callus asking her if she was alright and who the parchment was from, but she couldn't form the words to answer him. With the painstaking slowness of a quivering hand, she peeled it open

To the proprietor of the Witch's Tits and Tarts Tavern, Madame Kasha Volstruk,

The Lance requests the blessing of your audience at the Lucky Talisman Casino post haste. Be prepared to discuss the terms of the transfer of deed and title of The Witch's Tits and Tarts Tavern as well as the re-establishment of your contract to Mr. Tolgar. Should you fail to answer this summons our future invitations will be exponentially more forceful.

With the kindest regards,

Lance Authern on behalf of Mr. Tolgar

Without another word, she dropped the parchment and ran to the master suite, shutting and locking the door behind her.

Chapter Sixteen

Tools of the Trade

The darkness of the Umbra Court pressed in around them like a physical force. Where the Lunar Court held an eternal twilight beneath twin moons, here there was only the faintest bluish-gray glow emanating from crystalline formations that jutted from the ground at irregular intervals. The air itself felt thick and oppressive, carrying the sulfuric taste of dark magic.

Elirel stirred weakly in Oakira's arms, her eyes fluttering open. The teleportation had drained what vital energy she had left after maintaining the concealment spells for so long. Her normally radiant skin had taken on an almost translucent quality, the veins beneath clearly visible.

"Where..." Elirel's voice came out as barely more than a whisper.

"The Umbra Court, mother," Oakira said, trying to keep the tremor from her voice. "But we have a problem. The Seekers found us just as we were shifting."

Elirel's eyes snapped fully open, panic giving her a momentary surge of power. She gripped Oakira's arm with surprising strength. "Seekers? How many? How close did they get to us?"

"Two of them. A master in full silver and another in three-quarter weave," Oakira said, supporting her mother's head as she tried to sit up. "One of them yelled to place a dome, but they did not have time. I had to warn Kovag."

"No, no, no," Elirel moaned, her brief surge of energy already fading. "He sent two. I should not be surprised. They might be able to track the residual energy. The Umbra Court is no place for us to hide. Reaching out to him was foolish." She attempted to push herself up but collapsed back into Oakira's arms, her breathing labored.

Oakira felt tears welling in her eyes as she watched her mother struggle. "I had no choice. We can move again once you've rested. Just sleep now."

"You do not understand, child." Elirel choked out, her eyes growing heavy despite her obvious desire to stay conscious. "The Seekers... they're relentless. They will not stop until..." Her voice trailed off as unconsciousness claimed her once more.

Oakira held her mother close, feeling more alone than she ever had before. Around them, the purple crystals pulsed with an otherworldly rhythm, as if the very heart of the Umbra Court beat in time with her mother's weakening breaths. She knew they couldn't stay here long, the Umbra Court was home to the darkest of the Fae, and they would show no mercy to refugees from the Lunar Court.

But for now, all she could do was wait and hope her mother would recover enough strength to move them again. The willow wisp blossom, her connection to Kovag'Dresh, entered her mind. She could not be sure why it was bursting into the forefront of her thoughts right now, unbidden. Had she subconsciously wished he were here to lend her some kind of aid? No, against two Seekers? Even as powerful as he had grown over the years, they would toy with him. Right? More than likely he called for her, another call that she would not answer. Should she answer though?

The thought was quickly dismissed. Any use of their connection now would only make it easier for the Seekers to find them, and they had already gotten so close. Still, with her mother sleeping from arcane exhaustion, she wished she could call out to him... tell him everything. She realized now, with her mother helpless, just how alone she was and that it was a loneliness of her own making.

Oakira traced her fingers along her mother's pale cheek, remembering another time when moonlight had cast similar shadows across another face she had grown to cherish, despite being told not to become attached. The memory of that first night with Kovag beneath the ancient oak arose unbidden in her mind, as crisp as the autumn air had been that evening.

He had been so young then, barely into adulthood, with an innocence in his eyes that belied the strength in his arms. When she approached him for the pact, she had expected resistance, bargaining, or at least suspicion. Instead, he had listened with such earnest attention, asking thoughtful questions that showed wisdom beyond his years. His acceptance of the terms had been almost immediate, though she now wondered if he truly understood what he was giving up.

But then, that had been the plan her mother had set her to. Locate a mortal, so lost in themselves, in their troubles, that they would agree to anything. Oakira had been sitting in the branches at the crown of that oak tree, crying over that very plan when he fell against the trunk that night. She had felt such compassion for him then and she convinced herself that in the long run she was helping him. She was no longer sure if she could make the same choice if she had to do all over again.

The dark crystals of the Umbra Court pulsed again, casting eerie shadows that made her mother's sleeping form seem even more fragile.

Oakira closed her eyes, letting herself drift back to those early days when she and Kovag would spend hours together talking through their spiritual connection after each successful hunt, and the rarer times around the full moons when they would share themselves with one another. She had taught him about the arcane web, showing him how to channel the energy they collected. He had taught her about mortal customs, making her laugh with tales of tavern brawls and festival mishaps.

"You have become far too attached." Elirel had warned her one evening, after catching the way Oakira's eyes lingered out into nothingness with a fondness that told her Oakira was not present. "He is mortal, daughter. His entire life will pass in what you will consider a mere moment once you reach my age. Do not be foolish enough to let your thoughts become entangled with your tools. That is what you made him when you entered into that pact, my dear daughter. A tool."

Elirel shifted now, in her sleep, mumbling something incoherent, and Oakira felt a fresh wave of guilt wash over her. Her mother had been right, of course. Each time Kovag succeeded in his task, each time he grew stronger and channeled more power to them, it became harder to maintain their concealment. The ripples in the arcane web grew larger, more noticeable. She had been forced to distance herself, to make their meetings shorter and less frequent, though every time she left him, a piece of her seemed to stay behind.

Now, surrounded by the oppressive darkness of the Umbra, Oakira wondered if they had made a terrible mistake. Was their desire to challenge the Lunar Court worth all this suffering? Worth watching her mother waste away trying to keep them hidden? Worth the pain she saw in Kovag's eyes each time she pulled away from him? Worth the knowledge she carried that she withheld from him?

A crystal nearby pulsed with particular intensity, and Oakira instinctively pulled her mother closer, protective even in her uncertainty. Perhaps some dreams were better left as just that, dreams.

Hours crept by in the oppressive darkness, each pulse of the dark crystals marking time like a twisted heartbeat. Oakira had been forced to cast minor deterrent spells three times as various lesser Fae creatures, drawn by the scent of their weakness, attempted to investigate. Each casting made her wince, knowing it could potentially lead the Seekers to them, but she had little choice in the matter.

When Elirel finally stirred again, her eyes seemed clearer, though her skin retained its alarming translucency. She pushed herself up to sitting position with trembling arms, and Oakira immediately moved to support her.

"Tea," Elirel whispered, attempting to clear the hoarseness from her voice. "My set..."

Oakira reached into the space between spaces, drawing forth her mother's cherished tea set. It was a delicate thing of silver and moonstone, a reminder of their former status in the Lunar Court. The familiar ritual of preparing the tea helped calm her nerves, though her hands shook slightly as she measured out the dried moonflower petals.

"The Seekers," Elirel said as she watched her daughter work. "Tell me exactly what they looked like."

Oakira poured the heated water over the petals, releasing their ethereal glow. "The master wore full silver weave. It was polished like starlight. She moved like water; fluid and purposeful." She paused, remembering the way the female Seeker had nearly reached them before the shift. "Her companion wore three-quarter silver, leaving his left side in shadow. He..." She frowned, something tugging at her memory. "He seemed to be studying everything, even in those few seconds. His eyes never stopped moving."

Elirel accepted the cup of tea with both hands, bringing it close to her face to inhale the steam. "Physical description, daughter. They are Seekers, they all move in that fashion. What did they look like?"

"The master had amber hair, nearly as long as yours," Oakira said, watching her mother's face carefully. "The male..." She closed her eyes, trying to recall details through the chaos of their escape. "His hair was blonde, down to his knees. He moved differently than she did, more... deliberately."

Elirel's hands tightened around the teacup. "Amjani," she breathed, her voice barely audible. "She always was one of the most talented. And it sounds like she's partnered with Isque." She took a careful sip of tea, her hands steadying slightly. "This complicates things significantly."

"You know them?" Oakira's heart trembled at the tone in her mother's voice.

"I knew them, though thanks to your grandmother they do not know me any longer." Elirel corrected, some of her old strength returning to her voice. "Amjani hunted down a few of my pact mortals when I was forced to relinquish them at Lady Valene's command. She is... focused in her duties. If they are the ones hunting us, we need to be far more careful than we have been. Amjani never fails to catch her quarry, and Isque..." She shook her head slowly. "Isque sees everything, even things he should not be able to."

Elirel's hands had finally stopped shaking, but there was a new tension in her shoulders that made Oakira uneasy as she set down her tea cup.

"We may need to make a drastic choice," Elirel spoke with the matter-of-fact determination that always made Oakira nervous. "Your pact mortal."

Oakira's heart clenched. "His name is Kovag, mother. At least try to honor the name of our 'tool' as you like to refer to him."

Elirel's eyes met her daughter's with an intensity that seemed to pierce through the gloom of the Umbra. "We may need to... terminate our connection with him. Permanently."

Oakira's eyes narrowed. "What do you mean?" Though she already knew what her mother was proposing.

"The Seekers will be able to trace your connection to him," Elirel continued, her voice taking on a clinical detachment that frightened Oakira more than any sign of emotion could have. "We could either end him ourselves, or..." She paused, considering her words carefully. "Or we could leave enough of a trail to lead them to find him instead of us. Either way, his death would sever the connection and allow us to retreat deeper into the realms until we are strong enough to try and find a new pact mortal to aid in our cause."

A spike of raw emotion coursed through Oakira. She stood abruptly, her hands clenched into fists at her sides. "No."

"Oakira-"

"No!" The word erupted from her with such force that several nearby lesser Fae creatures scattered into the shadows. "I warned him not to use the arcane. They cannot trace what they cannot follow, and how can you even suggest such a thing? After everything he has done for us?"

"Everything he has done for us?" Elirel's voice took on an edge of steel. "He did what he was bound by the pact to do. For the last time, he is a tool, daughter, nothing more."

Oakira turned away, unable to look at her mother. "He is not just a tool. He's... " She struggled to find the words, to express what Kovag had become to her over the years.

"He is what?" Elirel pressed. "A friend? A lover? These attachments to mortals are precisely what I warned you against. They are not meant to be cared for like this. I should never have allowed you to visit the material world when you were a child. It has filled your head with nonsense."

"I will not do it." Oakira's voice was thick with unshed tears. "I will not allow it."

Elirel nearly sneered. "Do you think he still cares for you? After the years of your withdrawal from him? After the unanswered calls and pleas for your presence? And if he does, how do you think he would respond to your... withholding of information? Do you honestly think he could forgive you?"

Oakira shrunk back. Her withdrawal was partially necessary to protect them all, but mostly, it was her mother's bidding, not her own will. She barely remembered the sweet smile Kovag formed around his tusks. Now, she could much more easily recall the dour expression when she would leave him. "I do not know... but I won't do it, mother. Regardless."

There was a disturbing silence that followed. Even the crystals around them paused in their discordant pulsing as though they waited for something, expected something. Finally, Elirel spoke again, her voice softer but no less resolute. "You will doom us with your false love."

Chapter Seventeen

SCARS AND FALSE BEARDS

Kovag stared into the flames beneath the cooking fish, his mind wandering back to their brief and careful venture into Silverbreak. The crackling of burning wood mixed with the gentle flow of the river in front of him, creating a peaceful backdrop that contrasted sharply with the turmoil in his thoughts. Saffron lay curled up nearby, her tail occasionally twitching in her sleep. It had taken four days since they left Silverbreak, but she had finally managed to fall asleep without being in direct contact with him.

He had been so careful in approaching the city, using every trick he knew to remain unseen. He used a shimmer spell Oakira had taught him to lessen how much people noticed him. He was still a massive half orc navigating the streets, mind you. The spell just made people not seem to notice him as readily, as if he was the most average looking person they had ever laid eyes on. That was if they looked at him at all.

He had used that to his advantage and managed to pickpocket a fair sum on coin and valuables he was able to exchange with a less than cordial fence that seemed to none too happy about dealing with a half orc. Kovag had been made keenly aware that the 'anti-mongrel' rhetoric was more rampant here now than it had been in his youth. He was thankful enough, however, to see flyers placed on multiple notification boards that stated the Wolf Lords of the Emeraldom were seeking any and all tips on those responsible for pushing the anti-mongrel message of the Oskon Empire.

Once, when he was a boy, the three Wolf Lords had rode through Silverbreak on their way to a summit within the Brightborn Kingdom. Ulfgeir Etaunsson was a human male, but the largest Kovag had ever seen. He had long unruly brown hair and a red braided beard that rivaled that of any dwarf he had seen then and since. The second was, Jassin Elredsson, a half elven male with sinewy muscles and a massive scar that ran across his face. It was said that it was given to him by the third Wolf Lord, a half orc female named Dromla Denisdottir. She had broad shoulders and emerald eyes that caught Kovag's attention with so much zeal that he foolishly swore to his little sister he was going to marry the warrior woman.

Asking around about the scar on the half elf male's face was where he first heard the rumor that when someone became a Wolf Lord, they were given the gift and curse of lycanthropy. Apparently, sometimes the transformation proved problematic. The same shopkeeper, an elven man in his own right, claimed that had the elves of the Emeraldom not been stockier and more barbaric by nature, Jassin would have surely died. Then he went on a tirade of all the reasons Emeraldom elves were better than the elves of the rest of Yonara.

Kovag had passed by the farrier and chuckled to himself at the thought of leaving any coin for the Grayback woman to pay for the horse he had stolen. She had ruined any chance of that when he had become certain she was going to steal Saffron from him and collect the bounty.

He was beginning to feel a little guilty for putting a burden on the old halfling couple and thought he should turn around and leave the coin anyway. All care about that was lost though when he saw his mother's tavern listed on a public auction flyer, along with several other pieces of real estate. He had torn the parchment down and asked around about what had happened, finally coming upon an old woman that ran a produce stall just down the street from the old tavern.

The produce vendor's stall sat in the shadow of a crumbling stone building, its weathered awning fluttering in the cool breeze. Kovag approached slowly, adjusting the blanket around Saffron's at his hip. To any passerby, she appeared to be nothing more than a sleeping child wrapped against the light chill. The shimmer spell made him blend into the foot traffic, just another traveler with a tired youngster.

The old woman behind the stall barely glanced up as he approached, her gnarled hands continuing to sort through a basket of winter apples. Her gray hair was pulled back in a practical bun, and her weathered face spoke of decades spent working outdoors.

"Excuse me," Kovag said, his voice carefully modulated. "I was wondering if you might know something about the tavern down the way, the one that's up for auction?"

The woman looked toward him but her eyes seemed to slide past, unable to focus properly. She blinked several times, confusion creasing her brow. "I'm sorry, did you... what was the question?"

Kovag felt the familiar tug of the shimmer spell affecting her perception. With a subtle gesture, he let the magic fade, allowing himself to become fully visible and present.

The change was immediate. The woman's eyes sharpened, taking in his imposing frame and the bundle in his arms. Her expression softened with motherly concern.

"Ah, the old tavern," she said, her voice heavy with sadness. "Such a tragedy, that place. I've lived on this street for nigh on forty years, watched that family..." She shook her head slowly.

"What happened to them?" Kovag asked, though dread was already pooling in his stomach.

The woman set down her apples and wiped her hands on her apron. "The sickness that came through town, oh, must have been twelve, thirteen years ago now. Took so many good folk. It nearly killed the young girl there back then. Damned thing made the rounds again and took poor Brunhilda, that was the woman who ran the place. She fought it longer than most, but..." She made a small gesture of helplessness. "Left her daughter Morrigan all alone to manage everything."

Kovag's world began to tilt, his world spinning out of control.

"The girl tried her best," the woman continued, oblivious to Kovag's growing distress. "But running a tavern alone, she just couldn't keep up with the demand. She ended up marrying young Tommin, the baker's son. Sweet boy, that one. They were so happy when the babe was coming." Her voice broke slightly. "Both of them gone in the birthing. Little one too."

The world was no longer spinning because the bottom had fallen out of it. His mother. His sister. A nephew or niece he would never know.

"And Tommin, the husband?" he managed to whisper.

"Poor lad couldn't live with the grief. Found him in the river not three months later." The woman dabbed at her eyes with the corner of her apron. "Such a waste. All of them gone now."

"Some say that family was cursed. Before all of the recent tragedy, Brunhilda had lost her husband. Then that orcish son of her's just up and disappeared one day. Some thought it was him that was cursed, because after he left Mori got better and the tavern filled near to bursting."

Kovag's vision blurred as his chest constricted, making it impossible to breathe. Arcane energy crackled beneath his skin, responding to his emotional turmoil. The air around him began to shimmer with dangerous potential.

Then, suddenly, a wave of profound calm washed over him. He felt Saffron press deeper against his chest, her small hands somehow finding their way to his collarbone beneath the blanket. The touch was warm, soothing, and carried with it an inexplicable sense of peace that gradually quieted the storm that was about to burst forth.

As his breathing steadied, Kovag carefully recast the shimmer spell, watching the woman's attention drift away from them once more.

"Thank you," he whispered to the empty air, then turned and walked away from everything he had once called home.

Oakira had lied to him.

Kovag turned the fish mechanically, watching oils drip into the flames. His large fingers, usually so precise in their movements, trembled slightly as he recalled the elderly woman telling him how broken her sister's husband had been. After she and their son died, he followed shortly after by his own hand.

A fish scale caught the firelight and gleamed green, reminding him of Oakira's eyes. Once, that would have made him pine for her. That pining had slowly turned to longing, then grief and right now... rage. The technical terms of their pact had been to keep his mother's tavern turning a profit and to heal his sister of the sickness that had run through Silverbreak when they we younger. Nothing in it said they could not die. So, why had she lied to him. He directly asked her, and she had said they were fine.

His nostrils flared and his breathing became rapid. As his lips curled in a snarl, he rose and was fully in motion to kick the spit off the fire and start throwing the rocks from the edge of the pit.

The sound of Saffron whimpering in her sleep drew him from his dark thoughts. He glanced down at her, curled up in a tight ball and took three deep breaths. Slowly, he sat back down and watched her for a moment. He reached over and gently stroked her ear, the way he had learned would calm her. The whimpering subsided, but his worry didn't. The original plan was all that was left to him now. They were headed to the Ferrum Plains to seek out his old mentor, Bornar. That was if the old half dwarf was still alive. The man had acted as a haven for Kovag when he was in that city and he had connections. Most importantly, according to Erland, he knew how to get in contact with Matron Vadrida. Who in turn knew how to find Erland's sister, Maudrid.

The fish had begun to char slightly, and Kovag pulled it from the fire with a quiet curse. After allowing it to cool briefly he gently shook Saffron's shoulder to wake her. She stirred and stretched, rubbing her eyes. The smell of the fish caught her attention quickly and she took one of the skewers from Kovag with a grin.

Saffron nestled against Kovag's side as she devoured the fish with enthusiastic bites. The juices ran down her chin, dripping onto her already stained tunic. Some of the juice from his own fish found it's way into his beard, adding to the collection of flower petals Saffron insisted on weaving in almost daily. He didn't mind her handy work.

Their stolen horse, which Kovag had started calling 'Debt' in his head, meandered down to the river's edge. They had happened upon it on day two in their trek to the Ferrum Plains. The poor beast had the reins caught in a thick briar patch. Its hooves clicked against the loose stones as it made its way to the water. The sound of its drinking mixed with the gentle flow of the river created a peaceful melody that almost made Kovag forget about their dire circumstances and the lies that danced in his head. Almost.

A gust of wind whipped past them, carrying with it the unmistakable evidence of their recent travels. The pungent mix of horse, sweat, and whatever else they'd picked up along the way made Kovag's nose wrinkle. He glanced down at Saffron, really looking at her for the first time since their ordeal at the oak. The thin coat of fur around her forearms had started to turn less orange and her hair had become a nest of tangles that would make a bird envious.

"When's the last time you had a proper bath?" he asked, though he knew she wouldn't answer.

Saffron looked up at him, fish juice glistening on her chin, and tilted her head in that questioning way she had. She sniffed at her arm and made a face that told him she'd noticed their shared condition.

Kovag chuckled and used a corner of his cloak to wipe her chin. "Yeah, we'd make a shit shoveler run for the hills." He looked at the river, noting how the late afternoon sun sparkled on its surface. "Good news is, that water shouldn't be too cold this time of year. Want to go for a swim?"

She followed his gaze to the river, her ears twitching with uncertainty. Her tail curled around her waist, a sure sign she was nervous.

"Don't worry," he assured her, "I'll be right there. We'll stay in the shallows where it's safe." He pointed to a spot where the river widened and slowed, creating a natural pool. "Look there, it's perfect. Calm water, and you'll even still be able to touch the bottom."

Saffron's grip on his sleeve tightened, but she nodded slowly. Her trust in him won out over her fear, as it had done several times since he came into her life. Kovag felt that damn ache in his chest, the same one he had felt when she first put the flowers in his beard at the oak tree just a few days prior.

Kovag stripped down to his underclothes, keeping his back turned to give Saffron privacy to do the same. When he heard her small feet padding across the stones, he held out his hand without looking. Her tiny fingers wrapped around his, and he finally turned to lead her toward the water.

The first step into the river made Saffron halt. Her grip tightened on his hand, and her tail bristled. Kovag waited patiently, letting her adjust to the temperature and sensation before taking another step. Each advance into the river was met with similar resistance, both a reaction to the temperature and her fear of the moving water, but she had given herself over to the trust she felt radiating from him.

She could see the arcane aura about him again; the same one she had seen in the dungeon. They were nearly invisible swirls of green and silver light that danced and darted around like fireflies leaving trails in their wakes.

When the water reached Saffron's waist, Kovag lowered himself to sit, bringing the water up to his chest. The river's gentle current swirled around them, carrying away the first layers of dirt and grime. Saffron stood rigid, her ears pinned back, and her tail held out of the water as much as she could manage.

"See? Not so bad," he said, cupping water in his hands and letting it run down his arms. He watched as she observed his movements with intense concentration, her golden eyes tracking every detail. He felt his heart break as he wondered if she had ever been able to take a proper bath in her life. Not that this was considered a proper bath.

Hesitantly, she mimicked his actions, scooping up water and running it down her own arms. Her movements were precise, almost comically so in their attempt to perfectly match his. When Kovag splashed water beneath his armpits, she did the same. When he cupped the water to his face, she did too. When he ran his fingers through his beard, working out the tangles and remaining flower petals, Saffron's hands went to her own chin as well. With utmost seriousness, she began cleaning an imaginary beard, her small fingers combing through the air with determination.

The sight struck Kovag as so absurd that a deep laugh rumbled up from his chest. Saffron paused in her phantom beard-grooming, looking at him with confusion. Her head tilted to the side, trying to understand what was so funny about proper beard maintenance.

"I'm sorry," he managed between chuckles, "but, little one, I don't think you need to worry about that." He reached out and gently tapped her chin, causing her to finally realize what she had been doing.

Her eyes went wide with understanding, and for a moment, Kovag thought she might be embarrassed. Instead, a mischievous grin spread across her face, and she resumed cleaning her invisible beard with even more exaggerated movements. He even wondered if she was playfully mocking his small bit of vanity. Her performance was rewarded with another bout of laughter from Kovag, and though she made no sound, her shoulders shook with her own silent giggles.

For a brief moment, Kovag forgot about Oakira's lies, about the dangers that pursued them, about everything except this small moment of joy in a river with a child who needed and seemingly adored him. It was a dangerous feeling, he knew, but he couldn't help himself from cherishing it all the same.

The peaceful moment shattered when Saffron suddenly went rigid, her eyes fixed on something beneath the water's surface. Before Kovag could react with concern, her face lit up with unbridled joy. Without thinking, she dropped down into the river, sending ripples across the calm surface. She emerged gasping and spitting water, but nevertheless, triumphantly holding a small painted turtle.

She thrust the creature toward Kovag. Her eyes sparkled with excitement. The turtle's head retreated partially into its shell, but its legs still paddled helplessly in the air. Kovag couldn't help but smile at her enthusiasm. This was the most spirited he had seen her.

"That's a painted turtle," he explained, watching as she pulled the creature to her chest, cradling it like a precious treasure. "They're good luck, according to the dwarves. Something about carrying the world on their backs."

Saffron barely seemed to register his words, already scanning the riverbed for more of her new friend. She moved through the water with careful steps, all care for keeping her tail as dry as possible now forgotten as it swished back and forth with anticipation. Every few moments, she would freeze, then plunge into the water with surprising speed. Each time she crested the water with the same spitting and gasping.

"Hold your breath, Saffron." Kovag watched, amused, as her collection grew. A second turtle, smaller than the first, joined its companion in her arms. Then a third, this one with algae growing on its shell, was scooped up with equal enthusiasm. Each discovery was met with the same delighted expression, as if each turtle was the most wonderful thing she had ever seen.

Before Kovag could suggest they finish their bath, Saffron waded to the shoreline, her arms full of squirming reptiles. With single-minded determination, she began gathering stones from the riverbank, arranging them in a rough circle. Her small hands worked quickly, weaving fallen branches between the rocks to create a makeshift fence. She had to stop the construction several times and recollect the fleeing turtles.

"I don't think-" Kovag started to say but stopped himself. The look of pure concentration on her face as she worked was too precious to interrupt.

When she finished her impromptu turtle sanctuary, she carefully placed each of her new friends inside. The turtles, seemingly resigned to their fate, settled onto the damp earth within their stone enclosure. A fourth turtle, spotted while building the pen, soon joined its brethren.

Saffron stood back, hands on her hips, surveying her handiwork with unmistakable pride. She turned to Kovag, her chest puffed out slightly, clearly seeking his approval of her accomplishment. Water dripped from the fur on her lower arms, legs and tail, creating small puddles at her feet, but she paid them no mind. Her focus was entirely on sharing this moment of triumph with him.

Kovag felt that ache again, but did not have the heart to fight it off this time. "Well done," he said softly, "though we can't take them with us when we leave."

Her face fell slightly at this news, but she nodded in understanding. She knelt beside her turtle pen, reaching in to give each occupant a gentle pat on their shell.

Kovag motioned for Saffron to return to the deeper water. She cast one last longing look at her turtle companions before wading back to him, her tail dragging a V-shaped ripple behind her. He patted the surface of the water in front of him, indicating where she should stand.

"Your hair looks like a bird's nest had a fight with a bramble bush," he said gently. "We need to sort that out."

Saffron's ears flattened against her head, and she wrapped her arms protectively around herself.

"I promise I won't get water in your eyes. Although you already did a bang-up job of that yourself," he assured her, his deep voice barely above a whisper. "Promise promise."

She studied his face for a moment, then nodded hesitantly. He helped her turn in front of him, positioning her so she could lean back against his arm. With his free hand, he cupped water and let it trickle down the back of her head, careful to direct it away from her face.

As he worked the tangles from her hair with his thick fingers, being as gentle as possible, the wet fabric of her underclothes shifted. His hand froze as he noticed the network of thin, white scars crisscrossing her back. Some were old, barely visible, while others still held the pink tinge of more recent healing.

His throat tightened, and he felt tears begin to form at the corner of his eyes. He placed his large hand over several of the scars, covering them completely. "I'm so sorry," he whispered, his voice rough with emotion. "I'm sorry you went through all of that. Life is not supposed to be like that. There is kindness in the world."

Saffron turned in the water to face him, her eyes catching the light of the sunset. For a moment, sadness clouded her features, but then she reached out and traced one of the many scars that marked his chest and arms. Her small fingers moved from one to another, mapping out the story of violence written on his skin. Finally, she pressed her hand against her own chest and looked at him with such profound empathy that it nearly broke him.

The message was clear: she was sorry he had been hurt too.

Kovag swallowed hard against the lump in his throat. Here was this child who had endured so much, offering him comfort for his own wounds. He gathered her into a gentle hug, mindful of both their scars, and felt her small arms wrap around his neck in return.

The river flowed around them, carrying away dirt and grime, but unable to wash away the marks of their past suffering. Yet in that moment, sharing their pain somehow made it feel a little lighter to bear.

Kovag gathered Saffron in his arms and carried her from the river, her small form shivering slightly despite the warmth of the evening. He settled them both near the fire, its flames casting dancing shadows across their faces. Reaching into his pack, he pulled out the coarse horse brush that had thankfully been left in the saddlebag of Debt when they stole him.

"I'm sorry," he murmured, turning the brush over in his large hands. "It's not ideal, but it's all we have." He held it up for her inspection, watching as she ran her fingers over the bristles with inspecting consideration before nodding her approval.

Saffron settled cross-legged in front of him, her back straight and tail curled around her waist. The firelight caught in her damp fur, creating a subtle golden halo around her. Kovag began to work the brush through her hair with careful, measured strokes, starting at the ends as he'd learned to do so many years ago when he brushed his little sister's hair.

The familiar motion transported him back to evenings in their small home above the tavern, Mori sitting patiently as he brushed her dark hair. She'd always insisted he do it, even when their mother offered. "Kovag does it better," she'd say, beaming up at him with sisterly love in her eyes.

The memory struck him like a mule kick. His hand stilled, the brush caught mid-stroke in Saffron's hair. For nearly a week, he'd pushed aside the knowledge of their deaths, letting rage at Oakira's deception fill the void where grief should have been. But now, with this simple act of care, it all came crashing down around him.

The first tear fell silently, landing on Saffron's head. The second followed quickly, and then they came in earnest, his broad shoulders beginning to shake with silent sobs. He tried to continue brushing, to maintain some semblance of normalcy, but his hands trembled too badly to manage it.

Saffron turned at the sudden stillness behind her, her eyes widening at the sight of his distress. Without hesitation, she stood and wrapped her arms around his neck, pressing her forehead against his. A warmth emanated from her touch, spreading through him like summer sunshine. It didn't take away his grief, but somehow made it more bearable, as if she were helping him carry the weight of it.

The warmth he felt from her was the same he had felt in Silverbreak. The hum of the arcane coursed through him. She was calming him again, and he wasn't even sure she knew she was doing it.

Kovag just sat there, arms fallen at his sides and his forehead against hers. "I'm sorry," he whispered, though he wasn't sure if he was apologizing to Saffron, to his sister, mother or to himself. "I'm so sorry."

Saffron's tail wrapped around his arm, an additional point of comfort as the fire crackled and popped beside them, bearing witness to their shared moment of healing.

Kovag's tears had gradually subsided, leaving behind only the hollow ache of grief and the lingering warmth of Saffron's touch. When she pulled away from him, her face still full of concern, she pointed first to his mouth, then to the fire, and finally to the star-filled sky above them. She had pantomimed this move set once before and it had taken him nearly five minutes to understand what she was asking. She wanted a story. He felt like she was asking less for her and more to take his mind off of his grief.

He nodded, managing a small smile as she settled back down in front of him. The brush resumed its gentle strokes through her hair as he cleared his throat, searching his memory for a tale appropriate for the moment. His mother had told him many stories over the years, but one in particular stood out, a cautionary tale she'd used whenever he'd been too trusting of strangers.

"There once was a boy," he began, his deep voice barely above a whisper, "who lived in a small village near the edge of the mountains that surround the Spearfall ruins. He was kind and clever, but perhaps too trusting for his own good. He was a cobbler's son and had grown tired of sweeping around his father's shop." The brush moved in rhythm with his words, working out the last of the tangles around Saffron's ears.

"One day, when he should have been working, he played at the edge of the forest. He heard a voice and was astonished to find that it came from a small gray cat. He knew this cat. Everyone in the village knew of this cat. He was the familiar of the witch that lived in the woods. While others avoided him, the boy always tried to play with it."

As he spoke of the witch's cat, with its silver-tipped tail and eyes that glowed like amber coins, he noticed Saffron's ears twitching with interest. He described how the cat had convinced the boy to trade places with it, "just for a day," promising adventures and magical powers in return.

"But you see," he continued, setting aside the brush as the last knot came free, "the cat had tricked him. Once they switched places, the boy found himself trapped in the cat's body, while the cat, now in the boy's form, ran off to live his life."

Kovag glanced down, ready to tell her how the boy eventually outsmarted the cat, only to find Saffron had slumped against his knee, her breathing deep and even. The firelight played across her peaceful features, and he noticed she'd kept her tail wrapped loosely around his wrist, as if ensuring he wouldn't leave while she slept.

With careful movements, he gathered their bedrolls and arranged them near the fire. He gently lifted Saffron and placed her on the softer of the two, tucking his cloak around her. She stirred slightly but didn't wake, her tail curling around her own waist.

As he settled onto his own bedroll, Kovag looked up at the stars. Without Saffron to distract him his mind went right back to memories of his mother and sister. To memories of loving and trusting Oakira. His face was too confused in his own emotions to decide how to act. While tears fell freely again, his mouth twisted into a snarl of anger.

Chapter Eighteen

Should Have Seen That Coming

It had been several hours since the Guard Captain and a handful of his most trusted raced from the gates of Hus'rokn. They had set out early enough that there was thankfully still a decent amount of daylight to cover a good amount of ground between them and the city. There was no telling how far they might have to go to find the missing caravan or if they would even be able to.

"How far are we going to go Captain?" Serine was riding hard next to him.

He considered the sergeant's question. He reasoned there should be some sign of a scuffle on the main road somewhere but depending on who or what could have caused the delay, they might find the cargo untouched and all of the men dead or in the worst case the men decided to betray him and absconded with the cargo in hopes of selling it somewhere for themselves. Ethan didn't find that option likely, however. Most of the people he sent on the transports owed him greatly for his aid with various things in the past.

With all of that in mind he came to his senses and pulled up on the reins of his horse, bringing all of them to a light gallop and then a trot. He noted the collection of froth at the edges of the mouth on Serine's horse. He caught his own breath and patted the neck of his own horse.

"Sorry, old man. My worry got the best of me." He whispered. The horse reared its head back in annoyance and whinnied.

Ethan motioned for the other three of his men to gather closer and they all fell in a straight line while still moving forward. There was Hamlin, a stout dark dwarven man and a distant cousin of Serine. Surkras, a red dragonscale woman of towering height. Finally, Wolp, a satyr of the beastfolk peoples.

"There is a small stream a little off the road up about a mile. We'll water the horses there and take a short break. I know I rushed us out here without much explanation. None of you have ever dug into what cargo we bring in and I appreciate that. Not only for your trust in me but also for your ability to claim plausible deniability if shit ever went sideways. I told you all to be prepared to be away from Hus'rokn for a few days. I'll tell you now that this particular shipment, if taken by the wrong people, could be extremely dangerous. We're going to continue on until we find it, even if it keeps us away from home for a few weeks. Is that a problem for anyone?" He looked from side to side, surveying their words as well as their body language.

"No sir." Wolp nodded

"Had appointment with healer for boil on my cloaca. Few weeks of saddle pounding will probably make it worse. I expect compensation if it rots off." Surkras said with dripping sarcasm in her broken way of using the common tongue.

Hamlin wretched and spit off to the side. "Was that image bloody necessary?"

Everyone broke a smile, except Serine who was full business as always. "I'm at your service captain." Hamlin finally choked out.

Two nights in and they, so far, had found nothing. Well, they had found a few bodies but none of them belonged to the men that worked for Ethan. The Scarred Lands was a dangerous place in the various cities but out in the open plains if you weren't riding with protection or weren't capable of it yourself, you might as well do yourself a favor and start digging your grave so you won't be picked apart by scavengers.

They had found a grove and set up camp for the night. Captain Ethan was off in secluded thought while Serine sat with the other three of the crew. She wanted to speak with him but knew when he needed time alone. So, for now she traded stories with those around the fire.

Wolp had just finished telling of his recent entanglement. The poor goatman had to tear himself from a lovely elven woman's embrace and flee out the window when her husband arrived home early. He got rousing laughter from all but Serine, who found the act base. She took a drink from her waterskin and noticed Hamlin polishing a new dagger.

"When did you get that blade, cousin? I thought you were attached to the one your Da gave you?" Serine said it with genuine shock. Hamlin loved his old dagger. If he was off duty and not drinking, he was polishing and sharpening the old steel.

Hamlin gave Serine a side glance. "Lost the old one while I was on leave. I got a stray hare up me arse and decided to go hunting. Got the drop on a good-sized boar. Bastard's skin was tougher than I gave it credit for, and he kicked me off and ran away with the damn thing still in his side. Picked this one up in the Wylds when I got back a few days ago."

"Well, that's a bloody shame. I liked the gold etching on the cross-guard and pommel." She eyed the new dagger, and its style compared to Hamlin's older one. "Looks pricey. Are those rubies?"

Hamling stopped polishing the dagger and rubbed his thumb over three pea-sized well-cut rubies that were imbedded in the handle. "Aye, cost me several fistfuls of coin, but I figured I'd spoil meself after losing my family blade."

Serine nodded. It made sense. Well, it made sense that Hamlin would approach it that way. Serine was never one for expensive baubles, even if they were beautiful weapons. She was far more practical. A weapon only needed to be two things. Functional and reliable. As long as it met those two simple qualities then it could be a dinner fork for all she cared.

After two more stories of questionable behavior for members of the Guard in her opinion, told this time by Surkras, Serine needed a breather. Her eyes scanned behind her and caught sight of the Captain.

Ethan sat on the ground, leaning against his saddle and fiddling with a small puzzle box Arialyn had given him to occupy his mind after his wife left him to 'discover herself' a few months ago. He had been completely caught off guard by the whole thing, just let her go without a word. Well, there was one word, 'bitch'.

He had always been good with puzzles, but this blasted thing was testing the deep recesses of his mind as well as his ever-dwindling patience.

Serine meandered over from the fire where the other three were sharing rounds of ale while Surkras mentioned something about sitting on a gnome's face and, Serine consciously closed her mind off to what she said next.

She coughed as she approached the captain and then stood at attention a few feet away. "Permission to join you, Captain?"

Ethan cocked his head to the side and thinned his lips. "Serine, we're not out here on guard business. You can cut the formalities; in fact, I would prefer it. And it isn't like those three over there have ever cared for regulations. Relax."

She screwed up her face as if she couldn't understand what he was saying to her and then smirked. "Permission to act like a jackass, sir?"

Ethan huffed. "That's the spirit. Now, sit the fuck down, Serine." Just then one of the catches on the puzzle box clicked loose. "Progenitors cock! That's the first one in a week."

Serine sat down next to him. "Congratulations. Is there anything on the inside of the box?"

"She didn't say." Ethan twirled it in his fingers a few more times, checking to see if anything else had changed on the puzzle. He couldn't find anything obvious to push, pull or shift. Satisfied with the progress he had made, he wrapped it back up in an oiled cloth and leaned over to put it away in his saddlebag. He replaced the puzzle with a bottle and uncorked it, taking a long draught from it. The liquid perked him up a little and he blinked his eyes several times. "I know you won't sleep unless I order you to so you might as well take a drink." He handed the bottle over to Serine.

She took a sip and shuddered before handing it back to him. She sighed and shifted. "Thank you, Captain."

"Spit it out Serine. What's bothering you?" He recorked the bottle and put it away next to the puzzle box.

She shook her head and looked around as if something in the darkness might be stalking them. "I don't know. Something feels off, but I can't place my mind on what exactly it is. We need to proceed very carefully."

"We're in the open plains of the Scarred Lands, Serine. A little late to be careful."

"No, there is something else. Something feels ominous and directed at you in particular." She squinted and peered out into the darkness. Thanks to her dwarven ancestry, she could see out a bit further than the captain. She saw birds, and a few small primates chasing them up in the higher canopy but nothing of concern. She never understood how these little oases survived out here, but they were called the Resurgence Wilds for a reason she supposed.

"With you watching my back I'm sure I'll be fine. Now, if you're done damaging my calm, want to roll some bones?" He tossed a small leather sack of dice into her lap.

It was nearly dusk on the third day when they came across the signs of a scuffle involving a caravan. They were about two hundred yards away. The caravan in question was pulled off the main roadway just a bit. It sat between a tall hill and one of the many random oasis groves of peculiar trees that shouldn't be seen together, but that nevertheless often did, within the Resurgence Wilds. The caravan was overturned, and some crates appeared to be busted open and pilfered as best the Captain could tell from this distance. He couldn't make out any bodies, however. But that didn't mean there were none. Ethan pulled the spyglass away from his eye and surveyed the area more broadly.

"Surkras, check the outcrop of trees to the west. Wolp, get to the top of that hill and see if there is any other sign of movement, past or present. Serine, scout up to the caravan as close as you dare get. Follow the shadow line cast by the hill. Hamlin and I will hold here and wait for the all clear from Wolp and Surkras."

Hamlin spoke up. "Captain, are you sure you don't want me to scout up. No offense to my cousin, but I am more suited to that kind of work."

Serine turned in her saddle and eyed Hamlin with a look that let him know that offense, intended or not, was indeed taken.

Ethan shook his head while keeping his eye on the spot of the caravan on the horizon. "No, I want Serine on this. She is better at spotting the types of traps the scavengers around here like to use and Wolp will be able to see if anything is coming her way in plenty of time to warn her and us."

"But Captain." Hamlin blurted out a little more brazenly than he had intended."

Ethan did turn in his saddle now and glared at Hamlin. The dwarf threw his hands up to show he was backing down. "She's wearing steel banded leather is all I'm saying. Hardly quiet."

Surkras and Wolp immediately took off to their respective tasks while Serine spared a quick *'What the fuck were you just thinking?'* glance at Hamlin who simply shrugged it off.

After the flankers were out of easy sight and Serine had melded into the shadow the hill provided, Ethan turned his head briefly to Hamlin before putting his eyes back on the wreckage up the road.

"Felling itchy, Hamlin?" He asked.

"Sorry, Captain. I just don't much care for being out in the wastes. Shit always goes wrong out here." Hamlin nervously played with his jeweled dagger. "People and things go missing real easy. It can make a man mighty uncomfortable is all."

They remained silent for several minutes before Surkras let out a bird call from the grove, letting them know her area was secure and showed no sign of anything unusual. It was followed shortly after by Wolp giving out a feral dog yelp to indicate the same. They just needed to wait for Serine's call and then Ethan would move everyone forward to the caravan.

Ethan had told Serine to get as close to the caravan wreckage as she was able. The closer she got the surer she was that no one was lying in wait, and she saw no evidence of traps of any kind. She had managed to get within twenty feet of the overturned shipment when she saw crates with the familiar symbols of the Gauntlet, Helspires and even one from Void Fall Keep in the Brightborn Kingdom. This was their missing shipment for sure. *'Why the Helspires though?'* She squinted from the shadows and held her hand up to her brow to block out the slight glare that was bouncing off purple crystals that had spilled from one of the open crates. Her eyes went wide.

"Void ore?" She whispered to herself. "No wonder he wanted to keep this quiet. That explains the Helspires crates."

She frowned and made her way around to the other side of the busted crates. She caught sight of a blood trail that appeared to be five to seven days old by her best judgement. There were claw marks and pieces of a few bodies strewn about on the side of the caravan opposite the Captain and Hamlin. Whatever had been here either did the ambushing or came to feed of the remains that were left after the men were accosted. Maybe the beasts even interrupted the ambush. That would explain why none of the crates had been looted.

A twig snapped beneath her boot, and she froze and winced. A few carrion birds took flight. She opened her eyes slowly and took a better look at the body that remained mostly whole. She crept closer, keeping her head on a swivel, not wanting to be caught off guard if whatever animal did this decided to head back.

She froze again when she saw it.

"No." She leapt forward, rolled, and pressed her back to the caravan. She looked left and right for signs of movement and then peeked her head around the rear of the caravan and squinted toward Ethan and

Hamlin. She knew something had been off. She cursed, only able to see their blurry outlines off in the distance. Her hand plunged into her pocket. She had to try and warn him.

Ethan was growing concerned. It had been a solid thirty seconds since the Wolp and Surkras had given their all-clear signals. Serine had remained quiet.

"We're moving forward. Slowly." He spurred his horse forward with a light kick.

Hamlin followed behind him and sighed. "Should have sent me. It would have stopped this from happening."

Just then Serine blew hard into her warning whistle while her eyes remained locked on the dagger that remained buried in the chest of the body nearest her. A dagger with gold etching on the cross-guard and pommel. Hamlin's family dagger.

Ethan barely had time to register the searing pain piercing into his right shoulder before being knocked clean off his horse as Hamlin tackled him to the ground. They hit the ground with a hard crunch and Ethan was briefly thankful he wasn't wearing his guard issued plate armor. The fall would have probably broken more than the one rib he heard crack, at least he assumed it was his after an extremely sharp pain took his breath away.

Over at the caravan wreckage, Serine barely registered Ethan's surprised scream of pain over the thudding arrow that buried itself in the wood a few inches form her face. It was one of Surkras's poisoned arrows. Immediately after she recognized the owner of the would-be life ender, she heard Wolp let out a coyote call of warning. Serine had no time to consider if Wolp may have turned traitor as well and prayed to Volfmir, God of vengeance and grudges, that she was right in assuming he was trying to warn her. If she stayed in her current spot any longer Surkras's next arrow would hit true. She was shocked the dragonscale woman had missed in the first place.

She rolled to the hill side of the caravan that Wolp had been scouting. She could see now that Wolp was racing down the hill, doing his best to leap from small areas of rocky cover. If he was trying to avoid being in Surkras's sight that meant they only needed to worry about her and Hamlin. *'Hamlin, you bloody bastard!'*

Unable to see the captain and her traitor cousin from this angle she called out. "Captain!"

Back up the road Ethan had bridged his body and bucked Hamlin off. He rolled over and went to slam his knee into the dwarf's chest and pin him to the ground, but Hamlin was keen on the captain's ground tactics and quickly shrimped his body out from under him.

Ethan came up to his feet and drew his short sword. "You traitorous little fuck."

Hamlin bared his dagger and cursed. He had hoped to avoid this entirely but the Captain hadn't listened to his request to be the one to survey the caravan and now everything was going to be messy. One on one with his superior was going to be tricky. He made several quick feints in multiple directions. "Money talks, Captain."

"You kill me and you're going to have to kill your own kin. You know that?" Ethan snarled out.

Hamlin spat at the ground. "Distant kin." With that he dipped and leapt for Ethan's knee, hoping to sweep down and up with his dagger to hamstring the taller man.

Ethan reversed the grip on his sword and pivoted quickly to the side going down to his left knee and spinning around, bringing his shortsword down with intent to run Hamlin through from behind. Hamlin was just out of reach, however, and the sword only managed to slice across the dwarf's shoulder blade.

Hamlin growled and cursed again. He saw Ethan looking over his head at the caravan behind him quickly. "I hate to admit it, but Surkras will have them both dead before I can put you down. Then again, I did get the tougher target out of the deal."

"This is Alabaster's doing, isn't it? He finally linked the permits back to me didn't he." Ethan sneered at Hamlin while subtly looking for a weak spot in Hamlin's movements. Except he already knew it. It was his job to know the capabilities of his men after all.

Hamlin chuckled. "Ha! Alabaster's men never would have found you out. Not until he hit my price point and he's as broke as a street beggar. The Lance wasn't happy to hear that their biggest financier was near coinless. Their new man from the Helspires on the other hand is far more generous with his palm greasing. Gotta have your hands in as many pockets as possible these days. Times are rough, Captain." He spat out the word captain with violent sarcasm.

"Hamlin, you always talked too much." Ethan feinted right twice and then once to the left. That's when Hamlin exposed himself, shot in and overextended his right arm, trying to bring his dagger home in Ethan's gut. The Captain pulled back to his right and brought his knee squarely into Hamlin's face. Blood burst from his nose and mouth as he fell forward limp and unmoving. Wasting no more time on the backstabber, Ethan leapt atop his horse and raced for Serine and Wolp.

Serine had left her hand crossbow on her horse in favor of moving more stealthily. While that may have been a sound decision at the time, she was kicking herself now. She'd be a sitting duck until Surkras got a clear shot or she ran out of arrows. She heard Wolp whistle, and the satyr peaked from behind an outcropping of stone to signal to her where he last saw Surkras. He signed to her the she was off to his left, Serine's right with her back turned as it was. She nodded to him right as his body fell backward with an arrow suddenly protruding from the right side of his skull. Her mouth fell open, and she realized that meant Surkras was on the move and now to her left.

Serine drew her dual hand axes and took a deep breath before rushing around to the side of the caravan opposite where she believed Surkras to be now. It was just in time to avoid another arrow that would have taken her life. "Bloody coward! I'm going to see you rot away in the fucking dungeon!"

"Little sergeant can't bring herself to kill me?"

"How?!" Serine managed to get out once her brain registered that Surkras's voice was extremely close. She couldn't fathom how the far larger dragonscale woman had closed the distance that quickly and without making a sound. Serine dove forward and spun around to meet Surkras already moving forward with her scimitar in smooth arcs.

Serine steeled herself and began her own flurry of blocks, parries and slashes with her axes. Surkras was slowly but surely driving her backward but so far hadn't managed to breakthrough her defenses. She could hear the sound of hoofbeats pounding down the road and getting closer. She hoped it was the captain but dared not take her eyes off Surkras in order to find out.

Surkras on the other hand had a clear view of the approaching rider and the look on her face told Serine all she needed to know as well as give her the perfect second of distraction to go on the offensive. She brought both of her axes around Surkras's scimitar blade from either side and then pulled her arms taught, locking the blade between the beards of her axes. She yanked the advancing woman forward and used her own momentum to carry the blade down and into the dirt. With that she unlocked her axes and spun around planting one in Surkras's side and the other in her collarbone.

Surkras groaned as the two axes thudded into her flesh. She grabbed the arm that held the axe in her collarbone and held tightly, turning her head with what little muscle control she had left. If she was going to die, she would take Serine with her or at the very least leave her with a massive scar, so she remembered this moment for the rest of her life.

Serine saw Surkras's throat start to swell, and her head begin to nod rapidly. Had Surkras been of any other race of people in Yonara she would have thought the woman was about to wretch. Being a red dragonscale, however, she knew that Surkras was about to dowse her in flames.

"Serine!" She could hear the Captain call out behind her.

She thought quicker than she ever had and while her arm was held fast, she brought her foot up to step on Surkras's slightly bent knee and the jumped off it, forcing all her weight downward. Between the two embedded axes and the tight grip Surkras had on her arm, the sudden shifting weight pulled the dragonscale woman off balance and sent her head crashing into the ground. Fire engulfed her own face as her flame sacs let loose their pressure.

"Roll away!" Ethan called out.

Serine needed no further instruction and rapidly rolled several times to the side as the Captain trampled his horse over Surkras with several wet crunches.

Ethan wheeled around and leapt off his horse, "Are you hurt?"

The look of concern on her captain's face was deeper than she was used to seeing. She regained her feet and gave herself a quick once over. Other than a slice to her left forearm, that she just now started to feel after seeing it, she was fine.

"Aye, Captain." She then looked over to where Wolp had fallen several yards up the hill. "Wolp." She said with the flatness of a veteran city guardsmen regaining their dutiful composure.

The Captain moved his eyes to Wolp's body and sighed with regret as he began walking up to check on the satyr. Serine saw the blood soaking through the back of Ethan's leather armor. "Captain, your back."

"I'm fine, Sergeant." He said far more sternly than he intended. "Serine...Hamlin..."

"Better be dead." Serine said while running to Ethan's horse in a rage. She leapt into the stirrup, up and onto the stallion's back, already kicking it into a gallop back up the road.

Ethan raised his hand to call her back and then thought better of it. Family betrayal cuts deeper than most and he reasoned whatever she was about to do, she earned it. One thing he had learned about the Dwarven people in his lifetime was that no matter what mountain or plain their clan came from, no matter whether they believed in their grudge god Volfmir or not, every single one of them held on to grudges until they were resolved to their own personal satisfaction. He was reasonably sure Hamlin was still alive. Knowing Serine, she would want to watch him fade away in the dungeon. While he would rather kill the traitor and bee done with it now that he knew Serine was safe, he knew he would proceed as she wished.

He reached Wolp's body and found the man devoid of life, a shocked look on his face. The only solace Ethan took was knowing that Wolp hadn't turned on him. The satyr's stories had always made him laugh, even the most foolish ones. It would have been a shame to have those memories tarnished by betrayal. After confirming that Wolp was indeed dead, Ethan glanced over at the cargo and did a quick crate count. Surprisingly every crate was accounted for and other than a few that had spilled out a minor amount of contents, they all seemed to be intact.

Serine reined in Ethan's horse up next to her own and climbed down while grabbing a set on iron manacles from the saddlebag. She was close enough to see that Hamlin was still breathing, albeit labored. She pulled one of her axes back out and approached him slowly in case he was putting on a show. She got within five feet of him and kicked dirt toward him to see if he would rise or turn and try and attack. All he did was groan.

Even still, she moved cautiously until she was close enough to pin him down with her knee on his back. She slapped the manacles on him in record time and then kicked him over. Hamlin's face was washed in crimson. His nose was so caved in that his eyes were bulging, and his upper teeth were missing. She spit down at him without pity. "You rat prick. Why?"

Hamlin spoke but Serine couldn't understand him through the coughing and gurgling. She shook her head and sneered. That's when she became almost certain that he wasn't trying to speak at all. The traitor was laughing. The son of a poxy whore was actually laughing.

Serine could feel the heat rise in her cheeks. Something in her snapped. She dropped down to her knees near Hamlin's head and leaned down. "You tried to kill the Captain." She leaned down to his ear and whispered. "MY captain. A dungeon is too good for you."

With that she raised her hand axe high and clove Hamlin's face in two. She allowed herself to be briefly aware that she felt nothing for the loss of her cousin and then cast the feeling aside with the same disappointment she would have had if she had been craving pork for dinner and found out the butcher had none. The only regret she felt was for the momentary loss of control.

The wagon was busted beyond their ability to repair so they spent the remaining few hours of the evening carefully packing all five horses' saddlebags with void ore and what they could of some other orders that were in the shipment. They had also wrapped Wolp's body and laid it in the wreckage of the caravan as a makeshift pyre. Once they lit the fire, they both exchanged a few brief words of thanks and praise for the satyr before setting off up the road a fair bit and then pulling off into another outcropping and bedding down for the night. Serine had refused to do anything with the bodies of Hamlin and Surkras and figured the fresh corpses might keep the scavenger animals busy throughout the night and away from them.

They sat quietly for a time after tying up the horses and securing spots where each could keep a decent look out. They set no fires to keep them warm because they didn't want the added attention now that there were only two of them.

Serine stared up at the starry sky from her pallet, her face blank. Ethan had been shocked to find that she had killed Hamlin when he made it back up the road to her on foot. He didn't even ask her what happened. She had just looked at him and said 'Slipped.' He supposed that meant he didn't need to give her a less than half-hearted apology for ruining her cousin's face before she truly demolished it.

With everything they had been rushing to get accomplished before nightfall he had forgotten about the stab wound in the back of his shoulder. It was numb and he wasn't entirely sure if that was a better or worse sign than if it had been on fire as it had been earlier. He stood and peeled off his leathers and then his shirt. He grabbed a canteen and tried foolishly to turn so he could pour the water across the wound.

"I've got it Captain." Serine was already behind him, motioning for him to sit. She grabbed a small torch from her nearby pack and sparked it up with some flint and steel. Clearing a small space on the ground and leaving only dirt, she laid the torch down and then pulled out their first aid kit and began picking supplies from it.

"Assholes made sure not to pack any potions it seems." Serine wet a cloth with some whisky and blotted it against the wound. Ethan didn't flinch.

"Can't feel it?"

He sighed, "Not even a little. Arm still moves fine though."

"I knew something was wrong, Eth-Captain." She said while thread-ing a suture needle.

Ethan raised an eyebrow at her stumbling of words. "Ominous, I believe, was the word you used."

"I should have known." She had to stop her arms from folding into her lap as she felt a wave of failure wash over her.

"How could you have known that was going to happen. Shit! Felt that." Serine's needle had made the first pass through his flesh.

"Sorry." She pulled the thread taught. "I just should have, Captain." She sighed.

They remained quiet until she finished the stitches. Ethan had only felt about every fourth prick of the needle after the first. Again, he wondered if he should be thankful or worried by the numbness.

"Captain, we have some things to discuss. Not the least of which being what our next move is. But first, the void ore. I knew you were bringing some in for Arialyn, but I had no idea it was coming through the city in such large amounts."

With a heavy sigh he resolved to tell her everything. She was his most loyal guard, no, most loyal friend, and after what just happened, he knew he owed her the full truth.

"Serine, you've always trusted me. I've kept these sorts of things from you not because I don't trust you, but because it keeps you from potentially being used against me. Arialyn is doing great things with the ore. Callus's braces and that arcabus thing she uses. Those are just the ones that truly stand out. Most of the contraptions she makes can be made with other arcane infused stones, gems and the like, but none of them are as powerful or work as well as the ones with void ore. I know people say it can cause corruption, make them into abominations and wreak all sorts of havoc. In truth I have seen some of that myself. That's why I only bring it in for her and Callus, and they both gave me their word that any items they sold to people that contained void ore would be rendered safe. She has a way of, I don't know, cleansing the ore. You know I care for the people of our city. If I felt it was a threat to them or even the Wylds, I wouldn't have approached them about it."

She furrowed her brow and looked at Ethan with shock. "You approached them? Not the other way around?" She considered this further revelation for a moment.

"Callus's braces are a damned marvel. I saw him a few days after Mother Maudrid's murder, when he killed those two Talons of Misery members. His arm was useless, and he couldn't walk without a crutch. Even then I would barely call it moving. Arialyn made him new braces with an improved design than before and just like that-" He snapped his fingers to accentuate his point. "-he had full use of his arm and leg again. Then she refined the design again to the ones he wears now. Imagine the implications and the people she could help. If it wasn't for the widespread fear of the stuff, she could be improving the lives of so many. She's studying it daily and trying to find the best ways to make all kinds of contraptions without there being any unwieldy side effects. Hells, she thinks eventually she could make entire limbs for old war veterans."

He saw that he was reaching Serine. Not wanting to continue babbling and potentially lose her, he quickly moved on to their next topic. "As for our next move, Hamlin said Alabaster is on the outs with the Lance and someone from the Helspires had been brought in to replace him. We had our suspicions that Alabaster was going broke, but Hamlin confirmed it."

Serine barely kept up with the rapid change in the subject, but she was keen to understand why Alabaster, the Lance or whoever this new player was, would want to eliminate Ethan. It helped that she loved detective style work, so she moved along with his thought process.

"But what does that have to do with Kasha's place? If Alabaster had been behind this whole thing I could see the reason behind it. Hamlin tells him about the permits and your involvement. He would obviously want payback. Rather than murdering the Guard Captain within the city, he has you lured into the Resurgence Wilds so your death can be explained away by any of the hundreds of things that can kill someone out here."

Ethan nodded along. "Right, so if Alabaster is out then why would the new man care about Kasha's place and my involvement?"

They both ran through scenarios in their heads, trying to unravel the puzzle. A bell rang in Serine's head. "There was a man, a troll, that came in with an envoy of several men a little over a week ago. Guard did the usual checks but one of the men got a strange feeling about the envoy with him and asked me to come check things out. They seemed like hired thugs to me, but that made plenty of sense once I saw the three chests full of coin he was bringing in with him. He said he had business at the Lucky Talisman Casino, although the Gauntlet runs the casino, not the Lance. Everything was in order, so I let them through. I bet he is their new man. What the hells was his name?" She tapped her fingers furiously on her thighs. "Zuni...Zunibar! It was Zunibar Tolgar. Said his main trade was in 'this and that' as well as being an administrator of contracts. Whatever that is supposed to mean."

"The Lance and Shield sometimes hold meetings in Lance Adenus's secure rooms. Maybe that is why he was heading there. Could also be that he just wants to gamble or launder some coin through the casino. Three chests full though? If he is the Lance's new man, what could they possibly need that much backing for?"

He stopped for a few seconds furrowing his brow and thinking hard. His eyes snapped wide. "He's mad. Authern is absolutely mad. He's going to make a move to take over the syndicates. Listen, if he gets his hands on that kind of coin, and that troll bastard assuredly has more back in the Helspires, he can buy property out from under the Gauntlet's nose, bribe Gauntlet men to his side, hire sell-swords, shit, he could hire more than a few Kol'Theron companies if he wanted to. He eliminates the Gauntlet and adds the casino and their other holdings to his own. The Shield will have no choice but to fold or get into a war they have no hope of winning. He'll own Hus'rokn."

They looked at each other in a mixture of shock and delight that they may have just solved the whole mystery. "We rest up for a few hours and then we have no choice but to leave before dawn. I have to get word to Gauntlet Adenus." He noticed Serine remained quiet the whole time, her face undiscernible. "That is, if you're still with me. If you still trust me."

She had been looking at the ground and slowly rolling the torch in the dirt to keep the flame low. "I still trust you. Ethan..."

Her willing use of his name gave her his full attention, and he locked his eyes onto hers.

"But I will only remain your sergeant if you tell me everything from here on out. If not, then tell me now and when we get back to Hus'rokn I will resign from the guard." She fought to keep her eyes on him and was beginning to waiver, fearing that his silence was his answer.

"I have a condition to your request. It is nonnegotiable." He said flatly.

Serine held back her relief. "Yes, Captain?"

He broke into a smile. "Stop calling me captain if we're alone or not in uniform."

She smiled warmly and nodded as he moved over to her side.

"Let me clean the cut on your arm. I'm sorry I let my mind preoccupy me for so long. I should have returned the favor before ranting."

She held her arm out. He was so intently focused on her cut that he never noticed the flesh in her cheeks that suddenly matched her freckles. It faded quickly, however, as she realized that even with what they thought they'd figured out, it doesn't explain why the Lance and Zunibar would want *her* captain dead.

CHAPTER NINETEEN

IN PRINCIPAL

The portal's shimmering edges collapsed with a sound like breaking glass, leaving Amjani and Isque standing at the base of the ancient oak. The massive tree loomed above them, its gnarled branches reaching toward the star-filled sky like arthritic fingers. Amjani stumbled slightly as the portal's energy dissipated, her hand instinctively reaching out to steady herself against the oak's rough bark.

"Are you alright, dear?" Isque asked, his voice a low, honeyed murmur as he stepped closer. His blonde hair caught the sunlight like silver threads, and his eyes held a warmth in them that lingered just a touch too long for Amjani's taste.

Amjani straightened, brushing an invisible speck from her lunar weave armor. "How many times must I tell you to stop leaving your gaze on me that long. I'm just feeling lightheaded from using so much effort to teleport so often," she admitted, though her tone remained crisp and professional. "We've covered considerable ground today."

Indeed they had. Their investigation had taken them first to the smoldering ruins of Tsarra's mansion, where the stench of smoke and death still lingered in the air. The arcane essence there had been so thick, so chaotic from the fire and violence, that it had been impossible to get any meaningful readings. The few guards attempting to clear the rubble had proven useless, and ultimately expendable when they'd had no information to offer about their quarry.

From there, they'd managed to tracked down the blacksmith's home inland from the Emeraldom shore thanks to a hint of a trail at a dock on the shore of the Empire's side. That lead had yielded slightly more useful intelligence. Their target was indeed a half-orc traveling with a vulpine child, and they were headed toward Silverbreak. But the trail had grown cold after that, forcing them to expand their search pattern.

Now they stood beneath this sacred oak, drawn by the residual arcane energies that clung to its ancient wood like morning dew.

Isque circled the tree's massive trunk, his fingers trailing along the bark as he felt for arcane signatures. "There's definitely something here," he murmured, his casual demeanor replaced by focused concentration. "Old magic. Very old... and dying."

Amjani closed her eyes and extended her senses, feeling the ebb and flow of the arcane currents around the oak. The tree practically hummed with power, not the chaotic, destructive energy they'd encountered at the mansion, but something deeper, more primal. "A pact was made here," she said with certainty. "Not too long ago, but built upon much older foundations."

"This is where they must have made their pact. That is why he keeps coming back here." Isque asked, though his tone suggested he already knew the answer.

"Fae and Forgotten." Amjani's eyes snapped open. "It is them for sure."

Isque's attention was drawn to a peculiar arrangement not too far from the oak's base, a perfect circle of wildflowers, their petals in the beginning stages of decay. He knelt beside the formation, his fingers hovering just above the blooms without quite touching them. The air above the flowers shimmered with residual arcane energy, like heat waves rising from sun-warmed stone.

"Amjani," he called softly, his usual playful tone replaced by genuine curiosity. "Here."

She turned in her appraisal of the tree and moved slowly to Isque, keenly aware of the change in his flirtatious tone. "What is it?"

"Arcane Medicae," Isque murmured, studying the intricate pattern of the flowers. "But not the kind you would expect from a trained practitioner. This is... instinctual." He traced the air above the circle, following invisible currents of power. "The magic is old in its nature. It's something that runs in bloodlines, passed down through generations like eye color or the shape of one's ears."

Amjani crouched beside him, her amber hair falling forward as she examined the flowers more closely. "Who could have done this? The child?"

Isque fought the momentary distraction of Amjani's cascading hair. "Has to be." Isque shook his head definitively. He stood, brushing dirt from his knees. "It has to be the vulpine child. They're kind are known to possess latent arcane abilities that manifest when they form strong emotional bonds."

"A vulpine child with active magical abilities?" Amjani's eyebrows rose. "That woman at the blacksmith's described the girl as very young. Her people are not supposed to come into any arcane abilities until the years of young adulthood."

Isque nodded grimly. "Rare indeed." He gestured toward the flower circle. "This is quite remarkable."

"Lord Thruva would be pleased to have her enthralled to the Lunar Court. Which makes her valuable," Amjani said, her voice taking on a calculating edge.

Isque grew uncomfortable with Amjani's clear thoughts on the matter of the child. He already feared the instability of Thruva. Now Amjani wants to add to him the ancient magics of the vulpine people.

They stood in contemplative silence for a moment, both understanding the implications. A vulpine child with active magical abilities would be worth a fortune to collectors, researchers, or worse. The fact that she was traveling with a half-orc who'd made a pact with Oakira was dangerous work.

"We should move," Amjani said finally. "Silverbreak is just down the hill, and if they're seeking sanctuary there, we need to intercept them before they disappear into the town's population."

As they approached the outskirts of Silverbreak, both Seekers began weaving subtle illusion spells around themselves. Amjani's distinctive lunar weave armor shimmered and transformed, taking on the appearance of simple traveling leathers. Her elongated ears shortening to points, and her ethereal Fae features softened into those of a Emeraldom elf.

Isque's transformation was equally thorough, his blonde hair darkening to brown and his too-perfect features becoming more rugged, more mortal. To any casual observer, they now appeared to be nothing more than two elven travelers seeking lodging for the night.

"Ready?" Amjani asked, adjusting the illusion around her armor one final time.

Isque nodded and extended the crook of his arm. "Let's go to market, shall we?"

Amjani rolled her eyes and set forth toward Silverbreak.

The arcane trail through Silverbreak was faint, barely more than whispers of energy clinging to cobblestones and market stalls. Amjani followed the ethereal threads, navigating the streets and alley ways like a hound after swine. Behind her, Isque kept an eye on any tethers that Amjani might miss in her zeal.

The mortals they passed filled both Seekers with barely concealed revulsion. A merchant hawking his wares with gap-toothed enthusiasm, children playing in puddles of questionable origin, laborers stumbling to and from taverns reeking of cheap ale and desperation. Each interaction required careful control to maintain their illusions while suppressing the urge to simply sweep these lesser beings aside.

"I find it odd," Isque murmured as they paused near a fountain where the trail seemed to strengthen. "The pact mortal's arcane signature is present, barely, but the child..." He frowned, extending his senses more carefully. "There's nothing. No residual energy, no arcane footprint at all."

Amjani's jaw tightened as she felt the familiar irritation of Isque's inquisitive nature rising. "What are you getting at?"

"Well, if she has active magical abilities as we determined at the oak, she should be leaving some trace. Even untrained practitioners leak arcane energy." Isque's voice took on that analytical tone that always grated on her nerves. "Unless she's somehow containing it, or perhaps the emotional bond with the pact mortal is channeling her power through him, which might explain why his signature is so—"

"Enough," Amjani snapped, her disguised features twisting with annoyance. "Your endless theorizing serves no purpose. We track, we capture, we return. That is all."

The harshness of her own words surprised her, and she felt a pang of regret as Isque's expression shifted. She reached out instinctively, meaning to touch his arm in apology, but he had already turned away.

"Here," Isque's attention fixed on a weathered notice board. His hand hovered inches from the wood, and Amjani could see the subtle shimmer of arcane energy around his fingers. "There was a surge here. Significant emotional distress."

Amjani moved closer, studying the various postings, notices of lost livestock, announcements of market days, auctions and requests for laborers. Nothing that should have caused such a reaction.

The trail led them further into the market district, where it intensified near a produce stall tended by an elderly woman. Her weathered hands sorted through wilted vegetables while she hummed tunelessly to herself. Another surge of residual arcane energy marked this spot, stronger than the notice board.

Isque caught Amjani's eye and nodded toward the narrow alley beside the stall. They moved like predatory jungle cats and flanked the old woman. Amjani's hand clamped over the woman's mouth while Isque's fingers found pressure points that would ensure compliance without permanent damage, yet.

They dragged her into the shadows between buildings, where the illusion of their mortal disguises flickered and strengthened to hide what was about to occur.

"You will answer our questions truthfully," Amjani whispered, her voice carrying the subtle compulsion of Fae magic. "Any hesitation, any lie, will bring you pain beyond imagining."

The woman's eyes went wide with terror as she nodded frantically.

"In the past few days, have you spoken with a half-orc traveling with a child?" Isque's tone was conversational, almost gentle, which somehow made it more terrifying.

"Y-yes," the woman stammered. "A few days back, I think? He had a child bundled up... asked about the old tavern down the street."

"What did you tell him?" Amjani's grip tightened, her nails drawing thin lines of blood.

"About the family! The deaths! Poor Brunhilda and little Mori, and the husband who..." The woman's words tumbled out in a rush of terror. "He seemed so upset when I told him. Went pale as winter snow, he did."

Isque exchanged a meaningful look with Amjani. Personal connection, had to be. That explained the emotional surge.

"Anything else?" Amjani pressed. "Any detail, no matter how small?"

The woman shook her head desperately. "Nothing! I swear by the Bright One, nothing else!"

Amjani studied the woman's face, reading the truth in her terror. She had given them everything she could. Which made her a liability they couldn't afford to leave behind.

"Thank you," Isque said softly, placing his hand on the woman's forehead. "You've been most helpful."

The arcane fire that consumed her soul was swift and merciless, leaving behind only an empty shell that would be found hours later, apparently dead of natural causes.

They made their way down several blocks and followed the bend toward the abandoned tavern, their footsteps silent on the cobblestones. The illusions they wore flickered occasionally in the shadows, revealing glimpses of their true Fae nature before solidifying once more. Still no one seemed to notice, save one cat that hissed and then bolted in the opposite direction.

"A personal connection to the dead family," Isque mused. "The emotional surge was too intense for a casual acquaintance. Family, perhaps? Or close friends?"

Amjani's bit her lip in thought. "If the pact mortal is related to the deceased, it would explain why he sought out this particular location." She paused, considering. "Though it raises questions about why he would bring the child here, to a place of such obvious pain."

"Sentiment," Isque said with the dismissive tone he reserved for mortal weaknesses. "The mortal beings cling to their emotional attachments like drowning sailors to driftwood. Perhaps he thought to honor their memory, or seek some form of closure."

They rounded a corner and the tavern came into view, a modest two-story building with boarded windows and a door that hung slightly askew on its hinges. The structure bore the telltale signs of vagrancy, scorch marks from improperly set fires, rats, excrement and an overall air of abandonment that seemed to press down on the surrounding street.

As they approached the threshold, both Seekers felt it simultaneously, a pulse of arcane energy so distinct it might as well have been a beacon. Amjani's steps slowed, her senses extending to probe the arcane signature that lay buried just beneath the surface.

"There," she whispered, pointing to a spot just in front of the tavern's entrance. "Something's been placed here deliberately."

Isque knelt at the threshold, his fingers dancing through the air as he traced the invisible lines of power. The arcane signature was strong, purposeful, and unmistakably Fae in origin. He began to dig into the packed earth, his hard fingernails cutting into the earth like a knife through cheese.

His fingers closed around something small and smooth. "There we have it," he said smugly, brushing dirt from the object before tossing it up to Amjani.

She caught the piece of wood with two fingers, dropping it into her palm and turning it over. It was half the size of her palm, carved with intricate hidden symbols that seemed to shift and dance in the fading light. She raised an eyebrow as recognition dawned, and she looked off into the distance toward the ancient oak they had investigated earlier.

"This is from the same tree," she murmured, her voice carrying a note of professional admiration. "The arcane signature is identical."

As she studied the carved symbols more closely, the hidden Fae script began to reveal itself, the words appearing like ink bleeding through parchment. Her lips moved silently as she deciphered the text.

'By this pact the child shall be healed and the tavern shall flourish under the matron of the house. By this pact you belong to me and will deliver unto me power.'

Isque leaned closer, reading over her shoulder. A slow laugh bubbled up from his chest, rich with dark amusement. "Oh, that is deliciously brutal," he said, his eyes sparkling with appreciation for the craft involved. "She made a pact with the fool under Fae law but left herself loopholes like the Forgotten would."

Amjani's expression grew thoughtful as she continued to examine the carved wood. "Oakira betrayed her pact mortal in principle but not in word. Quite devious..." She paused, considering. "Or perhaps just a pact made with a highly inexperienced hand."

"Either way," Isque said, as he inhaled the scent of musk and sweat from Amjani's neck with a veiled shutter, "it tells us everything we need to know about our quarry's motivations. And his weaknesses."

Amjani closed her eyes and sighed with a mixture or vexation and highly restrained desire. "Isque."

"Yes, Master Seeker?" His words came out as a purr.

"I know that the hunt can make you... enraptured. However, if I feel it poke my ass again I will give you what you seek and then rip it from you and place it on my shelf." She gave him no chance to be enticed by her words and reared back with her fist.

She was already two blocks away before Isque had caught his breath enough to return to a standing position.

YOU READ THE CARDS WRONG

They had each in turn gone to Kasha's door, trying to get her to talk and find out exactly what the letter could have meant and who Mr. Tolgar was. She had said nothing to Callus and Egrim, but she spoke quietly through the door to Arialyn and asked her to make them give her some time.

Callus read the note again, breaking down every detail he could. Everything from the writing style, the penmanship and even the paper used. Callus was fuming but was trying to put his tactical mind to good use.

Egrim set Morrigan down after reassuring her again that he was okay after the blast of the door.

"See, Arialyn took care of it. I'm all healed up again. Good as new." He sat her down in a chair near Lemmy who seemed to understand he was needed to keep her calm.

Egrim walked over and snatched the paper out of Callus's hands, reading it rapidly once more. He handed it back and walked quickly to the backroom.

Arialyn whispered up to Callus, "You're going to the casino, aren't you?" It was less of a question and more of a statement, she already knew the answer.

"I would prefer to be a little more prepared before barging in, but I don't think Egrim is going to wait for that. Adenus and the Gauntlet can't have anything to do with this. It isn't how he operates. He'd have come to Kasha directly and talked to her. The Lance has to just be using one of his secure rooms at the casino." Callus thumbed at the noose bracelet as Egrim came back into the main room.

"Am I doing this alone?" Egrim asked while staring daggers out the door and into the street. A salesman peaked in and nearly wet himself before realizing now was not the time.

"Fuck no. But you're not going to get that big ass club passed security. Let me do the talking. I doubt Adenus is in on whatever this bullshit is. If we walk into his establishment and start trouble right away without being physically provoked, he'll act on us too. Let me find Adenus first. He and I have a long history and he's probably grown fond of the coin you've won him in the Shale Grounds-" Callus realized his mistake too late.

"I fucking knew it!" Arialyn blurted out.

Callus turned to her slowly, ready to explain himself, but she waved him off.

"I didn't say I cared. Just voicing that I was right." She said it with a smirk.

Egrim dropped the club. "You get us access and talk to Adenus. We find them, and we break them."

"See, look at you. Planning already. I'm proud of you." Callus slapped the big man on the back.

"Fuck you."

"You really need a deeper vocabulary."

As the two left, Arialyn began setting crates to block the door until it could be fixed properly.

The Hus'rokn people moved out of the way like animals instinctively fleeing a storm as the pair walked down the street. There were a few disappointed fans of Callus that weren't greeted as warmly as they were used to by the Towering Tactician.

After close to half an hour they reached the base of the long stone stairs that led up to the Lucky Talisman Casino. The stairway started out being wider than one of the Hus'rokn city blocks and narrowed down to about half of one at the top. The casino itself was one of the most massive structures in the city. It wasn't very tall, only two-stories, but was spread out over a vast amount of land. It was built of vibrant white stone with false gold etchings of coin and reliefs of naked men and women in various poses, coins showering over them as if they were water.

Inside the first story held all the things you might expect on a casino floor. Card and dice tables, pit rat fighting stalls, and roulette which was Callus's personal favorite. Although he very rarely partook in the game.

In the backrooms of the first floor there were stranger games meant for more base clientele and those of higher station that sought to test out their darker intentions. They resembled carnival games with a seedy twist. They were the first games the casino used to lure people in, way back during the founding of Hus'rokn. These games were like historical treasures that a society of scholars might suggest should never be upgraded or interfered with, unless you were willing to pay a hefty fine.

There was the cock ring toss, usually on an erect and very willing bugbear. Criminal stone hurling, where one would literally hurl stones at a criminal until they died. Bets were placed on how many stones a thrower would take to kill the poor sod. The name, however, was a bit of a misnomer since the entire city of Hus'rokn from its founding all the way up to present was run by criminals. So, in this case, the role of the criminal was usually reserved for traitors, and those whose debts finally exceeded the Gauntlet's leniency. There were plenty of other 'historical' games, but they only got weirder, darker and more deviant. Even Adenus didn't go back there. He just enjoyed the coin it brought in.

On the top floor were the basic rooms, suites, meeting rooms and those reserved for private gambling. The Gauntlet offices were also here along with their vault that held their coin, collateral and expensive items that high class customers wanted to make sure were secured while they stayed.

Callus and Egrim reached the front gate and passed through without incident. That first gate was just a precursor and was usually wide open with only two to four Gauntlet men outside to make sure no one passed through with any obvious weapons or devious intent. Of course, there was no one in this city dumb enough to come here with anything more than hollow bravado in the nature of causing trouble. The irony was not lost on Callus at the moment.

As they made their way further in, Callus's nose was swiftly assaulted by the smell of something awful. It reminded him of the sickly-sweet smell of recently rotting flesh. He quickly turned and there was a brief moment were he swore he saw a figure in dark robes move swiftly in his periphery. He looked in that direction and saw no sign of anything. Just as quickly as it came, the smell was gone.

In between the front gate and the main doors was a beautifully lavish courtyard with a plethora of gardens, statuary and fountains whose waters flowed by arcane means. Gauntlet men and paid off-duty city guards patrolled the area in a half lazy manner that Callus saw as a facade. Every one of them was scanning every individual that walked by. One of them noted Egrim's posture and moved ahead of the pair to whisper something to the large Gauntlet Orc that stood in front of massive doors. Callus could never remember the fellow's name. The orc eyed the two of them and whistled to the other two Gauntlet men by the door who then broke away from their posts to join him.

Callus breathed out the disappointment and without breaking eye contact with the orc, whispered to Egrim. "Fucking relax your damn shoulders."

Egrim groaned, now recognizing the problem. He was terrible at hiding his anger, always had been.

Once they were roughly twenty paces from the door the orc held his hand up. As Callus and Egrim stopped he tilted his head to the side with a sign of recognition crossing his face. "Callus, welcome back to the Lucky Talisman. It's been awhile."

"Indeed, it has." Callus put on an upbeat tone of voice. "But if I am indeed welcomed back then I have to say I am a little surprised to be stopped at the front door in this manner."

The orc eyed Egrim. "Your companion here has an air about him. An awful lot of aggression in his posture."

Egrim fought hard to hold back a snarl and thankfully succeeded.

Callus slapped Egrim hard enough on the shoulder to move the man a step. It was a dig and Egrim knew it. He grunted in Callus's general direction. "Please excuse my friend. He had a rough day. Went to sleep in the arms of a beautiful lady and woke up to the sight of an elf that had been slapped in the face with an orchard of ugly trees. Said his cock damn near ran away from him. That's what drinking yourself into oblivion will get you, am I right?"

'You son of a bitch.' Egrim thought.

The orc groaned and nodded. "Rough break. Renny was in that spot last week, weren't you Renny"

Next to the orc, a white dragonscale man's eyes went wide with a look that pleaded with the orc to say no more.

"Renny went on a bender and swore he took a sweet little elven woman to bed. Woke up to a sore cloaca and human woman with massive tits stroking her own cock."

The other Gauntlet, a dwarven woman, nearly doubled over in laughter at the short retelling of the tale again.

The orc shrugged. "I don't know what upset him so much. Giant tits and a cock? Best of both worlds if you ask me. But to each their own."

The dragonscale man deflated in front of all of them.

The orc tapped at a stone on the front of his leather vambrace. "Still, let me check with the boss. He needs final approval on anyone we stop."

Callus bowed slightly. "We understand."

The orc spoke in hushed tones and neither Callus nor Egrim were able to make out his words. After a few exchanges with the stone, he looked up with a smile.

"Adenus says you're both clear. He also says the next time the two of you want to tangle with each other in the Shale Grounds to give him some warning and try not to end it in a draw. No one got to make any coin on that one and it was a hell of a fight. His words not mine."

Callus and Egrim both had to fake a smile as they passed through the door and into the attention-grabbing and mind-altering lights of the Lucky Talisman. Gilded chandeliers hung from the vaulted ceiling of the foyer, their crystals refracting light in dazzling patterns across the gaming floor. The cacophony of clicking dice, shuffling cards, and the constant murmur of desperate hopes and jilted jeers filled the air.

Egrim's gaze swept across the room, taking in the various gaming tables where masked dealers efficiently managed the entire affair. Their faces were hidden behind ornate masks of gold and silver, each uniquely decorated but all bearing the same emotionless expression.

"Why do they all wear masks?" Egrim asked, his voice raised slightly so Callus could hear him over the crowd.

Callus guided him past a roulette table where a nobleman was cursing his luck. "Protection," he replied. "Can't hunt down what you can't recognize. You'd be amazed how many sore losers try to find the dealer that 'cheated' them out of their fortune." He smirked and added, "Plus, Adenus has always had a flair for the dramatic. The masks add to the mystique."

They continued through the main floor, weaving between tables and patrons. As they passed the heavy wooden doors that led to the backrooms, one swung open briefly. Egrim happened to glance inside at precisely the wrong moment. His face went pale, and he stumbled, catching himself on a nearby pillar.

"What's wrong?" Callus asked, noting his complexion turning paler than usual for the human.

Egrim shook his head violently, his braided beard swaying with the motion. "Don't ask," he managed to croak out. "Just... don't." He straightened himself but kept his eyes firmly fixed ahead, deliberately avoiding looking at the doors again.

Callus raised an eyebrow, wondering what could have possibly disturbed the usually unshakeable man so deeply. He'd seen plenty of the backroom "entertainment" before, but he supposed some of the more creative games might be shocking to the uninitiated.

"Come on," Callus said, clapping Egrim on the shoulder. "Let's find our way upstairs. We need to take care of business and then get you a drink." He gestured to a passing server who carried a tray of various spirits. "You look like you could use one."

They moved toward the grand staircase that led to the upper floor, leaving behind the sounds of celebration and despair that echoed through the main casino below. Once at the top Callus turned left and pointed ahead. "Adenus's office is just up here and to the right. We won't have to wait unless he's... enjoying himself. You know what I me-" Callus suddenly felt like he was talking to no one and as he turned to regard Egrim, he realized that was exactly the case.

Egrim had seen and followed the wall signage to the right at the top of the staircase. The signs the pointed to the private meeting rooms. Callus saw the him walking slowly and confidently toward two Lance men that stood on either side on the double doors of one of the room. "Motherfucker." He sighed and broke into a jog.

Alabaster had dressed in his finest whites for the meeting, trying his best to make sure he didn't appear weak. He couldn't afford that right now. Hells, he could barely afford anything right now. He did manage to squeak out a little coin to get Marvin something that stood out more than his usual drab colors. Something Marvin had nearly cried in excitement over.

They entered the private meeting room on the second floor of the Lucky Talisman and Alabaster immediately had to put on the most brave face he could muster since moving to this city. He thought he hid his outrage well enough, although the slight stutter step he made when seeing the meeting that was already in progress most likely gave that away.

He had arrived at the casino earlier than scheduled, trying to prove his dedication to the partnership with Lance Authern. His shock as he entered the room was four-fold. One, this Zunibar Tolgar, a large troll fellow in a better state of dress than him, was already fucking here. A full week earlier than what had been reported to him.

Two, he was pretty sure that he was wearing clothing tailored by Desmond Laticien, the most sought-after tailor in the lower half of the Scarred Lands.

Three, the son of a bitch was sitting in the chair he normally sat in for finance meetings.

But perhaps the most shocking was four. Around the walls of the room stood eleven members of the Talons of Misery. The only blessing Alabaster took from the whole scenario playing out in front of him was that he recognized only two of them. Frezup, a sleek and snooty half-elven man with slicked back blonde hair, far too round features for a man with elven parentage and his usual black leather armor. And then Dunmaris, a gruff looking hobgoblin man of a much thicker build that looked far older than he truly was and wearing nearly identical armor.

The other faces were all new and that hopefully meant they were not keen on ending his life right here and now for his past transgressions against the Talons. He found it very peculiar that they all still wore their embossed bracers with a hawk's talon clutching a bleeding rose within the city. All gangs and mercenary companies, save the Kol'Theron companies, had always been restricted from wearing their signature gears within Hus'rokn. Authern must have convinced Adenus and Rosamunda to make an exception for his new business partner.

Adding to his outrage, Authern had a total of five other Lance men and women around the room and all he had brought with him was Marvin. He had not wanted to come to this meeting showing any kind of force and now he was regretting that decision. Truth be told, however, he was not able to steadily pay most of his people anymore. As it was, he only had Marvin because he was under an indentured service contract. Beetle was another matter. The orc had a devotion to Alabaster simply because he offered him a place to live off the street. The devotion was very strange coming from someone that followed the tenants Odhrum Voidspawn. Alabaster would have shunned the orc, but he found his talents to be very valuable.

Beetle was outside keeping an eye on things in his usual creepy fashion, but that didn't really help him in here unless things got out of hand. In which case he knew Beetle could at least help offer a better chance at escape with some of his little tricks. Deep in Alabaster's front pocket was one of Beetle's messenger bugs. He couldn't have it up near his face for obvious reasons, so it was only there for Alabaster to call out for help.

Nevertheless, Alabaster put on a show for his would-be partners with a slight bow of his head. "Lance Authern, good to see you again as always."

Lance Authern was a half-giant, literally. He stood at around seven and a half feet tall and weighed exactly as people would imagine he might. He earned the nickname The Howler because of the howling sound his great axe made when cutting through the air. The man was pale as a ghost, but you'd never know with all of the intricate tattoos he had covering nearly every bit of flesh you could see. They looked like strange occult-like designs but in truth they were just random patterns that he had found pleasing to his own eyes.

He advanced on Alabaster with one of the fakest showings of pleasant platitudes Alabaster had ever seen. He held a cigar in one hand nearly the size of Marvin's head and shook Alabaster's hand with the other. The grip of the man let everyone know he could rip your arm off with just a slight twist.

"Welcome, Alabaster." Authern extended a sweeping hand to the assembled crew of Zunibar. "This is Mr. Zunibar Tolgar, our new business partner."

Alabaster again, hid his annoyance. Zunibar was supposed to be a new *potential* business partner. It seemed Authern had already made up his mind on the matter without a care for Alabaster's wishes. He stowed his irritation.

"Mr. Tolgar, a pleasure. I'm Mr. Alabaster Jakel. How was your travel from the Helspires? Uneventful I hope."

Zunibar stood nearly as tall as Authern but not quite as wide of frame. His skin was an olive green like most trolls, and his nose was more than a bit bulbous. Had Alabaster not been so caught off guard by the change of course from what he was expecting for this meeting, he would have had a very hard time not staring at it.

Zunibar straightened his vest and jacket as he stood and walked over to extend a hand to Alabaster. "Yes, it was much faster than I had anticipated. I was not required to be as careful in my travels with my new guard here. The Talons of Misery have quite the reputation in the Scarred Lands."

Alabaster shook the troll's hand and prayed that Frezup and Dunmaris hadn't noticed who he really was. Other than reinventing his business image and slightly changing his personality he had done nothing to modify who he truly was, including his appearance. Counting him, there were exactly no other onyx colored and hornless tieflings in the Scarred Lands, possibly in all of existence. Who was he kidding? He was incredibly fucked. As soon as Authern finds out who he truly is and what went down in Toz'Unro with the Brightborn reconnaissance team, he'd be a dead man. For the leader of one of the Three to find out they had been working with a rat, he might as well start tying the noose for the man himself. He stole a glance to read the faces of the older Talons and found them unreadable. That in and of itself made his bowels churn.

Authern motioned for Alabaster and Zunibar to sit. As they did, a robust looking human servant brought them all fresh cups of mead and a tray of meats and cheeses. Even Alabaster scoffed inwardly at the gesture as pretentious. Ironic since under the name of Alejak he had done very similar things during his meetings in Toz'Unro at the Hornless Devil just to make himself look more important. It was one of the things that had driven Callus crazy, which of course made him go even further with it when the Hobgoblin Reaver was around.

Marvin took his place, standing at Alabaster's left side and a footstep behind the chair back. While Marvin had royally fouled up the information on Callus Kordec, he actually was a fairly decent purveyor of secrets. He was quite fluent in the speech of body language, and it would be his job to inform Alabaster, if they made it out of this room alive, what information he gathered. Things such as who looked uncomfortable, who clenched a fist when a certain word or name was spoken, etc. Most importantly, who looked at Alabaster Jakel like they were ready to kill him and were probably planning on it soon.

The ale cups looked far too small in the hands of his host and possible future partner for Alabaster to relax even the slightest. The atmosphere in the room carried the forced calm of a room full of people that know something you don't.

Zunibar raised his cup. "To current and future riches in this beautifully lucrative partnership."

Authern and Alabaster each raised their cups and toasted with the troll.

Zunibar looked to Lance Authern for permission, "May I start off the official portion of the meeting with a question or two, Lance Authern?"

Authern smiled wide and held his cup up again in a polite sign of acceptance. "By all means, you are my honored guest."

Zunibar straightened in his chair, creaking wood making Alabaster wonder if the damn chair would hold much longer. "Mr. Jakel, if I may, what are your plans for this, what was the damned place called, Tits and Tarts?"

Alabaster nodded along. "Correct."

"What are your plans for this building? I understand you had the proper permits in order and yet you were somehow bamboozled out of the property and all the coin that you had put down in it. Is that correct?"

Alabaster held back a sneer. Someone jumping straight to the point of the meeting without any jousting back and forth on trivial matters was unseemly. He smiled wryly. "It is prime real estate, at the perfect intersection of the main thoroughfare from the main gate of Hus'rokn and the Trade Gate to the Wylds. Couple that with one of the other roads of the intersection being the road that leads directly here and you have the perfect spot for a tavern and trading post. By my estimates I would have recouped my purchase within the year and had a steady income of two hundred thousand to three hundred thousand yearly after that."

Zunibar spread his lips in a grin of surprise and nodded along with Alabaster's assessment. "And now that you have had this property stolen out from under you, in a dreadful manner to be sure, how do you plan to proceed moving forward?"

Again, Alabaster held back a sneer, but it was becoming much harder to do so. The fear of death was the greater cause for hiding how he truly felt about the questioning. "The usual tactics of fair market businessmen such as ourselves. Strongarming and fear."

Zunibar waved off the assumption that he resorted to such things himself. "Why not just offer to purchase the property from this, Kasha Volstruk?"

Alabaster's eye twitched. He didn't like that Zunibar knew her name. This meant that either Authern had filled Zunibar in on his personal business or Zunibar investigated the Hus'rokn Property Management files. Either was an insult to him.

"She has been... uncooperative in my attempts to persuade her." Alabaster smiled through clenched teeth.

"As it happens, Mr. Jakel, I can do you a huge favor. You see, Ms. Volstruk and her mother were under an indentured contract with me on my estate back in the Helspires many years ago. Her mother spiced herself into oblivion and Kasha escaped my home. As such, she never finished out her mandatory twenty years. Our just Lance Authern here has agreed to honor the Helspires contract within the city boundaries of Hus'rokn. This means that she is not allowed to own property and since she is in fact my property that makes the Witch's Tits and Tarts Tavern my property. How about I sell it back to you for, say, half the price she paid? That seems dually fair to my eyes."

Alabaster sighed and looked down and away trying to rapidly think of something, anything to get his property back. The loan was the first option. It would seem now that was certainly off the table.

"I..."

Zunibar took in an immediate sarcastic gasp. "You cannot, can you Mr. Jakel. Because you are in fact a near copperless rat, a pretender, weasel and liar. Isn't that right, Alejak of Toz'Unro."

With that, Alejak heard a violent thud and Marvin hit the floor, retching. His own arms were yanked behind him and his face pushed into the solid wooden table. He heard Frezup's familiar laugh behind him.

Authern shot up from his seat at the head of the table. "To think I have been doing business with a damn rat this entire time! How long did you think you could keep this from the Lance? You know what happens to rats around here."

Alejak groaned. "Everyone is a rat for the right price. What I did in Toz'Unro had no bearings on anything this far east in the Scarred Lands."

Frezup lifted Alejak's face up to spit in it and slam it back down on the table. "You sold the gang's trade caravan routes to the Brightborn."

Alejak spit blood onto the table and choked out a laugh. "Not all the gangs. Just the Talons. Well, the Cobalt Crew too, but no one liked them anyway."

Another slam of his head off the table and his ears rang like bells.

"Why?" Frezup leaned in close, frothing at the mouth.

"Callus and Raseg. I wanted to fuck the shit eating grins off their faces, and they were with your crew." Alejak was pretty sure three of his teeth were loose now. No, he just swallowed one. So, two loose teeth.

Zunibar cocked his head to the side. "Callus? Kordec? The gladiator?"

"Do you know any other Callus you fat fuck?" Alejak didn't care at this point. He was going to do die anyway so he might as well be an ass while doing it.

Zunibar chuckled. "I wondered what happened to him after that debacle in the arena. He became a lowly gang punk? No offense intended to present company."

There was a mixture of offended glances and snorted laughter from the crew of Talons.

Authern walked around the table to stand at Alejak's side while one of his men switched places with Frezup and restrained him. "I liked you, as much as I like anyone at least. So, before you die, I'll give you few tidbits of information to grant you some solace before I take your head. The Guard Captain, he's the one who fucked with your permits. We bribed a few of his men to disrupt one of his less than secret shipments and get him out of the city. Adenus and Rosamunda like the man, so I couldn't exactly kill him within Hus'rokn. He should be on a wild goose chase in the Resurgence Wilds right now. At least until some of my men catch up with them. Then he'll be silenced permanently. He was a thorn in my side anyway. Having a somewhat honest man at the head of the City Guard, especially one the people respect, puts a wrench in the gears of my organization's... body count. We must maintain at least a thin veil that we don't do what we do of course. Rosmunda, all praise to the sitting Governor," the words dripped with sarcasm, "doesn't care for our chief export of contract killing. Nevertheless, fear not. I took pleasure in ordering his death. He and his sergeant won't make it back here. Kasha Volstruk has received a delightfully stern note from us, and if she doesn't show her pretty little face here within the next half hour she will be collected. Just wanted you to know that I was righting the wrongs done to you. Mr. Tolgar assures me that she will be a free use slave for the pleasure of all the Lance for a time no shorter than a week per year of her absence from her contract. So, she will be aptly punished for the trouble she caused you."

Alejak chuckled. "Free use? You really do go low don't you Authern. Just take my head and be done with it."

Marvin was leaning against the table now, looking even more woozy than Alejak. Even still, he could see the halfling doing his work and subtly scanning the room. He knew the end was at hand when Marvin's eyes went wide, and a cold blade rested against his neck.

"Thank you, Marvin. That'll be all." He shocked himself with how much he was going to miss the little man.

"Wait! Wait, just a moment my dear Lance. Steady your blade if you will." Zunibar motioned for the Talon men to raise his head toward him.

Alejak's right eye was nearly swollen shut, but he still managed to glare at the troll bastard.

"Do you happen to know the whereabouts of Callus Kordec?"

Dunmaris interrupted before Alejak could answer. "Lord Tolgar, last we heard he killed our former President and one of our Skirmish Bosses across the Trade Gate in the Wylds, but he left here and went west to the Brightborn Kingdom with a gnome bitch that started that whole cock up in the first place."

Alejak started laughing. "Whoever gave you that last bit of intel either lied to you outright or was more afraid of Callus than he was of you chucklefucks."

The Talon holding him down wrenched his arm further back and upward and he felt something pop.

"Then tell me where he is Alejak. I bet I can fill his pockets with enough gold coins to have him be my own personal captain. Give me reliable information and I will see if I can convince the Lance here to let you live. If he agrees then you will enter into a contract of indentured servitude with me for thirty years. That seems fair to me in exchange for your life."

Alejak's laughter erupted, he sounded mad as a true jackal now. "He's here you twat. Been here for several months." He said it as confidently as if he hadn't just found out the same information just recently.

Frezup and Dunmaris shared a look of pure outrage. Alejak knew of the Talons of Misery code to kill anyone that marred the face of one of their own and Callus had killed many of them. He wished he could see how that would play out, the very men Zunibar hired to protect him now wanted the head of the hobgoblin he wanted to convince to oversee them all.

"You will take my men to his location and tell him I want a meeting." Zunibar could have had one of the Gods command him to do it and it wouldn't have mattered anymore.

Alejak's laughter grew even louder.

"He's lost his mind." Dunmaris said flatly.

Alejak laughed throughout his entire next statement. "Just so I am clear. You want me to take your men to meet with Callus Kordec, The Ruiner, and ask him to link up with a man that ordered one of his closest friends killed in the Resurgence Wilds and sent threats to his childhood best friend with plans to make her a sex slave to be assaulted daily?"

Zunibar's face darkened at Alejak's words of revelation. "Authern, did you know any of this?"

The Lance's knuckles went white on the handle of the axe he held. With all of this new information, Marvin, at least could see the Lance was trying to see how to play his hand now. "Yes, I knew he was close to the Guard Captain, but it isn't like you, or your men strode in here asking about the damn hobgoblin until now. His relation to the Volstruk woman, however, I was unaware of."

Alejak was able to see Marvin's eyes briefly hon in on someone else across the room before going back to looking stunned and dizzy. Alejak spit blood across the table and began to laugh like a man gone mad.

"You're all dead. He is going to kill every damned one of you."

As if Alejak had summoned Callus from the heavens, the meeting room door opened and the two Lance guards that had been stationed outside were dumped onto the floor, motionless.

CHAPTER TWENTY-ONE

STAR CHERRIES AND IRON

Kovag pulled back Debt's mane gently, bringing the horse to a halt several yards from where the road curved toward Ferrum Plains' eastern gate. The morning sun cast long shadows across the dusty path, and he could feel Saffron fidgeting in front of him, her small fingers working at the braid he'd woven into her hair the night before.

Something had caught his eye, a flash of crimson and gold that didn't belong in dwarven territory. He blinked, a pale green wave of energy enveloping in his Fae touched eye. The world sharpened and stretched before him, bringing distant details into crystal clarity. His jaw clenched as his vision confirmed his fears, four riders in Empire colors were passing through the city gates. One of them set the hairs at the back of his neck on end, but he couldn't place why.

Saffron must have felt the tension in his body because she tilted her head back to look up at him, her amber eyes inquisitive. He forced his expression to remain neutral, though his heart hammered in his chest.

"Here," he murmured, placing his finger gently against her temple. He watched her eyes widen as the spell took effect on her again, her small hands gripping the saddle horn tighter as the sudden change in vision made her dizzy. "See those men in red and gold entering the city?"

She nodded, her ears flattening against her head. She felt an odd sense of familiar dread, but she couldn't place it. Something in those colors terrified her, encased in a safe somewhere that her brain refused to unlock.

"If you see them anywhere near us, anywhere at all, I need you to let me know immediately." His voice was barely above a whisper, but he knew her sensitive ears would catch every word. "They are probably just diplomatic envoys, but we should be cautious. Squeeze my arm twice if you understand."

Her small fingers found his forearm and squeezed twice, her tail curling tighter around her waist, a sure sign of her apprehension. What was worse, she could sense Kovag's unease, and that made her very core shiver.

Kovag pulled her closer against his chest, adjusting his heavy cloak to completely envelope her. He willed the shimmer spell around them both again, feeling the arcane ripple around them as the spell settled over their skin. As long as the Empire men weren't skilled arcane practitioners their eyes would slide right past them like everyone else.

"Remember," he whispered into one of her twitching ears, "you're safe with me. Quiet as a meadow mouse." He felt her nod against his chest as he urged their Debt forward, keeping to a casual pace that wouldn't draw attention.

As they approached the city gates, Kovag's mind raced. Empire men this far into the Brightborn Kingdom meant trouble, the kind of trouble that could make their planned stay in Ferrum Plains dangerously complicated. The occasional envoys that the Oskon Empire sent here always gave as much of a sign of strength as they could without pissing off the Jarl and local Brightborn military. Four men was hardly a sign of force. That meant these men were here for something else entirely, even though he was trying to convince himself otherwise. He briefly considered changing course, but they needed some true rest, information, and most importantly, they needed to find Bornar. He just hoped the old half-dwarf hadn't kicked the bucket or wound up in jail again.

Kovag guided their horse through the bustling streets of Ferrum Plains, weaving between merchant wagons and groups of travelers. The familiar scents of the dwarven city, coal smoke, fresh bread, horse dung and metal shavings, filled his nostrils, but the layout seemed different than he remembered. New buildings had sprung up where he recalled open squares, and some of the old landmarks had vanished entirely. He realized it had been longer than he thought since he had been back here. Had it really been four years? No, had to be three.

Saffron's pressed closer against him beneath the cloak as they passed particularly loud groups of travelers. Her tail occasionally brushed against his arm, letting him know she remained alert and watchful. The shimmer spell held steady around them, but he still felt exposed asking for directions. He had to stay in one place too long to pry the information from the people he asked because the spell made them disinterested in answering his queries.

After several more minutes of aimless navigation, Kovag halted Debt to a stop near a weathered fruit cart. The merchant, a stout dwarf woman with elaborately braided silver hair, barely glanced in their direction before returning to arranging her wares.

"Excuse me. I'm a bit turned around. Green Bastard's Blades," Kovag said, keeping his voice low and neutral. "Where might I find it?"

The merchant's hands stilled over a pile of bright red star cherries. She looked up at him with shrewd eyes, her expression calculating. "Might be I know the place," she said, running a finger along one of her braids. "Might be I could remember better. Got a business to run-"

The woman's voice began to trail off as her eyes began to look through him. Kovag felt Saffron's silent giggle against his chest as he let out an annoyed grunt. He reached into his coin purse, painfully aware of how light it had become. "Fine."

The dwarven woman blinked rapidly and shook her head before her face split into a wide grin, revealing several gold teeth. "Now you're speaking proper business." She gestured to her wares with a flourish. "Finest star cherries this side of the Great Scar."

"Perhaps that's because they don't grow on the other side." He responded gruffly. Kovag purchased a small bag, the price was fair, the annoyance was not. Saffron's tail swished with interest as the sweet aroma wafted up from beneath the cloak.

"The Green Bastard, eh?" The merchant tied off the bag with her gnarled fingers. "Take a right up three blocks. Look for the sign for the Stone Way down past the Temple District. That'll get you to the Forge Quarter, should be simple to find from there. Pretty sure it still has that right ugly mug painted on it too." She handed him the cherries with a knowing smirk. "Though I'd wager you already knew that part."

Kovag took the bag with a nod of thanks, careful not to let his cloak shift too much as he stored it away in a pouch that hung from the saddle horn. As they moved back into the flow of traffic, he felt Saffron's small fingers working their way toward the cherry bag. He allowed himself a small smile, remembering how Mori used to do the same thing when they were children.

"Later," he whispered, gently moving her hand away. Her disappointed huff was barely audible over the city noise, but he felt it all the same.

Saffron waited until she felt Kovag's attention drift to navigating the crowded streets before making her move. Her small fingers crept toward the pouch with all the stealth she could muster, which wasn't much. The leather creaked under the cloak beneath her touch, and she froze, certain she'd been caught. When Kovag didn't react, she continued her careful mission.

The sweet scent of the star cherries called to her like a siren's song. She managed to work the bag open, wincing at every tiny sound. Her tail, betraying her excitement, swished against Kovag's arm in a steady rhythm. If she'd been able to see his face, she would have noticed the slight upturn at the corner of his mouth as he pretended not to notice her less-than-subtle theft.

Just as her fingers closed around one of the bright red fruits, Kovag pulled Debt to an abrupt halt. Saffron nearly lost her balance, barely catching herself before she could tumble forward. She quickly withdrew her hand, trying to look as innocent as possible beneath the heavy cloak.

Ahead of them, the Empire soldiers they had seen at the gate were questioning merchants along Stone Way. Their crimson and gold uniforms stood out starkly against the earth tones of the dwarven architecture. Kovag's body tensed, and Saffron sensed his unease. She tapped his thigh rapidly, wanting to know what was happening.

"Just going around an obstacle. Quiet as a meadow mouse." His voice was calm, but she could sense his emotions keenly. The strength with which she felt them caused her to tilt her head to the side, curious at the new development. A development that peeked her curiosity.

Without a word, he guided their horse down a side street, taking a circuitous route that added nearly half an hour to their journey. Saffron's stomach growled quietly. She slowly opened the bag of star cherries again and bit into one. Her mouth fell open. These were the sweetest thing she had ever tasted. It wasn't long until she devoured them so eagerly that Kovag could hear her smacking over the crowded streets. Even with the dread he held for the Empire men somewhere behind them, he still smiled. He even felt her retie the pouch shut.

When they finally emerged onto the street that housed the Green Bastard's Blades, Kovag's shoulders relaxed slightly. The shop stood before them, a weathered wooden sign creaking gently in the breeze. True to the merchant's words, it still bore the crude painting of a scowling olive green half orc-half dwarf face that Kovag knew so well.

The forge was active, evidenced by the smoke rising from the chimney and the rhythmic sound of hammer striking anvil. The familiar scents of oil and coal filled the air, mixing with the aroma of freshly worked iron.

Kovag dismounted, carefully holding Saffron to his chest. He looked around and once satisfied no one was paying attention to them, he set her down while still shielding her with an outstretched draping of his cloak. She felt him slip something into her hand. She looked down to find a perfectly ripe star cherry sitting in her palm. When she glanced up at him questioningly with a mouth stained red from the star cherry juice, he winked.

"Next time," he whispered, "try not to let your tail give you away quite so much."

Saffron's ears flattened in embarrassment, but she couldn't help grinning as she stood on her tiptoes and held the star cherry up to Kovag. He paused before grinning himself and bending low to bite the tiny fruit from her fingers. "A generous offering, Saffron, The Unyielding Doomicorn of Yonara."

She gave Kovag a mocking bow, one that royalty would give to someone of lesser station out of obligation. He took her hand and cracked open the door to the Green Bastard, looking around to make sure the smithy was empty or near enough that he could still hide Saffron. He dropped the shimmer spell with a subtle shift of his will.

The smithy's interior lay dim and quiet, save for the gentle crackle of the forge in the rear of the building. Kovag ushered Saffron inside, his large hand gentle on her shoulder as he guided her through the doorway. He turned to secure the lock, wanting to make sure he had a private audience with his old friend and mentor.

The whisper of movement was his only warning.

In one fluid motion, Kovag spun and threw up his hand, catching the head of a blacksmithing hammer. He flipped it around and gripped the handle, ready to use it if need be. He was a pugilist at heart, but it never hurt to use a weapon if it became available. Saffron pressed herself against his leg and he placed his other hand in front of her.

"Bornar, you crotchety bastard!" Kovag called out, keeping the hammer raised. "It's Dresh!"

A gruff voice emerged from the shadows near the forge. "Dresh? You stupid fucker!" Heavy footsteps approached as a stout figure emerged into view. "Locking my door is a sure way to end up with more holes than a beggar's boots!"

Bornar's visage caught the forge light as he stepped forward, his long braided grey mohawk falling into a ponytail that fell over his shoulder. Despite his threatening words, a broad grin split his bearded face, metal beads clicking together as he moved.

"Been too long, you great green fool. Thought that blasted Fae witch got you killed." Bornar said, closing the distance between them. The small tusks that were a clear sign of his half orc heritage gleamed as he clasped Kovag's forearm in a warrior's greeting, pulling him into a rough embrace that made his leather armor creak.

Kovag tossed the hammer to a nearby table and returned the gesture, though he kept one hand protectively near Saffron. "Good to see you haven't lost your warm welcome, old man."

"Warm as a forge fire," Bornar chuckled, stepping back. His eyes fell to Saffron, who had partially hidden herself behind Kovag's leg, her tail wrapped tightly around her waist. "And who's this little shadow you've brought into my shop?"

Before Kovag could answer, Bornar's expression shifted, his eyes narrowing as he glanced between them before they grew huge. "There must be quite the story behind this. I haven't seen one of her kind since the Mongrel War, and I was sure that..." He stopped in his thought, not wanting to scare Saffron.

He moved to the windows, pulling the heavy shutters closed. "She can't be seen. Fucking Empire has been in my damn city for a bleeding week. They claim to be here to improve diplomatic relations, but they're asking too many questions for diplomats."

Kovag felt Saffron's grip tighten on his leg. "That's part of why we're here," he said quietly. "I'm trying to find more vulpine, and Erland said his sister, Maudrid, is the best person he knows to help. But the network has made it so he doesn't know exactly where she is. He said Matron Vadrida would and that you would know which temple I can find her in and how to ask for her proper. Sounds like quite the damn runaround now that I say it all out loud."

Bornar sighed. "We can get to that, but you look like you need a drink and to take some weight off for a beat. Those damn Empire men are snooping around the area too, so best you stay here for the night at least."

He waved them to the back, leading them through the smithy, past racks of cooling blades and other half-finished works. The backroom was sparsely furnished with a worn wooden table and three mismatched chairs, clearly a space meant for private business dealings.

Saffron's eyes darted around the room, taking in every detail while maintaining her death grip on Kovag's leg. Her tail swished anxiously behind her, betraying her unease in the confined space.

"Sit," Bornar grunted, pulling out one of the chairs. "You look like shit warmed over."

Kovag settled into the offered chair, lifting Saffron onto his lap when she made no move to take her own seat. "Feel like it too," he admitted, his voice heavy with exhaustion. "Sleep has been... an absent lover as of late."

As Kovag recounted their journey, Bornar's expression grew increasingly grim. His thick fingers absently stroked one of the metal beads in his beard, a habit Kovag remembered from his short days as one of Bornar's apprentices back when the old man helped teach him how to fight proper.

"And that Fae witch of yours?" Bornar asked when Kovag finished his tale. "The one with the tree fetish. Has she been any help?"

Kovag's jaw clenched, and Saffron looked up at him, sensing the sudden shift in his emotions. "Other than pointing me toward the monster who happened to have Saffron, no." His voice carried an edge that made even Bornar raise an eyebrow. "Our communication has been limited."

"Limited?" Bornar's eyes narrowed. "That's not like her, from what you've told me before. Don't you two normally," he briefly looked at Saffron and chose his next words carefully. "... commune during the full moons."

"It's been years since I've been here, Bornar. Things change." Kovag replied flatly, his hand unconsciously moving to rest protectively on Saffron's shoulder.

Bornar studied them both for a long moment, his expression unreadable. "Aye, that they do."

He rose from his chair. "And some things don't change at all. Like you finding trouble bigger than that thick skull of yours can handle."

He moved to a cabinet in the corner and pulled out a dusty bottle and three cups. After a pause, he returned the third cup and poured two measures of amber liquid. "You still take your whiskey with water like a milk-drinking apprentice?"

"Not today," Kovag replied, accepting the full measure with his free hand. Saffron wrinkled her nose at the sharp smell and stuck out her tongue as though she were trying to get the scent out of her system.

Bornar poured another measure of whiskey for them both, the smooth liquor catching the dim light from the forge's glow through the doorway. Saffron had dozed off in Kovag's lap, her tail occasionally twitching in her sleep.

"You missed quite the show last month. Ended up back behind iron," Bornar said, his voice pitched low to avoid disturbing the sleeping child. "Some merchant's whelp thought he'd make a name for himself by challenging the old half-breed smith." He gestured to a barely healed cut above his eye. "Caught me with a cheap shot, but that was all he managed before I introduced his face to a tavern table."

Kovag raised an eyebrow. "And that landed you in jail?"

"Turns out his father has the Jarl's ear." Bornar shrugged, the metal beads in his beard clicking softly. "Week in the cells was worth it though. Should've seen the look on the boy's face when I went straight back to drinking." He took a long drink. "Some lessons need to be taught the hard way."

The warmth of the whiskey spread through Kovag's chest, but it did little to ease the weight of his next words. He glanced down at Saffron's peaceful face, then back to his old friend. "I need to get her to her own people."

Bornar's expression shifted, understanding dawning in his eyes even though his head shook with unease. "As I said, boy, the last I saw of her kind was in the war and they're all dead," he said, matching Kovag's careful tone. "If any did survive they are going to make damn sure they can't be found."

"She can't stay with me. My life is far too dangerous for a child." Kovag looked down at her, his face briefly dropping the mask of certainty.

Bornar sat forward in his chair. "Maybe, but your heart is telling you differently isn't it." It was a statement and not a question.

"You were there during the war," Kovag pressed, his free hand unconsciously stroking Saffron's hair. "Surely you must have heard something about where any survivors might have gone? Safe places? Tribes?" Kovag's face was pleading.

The older man studied him for a long moment, his weathered face creasing with concern for his former apprentice. "There were rumors once," he said finally, "of sightings of some of the beastfolk in and around the mountains surrounding the Spearfall ruins. Deep in the forests where even the Wolf Lords rarely venture."

He leaned forward, his voice dropping even lower. "But no one knows how to get there. You know that. The old magics that guarded that dead kingdom still hold. People walk into those cursed forests and find themselves turned around and right back where they started. There have been entire expeditions to get there by land and sea. None make it. Kovag, with the repercussions from the war, even the Emeraldom won't be safe for you to travel openly with her. The price for her kind has got to be more than either of us have made or will ever make in our lifetime, and that's if she isn't the only one left."

The old man squared his eyes with Kovag. "Sometimes the safest place isn't the right one, boy."

Kovag's jaw tensed as he looked down at Saffron curled up against him, innocent and unaware. "And sometimes the right place isn't where we want it to be," he murmured, as if trying to convince himself. "She should be with her people, someone who can protect her. Someone who won't bring danger with every step." His fingers twitched against the fabric of her cloak. "If she stays with me... I'll get her killed."

There was a beat of silence before Bornar spoke again, softer this time. "Or maybe the only reason she's still breathing is because she's with you."

Bornar ran his thick fingers through his beard, the metal beads clicking together in a familiar rhythm that reminded Kovag of hours spent at the forge. The old half-dwarf's eyes settled on Saffron's sleeping form, his expression softening almost imperceptibly.

"Matron Vadrida," Bornar said, taking another slow sip of his whiskey. "She's at Thromgrid's temple on the west side of the city. That woman's got more connections than a spider's got legs, and she hates the Empire more than I hate a dull blade. She'll get you in touch with Maudrid. She knows where half the network is located. When you get there tell one of the priestesses, 'I'm looking for solace among the flowers of the dawn.' They'll fetch her."

Kovag nodded. "Thank you, old man."

Bornar nodded, a grim smile playing at the corners of his mouth. "Vadrida fought in the war too. Bloody war priestess, she was. I was there. She led several of us over that final hill as though she were Volfmir the Grudge Keeper himself. A miracle Erland survived that battle. He's the one that leaked the intel on where to attack that day. It was total chaos on their side. I found him surrounded by Brightborn Irregulars with their blades drawn on him. He was standing over his own captain, his sword through the man's chest. The Irregulars didn't know what to make of it. If Vadrida hadn't come barreling in to clarify he was our mole, they would have killed him. The things tha poor fool witnessed on the Empire side of things..."

Bornar went silent for a few moments, visions of that terrible war passing by in his head. "Anyway, Vadrida will get you what you're looking for or at least the next best thing to it. She'll consider it a personal victory to keep something precious out of Empire hands."

Kovag felt Saffron stir slightly in his lap, her tail twitching as she dreamed. The weight of her attachment to him felt heavier than any armor he'd ever worn.

"Where can we get some rest? You still have that hay pile you call an apprentice bed?" Kovag teased, trying to lighten the mood for his own sake.

Bornar chuckled and nearly snorted his drink. "Do I look like I've had any apprentices lately? She can take my bed. Gods know you won't fit in it. We get the floor, lad."

CHAPTER TWENTY-TWO

SHE'S GOING TO BE PISSED

Lance Authern, Zunibar and a room full of Lance and Talons of Misery looked at the two figures in the now open doorway with faces that ranged from shock to fear and outrage. Eyes shifted back and forth between the two unconscious bodies lying on the floor and a well-muscled, middle-aged hobgoblin and one hulking human that stood a head taller than the retired gladiator.

Callus rolled his neck and began with the most obviously over-the-top false apology he could muster as though he was reading from a note without looking up.

"My apologies to the illustrious Lance and Mr. Tolgar, whoever the fuck that is." He looked up from the note to confer with Egrim, who was too busy burning everyone in the room with his eyes. "Who in the hells goes around blowing up doors and then asking someone for a meeting? Terrible branding if you ask me."

Egrim took a step forward with fists clenched so tightly that one of his fingernails had drawn blood that was starting to drip from his palms.

Callus placed a hand on the big man's chest and was met with a low growl.

"Let's give the gentlemen a chance to defend their actions. Wait, is gentlemen the right word? No. Fools? Ah, I have it. Dead men."

With that, Callus finally looked up and scanned the room fully. He felt heat rising in his flesh, recognizing Frezup, Dunmaris and the gears of the Talons of Misery. His eyes darted briefly at a young grimalkin, Herodin, that he had a vague recollection of. All the others must have been newly recruited street scum. Authern stepped to the side, making his greataxe plainly visible, and revealed Alejak, face down and bleeding on the table. The heat in Callus's flesh hit his face and his eyes turned to fire. Several items clicked into place all at once. How stupid had he been? How many damn onyx skinned tiefling's did he fucking know of in this world. "You! You're Alabaster?!"

As nonchalantly as if he were making tea and welcoming a guest into his offices, Alejak smiled through his bloody mouth. "Hello Callus. I'm afraid you caught me at a bad time. Could we perhaps reschedule?"

Callus rushed to the table and slammed his hands down on it. Nearly everyone in the room produced weapons, except Zunibar who simply reclined in his chair.

Egrim was glad to see Callus now on the same page as him. This wasn't a mission of politics and speeches, it was a mission of blood and vengeance. Better that Callus was in agreement than trying to stop him.

Authern held his hand up to steady the other Lance members. Frezup and Dunmaris moved to flank Zunibar on either side of his chair. Callus wrinkled his nose as the smell of sickly sweet death wafted by him again. He noted Egrim's eyes catch something as it moved around the room and then settled somewhere behind Alejak before moving to the troll who began to speak.

"Callus Kordec and..." Zunibar raised his brow to Egrim, expecting the man to announce himself.

"Someone who is going to start ripping heads off momentarily." Egrim spat out like cold steel.

Zunibar's lips flattened. "That would be most unfortunate. For you. I'll be speaking to the retiree only now. Mr. Kordec, I am Zunibar Tolgar. I am sure you have at least a passing knowledge of Lance Authern here. I am pleased, that to my recently acquired wisdom, I have reunited you with some old friends." Zunibar motioned with his hands to the Talons around the room and then to Alejak.

Callus punched the table, making a few cups spill over. "If you lot had stayed in Toz'Unro you could have lived the rest of your filthy lives enjoying the debauchery you sow. But you had to come here. I told you to stay the hells away from me Frezup. Was that note not clear?"

With a sneer Frezup crossed his arms and shrugged. "We're not here for you Reaver. We are under contract with Mr. Tolgar. Now, if he sends us after you that's a different story all together. For now... he hasn't set you as a target to be dealt with. This sack of worg shit on the other hand." He spat on Alejak.

"In my eye, really?" Alejak felt far calmer than he should be in his position. Perhaps because the messenger bug had informed Beetle of his predicament and he knew that the cadaverous man was somewhere in the room right now. Beetle stood with no one the wiser except for the human with Callus whom the messenger bug told him was more than he seemed. In any case, while not great by any stretch of the imagination, his odds of getting out of here alive had improved.

The loud clearing of Zunibar's throat broke in. "Mr. Kordec, allow me to explain a few things to you. Alejak, whom you clearly have no love for, was just about to be executed for trying to enter into a business arrangement under false pretenses of actually being of any value and having any wealth to contribute. Not to mention he is a rat among a room of wolves. I get the suspicious feeling that you might enjoy seeing that event."

Egrim and Callus interrupted the troll in unison. "The fucking note."

Authern took a step toward the pair of interlopers. Egrim grabbed the chair nearest him and slung it against the wall, removing its obstruction from his path.

Zunibar's voice boomed out again. "Lance, is everyone in this room other than me so eager for violence? This is just business. Let cooler heads prevail until we have no further recourse. Please."

Authern halted his movement much to Alejak's amusement. The Lance allowing someone else to tell him what to do? Authern must really need Zunibar's funding. But for what?

"I have learned a great many things this day. You are close to Ms. Volstruk, so I am told. Allow me to enlighten you on some things from her past that you may not be aware of. She failed to serve out her time on an indentured service contract with me in the Helspires. Lance Authern, presiding over the indentured service market in Hus'rokn, has been gracious enough to honor the contract here. Thus, making it fully legal in this city. In light of the knowledge that she means so much to the former Scarred Lands Champion that used to entertain me greatly in the Helspires, I am willing to release her from said contract if she hands over her establishment to me without a fuss."

Alejak let out a bloody laugh again.

Marvin swallowed hard and blurted out the words as fast as he could. "Lies! They want the tavern and to turn her into a sexsl-" His words were cut short by the massive hand of Lance Authern smashing down on his head with a crunch.

Neither man could hold back anymore. They would have blood. Callus summoned the Hangman's Spears and hurled it at Zunibar, but the spear collided with a quick arcane shield thrown up by Dunmaris. The spear vanished and reappeared in Callus's hand.

Egrim grabbed the table and flipped the fifteen-foot solid wood like it was a toy. It collided with the left side of the room, pinning a handful of Talons and Gauntlet between it and the wall.

The Talons holding Alejak quickly forgot about him and moved to join the fray. Beetle's visage shimmered into view, and he used the opportunity to place a hand on Alejak and the crumpled form of Marvin. With a burst of deathly fumes, the trio vanished. The few Talons around that area began to cough and vomit from the stench.

Callus engaged a young advancing Talon and slammed the pommel end of his spear into his throat, forcing him to the ground spitting blood and gasping for air while Egrim dodged to the left of Authern's greataxe swing and drove the half-giant off his feet and through a chair.

Callus spun around two Lance men, tripping one and slicing the other's calf as he aimed his Ring of Anguish squarely at Zunibar's throat. Three silver bolts shot forth. Had they been just a second earlier leaving the arcane ring they would have hit true. Fortunately for Zunibar, a high-pitched wail rang out in the room causing everyone to drop what they were doing and cover their ears. An arcane blinding spell went off from all four corners of the room right after, momentarily taking everyone's sight from them.

Every person in the room screamed in soundless pain and staggered. As everyone's vision slowly came back, they each became keenly aware of the daggers at their throats and the masked men and women of the Gauntlet.

"Lance Authern! You carry this sort of business out in MY casino?! Mine?!" The ringing had stopped enough for Callus to recognize the voice of Gauntlet Adenus. The tall and slender dark elven man moved among the group in contained rage.

"Adenus, this is no concern of yours." Authern hollered out, shoving the Gauntlet dagger away from his throat and standing slowly.

"You made it my business when you decided to enact violence in my establishment. You were never good at thinking things through. Mr. Tolgar, you will be escorted to collect your chests and then you will leave. You are barred from the Lucky Talisman. Callus, the same goes for you and Egrim. Leave. Now!" Adenus looked squarely into Callus's eyes in a way that told the hobgoblin they would be talking more soon.

Zunibar opened his mouth, attempting to protest and stopped when the orc Gauntlet pressed the blade harder against his throat. His lip rose but he relented with a nod.

Once Callus and Egrim were out of the room the Gauntlets that escorted them lowered their blades. Callus looked into the room, locking eyes with Zunibar. "If you come for Kasha you had better come with everything you have. Better bring a God with you too if you want any chance of living."

Callus turned to walk but Egrim stood there, eyes locked on Zunibar. "I'll be the last thing you see."

The Gauntlet perked up at the mention of Kasha. "What does this mess have to do with Ms. Volstruk?"

Adenus snarled at the dark elf. "Property acquisition and agreed upon terms for a re-establishment of an indentured service contract. Nothing that involves you. This is my domain."

"Callus." Adenus called over his shoulder with a smirk that Callus was unsure if he liked.

"Gauntlet?"

"Correct me if I am wrong, but Kasha filed paperwork to run card and dice tables in the new building. Is that right?" Adenus said flatly.

Egrim knew of no such paperwork or even plans to bring gambling into the Tits and Tarts. But Callus knew what Adenus was up to.

"She did. Just a few days ago if memory serves." Callus's smile let Egrim know this was going to work in their favor.

Adenus folded his arms behind his back, nodded and whistled. "Well, then it seems we are in a little bit of a muddy area Mr. Tolgar. You see, the Gauntlet runs the gambling in Hus'rokn. ALL of the gambling. That means that your proposed acquisition of the Witch's Tits and Tarts interferes with my business. Since the current owner of the Tits and Tarts is then technically under my protection, this puts the Lance and Gauntlet at odds. When such matters occur the Three, meaning myself, Authern and Rosamunda of the Shield, must meet to discuss how to handle the issue at hand. Remind me Lance Authern, when was our last meeting?"

"You are reaching pretty hard, Adenus." Authern's jaw was beginning to twitch.

"When?"

"Four days ago."

"Excellent. Since we meet once a month, I look forward to coming to favorable terms for the both of us in twenty-one days. I trust that you and your men can see yourselves out. Oh, bring weapons into the Lucky Talisman again and I will treat it as an act of aggression against the Gauntlet. You can't afford that kind of heat, Authern."

Callus and Egrim were outside the main gate when Egrim finally asked. "What in the hells just happened?"

"Adenus saved Kasha's business, at least for now, but she is going to have to actually have card and dice tables in the Tits."

Egrim shrugged. "That's not so bad."

"And he'll get fifteen percent of her overall profits." Callus nearly winced as he said it.

"I'll let you handle the fallout on this one."

"Figures."

CHAPTER TWENTY-THREE

NEVER HIT THE TITS

Arialyn stood outside Kasha's suite door, her hand hovering near the wood but not quite touching it. She slumped her shoulders and let out a sympathetic sigh at the sound of quiet sobbing from within. She glanced down at Morrigan, who clutched Lemmy firmly to her chest. He bobbed his head in the direction of the door.

"Kasha?" Arialyn called softly. "Please let us in. Tell me what's going on, please."

There was no response, just the continued sound of muffled crying.

Morrigan, at Lemmy's insistence, stepped forward and knocked gently with her small knuckles, barely audible over the sobbing inside. After a few attempts she scratched at the door with the sharp nails most tieflings had. The scratching stopped abruptly when the crying quieted.

"Morrigan's worried about you," Arialyn added.

After a long moment, they heard the lock click. The door creaked open just enough for them to see Kasha's tear-streaked face, her makeup smeared across her cheeks. Her eyes were puffy and red, making the hazel irises stand out even more starkly than usual.

Kasha looked down and then motioned with her hand, stepping back to let them enter. The suite was immaculate as always, except for the overturned wine goblet that stood out like a bloodstain on the polished wooden surface. Kasha sank onto the edge of her bed, wringing her hands in her lap.

Arialyn looked at Morrigan, "Sweetness," trying to keep her voice neutral, "Would you take Lemmy to go play in the corner for a bit? I think I need to talk with Kasha in private. You can have fun with her makeup..."

Kasha looked at Arialyn with a silent plea to not give her that idea. Arialyn smirked and rolled her eyes playfully.

Morrigan nodded, carrying Lemmy over to the corner near the vanity. She grabbed a few cosmetics off the vanity top. She tilted her head to the side while looking at Lemmy, wondering what Lemmy would look like with lipstick.

Once Kasha saw the quizzical look on the girl's face she smiled lightly and relented. Arialyn sat beside Kasha and took one of her trembling hands. "Who's Tolgar?"

She breathed deep and sighed before deciding what to say. "His name is Zunibar Tolgar. He's..." She paused, squeezing Arialyn's hand tightly. "He held a indentured service contract on my mother and I when I was, hells, I was probably less than Morrigan's age."

"Like a slave contract?" Arialyn's voice carried a dangerous edge. "Like an actual term contract? From where?"

Kasha glanced over at Morrigan playing quietly. She felt a brief moment of envy over the innocence and joy on the girl's face. Then she remembered how Egrim said they had lost Morrigan's mother and realized they actually had a lot in common. "The Helspires."

Arialyn perked up at that. "Well, we aren't in the damned Helspires are we? So that contract is not enforceable here and even if it was-" Arialyn saw a dark wave pass over her friend's face. "You didn't finish out the time on it did you?"

With another heaving sigh that fought back a new wave of tears Kasha told Arialyn the full story of Zunibar, her mother essentially giving up and her escape with the goblin man. She was not ready to relive the time between then and arriving in Hus'rokn, where she was adopted into Sylus Mordath and his Traveling Spectacles.

"It's been nearly thirty years. I know we aren't in the Helspires, but that monster is a truly resourceful man and I don't trust that he won't find a way to make it happen. In the letter he claimed I needed to sign the title of the tavern over to him. That's something only enforceable if I am recognized as a slave again. I'm afraid he has already found a way."

Arialyn sat quietly for a moment, her fingers drumming against her thigh as she processed what Kasha had told her. The gears in her mind turned rapidly, considering angles and possibilities. Her eyes darted to Morrigan, who was now carefully applying rouge to an indignant Lemmy's beak.

"Kasha," she said finally, keeping her voice low, "Callus and Ethan both have connections with Adenus and the Gauntlet." She squeezed her friend's hand. "I'm certain they could speak with him about it. Probably find out exactly what this asshole is planning."

Kasha wiped at her eyes with the back of her hand, smearing what remained of her makeup further. "I hadn't thought of that. But would Adenus even care about something like this?"

"Are you kidding?" Arialyn gave a soft laugh. "You run one of the most profitable establishments in this area of the city, and you're reopening in a larger space. That means even more income. Of course he'd care."

Kasha nodded and then looked Arialyn dead in the eye. "Wait, where are the boys right now?"

Arialyn winced slightly. "They may have already left for the Lucky Talisman... about an hour ago, after you wouldn't answer us at the door."

Kasha's head snapped up, her eyes wide. "What? Why?"

"Seriously?" Arialyn shifted, "They both read the letter. Did you really think either of them would read that and not go charging over there? They may not know the specifics, but they certainly know that some worg's asshole is trying to take the tavern and claim some kind of rights to you. I'm pretty sure anyone that tries to get in their way is going to meet an early grave."

"Oh Gods," Kasha breathed, her tail twitching anxiously. "This could get really bad."

There was a brief moment of silence as they both absentmindedly looked toward Morrigan, who was now sitting and giggling as Lemmy kept trying to hop away with the lipstick. "Neither of us could have stopped them from leaving. We can only hope that Callus is able to get Egrim to hold off breaking people in half until it will be most effective."

Kasha's shoulders slumped slightly, some of the tension leaving her body. "I just... after all this time I never would have dreamed that prick would find me. I don't want either of them to get hurt or into trouble. With the Lance involved almost anything could happen to them."

There was a sudden crashing sound from downstairs. Simultaneously, Arialyn and Kasha jumped to their feet, Morrigan ran over to stand behind Kasha, and Lemmy squawked, flying to the top of the armoire. Seeing the white raven atop the wardrobe with lipstick and rouge would have been an entertaining sight had they not held the knowledge that no one should be downstairs right now.

"Maybe it's the boys?" Kasha whispered.

Arialyn shook her head. "Back too fast."

Quietly, Kasha moved Morrigan over to her personal washroom. She closed the door with remarkable stealth while holding a finger over her mouth and remembering what Egrim had told her to say to Morrigan if something like this ever happened. "Quiet as a meadow mouse."

Morrigan's face looked panicked. When Egrim had used the phrase with her, violence usually followed. Only Egrim wasn't here and that made her panic even worse. Lemmy flew into the washroom and landed on the edge of the tub, bobbing his head toward the inside. Morrigan climbed in on shaky legs as Kasha closed the door. Lemmy perched on the edge of the tub and tugged a hanging towel off a rack, trying to drape it over Morrigan.

When Kasha turned around, she saw Arialyn already peeking out of the cracked door with her arcabus in hand. There was another crash. Whoever was down there was not making any attempt to conceal themselves. This was clearly meant to be a statement and one that was now given voice.

"Oh, Madame! Our client asked us to have a polite discussion with you. Come on down before more of this tavern ends up in shambles." The voice was scratchy and definitively male with a hint of an Empire accent.

Arialyn's eyes went wide as one of the people downstairs strode out far enough into the main room to be visible through the mezzanine railing from her spot at the door. Her mouth fell open.

"Talons? Fucking Talons?" She whispered up to Kasha.

There was another crash, this time of glass. "A shame you're all alone in here. We saw your men leave. This could get very disturbing if you make us wait any longer. Was that Callus bloody Kordec I saw?"

Another voice called out. This one more aggressive. "Get your filthy cunt down here now!"

Arialyn pulled back the hammer on her arcabus. She looked up to see how Kasha wanted to handle this and immediately knew how this was going to go. Kasha's eyes erupted in a frosted mist and her fists illuminated with the same arcane energy.

Arialyn stepped in front of the fuming frost witch while reaching into a pouch on her belt. She flung the door fully open and hurled a small spherical object over the rails and down to the main room floor. It bounced a few times and the visible Talon barely had time to gawk at the device before it exploded with a mix of sparks and a humid smoky mist, causing the eyes of anyone downstairs that was looking at it to be immediately blinded. Those that had not been temporarily blinded would still have to gaze through the thick fog to search for the source of the apparatus.

Kasha rushed to the railing and Arialyn sprinted halfway down the stairs. The fog was already dissipating, until Kasha's outstretched hands sent motes of hoarfrost into the cloud. The fog seemed to almost solidify, hanging in the air. Inside the cloud, at least a couple of Talons cried out from the freezing burns that clung to their flesh.

Arialyn brought her goggles down over her eyes. She flicked a small switch, causing a yellow flash to move across the lenses. Now she could see that there were three of the Talons inside the cloud and at least another two behind and outside of the fog's radius.

She leveled the arcabus, one by one, at the three in the frozen cloud and rapidly pulled back on the trigger. Six arcane bolts fired out into their assailants. Or were they now victims at this point? Two of the Talons slumped to the floor, dead. The other had been sprinting towards the makeshift box-front door and Arialyn had only managed to clip him in the shoulder.

Bursting forth from the cloud, a human man with a severely scarred face caught sight of Arialyn and rushed up the first few steps before a shard of ice pierced him in the thigh. It gave Arialyn time to turn her arcabus and fire it into the man at nearly point-blank range.

She stole a brief chance to look at Kasha with gratitude and saw her nearly stumble. Arialyn knew from many of their talks, that Kasha was not skilled in using her arcane abilities for combat. What she had done must have sapped a lot of energy from her, still the tiefling madame moved to the stairs to further assist in the defense of the Tits.

Arialyn stepped carefully over the fallen Talon, his blood already pooling on the wooden stairs. Her goggles whirred softly as she adjusted the focusing mechanism, scanning through Kasha's frozen mist for any sign of movement. The remaining two Talons had vanished from her enhanced vision, likely taking cover behind overturned tables or the bar itself.

Behind her, Kasha's labored breathing echoed in the eerie silence. The frost witch gripped the railing halfway down the stairs, her normally vibrant red skin now pale from the exertion of her magic. Her hazel eyes darted frantically around the room, trying to pierce the supernatural fog she and Arialyn had created together. She spared the smallest moment to acknowledge how well they already worked together.

The sharp twang of a crossbow string broke the quiet. Arialyn barely registered the sound before white-hot pain lanced through her left shoulder. She stumbled back a step but kept her footing, years of working with volatile materials having taught her to maintain her balance even when injured. Without hesitation, she squeezed off two shots in the direction the bolt had come from, the arcane ammunition leaving trails of purple light through the mist.

A grunt of pain rewarded her quick response, but she couldn't tell if she'd hit her target or just gotten close enough to startle them. Blood trickled down her arm, the warmth of it a stark contrast to the frozen air around them.

Kasha suddenly launched herself from the stairs with a primal scream. Her body crackled with energy as she descended through the cloud, her horns trailing sparks of lightning. The frosty mist conducted the electricity, transforming the defensive cover into a deadly weapon. Two distinct male screams pierced the air as the lightning found its marks.

Through her goggles, Arialyn could now see the paralyzed forms of both men. One was slumped against the bar, a crossbow fallen from his rigid fingers. The other had been caught trying to reach the front door that had been barricaded temporarily with crates, his body frozen mid-stride by the electrical assault.

Without mercy or hesitation, Arialyn raised her arcabus and fired twice more. The first shot caught the man by the bar in the chest, the arcane bolt burning through his leather armor. The second found the runner's head, ending his flight permanently. The smell of ozone and burnt flesh filled the air as the frost cloud began to dissipate.

"Five." Arialyn muttered, counting the bodies as she made her way over to Kasha. "That's all that I saw." She glanced at Kasha, who had collapsed to her knees, completely drained from the magical exertion. "Kasha!" She ran to her friend's side and let Kasha lean against her.

Kasha nodded weakly, her tail wrapping protectively around herself. "I haven't... haven't used that much... in a long time. Lighting sconces is much different than throwing shards of ice."

Kasha's chest heaved as she leaned heavily against Arialyn, her tail hanging nearly flaccid from her exhaustion. The magical exertion had left her feeling as though she'd run for miles, her muscles trembling with fatigue. She tried to focus on steadying her breathing, counting each inhale and exhale as Mother Maudrid had once taught her.

A sudden grunt of effort shattered the post-battle silence. Both women's heads snapped up to see one of the decorative potted plants tumbling down from the mezzanine. It landed with impressive accuracy atop one of the dead Talons, dirt and pottery shards exploding around his already lifeless head.

Following the trajectory of the impromptu missile, their eyes found Morrigan standing at the railing above, her small hands gripping the wooden barrier as she peered down at her handiwork. Her face bore an expression of fierce determination that looked almost comical on her young features, her tail swishing behind her with satisfaction.

Despite the gravity of the situation, a small laugh bubbled up from Kasha's throat. It was slightly hysterical, born more from relief and exhaustion than genuine humor. Arialyn joined in, her own chuckle tinged with the same edge of post-battle nerves.

"Thank you, sweetness," Kasha called up to Morrigan, her voice still shaky but warm. "Quick thinking." She knew full well the man had been dead long before the pot struck him, but the girl's desire to help, to be part of protecting their home, touched her deeply.

Lemmy appeared beside Morrigan, his white feathers still bearing traces of the makeup session from earlier. He cawed triumphantly, as if claiming partial credit for the plant attack, then began preening his wing with exaggerated nonchalance.

Kasha pushed herself to her feet, using Arialyn to stabilize herself. "Why would the Talons be here?"

"They must have finally found out Callus was still here somehow. He was certain they were smart enough to let it go at this point." Arialyn said while bringing a chair over to Kasha.

"But one of them said they were here for me at the behest of a client. Zunibar must have hired them." Kasha wobbled as she sat down, or more accurately fell into a chair.

"Callus should be back soon. I'm sure he'll have better details than we can get from whatever this worg shit attack was supposed to accomplish. So," Arialyn whispered to Kasha while looking up at Morrigan, "Do you think Egrim is going to be proud that she tried to help or pissed that she didn't stay hidden?"

Kasha managed a weak smile, though her eyes remained serious as they swept across the carnage in her tavern. She glanced meaningfully at Morrigan, "Perhaps we should all agree that certain little ones were safely hidden away the entire time? The Captain is going to have a field day with this one when he gets back."

The makeshift barricade of crates at the front door made a grinding sound as the wood began to grate against the floor. Arialyn whirled around, her arcabus raised and ready. Through the widening gap, Callus's scarred face appeared for a split second before jerking back out of view.

"Dammit!" his voice boomed from outside. "Hells woman! It's just us! Are you trying to deny the world of this gorgeous face?"

Arialyn lowered her weapon with a shaky exhale while Kasha slumped further into her chair. Together, they watched as Callus and Egrim shouldered their way through the gap, pushing the crates aside with ease. Both men froze at the sight before them. Five dead Talons scattered across the floor, frost still clinging to their bodies, and the acrid smell of arcane charred flesh hanging in the room.

Callus growled under his breath; his eye narrowing as he took in the scene. His gaze snapped to Arialyn, zeroing in on the blood staining her shoulder. In three long strides, he crossed the room to her side. "You're hurt."

"It's just a graze, Love" Arialyn insisted, though she didn't resist when he began examining the wound. "The bolt barely caught me." Callus pushed her goggles up and pulled her in close with a kiss.

Meanwhile, Egrim's eyes searched first to find Morrigan. She still stood at edge of the mezzanine railing, eyes wide but mostly calm.

"Are you alright?" He had barely gotten the words out before she was down the stairs and in his arms. He held her close and shut his eyes in gratitude. His eyes then opened on Kasha leaning forward in a chair. Exhaustion painted across her face.

He moved quickly to her side, just beating Callus, and set Morrigan down on the table edge. His face was a storm of concern that he didn't bother to hide from her.

"Kasha?" he asked, kneeling beside her chair. His large hand engulfed hers when she reached for him.

Callus stopped in his movement to his friend and smiled slightly at the bond he was seeing take better form. He moved back to Arialyn and lifted her up onto the bar top to examine her shoulder better.

Kasha smiled weakly. "I'm fine, Egrim. Not injured, just tired," Kasha admitted, her tail uncurling and relaxing slightly from his presence. "I haven't used that much arcana all at once in a very long time, and never for... this." She motioned at the bodies on the floor. She and Callus shared a brief glance at one another, knowing that wasn't entirely true but neither giving that truth voice.

Morrigan leaned over and placed her head on Kasha's shoulder. The sudden acceptance from the young girl almost made her forget how spent she was.

Egrim should have been enraged, and he was. He just wasn't allowing himself to feel it right now. He grabbed a cloth from the bar top and dabbed it across Kasha's brow.

Callus blotted the blood away from Arialyn's shoulder so she would have a clear view of the damage. It indeed was just a deep laceration. She brought her hand over it and focused on mending the wound as the familiar blue pulse came forth from her palm.

Arialyn spoke first. "What are they doing here Callus? Why now?"

Callus looked over at Kasha. She met his eyes with resignation, knowing that he was about to confirm what she feared. "They work for a troll named Zunibar. He claims to have an indentured service contact on Kasha and therefore ownership of the Tits and Tarts. Which would mean nothing here, except that the Lance is backing him on it and they have control of those kinds of contracts in Hus'rokn."

Kasha winced as he confirmed that Zunibar was in fact in Hus'rokn. She felt the overwhelming panic begin to surge up inside her again, but

Egrim laid his hand on her shoulder, and she felt the wave suddenly even out. With a deep breath she forced herself to speak about it again.

"My mother and I were under contract with him in the Helspires. She died and I ran away. I am, technically, in breach of that contract but it should have only been valid in the Helspires."

She saw Callus's shoulders drop for a moment. If she hadn't known him for so long, she didn't think she would have noticed.

Arialyn looked back and forth between the two of them. "You didn't know any of this?" She was taken aback. She had heard so many stories of Callus and Kasha growing up together that she felt she had been there for a few of them. The idea that one of them kept a secret from the other was mindboggling to her.

Kasha spoke up quickly, partially worried about what Callus might say or that he would overthink why she hadn't told him. She managed to sit up a little straighter. "I never told him. I never told anyone but Sylus, and that was only after I had overheard him talking about taking the Traveling Spectacles there when we were younger, but before you earned the right to challenge for the championship there. I pulled him aside and told him I couldn't go. I offered to stay behind until you all were done touring, but he refused and said the Traveling Spectacles didn't need Helspires coin then."

Callus met her gaze. "That's why you didn't come with us when I fought for the Unified Scarred Lands Championship?"

Kasha nodded wordlessly.

"Why didn't you tell me then? I would have refused it. Or found the bastard and killed him." Callus looked down at his hands.

"Well, there's one reason right there. There is no telling how much trouble that would have brought upon you, Sylus, Mother Maudrid and the rest. I didn't want anyone to get harmed or potentially die because of me. But more importantly to me, Callus, you were my best friend. Was I supposed to do something that would have denied you what you wanted most? What kind of friend would I have been?" Her eyes were sad now. Thoughts of how many lives would have been saved if she had told him. Perhaps that would have convinced him to stay. Then Sylus and the others might still be alive.

Callus could see the doubt on her face, and he knew where her mind was going. "Don't do that. It wasn't your fault. It took me years to realize it wasn't mine either, and I won't let you do that to yourself. Maybe I would have refused the fight and stayed. Maybe I would have gone there and killed the troll and caused all sorts of trouble for everyone. Maybe, had I refused, Kathal Mortis would have sent men after Sylus and me to set an example to those that refused his requests. There are too many variables for blame to be assigned to anyone. Whatever the choices and their repercussion, we are all here together now. Let's focus on what needs to be done now. We now clearly know who our enemies are, and we have help in fighting them."

"Help?" Arialyn and Kasha said in unison as they looked at each other, slightly confused at Callus's statement.

Callus and Egrim told them everything they had learned and all that had happened at the Lucky Talisman. They told them of the involvement of the Lance, that Alabaster was actually a tiefling named Alejak from his own past, the Talons being under contract with Zunibar, Alejak vanishing after one of his men told them the full truth of Zunibar's plans and the subsequent skirmish. Finally, and with some reluctance, they told the ladies of Adenus stepping in and coming to their somewhat conditional rescue.

There was a long moment of silence as they processed the amount of information that was handed to them. Kasha groaned. "So, we have at least a month to get this sorted but I now have to include dice and cards in my tavern?"

Callus nodded. "I'm sorry, Kasha. There really wasn't anything else we could have done. It was the only way Adenus could have saved the tavern, short of letting us attempt to kill everyone in that room. And for the stability of The Three, he couldn't allow that. Thanks to him Zunibar and the Lance are forbidden from coming after you." He looked at the death around them and spared a moment of pride at the handiwork of the two most important women in his life. "This attack was probably ordered before Adenus stepped in."

"I need a drink." Kasha said, holding her fingers to her temples.

Arialyn popped up and rolled her now healed shoulder. "I'm on it."

She had just set down ales for all, but Morrigan who was given a chilled sugared tea, when a knock came at the door frame.

Adenus stood in the doorway, his elegant dark elven features a mask of controlled irritation. Three Gauntlet men flanked him, their hands resting casually on their weapons. His calculating eyes swept across the room, taking in the carnage with an appraising assessment.

Morrigan leaped to her feet atop the table, brandishing a butter knife that seemed to materialize from thin air. Her tail whipped back and forth as she assessed what she clearly thought was a threatening stance.

"For fuck's sake," Egrim muttered, plucking the impromptu weapon from her small hand. "Where in the hells do you keep getting these?" He examined the knife with bewilderment, recognizing it as one from their private quarters upstairs.

Morrigan's only response was to cross her arms and pout, though her eyes remained fixed warily on the newcomers.

"I see you're making an even further habit of wanton violence in established businesses." Adenus drawled, stepping carefully over a fallen Talon. His boots made no sound on the wooden floor despite the scattered debris.

Callus leaned back against the bar, a hint of a smirk playing at the corners of his mouth. "As I recall, you've made quite a bit of coin off our 'wanton violence' in the past." He gestured toward Arialyn and Kasha with his ale. "Though I'm afraid we can't take credit for this particular scene. The lovely ladies handled this one flawlessly it seems."

Adenus's eyebrows rose slightly as he regarded the two women. Arialyn stood proudly, her hand relaxing away from her arcabus, while Kasha remained seated but lifted her chin defiantly. Adenus's expression shifted from irritation to something approaching admiration.

"Five Talons," he mused, nudging one of the bodies with his foot. "And here I thought I was doing you a favor by keeping them away." His eyes settled on Kasha. "Though I suppose this does make our new arrangement more... mutually beneficial. A proprietor who can handle herself is always good for business."

"Speaking of business," Kasha said, her voice still tired but carrying an sharp edge, "I don't recall agreeing to your terms yet."

"My dear," Adenus smiled, showing perfect white teeth, "you just demonstrated exactly why I want to work with you. Besides," he spread his hands in an elegant gesture, "would you rather deal with me, or with our mutual troll problem?"

Kasha sighed deeply, her hand tightening around Egrim's. "Thank you, Adenus. Truly. But why exactly did you step in? What do you hope to gain from this arrangement beyond the obvious percentage?"

Adenus's lips curved into a knowing smile as he carefully maneuvered around the carnage to find a clean chair. He sat with characteristic grace, adjusting his deep purple vest. "My dear, I've had a vested interest in your associates for quite some time." His eyes flicked to Callus. "I was there, you know, when this scarred brute first stepped into the minor arenas around here. Barely more than a boy but already showing such... promise."

Callus shifted his stance at the compliment, while Egrim suddenly became very interested in his ale. The dark elf's smile widened. "And now, these two fine gentlemen have been providing me with quite entertaining matches in the Shale Grounds. The betting has been most profitable. Oh dear, did I just let a secret slip?"

Callus shook his head. "They figured it out already."

Adenus seemed genuinely upset. "Hells, I was hoping to get a little payback for the broken furniture by causing some discord with the women folk."

"We, admittedly, could have been a little more subtle." Callus stated while glaring at Egrim.

"The planner over here wanted to talk with you first. My anger got the better of me. I will not apologize but I will concede that you are owed compensation. Let me know what you require." Egrim said flatly.

Adenus leaned back in his chair, clearly enjoying the moment. "I am sure we'll figure something out young man. However, back to my interest in this partnership. I have a growing suspicion and need to take a more active approach in monitoring certain movements of the other individuals involved in this debacle of a scenario. That, my dear Madame Kasha Volstruk, is my main concern. For now, I must leave it at that. In any case, shall we discuss the details of our new arrangement?"

After several minutes Adenus and Kasha agreed to the terms of their new arrangement. While Kasha would have preferred not to have the gambling tables in the Tits, she did appreciate the additional security that Adenus was offering. She was able to get him to agree, however, that none of the Gauntlet would be stationed inside the Tits and Tarts. They would just patrol the area. She feared a continued visual presence might deter some patrons. Adenus acceded to the previously mentioned request with the exception that she must allow him to station someone on his payroll within the building.

Adenus leaned forward in his chair, his elegant fingers steepled before him. "I'm sending Merle to you tomorrow. He's a one-handed dwarf, impossible to miss really. Don't let his missing appendage fool you though - he's as capable as they come." His lips curved into a slight smile.

"He's not Gauntlet, but he's done work for me in the past. Trustworthy, which is becoming a rarer commodity these days."

Kasha nodded. "What exactly does he do?"

"Everything from tending bar to handling difficult situations." Adenus replied. "He has a rather ingenious crossbow of his own design. Five-shot capacity, auto-loading mechanism. Quite impressive, really."

Callus and Egrim exchanged glances, clearly recognizing the implied utility of such a weapon in a tavern setting. Arialyn's eyes lit up at the mention of the mechanical innovation, and Kasha could practically see her nipples harden beneath her overalls, which considering the fabric, was quite impressive. She couldn't help herself, "Need a cold shower?"

Arialyn narrowed her eyes. "Maybe... "

Rising from his chair Adenus straightened his vest. "Now, as for you two," he said, fixing Callus and Egrim with a stern look that didn't quite mask his underlying high spirits. "When the time is right, I'll lift your ban from the Lucky Talisman. I must maintain appearances, you understand. His voice took on a harder edge, "However, if you ever cause that kind of chaos in my establishment again, my fondness for you won't matter."

Both men nodded solemnly, though Callus couldn't quite suppress his smirk. Adenus's gaze then fell on Morrigan, who was still perched on the table, watching him with suspicious eyes. A butter knife had somehow materialized in her hand again, much to Egrim's visible exasperation.

"My, my," Adenus chuckled, his eyes crinkling at the corners. "Quite the threatening presence you have there, Madame Volstruk." He gestured toward Morrigan with an elegant hand. "Perhaps you should consider hiring her as your chief bouncer. She certainly has the proper intimidation technique down." His voice carried a playful lilt that even Morrigan seemed to pick up on, as her stern expression cracked into a small smile.

Kasha laughed, some of the tension finally leaving her shoulders. "I'll keep that in mind. Though I think she might need to work on her weapon selection."

Egrim palmed his face, now worried that Morrigan would begin pocketing something that would actually cause real damage.

"Nonsense," Adenus replied with mock seriousness. "In the right hands, a butter knife can be quite deadly. Though perhaps we should wait until she's tall enough to reach the bar before discussing employment opportunities." He winked at Morrigan, who responded by sticking out her tongue, though her eyes sparkled with thoughts of what to replace her butter knife collection with.

Chapter Twenty-Four

The morning sun had barely crept over the city walls when Kovag and Saffron prepared to leave Bornar's forge. As expected Kovag slept terribly. He was used to his soft bedroll out in the wilderness of Yonara and with the occasional tavern or inn. The stone floor in a smithy was a bit uncomfortable, even for him. They were around the back of the forge where wandering eyes were never seen.

"Sorry, Debt. This is all I have at the moment. I'll get you something at the temple." He held a large potato up. After a brief snort Debt bit into the potato and devoured it in three bites.

The old half-dwarf clasped Kovag's forearm firmly, metal beads in his beard clicking as he pulled him close. "The temple has a small stable around back. Might be you could get the horse brushed out and wiped down. Watch yourself, boy." Bornar muttered. "Keep the little one safe. If you choose to... unburden yourself, come on back. We'll catch up some more. I could use another pair of strong hands on the iron and steel for a bit. It'd be nice to have someone to keep me out of trouble for a bit or at least be laughing in the cell next to me."

Saffron, perhaps sensing the gravity of the farewell, stepped forward and extended her forearm as well. She looked confident in her farewell. The gruff smith's expression softened as he gently clasped her forearm and patted her head awkwardly.

Kovag lifted Saffron against his chest and threw on his cloak, covering her from prying eyes again as they exited and climbed onto Debt. With that they moved out from the covered alcove and into the streets of Ferrum Plains again.

They hadn't made it five streets before Kovag spotted the crimson and gold uniforms again. The Empire soldiers were methodically working their way through the districts, showing something to merchants and asking questions. His jaw clenched as he pulled Debt into a side alley. They couldn't be looking for them specifically, could they? Had enough time passed for them to send hunters out looking for them?

"Twice in less than a day," he whispered, more to himself than to Saffron. "In a city this size?" He felt Saffron's small fingers squeeze his arm twice, their signal. She had spotted them too through the small opening she held at the front of his cloak.

Kovag guided their mount through a maze of back streets and service alleys, taking the longest possible route to the Temple District. Saffron's tail swished anxiously beneath his cloak as they wound their way through the city, but she remained still as instructed. It helped when he placed his hand over the cloak and held her more secure. Kovag was a large enough man that with the size of the cloak and the arcane shimmer he held over them, most would just assume he held his stomach for fear of a night of drinking returning to haunt him.

When they finally reached the Temple District, Kovag immediately recognized the symbol of Thromgrid, two clasped hands forming a heart stamped onto a keg, carved above a modest silver-doored temple. A young woman in flowing robes swept the steps haphazardly, humming a gentle song while sipping from a flagon.

The partaking of drink, joy, love and all the things that brought happiness were tenets of Thromgrid. Had Kovag not already placed his limited faith in Ehrmus the Glorious, he would have placed it with the Goddess of love and drink. Perhaps a change of belief was in order?

"Excuse me," Kovag called softly, keeping Saffron hidden beneath his cloak. "I'm looking for solace among the flowers of the dawn."

The woman paused her sweeping, studying him with kind but wary eyes. She glanced nonchalantly about the street in a manner that told Kovag it was truly anything but nonchalant. "Wait by the garden gate 'round back," she whispered. "I'll fetch her."

As they moved around the temple's stone walls, Kovag felt Saffron press closer against him. Whether from fear or the chill in the breeze, he couldn't tell, but he tightened his arm around her protectively either way. The weight of the Empire's presence in the city pressed down on him like a bear fighting for its next meal. Reflexively, he hoped Oakira might be taking the time to look in on him now. The thought quickly turned to vinegar in his mouth as recent revelations popped back into his mind.

The garden gate creaked softly as Kovag guided their horse through it. A horse walking through a gate would be a strange thing except this gate was easily three times as wide as necessary for just people to pass through. That's when he noticed the wagon tracks and made the correct assumption that the ale wagon made it's delivery through here, hence the larger gate. The temple's garden was a secluded sanctuary, sheltered from the busy streets by high stone walls covered in flowering vines. He kept his eyes moving, scanning for any sign of unwanted attention while they waited and spotted the small stable in the corner. Three stalls was indeed quite small for a stable.

The sound of a door opening drew his attention. The sheer presence of the woman that emerged from the temple's door told him she had to be Matron Vadrida. He found himself stunned briefly. The elderly dwarf woman he'd expected was instead a mature beauty whose silver robes clung to curves that would have made a succubus envious. The fabric was gossamer-thin in the morning light, leaving little hidden.

"My eyes are up here, dear," Vadrida's voice carried both amusement and reproach. "Thromgrid may insist we revel in all of life's pleasures, but staring is still considered rude in polite company."

Kovag felt heat rise in his cheeks and quickly averted his gaze. "My apologies, Matron. Bornar sent me. Said you might be able to help with a... delicate situation."

She laughed, a sound like silver bells. "If you're seeking treatment for 'love sores,' I'm afraid you've come to the wrong priestess." Her expression playful but goading.

Kovag's mouth fell open.

She began to giggle almost like a child. "I am teasing you, young man. How can I be of service?"

He shut his mouth and smirked before looking around the garden and checking for anything of concern.

"I assure you it is safe within these walls. Speak." She exhaled and folded her arms over her chest. Barely.

Slowly, Kovag opened his cloak just enough to reveal Saffron's face.

Vadrida's playful demeanor vanished instantly. Her eyes, which had been twinkling with mirth moments before, hardened into chips of steel. She moved closer, her gaze fixed on Saffron.

"By Thromgrid's loving heart," she breathed, her voice tight. "Where did you find her?"

"The Empire," Kovag answered grimly, closing his cloak again as Saffron pressed herself closer to his chest. "And I have reason to believe they're looking for her. There are soldiers in the city. They may not be looking for her specifically, but they will want her all the same."

"Yes, I know," Vadrida said, her tone sharp as a forge-fresh blade. "They claim to be here to improve diplomatic relations with charitable donations at all of the temples and several businesses. The Jarl is keen on taking their coin. The damn fool. But such things don't require the sorts of questions they have been asking." She glanced at the garden gate, then back to Kovag. "Put your horse away and bring her inside. Quickly. We have much to discuss, and these walls have fewer ears than even Bornar's forge."

Kovag slid off Debt, clutching Saffron against him and guided him into the stall. There was a feed bag, and some feed set aside in the corner. He quickly filled it and strapped it to Debt's muzzle. "I promise I'll brush you out later."

He turned quickly and followed Vadrida inside, Saffron still clinging to his chest like a scared kitten. He could feel her claws digging in and winced a little.

Vadrida led them down a pristine hallway, its white marble walls adorned with intricate carvings depicting scenes of joy and celebration. The sound of flowing water echoed from a fountain across the corridor, its gentle splashing providing a soothing backdrop to their hurried footsteps.

"These chambers," Vadrida explained in her melodious voice as she opened an ornate door, "are reserved for followers requiring special rites or treatments. Only the attending priestess and I are permitted entry." She ushered them inside, closing the door with a soft click that seemed to seal them away from the world outside.

The room itself was a testament to Thromgrid's appreciation for life's pleasures. Rich tapestries in warm colors adorned the walls, and comfortable cushions were arranged around a low table made of polished ash wood. Delicate silver censers hung from the ceiling, releasing thin wisps of sweet-smelling smoke that danced in the morning light streaming through high windows.

Kovag gently set Saffron down, and she immediately darted behind his legs, peering out at the unfamiliar surroundings with wide golden eyes. Her initial wariness, however, quickly gave way to curiosity as she took in the room's many fascinating details.

A collection of crystalline bottles caught her attention first, their contents shifting with rainbow colors as the light struck them. She crept out from behind Kovag, her tail beginning to sway with interest rather than anxiety. Her small fingers reached out to touch one of the bottles, then quickly withdrew as if expecting to be scolded.

When no reprimand came, her confidence grew. She moved from object to object with increasing boldness, running her fingers along the intricate patterns carved into a wooden chest, pressing her nose close to examine the detailed embroidery on a wall hanging, and tilting her head to better sniff the incense smoke curling through the air.

Kovag watched her exploration with a mixture of amusement and concern, noting how she kept checking back to ensure he remained nearby. Each time she looked his way, he gave her a reassuring nod, encouraging her curiosity while remaining alert to any sudden movements that might startle her.

Vadrida observed them both, her earlier playfulness replaced by a calculating expression that reminded Kovag of Bornar's tales of her in the Mongrel War. "She's quite remarkable," she said softly, her eyes following Saffron's careful investigation of a silver bell. "Though I suspect you are already keen on that."

Kovag settled onto one of the cushions, his size making the ornate furniture seem almost comically small. He opened his mouth to explain how he'd found Saffron, but Vadrida held up a delicate hand, silencing him.

"The less I know about where you found her, the better it is for everyone involved," she said, her voice carrying the weight of experience within the network. "What I don't know cannot be pried from me."

She moved to a cabinet adorned with Thromgrid's holy symbol and retrieved a crystal decanter filled with rose-colored wine. The sweet aroma that wafted from it as she poured reminded Kovag of summer berries and honey. Saffron's nose twitched at the scent, and she paused in her exploration of a particularly interesting tapestry to watch the liquid flow into delicate silver cups.

"I haven't seen any vulpine since the war," Vadrida continued, passing Kovag a cup that looked absurdly small in his hand. "But I learned a little about them from an... unconventional priestess of the Bright One." A fond smile played across Vadrida's lips. "She had a way with the beastfolk refugees. Understood them better than most."

She took a slow sip of her wine. "The Order claimed her practices were 'unsavory,' but I saw firsthand the good she did during the war. She had a particular gift for helping the beastfolk children we managed to save." Her eyes drifted to Saffron, who had crept closer to investigate the wine's aroma. "They're naturally gifted healers, you know. Their magic manifests strongest when they form close bonds with others. Eventually that bond," her eyes shifted between the pair as though she saw something in the air, "becomes their pack."

Kovag's mind flashed to the patch of flowers and his mysteriously healed shoulder. He watched as Saffron reached for his cup, her curiosity getting the better of her. He tilted it slightly, allowing her to take a small sip. Her face scrunched up at the sweetness, and she stuck out her tongue, causing Vadrida to laugh softly.

"Mother Maudrid would have liked her," the priestess said, her voice tinged with something that might have been regret. "She always said the vulpine had more life in their little fingers than most people had in their entire bodies."

Kovag leaned forward eagerly at the drop of Maudrid's name. "Yes. That is who I was told to seek you out for. Erland gave me your names.

"Erland?" Matron Vadrida questioned?

"Yes, Erland," he confirmed, watching Vadrida's face carefully. "He helped us get out of the Empire. I've worked with him a few times, getting in and out unseen for other... dealings."

The Matron's silver robes whispered against the cushions as she leaned back, a knowing smile playing across her lips. "The gods work in mysterious ways, dear one. It seems someone above has been guiding your steps quite deliberately." She glanced meaningfully at Saffron, who had discovered a shelf of colorful glass prisms and was watching them cast rainbow patterns on the wall.

Kovag shifted forward, lowering his voice despite their privacy. "He said that you could tell me how to find Maudrid and that she might know where I can find what remains of her people. I need to get her to safety." His fingers tightened around the delicate wine cup. "Bornar said he heard rumors about sightings near Spearfall, in the mountains..."

Vadrida's expression softened with something like pity. "Ah, those old tales. I've heard them too, but that's all they are, stories whispered around campfires to give hope to the hopeless beastfolk right after the war. There haven't been any fresh 'sightings' since a few years after the war ended." She set her cup down with a gentle clink. "And even if they weren't, I'm afraid it's too late for such considerations."

"Too late?" Kovag frowned, glancing at Saffron who had paused in her exploration to look back at him, as if sensing concern. With her eyes on him now he spoke as softly as he could, afraid for her to hear his words. "Perhaps then I could leave her here with you. She could be safe here?"

"No!" Vadrida's sharp response made Saffron jump, her tail bristling. The Matron immediately softened her tone. "No, that would be cruel beyond measure now. She's formed a pack bond with you."

Kovag's heart sank. "Sorry, what?"

"An arcane spiritual connection," Vadrida explained, her voice soft with reassurance. "It's what I mentioned earlier. Its unique to the vulpine, a survival trait that evolved into something deeper, more meaningful. When they form strong emotional attachments, it creates a magical tether between them and those they consider their pack." She gestured to how Saffron kept checking his location, even as she explored. "I can see the arcane thread between you without the need of my goddesses aid. Breaking such a bond... the pain would be extraordinary. For both of you."

Kovag watched as Saffron returned to investigating a particularly interesting tapestry, his chest tight with an emotion he couldn't quite name. He had tried so hard not to let himself grow attached, but it seemed the choice had already been made for both of them.

He checked to make sure Saffron was occupied again. Thankfully her attention was back on the tapestry, though he could see her ears twitching back toward them for quick seconds at a time. "She will not be safe with me. The work I do is very dangerous."

Matron Vadrida's eyes became scrutinizing and then widened with appreciation for his situation. "You made a pact with someone quite powerful, didn't you?"

His eyes fell to the floor, and he felt a low growl come forth unbidden form his throat. "Yes."

The chamber fell into silence, broken only by the soft tinkling of glass as Saffron went back to playing with the prisms. Kovag's mind whirled with the implications of the pact bond and he felt his breath taken with a mixture of fear and the warmth he wished he couldn't feel right now.

The door burst open without warning, causing Saffron to drop the prism she'd been holding. A young halfling woman in initiate's robes stepped inside, her eyes fixed on the floor as she muttered something about fresh linens. She glanced up, finally registering the room's occupants, and immediately dropped her gaze again, her cheeks flushing crimson.

"Initiate Rosebud!" Vadrida's voice cracked like summer lightning. "These chambers are restricted, as you well know."

The halfling's shoulders hunched as if trying to make herself even smaller. "I... I'm so sorry, Matron. I thought... the room was empty, I didn't..." She backed toward the door, nearly tripping over her own feet. "Please forgive me, I'll go right away."

The door clicked shut behind her retreating form, and Vadrida sighed heavily. "My deepest apologies," she said, turning back to Kovag. "The younger initiates sometimes forget their training in their eagerness to serve."

Kovag barely heard her, his eyes fixed on Saffron. The girl had retreated to his side at the interruption, pressing against him as she always did when startled. Her presence felt different now that he understood the nature of their connection. He thought of his own family that he'd left behind. Now dead in the ground. Then of the family he would never be able to have with a woman to love and children to teach and laugh with when he'd made his pact with Oakira. How quickly he'd given up those bonds for false assurances, power and purpose. All for the chance to feel loved by a being that was incapable or unwilling to love him in return.

Vadrida moved her chair closer, her voice dropping to barely a whisper. "Do you care for her?"

The question caught him off guard, though perhaps it shouldn't have. He watched as Saffron cautiously returned to her exploration, picking up the dropped prism and trying to piece it back together like a puzzle. Every protective instinct in his body surged as she handled the delicate object, ready to comfort her if it proved too broken. His answer came without hesitation, just as quiet as Vadrida's question.

"Wholly."

The word felt like both a confession and a promise, and he knew in that moment that whatever path lay ahead, they would walk it together.

Kovag's eyes stayed on Saffron as he spoke to Matron Vadrida. "Tell me everything you can about her people, please." He spoke with a sudden quiet zeal of urgency, as though this was his only chance. It made Vadrida's smile widen.

"Mother Maudrid spoke often of the vulpine," Vadrida said, her eyes distant with memory. "They carry within them a wellspring of arcane power, though it manifests differently in each individual. Some are stronger than others, but all share an innate gift for healing." She gestured to Saffron, who had managed to fit the broken prism mostly together before returning to examining the others. "She said that some of their abilities remain dormant until needed, emerging instinctively at moments of necessity. Only with time and training do they learn to control them at will."

Kovag watched as Saffron arranged the prisms in a pattern, creating dancing rainbows across the wall. "She hasn't spoken since I found her," he said softly. "I assumed it was because of what she endured in the Empire. Trauma, maybe?"

Vadrida shook her head, silver robes whispering with the movement. "It's more fundamental than that. Vulpine children only begin to speak once they recognize having a complete pack bond. Until then, they remain silent, communicating through gesture and touch." Her expression grew thoughtful. "She's formed a strong connection with you, but she likely doesn't yet feel the security of a full pack."

The priestess's face darkened as she continued. "Their gifts are why the Empire coveted them so deeply. Before the war the nobility would use them for their arcane medicae abilities. They were trying to find ways to prolong their lives. But since they only come into these gifts once they have formed bonds with a pack, well, you can imagine how hard it is to form a bond when someone is essentially keeping you as a slave. So, the Empire experimented with trauma bonding."

Her voice dropped lower, heavy with disgust. "Though the nastiest of the whole business came when they'd reached maturity. Well, then they would," she glanced at Saffron to ensure she was still preoccupied, "seek them for more base purposes, and most know the Empire's ways of dealing with those that don't follow orders, even in their own ranks."

Saffron remained absorbed in her rainbow patterns, seemingly oblivious to the heavy conversation behind her. But her tail had stopped its gentle swaying, and her ears were tilted back slightly. Kovag knew she was paying closer attention than she appeared to be.

"Where is Mother Maudrid now?" He sought to quickly change the subject, knowing that Saffron had begun eavesdropping.

Matron Vadrida sipped her cup before refilling each of theirs. "She is in the Wylds next to Hus'rokn. She has a shop there and deals in minor witchcraft. Although I haven't spoken with her in several months now."

She considered her next words carefully. "The girl is bonded to you, but seeking out Mother Maudrid for more knowledge that could aid you with the girl is a wise decision. At the very least, she could give you some guidance on raising the girl and the Empire is not welcome in the Scarred Lands. They did everything they could during the war to keep the Scarred Lands out of it. A land filled nearly exclusively with the races you seek to wipe from existence, fractured as they are, would quickly rally all of their chaotic banners together in an instant if it meant spilling Empire blood."

Her words struck him. *'Raise the girl.'* His mind raced with sudden panic. "I...I can't."

Matron Vadrida reached out and patted his leg with both comfort and playful chiding. "Sure, child. Keep telling yourself that."

She held her cup up to Kovag. "Stay the night, please. You will both be safe here. I can procure some supplies, and you can leave in the morning if it is safe. If not then you can stay here until it is."

Kovag's dreams carried him back through the years, to a time when his pact with Oakira was still fresh and his understanding of the arcane muddled. He felt again the searing pain of a Solar Fae's nearly divine magic burning through his flesh, remembered the taste of copper in his mouth as he'd finally managed to end the creature's existence. The familiar pull of its power being drawn away, not into him, but through him and to Oakira, leaving him feeling hollow and spent.

He'd collapsed in an alley behind Green Bastard's Blades, his blood leaving dark stains on the cobblestones. The moons were wrong, he knew that even then. Oakira wouldn't be able to reach him, to help him. All he felt from her was a thrum in the willow wing blossom, she was concerned and that worried him even more because until this point he'd only ever felt her confidence.

The gruff voice of Bornar cut through his memory-dream, just as it had that night. "By the Forge Father's shining ass, you're making a mess of my alley." The half-dwarf - half-orc's face had appeared above him, beard braids clicking with metal beads as he'd knelt to examine Kovag's wounds. He could feel the arcane vapor fading around Kovag. "Arcane user, eh? Big fucker for a straight magic wielder. Must be terrible shit at actual fighting if something got close enough to do this to you."

His dream shifted to the following weeks. Bornar standing over him in the training yard behind the forge, wooden practice sword in hand, watching as Kovag struggled to his feet for what felt like the hundredth time that morning. "Being big ain't enough, boy. Magic's great until it ain't there anymore. Then what? You gonna ask whatever's trying to kill you to wait while you catch your breath?"

The lessons had been brutal but effective. Bornar had stripped away every crutch Kovag had developed, forced him to learn the basics of swordplay, hand-to-hand combat, and his personal favorite, dirty fighting.

"In a real fight honor gets you killed just as easily as inexperience." In the end Kovag favored using only his fists. Even the biggest swords felt like toys in his large hands. Bornar had offered to make him a custom great-sword, but Kovag had refused the generosity, the man had done enough for him.

Six months of straight training and another year of using the Green Bastard's Baldes as a base of operations. A year and a half of falling and getting back up, of learning to read an opponent's body language, of trying his best to understand that true strength came from more than just size or magical ability. Bornar had shaped him into something more than just Oakira's instrument, though Kovag hadn't fully appreciated that fact until years later.

"Magic's just a tool, boy. Like any tool, it can fail you. But if you know how to fight without it, then it becomes a weapon instead of a crutch. You're still shit at keeping a level head, but that thick skull of yours might be enough to keep you alive. At least until you pick a fight with someone stronger and more seasoned."

A piercing scream jolted Kovag from his slumber. His eyes snapped open to find an Empire soldier standing over him, blade already descending. Pure instinct took over as he launched himself upward, his elbow connecting with devastating force against the man's jaw. The satisfying crack of bone preceded the soldier's flight across the room, his body crumpling against the far wall as he held his face and groaned.

Sheer adrenaline cleared his waking vision to a horrifying clarity. He was standing and about to charge when he took in the full gravity of what his eyes told him.

One of the soldiers held Saffron against him, a boot knife at her throat. Another held a crossbow leveled at his chest from less than fifteen paces, too close for him to dodge or even throw up an arcane shield in time. Then there was the lead man, an officer by Kovag's assessment.

"You couldn't have waited to grab the brat until a blade was in the big fucker's throat?" The officer chided the soldier restraining Saffron.

Kovag shifted his stance, surveying how to get this done without allowing Saffron to come to harm in the process.

"Enough!" The officer barked, as the other man pressed the blade against Saffron's skin. "One more move and we bleed the girl."

Kovag froze, his heart thundering in his ears. There was no way to get this done without losing her. At least not without using the arcane, and Oakira had warned him that it would bring the Seekers right to him.

"We never dreamed of catching this one," the officer said, his cultured Empire accent falling away into the guttural tones that Kovag knew well. "We were here searching for others, well, they were." He motioned to the other soldiers. "Imagine my surprise when we received word that one of the most highly valued pieces of stolen property was here in the very city we stand in." The officer's elven face melted away, dripping fleshy chunks to the floor. Spiked horns burst forth from multiple places on his face and forehead as his skin, his true skin, revealed itself as the deep red only seen in the Forgotten.

"Lord Ulrannoth does not like having his sacrifices stolen. Especially from a Fae touched brat." As the officer finished speaking the Empire men became fully aware of who they had been traveling with.

Kovag heard a scream and then saw the face of the young Initiate Rosebud standing in the open-door frame, her hands over her mouth in terror. Behind her was a grisly scene on the marbled stone floor. Matron Vadrida's lifeless eyes bore into him as though she were still trying to warn him far too late.

The crossbowman began to shake, slowly lowering his weapon. The broken jaw soldier frantically pressed himself further into the wall, as if willing himself to pass through the solid stone. A split second later he simply passed out. The man holding Saffron turned the knife toward the Forgotten, while backing up with her still in his grip.

"You did a number on Tsarra's mansion, burned the whole place to the ground. The Governor of Kath Thalore feared the girl might have died in that fire. He of course, simply thought Tsarra was borrowing her for some...fun. The fool had no idea." His lips curled into a cruel smile. "He would have been pleased to find the Empire's property unharmed. It's a pity he will have to go on believing she perished. Ulrannoth will not be denied."

Tremors racked Saffron's body. Her expressive tail went completely rigid with sheer dread. Kovag felt her fear spike through their bond, and something inside him snapped. Oakira had said to lay low, not use the arcane.

She had also lied to him. *'Damn her.'*

His lip twitched, giving his tusks an even more intimidating aura. The willow wing blossom pulsed once, powerfully. *'Let them come.'*

The crossbowman's hands could hold on no longer. The weapon slipped from his grasp, clattering against the marble floor. The impact triggered the mechanism with a sharp thwack, sending the bolt streaking across the room to punch through the Forgotten's thigh with a wet thunk.

The demon roared in pain and fury, dark ichor mixing with blood spraying from the wound. In that instant of chaos, Saffron's teeth found their mark again, sinking deep into her captor's wrist. The soldier yelped, releasing her and stumbling backward as she dropped to the floor.

The arcane flared to life within Kovag as he willed himself to be in a new place, appearing directly behind the Forgotten in a shimmer of displaced air. His massive hand closed around a fistful of the demon's hair, yanking the creature's head back as he drove an arcane burst into its spine. The impact sent green sparks and shockwaves through the room, cracking the marble beneath their feet.

Saffron scrambled beneath the ornate bed, shaking as she pressed herself against the far wall. Her hands pressed down on her ears and she held her eyes shut so tight her face began to ache.

The Forgotten's clawed hand shot backward, seizing Kovag's forearm in an iron grip. Lightning erupted from the demon's palm, coursing through Kovag's body in an agonizing wave. He growled through clenched teeth, his muscles spasming as the electrical assault threatened to drop him to his knees. His grip on the creature's hair loosened, and he staggered back.

"Attack him, you fools!" the Forgotten snarled at the remaining soldiers, dark blood streaming down his leg. "The wrath of the Empire won't hold a candle flame to the inferno of the Legion's disapproval!"

The soldiers, caught between terror of the demon and fear of disobedience to the man they had previously known as their superior officer only seconds ago, moved forward with panic. But as they advanced, Kovag's Fae-touched eye blazed with to life. The green radiance washed over the four combatants, and immediately their movements became sluggish, as if they were moving through thick honey. Their weapons felt impossibly heavy in their hands, their steps uncertain and clumsy.

The Forgotten growled in frustration, shaking off the arcane malaise that Kovag had washed over them all. With an outstretched hand it conjured forth a terrifying greatsword from the ether, its blade wreathed in hellish flames. He brought it down in a devastating overhead chop that would have cleaved Kovag in half. But Kovag rolled aside at the last second, the burning blade carving a molten furrow in the marble where he'd stood.

Using his momentum, Kovag spun and drove his elbow upward with bone-crushing impact. The force connected with the Forgotten's face in an explosion of dark ichor and splintered bone. The demon's left cheekbone caved inward, and one of his pointed facial horns snapped off into Kovag's elbow.

The Forgotten staggered, momentarily stunned by the devastating blow. Kovag seized the opening, pivoting to face the soldier who had held the knife to Saffron's throat. The man was still moving with cursed slowness, his blade raised but trembling in a wide arc. Kovag's boot caught him squarely in the stomach like a battering ram.

The soldier's spine snapped with an audible crack, his body folding forward at an impossible angle before he crumpled to the floor, twitching once before going still. He whirled and caught the crossbowman mid tackle, using the man's own momentum to hurl him head first into the wall. He would have found the sight of the man's head finding a new home in his own chest cavity quite amusing under different circumstances.

The Forgotten shook his head, his left eye hanging from the socket on his ruined face as he raised the flaming greatsword once more. The flames grew brighter and all in the room, still living, could feel the heat intensify.

Kovag leapt and rolled to the soldier with the broken jaw, still unconscious. In one fluid motion, he grabbed the man by his leather armor and twisted around, positioning the soldier between himself and the advancing demon just as the greatsword came down in a violent arc.

The blade cleaved through the soldier's torso like parchment, separating him cleanly at the waist. Hot blood sprayed across Kovag's face as the man's lower half tumbled away, his legs collapsing in a heap. The Forgotten's eyes widened in surprise at the sudden lack of resistance, his momentum carrying him forward.

Kovag seized the opening, ducking low beneath the demon's guard and driving his shoulder into the creature's midsection. His massive arms wrapped around the demon's legs as he attempted to drive him to the ground, muscles straining with the effort. But the demon's stance remained solid as stone, his clawed feet finding purchase on the blood-slicked marble.

The Forgotten drove a knee into Kovag's face with such impetus that his left tusk exploded in his mouth. He then brought the pommel of the greatsword crashing down between Kovag's shoulder blades. Lightning shot down his spine, every nerve screaming in agony as he was driven to his knees. His vision blurred, stars exploding behind his eyes as pain coursed through him .

Through gritted teeth, Kovag channeled his fury, summoning eerie lunar flames to erupt across the Forgotten's chest, in a rebuke of silver fire that ate through flesh and armor alike. The demon shrieked, staggering backward against the otherworldly flames.

But the creature's rage only intensified. His boot caught Kovag in the chest, launching him across the chamber with several cracked ribs as reward. His body slammed into the stone wall with a near deafening crack, loose mortar raining down as spider web fractures spread through the ancient blocks.

The Forgotten turned toward the bed, his burning chest still wreathed in dying lunar flames. "The girl will come with me," he snarled, limping forward. "My Lord has been far too patient."

Kovag's eye blazed to life again, green radiance flooding his vision as raw power coursed through him. He thrust his hand forward, and a lure of crackling fire erupted from his palm, wrapping around the demon's sword arm like a burning chain. The Forgotten spun involuntarily as the arcane tether yanked him away from the bed, his feet sliding across the slick floor this time.

Using the momentum, Kovag launched himself from the wall, his boots gaining traction on the cracked stone as he propelled himself forward. The Forgotten's eyes widened in the instant before Kovag's fist, wreathed in his radiant green energy, sank into the demon's throat.

The impact was ruinous. Cartilage and bone crumpled beneath the blow, the creature's windpipe collapsing with a flood of dark ichor and blood that fountained from its mouth. He toppled backward like a falling tree as his flaming greatsword clattering away across the marble.

Kovag bit down, his tusks grinding against his teeth. His hand reached for the source of the pain before his eyes found it. A large slice across the left side of his rib cage. He'd been so focused on connecting that final blow he hadn't shifted over far enough to miss the outstretched sword. Luckily, the flames cauterized the wound as it found his flesh.

He turned slowly, his breath coming in ragged gasps as the rage began to ebb. He squatted down by the bed where Saffron had taken shelter from the chaos. She lay curled into a tight ball, her tail wrapped protectively around herself, eyes still squeezed shut against the horrors she'd tried to not witness. The sight of her safe, if terrified, loosened something in his lungs he hadn't realized was tight.

The sharp peal of alarm bells shattered the moment. His head snapped toward the door where Initiate Rosebud stood trembling, urine spreading across the front of her robes and pooling at her feet. Before she could regain herself from the massacre that had played out before her, he was upon her. Kovag's hand shot out and seized her by the throat, dragging her into the blood-spattered room and liftin her off the ground.

"How many?" he growled, his voice rough with fury. "How many did you tell?"

The halfling's eyes were dilated orbs of horror-stricken panic as she stared at his blood-flecked face, at the lunar fire still smoldering on the Forgotten's corpse; at the gruesome remains of the other soldiers. "W-what are you?" she whimpered.

Kovag's lips twisted. "I am wrath." The words came out in a primal snarl as he squeezed, feeling the delicate bones beneath his fingers give way.

He let her body drop and rushed to the bed, reaching underneath to gather Saffron into his arms. He stared down at the Forgotten body. Normally he'd siphon its power to Oakira. However, doing that now would be a definite beacon to their location and, if he was honest, he didn't feel like giving her any more power.

Saffron clung to him instantly, burying her face in his chest. As they passed through the temple's rear hall, his eyes fell on Matron Vadrida's body. Regret stabbed through him, she'd died trying to protect them, and he hadn't even heard the fight.

Outside, Debt was nowhere to be seen. The bells continued their frantic call as shouts echoed from nearby streets. Kovag's gaze locked onto a rooftop a block away, his mind reaching for the arcane power that hummed through his body. The willow wing blossom pulsed once, and reality bent around them.

They materialized on the rooftop in an instant. Kovag immediately dropped to one knee, his hands frantically checking Saffron for injuries. His fingers probed gently at her throat where the knife had been held, finding only the slightest scratch. Relief flooded through him, making his hands shake as he pulled her against him.

Saffron trembled in his arms for several moments, afraid to move. She could feel his muscles tense each time he breathed in and her eyes darted up to his face, widening as she noticed his bloodied lip where his left tusk sat broken. Her gaze then fell to wound on his side, and her expression shifted from terror to concern. Throughout the entire ordeal she has remained terrified but tear-less. Now, however, she now felt moisture collecting in her eyes and falling down her cheeks.

She pressed herself closer to him, feeling his arms close in even more protectively than before. A gentle warmth spread through his body, focusing particularly around his jaw where the tusk had shattered. The pain subsided almost instantly, replaced by a tingling sensation that felt soft and natural.

"Thank you," he whispered, his voice barely audible above the distant sound of the alarm bells.

She pulled back slightly, tilting her head to one side in confusion at his healed over broken tusk and lip. She put her small fingers to his mouth and prodded the healed flesh. She pointed to herself, her expression questioning, as if asking if she had been the one to mend him.

"I think so," His voice soft and watching her face carefully. "Like at the oak tree."

Her small fingers reached for his side. She closed her eyes in concentration, her face scrunching up with effort. Under different circumstances Kovag would have smiled. After a moment, she opened them again, disappointment evident across her face when nothing had happened. She shook her head with determination and tried again, squeezing her eyes shut even tighter, but still nothing.

"It's okay," Kovag assured her, examining the wound himself. The greatsword had sliced cleanly along the edge on one of his ribs and thankfully not the broken ones. "I'll be fine."

He made to rise and found himself dizzy, falling back into a sitting position on the roof top. He surveyed the roof quickly and was thankful to see that it was fully flat and had an outer crown of about three feet that could keep them hidden. "I need a short bit of rest. I am drained. Just an hour or so and we will get moving again to the Wylds. Stay low with me and when I can, we'll head out."

He laid back and closed his eyes, his breathing ragged from exhaustion. Then he bit his lip, stifling a surprised shock of pain that came from his elbow. He shot up into a sitting position. His eyes locked of

Saffron holding the broken piece of the Forgotten's tusk that he had fully let out of his mind.

She held it up triumphantly like a trophy, somehow managing a wide smile even after all that death and chaos. He glared at her for the briefest moment before shaking his head with the faintest smirk and laying back down.

The perpetual darkness of the Umbra Court pressed against Amjani's vision like a physical force. Even with her gifts, the shadows here seemed to have a life of their own, writhing and dancing at the edges of her sight. She pressed her hand against a nearby obsidian wall, its surface cool and somehow both solid and fluid at the same time.

"This is impossible," she muttered, more to herself than to Isque. "The amount of power required to maintain a protected portal spell should be draining Elirel to the point of collapse. Yet here we are, chasing shadows within shadows."

Isque nodded absently, his mind elsewhere. The image of that ring on Lord Thruva's finger kept intruding on his thoughts. Raw void energy wasn't something to be trifled with, even by an Arch Fae. The last time anyone of a matching power had attempted to harness pure void, it had resulted in the Void Scar. He suppressed a shudder, remembering the histories he'd studied of that catastrophe.

"Isque, are you even listening to me?" Amjani's sharp tone cut through his contemplation.

"Of course, my darling," he replied, forcing a playful smile. "You were expressing your professional admiration for Lady Elirel's impressive stamina."

Amjani's hand shot out, grabbing him by the throat. "This isn't a game, Isque. Something isn't right here. The power signatures we're tracking... they're too strong. Either Elirel has found a way to supplement her power beyond what should be possible, or..."

"Or we're being led exactly where they want us to go," Isque finished, gently removing her hand from his neck. Her touch lingered longer than necessary, and she looked away quickly. He smiled at her while filing that little lapse of hers away for later consideration.

A whisper of movement caught their attention, and both Seekers froze. The shadows ahead seemed to coalesce into something almost solid before dispersing again. Amjani moved forward cautiously, her silver lunar weave armor absorbing what little light existed in this realm.

Isque followed, his mind racing between the immediate danger and the larger implications of what he'd seen in the Lunar Court. If Lord Thruva was experimenting with raw void energy, and Elirel was somehow maintaining impossible levels of power... the pieces were there, but he couldn't quite see how they fit together.

"We need to split up," Amjani announced suddenly.

"That seems unwise," Isque replied, genuinely concerned. Not just for her safety, but for how it might impact his own hidden agenda. Duke Dalmoth instructed him to keep the abomination alive.

"We're running out of time," she insisted. "Whatever Elirel is planning, whatever power she's gathered, we can't let her complete it. You take the lower passages, I'll continue along this level."

Isque watched her form shift around in the darkness, the silver of her armor absorbing his vision as she looked for a path forward. He touched the coin in his pocket, wondering if he should contact Duke Dalmoth again. But something held him back, a growing suspicion that they were all pieces in a game far larger and more dangerous than even his master realized.

Isque reached out and caught Amjani's wrist before she could move away. "Tell me you're not concerned about that void ring. Tell me it doesn't make your skin crawl that an Arch Fae is wearing raw void energy like a fashion statement."

Amjani's face contorted with fury as she spun back to face him. "By the eternal moons, Isque! We have a mission to complete, and you're still fixated on-"

Her words cut off as a deep rumbling shook the obsidian walls around them. The previously dormant umbra crystals that lined the corridor began to pulse with sickly dark light. Before either Seeker could react, the crystals exploded outward, revealing two massive crystalline behemoths, their forms writhing with shadow essence.

The creatures towered over them, easily twice their height, with limbs of jagged crystal and cores of pure darkness. They moved with impossible speed for creatures of their size, but the Seekers were faster.

Amjani's twin silver blades appeared in her hands as if they'd always been there, the lunar weave of her armor humming with the arcane. Isque mirrored her movement, his own blades catching what little light existed in the umbra realm.

They moved in perfect synchronization, years of training making them deadly dance partners. Amjani ducked under a crystalline swipe while Isque leaped over her, his blades scoring deep cuts into the behemoth's shadowy core. The creature roared, a sound like breaking glass and rushing wind. There was confusion in the wail of the creature that clearly was not used to being dealt wounds from blades.

The second behemoth charged, but Amjani was ready. She slid between its legs, her blades carving upward through its crystalline form. Isque spun away from his opponent, trading places with her in a fluid motion that brought them back-to-back.

Their blades flashed in the dull light, silver arcs cutting through shadow and crystal. When both behemoths lunged simultaneously, the Seekers split apart, each taking their target in a final, decisive strike.

They met in the middle as their foes collapsed, face to face, chests heaving from the excitement more than exertion. Amjani found herself staring at a bead of sweat trailing down Isque's neck, while he couldn't tear his eyes away from her parted lips.

The tension between them crackled like lightning, more dangerous than any behemoth. Amjani's hand twitched, wanting to reach out, to forsake her oath just once, to touch...

A wave of raw power suddenly washed over them, strong enough to make their teeth ache. The arcane signature was unmistakable; their quarry's pact mortal had just tapped into something significant.

The moment was shattered. Amjani's face hardened back into the mask of a Master Seeker. "We need to move. Now. You trace the mortal thread, and I'll follow the tether."

Isque nodded, pushing down the lingering heat in his blood. "After you, Master Seeker."

Isque closed his eyes, letting his consciousness drift into the arcane web. The residual energy from the pact mortal's surge still rippled through the ethereal threads, making them hum with an intensity he'd never felt from a mere mortal before. The power signature pulsed like a heartbeat, strong but rapidly fading.

"Brightborn Kingdom. Ferrum Plains, I believe." he muttered, opening his eyes. "That's all I can get. The surge was powerful but brief. Foolish, he must have been in trouble." He turned to Amjani, watching as she traced her own thread of investigation.

Her face was stern, the delicate features drawn tight as she followed the separate signature. The lunar weave of her armor seemed to shimmer in response to her mental probing, and Isque found himself captivated by the way the silver light played across her skin. The dark voice whispered to him from the golden coin beneath his armor. *'Patience. She will be yours.'*

"Southern Umbra Court," she announced, her eyes snapping open. "Elirel and the abomination are hiding in the deeper shadows." Her lip curled in disgust at the thought of their quarry seeking refuge in the darkest corner of the Fae realm.

Isque nodded, careful to keep his expression neutral despite the conflict raging in his mind. Duke Dalmoth would want to know they were closing in, but there was no way to contact him without arousing Amjani's suspicion. They were too close now, the space between them charged with more than just the lingering energy of the arcane surge.

"Together then?" he asked, allowing just a hint of suggestion to color his tone.

Amjani shot him a withering look, but there was a slight flush that crept up her neck. "No," she disagreed, her voice clipped.

"No?"

"I spoke plainly enough Isque. You trace the thread in the Brightborn Kingdom. See what you can find, who can be pressed for more. I'll seek Elirel and her brat. When I get close, I will summon you." Her voice brokered no argument.

He inclined his head. "As you command, Master Seeker."

Amjani's eyes fluttered as she created a portal to the Ferrum Plains. Isque stepped through and it quickly shut. She felt a relief in his absence. The temptation was growing stronger. How had he managed to get beneath her skin? Her thoughts then went unbidden to her duty and devotion to Lord Thruva and Isque's incessant worry about the damned void ring. With a groan she turned and began to stalk her own thread.

CHAPTER TWENTY-FIVE

THE PRICE OF CLARITY

They had pushed the horses beyond their limits. Serine had tried to reason with Ethan more than once during their frantic retreat, but this time her patience snapped.

"Ethan, if we don't ease up, none of these animals will survive the journey. We'll end up walking the rest of the way back." She caught herself before adding 'Captain' as per his request. "It's nearly dark."

He swore under his breath and yanked back on the reins. His mount's legs trembled beneath it, sides heaving. Even Ethan's own chest burned from the relentless pace. The familiar cluster of trees where they'd rested on their way to the doomed caravan stood just ahead.

"Damn it all!" His anger crested, threatening to boil over completely. "We rest there for a few hours, then move. Authern doesn't believe in patience. There's no telling how quickly he'll strike." They guided the exhausted horses toward the grove at a careful walk.

Ethan dismounted and ran his hand along his horse's neck. The animal's coat glistened with sweat, each breath a labored effort. "Sorry, friend. I know I pushed you too hard." The horse's weak nicker carried no reproach, only exhaustion.

"Let's get them to the water." Serine said, already guiding her mount and one of the pack animals toward the small spring they'd used on their way out. She scanned the surrounding terrain while she walked. The Resurgence Wilds were living up to their name. New growth sprouted between scattered groves, but the sparse tree clusters made surveillance easy enough. Anyone approaching, at least while the sun still peered over the horizon, would stand out like a grimalkin in the Empire.

Ethan gathered the remaining horses and led them to the pond's edge. Every instinct screamed at him to unload their gear, to give the animals proper relief, but he forced himself to leave everything secured. "We can't get comfortable. A few hours to rest and water, then we move under cover of darkness."

The horses lowered their heads to drink, their relief almost a palpable thing. Serine retrieved what remained of their meager healer's kit. "Let me check those stitches."

He pulled off his shirt without protest, exposing the wound she'd sewn together earlier. Her touch was careful as she examined the area around the injury. She trickled what was left of the ale over the sutures "Still looks clean. No sign of infection yet. How's the numbness?"

"Well, I know that should have burned and it didn't. So, still numb I'd say," he admitted. "But I can still move it freely and it hasn't gotten stiff. That's a win I suppose." He turned to examine the cut on her arm that he'd bandaged as well. "Looks like I did a better job. Yours is already looking better." He said it with all the good humor he could muster under the circumstances.

Serine smirked, then asked the question that had been gnawing at her mind as they rode hard for Hus'rokn. "What do you think Adenus will do when we tell him about what you think Authern's up to?"

Ethan's expression grew thoughtful as he rewrapped her arm. "He'll more than likely verify it himself using his own channels. Then he'll set something in motion, that's for certain. But he'll have to be careful about it because of the Warlord's Compact. He can't be directly responsible for whatever happens. Fuck, that might even be what Authern's trying to goad him into. If Adenus acts first, then he has every right to go scorched earth on the Gauntlet."

"What in the hells happens with an empty seat with The Three?" Serine's brow furrowed with concern.

"That's the real question, isn't it?" Ethan shook his head. "I have no idea how that will play out. The power vacuum could cause as much chaos as Authern's attempted takeover." He glanced at the horses, gauging their recovery. "But that's a problem for after we get back to Hus'rokn. Right now, we just need to focus on getting this information to Adenus before Authern makes his move."

Again, they set no fire. Not much of a reason to with the brief rest Ethan had decided they'd take here. Serine sat about five feet from him, her back against a fallen log with a book in hand. He pulled out Arialyn's puzzle and began working at it.

"What are you reading this time?" He asked as another click sounded from the puzzle box. He glanced down to note the change in the contraption and the new possibilities that opened to him.

Serine's cheeks flushed slightly. "Phalanx Tactics, by Frenz Lorzna."

Ethan looked up from the box with a raised eyebrow. "Bullshit."

She seemed startled by his blunt challenge. "It is!"

He shook his head with a smirk, the first hint of anything other than anger and worry since they'd been betrayed. Another click sounded from the box. It had been months with so little progress on this damn thing and now it was responding to his touch while he wasn't even fully focused on it.

"So, if I scoot over and look I'm not going to see one of those smutty novels the other women in the guard are passing around?" He watched her with a playful expression.

Her blush was unmistakable this time as she scowled and pulled her knees up closer to her chest. "Captain..." The tone she used was pleading with him to drop the subject.

"I like when you aren't so rigid about things, Serine. I find it—" Another click came from the box and he felt it unlatch in his hand, just waiting for him to release his grip so it could fully open.

He remembered Arialyn's words. *"By the time you manage to get this open you may not need what's inside anymore, but just in case, I'd open it privately. Or at least where no one else can see what's inside."*

Thankfully Serine's embarrassment got the better of her and she had turned away slightly. She heard him cut off whatever he was going to say but wanted to shrink inside herself so badly that she chose to pretend she hadn't really heard him at all and hoped he would change the subject.

Ethan peered at Serine with a side eye, making sure she wasn't watching. He felt like a kid opening one of the secret gifts on the sacred nights in the month of Snows Hunger. He brought his knees up and rested his elbows on them as he slowly opened his hands. His eyes were squinting, not fully trusting that Arialyn wasn't trying to get back at him for giving Callus an outlet for fighting and trying to persuade him to join in his 'dubious illegal activities' as she said.

The puzzle box held one final click as it fully opened, and Ethan found himself wincing with expectation. No shock or flash came. He slowly opened his eyes and found a small, folded piece of parchment inside. Grabbing it, he set the box to the side and unfolded the parchment. His eyes went as wide as gold coins as he read the paper not twice, or thrice, but five times, each time slower than the last.

'She is in love with you, jackass.'

He blinked rapidly and read it several more times. He kept his head down, but his eyes slowly moved to Serine. The fire made the blush in her cheeks contrast heavily with her blonde hair. She tucked a stray strand of it behind her ear as she continued reading. Surely Arialyn was wrong. Serine had never treated him as anything other than her commanding officer that she held in high regard with trust and respect. Right?

He didn't need this right now. He should be focused on how to get to Adenus without anyone in the Lance seeing him and then how he could help him subvert Authern and make sure that the Lance didn't gain any more power in Hus'rokn.

Instead, his mind raced and tried to reevaluate every interaction he and Serine had shared. There were too many to count. They had come up in the City Guard together, all the way from being footman. They had been close then too, hanging out in the taverns together, getting into trouble in their off time. He had even asked her to be the best-woman at his wedding. She had refused. Claimed she would be too embarrassed to be up on the dais like that. Then he had been promoted to Guard Captain by the Shield Rosamunda several years back and she had started to speak to him as someone of lower rank was required to, only she had continued to do it even when they were off.

She had stopped meeting him at the taverns as often and the trouble they used to find themselves in ceased all together. She had helped keep him together for the first few weeks when his wife left. Even let him stay at her place when he had let the ale drown out his anger and frustration a little too deeply. It had been awkward in the mornings when he sobered up. Hells, she had just now stopped calling him captain. And he had to practically plead with her for it to stop.

Ethan's mind wandered back through the years, memories shifting like pieces of a puzzle suddenly clicking into place. The parchment trembled slightly in his hands as he recalled those late nights at the

Copper Kettle when they were both still footmen. Everyone else would stumble home or pass out at their tables, but Serine would always stay. Even when her eyelids drooped and she'd stifle yawn after yawn, she'd order another ale and keep him company until he was ready to leave.

He'd always assumed she was just being a good friend, looking out for a fellow guard who had a tendency to drink too much and start fights with the wrong people. But now... now he remembered the way she'd watch him when she thought he wasn't looking. The way her laugh would come just a beat too late when he'd flirt with the serving girls, as if she had to force herself to find it amusing.

His wedding day. Gods, his wedding day. He'd been so focused on his bride, on the ceremony, on trying not to trip over his own feet that he'd barely noticed anyone else. But he remembered Serine's tears during the vows. At the time, he'd thought she was just emotional, she'd always been sentimental about important moments. But those tears hadn't looked like joy. They'd looked like... loss.

When he'd been promoted to Captain, though, those tears had been different entirely. Pride, genuine happiness, the kind of tears you shed when someone you care about achieves something they've worked for. She'd hugged him then, briefly, professionally, but he remembered how tightly she'd held on for just a moment longer than necessary.

The shift trading. How had he never noticed the pattern? Before he'd promoted her to sergeant, Serine had somehow always managed to work the same shifts he did. He'd chalked it up to coincidence, or maybe their similar work ethic. But now he realized she must have been constantly negotiating with other guards, probably owing favors left and right just to be partnered with him on patrol.

And those recent mornings at her house... Ethan's chest tightened as he remembered waking up on her couch, head pounding from too much ale and too much anger at his wife's departure. Serine would already be up, making breakfast, acting like it was perfectly normal to have her commanding officer passed out in her living room. But there had been something in her eyes those mornings, something careful and hopeful and terrified all at once.

The way she'd linger by the door when he'd gather himself to leave, like she wanted to say something but couldn't find the words. The way she'd always have his favorite tea ready, or how she'd hand him back his dress jacket folded to perfect regulation. Small gestures he'd attributed to her natural thoughtfulness, but now...

It was all so clear to him now. As he looked at her, really looked at her, he wondered how he'd been so blind for so long. Arialyn was right. He was a jackass.

He began to search his own feelings. The realization hit him in the chest like a warhammer. He'd only ever looked at Serine as a friend and a colleague. Not because he didn't want to see her in any other light, but because he had never given himself permission to do otherwise.

Early days in the guard were full. Hus'rokn had no military, but the City Guard was expected to train in fending off sieges should the time ever come that some upstart warlord or the Empire decided they wanted the city's advantageous position. There was no time for any sense of romantic feelings between cadets. The rules were too strict and the training too harsh. You trained sunup to sundown four of the five days of the week. Hadra to Bridra you felt like your body was going to give up on you and on Progendra you either slept or got drunk. Then he had gotten married, foolishly in retrospect, after his first promotion to Corporal.

All this time and Serine never even tried to let him know. Never tried to tell him. Never tried to steal a kiss. Never even admitted anything to him while he had been three sheets to the wind. What man would not yearn for the touch of a woman that he had called friend for so long? A woman that knew his secrets and still had his back. Serine had never been anything other than loyal to him. He wasn't sure if he was in love with her but he knew he cared for her deeply. If nothing else, he knew now that he wanted his friend back fully. With the uncertainty that was about to unfold when they returned to Hus'rokn, he didn't need a sergeant, he needed his best friend. If more came from that, then so be it.

Ethan rose to his feet, Arialyn's note clutched in his trembling hand as he took the first few steps toward Serine. That was strange, his hands never trembled. She noticed his approach and quickly closed her book, offering him a nervous smile that made his hand now shake so badly he had to clench them, worried she would notice.

The whistle of the crossbow bolt came a heartbeat before it struck. Serine's eyes went wide as the bolt buried itself in her collarbone, mere inches from her neck. Blood immediately began to soak through her undertunic.

In that same moment, a burst of white energy slammed into Ethan's chest. The arcane force lifted him off his feet and threw him backward. He crashed into a tree trunk with enough force to drive the air from his lungs. Through blurred vision, he saw two men in Lance colors charging from the shadows, their weapons already drawn.

"Serine!" He scrambled for his sword, which lay next to the open puzzle box where he'd been resting. A second bolt thudded into the wood near his hand as he grabbed the weapon's hilt.

Twenty yards back, partially concealed by the trees, stood a robed woman with her hands wreathed in prismatic energy. Beside her, a crossbowman was already loading another bolt. The woman's hands moved in an intricate pattern as she prepared another spell.

Serine snapped the bolt in her shoulder in half with a grunt of pain and snatched up her hand axe. Blood ran down her arm, but her grip remained firm. "Two on the approach," she called out, her voice tight but steady. She aimed and let loose her hand axe at the man closest to her. It easily cleaved in the leather armor the man wore, and he went sprawling to the ground after another step. "Ranged fighters on the hill."

The second man darted toward Ethan, a wicked-looking curved blade in each hand. Another burst of arcane energy crackled past Ethan's head as he brought his sword up to meet the dual-wielder's attack. The air hummed with the residual magic, making the hair on his arms stand on end.

"Take the mage!" He shouted as he blocked another strike from the curved blades. "I've got the other two!"

Serine wanted to argue, just an hour ago he had admitted that his shoulder was still numb. What if it failed him. But if she didn't deal with the spellcaster quickly, they'd be picked apart at range. She feinted toward the crossbowman, ripped her hand axe from the dead man and then broke into a sprint toward the mage causing the crossbowman to release the bolt early. It flew wide from Serine's position and ricocheted off a nearby stone.

An arcane shot whistled past her ear as she charged. Behind her, she heard the clash of steel and Ethan's grunt of exertion as he engaged the swordsmen. The mage's hands began to glow again, and Serine knew she had to reach her before she could complete another spell.

Ethan's blade crashed down toward the dual-wielding attacker, who barely managed to catch the strike between his crossed blades. The impact sent tremors up Ethan's arms, but the numbness in his shoulder masked most of the pain. In one fluid motion, he dropped and rolled to the side, scooping up a handful of loose dirt. The assassin followed, curved blades whistling through the air where Ethan had been a second before.

With the grace of a well-rehearsed move, he hated to admit he had used several times before, Ethan flung the dirt directly into his opponent's eyes. The man cursed and stumbled backward, furiously trying to clear his vision. Ethan didn't waste the opportunity. He lunged forward; his blade extended in a piercing thrust. Steel met flesh, and the Lance's head tumbled from his shoulders before his body had even begun to fall.

Across the clearing, Serine dove into a roll as flames erupted from the mage's fingertips. The heat was intense enough that she could smell her own singed hair. As she came up from the roll, white-hot pain lanced through her left side. She hadn't noticed the crossbowman's bolt until it was already buried itself in her flesh.

Her eyes darted to the crossbowman, who was already lowering his weapon to reload. The practiced movements of his hands told her he'd have another shot ready in seconds. But before he could slot the fresh bolt into place, a curved blade, one of the pair from the man Ethan had just killed, spun through the air like a deadly disk.

The improvised throwing weapon bisected a portion of the crossbowman's face. Blood sprayed in an arc as the blade carved away his nose and a good portion of his cheeks and lip. His scream was wet and gurgling as he dropped his crossbow and clutched at his ruined face.

"Serine! Take her down!" Ethan's voice carried across the clearing, thick with concern and urgency.

She gritted her teeth against the pain in her side, tightening her grip on her hand axe. The mage was already weaving another spell, her hands trailing streams of arcane light. Serine knew she had to end this quickly, one solid hit from the mage could finish either of them off.

She could hear Ethan's footsteps thundering up behind her. The crossbowman's agonized wails echoed through the trees, but Serine forced herself to tune them out. She focused entirely on the mage, whose eyes had begun to glow with gathering power. Blood ran freely down Serine's side, but she pushed through the pain, closing the distance to her target with pure grit.

She reached the mage and brought her hand axe down, but the woman had not been preparing another offensive spell, instead she had thrown up a shield. Serine's axe vibrated so hard that she nearly dropped it.

Ethan ran over the body of the screaming crossbowman, stabbing down into his chest as he passed over him without even giving him the courtesy of meeting his eyes with the deathblow. The wailing stopped immediately. He quickly assessed the arcane shield and noticed that the mage had not accounted for her elevated terrain. The base of the shield was not supported by or buried into the ground. That meant there was nothing holding it up except the woman herself. He lowered his shoulder and barreled into the mage causing the pair of them to tumble over each other and down the hill, hitting stones and broken limbs from the trees above.

Serine watched as the mage tumbled down the hill with Ethan, her arcane shield flickering and failing as her concentration broke. Without hesitation, Serine leapt down after them. The mage had landed face down, stunned by the impacts. Before she could recover, Serine planted her boot firmly on the woman's back and brought her hand axe down with all her remaining strength. The blade cleaved through the base of her skull with a sickening wet crack. The mage's hand twitched for the briefest of seconds until Serine twisted the axe a touch.

Ethan scrambled to his feet, sword at the ready. Their eyes met briefly before both instinctively moved together, pressing their backs against each other. They began to rotate slowly, scanning the darkness between the trees for any sign of additional attackers.

"That motherfucker." Ethan spat, his voice thick with rage. "If Adenus doesn't gut him, I swear by the Hanged One I'll do it myself." His eyes swept the tree line methodically. "My side's clear. Serine?"

The silence that followed made his blood run cold. He felt her weight shift against him, then begin to slide downward. "Serine?" he asked again, his voice cracking as he felt her slump against his waist.

Ethan spun around just in time to catch her before she fully collapsed. Her face had gone pale, and her breathing came in short, ragged gasps. That's when he saw it, the crossbow bolt protruding from her left side, positioned perfectly to pierce her heart. Blood had soaked out and over her armor and undertunic, spreading in an ever-widening circle.

"No, no, no," he whispered, carefully lowering her to the ground. His hands shook as he assessed the wound. The bolt's position made his stomach turn. It was exactly where a trained killer would aim to strike a dwarf's heart. "Serine! Serine, look at me."

Her eyes found his, still alert despite the pain and blood loss. She tried to speak but only managed a wet cough. A thin line of blood appeared at the corner of her mouth.

"Don't try to talk, stay still." He felt panic beginning to set in. They had nothing that could help this and if they had they would have already used it for their previous wounds.

He frantically ran to each other the Lance bodies, praying to the Bright One that he would find a healing potion of some kind. There was nothing except bandages and antiseptic solutions. Those were absolutely useless to him.

He rushed back to Serine. Her eyes were closed. With another prayer, he lifted her head into his lap and smacked at her cheek. "Serine, please."

Her eyes opened lazily. She smiled through the blood on her lips. She tried to lift her hand but the best she managed to do was make a grasping motion. Ethan reached down and grabbed her hand, bringing it to his face. "Please, Serine. I just realized it all. I'm so sorry. I need the chance to-"

The corners of her lips edged to the biggest smile she could manage. They moved and he had to lower his ear directly to her mouth to hear her words. "Permission... to kiss... my cap... captain."

Ethan's eyes flooded with tears that fell to Serine's cheeks. He placed his lips to hers. They were already growing cold. He pulled away just far enough to see a faint smile cross her lips before they parted again. He leaned further back, and his heart fell as the life left her eyes. He leaned down and kissed her again and then again. "I'm sorry. I'm sorry."

He held her lifeless form in his lap, his body rocking back and forth as though he was trying to comfort her to sleep, but it was the waves of grief crashing over him that forced his movement. His mind tortured him with memories of every shared laugh, every knowing glance, every moment he should have seen differently that had been right in front of him this entire time. The weight of lost possibilities crushed down on his chest until he could no longer breathe.

His eyes drifted to one of the Lance assassins, the one whose head he'd taken. Something dark and primal stirred inside him, replacing the crushing weight with a burning rage that demanded release. He gently laid Serine's body on the soft earth, his movements careful and reverent. Then he stood, his fingers tightening around the hilt of his sword until his knuckles went white.

The first body he reached was the headless swordsman. Ethan's blade came down again and again, each strike accompanied by a guttural roar that seemed to come from somewhere deeper than his throat. Blood sprayed across his face and chest as he reduced the corpse to ribbons. He moved to the crossbowman next, his sword rising and falling in a brutal rhythm that sent gore splattering across the trees and stones.

The mage's body received the worst of his fury. He hacked at her remains until his arms burned and his sword arm shook, screaming wordlessly into the night. When he finally stopped, he stood panting in the middle of the carnage he'd created, covered head to toe in blood and viscera. His eyes held a wild, dangerous light that hadn't been there before or perhaps it was a lack of light.

He returned to Serine's body with his pack. He sat down next to her and began to clean his sword and one of her hand axes with lifeless mechanical precision. He kept to the strict regulation code of the

City Guard on properly cleaning and maintaining one's duty weapon, something he had not fully bothered to do in a long time.

Ethan set about his tasks like a cleric performing a sacred ritual. He retrieved Serine's bedroll from their gear, his hands steady despite the tremor that had moved from them to now take up residence in his chest. The soft fabric unfurled beside the pond's edge, creating a makeshift altar in the moonlight.

He returned to where she lay and knelt beside her still form. He thought to talk to her but he couldn't find the right words to convey any of his feelings.

With infinite gentleness, he lifted her into his arms. She felt impossibly light, as if death had stolen more than just her breath. He carried her to the water's edge and began the painstaking process of removing her armor. Each buckle, each strap was handled with the reverence due a fallen comrade. The banded leather came away piece by piece, revealing the extent of her wounds beneath.

The crossbow bolt still protruded from her side. Ethan's jaw clenched as he carefully worked it free, his movements slow and deliberate. The wound had stopped flowing but once the bolt was removed it began to move again in a slow trickle. He peeled the fabric of her stained undertunic away. He looked briefly at her and felt a sense of shame wash over him for seeing her naked without her ever have granted him permission. A permission that he now knew she had probably yearned to give him. The shame faded as he saw the small tattoo of what appeared to be a fluffy rabbit on her hip.

"You were keeping all kinds of secret from me it seems." His chuckle came of hoarse and painful.

He waded into the pond until the water reached his waist, then lowered her body into the cool embrace of the spring. The blood began to wash away in pink ribbons that dispersed into the darkness. With cupped hands, he poured water over her face, cleaning away the dried blood from her lips. Her blonde hair fanned out around her head like a golden halo.

"You were always so proud of your appearance," he murmured, running his fingers through her hair to work out the tangles. "Said a proper guard should look the part, even off duty." His voice cracked on the last words.

He cleaned each wound methodically, washing away the evidence of her final battle. The freckles across her nose stood out starkly against her pale skin. He couldn't stop staring at them now as he began to count each one.

His eyes burned with the strain of tears that wouldn't come. His body had exhausted its capacity for weeping, leaving only a hollow ache where his heart should be. He lifted her from the water and carried her back to the bedroll, laying her down with the same care he might show a sleeping child.

Her armor lay scattered where he'd placed it. Ethan gathered each piece and began the ritual of cleaning and polishing. The banded leather responded to his ministrations, the surface gleaming despite the battle damage. He worked with the same attention to detail Serine had always demanded of herself, buffing away every scuff and stain until the armor met regulation standards even though this wasn't her guard armor.

When he finished, he dressed her like each movement was a prayer of forgiveness. Each strap was secured exactly as she would have done it. Finally, he placed her polished hand axe on her chest and folded her arms over it, her fingers curled around the familiar grip.

He wrapped her in the bedroll and lifted her onto his horse, securing her body to ensure she wouldn't slip. He didn't even spare a glance at the other horses and their saddlebags that bulged with void ore and contraband worth more gold than most people would see in a lifetime. He mounted up behind Serine's body. She was the only cargo he cared about now.

His eyes fixed on the horizon where Hus'rokn waited. The playful light in them gone and hardened into something colder, more focused - absent. Gone was the practical guard captain who'd navigated the complex politics of the city with careful politicking. In his place sat a man who'd crossed a line from which there was no return, whose only remaining purpose was vengeance.

Without a word, he spurred his horse forward, leaving behind a fortune in void ore and the butchered remains of their enemies. The night swallowed him as he rode, a harbinger of the violence to come.

CHAPTER TWENTY-SIX

BURNT BRIDGES

The stench of stagnant water and mildew pulled Alejak back to consciousness. His head throbbed with each heartbeat, and the metallic taste of blood lingered in his mouth. Through blurry vision, he made out the vague shapes of rusted maintenance equipment and moldering wooden shelving units.

He tried to sit up but immediately regretted the decision as waves of nausea crashed over him. Instead, he remained prone on what felt like damp stone, trying to piece together his last memories. The meeting at the Lucky Talisman played back in fragments – Zunibar's smug face, Authern's betrayal, and then... Callus. His stomach churned at the thought. Had the hobgoblin really been there? Or was that just his addled mind conjuring up his worst nightmare in his final moments?

"If this is the afterlife," he muttered through swollen lips, "I demand a bloody refund."

A skittering sound echoed through the chamber, and Alejak's hand instinctively went to where his dagger should have been. Of course, it wasn't there. But then a familiar scent cut through the sewage, the unmistakable odor of decay and that strange tangy scent of insects that always accompanied Beetle. Alejak still hadn't figured out how insects could have a scent.

Alejak's tensed muscles relaxed slightly. "Beetle?" His voice came out as more of a croak than he'd intended.

"Master lives." The words seemed to emanate from the shadows themselves, followed by that unsettling throaty giggle that only Beetle could produce.

"Living? Is that what you call this? Where exactly am I... living? How long have I been out?" Alejak asked, finally managing to prop himself up against a wall. His vision was starting to clear, revealing what appeared to be a sealed-off section of the city's sewer system.

"Safe place. Maintenance storage. Master sleeps a few days. No one come here anymore." Beetle's voice moved around the room as he spoke. "I brought small one too."

Alejak's memory sparked. "Marvin? He's alive?"

"Mostly." Another giggle. "Skull not as broken as looked. He sleep now."

Relief washed over Alejak, though he'd never admit it aloud. Marvin was a useful tool, and tools were hard to replace. That's what he told himself, anyway. He touched his face gingerly, wincing at the swollen flesh around his eye.

"Did I..." he paused, still uncertain about his recollection, "Was that Callus I spoke to. Truly?"

"Yes." Beetle's voice hardened. "The Reaver lives. Saw him. Smelled him. Death himself follows him now."

Alejak let his head fall back against the wall with a soft thud. "Death... himself?" Was his head still so rattled that he was missing something that should have been obvious or was Beetle talking in riddles again?

"My Lord Odhrum's uncle watches over the hob. I see noose as much as smell it." Beetle chittered with disdain.

"Wonderful. Because this situation wasn't complicated enough already." He closed his eyes and took a deep breath, immediately retching as the sewer's stench filled his lungs. "Well, my peculiar friend, it seems we need to devise a new strategy. Preferably one that doesn't end with my head on a pike."

Beetle's unsettling laughter echoed through the maintenance chamber, bouncing off the damp walls in a way that made Alejak's headache intensify. "More complicated, master. Much more."

"How could it possibly be more complicated?" Alejak groaned, massaging his temples.

"The large one. Human with Reaver. He saw me." Beetle's voice dropped to a whisper. "Even when I wasn't to be seen."

Alejak's unswollen eye widened. "What do you mean 'wasn't to be seen'?"

"Hidden. Cloaked in death's shroud. But his eyes..." Beetle's chittering grew more intense. "His eyes followed me. Something wrong about him. Something not... right. Can't smell him properly. Like trying to smell smoke underwater."

"Marvelous," Alejak threw his hands up in exasperation. "So now we have a potentially otherworldly giant working with my least favorite hobgoblin. Please tell me you have some good news? Anything at all?"

The silence that followed made his stomach sink.

"Lance Authern claimed your estate," Beetle finally said, his voice dancing with dark amusement. "False documents. Large debt. Very creative. Gave it all to the troll-man. They throwing party soon."

"And my men? My so very few men..." Alejak asked, already knowing the answer from Beetle's growing grin in the shadows.

"Dead. All dead. Troll-man very thorough. Very cautious." Beetle giggled again. "You've been asleep days. Little Marvin barely breathing."

Alejak slumped further against the wall. "I asked for good news, you morbid bastard."

"Oh yes!" Beetle's excitement sent a wave of insects scurrying across the floor. "Little Marvin saw something. Before man broke him. Something about Lance and troll-man. Something useful."

"And?" Alejak prompted, trying not to show his desperation.

"Can't tell you." Beetle's giggles grew louder. "Marvin must wake first. If he wakes. When he wakes? Who knows?"

"Beetle," Alejak said through clenched teeth, "I swear by the Voidspawn you worship, if you don't stop laughing at my misfortune, I will find a way to make you regret it."

"Master threatens," Beetle cooed, "but master needs Beetle now more than ever." His voice grew serious for a moment. "Things are changing. Old powers stirring. Can smell it in the air. Like lightning before a storm. The Voidtongue, Fogjeck, whispers on behalf of my Lord's bitch mother. Dark days. Darker than dark."

"Wonderful," Alejak muttered. "Cryptic warnings. That's exactly what I needed to complete this perfectly horrible situation."

Beetle's snicker echoed through the dank chamber. "Said it plain as plain, Master. In my own way."

Alejak fought back the urge to snap at his peculiar servant. Instead, he forced his voice to remain level. "Help me over to Marvin. I need to see how badly they damaged my property."

Beetle's spindly frame supported Alejak's weight as they shuffled across the wet stone floor. Every step sent jolts of pain through Alejak's battered head and back, but he kept his face carefully neutral. They reached Marvin's unmoving form, and Alejak lowered himself to sit beside the unconscious halfling.

His eyes swept over Marvin's injuries, noting the ugly purple bruising that spread across the left side of his face. The halfling's breathing was shallow but steady. Alejak reached out and gently tapped Marvin's less-damaged cheek. "Wake up, you observant little fool. I need whatever information is rattling around in that cracked skull of yours."

Marvin remained motionless.

Alejak tapped again, harder this time. "Come now, Marvin. You've had worse." That was a lie, but Alejak needed him conscious.

Before Alejak could try a third time, Beetle's nearly skeletal hand appeared holding a water skin. Without warning, he upended it over Marvin's face. The halfling sputtered awake with a gasp, his eyes wide with shock from the icy water.

"Beggar's purse, Beetle!" Alejak glared at the walking infestation, water droplets spattering his own face from the splash.

Beetle's shoulders rose and fell in an exaggerated shrug, his perpetual grin somehow growing wider. "Little Marvin awake now. Efficient, yes?"

Marvin coughed and tried to sit up, only to fall back with a groan. His eyes darted around the chamber in confusion before settling on Alejak's battered face. "Mr. Jakel?" His voice was barely more than a whisper.

"If that name still means anything, yes," Alejak said, carefully keeping the relief out of his voice at seeing Marvin conscious. "And you can thank our friend Beetle here for your refreshing awakening." Alejak stifled a sharp breath at seeing the fixed pupil of Marvin's right eye. He knew from experience that was a very bad sign.

Alejak leaned forward, ignoring the protest of his bruised ribs. "Marvin, focus quickly. What did you see in that room that we can use? Beetle tells me you saw something we might be able to use against Authern and that fucking troll?"

Marvin's body suddenly went rigid, his eyes rolling back slightly before fluttering rapidly. The seizure lasted only seconds, but it felt like an eternity to Alejak's annoyance. When Marvin's body relaxed, he shook his head so slowly it might as well have been in a vat of oil.

"A Talon," Marvin croaked, his voice still rough. "When Frezup said they weren't there for Callus... but would hunt him if Zunibar ordered it..." He paused, collecting his scattered thoughts. "There was a tan-furred grimalkin among the Talons. The way he looked at Frezup and Dunmaris... like they'd lost their minds even suggesting going after Callus."

Beetle's unsettling giggle echoed through the chamber. "Oh yes, yes. The pretty kitty. Herodin is his name." The emaciated orc's dark eyes gleamed in the shadows. "Did some crawling while master and little welp sleep. Third in command, he is. After Dunmaris in the pecking order."

"And how, pray tell, does this help me?" Alejak pinched the bridge of his nose, feeling the pain shoot through his face and being immediately reminded that his nose was shattered. "A Grimalkin who's smart enough to be scared of Callus is hardly useful information."

Marvin's body seized again, shorter this time but no less concerning. When he recovered, a slight smile played across his split lips. "Mr. Jakel... if we can remove Frezup and Dunmaris..." He coughed, wincing at the pain. "Herodin might be... amenable to discussion. The way he looked at them... there's no loyalty there. Just contempt."

Alejak sat back, his mind already working through the possibilities. A crack in the Talons' leadership could be exactly what he needed. "Beetle, how sure are you about this Herodin's position?"

"Sure as death," Beetle chittered, his insects skittering across the floor in excited patterns. "Watched him give orders. Others defer. But always looks over shoulder. Always watching for Frezup's shadow."

A slow smile spread across Alejak's face, pulling at his split lip. "Well then, my minions, perhaps we're not completely without options after all."

Alejak stared into the darkness of their makeshift sanctuary, his mind churning through possibilities like a mill grinding wheat into dust. Each potential plan seemed to crumble before it could fully form in his mind's eye. The damp air somehow made his swollen face throb with every heartbeat.

"Beetle," he said finally, his voice carrying a resignation that made the necromantic orc cock his head in curiosity. "How good are your insects at tracking someone without being noticed?"

Beetle's perpetual grin widened. "Master asks obvious questions. Like asking if water is wet. You know answer already."

"I need you to find Callus." The words tasted like bile in Alejak's mouth.

Marvin made a strangled sound from his position on the floor. "Mr. Jakel, I thought you hated-"

"Oh, I do Marvin, and he probably hates me more." Alejak closed his eyes and leaned his head back against the slimy wall. "We're going to have to convince the most violence-prone hobgoblin in the Scarred Lands that helping me is in his best interest."

Beetle's chittering laughter echoed off the walls. "Master has head injury worse than thought. Reaver will kill you. Slowly. Painfully. Will enjoy it."

"Possibly. Highly probable even," Alejak admitted, opening his good eye to glare at his servant. "But Authern and Zunibar made the critical mistake of going after someone the Reaver cares for. Ergo, he hates them more than he hates me right now. And unlike me, he has the strength to actually do something about it."

"And the Talons?" Marvin wheezed. "Even if Callus doesn't kill you immediately, they'll-"

"They'll what?" Alejak interrupted, a hint of his old arrogance creeping into his voice. "Kill me? Take everything I own? They've already done that, thanks to our troll friend and that limp prick Authern." He gestured at their surroundings. "We're in a sealed-off sewer maintenance room. I think we've hit rock bottom, gentlemen."

Beetle stiffened a little. "Rock bottom? This place cozy." He meant it and both Alejak and Marvin could see it.

Marvin opened his mouth to speak but Beetle swiftly placed his hand over the halfling's open mouth. "Adults talking."

Marvin held back vomit. "The smell is in my mouth."

Beetle's unsettling eyes set on Alejak. "Master plans to offer information about pretty kitty to angry hobgoblin? Trade Herodin's weakness for protection?"

"No," Alejak said, his split lip curling into a painful smile. "I'm going to offer Callus something far more valuable than information about a scared grimalkin." He paused, savoring the moment despite their dire circumstances. "I'm going to offer him the chance to destroy both the Lance and Zunibar in one fell swoop. And all it will cost him is keeping me alive long enough to help him do it. But first, I need you to set up a private meeting with this Herodin fellow so I can get the measure of him."

Lance Authern watched as Berekr waddled into the meeting room at Butcher's Row, the rotund dwarf's bald head gleaming in the lamplight. The smell of fresh blood and raw meat wafted up from the slaughterhouse below, a scent that always put Authern in a contemplative mood.

Authern cleared his throat. "Tell me the good news, lieutenant." His massive frame cast a long shadow across the polished table.

Berekr's face split into a lecherous grin as he settled into his customary seat at Authern's right hand. "Those fuckers should be pushing up daisies in the next few days, if they aren't already fertilizing the Resurgence Wilds." He adjusted his fine silk vest. The vest was far more visible than it would have been on most dwarves due to Berekr's complete lack of facial hair, an oddity among dwarves that had always amused Authern.

"You trust the turncoat?" Authern glared.

"Fuck no. That's why I sent four of our own to smash them on the way back in case Hamlin cocks it all up." Berker snorted with minor offense. "Trust him? I don't trust anyone."

Authern nodded slowly, his fingers drumming against the table's surface. "Good. As long as it'll look like bandits if anyone decides to go snooping around. Adenus, for one, is a little fond of the dear Captain, and he is already pushing himself further into my business."

"Of course," Berekr spat on the floor, a habit Authern had long since given up trying to break. "What kind of amateur shit do you take me for? Whatever odds and ends that twat of a captain brings in, the wagon's loaded with enough valuable cargo to make it look like a proper robbery gone wrong. No one's going to question two more bodies in the Resurgence Wilds. Plus, as long as they don't manage to get killed in the scuffle, Hamlin and Surkras will be eyewitnesses to the alleged incident. Then you have Hamlin in your pocket when we need them for the... business venture."

"Excellent." Authern leaned back in his chair, the wood creaking under his weight. "We need to be careful with our next moves, especially with Zunibar watching our every step."

Berekr's face twisted into a sneer. "That fucking troll thinks he's so clever with his fancy clothes and proper manners. Makes me sick."

"That 'fucking troll' has enough coin and influence to make or break our plans.," Authern warned, his voice dropping to a dangerous whisper. "He's craftier than he lets on. You weren't there to see how quickly he adapted when the situation with Callus came to light."

"Bah," Berekr waved his hand dismissively. "He's just another rich bastard trying to play at being a proper criminal. Give me a week with him, and I'll show you how soft he really is."

Authern's massive hand shot out, grabbing Berekr's vest and pulling him close. "That's exactly the kind of thinking that you'll stow away in that alcohol pickled brain of yours until the time is right. We need his investment to take the city. Without him, we are vastly outnumbered." He released his grip, smoothing Berekr's vest with an apologetic pat. "We play this smart, or we don't play at all. Once the time is right, I'll need you to start greasing the palms of any Gauntlet and Shield members that are unhappy and looking for a change. Hire a few mercs and then we can take them all out in a single night. If we need to, we can reach out the Kol'Theron and see which companies bite."

Berekr straightened his clothes, his face flushed with embarrassment and anger. "Fine. But when this is all over and he is no longer useful, I want first crack at that fat ass troll bastard. Been too long since I've had a proper bit of fun."

The silence hung heavy in the room, broken only by the rhythmic tapping of Authern's fingers against the polished wood. His jaw clenched tighter with each passing minute that Zunibar failed to appear. The half-giant's patience, already worn thin from the debacle at the Lucky Talisman, threatened to snap entirely.

Berekr seemed content to occupy himself by picking at his teeth with a small knife, occasionally flicking whatever he found onto the floor. The sound of each tiny splat made Authern's eye twitch.

A knock finally came at the door, and Authern's voice boomed through the room. "Enter!"

The door swung open to reveal Petra, one of his more effective enforcers. Her copper-red hair was pulled back in a severe braid that emphasized her sharp cheekbones and full lips. The kind of beauty that made marks lower their guard right before she separated them from their coin and their lives. Her leather armor bore the Lance's insignia proudly over her left breast.

"Lance Authern, Mr. Tolgar has arrived." She barely kept the amusement from her voice. It seemed most of the Lance was only passively tolerating this new partnership.

"Send him in." Authern straightened in his chair.

Zunibar entered with Frezup and Dunmaris flanking him like guard dogs. The troll's nose wrinkled in obvious distaste, and his usually impeccable clothing showed signs of hasty adjustments, likely from trying to avoid the more pungent areas of the slaughterhouse below.

"Before we begin," Zunibar remained standing despite the chair that was pulled out for him, "I must question the wisdom of conducting business in such a... fragrant location."

Authern's lips curled into what might have been a smile on a less threatening face. "Butcher's Row has been the heart of the Lance's operations since Hus'rokn was little more than a collection of hovels and battle-weary Warlord camps. The original Lance, may the Progenitor watch over his soul, saw the potential in this ranch. Turned it into something more useful, a place where both legitimate business and our more discrete operations could coexist."

He gestured broadly at the walls around them. "What was once the edge of civilization is now the center of our southern holdings. The city grew around us, Mr. Tolgar, but we were here first. The blood in these stones runs deeper than any other foundation in Hus'rokn."

Zunibar's expression remained carefully neutral as he finally took his seat. "How charmingly rustic. Though I do wonder if perhaps it might be time for the Lance to consider more... contemporary accommodations."

Authern nearly bit the inside of his cheek to stop from lashing out at the troll. "Once we accomplish our end goal, we will have the run of the entire city and we'll be based wherever the hells I want us to be. For now, I stand on tradition that will not be questioned in our own building. Try and remember you are our guest, Zunibar."

The foregoing of the formality of calling him Mr. Tolgar was not lost on Zunibar. The troll considered that if they had not been in Butcher's Row he would have had the Talons strike then and there.

Zunibar adjusted his perfectly tailored jacket and leaned forward, making the chair creak ominously. "My dear Lance Authern, since we are speaking plainly, let me be blunt as well. I am your guest because you require my considerable resources to achieve your admittedly ambitious goals. Perhaps we should both remember our respective positions in this arrangement?"

Authern's fingers dug into the armrests of his chair, the wood splintering beneath his grip. His face remained carefully neutral even as his mind conjured vivid images of Zunibar's severed head being put to particularly degrading uses.

"Of course," Zunibar continued, his tone softening slightly, "I meant no offense regarding your traditional accommodations. Sometimes my desire for refinement gets the better of me."

Authern nodded slowly, imagining how satisfying it would be to hear the troll's neck snap. "None taken," he growled through clenched teeth.

"However," Zunibar's expression hardened, "after the debacle at the Lucky Talisman, we need to address a rather pressing concern." He gestured to Frezup and Dunmaris. "My men have shared some rather disturbing stories about their former bosses' demise at the hands of Callus Kordec."

Berekr snorted. "The crippled hobgoblin? He's-"

"A force to be reckoned with," Zunibar cut him off sharply. "I witnessed his prowess firsthand in the Helspires arena. But more concerning is his companion, this Egrim." Zunibar snarled softly. "No one threatens me and lives to boast about it."

Authern leaned back, studying the troll's face. "You want them dead before we proceed?"

"Precisely." Zunibar's lips curled into a cruel smile. "When I eventually collect Ms. Volstruk, and make no mistake, I will collect her, Callus will interfere. Better to remove both problems now, while they're still reeling from our previous encounter."

Frezup cleared his throat. "With respect, Mr. Tolgar, Callus isn't someone you simply remove. He's earned every one of his titles - The Ruiner, The Towering Tactician. He-"

"Is still just flesh and blood," Zunibar interrupted. "And flesh and blood can be ended with sufficient application of force." He turned back to Authern. "Consider this my first official request as your financial partner."

Authern's hand sliced through the air, cutting off Zunibar's declarations. "The Warlords Compact explicitly forbids any action against Egrim at present." The Lance leader's tone brokered no questioning. "More importantly, he's employed at the establishment Adenus now has a stake in."

Zunibar's face darkened, but Authern continued before the troll could interject. "If we move against him now, Adenus will know exactly who orchestrated it. He'll see it as a direct violation of his current holding over the Tits and Tarts. That dark elf bastard will bring Rosamunda into it, and then we'll have both the Shield and the Gauntlet bearing down on us with numbers we can't match."

"You seem remarkably concerned with the opinions of your fellow criminals," Zunibar sneered, adjusting his expensive cuffs.

Berekr spat on the floor again. "It's not opinion, you overdressed fuck. It's survival."

Authern shot his lieutenant a warning glare before turning back to Zunibar. "When the restriction lifts, or we reach an arrangement with Adenus at our next meeting, I'll personally oversee the execution of Ms. Volstruk's dog." His lips curled into a cruel smile. "Callus, however, is a different matter. If handled properly, we can remove him without directly opposing Adenus. Though I'll want compensation for the men we'll inevitably lose in the process."

Zunibar stroked his chin thoughtfully. "Perhaps instead of compensation, I could offer a more practical solution." He gestured to Frezup and Dunmaris. "My Talons could accompany your men. Share the risk, as it were."

Dunmaris's eyes lit up with eager bloodlust. "Retribution is the sweetest of wines."

Frezup shifted uncomfortably, his fingers drumming against his leather armor. He didn't relish the idea of coming face to face with Callus in close quarters combat. After a moment's consideration, his face hardened with resolve. "Herodin and a few others can go with your men, Lance Authern. He knew Callus for a little while and has a better understanding of the way he thinks than anyone else here."

"And they're more expendable than you, eh Frezup?" Berekr cackled, flicking something from his teeth in the half-elf's direction.

Frezup's hand twitched toward his blade, but Zunibar's sharp look kept it at his side. "A prudent leader knows when to delegate," he said through clenched teeth.

Authern nodded slowly, considering the arrangement. In truth, having the Talons take the brunt of Callus's inevitable fury suited him perfectly. Let them thin themselves out while he focused on the larger game at play.

Zunibar rose from his chair with deliberate slowness, the wood groaning beneath his considerable weight like a dying dragon's final breath. The tortured sound sent an involuntary shiver down Berekr's spine, his shoulders hunching as if someone had walked over his grave.

Frezup's lips curled into an amused smirk at the dwarf's obvious discomfort. "Bit jumpy there, aren't we?"

Berekr's face flushed red as he whipped around to glare at the half-elf. "Fuck off, you knife-eared bastard. At least I don't piss myself every time someone mentions Callus Kordec."

The two men locked eyes across the table, their mutual disdain crackling in the air like lightning before a storm. Frezup's hand drifted toward his blade while Berekr's fingers tightened around the small knife he'd been using to pick his teeth.

"Gentlemen," Zunibar's falsely cultured voice cut through their brewing confrontation like a blade through silk. "Perhaps we could save the posturing for our enemies?"

Both men reluctantly backed down, though neither took their eyes off the other. Zunibar smoothed his jacket, adjusting his rings with the careful attention to resume his pristine appearance.

"Lance Authern," he continued, his tone shifting to something approaching warmth, "I trust you haven't forgotten about our dinner engagement late tomorrow evening? A proper celebration of our new partnership, as it were."

Authern stood. "I hadn't forgotten."

"Excellent." Zunibar's smile revealed teeth that seemed just a touch too sharp. "I'll be providing everything we need for the evening. All you need to do is bring your most trusted men. Consider it my way of showing proper respect for our new arrangement and the future ruler of Hus'rokn."

The half-giant nodded slowly, though something in Zunibar's tone made his jaw clench. There was an underlying current to the troll's words, a suggestion that this dinner was more than mere celebration. "I'll be bringing the best of my men?"

"Oh, as many as you feel comfortable with. I have far more coin than I need so I can accommodate whoever attends quite easily," Zunibar replied with casual indifference. "I want your people to feel welcome in our new partnership. After all, trust is built through shared experiences, wouldn't you agree?"

"Of course." Authern's fingers drummed against the table's surface, each tap echoing through the room like thunder.

Zunibar gathered his expensive, and unnecessary, walking stick and adjusted his cuffs one final time. "Until tomorrow evening then." He gestured to Frezup and Dunmaris, who fell into step behind him like well-trained hounds.

The moment the door closed behind them, Berekr hawked up a particularly impressive glob of phlegm and spat it directly at the wooden barrier. The wet splat echoed through the suddenly quiet room.

Authern's knuckles cracked like breaking bones as he slowly clenched and unclenched his fists. *Just a little longer,* he reminded himself, watching the spittle slowly slide down the door. *Keep the troll alive just long enough to secure his resources, then we can settle accounts properly.* The thought of Zunibar's eventual demise was the only thing keeping his temper in check.

Chapter Twenty-Seven

GRAND REOPENING

Kordra 7:35pm

Everything since the midday opening had been perfect. At least in the eyes of Egrim, Lorisse and the rest of Kasha's girls. The tarts were baked to perfection, there had been no issues with the ale taps or Arialyn's arcane cooler and Egrim had not had to do anything more than give a few growls to individuals that were starting to get a little rowdier than was acceptable.

A surprise shipment of Bloody Ale Company Red, delivered by Callus and Arialyn, had even arrived early in the morning, courtesy of Carl Just Carl as a congratulations on the new place. Callus and Arialyn stayed from the midmorning opening until the start of evening. They had orders to polish off and deliver tomorrow. Mufz and the other girls were fully booked for the day and had just enough time between appointments to bathe and get the sheets and scents changed out in their rooms.

Stig, the human male that had taken the last room barely had time to breathe between his appointments. In truth, he was fairly average in the department of attractiveness and anatomy, but his charismatic personality and the little-known fact that there were only three men in the sex trade within Hus'rokn made him very popular. Lorisse had remarked to Kasha that she feared his cock would fall off before the night was over.

Even the two gambling tables that Kasha had been mostly forced to agree to were performing well. Adenus had graciously supplied the Tits with two of his masked dealers until such a time that Kasha could hire her own. She had ordered the table be placed in the corner under the stairs so it was out of sight from most of the main room but still visible from behind the bar, her place at the top of the mezzanine and Egrim's 'perch' near the front door.

Despite the smoothness of the day, which had moved on into late evening now, Kasha was obsessing over the most miniscule details that either no one else would notice or that were, in fact, perfect in the first place. Thrice now, Egrim and Lorisse had checked in with her and tried to calm her down. Each time they were met with rushed appreciation but a quick dismissal of their worries.

Currently, Kasha stood at mezzanine directly outside her Madame's suite, throwing flicks of arcane energy to recharge all the sconces. The bard, a lyre player, she had hastily hired after the advertised act bailed at the last minute was strumming away beautifully. Her name was Jezel. She carried the sort of attractive flair that grew even more when you heard her sing. Mufz had said her eyes commanded the room more than her voice, though either would get her into her room free of charge.

Lorisse was behind the bar directing the other girls and passing orders to the kitchen for more tarts. Merle, the new Gauntlet appointed bartender, was quickly filling pints and mugs with their various ales and the exotic mixtures he came up with on the fly. The dexterity of the dark dwarf was astounding. What made it even more impressive was the fact that not only was he one handed, but he only had the middle finger and thumb on his remaining right hand. A wood working accident he claimed. Egrim, on the other hand, believed they were too perfectly cut and that he probably ended up owing one of the gambling dens, possibly even Adenus, more than he could afford. Each of the other girls ran about bringing orders to their tables and practicing the perfect ratio of flirtatious banter and upselling.

Kasha had given all the new girls three separate mini classes on the artform last week. A two to one ratio was something she picked up over the years of running the old location. Playful seductive comment, recommend ale and tart pairings or an ale that would go with a particular mood followed by more flirty words or a suggestive gesture. They had of course installed the old location's warning signage over the new bar, *'Eyes encouraged, hands discouraged...with violence.'*

Another sign had been added right as you began to climb the stairs. *'Nonconsenting ungentlemanly touch will result in loss of coin, cunt and cock.'* Two of the girls and Stig were busy with clients. Mufz leaned against her door smoking a bit of rolled pipe weed. Her skin was a soft yet bright green with eyes to match. Her facial features were more rounded and softer in comparison to that of most Goblin people. It gave her a much more innocent look. How she managed to keep her hair in two perfectly round puffed-up buns was a mystery. She wore a mixture of silks and soft leather strapping, leaving just enough to the imagination. Of course, as her name seemed to not so subtly imply, her muff was poking out of the sides of her lingerie.

She walked over and stood next to Kasha, regarding the crowd as well. "Pretty successful opening, Madame."

"Indeed. And your openings?" She retorted with a smile and snort.

Mufz huffed in amusement. "I might need to talk to the fire marshal about a daily occupancy limit."

The laughter that followed allowed Kasha a moment to forget the stress of the day, a very brief moment. A loud scream came from Rekai's room. She was a gorgeous darker skinned human woman with vitiligo so beautiful you would have thought it purposefully painted by a goddess. She burst forth from the room stark nude and holding her busted and bleeding lip. Egrim had already scaled the stairs by the time she yelled for him.

The man responsible for the egregious offense had barely made it to the door when Egrim had a hand wrapped around his neck. He recognized him immediately. The bastard had come in with a handful of other men. They seemed to be the usual working-class men, orcs and dwarves that they would expect to make up most of their clientele. This particular human had an air about him that Egrim didn't like, but other than that he had seemed appropriate at the time. Still, he was going to boot the bastard right back out the door then and there, but Kasha had asked him to try and be sparing with removing people until they gave him just cause. Still, he felt guilt wash over him now that one of the girls had been harmed under his watch. That was going to sit heavy on his conscience for a while.

"She said I could-" The man belched loudly, "Ugh – said I could be rough you fucking brute!"

Egrim spun around and held the naked and pathetic excuse for a man against a support pillar attached to the rail overlooking the main room. He had the man's left arm pinned behind his back and was pushing him face first against the pillar. Jezel had stopped playing and all eyes on the lower floor were now staring wide and waiting to see what the enraged bouncer would do to this man.

Egrim looked over his shoulder at Rekai. She had tears in her eyes and was standing there covering herself in a hastily thrown on robe. "HE'S LYING!"

It was then that Egrim made note of the blood dripping from Rekai's nose. He snarled and pulled the man's head back and then abruptly slammed it forward into the pillar with a muted thud.

"Fuck!" The man tried to wiggle free. Egrim slammed him into the pillar again and leaned into his ear, "Can you fly?" He then swiftly moved with him to the right of the pillar and looked over to Kasha. The look of shock left her face, and she took on a sterner appearance, giving him a nod. She knew now that she should have allowed Egrim to operate his portion of the Tits at his own discretion. It may have been too late to stop this from happening tonight, but it was the perfect opportunity to show everyone what would happen if they tried anything like this in her establishment again.

Kasha stood straight and clasped her hands below her breasts as her voice rang out. "The Witch's Tits and Tarts Tavern will not tolerate this kind of behavior. Those who violate our rules will be dealt with in the harshest manner. Egrim, if you please."

With that, Egrim spared a momentary glance down at the floor to make sure it was clear and shoved the man over the railing. A brief scream was quickly drowned out by a loud crashing thud as the wretch's body hit the floor. A few patrons gasped and one man cursed as he slid several silver coins to the barkeep, Merle. He had clearly hastily bet that Egrim would simply throw the man out. Merle hadn't had long to get to know Egrim, but he had seen the giant of a man in the Shale Grounds and knew throwing the man out would not be satisfying enough.

Egrim finished peering down at the unmoving body and made purposeful eye contact with every one of the men that had come in with the fool, warning them that they would meet the same outcome if they dared to do anything other than continue being polite patrons.

Spurred on with a look of pleading from Kasha, Jezel kicked back into a rousing song to bring merriment back to the Tits.

Egrim spit down on the unconscious man's body and turned to Rekai, pulling a cloth from his pocket. He gently dabbed at the blood coming from her nose and then picked her up. She wrapped her arms around him, and he carried her back to her room, setting her on the bed. "I'll get you some ice and help you get cleaned up once I throw him in the street."

Egrim turned to leave but was halted by Rekai's hand on his arm. "Thank you, Egrim."

He looked away shamefully. "Don't thank me. I shouldn't have let him in."

As he left the room Kasha stopped him briefly. "This was my fault. From now on, do as you see fit. I trust your instincts. If you get a feeling about someone, do what you need to."

He nodded as she passed him and went to see Rekai. Once downstairs he walked over to the man and kicked him with his boot. The man gave a low groan that seemed to be more from air escaping collapsed lungs than a man feeling pain. "Keep breathing, asshole. I won't even bother to try and hide your body. You're not worth it."

He lifted the ragdoll of a body up over his shoulder and carried him to the back door. Merle cackled as he past. "Right good work there."

Merle followed Egrim quickly and opened the back door for him after unbarring it. Egrim didn't bother making it all the way into the alley. He simply shrugged the man off his shoulder and let him collide with the few raised stone stairs and roll a bit. Merle reached up and gave him a pat on the back as he rolled and popped his neck, heading back toward the bar.

Egrim took a quick moment to change his shirt. Kasha might have a stoke if he walked back in with a blood-stained shirt. When he made his way back to the bar, he saw Merle lining up a few pints. By the looks of it four in total. Merle pushed them toward him. "From Rekai and the others."

He smirked and downed one. "Rekai needs some ice and probably a hot bath."

Merle spoke up, "Kasha is already seeing to Rekai, mate. The last two men that were lined up for her are already so infatuated with her they both sent up a bottle of mead to her and asked if they could get a raincheck...no, railcheck? Ramcheck?"

"Merle."

"Sorry, just trying to be clever, but you get my meaning."

Egrim nodded and looked over the crowd. The Tits was returning to normal, but not before Jezel lifted her own glass from the small, raised stage and called the Tits and Tarts to attention. "To the hero of the night."

Several cheers arose and glasses raised. Egrim forced the smallest of smiles and inclined his head. He didn't feel he deserved to be lauded, especially as a hero. Jezel picked her lyre back up and began to play again.

Egrim had almost allowed himself to think the night was going to get back on track when an orcish man from the table of men that entered with the now near corpse in the alley, rose and began walking toward him. The orc wore simple, but tailored, brown linen clothes and looked up at the mezzanine to Rekai's door before stopping at the bar.

Egrim studied the man's approach out of the corner of his eye. He moved differently than he had when he entered earlier. Before he moved like any other laborer man. Now, he moved like someone that knew how to handle themselves, or at the very least thought he did.

Merle's eyes went from Egrim to the approaching orc, seeking to ease the already mounting tension. "What can I get you, sir?"

The orc pushed in between two people on stools at the bar and leaned against it. He scratched his chin and pursed his lips. "I suppose I'll have whatever this big bastard of a man is having."

Egrim turned his eyes on the orc and gave him a hard stare. "Dark ale."

This was code to Merle. Kasha was far too posh to ever call any of her ales by the style they were, like many of the bars and taverns in Hus'rokn. Every ale, beer and mix had its own recipe and original name. Dark ale truly meant for Merle to give the fool a special concoction that was sure to make the orc shit himself in the next half hour.

Unaware of the implications the orc nodded. "Darker the better."

Merle smirked and disappeared behind the bar to begin the hasty creation.

"I'm Parzin. Please allow me to apologize. While that fool came in with us, I assure you he is not with us. If you catch my meaning."

Egrim kept his gaze squarely on the orc. "I would advise that you keep that stance on the relationship then."

Merle rose and set the 'dark ale' down and slid it over to Parzin. He lifted it and took a sip. His face immediately shifted as he tasted what was assuredly the most gods awful thing he had ever had in his mouth. "By the…"

Egrim smirked at Parzin.

Parzin's eyebrow rose. "I suppose that is fair play." He pushed the cup back toward Merle, who quickly poured it out.

"I heard a fellow remarking to another about Bloody Ale Company Red. I'd like one of those, barkeep." Parzin smacked his mouth repeatedly as he tried to remove the taste.

Merle placed his hand on the bar top. "Gold club members only." There was no gold club.

It was at this point that Parzin dropped the nice guy routine. "Alright you two limp cocks, you've had your fun. I have a message to deliver to your whore queen."

Merle shut his eyes for a moment, expecting to hear something breaking. Wood or bone most likely. No noise came. No cacophony of violence and screams of pain. He opened one eye slowly first. To his surprise, Egrim just stood there, as if frozen. He just continued to stare at Parzin. This went on for a time that had begun to get uncomfortable.

"Are you going to fetch your Madame or keep eye fucking my face?" Parzin snapped.

Merle couldn't believe the size of the balls on this orc.

Egrim's eyes narrowed a little. "In a second. First, I want to study all the features of your face."

"What the hells for?"

"I would want someone to remember what I looked like from before my accident."

Parzin tilted his head in confusion. Egrim waited just long enough to see the look of understanding ignite in his eyes. In one swift and coordinated motion Egrim pushed the dark ale cup back toward Parzin and slammed his face directly into it, shattering the hardened clay into pieces. Some of which were now embedded in his face.

Swiftly, Merle unlatched a hidden compartment next to one of Arialyn's arcane cooling boxes. Inside he had his one-handed auto loading crossbow, primed and ready. He brought it out and had it leveled at the table Parzin had come from before those that remained there could fully stand.

Thankfully Jezel read from Egrim's face that now was the time to keep playing, and so she did so with even more gusto to keep the attention of as many of the patrons as she could.

Parzin stood woozy and leaning on the bar top, blood dripping from his face.

"You're a Talon aren't you? Knew you couldn't get a foot in this door wearing your damn gear." Egrim grabbed him by the collar and roughly moved him toward the front door. The three remaining men at the table took steps toward Egrim and Parzin but stopped when crossbow bolts flew past each of their faces and thudded into the wall behind them in impossibly quick succession.

This time there was nothing Jezel could do to keep the attention of the patrons. A few even dropped their drinks and ran out the door. The main room was eerily silent, save for the sound of Kasha's heels as she slowly descended the stairs.

"More buffoonery from the same cluster of jackanapes, Egrim? What was it this time?" She stopped at the base of the stairs just shy of Egrim and Parzin.

Egrim's eyes remained on the three other men, but he held firmly to the wobbly and nearly unconscious orc's collar. "The Talons of Misery came to say hello, but so far are only receiving their namesake in return. This one had a message for you." He shook Parzin's collar. The rapid movement seemed to reawaken the orc.

Parzin's vision was blurred but he made out the form of Kasha. "Zunibar says to enjoy your freedom while you can, bitch."

Egrim didn't have time to adjust Parzin's attitude again. Kasha beat him to it and left a burning icy hand mark across the orc's face. Egrim was mildly surprised to feel Parzin go completely limp. He almost lost his grip of the orc.

Kasha looked to the other men. "See that your boss gets my reply."

Egrim dropped Parzin where he stood. "Collect your man and get the fuck out."

The three looked at Merle with sneers before moving any further. Merle shook the crossbow in the direction of Parzin, and the men moved to pick him up from the floor. Egrim gave each of them looks that would turn the bowels of most men to water.

Once they were safely out the door one of the men hollered back inside. "You might be protected by the Gauntlet, but your friends don't share that luxury."

CHAPTER TWENTY-EIGHT

UNWELCOME REUNION

Kordra 7:56pm

"So, I arc the core to this little node here?" Callus asked with slight confusion.

Arialyn giggled. "For the third time, yes."

"But that seems counterintuitive. Shouldn't that make the gear move clockwise?" He scrunched up his nose and squinted hard at the small sewing thread-like cord of arcane energy that tethered from the arc spanner to the core of the contraption. In spite of his uncertainty, he did as she instructed and moved the tool to the node.

"Stop shaking so much," she said, gripping his hand between hers and steadying it for the connection.

With a small spark the thread of arcane energy tethered the two together and then faded from visibility as it should when stable. Arialyn relaxed her hands around his and took the arc spanner from him as he stepped back. She placed a thin metal cover over the area they were working on, closing the box-like structure. She then flipped a switch, and the machine came to life. The gears inside hummed and the smooth phallic like exterior horizontal piston began to pump back and forth.

"Good job, my love." She turned to him from her stool and kissed him on the cheek.

"Thank you..." He looked on as she flipped another switch, and the piston moved faster with an increased whirling sound. His mouth fell open at the realization of what this machine was for. "What the fuck. Why didn't you tell me what in the hells I was helping you make?"

"You said you wanted to learn my craft. I said wait until the next project and then you threw your hands down like a bratty child and said, and I quote, 'I don't want to wait anymore, show me now' end quote."

Callus blushed slightly. "Who was this for again?"

"She asked me not to divulge that information." She then looked about as if there was someone around to hear her secret and then whispered. "Someone from the Trade Authority. They paid extra for anonymity. I think it's for the Trade Princess."

Callus shook his head as the machine continued to pump into the air. "I don't want to know."

Arialyn snickered. "I wonder if she'll use it in her wereboar form?"

"Did you have to put that bloody image in my head?" He said with a sigh.

"Yes. Yes, I did." Arialyn beamed.

"You know, on second thought, you should get this patented with the Trade Authority. Like, yesterday. Then I could be a house hus-band." His lips went tight at the word slip.

"A what?" Arialyn's eyes went wide.

"A house...hobgoblin..." He put his hands behind his back and kicked his foot sheepishly.

Her eyes narrowed. "That is absolutely not what you said, dear sir."

He sighed playfully. "I was going to wait until we went back to the Tits later tonight."

The biggest smile that Arialyn had ever seen, came across his face . He pulled a green cloth from his vest and went down on one knee. The arc spanner dropped from Arialyn's hands as they flew to cover her mouth in shock. He tenderly uncovered the layers of cloth to reveal a glimmering torc bracelet with a single blue sapphire centered at its midpoint.

"I had to do some digging into my people's bonding rites. It is supposed to be gold, but I know you aren't fond of that metal. I searched for a long time to find a sapphire that was close to the shade of blue you like the most." He was rambling and stumbling a little over his words.

"Callus, shut up and ask me before I jump on you." Arialyn was ready to spring on him.

"Arialyn Foghand, you hold my heart, my mind, body and soul. You gave value to my life and helped me see past my failures to my strengths. You are my home. I, Callus Kordec, seek the binding of your heart, mind, body and soul to mine for all of our days, living and after." He reached up, taking her hand and setting the torc above her wrist, waiting.

"I, Arialyn Foghand, accept the bond you offer. I pledge myself to you as you do to me for all of our days, living and after." Her eyes swam in tears of joy.

Callus looked at her with surprise. "How did you know the words?"

"I accidentally found the torc when I was putting clothes away. I wanted to surprise you too." She placed her hand over as he held the torc above her left wrist. "Now put it on me!" She bounced on the balls of her feet.

Callus maneuvered the bonding torc onto her wrist and braced for the gnome ballista that was about to come his way. Arialyn leapt into his arms and kissed him deeply. The kiss lasted for several moments. It was perfect. Until they both became aware of the whirling sound of the pleasure machine on the workbench again.

They shared an amused chuckle before Callus shook his head. "Let's try and block this part out of the memory of this moment."

Arialyn smiled. "Not a fucking chance."

He was seconds away from carrying her to bed when the sound of someone tripping and cursing came from upstairs. When going through the one hundred and forty-nine-point list of things to do when setting up the Amethyst Artificer, Arialyn had placed setting traps as priority number three. The concealed coin lock box and having Callus take her on the counter were numbers one and two respectively. They had been through far too much not to be prepared for thieves or anyone from their respective pasts. Whatever unfortunate soul set off that particular trap would be dying from several poisoned tipped darts, if they were not dead already.

Callus released Arialyn onto her stool. He flicked his wrist and summoned the Hangman's Spear while she grabbed her arcabus from a hook under the workbench. They both kept quiet and moved. Callus pressed his back against the wall that separated the shop from the stairs and Arialyn positioned herself behind a crate, ready to peek out and fire at the first thing that came down the stairs.

Whoever was breaking in was smart enough to time their actions reasonably well. Two people came rushing down the stairs as someone simultaneously breached the back door. There was yelping and scream-ing as the first people entering from the back entrance were electrocuted or blasted in the face or crotch with fire and a force burst bolt of ball bearings. The target of that last one depended entirely on the height of the individual or individuals breaking in. Either way the three that breached the back entrance screamed in agony until Arialyn tossed a small fist sized cube contraption over the island workbench. Once it landed, it exploded in a short radius and sent a rapidly evaporating acid into the air around it. No shrieking followed.

"Dammit woman! They were already dead!" Callus hollered out.

Arialyn shrugged from behind the crate.

Callus saw a faint smile cross her lips. Was he rubbing off on her? He felt a brief rush of pride before immediately returning his attention back to the remaining threats. All that he saw for now was the four walking corpses that came in from behind the first breach team. There was also still the pair of footfalls rushing down the stairs.

Arialyn fired the arcabus at the lead person descending the stairs and they crumpled, falling down the remaining steps in a heap. Callus rolled from the wall to place himself directly in front of the second person on the stairwell and drove his spear through their chest, withdrawing it quickly and turning his attention to the four coming through the back door.

Arialyn rolled out from behind the crate and fired at the first man. The arcane bolt bounced off a tower shield that had been positioned almost perfectly in front of the team. The poor fool had left about a foot long gap from the floor.

Callus leapt and rolled over the island workbench and landed in a crouched position, sweeping the feet from under the one holding the tower shield. The eyes of the bugbear directly behind him didn't have time to dilate in shock before he dropped to the floor with an arcane bolt through his chest. Callus rolled on top of the man with the tower shield, planting his knee on the shield and effectively pinning him to the floor. He aimed his fist at the third man and sent three silver blasts of arcane energy from the Ring of Anguish, pushing him back into the halfling behind him.

Arialyn vaulted from the ground to her work stool, then to the island workbench and unleashed a volley into the halfling and the man stumbling over him. They fell lifeless as Callus remained kneeling on the tower shield. He raised the Hangman's Spear up with both hands and thrust it downward with so much force that it pierced the shield and skewered the man beneath.

Arialyn peaked out the broken back door carefully and saw no one else waiting in the alley. While she did that Callus did a quick inventory of the bodies around them. All of them were Lance men. He felt rage rising in him, the calm calculated attitude of the Towering Tactician fading quickly

Arialyn turned around and gave Callus a nod, telling him the back was clear now.

"Fucki-" She abruptly stopped as Callus held a finger to his lips.

His ears perked up to see if he could hear any further movement coming from their room above them. After a count of five he was satisfied and sighed with a growl.

Arialyn continued her thought. "Fucking Lance wasn't expecting an arcabus up their asses, were they?"

"That's exactly why we never flash it around for others to see." Callus's eyes shifted out of the back workshop to the front of the shop proper as a gentle rapping came from the front door.

He and Arialyn moved silently from the back room to the shop counter and waited again. After another moment the gentle rapping turned into a hard knock.

Just outside the door they heard a muffled voice. "This doesn't seem smart."

A split second later the door swung open, and the Hangman's Spear pierced the skull of the dark elf woman behind it with so much force that her body flew back about five feet. The spear vanished once her body hit the ground.

Another voice, one somewhat familiar to Callus, spoke from somewhere off to the side of the front door. "That's exactly why I had you do it, dipshit. Callus, it's Herodin. I'm here to parlay."

Callus called out from inside. "Parlay? You panty wastes broke into my fucking home. If you think any of you are walking away from this then you clearly don't know who I fucking am!"

Herodin nearly pissed himself as he heard the footsteps pounding through the shop and to the front door.

"Wait! Do you see any Talon bodies in there? Other than the one you just made out here?" He nearly squeaked the words out and felt more than a little humiliated by the crack in his voice. The handful of Talons around him would have laughed had they not been trying to hold their own bladders as well. While only Herodin had been in the Talons during any of Callus's time with the gang, all of them had heard the tales of the Hobgoblin Reaver.

The footsteps halted. "You, and only you, come in. Keep your eyes closed. If I see a weapon in your hand-"

Herodin dropped his short sword and dagger with a clang before Callus could finish his sentence. He held his hands up and slowly felt his way into the door frame. His eyes were closed so hard they were beginning to water.

"Five steps forward." Herodin followed Callus's instructions.

"Open your eyes."

He opened one eye at a time and almost jumped with fright. He expected to find Callus in front of him with some kind of weapon. What he didn't expect was to see an aura of death radiating off of the spear that was leveled at his chest. The Grimalkin people were known for having an inherent sixth sense that saw glimpses of energy from the darker realms. This realization caused a few drops of the aforementioned bladder issue to come forth.

Callus pushed the spear tip to rest against the grimalkin Talon's chest. Herodin swallowed hard.

"You have one minute to make me care enough to let you live." Callus looked at Arialyn as she made a tsk tsk sound and gestured with her free hand at the mess that had been made of their shop and home.

"The lady says thirty seconds."

Herodin took a quick a deep breath and began to dump as much information as he could on one exhale. "Zunibar is allied with Lance Authern, you know that. What you don't know is why. Alabaster Jakel, who we only discovered was Alejak when we arrived here, was supposed to be working with Authern to get a leg up on real estate and other business arrangements in Hus'rokn. In return, Alejak was supposed to help finance the Lance in their takeover of the rest of the Three. Only Alejak kept the fact that he was broke close to his chest. He was banking on the property Ms. Volstruk purchased to be the coin cow he needed to help return the favor in proper coinage to Authern. When that fell through Authern discovered Alejak was broke and sought out a better partner-"

"Time is up." Callus pushed the spear tip in a fraction and drew blood.

"We want them both dead!" Herodin blurted out with a whimper.

Callus stopped and tilted his head appraisingly. "You may continue."

Herodin felt a trickle of blood dripping down his chest. He closed his eyes and took another deep breath. His words tumbled out in a desperate rush, his fur matted with sweat as the spear remained pressed against his chest. "After you and the lady killed Lindri and Raseg, everything fell apart. We tried holding onto what territory we had left in Toz'Unro, but our numbers were too thin."

Callus's expression remained stone-cold, but his eyes narrowed slightly at the mention of that night.

"Frezup, he got desperate. Started recruiting anyone with a pulse and a willingness to kill. But that's where it all went tits up." Herodin's voice cracked. "Some of those recruits were plants from other crews. One night, they turned on us. Opened the doors to our safehouse while we slept."

Arialyn kept her arcabus trained on the door, listening while watching for any movement from the remaining Talons outside.

"Only seven of us made it out alive. Frezup, Dunmaris, me, and four others." Herodin's chest heaved against the spear point. "We became nomads after that, picking up work where we could. Added a few new faces along the way. Then Zunibar found us in the Helspires, offered us steady work and relocation."

"And now you're here," Callus said flatly.

"That's the thing." Herodin licked his lips nervously. "When we realized you were here, Dunmaris wanted you dead for what you did to so many of us, but Frezup said we should leave you be unless we were ordered to go after you. Well, that pompous troll fucker gave them the order. Frezup had no choice but to relent or look weak." He glanced at the spear, then back to Callus's face. "But listen, the rest of the new crew wasn't there in the old days. They've heard the stories. They know what happens to people who cross the Bloody Ruiner, and I got to witness some of it firsthand before you left. We'd rather live. So, we'd like to make an arrangement."

Callus pressed the spear a fraction deeper, drawing another drop of blood as he studied Herodin's face. "Is this a ploy, little kitty. Is there really that much dissent in the crew?"

"More than dissent," Herodin relaxed his shoulders a little, sensing Callus was more open to listening now and whispered. "Several of us were already waiting for the opportunity to make a break on our own or turn on Frezup and Dumbass. So, I told the others that you may be a fallen god of the arenas, but a god of brutality, nevertheless. Tales of your fight against Lindri and Raseg are frightful. Some think them exaggerated a bit, but I don't, and the lads would rather not put it to the test. Half the crew would turn on Frezup in a heartbeat if it meant surviving this contract. We've seen enough death and things need to change if we're going to survive. When Zunibar told Frezup to send us out here to kill you he told me to lead our guys in a joint hit with the Lance. I scouted out your place, lovely home by the way, and made sure that the Lance men ran right into each of your traps. Brilliant contraptions, m'lady. I held my lads back knowing you would pick off the traps survivors."

Callus frowned at Arialyn as he saw a smile on her face at the praise of her work.

Callus looked passed Herodin to the body of the dark elf Talon woman that lay dead just off their porch. "What about her? You didn't hold her back."

"She was loyal to Frezup. I figured you'd kill whoever knocked at the front door without a second thought. That's why I told her to knock. She did manage to do it politely. I'll give her that." Herodin tried to smile, feeling clever about the trick, it failed to reach his mouth.

The Hangman's Spear hummed with an otherworldly energy that made Herodin's fur stand on end. "And why should I believe you?"

"Because with you *we* stand a chance of doing this. Without you we're definitely fucked. Hells, I won't be walking out of here if you don't agree. I know that."

They way Herodin said the word *'we're'* made Callus's feel like he wasn't talking collectively about the Talons. His eyes narrowed. "Who is we?"

A cough from the front door drew their attention as Alejak stepped into view, his onyx skin gleaming in the dim light. His usual pompous smile spread across his face as he straightened his immaculate coat.

"The 'we' would be myself, actually," he said with deliberate slowness.

Callus moved faster than anyone expected. His fist slamming against Alejak's already shattered nose with a satisfyingly wet crunch, sending the tiefling stumbling backward and onto his ass. Blood sprayed across his already bloody white shirt.

The smell of decay and rot suddenly filled the air around them. Callus whirled to see Beetle materializing next to Arialyn, his sunken eyes reflecting no light as a miasma of corrupt death magic swirled around him.

"Fuck!" Herodin's voice cracked as his fur stood on end. "This wasn't part of the deal!"

Alejak held up a hand while doubled over, blood streaming between his fingers. "Beetle," he said with careful pronunciation despite his broken nose, "stand down immediately."

The sickly orc vanished in a cloud of necrotic energy, reappearing beside his master. He helped Alejak straighten up, his spindly fingers leaving dark stains on the tiefling's ruined clothing.

"You're dead," Callus growled, pulling the Hangman's Spear back for a thrust.

Alejak dabbed at his nose with an embroidered handkerchief, his usual theatrical grace somewhat diminished by the injury. "Now, now, let's be reasonable. I'm here to propose a mutually beneficial arrangement." He paused for dramatic effect, though the blood running down his chin somewhat ruined the moment. "Why Alejak, what do you hope to gain from working with my old enemies? Why, thank you for asking, my overly muscled hobgoblin friend. Allow me to explain. Primarily, that at completion, Zunibar will be dead and with him his claim on dear Ms. Volstruk. That would of course being your chief gain in all of this. Secondary would be eliminating Lance Authern. A man that seeks to take over the entirety of Hus'rokn and will with the funds Zunibar is going to provide for him. He has the coin to hire a third of the Kol'Theron companies to assassinate the city guard and then lay siege to the Gauntlet and Shield headquarters for over a year if he wanted. Also, and this will really get your mind set to murder, he orchestrated an ambush on a shipment your Captain friend was bringing into the city. Apparently, they were none too happy with him sticking his nose in their business so often. It seems having a Guard Captain that even mildly walks the straight and narrow isn't good for Lance business. In any case, Captain Ethan is most assuredly dead now."

Callus's spear wavered a fraction of an inch at the news. There was a part of him that ached at the thought of Captain Ethan's body rotting in the sun of the Scarred Lands. The man had been an avid fan of Callus's since he was a boy and since then had given Callus an outlet to resume combat in the Shale Grounds. More importantly, the man had become a true friend.

Arialyn felt a tear trail down her cheek, but kept her arcabus trained on Beetle, who simply stood there with his unsettling gaze fixed on her as a small smile grew on his lips.

"Tell your man-thing that if he doesn't stop eyeballing me in my home, Callus will be the least of your worries." Arialyn aimed right at Beetle's throat.

Alejak groaned through the pain in his nose and waved Beetle off. "Beetle, please wait outside."

The orc monstrosity grunted and backpedaled out the door.

"We remove those two rather unfortunate individuals from the equation, I collect a modest portion of Zunibar's considerable wealth, and then I disappear from Hus'rokn, and more importantly, from your lives. Forever." He attempted his usual calculated smile, but it came out as more of a grimace. "I must say, you haven't lost any of your speed. How long have you wanted to do that to me?"

"Too damn long."

"Zunibar is currently staying in my mansion. The bastard is planning a dinner party later tonight and inviting Authern and his top men of the Lance."

Arialyn raised an eyebrow. "How do you know that?"

Alejak smiled politely. "Beetle's tiny friends see everything in this city."

Arialyn shuddered as Alejak continued. "It is the perfect place for an ambush. All of them will be in the same place at the same time, however, their numbers will be too great for us, and what Talons Herodin is confident will join us. I figured the Towering Tactician might be able to devise a plan that sees us all living and getting what we need out of this arrangement."

"Why would we need you for any of this? You're no fighter. All you do is scheme and lie. I can kill you right now and move forward with Herodin easily." Callus fought the nearly overwhelming urge to thrust the spear straight through the hornless tiefling.

Herodin groaned at the news he knew was going to be revealed next and prayed that his head would not be added to the pile of body parts in this shop.

Alejak's face gave way to a ruthless smile. "Because I took a page out of your dear Captain's book and had Beetle, let's say, 'acquire' the deed to the Amethyst Artificer from the Wylds Trade Authority and if you do not I'll make sure this building is sold or demolished."

"You motherfucker!" Arialyn took a step forward, her face crimson red with anger.

Alejak wagged his finger. "If I die at any time before our problem is dealt with, I can assure you the same will occur."

"He's lying." Arialyn was hoping.

Callus measured Alejak's face. "No. He isn't. When this is over. You and I will have this finished. One way or another. You have too much to answer for, Alejak." Callus said flatly.

Alejak dabbed at his nose with the handkerchief and gave Callus a coy look. "My dear friend, all I did was leave a few deceased creatures around Ms. Volstruk's establishment and attempt to burn it down once. I was only endeavoring to scare her out of the deed. I have no further interest in the place now with all that has transpired."

"You still have things from our past in Toz'Unro to answer for," Callus growled, his knuckles turning white on the Hangman's Spear.

A laugh escaped Alejak's bloodied lips, though it held no warmth. "What exactly? For making things difficult for the Talons? For providing the Brightborn Kingdom intelligence about the gangs?" He spread his arms wide in mock confusion. "Why should any of this matter anymore when you yourself killed half the Talons within the last year?"

Callus took a step forward, but Alejak continued undaunted. "The only reason I even made things difficult for the Talons was because of you, Callus." His voice dropped its theatrical quality, revealing a bitter edge. "I despised you because you had everything and lost it all, yet people still feared and praised you. They still looked at you like some sort of prince. You still acted like you had the right to have that level of respect. You bloody well did not, and you know it."

Alejak's eyes narrowed as he wiped more blood from his face. "Meanwhile, I was at the top of Toz'Unro society in my sweet Hornless Devil, and while people respected me to my face, they tore me down behind my back. And you?" He jabbed a finger in Callus's direction. "You were the worst."

Arialyn kept her arcabus trained on the door, but her eyes flicked between the two men as the tension built.

"Tell me, Callus," Alejak's voice softened to almost a whisper, "What exactly do you have to gain by killing me now? The past is gone." He gestured around the shop. "You have a home, a business, and..." His eyes settled on Arialyn for a moment before returning to Callus, "a woman foolish enough to love you. Why risk all of that for old vengeance that no longer has a purpose?"

The words hung in the air between them, heavy with the weight of their shared history. Callus's jaw clenched as he processed Alejak's words, the truth in them warring with years of built-up hatred for the man.

"He has a point." Herodin spoke up and immediately regretted it with the glare Callus sent his way.

"What do you say, Callus?" Alejak held his hand out. "Shake on it?"

Beetle's sunken eyes scanned the empty street, his gaunt frame casting long shadows in the dim light of the streetlamps. A cockroach scuttled near his feet, its antennae twitching as it relayed the conversation from inside the shop to its master. His blackened fingernails scratched absently at pustules on his pale green skin as he listened.

A sudden cackle echoed through his mind, causing him to twitch violently. He heard the name again, *'Fogjeck. Voidtongue.'* He shook his head and sent a few of his little minions skittering to find new places on his person to hide. The name came again, and he could see a figure in his minds eyes wreathed in the deep purple of the void. Then came whispers of a language he didn't know echoed in his head. Something in the words pulled his thoughts to the gnome woman inside. He pressed his spindly fingers together and whispered a prayer to Odhrum Voidspawn, feeling the familiar comfort of decay and suffering wash over him. The miasma of death that constantly surrounded him swirled and thickened with his devotion. The whispering faded away.

Through his insect spy, he heard Alejak's voice clearly: "Stay there and be ready to get me out of here quickly."

The silence that followed was deafening. Then chaos erupted.

The five Talons waiting outside burst through the shop's open door, weapons drawn. The sound of shattering glass and splintering wood filled the night air. Beetle watched with detached fascination as arcane bolts of energy punched through the windows, illuminating the street in brief flashes of violent light.

Screams and crashes echoed from inside, accompanied by the distinctive sound of Arialyn's arcabus discharging repeatedly. The roach's perspective became chaotic as it scrambled to avoid being crushed in the melee, but Beetle could still make out fragments of the battle - boots stomping, furniture breaking, flesh meeting flesh.

Then Callus stumbled through the doorway, his massive frame silhouetted against the shop's interior light. Blood poured from wounds in his stomach and throat, staining his clothes crimson. The hobgoblin took two unsteady steps into the street before collapsing face-first onto the cobblestones.

A pool of dark liquid began spreading beneath him, reflecting the dim street lanterns above. Beetle tilted his head, studying the fallen warrior with clinical interest. He had seen many deaths in his service to Alejak, but few had been as exaggerated as this one.

Chapter Twenty-Nine

DO YOU FEEL IN CONTROL?

They had made a hasty retreat from the Ferrum Plains, but not before Kovag had managed to swipe a few extra provisions from the far edge of the city and barter with an aged dwarven man for a watered-down healing potion. It had only cost him two bottles of dwarven black mead, both of which he had stolen from the old dwarf's cart a few minutes earlier anyway. The cut potion had done nothing for the pain and had barely closed the wound from the Forgotten's horn, but at least there would be less of a chance of a repeat of the crossbow bolt infection from a few weeks back.

Saffron had ridden on Kovag's shoulders for nearly three days before they happened upon a small massacre. It didn't take long for Kovag to discern what happened. It appeared that a small family had been set upon by bandits. The family's wagon had been burned heavily and the wheels rendered useless. The rain from the day before stopped him from determining if the fire damage was arcane or mundane in nature.

There were five bodies littered across the ground that had been picked at to varying degrees by the scavenger animals of the eastern Brightborn woods. From what he could tell they had arrow, sword and axe wounds and at least two of the bodies belonged to the bandits. All supplies were either taken or ruined by the weather. What they found several yards into the tree line was a godsend from whatever benevolent god or goddess gave a damn about what was happening to them. The horse that had been tied to a tree, and on its back a bedroll and tent just large enough for both to sleep in. Kovag had named the mare Lucky. Saffron had scrunched her face at the name but he held firm on it.

After five days on horseback, they had finally made it the border of the Brightborn Kingdom. The evening sun cast long shadows across the plateau as Kovag stood with Saffron at the edge, his massive frame silhouetted against the dying light. Lucky grazed contentedly behind them, seemingly unbothered by the desolate view that stretched out past the plateau. Kovag had wondered if the state of Lucky's previous owners would affect Saffron, but she seemed unbothered by it. At the very least she did not cry and whimper in her sleep any more than she had before they had come upon them. He thought again about everything she had seen since he rescued her and what terrible things she experienced before.

He pointed toward the horizon where the wastes of the Scarred Lands gradually transformed into scattered vegetation at the furthest point the eyes could see. "Look there. That's the Resurgence Wilds. It's where life is finally returning to the Scarred Lands."

Saffron squinted, her eyes focusing into the growing darkness from the sunsetting behind them as she followed his gesture. Her tail swayed with curiosity, and she tugged at his cloak, silently asking for more information.

"They say that long ago," he continued, dropping to one knee beside her, "this was all green and full of life. Then came Varl's Wall and the corruption of the void by the Cult of the Void Heart." He paused, considering how to explain such complex history to a child. "Bad magic changed everything, burned it all away. But now, after thousands of years, plants are growing again. Animals are returning."

Her ears perked up at the mention of animals, and she pointed eagerly at a lone bird circling above the sparse tree line.

"Yes, exactly like that," Kovag smiled, though it didn't quite reach his eyes. "The Wilds are dangerous; everything that thrives out there had to learn to survive in harsh conditions. Our crossing will be dangerous. But they're also proof that even the worst wounds can heal, given enough time."

He glanced down at Saffron, who was still watching the bird with rapt attention. The parallel wasn't lost on him. She too was healing, slowly but surely, from wounds both seen and unseen. Her fascination was infectious, and he wondered, not for the first time since his education from Matron Vadrida, if this was her pack bond he was feeling.

A cold wind picked up, carrying with it the acrid smell of the Scarred Lands. Saffron wrinkled her nose and stepped closer to Kovag, pressing against his side. He wrapped a hand around her shoulders, grateful for the small tent they'd salvaged. They would need its shelter tonight, meager as it was, before venturing into the Resurgence Wilds tomorrow.

"Come on," he said, steering them both away from the edge. "Let's get camp set up before it gets dark. Those clouds look like rain."

The rain had started as a gentle patter but quickly built into a steady downpour that created a rhythmic drumming against the tent's canvas. Kovag sat just inside the entrance, his broad shoulders nearly filling the opening as he watched Saffron dance in the falling water. He'd never seen her act this free, she twirled with arms outstretched, face turned upward to catch the drops on her tongue.

A pang of sadness touched his heart as he wondered how long she had been kept from such simple pleasures. Had she ever felt rain before?

Had she ever been allowed to simply play, to experience the world as a child should? The thought of her locked away in that dungeon and whatever came before made his jaw clench.

He could feel her pure delight washing over him like the rain itself. Her tail moved in wide arcs, spreading water droplets in sparkling circles as she spun. The firelight caught the moisture in her fur, making her seem to glow in the gathering darkness.

He had already decided to keep her with him back at the temple, but then it was a decision made for her protection alone with the assistance of Matron Vadrida's lesson on the pack bond. However, now, as she danced and moved carefree as she always should have been allowed to, he was making the decision for himself as well. Oakira took the chance of a family away from him. Now he would take that chance for himself.

Behind Saffron, the twin moons hung full in the night sky. Every full moon since the pact he had done as Oakira had bade him and stood skyclad under the moons. Even when she remained silent, he had remained true to the request. Now though, with what he'd learned of his mother and sister, he decided that for the first time he would push back and deny her that simple act.

Something tickled at the edge of his consciousness, a warning. His Fae-touched eye shifted to peer just beyond the circle of firelight, where the shadows seemed to move against the rain's pattern. His blood ran cold.

A warabura crouched there, its feline muscles bunched beneath scaled hide, its monitor lizard-like head low to the ground as it prepared to strike. Its tail, tipped with a deadly paralytic barb, whipped back and forth in perfect mimicry of Saffron's joyful movements.

"Down!" Kovag roared, his hand shooting forward as the beast launched itself toward the dancing child. Silver-green energy coalesced around his fingers, condensing into a bolt of pure force that streaked through the rain.

Saffron jumped, his sudden warning frightening her. She barely dropped in time to be missed by Kovag's own arcane force. The eldritch bolt struck the warabura mid-leap, catching it in its exposed belly. The beast let out a horrific screech, part big cat's roar, part reptilian hiss, as the force sent it tumbling through the air past where Saffron had stood moments before.

Kovag knew the creature's reputation well enough to know that one hit would just piss it off. The warabura was already rolling to its feet, its unnatural yellow eyes fixed on Saffron with predatory focus. Its jaw unhinged, displaying rows of venomous fangs that dripped a sickly green fluid into the mud with a hiss as they touched the collecting rainwater.

Kovag slammed his fist against his chest with a primal roar, drawing the warabura's attention away from Saffron. The beast locked onto him, its scaled hide glistening in the rain and firelight. Kovag's muscles tensed so hard he could feel their desire to cramp as he launched himself at the beast with burst of arcane infused speed.

The warabura's tail lashed out, the paralytic barb whistling through the air where Kovag's throat had been a moment before. He twisted away, feeling the wind of its passage. The creature's heavy claws raked across his forearm as he deflected its strike, splattering blood to mix with the mud.

'Being big ain't enough, boy.' The old smith's voice echoed in his mind as he ducked under another swipe of those deadly claws. The warabura's jaw snapped shut inches from his face, venomous fangs gleaming. The acidic smell of its breath made his eyes water.

Kovag saw his opening as the beast overextended itself. He dropped and rolled, feeling its scaled belly brush against his back. In one fluid motion, he came up behind it, his arm snaking around its throat. The warabura thrashed wildly, its tail whipping back and forth as it tried to strike him with its barb. Kovag grabbed it mid-strike and wrapped it around his forearm before ripping it out at the root. Swiftly he locked his arms back together around the beast's neck.

He squeezed, muscles straining as he fought to maintain his grip on the slick thrashing creature. The scales cut into his skin, but he didn't allow himself to feel it. With a final surge of strength, he twisted sharply. The crack of its neck echoed across the plateau, followed by the dull thud of its body hitting the mud.

Kovag stood, chest heaving, and let out a victorious roar that shook the very air around him. His triumph quickly turned to ash in his mouth as his eyes fell on Saffron's small body lying motionless near the fire.

"No," he breathed, his heart standing still. He crossed the distance in two massive strides, dropping to his knees beside her. The rain plastered her fur to her skin, making her seem even tinier than usual. Her tail lay limp in the mud, no sign of its usual expressive movement.

His hands trembled as he reached for her, terrified of what he might find. As he rolled her into his arms he saw it. The beast had managed to tag her with its tail. Their bond felt muted, distant, like a candle flickering in a strong wind. She was paralyzed but not dead. Not yet, but she would be soon.

"Please," he whispered, gathering her into his arms. "Please, not like this." The willow wing blossom in his chest pulsed with a desperate energy as he called out to Oakira.

"OAKIRA!" He roared.

"OAKIRA!" No response came.

Panic clawed at Kovag's chest as he held Saffron's limp body. The rain pelted them both, washing away the mud and blood. Their bond felt like a fraying thread, growing weaker with each passing moment. He realized only now that he could truly feel it, this tether that had been present in the back of his mind for weeks.

"Oakira, I need you!" His voice cracked with desperation. "I will never forgive you for this! Not for this!" The words tore from his throat, raw and primal. Thunder rolled across the plateau as if in response to his anguish, but she did not appear.

The storm raged around them as Kovag gently laid Saffron on the ground. Her golden eyes were seemingly lifeless. She stared up at him, conscious but unable to move. He could feel her terror pounding in his mind, and something in him shattered.

Rising to his full height, Kovag gathered arcane energy into his right hand. The power crackled and sparked, casting an eerie green glow across his rain-slicked skin. His Fae-touched eye ignited in a furious blaze as he plunged his fingers into his own chest, seeking the willow wing blossom that connected him to Oakira.

Pain exploded through him as his fingers found the ethereal flower. The sensation was beyond physical, reaching into the very essence of his being. He knew the surge would ripple through the arcane web, knew Oakira would feel it wherever she was.

"If you won't help me," he snarled through clenched teeth, "then you'll feel this pain with me." His fingers tightened around the blossom, sending waves of agony through both himself and the connection.

Blood began to trickle from his nose as he poured more power into his grip. The willow wing blossom pulsed erratically, its usual gentle thrum becoming a desperate flutter. Lightning split the sky above them, and for a moment, Kovag's shadow stretched grotesquely across the muddy ground.

Through the haze of pain, he felt Saffron's presence in his mind growing fainter. Her life was like a candle in a hurricane, threatening to go out entirely. Tears mixed with the rain on his face as he realized he might lose her, might fail her just as he had failed his family.

His grip tightened further on the blossom, and he screamed his defiance into the storm. The sound carried all his rage, his fear, his love for the child dying at his feet. Power surged through him, wild and uncontrolled, as he forced every ounce of his pain through the connection to Oakira.

The willow wing blossom shuddered in his grasp, and somewhere in the vast expanse of the Fae realm, he knew Oakira would be screaming too.

Oakira's hands trembled as she wrung out the cloth, watching the water cascade back into the ornate obsidian basin. Her mother's usually pristine silver hair hung limp and dull around her shoulders, another testament to the toll their constant relocation had taken. The last few teleportation circles had drained Elirel faster than before, and Oakira could see the exhaustion etched into every line of her mother's face.

"They are getting closer," Elirel whispered, her voice barely audible over the gentle splash of water. "I can feel them, daughter. The Seekers are like shadows at the edge of my consciousness."

Oakira's hands stilled. "Mother, please. You need to rest."

"Rest?" Elirel laughed, but there was no humor in the sound. "That surge of power your pet mortal sent through the web might as well have been a beacon. They will find us now; it is only a matter of time."

The willow wing blossom in Oakira's chest pulsed gently, and she pressed her hand against it. "Stop calling him that," she said softly, resuming her ministrations. "He is-"

"He is a liability," Elirel cut in, her tone sharp despite her weakened state. "One we can no longer afford. If you will not eliminate him, I will."

"No!" Oakira's voice echoed off the obsidian walls. "He is only trying to protect what little he has left. The twin moons are full tonight. I will go to him and explain just how careful he needs to be. They must lay low-"

A familiar pull tugged at her chest, Kovag's voice calling out to her across the realms with immense pain and need. She rose, ready to answer his summons, but Elirel's hand shot out with surprising strength, gripping her wrist.

"Foolish girl," her mother hissed. "You would throw away everything we have sacrificed for a mortal's desperate plea? Let whatever it is take him. It will spare me from having to deal with it."

Before Oakira could respond, pain exploded through her chest. She collapsed to her knees, a scream tearing from her throat as she felt Kovag's fingers close around the willow wing blossom. The agony was beyond anything she had ever experienced. It felt as though he was trying to tear out her very essence.

"Oakira!" Elirel's voice seemed to come from far leagues away.

Through the haze of pain, Oakira caught glimpses of what Kovag was seeing, a small, paralyzed form on rain-soaked ground, a bond fading like morning mist. She understood then, with dangerous clarity, why he was willing to destroy their connection and call down any that would feel the power. A last ditch move of mutual destruction if she would not answer him in his time of need. He had never even threatened to do something like this before.

"The child," she gasped between waves of agony. "He is trying to save the child."

Elirel's face contorted with disgust as she spat at the umbra floor. "This is what your feelings have cost you, daughter. Your sniveling beast of a pet has overstepped. He has made the choice for you." Her silver hair whipped around her face as she gathered her power, preparing to project herself across the realms.

"Mother, please-" Oakira's plea was cut short by another wave of agony as Kovag's grip tightened further on the willow wing blossom.

Elirel's consciousness tore through the veil between worlds, her ethereal form materializing before Kovag in the storm-swept plateau that overlooked that wasteland. Rain passed through her incorporeal body as she towered over his kneeling form, her eyes blazing with lunar fury. The moons seemed to almost radiate brighter in her presence.

"You simpering fool," she snarled, her voice carrying even over the thunder. "Your pathetic attachment to this broken child will be the death of my daughter. Your reckless display of power draws the Seekers closer with every passing moment."

Blood dripped from Kovag's chest where his fingers pierced his flesh, mixing with the mud beneath his knees. His Fae-touched eye burned with an intensity that matched Elirel's own as he looked up at her. "Then help her," he growled through clenched teeth, nodding toward Saffron's unmoving body.

"You have been a liability for far too long." Elirel raised her hand, gathering deadly power that crackled with dark lunar tendrils. "I should have ended this farce years ago."

A bitter laugh escaped Kovag's bloodied lips. "Do you truly believe you're fast enough?" His fingers flexed around the willow wing blossom, sending fresh waves of agony through both himself and Oakira. "I'll tear it out before your spell leaves your hand. I'll die for breaking the pact, but the arcane discharge will bring the Seekers directly down upon you both."

Elirel's hand wavered slightly, the energy flickering as she weighed the odds. Her lip curled in contempt as she regarded him. "Look at what you've become, a broken tool threatening to shatter itself out of spite. You were a flawed choice from the start."

"Then maybe you should have come out from behind your veil of cowardice and made the pact yourself instead of using your own daughter, you bitch." Kovag spat back, blood trickling from the corner of his mouth. "Now save her, or we all burn together."

Elirel's eyes burned with intense hatred at Kovag's accusation, her spiritual form seeming to grow larger with ferocity. But as quickly as the rage came, it subsided. Her gaze shifted to Saffron's motionless form, studying the child with cold and uncaring calculation.

Kovag felt the bond between himself and Saffron growing impossibly thin, like a spider's web ripping apart in a storm. The strength of his own heart felt nearly as thin in his chest as he watched Elirel consider the dying child. Blood now dripped from his eyes and mouth, adding to what fell from his nose and where his fingers pierced his flesh. He glared defiantly at Elirel and shrugged the pain away as he was racked with another bloody cough. Droplets of his life-force splattered through Elirel's form.

With a dismissive wave of her hand, as though the act was beneath her notice, Elirel sent a wave of silver lunar energy washing over Saffron. The vulpine girl's chest heaved as she coughed violently, her tail twitching back to life. Kovag felt their bond surged back fully, nearly overwhelming him with the intensity of her returned presence in his mind.

"Release the blossom," Elirel commanded, her voice carrying the weight of a millennia of authority.

Kovag's fingers remained firmly wrapped around the ethereal flower. "Not until you're gone," he growled through clenched teeth. "You're a serpent and I have already been bitten by your kind more than once."

Rage flashed across Elirel's drained features. Her hand lashed out, striking Kovag across the face with enough force to shatter stone. The sound cracked like thunder across the plateau, but Kovag didn't budge. His massive frame stood, his back straightening. He was eye to eye with Elirel now with fingers still gripping the blossom within his chest.

Shock registered on Elirel's face for a brief moment before her expression hardened into something terrible. She leaned in, her incorporeal form inches from his face. "Listen well, you misbegotten mongrel," she hissed. "If any harm comes to my daughter because of your foolish display of defiance, I will unmake the very weave of your soul. I will unravel you thread by thread until there is not enough left of you to fill a thimble."

Rain continued to fall through her ghostly form as she straightened up, her hair writhing like living mercury. "And that, I promise you, will be a mercy compared to what I will do to your little orphan."

Kovag smiled through the blood on his lips. "Better run along back to wherever the fuck you're hiding then."

Elirel raised her hand to strike him again but he pushed his forehead directly to hers with a snarl. "Hit me again and my hand might just slip."

Her visage dispersed. Kovag pulled his hand from his chest and felt like his lungs collapsed as breath left him in a gasp. He staggered toward Saffron and nearly stumbled into the fire twice before reaching her. His attempt to kneel by her quickly turned into a face first fall.

Saffron sat up in a panic, gasping and clutching at her throat. She scrambled to her feet, eyes wide as the moons above and spun around searching for the owner of the voice she heard speaking with Kovag as everything began to grow dark. Her lungs burned, her heart surged, and her eyes felt like they were on fire from being opened to the pelting raindrops from above as she had lain paralyzed.

Saffron's spirit sank as she turned to see Kovag lying in the mud where she had been moments before. Despite the blood staining the ground around him and the exhaustion etched into his features, a thin smile played across his lips. "Saffy," he whispered, the sudden nickname falling from his mouth like a triumph.

He pushed himself up into a sitting position, his body trembling with the effort. The sight of his weakness broke her stillness, and she rushed to him with tears streaming down her face. All of it crashed over her at once, the terror of the warabura's attack, the hateful voice that had seemed to despise Kovag so deeply, and the horrifying sight of blood seeping from his chest where his own fingers had pierced his flesh.

She collided with his chest, her small hands clutching desperately at his rain-soaked clothing. Kovag's arms enveloped her, and she felt the familiar safety of his embrace close over her like a home. His large hand stroked the wet fur on her ears as she sobbed, her tears mixing with the rain and blood around them.

"I'm fine," he murmured, his deep voice rumbling through his chest against her ear. "You're fine. We're going to be fine." The words seemed as much for him as for her. His hand continued its gentle motion through her fur, each stroke helping to calm the trembling that wracked her core.

"I'm sorry, Saffy." he said, his voice thick with emotion. "I should have seen the beast sooner." Tears began to form in his eyes, catching the firelight as they rolled down his cheeks and to her hair.

Saffron pulled back just enough to look up at his face. She shook her head vigorously, refusing to let him blame himself. Her hands reached up, gently wiping away his tears with a tenderness that made his breath catch in his throat. Through their bond, she pushed all her feelings of safety and trust, trying to show him that she didn't blame him, that she knew he had saved her.

Kovag's arms tightened around her, and she felt his tears fall onto her head as he pulled her close again. They sat there in the rain, holding each other, both grateful for the simple fact that they were alive and together. The fire sputtered and hissed behind them, but neither moved to tend it, too focused on the comfort they found in each other's presence.

Chapter Thirty

TO THE DEALER
GO THE SPOILS

Kordra 10:42pm

The mood was one of resounding success. An overly large banquet table was filled to capacity with food and drink to the point that no one could see the exquisitely crafted white wood beneath it all. The same wood that Alejak's office desk had been made from. Of course, this banquet table no longer belonged to the hornless tiefling, nor did the mansion that contained it.

Zunibar sat at the head of the table sipping from a wine goblet that looked like a toy in his large hand. Next to him Authern watched with a raised eyebrow as Herodin regaled the Talons and Lance men, for the third damn time, with the tale of how they killed Callus and his woman.

Herodin was overly animated in his movements. Acting out what he himself had done and mimicking the actions of the others that were there. "By the time we got the big bastard under control he had made a bloodbath out of the Lance men. So, we got him on his knees right-"

Berekr slammed his meaty fist on the table, causing several goblets to wobble precariously. "How many more bloody times do we have to hear this story?" His face had grown redder with each of Herodin's retellings, though whether from drink or irritation was hard to tell. "You may have achieved the goal, but we lost every Lance man that went with you lot, while you only lost one of yours. Seems a little fucking suspicious, don't it?"

Herodin's whiskers twitched with barely contained amusement as he turned to face the rotund dwarf. "Why, Berekr, I didn't know you'd developed feelings for your compatriots. Here I thought you only had those sorts of emotions for the working boys in the back streets."

The room erupted in laughter from the Talons joining in the mockery. Even Zunibar chuckled into his oversized wine goblet, though his eyes remained calculating as they darted between the two men.

Berekr's face darkened further as he pushed himself up from his chair, the wooden legs scraping against the floor. "Listen here, you mangy little shit-"

"Berekr." Authern's voice cut through the revelry like a hammer on a bell. The half-giant didn't raise his voice, but the single word carried enough weight to silence the room. "Take a breather outside. Now."

The dwarf's jaw worked as he visibly struggled with the command, his hands clenching and unclenching at his sides. Finally, he let out a string of vulgarities that would have made a brothel madame blush and stomped toward the door, slamming it behind him with enough force to rattle the windows.

Herodin waited until the echo of Berekr's heavy footsteps faded before continuing, his tail swishing with excitement. "Now, where was I? Ah yes, the best part." His eyes gleamed as he surveyed his captive audience. "So, there we had the mighty Hobgoblin Reaver on his knees, and that's when we really started having fun with his little gnome woman."

He pantomimed pulling someone's hair back, his voice taking on a cruel edge. "You should have heard her screams when we started breaking those clever little fingers of hers. One. By. One." He punctuated each word with a snapping gesture. "But the real art was making sure Callus could see everything. The way he thrashed against the chains, begging us to stop, now that was music."

Several of the men around the table leaned forward, entranced by the performance. Zunibar's expression remained neutral, but his grip on the wine goblet tightened imperceptibly.

"And then," Herodin continued, his voice dropping to a dramatic whisper, "we doused him in lamp oil. The look in his eye when that first torch touched him was priceless. Went up like a festival bonfire, he did."

The raucous cheers filled the expansive dining room as the assembled criminals raised their glasses to Herodin's tale. Wine flowed freely, and the dancers Zunibar had hired began to weave between the tables. Their silken scarves trailed behind them like colorful smoke, drawing appreciative glances and crude comments from the assembled men and women. One girl squealed with a mixture of excitement and fright as a Talon scooped her up and carried her to an adjacent room.

Herodin soaked up the acclaim, his whiskers quivering with poorly hidden pride as he received praise from the surrounding crowd. His performance had hit all the right notes - violence, cruelty, and just enough detail to hide the initial betrayal of the Lance. He'd learned long ago that the best lies were the ones that left room for the listener's imagination to fill in the gaps. The respect of the others was something he never felt so keenly.

A heavy hand landed on his shoulder, and Herodin turned to find Dunmaris standing behind him. The hobgoblin ranger's face was unreadable as ever, but there was something in his eyes that made Herodin's fur stand slightly on end.

"Walk with me," Dunmaris's grip tightening ever so slightly on Herodin's shoulder. This wasn't a request.

They moved away from the main table, past the dancers and toward one of the room's darker corners. The music and laughter provided perfect cover for quiet conversation, though Herodin noticed how Dunmaris positioned them so he could see the entire room.

"Didn't know you had that kind of violence in you," Dunmaris said, his voice barely above a whisper. "Always took you for more of a... practical sort."

Herodin forced a smile, though his tail twitched nervously behind him. "We all have hidden depths."

Dunmaris leaned in closer, his breath hot against Herodin's ear. "Indeed, we do. Perhaps later you can tell me how you managed to spare almost all of our brothers while the Lance men met such unfortunate ends?" The last words carried a humorous edge. Dunmaris had never praised him before. This was... unnerving. "I knew many would die. Good on you for making sure it was mostly just them. Anything that pisses that squat dwarven fuck under Authern off makes me happy."

The grimalkin's mind raced as he maintained his casual demeanor. "A bit of luck," Herodin replied carefully, his eyes fixed on the dancers. "And perhaps the Lance men weren't as skilled as they thought they were."

Dunmaris's low chuckle held no humor. "Luck, is it? We'll discuss your particular brand of luck later tonight. In detail. Oh, maybe stop pissing off the rest of the Lance by retelling the story of the slaughter." He patted Herodin's shoulder once more before moving away, leaving the him to wonder if he'd just signed his own death warrant.

Herodin watched Dunmaris rejoin the main table, accepting a fresh glass of wine from one of the serving girls. The ranger's eyes met his across the room, and Herodin felt a chill run down his spine.

Berekr's return to the dining hall went largely unnoticed amid the cacophony of celebration. He waddled his way through the crowd of revelers, his round face still flushed from earlier anger. Upon reaching Authern, he stretched up on his tiptoes to whisper something in the half-giant's ear.

Authern's initial reaction was to wave him off with clear annoyance, but as Berekr continued speaking, his expression shifted. The irritation melted away, replaced by a self-satisfied smirk that spread across his features.

With a dismissive wave of his massive hand, Authern gave Berekr permission to proceed. The dwarf's chest puffed out as he turned to face the raucous gathering.

"Quiet down, you lot!" Berekr bellowed, his voice barely audible over the din of music and drunken storytelling. When no one paid him any mind, his face darkened to an even deeper shade of crimson. Without warning, he drew a dagger from his belt and hurled it across the room. The blade whistled past the bard's ear and embedded itself in the wall with a solid thunk.

The musician let out a high-pitched shriek and dropped his lute, the instrument clattering to the floor. The sudden absence of music brought the revelry to an abrupt halt as all eyes turned toward the source of the commotion.

"That's better," Berekr said, smoothing down his fine coat with exaggerated movements. "Now then, we have an unexpected guest. One who has decided to grace us with his presence on this momentous evening." He paused for dramatic effect, clearly enjoying the attention. "May I present Gauntlet Adenus of the Lucky Talisman."

The double doors at the far end of the dining hall swung open, revealing the tall, elegant figure of the dark elf crime lord. Adenus stood framed in the doorway for a moment, his expensive clothing and multiple rings catching the light from the chandeliers above. His piercing eyes surveyed the room appraisingly as he crossed the threshold, his motions displaying the fluid elegance of a smooth politician. His choice of attire meant he was here on business, and pleasant business at that.

The assembled criminals parted before him like water around a stone as he made his way toward the head of the table. Some bowed their heads slightly, others simply stared, but all maintained a respectful silence. Even the dancers pressed themselves against the walls. They took the time to cover themselves as best they could with the silk scarves Zunibar had allowed them, for now, to keep on. Adenus noticed the fear on the women, many showing signs of fresh bruises, but did his best to feign no interest in their plight. It wasn't easy for him.

Zunibar leaned forward on the table as he regarded the newcomer, his expression unreadable. Authern's smirk remained firmly in place as he stood to greet a fellow member of the Three, though a portion of his vision remained on his greataxe leaning against the table.

Authern poured a glass of dark red wine, the liquid catching the light like fresh blood as pushed it across the table toward Adenus. "To what do we owe the pleasure?" He said with the falsely rehearsed warmth of someone who had learned to tolerate the displeasure of this man's company.

Zunibar tensed, his fingers tightening around his own goblet until the glass groaned in protest. "The Gauntlet had better have an excellent reason for darkening my doorway." The troll's voice rumbled. "Especially after making it clear I wasn't welcome in his precious casino."

Even Authern's perpetual smirk faltered at the blatant disrespect. The half-giant shot Zunibar a warning glance, but the troll seemed beyond caring about tenuous peace in the room.

Adenus's lips curved into a coy smile, the kind reserved for dealing with particularly difficult children. He made no move to touch the offered wine, instead clasping his hands behind his back as his gaze swept the room. "I heard the most unfortunate news about our mutual acquaintance, the former Scarred Lands Champion." His voice carried just enough genuine concern to make several of the assembled criminals shift uncomfortably. "The grisly display of two hanging burnt corpses outside is quite... dramatic. Though I must say, the bodies make a rather glaring statement."

Zunibar straightened, wondering if things were about to get violent. He had to assume the Gauntlet wouldn't dare incite a fight while so terribly outnumbered. A bead of sweat traced its way down his temple despite the room's comfortable temperature.

Authern leaned back in his chair and sighed. "There was nothing in our agreement that prohibited taking revenge for the hobgoblin's slight against us." His tone remained casual, but there was an edge to it now, a subtle warning. "In any case, none of the Three have jurisdiction past the Trade Gate."

"Of course not," Adenus agreed smoothly, his eyes glaring with suppressed exasperation. "Though I do find it curious that none of my people were informed of this execution. After all, we did have certain... arrangements with the deceased." His gaze flickered briefly across the room, as if he were counting heads to collect.

The tension in the room grew thick enough to cut with a knife as the implications of Adenus's words hung in the air. Several of the Lance men's hands drifted toward their weapons, while the Talons exchanged uncertain glances.

"The Ruiner made me a fair amount of coin in the Shale Grounds. I will seek financial compensation when next the Three meet." His words hung heavy in the air.

Authern tilted his massive head, the candlelight catching the intricate tattoos that covered his pale skin as he weighed his options. The muscles in his neck tensed visibly as he fought against his natural inclination toward violence. After what felt like an eternity to those holding their breath around the table, he inclined his head in a measured nod.

"Fair enough," he rumbled, his voice dripping with the forced pleasantness of a predator choosing not to strike. "The Gauntlet's interests should have been considered."

Adenus's inclined his head in gratitude. "I'm gratified to hear you say that," he purred, finally reaching for the offered wine. "In truth, this matter of compensation was merely a pretense for my visit tonight." He took a delicate sip, savoring the vintage with apparent appreciation, even going so far as to nod his head in respect at the choice of wine. "My true purpose was to extend an olive branch, to sue for peace once more between our organizations."

The assembled criminals exchanged glances, some skeptical, others clearly interested in the mention of peace, and what it might mean for their own prospects.

"My recent... reticence regarding Mr. Tolgar's presence in my establishment may have been... hasty," Adenus continued, managing to sound apologetic without actually admitting any wrongdoing. "The tensions between our organizations serve none of us well, particularly in these changing times."

Zunibar shifted again in his chair. His expression remained guarded, but there was a gleam of interest in his eyes at the dark elf's words.

"In fact," Adenus added, setting his wine glass down gingerly, "I've brought a peace offering of sorts. Three of my finest dealers await outside with their portable tables, ready to provide entertainment for your celebration." His smile sparkled as he surveyed the room. "Along with a gift of one hundred gold coins for each man and woman present. Assuming, of course, that our gracious host is amenable to allowing them entry into his new home?"

The last words hung in the air like a whore's perfume, sweet but potentially poisonous. Several of the Lance men and Talons straightened at the mention of gold, their earlier suspicions temporarily forgotten in the face of potential profit. Even Berekr's perpetual scowl softened slightly at the prospect of such generosity.

Authern's calculating gaze moved from Adenus to Zunibar and back again, clearly weighing the political implications of accepting such a gesture. His fingers drummed thoughtfully on the table as he considered the offer, the sound barely audible over the renewed whispers of excitement among the gathered criminals.

Authern's finger traced the rim of his wine glass as he considered Adenus's offer. "A fine gesture indeed," he said, his voice straining to hold its neutrality. He turned to Zunibar, clearly deferring to his new business partner's judgment.

Zunibar stared at Adenus, studying his intent. "And what exactly do I get out of this generosity?" His words were heavy with suspicion.

Adenus's opens his hands in front of him in placation. "Actually, I have a surprise waiting on the front lawn for you." He gestured toward the window with an elegant flourish of his ring-adorned hand.

Zunibar's laugh filled the room, a deep rumbling sound that held no real mirth. "Following you outside doesn't seem in my best interest, Gauntlet." He said as he set his wine goblet on the table, preparing for this impromptu meeting to get nasty.

"The level of trust isn't there yet, I understand completely," Adenus nodded, his tone sympathetic. He moved to the nearest window. "Perhaps you'd prefer a quick sneak peek?"

Zunibar's chair scraped against the floor as he rose and joined Adenus at the window. His eyes narrowed as he peered into the darkness beyond the mansion's gates.

There, illuminated by the ethereal glow of oil and enchanted lanterns, stood an ornate carriage. Before it, three of Adenus's dealers held their portable tables like precious oversized briefcases, their Gauntlet escorts standing at attention nearby. But it was the two figures before them that drew Zunibar's attention. A hooded woman with red skin that caught the lamplight like fresh blood, and beside her, a large human man forced to his knees, his blood-soaked hooded head bowed in apparent defeat.

Zunibar turned back to Adenus, a predatory smile spreading across his features. "Why the sudden change of heart?" His voice had lost some of its earlier hostility, replaced by genuine curiosity.

"I would be happy to explain everything on our way down," Adenus replied smoothly, gesturing toward the door. "And of course, you're welcome to bring as many of your men as you feel necessary." He paused, "After all, what are new partnerships without a proper foundation of trust?"

Zunibar inclined his head, his hands nearly shaking with excitement. After all these years, the prize that had slipped through his grasp would finally be his again. His mind raced with the delicious possibilities of what he would do to Kasha, how he would make her pay for every moment of defiance.

He turned to Frezup. "Gather some men. I want this done properly."

Frezup nodded sharply and called out to Dunmaris. "Take four of our brothers and escort our generous host."

As Adenus waved his hand from the window, the three dealers gathered themselves. The largest one handed his portable gambling table to one of the other dealers and retrieved a coin chest from the back of the carriage while the smaller of the three headed directly for the front door.

Dunmaris scanned the room, his eyes settling on Herodin and a few others. Before he could finish calling them forward, Herodin's face suddenly twisted in distress. The grimalkin held up a hand, his fur standing on end as he bolted for a side room, retching sounds following in his wake.

One of the other Talons, a scarred human who had been eyeing the dealers with particular interest, stumbled dramatically, wine sloshing from his cup. "Can't hold his bloody drink!" he announced with an exaggerated laugh before slumping against a wall. "We'll get him straight." The man grabbed another Talon and pulled him with him to the side room with Herodin.

Dunmaris growled in annoyance, grabbing a few other Talons to replace three drunkards. "Useless fucks," he muttered. He couldn't fathom how in the Hells that cursed cat man had managed to come through his previous mission unscathed.

As the group descended the mansion's grand staircase, the three masked dealers passed them going up. One of them was notably larger than the others, his broad shoulders perfectly suited for carrying the coin chest.

A younger Talon, fresh enough to still speak without thinking, nudged his companion. "Look at the size of that bastard," he whispered, though not quietly enough. "Might want to find a different profession."

Dunmaris cuffed him sharply across the back of the head. "Keep your observations to yourself," he hissed, though his own hand had drifted closer to his weapon.

Adenus laughed softly. "That dealer's mind is half shattered, half genius. Great with numbers but atrocious with everything else."

Zunibar barely seemed to notice the exchange, his attention fixed firmly on the front door and what waited beyond it. His fingers flexed unconsciously, already imagining them wrapped around Kasha's throat.

The group came to a halt several paces from the carriage, the night air carrying the coppery scent of fresh blood. Adenus turned to face Zunibar and placed his hands elegantly behind his back.

"Now, to that change of heart you inquired about upstairs," Adenus's voice remained sweet but now had a hint of an edge.

Zunibar barely seemed to hear him, his attention fixed on the hooded figure with red skin. Her gentle sobbing carried on the night breeze, and his massive hands clenched into fists at his sides. After years of searching, she was finally within his grasp again.

"Our dear Ms. Volstruk," Adenus continued, his tone of disappointment evident, "decided to test my patience on her very first night of operation. Skimming from my tables. Can you imagine?" He clicked his tongue in disapproval. "I would almost admire the audacity if I wasn't so thoroughly insulted."

The troll's eyes finally snapped to Adenus, narrowing with sudden understanding. "The gaming tables you had arranged to put in her establishment?"

"Precisely." Adenus smoothed an invisible wrinkle from his sleeve. "No one crosses the Gauntlet. Not without consequences. Even the ones I am fond of." His eyes gleamed with foreboding in the lamplight as he studied Zunibar's reaction. "However, I see an opportunity here. The same arrangement I had with her. Two tables and fifteen percent of the profits. That could transfer quite easily to you, as the property's new owner."

Zunibar didn't even pause to consider. "Done," he said, his voice dripping with lusty anticipation as his gaze returned to the hooded figure. "Now, if we're finished with the negotiations..."

"Of course," Adenus said with a slight bow. "She's all yours." He gestured to his men near the carriage. "Though I should mention, she did put up quite a fight. My men had to be... forceful in subduing her, and that brute she keeps with her, well, a few of my men will not be able to enjoy fine foods for a while."

The troll's laugh rumbled through the courtyard like distant thunder. "Good. I prefer them with spirit. Makes breaking them all the more satisfying." He took a step toward the carriage, his hulking shoulders straightening with excitement.

Behind him, Adenus smirked in a manner that would give even the most hardened criminal pause for thought.

Zunibar's hand engulfed the hood, yanking it back to reveal Kasha's face. A dark purple bruise bloomed around her right eye, the skin swollen and angry. His lips pulled back in a predatory grin as he studied her features, drinking in the mixture of defiance and fear in her gaze.

"Just like your mother," he rumbled, his breath hot against her face. "Though she never had quite the same fire in her eyes. I do hope you're a better fuck than she was." His tongue flicked across his lips, making the words even more obscene.

A pained groan drew their attention. The hooded figure on his knees struggled to rise, muscles straining against themselves. Even through obvious agony, he tried to move toward Kasha, his shoulders trembling with the effort.

"Ah yes, her protector," Adenus groaned. "My men had to get rather creative with his kneecaps. Amazing what a few well-placed hammer strikes can accomplish."

Zunibar's eyes gleamed with cruel amusement. He jerked his chin toward Dunmaris. "Let's see what's left of him."

"Parzin," Dunmaris barked at the orc, his face still a wreck from the assault from Egrim and Kasha earlier in the evening. "Remove the hood."

He smiled even though it caused him significant pain. "With plea-sure, boss."

Kasha thrashed against Zunibar's grip as the troll's fingers found the cloth gag in her mouth. He pulled it free with deliberate slowness, savoring the moment. The instant it cleared her lips, she gathered what moisture she could and spat directly into his face.

The glob of saliva struck his cheek, drawing surprised inhales from the watching Talons. Tears streamed down Kasha's face, but her eyes burned with hatred as she glared up at her tormentor.

Zunibar's laugh started low in his chest, a rumbling sound that grew until it echoed off the mansion's walls. Without warning, his hand shot out, catching Kasha across the face with a crack that seemed to split the night air. The force of the blow snapped her head to the side, fresh blood trickling from the corner of her mouth.

"Oh yes," Zunibar purred, grabbing her chin and forcing her to look at him. "You'll do nicely. We have so much lost time to make up for."

INSIDE THE MANSION

Authern watched the Gauntlet dealers set up their tables with meticulous care. Each chose a different corner of the dining room, creating a perfect triangle of gambling opportunities for his increasingly inebriated crew. A smirk danced across his tattooed features as he considered how far the mighty Adenus had fallen. The dark elf's capitulation felt sweeter than the aged wine in his glass.

The largest of the dealers, the one Adenus had called "half-shattered," fumbled with his cards in an almost comical fashion. The display only reinforced Authern's sense of superiority. Even the Gauntlet's best aren't what they used to be.

Around the room, Lance men and women had given themselves over to celebration with abandon. Their usual discipline had eroded under waves of alcohol and victory. One of his lieutenants attempted to demonstrate a sword technique, nearly impaling herself on a decorative suit of armor. The resulting crash of metal drew raucous laughter from her companions and Authern was thankful that Zunibar wasn't inside to complain about the suit of armor that was now in pieces.

Berekr seemed to be orchestrating the chaos with particular glee, his right hand moving about as though he directed everything. The rotund dwarf waddled between groups, topping off glasses and encouraging increasingly outrageous behavior. His face had grown red not from anger this time, but from the sheer joy of watching the revelry descend into debauchery at the expense of their temporary business partner.

As if to punctuate his disdain for their new partner, Berekr made an exaggerated stumble near a delicate crystal vase perched on an ornate pedestal by the hearth. His arms windmilled wildly, a display worthy of a street performer, before he "accidentally" sent the piece crashing to the floor. The sound of shattering crystal drew cheers from the drunken crowd. A few of the remaining Talons eyeballed the dwarf but seemed to care little for the damage he had caused. It seemed to Authern that Zunibar's own hired men barely cared for the troll either.

Authern fixed his lieutenant with a stern glare, one that was meant to rebuke him. But he couldn't maintain it, not when he shared Berekr's sentiment so completely. His gaze drifted back to the window, where Zunibar could still be seen in the courtyard below. A cold smile crossed his features as he imagined how simple it would be to eliminate the troll once his usefulness had run its course.

The Lance were killers, after all, and Zunibar was just another target waiting to be crossed off their list. For now, though, he would let him play his part in their little drama. The half-giant raised his glass in a mock toast to the window, knowing that soon enough, very soon, the troll's newly acquired mansion would have a different occupant.

One of the dealers called out, his voice carrying an odd timbre that seemed to draw the drunkest Lance members like moths to a flame to let the potential players know the games would begin shortly. Authern's smile widened. Let them gamble and drink. Soon enough, they'd have real work to do.

He briefly fantasized over his plans to take over the city. Which locations to hit first. How to best take down each one. Taking out Adenus first would be the smartest move, but Rosamunda would probably be the easiest to remove from power. Then there was which of the Kol'Theron companies to hire? There were twelve sanctioned companies in Kol'Theron. Never more and never less. The Half Boulder Horde was said to be brutal and revel in violence. They sounded like his kind of people. The Shattered Sisters were supposed to be experts in infiltration. The Iron Vow was said to be the newest and therefore most likely the cheapest. Not that the coin mattered too much since he wasn't the one footing the bill up front. Then there was the Bloody Ale Company, one of the oldest of the companies and said to operate more like a small military. Authern closed his eyes and sighed, forcing himself to stop planning for the moment and get back to enjoying himself.

While the largest and smallest of the dealers began finishing the finer touches of their tables the other approached Authern and spoke with a rasp in his voice. "Please excuse me Lance Authern, how many will we be serving tonight? Gauntlet Adenus gave us instructions to hand out the gold to each person individually."

"Are you asking me for a damned headcount?" Authern said with a hardened stare. The dealer shifted, but not backward as Authern would have expected. The Lance made a mental note to either steal this man from the Gauntlet or kill him for having such a backbone.

The dealer just repeated himself, "How many will we be serving tonight?"

Authern kept his eyes glued on the slits in the dealer's mask as he sipped his wine. "Why do you all wear those ridiculous masks? Was it so common beforehand for gamblers to find you lot in an alley later and gut you all for poor betting practices?"

The dealer remained still and Authern briefly wondered if there was a fire in the man's eyes. Satisfied with goading the man to this point he relented. "Twenty-three of my men." Just then Herodin and two other Talons came back from the side room, wiping their faces of vomit. "Those three useless fucks over there and however many of

Zunibar's other cutthroats followed him outside like good little dogs. Now, bother me again and I'll relieve you of your bowels and send them back to your master in a bag."

With a slow bow the dealer turned around and made his way to the chest. He only made it through the first three Lance members before the procedure was thrown out the window as they all rushed the chest and began to just grab what they could of the stash. The dealer stepped back in clear annoyance at the turn of events.

It was only a few minutes later that the dealers began to start their games. The players seemed to be almost evenly split between the three tables. The largest dealer began the first round of the dicing table. While the dealer that had attempted to hand out the gold finished the setup of the roulette table and was letting two of the Lance men argue over whether red or black stood a better chance of being the winning color.

At the card table, the smallest of the masked dealers shuffled the first deck of cards. Her physique was small but feminine and her movements quick and efficient. Berekr stumbled over, his face so flushed he looked damn near red skinned. He planted his stocky frame directly across from the dealer, leaning forward with what he clearly thought was charm.

"Well now, aren't you a tiny thing," Berekr slurred, his eyes roving over the dealer's masked face. "Bet you're pretty under there. Why don't you show old Berekr what you're hiding?"

The dealer remained silent, continuing to shuffle. Her hands never faltered despite the dwarf's increasingly lewd suggestions.

Herodin approached unsteadily from the main dining table with another glass of wine, his fur still damp from washing his face. He caught the subtle tension in the dealer's shoulders as Berekr's comments grew more explicit and threatening.

"How about a game?" Herodin interrupted, his ear twitching as he positioned himself between Berekr and the dealer. "Wyvern Red Eye, perhaps?"

"Piss off, cat," Berekr growled, shoving Herodin aside. "Can't you see I'm working my magic here?" He turned back to the dealer, his voice dropping to what he probably thought was a seductive whisper. "Don't worry about later, love. I won't hurt you much if you cooperate, but those under garments will be coming off one way or another."

The dealer's hands stilled for just a moment before resuming their shuffling.

"Magic?" Herodin snorted, loud enough to deliberately draw attention. "Is that what you call it? Last I heard, your 'magic wand' couldn't even cast a simple raising spell anymore."

Several nearby Lance men burst into laughter. Berekr's face darkened to a dangerous shade of purple as he spun to face Herodin.

"You mangy little shit," he snarled, spittle flying from his lips. "I'll take every coin you've got and then I'll take your nine lives one by one."

Herodin's whiskers twitched with amusement. "Big words from a small man with performance issues. Care to back them up?"

The dealer began laying out cards swiftly, her movements suggesting she'd rather be anywhere else but trapped at this table between the two antagonists.

"Prick spittle," Berekr spat, slamming his pile of newly acquired gold onto the table. "I'm going to enjoy this almost as much as I'll enjoy this one's cunt later." He leered at the dealer again, who somehow managed to maintain her professional composure despite the Berekr's vile implications.

Herodin settled into his chair, positioning himself to keep the dealer partially shielded from Berekr's view. His casual demeanor belied the tension in his shoulders as he prepared for what was surely going to unfold momentarily.

Herodin stared at his cards in disbelief as the dealer revealed the winning hand. Half of his newly acquired gold slid across the table toward Berekr's greedy fingers. The dwarf's laughter echoed through the dining hall as he scooped up his winnings.

"Look at that," Berekr crowed, his words slurring worse with his excitement. "The pussy lost to the better man." His beady eyes shifted to the masked dealer. "Though I bet you helped me win, didn't you sweetheart? Can't stop thinking about what it'll be like later when I bury my face between those lovely thighs of yours. Are they milky pale or dark like the sweetest chocolate?"

The dealer's hands trembled slightly as they collected the cards, but they maintained their silence. Herodin's tail twitched indignation.

"Please," the grimalkin scoffed, his whiskers quivering. "The only thing that face of yours should be buried between is the pages of a book on proper hygiene. Though I doubt you can read, so perhaps that's a lost cause."

Those around the card table grew quieter as Berekr's hands griped the table. The dwarf pushed his chair back, scraping against the floor as he rose to his full, if unimpressive, height.

"What did you say to me, you mangy little shit?" Berekr's hands twitched toward his dagger.

Herodin's ears flattened against his head as he held up his hands in mock surrender. "Perhaps I went too far," he said quickly, though his tone carried more amusement than actual contrition. "How about we make it even? One more hand, all or nothing?"

From his position near the window, Authern's eyes narrowed as he observed the exchange. Something about Herodin's demeanor had just changed. The stumbling drunk from earlier had been replaced by someone far more focused, his movements intentional despite his theatrical display of submission.

The half-giant's gaze swept the room, seeking out the other two Talons who had helped Herodin earlier. He found them, and to his surprise three more of them that he hadn't seen present earlier, standing near the main dining table, their attention fixed on the elaborate spread of food with unusual intensity. Their hands picked at the various plates with disinterest, as if they were waiting for something.

Authern's fingers tightened around his wine glass as pieces of a puzzle he couldn't quite see began to shift in his mind. But before he could pursue the thought further, Berekr's voice boomed across the room.

"All or nothing?" the dwarf sneered, dropping back into his chair. "I'm going to enjoy taking everything you have, pussycat. Then maybe I'll let you watch what happens next with our lovely dealer here."

Herodin pushed his remaining coins across the betting surface with deliberate slowness, his earlier drunken facade falling away like autumn leaves. He held up a single finger, his eyes locked onto Berekr's reddened face. "Actually, I'd like to sweeten the pot." His voice stone-cold sober.

The change in the grimalkin's demeanor was so stark that even through his drunken haze, Berekr felt the first stirrings of unease. Herodin's eyes dilated fully, taking on a predatory gleam that seemed entirely too sober, too focused.

"I have something worth more gold than everyone at this table combined," Herodin said, reaching slowly into his coat. The movement drew every eye in the immediate vicinity.

When his hand emerged, it held an intricate device of polished metals and finished void gems that he placed carefully in front of the masked dealer. The arcabus gleamed in the lamplight, its void ore chamber pulsing with an ethereal purple glow.

Berekr's alcohol-addled mind struggled to process what he was seeing, but before he could fully grasp the significance, the dealer's small hands wrapped around the weapon with intimate familiarity. The mask fell away, revealing Arialyn's fierce purple eyes and satisfied smile.

The arcabus discharged with a sound like crystal shattering. Where Berekr's head had been, there was now only a fine red mist that painted the faces of the man behind him. His body remained upright for a moment, wine glass still clutched in his stubby fingers, before toppling backward with a meaty thud.

In the heartbeat of stunned silence that followed, the largest dealer quickly rolled his shoulders and flicked his wrist. The Hangman's Spear materialized in Callus's grasp with a whisper of death, and in one fluid motion, he drove it through the chests of two Lance men who had been reaching for their weapons. Their bodies slid from the shaft with wet sounds that were lost in the sound of the attendees realizing they were under attack.

At the third table, the last dealer pulled his mask off and glared into the eyes of Authern. Authern's face somehow managed to become even more shocked by the sight of Guard Captain Ethan.

The captain yanked his table back toward him onto its side while pulling a concealed cord that had been hidden under the roulette wheel. Flames erupted from hidden chambers that rested underneath it, engulfing eight Lance men in an inferno of alchemical fire. Their screams filled the room as they thrashed and burned. One of the Talons tossed a sword through the air, and Ethan caught it, immediately spinning to separate another Lance man's head from his shoulders.

Back at Callus's position, his finger found a small switch beneath his table's edge. He spared the quickest look of total infatuation at Arialyn for the genius creations she had hastily produced for the event before he dove away as the device detonated with thunderous force. Metallic shrapnel and splinters peppered screaming Lance members in every direction.

Chapter Thirty-One

FUNERALS & RESURRECTIONS

Kordra 8:32pm

"What do you say, Callus?" Alejak held his hand out. "Shake on it?"

Callus stared at the outstretched hand, his jaw clenched tight enough to crack stone. Every instinct screamed at him to end Alejak right there, to feel the satisfying snap of the man's throat beneath his fingers. But the deed to their shop, their home, hung in the balance. More importantly, the threat to Arialyn's security and happiness stayed his hand.

He caught Arialyn's eyes briefly. The slight nod she gave him carried what felt like years of shared understanding. They'd survived worse, and they'd survive this too. But Alejak? He'd have to die when this was done. No one threatened what was his and lived to gloat about it.

With deliberate slowness, Callus reached out and clasped Alejak's hand. In one fluid motion, he yanked him forward, twisting his arm at an angle that sent lightning bolts of pain through Alejak's shoulder. The hornless tiefling's eyes widened as ligaments stretched to their breaking point.

"Listen carefully," Callus growled low, his face inches from Alejak's. The scent of blood from the tiefling's broken nose filled Callus's nostrils. He inhaled it with deep satisfaction. "If I catch even a whisper of betrayal from you, I won't just kill you. I'll take you apart piece by piece. I'll make sure you stay conscious through every moment of it."

Alejak let out a strangled yelp, his previously cocksure composure cracking under the pressure. But then, remarkably, a smile spread across his bloodied face. It was an ugly thing, full of spite and calculation.

"My dear Hob," he managed through gritted teeth, "believe me when I say that my hatred for Zunibar and desire to see Authern's head decorating my office far outweigh any lingering animosity I might harbor toward you." His eyes glittered with malice. "You can trust in my self-interest, if nothing else."

Callus held the painful grip a moment longer, letting the threat sink in. Then he released Alejak's hand, watching with grim satisfaction as he massaged his abused shoulder.

"Now then," Alejak said, straightening his coat with his good arm, "shall we discuss the finer points of our arrangement? Time is rather of the essence."

Callus's eyes narrowed as a thought occurred to him. "Herodin, did they ask for proof?"

The grimalkin's fur bristled slightly, his tail going still. "Yes... they wanted bodies."

The emphasis on the plural didn't escape Callus's notice. His face darkened. "Bodies?"

Herodin's ears flattened against his skull as he chose his next words with extreme care. "They were... specific about the order of things." He swallowed hard. "We were supposed to make you watch while we killed her first."

The temperature in the room seemed to drop several degrees. Callus's hands clenched, his knuckles cracking audibly. The thought of Zunibar and Authern plotting Arialyn's torture and death made his vision blur red at the edges.

Arialyn's slender hand came to rest against his arm, the gentle pressure an anchor for him to seize hold of. Her fingers trembled slightly, but her touch was firm and reassuring. That simple contact was enough to quell the rage threatening to overwhelm his senses, pulling him back from the crimson haze that had started clouding his judgment.

Herodin's tail suddenly perked up, and his whiskers twitched with unexpected enthusiasm. "But you know, we've already got suitable replacements in the back room." He gestured toward the dead Lance members. "One bugbear and one halfling, courtesy of your earlier hospitality."

Callus and Alejak both brought their hands to their faces in simultaneous facepalms. Alejak immediately regretted the action, letting out a pained yelp as he jarred his broken nose. Callus couldn't help but laugh at the tiefling's misfortune. "Jackass."

"You do realize," Arialyn said, rolling her eyes, "that my love here isn't a bugbear, and I'm certainly not a halfling?"

Herodin shrugged, his whiskers twitching with amusement. "Well, no. But they didn't specify what condition the bodies needed to be in." A predatory grin spread across his feline features. "We burn the bugbear until his fur's gone, mess up his face real proper-like. And since they wanted you tortured anyway," he nodded to Arialyn, "we've got free rein to make that halfling completely unrecognizable."

Arialyn's eyes lit up with sudden inspiration. "I've got Callus's old braces upstairs. If we attach those to the bugbear and damage him appropriately..." She trailed off, her mind already working through the technical details.

"That..." Callus said slowly, "might actually work."

Alejak dabbed at his nose with the now thoroughly bloodied handkerchief. "A delightfully gruesome plan for getting the Talons back into my mansion without the need for a more discerning look, but what of the rest of us? I assume you have something equally devious in that tactical mind of yours?"

Callus's expression remained stoic as he considered his next words. "I do. But it involves asking someone to play very loose with their own rules."

"Are you going to enlighten the rest of the class?" Alejak's theatrical tone had returned, though somewhat nasally.

"No." Callus said plainly before he turned to Herodin, who visibly flinched at the sudden attention. "We need to make this place look like there was a proper fight. Something that shows how you lot got the upper hand."

Herodin's whiskers twitched nervously. "What's the story then?"

"Tell them you found us sleeping. That's how you managed to get the drop on us." Callus's voice was flat, matter-of-fact.

A grunt escaped Alejak's throat, fresh blood trickling down his chin. "My dear brute, even Zunibar isn't dim enough to believe that explanation. Not with the number of Lance corpses decorating your floor."

Before Callus could respond, Arialyn stepped forward. "The last two people who underestimated us were far more threatening than you lot." Her eyes flickered meaningfully to a spot just outside the shop's entrance. "They died right there on the streets."

A heavy silence fell over the room as Alejak processed her words. His cocky mask faltered for a moment as he recalled the stories he'd heard about Lindri and Raseg's deaths. He gave an elaborate bow, though the effect was somewhat diminished by his blood-stained clothing. "Fair enough, my lady. Far be it from me to question the capabilities of Yonara's most charming arcanomancer."

Callus shouldered the Hangman's Spear and fixed Herodin with a stern look. "You're coming with me to my next stop. You'll need to understand the full scope of what we're planning."

The grimalkin's tail drooped slightly. "I was afraid you'd say that."

"Good," A predatory grin spread across Callus's face. "That means you might be smart enough to survive what comes next."

Alejak nodded steadily, knocking a clot of blood from one of his nostrils. "Well then, I say we get moving." His voice fell flat and it seemed to him that all of the Talons had already decided Callus was in charge of the entire affair.

Callus smirked. "Everyone ready? Make it look good. Shit, wait." He quickly jogged to the workshop and returned with a jar of some sort of reddish-pink fluid. It was thick and didn't look much like blood but would pass for it in the dark of night for anyone out in the street that happened to see what was about to go down.

Everyone moved to react and then swiftly paused when Arialyn aimed her arcabus at Herodin. "Anything that gets destroyed in my shop comes out of your share of the take. Understand. With interest."

Herodin looked around at the shelves and noted how everything they contained seemed very expensive but agreed reluctantly. "Yes ma'am."

Alejak whispered to Beetle through the roach under his coat. "Stay there and be ready to get me out of here quickly."

Through the two-way mirror of his private office, Adenus watched the bustling casino floor of the Lucky Talisman with raptor-like attention.

His eyes narrowed on a particular dicing table where a short-nosed goblin had been winning far too consistently for the past hour.

A soft moan escaped his lips as he observed the goblin's practiced sleight of hand. The sound had nothing to do with the high elf woman between his legs and everything to do with catching someone stupid enough to cheat in his establishment. He reached for the crystal talisman that hung around his neck, pressing it between two fingers.

"Table seven," he whispered into the crystal, his voice oozing with pleasure. "The goblin with the short nose. Loaded dice. Deal with it."

The woman's ministrations continued as Adenus watched one of his Gauntlet men approach the table. The man, a burly human with a slicked back mohawk, positioned himself perfectly behind the unsuspecting cheater. In one fluid motion, he brought his club down on the back of the goblin's head. The sound was lost in the general noise of the casino, but Adenus could practically feel the impact from his vantage point.

Another Gauntlet member, this one moving with smooth feminine grace, emptied the unconscious goblin's pockets while the first grabbed him by the belt. They dragged the limp body toward the back rooms where cheaters were 'dealt with' according to Gauntlet policy.

Adenus allowed himself another moan of pleasure, this time everything to do with the high elf between his legs. She stood gracefully, adjusting her Gauntlet colors with a flare that showed she knew exactly how talented she was. She untied her golden hair and let it fall back over her thin shoulders as she looked at him expectantly.

"Are you satisfied, Gauntlet Adenus?" she asked, her voice laced with a seductive melody.

Adenus reached out and pulled her close, pressing his lips to her forehead in a strange, almost paternal, gesture. "Take the rest of the day off, Sylvari. You've earned it. You can assist in the discipline of the goblin before you leave if you wish."

Sylvari smiled wide and with sinister intent, "You always know what to say to make a girl cream herself." She bowed slightly and left the office without another word, the door clicking shut behind her. Adenus returned his attention to the casino floor, already scanning for the next fool who thought they could outsmart the house. The Lucky Talisman always won in the end.

Adenus turned his attention to more pressing matters. The delicate balance of power in Hus'rokn was shifting, and he would need to act swiftly and decisively to ensure the Gauntlet's continued dominance. He reached for a stack of parchment on his desk, several reports detailing the recent movements and machinations of his rivals, Lance Authern and Shield Rosamunda.

He and Rosamunda had a long tenuous understanding with each other. Just as the original Three Warlords that founded the city had known, they knew the balance between the Three in Hus'rokn was paramount to its survival. The Lance's previous leader, Lance Wibbrem had also understood this. The original Three had known times were changing. Centuries of pillaging the Scarred Lands had left nearly nothing of worth in the land east of the Great Scar. They had thought to go west but the advanced weaponry of the Brightborn Kingdom would crush them.

At best, they could have hoped for a siege at one of their outlying outposts. However, the dwarves were geniuses of architecture and re-source management. The Three would have starved before those under siege. So, they settled and established Hus'rokn several centuries back.

To lure people to settle in the city, they devised a clever method of a mock three-party political system. The people could vote but in truth, the Three would always decide which of them would be the false figurehead and assume the title of Governor. They had planned the city's development step by step, adding puppet departments that mostly operated on their own but truly answered to whichever of the

Three it had made the most sense to have control of them. The most independent department had been the City Guard. They were originally meant to help maintain peace between the Three, but that responsibility died over the centuries. Now the City Guard's captain was installed by whoever was acting Governor at the time instead of by the people and their power over the Three was next to nil. Open warfare on the plains of the Scarred Lands turned into secret criminal enterprises hidden in the shadows of the city.

The recent mysterious resignation of Lance Wibbrem that led to the sudden change of Lance leadership to the new Lance, Authern, was a cause of concern to both Gauntlet Adenus and sitting Governor and Shield leader Rosamunda. Authern had been Wibbrem's second in command and even then, had been an unwieldy and power hungry 'donkey shit covered cock' as Rosamunda had once said.

Adenus and Rosamunda had met in secret a few times, exchanging information about Authern's movements behind the curtain, as it were. The Warlord's Compact stated in its very first clause that to ensure stability, no house could directly interfere with another. The fear being that eliminating one of the Three would cause an imbalance between the remaining two, each one worrying if their house was next. Open war in the streets would surely follow.

Adenus couldn't help but wonder lately if perhaps the old ways needed to be rewritten. He began to read through the reports on his desk, his sharp mind already formulating plans and counterstrategies. His eyes flickered to the hidden wall safe in the corner. Not for the first time in his eighty years of running the Gauntlet did he wonder if now was the time.

The Veiled Gauntlet protocol sat in that safe. A last resort he didn't want to use unless the situation became most dire. Or... if the right opportunities presented themselves. He wouldn't allow the Gauntlet to fall, and he would do whatever it took to protect his organization and the empire he had built within the walls of the Lucky Talisman Casino.

Adenus's eyes were beginning to cross on this current report of alleged demonic orgies in the sewers when a rhythmic coded pattern of knocks echoed from his office door. His fingers found the hidden button beneath his desk, and the door swung open to reveal Sylvari standing beside a hooded figure.

"Found a stray on my way out," Sylvari purred, her eyes glittering in the faint illumination as her lips curved upward. "Thought you might want to see him."

The hood fell back, revealing Captain Ethan's face covered in a mask of old dried blood and dirt. Adenus's usual mask of control nearly slipped at the change in the man's face and the deep shadows under his eyes. A darkness seemed to permeate the man's aura. He had never known the Guard Captain not to keep up his appearance in all the years he had been on Adenus's payroll. The Hus'rokn Guard was technically under the employ of all the Three, but Adenus had been the Governor that had appointed the young captain.

Adenus has taken a special interest in Ethan while he was in the academy. He was the right amount of starch ass and rebel to be of use, and in truth Ethan had somewhat befriended the dark elf. Adenus had even called him the thumb of the Gauntlet.

"You can tell someone everything is golden or be shoved uncomfortably up someone's ass." Were the actual words he had spoken to Ethan at his promotion.

"Come in," Adenus said, maintaining his composure as Sylvari closed the door behind the man.

Adenus gestured to the chair across from his desk. "Sit. You look like death warmed over."

"I'll stand. Is the room secure?" Ethan's voice was heavy in a way Adenus had never heard before.

Adenus let out a soft laugh. "You know it always is, Captain."

The look Ethan gave him spoke volumes. This wasn't the time for casual assurances. Something had gone terribly wrong, and Adenus needed to be absolutely certain they couldn't be overheard.

With a resigned sigh, Adenus settled into his chair and waved his hand toward an ornate crystal sphere sitting on a nearby bookshelf. The air around them shimmered as a nearly invisible dome of energy encased them. Ethan recognized the field, a powerful ward that would contain not just sound but any disturbance within. They could set off explosives inside and all anyone outside of the dome would notice would be a slight rumble of vibration.

"Now even the Progenitor could not hear us," Adenus said, his expression growing serious as he studied the captain's battered appearance. "What brings the Guard Captain to my door looking like he's been dragged through the muck and mire?"

The silence that followed felt heavy enough to crush stone. Ethan's hand unconsciously moved to the bandaged wound on his shoulder. His eyes held the edge of a haunted man that had undergone a major shift in his outlook on life. Adenus had seen this look several times in this life. More often than not it was when someone taken to the backroom finally resigned themselves to their fate. The eyes of a man that knows he is about to die and doesn't want to give his killer the satisfactory taste of fear was somethings he found most fascinating.

Ethan's eyes, however, carried the slightly different look of a man who has decided not to show the people he is going to kill the satisfaction of his own thrill in the deed. These were the dead eyes of a man who seeks vengeance and has resolved to do whatever is necessary to make it happen. These were dangerous eyes.

Ethan's words emerged calculated and icy, each syllable steeped in the bitterness of betrayal. He recounted how he, Serine, and three of his most trusted guards, so he had thought, had gone to investigate a missing caravan. His lip raised in a silent snarl when he spoke Hamlin's name.

"Hamlin sold us out," he said, his jaw clenching. "Bastard was on Authern's payroll the whole time. Leaked my involvement with Madame Volstruk's real estate affairs and I suspect my tighter alliance with you. Led us right into their trap."

Adenus leaned forward, resting his chin on steepled fingers as Ethan described how the Lance's men had later ambushed him and Serine in the Resurgence Wilds. How Serine had taken an arrow meant for him but still managed to help finish the assassins off.

"We pieced everything together before the attack," Ethan continued. "Authern's been meeting with a troll from the Helspires named Zunibar. The troll's got enough coin to bribe, buy and kill the people necessary before striking and or laying siege to the areas in Hus'rokn that would resist the longest. They're planning to take both you and Rosamunda out. I believe they will come for you first as the Gauntlet is the greater martial threat."

Adenus's eyes flickered to the wall safe where the Veiled Gauntlet protocol lay waiting. His worst fears confirmed, the weight of maintaining the delicate balance and traditions between the Three suddenly felt crushing.

"I'm taking Authern's head." Ethan stated as though the matter was already resolved.

Adenus's eyebrow raised with interest. "I am sorry for the loss of the Sergeant, Captain. However, taking the head of one of the Thr-" Before he could finish his thought another rhythmic pattern of knocks interrupted him. He cursed under his breath. "Rather popular today," he muttered, waving the arcane dome of silence away and reaching for the button beneath his desk. As the arcane silence dissipated, he added, "Stay alert, Captain."

The door swung open to reveal two cloaked figures standing beside Grokmar, the scarred Gauntlet orc who'd admitted Callus and Egrim the day of the brawl. The larger of the two figures pulled back his hood, revealing the hobgoblin's familiar face. The smaller figure remained covered, but Adenus could see the gray fur of a grimalkin beneath.

"Peculiar moment to arrive," Adenus remarked, a bewildered under-tone in his words. "I've just received some troubling news concerning a man you tried to assault several days ago, Lance Authern." He motioned them inside as his fingertips tapped pensively against the desktop.

Callus's eyes widened slightly at the sight of Ethan, alive but clearly changed. The Guard Captain's usual warm demeanor had been replaced by something nearly sinister, a shadow that seemed to hang over him like a burial shroud. Old blood matted his hair, and his clothes bore the telltale signs of recent combat.

"You're alive!"

Ethan gave Callus a weak smile and a slight nod that told Callus the answer to his next question. "The Sergeant?"

Ethan's hand moved to his belt, retrieving the familiar puzzle box. He tossed it to Callus with a slight shake of his head, his eyes holding to the burden of fresh loss. Callus caught it one-handed, noting immediately that it had been opened. He knew what had been inside, the note that told Ethan of Serine's true feelings for him. A great shame he had learned it all too late.

Callus nodded sadly, understanding all too well what it meant to lose someone close. "The Lance?" he asked, though it wasn't really a question.

Ethan's curt nod provided all the confirmation needed, along with an unspoken threat of the retribution to come.

"Before this touching reunion continues," Adenus cut in, each word measured with his characteristic exactness, "I'd like to know who your

feline friend is." His eyes fixed on the smaller cloaked figure with intensity. "I don't appreciate uninvited guests in my private office."

Callus raised his hand in a calming gesture. "Both of you, still your blades. A lot has changed, and you need to let me explain so that we have the greatest chance of success for what I have planned."

The grimalkin hesitated for a moment before pushing back his hood, revealing Herodin. The reaction was immediate. Ethan's face contorted with rage as he recognized one of the Talons. The mercenaries he knew worked for Zunibar, and by extension, Authern. He lunged forward, but Callus moved with an unsurprising speed for the Captain, positioning himself between them.

"He's with us," Callus said quickly, one hand pressed against Ethan's chest to hold him back. "Hold, my friend. I need you to hear me out on this."

The muscles in Ethan's jaw worked as he fought to contain himself, his hand already on the grip of his sword. But something in Callus's tone, the urgency, the implicit trust they had built, made him pause. The hobgoblin had earned that much respect from him over the last several months.

"This had better be good," Ethan growled, his eyes never leaving Herodin's nervous face. The grimalkin's tail twitched anxiously and he, held his hands up as he tried to make himself appear as non-threatening as possible.

Callus glanced around the office with a guarded expression. "Is the room secure?"

Adenus released an exasperated sigh and waved his hand at the crystal sphere once more. The familiar shimmer of arcane energy encased them again, though this time the elf's irritation was evident in the way the dome rippled into existence.

"I can only use that damned thing a few times a day. Now then," Adenus said, leaning back in his chair, "enlighten us as to why you're consorting with one of the Talons? A group of savages that I specifically banned from my establishment mind you."

Callus's gaze shifted between Ethan and Adenus. "The hornless tiefling you know as Alabaster Jakel?" He paused, noting how both men bristled at the name, as he knew they would. "His real name is Alejak. I met him years ago in Toz'Unro. He was an information broker and mediator there, ran a place called the Hornless Devil. He was a thorn in the side of the Talons of Misery back when I ran with them."

Ethan's brow furrowed, his hand still clutching the grip of his sword. "What's this information have to do with the Lance and Zunibar?"

"Everything," Callus replied, gesturing to Herodin. "Zunibar used the knowledge of you sweeping the purchase of Kasha's new building out from under Alejak to follow a trail that proved he was actually broke and therefore couldn't provide the Lance with the coin they were seeking from him. So, Zunibar got cozy with Authern, leaving Alejak with nothing but wounded pride and nearly an execution before we broke up their meeting." A grim smile crossed his face. "Now he wants them both dead, and he's not particular about how it happens."

Herodin's whiskers twitched nervously as all eyes turned to him. "Most of us Talons," he said, his voice careful and even, "we're sick of Zunibar treating us like his personal army. We signed on with the Talons, not some troll from the Helspires who thinks he can buy us outright and our current leadership is losing their damned minds."

"And the rest of the Talons?" Adenus asked.

"They'll follow whoever has the coin," Herodin admitted. "Callus will tell you, most of the Talons are new recruits. Only been around for the last several months. Only I, Frezup and Dunmaris were there when Callus was. Frezup and Dunmaris may be willing to be treated like servants and treat the rest of us as cannon fodder to be thrown into a suicide mission, but those that are following my lead on this have other plans. We have a different vision for what the Talons should be.

So, we'd rather take our chances grabbing what we can of Zunibar's fortune and disappearing than keep following his orders."

Callus noticed how Ethan's hand had finally moved away from his sword, though the Captain's eyes still held that soulless gleam. "So," Callus continued, "we have a chance to solve several problems at once. But we'll need a way into the Alejak's old place. They are holding a celebration there right now. Now that you're here Captain, we can add your sword I am certain. Adenus, any chance you would want to bend the rules of the Warlord Compact a little?"

Adenus's lips curved mischievously as his fingers drummed thoughtfully on his desk. "Now that," he said, his eyes drifting to the wall safe, "is an interesting proposition indeed. What do you propose?"

Herodin looked at Callus for permission to proceed. With a nod, he did. "They sent us and some of the Lance to kill Callus and his lady."

Callus glared at him. "Arialyn."

Herodin cleared his throat and restarted with a squeak. "Yes, sorry. Arialyn. But Alejak found me before we headed there and told me his proposition. So, when we arrived at the Amethyst Artificer, I scouted the place and told the Lance where to enter, making sure they would run into Arialyn's traps."

"Get to the bloody point." Ethan interrupted with exasperation.

"Yes, the point. Right 'O." He let out a nervous laugh. "Callus and Arialyn made short work of the Lance men which just drove my point home even further with the Talons that were there with me. Anyway, we have Lance bodies that we have made resemble the ruined corpses of Callus and Arialyn. That gets the Talons back into the mansion but that doesn't get the rest of the crew in."

Adenus and Ethan exchanged glances, a silent understanding passing between them. The Captain's shoulders slumped as he attempted to run a hand through his blood-matted hair.

"Short of storming the mansion with the city guard, I've got nothing on such short notice," Ethan said with heavy frustration. "And after Authern ordered my execution, I can't be sure who among the guard is still loyal." His hand unconsciously moved to the lock of Serine's hair at his belt.

Adenus rose from his chair with a groan, suddenly looking much older than he just had. He moved to a crystal decanter on a nearby shelf. The soft clink of glass on glass filled the silence as he poured himself some Elven Cherry Red. He returned to his seat, the leather creaking softly beneath him as he settled in with a weary sigh.

"Callus, I can see by the way you're standing that you already have a plan to get into the mansion and since you're here I know it involves me. So, let's hear it."

Callus bowed lightly. "Always a pleasure to have my genius acknowledged. All we need from you is two," he regarded Ethan, "make that three of your dealer's uniforms as well as three portable gaming tables that you won't mind not getting back. Oh, and the best thespian performance you can muster."

Adenus sat gravely still as they devised the full plan and weighed the odds that it would work as intended. By his estimations it actually seemed like a highly winnable scenario. He was a gambler after all. "So, it's settled. Tonight begins one of the biggest changes in Hus'rokn history. Does Madame Volstruk know of this plan yet?"

Callus shook his head. "And I can't be seen anywhere near there, just in case someone notices me."

Adenus nodded and sipped his wine. "I'll take care of it."

"Tell her I said thanks for the flower crown, and she'll know I sent you with the plan." Callus then tapped Herodin on the shoulder and the pair pulled their hoods back up and exited the office.

Adenus poured another glass and pushed it across the desk toward Ethan. "That grimalkin is riddled with anxiety."

Ethan glanced at the wine but didn't move. Adenus raised his glass. "At least partake in a toast to the memory of Sergeant Serine with me. Plus, you'll want to sit down with what I am about to show you."

The Captain relented and eased himself into the chair opposite the desk. They held their glasses up in a moment of silence and then tapped them together before downing the glasses entirely.

"By tomorrow," Ethan said with a razor sharp edge, "There won't be a Lance left in Hus'rokn. Not Authern, not his snarky assed lieutenant Berekr, not even the bloody stable boys who muck their horses."

"My dear Captain, if you aren't careful, I may become fully erect."

Ethan ignored the statement. "Serine once told me I couldn't keep living half in and half out of your world. She said I needed to become a true Guard Captain or step fully into the world of crime. True law enforcement can never occur in this city. It wasn't built that way. The best thing I can do is try and manage it from the other side. Better the devil you know than the one you don't."

Adenus nodded in approval with look of satisfaction. Ethan had played his role as captain well. He had been exactly what Adenus and the city needed, the happy mask that covered the scared monster beneath. Times were changing, however, and if they were going to survive them then Ethan needed to be something else entirely.

Adenus began to pour another glass and then stopped as he looked at the hidden wall vault again. "The time is finally right I believe." He pushed the bottle toward Ethan. "You're going to need another sip or two of this.

He then moved to the large solid wood bookcase in the corner. With a few hidden movements that Ethan wasn't able to follow, a small door swung open and out from it Adenus pulled a thick black book.

He set it down in front of the Captain, so it faced him when he opened it. "Read the first page and then let's talk about the future."

Ethan frowned, picking up the book. His eyes trailed across the page, his expression changing. By the time he finished he was smiling.

LANCE CAPTAIN

Kordra 11:10pm
INSIDE THE MANSION

Herodin lunged forward, his claws digging into the polished wood as he helped Arialyn flip the portable table. The sound of splintering furniture and screaming filled the dining hall as they took cover behind their makeshift barrier. The acrid smell of alchemical fire from Ethan's table mixed with the metallic tang of fresh blood from those torn apart by Callus's shrapnel.

"I love a good entrance," Herodin said, his ears flinching at the chaos around them. "But I'd like some credit for the assist with Berekr."

Arialyn's arcabus hummed with power as she took aim at a Lance woman who was fumbling to draw her sword. "No one ever gives credit to the deliveryman." The weapon discharged with a crystalline crack, and the woman collapsed with an arcane mist billowing from her chest. She flicked a gold coin from the floor at Herodin. "Here's your tip, though."

Across the room, the five Talons who had pledged themselves to Herodin's plan sprang into action. They had positioned themselves perfectly during the gambling, and now they carved through the stunned Lance members with brutality. The Lance fighters, many of them still processing the shock of seeing the dead walk and fighting, struggled to mount any kind of coordinated defense. Per their trade, most were well trained assassins, but their art was one drawn best when they were delivering the surprise and not the other way around. This was something Callus had planned on. In his experience, assassins never did well when they started off on their back foot.

The Hobgoblin Reaver bent at the knees and ducked backward to avoid an axe swing aimed at this chest. He brought the butt of the spear around and slammed it into the attackers temple, knocking him out cold. There was a quick correction of posture, a thrust to the side followed by a spinning elbow and slash with the edge of the spear blade before Callus slammed his boot into the neck of the one he'd knocked unconscious a split second ago. Just like that, three more bodies lay around the retired gladiator. He turned just in time to hurl the spear at a Lance man aiming a crossbow at Arialyn. It tore through the man's chest and stuck in the wall behind him before vanishing and reappearing in his hand.

The bolt had come loose before the man died, however, but the spear had forced the man's aim to shift. Herodin ducked as the crossbow bolt whistled past his ear. He took in a large breath before eyeing Arialyn. "I don't suppose you could make one of those fancy arc-aboom-ajigs for a new friend?" His eyes dilating to the their visible edges from the massive adrenaline dump of the fight.

"You can't afford it," she promised, her purple eyes gleaming as she sighted another target. "And 'friend' is pushing it by far."

A Lance fighter charged their position, sword raised high. His steps were unsteady from the wine he'd consumed earlier, and his eyes were wide with panic. Herodin popped up from behind the table. His blade found the gap between the fools ribs. "Don't suppose you'd help me get my scattered gold from the floor after this is over, then?" He smirked, letting the body fall. "Is that something a 'not friend' might do?"

Arialyn's reply was cut short as more Lance members rushed their position. She fired twice in rapid succession. The first shot tore through a man's upper leg, sending him sprawling to the floor screaming in agony. The second clipped the shoulder armor of a Lance orc and ricocheted above the hearth. She groaned with disappointment and grabbed a small spherical object from the underside of the overturned table. "These, on the other hand, can be yours for just twenty gold a piece."

She hurled it at the charging orc's face. The orb had been made of glass and shattered on impact. A greasy oil caked on the orc's face and then suddenly ignited in flames.

Herodin's eyes went wide, and his whiskers twitched with morbid curiosity. "Diabolical. I'll take three."

Across the room, Ethan ducked low and rolled to avoid a high swipe from a mace, his blade cut through the air and sliced cleanly through the back of the Lance woman's knee. Her scream of torment was cut short as Callus's spear erupted through her neck in a spray of crimson. The hobgoblin yanked his weapon free with savage force, blood and viscera spraying across his face as he pivoted toward their true target.

The spiral on his Hanged One gifted Ring of Anguish pulsed with orange light as it channeled its power. Three orange beams of necrotic energy lanced through the air toward Authern, but the half-giant was agile for his size. He dipped to the side, the deadly arcane bolts scorching the wall behind him.

"Getting slow in your retir-," Authern taunted, before a sudden dagger slicing through his calf transformed his mockery into a pained gasp. He whirled to see the captain, brow furrowed in concentration, lunge in and managed to get another slice in before Authern brought the pommel end of his great axe across in an arc. The impact caught

Ethan in the ribs and sent him hurling into the nearby wall, knocking loose a body sized portion of plaster.

Proud of the distraction he'd caused for the Captain and the expertise he saw in the sly maneuver, Callus caught the movement at his side too late. Two throwing knives came flying in his direction. One blade skittered harmlessly off the edge of his shoulder, but the second buried itself deep in the meat of his lower back.

Before he could process the pain, a weight slammed into him from behind. Frezup's momentum carried them both through the closed door of a neighboring room, the Hangman's Spear clattering from Callus's grip before vanishing in a whisper of shadow. They rolled across the blood-slicked floor, each fighting for dominance.

Frezup's dagger glinted in the firelight as he tried to drive it toward Callus's throat, but Callus caught his wrist, straining against the Talon leader's surprising strength. His other hand, adorned with the Ring of Anguish, was similarly locked in Frezup's iron grip. Callus cursed, "I see you're still addicted to those little strength potions you loved so much. Don't they make your balls shrink?"

"Nice trinkets you've picked up," Frezup snarled through clenched teeth, ignoring the verbal barb. His eyes darted between Callus's ring and where the spear had vanished. "Don't remember you having such fancy toys when you were one of us. New friends in high places?"

Callus headbutt him in the nose, drawing a flood of blood from Frezup's face. "You wouldn't believe me if I told you."

The headbutt threw Frezup off balance, and Callus seized the opportunity, rolling on top of him.

"You fucking traitor," Frezup cursed, his face twisted with effort and streaming blood. "All this for some gnome whore."

Callus leaned in close, his voice growling low. "See, now I have to make this really hurt and for the sake of the Gods, can you assloads come up with something new to say?"

With a swift motion Callus shot his elbow down, separating Frezup's jaw from the rest of his skull. There was a gurgle of blood and Callus wrenched his hand free from and broke Frezup's arm in three places. Frezup reached up with his good hand and tried to claw at Callus's eyes. The Towering Tactician bit down on the hand and then repeated the process, breaking Frezup's remaining arm.

The Ring of Anguish flared with sudden light. Callus smiled through blood-stained teeth. "Even pumped up on potions you never stood a chance. Do people forget so easily the man I am? I am still Callus fucking Kordec."

With that, Callus slammed his fist into Frezup's face, the ring unleashing its necrotic energy point blank. The impact was devastating, Frezup's features immediately began to decay, flesh withering and blackening as the life drained from his eyes. The half elf's cries were brief but haunting in their pitched wailing. Within a handful of seconds, he was dead.

Callus pushed himself up from Frezup's corpse, his joints briefly protesting the movement. The knife in his lower back shifted painfully. He staggered slightly as he made his way back through the splintered doorframe into the main dining hall.

The scene before him was a masterpiece of carnage. Lance members lay scattered across the floor like broken dolls, their blood mixed with spilled wine and shattered glass. One of the allied Talons, he thought it might have been the young human woman that Herodin said joined up with them in the Helspires, lay face-down near the overturned card table, her neck bent at an unnatural angle.

The remaining four Talons and Herodin had formed a loose semicircle, weapons ready but not advancing. Their attention was fixed on the center of the room where Ethan and Authern faced each other like rival predators. The half-giant's massive greataxe gleamed wetly in the lamplight, while Ethan's sword oddly shook in his grip.

Callus straightened up, ignoring the fresh wave of pain from his back. The Hangman's Spear materialized in his grip as he stepped forward, its weight familiar and reassuring.

Authern looked at the Guard Capatin. "I'll have Adenus's head for this betrayal. This means open war in the streets. You realize that?"

"No war in the streets," Ethan said, his voice sharp with an edge that even Callus had never heard before. "Your men are dead. Those who weren't here tonight will understand what's coming or fall in the gutters. An inferno of change is coming, and you won't be around to watch what I build from its ashes."

A deep rumble of laughter echoed through the blood-stained dining hall. Authern's chest heaved with genuine amusement as he leveled his gaze at the Captain. "Is that what this charade is? Are you actually challenging me for the title of Lance?" He gestured around the carnage-filled room with his greataxe.

Ethan didn't dignify the question with a verbal response. The Captain lunged forward, his blade weaving a complex pattern designed to test Authern's defenses. The half-giant barely managed to bring his greataxe up in time, deflecting the probing attacks with the weapon's thick shaft.

The sound of steel on steel rang through the room as Ethan pressed his advantage, forcing Authern to give ground. The captain's face was a blank mask, each strike calculated. This wasn't the excitable young man who had once fanboyed over meeting Callus at the Trade Gate. That man had died in the Resurgence Wilds and with him all caution for his own life.

Arialyn's fingers tightened around her arcabus as she watched the deadly dance unfold. "Should we..." she whispered to Callus, leaving the question unfinished.

Callus shook his head slightly.

"Was this part of the plan? Ethan as Lance?" Arialyn asked, shocked at the change she saw in the Captain. He had been a blank slate when they met up before coming here but this was something greater. She realized just how much Serine friendship had been keeping this man alive.

Callus shook his head again. "I had a suspicion."

Authern's greataxe whistled through the air as Ethan pressed forward with another series of targeted strikes. The half-giant's initial surprise at the captain's skill had faded, replaced by a calculating focus that made his earlier fury seem like mere theater. He deflected each attack with near carelessness, his massive weapon moving gracefully.

"Your form is impressive," Authern remarked, his tone almost conversational as he parried another thrust. "But you telegraph your combinations. They weren't big on solo tactics in the academy, were they?"

The truth of those words became apparent as Authern suddenly shifted from defense to offense. His greataxe became a blur of motion, each swing moving with devastating power. Ethan backpedaled, his sword barely deflecting the onslaught. Sweat beaded on his forehead as the half-giant's superior reach forced him to give more ground.

"Getting tired, Captain?" Authern's blade crashed against Ethan's sword, the impact sending vibrations up the smaller man's arms. "Or perhaps realizing that playing soldier didn't prepare you for real combat?"

Ethan's face remained an impervious mask as Authern's next strike caught his blade at an awkward angle. The sword went spinning from his grip, clattering across the floor and sliding under an overturned chair. Instead of panic, though, a slight smile played at the corners of Ethan's mouth as he ducked beneath another powerful swing.

Callus shifted forward, preparing to save Ethan's life with the hangman's noose. He was already halfway through the mental summoning when he noticed the calm expression on the Captain's face. He ceased the summoning.

"Why do you find your impending death so amusing?" Authern growled, his axe cleaving through the air where Ethan's head had been moments before. "Planning to dodge until old age takes me?"

Ethan rolled away from another strike, his movements fluid despite the growing fatigue in his muscles. "You should be feeling it right about now."

Authern raised an eyebrow and took a confident step forward. The smirk on his face vanished instantly as his limbs refused to support his weight. His body crashed down onto one knee, the greataxe wavering in his suddenly unsteady grip.

Understanding dawned in his eyes as he turned his head and stared at the shallow cuts on his calf where Ethan's blade had sliced him at the beginning of the fight. The half-giant's mouth worked silently for a moment before he managed to rasp out, "Poison?"

"They also taught us how to properly assess our enemy in the academy," Ethan said casually, brushing debris from the dealer uniform as he retrieved his sword from beneath the overturned chair. "I knew I wasn't a match for you in single combat. The paralysis starts in the extremities." He approached Authern's kneeling form with slow measured steps. "But, by now, you probably can't even speak."

Authern's lips moved, but no sound emerged. The greataxe slipped from his nerveless fingers and clattered to the floor. Real fear crept into his eyes as he realized he couldn't move his arms or legs. He swayed precariously as the poison worked its way through his system.

"But here's the interesting part," Ethan continued with cold satisfaction. "The formula preserves all sensations. You'll feel everything. Serine would be disappointed in me for this. She could never abide torture. But she isn't here anymore. You saw to that." His blade flashed three times in quick succession, opening deep cuts across Authern's broad chest. "That hurt, didn't it?"

Blood soaked through Authern's leathers as he toppled backward onto his haunches, unable even to raise his arms in defense. His eyes, now the only part of him still under his control, widened in terror as Ethan's blade descended again and again.

The captain's movements were deliberately placed to cause maximum pain while avoiding immediately fatal wounds. Blood sprayed across the floor in crimson arcs as Ethan carved his revenge into Authern's flesh. Only Callus managed to not look away from the carnage. Finally, Ethan stepped back, watching dispassionately as the half-giant's life drained away.

"I'm sorry, Serine," Ethan whispered. The former Lance leader's eyes had grown glassy, fixed on some distant point as his body slumped further toward the floor.

Behind him, Callus watched in silence as the man who had once been an eager young guard captain methodically dismantled one of the most feared crime lords in Hus'rokn. The dining hall was quiet except for the wet sound of blood dripping onto polished wood and the ragged, weakening breaths of the dying Authern.

Ethan waited until Authern's last breath before severing his head from his body. His blade had become so damaged in his defense from the greataxe that it took him three strokes to get the head free.

Callus stepped up next to the guard captain. "Was this your plan all along? Taking his spot as Lance?"

Ethan nodded. "No more half in and half out." He moved to the balcony and pushed the door open. He held the head of Authern up and called out to the courtyard. "I have challenged and slain Lance Authern. I have earned the right to name myself Lance and acquire all the former Lance's assets."

Back inside Callus shook his head. "Something in him broke when they killed the Sergeant."

"He's still in there. I see it." Arialyn sighed. "You look like shit," she said, trying to mask her concern with humor.

Callus smirked, though it pulled at a fresh cut on his lip. "What, this?" He gestured vaguely at his blood-spattered uniform and the knife still protruding from his back. "Just a friendly chat with an old colleague. Not every fight has to end with me half-dead, you know. This is how things go when I have time to plan."

Arialyn's expression softened for a moment before hardening again as she noticed the wound. "Hold still, jackass." She moved behind him, examining the throwing knife with concerned eyes. "This is going to hurt."

"Everything always does with you, squirt," he replied. He immediately regretted the use of the nickname with a grunt as she yanked the blade free a little harder than necessary. "Though usually in more entertaining ways."

"Call me squirt again and I'll put it back where I found it."

Kordra 11:10pm
IN THE COURTYARD

It had taken everything Egrim had not to launch at Zunibar the second he saw him, but he had managed to hold back right up until the fucker slapped Kasha. Plan be damned, he was about to kick this show off on his own. So, it was a good thing that inside the mansion an explosion went off signaling the time was now.

Parzin, the Talon that Dunmaris had sent to take the hood off Egrim was the first of the men outside to have a taste of 'the plan.' There was a sickening crunch and wet gurgle from his throat as Egrim reacted and buried his fist into the man's throat. His fist was so large in comparison that he managed to strike his jaw, throat and top of his rib cage in one strike. All three shattered on impact.

Adenus used the opportunity to take five sharp steps back, putting him just outside the threshold of the gate to the estate and technically outside the threshold of responsibility in the affair. "Best of luck, Mr. Tolgar."

Zunibar's eyes went wide with the realization that this had all been a set up. He turned back to Kasha and the illusion of her bruised and battered face fell away. The mask of terror fell away as well, a facade she had played very well. It had been replaced with focused hatred.

"I'm not a scared little girl anymore." She raised her hands swiftly and drew a sigil in the air so rapidly that Zunibar barely saw her fingers move. A gout of flames erupted in his face.

Kasha's thrill of triumph was lessened significantly by the shimmering field that abruptly appeared and safeguarded Zunibar. He sneered at her with a smile breaking the corner of his mouth and tapped a finger against a ring on his left hand. "Perhaps not scared, but still a foolish morsel. Kill them." He didn't need to call out the command because the Talons and the Lance guards in the courtyard were already in motion.

A body of one of the Lance men went sailing over Zunibar's head as Egrim hurled him like a stone. The first man to get within ten feet of Kasha cried out breathlessly as a necrotic mist surrounded him. Beetle seemed to shimmer into existence behind the man. The sickly thin orc stuck a curved blade into the throat of the man. A crossbow bolt ricocheted off of the arcane force field around Zunibar, and he looked to the gateway to see Alejak cursing his misfortune.

"Peculiar companions you've selected, my sweet little strumpet." Zunibar muttered through clenched jaws, retreating several paces and permitting the fighters of the Talons and Lance to subdue the fools confronting him. "Teaming up with the copperless limp cocked fool that's been trying to kill you? Strange bedfellows indeed."

Ice spikes, crossbow bolts and the clash of metal on metal resounded off the walls of the mansion's courtyard. Egrim dodged to the side of a Lance member that was thrusting with a pike. He grabbed the haft just below the pike and chopped down with his other hand, snapping it in two before twirling around and slamming the pike tip through the man's sternum. He then used the man himself as an improvised weapon and swung him into a Talon woman that had attempted to slip in behind him with a shimmering blade. She took the hit and rolled with it, though her breath was lost from her.

Alejak rolled back and ducked against the outer wall of the estate to reload, cursing Zunibar's arcane shield.

Adenus waited for the tiefling to turn and fire back into the courtyard again before gently placing his foot to his back and pushing him in. "This must be done on the grounds Jakel or else I will have to intervene."

Alejak's bolt went wide of a Talon with the added forward momentum Adenus's boot had given him. He turned to the dark elf and sneered as Adenus closed the gate. A sword came for his head, and he yelped, ducking and rolling away before breaking into a flat sprint away from the bulk of the fighting. The Talon, a dwarven man, gave chase but the life left his body as a bloody mist was pulled from every orifice he had. It all surged directly to Beetle who laughed with an ear-piercing cackle.

Kasha marched forward, step by step, slinging spell after spell at Zunibar, sweat already coating her face. Each spell either bouncing away or dissipating as it hit his shield. Even still, the force of each spell pushed him backward a foot at a time. She was raging, screaming with the effort she put into every casting, every thought of what she was going to do to him once the shield failed driving her onward through her exhaustion.

Egrim tore a shield from the arm of a Lance man. The force of the pull brought the arm of the man with it as sinew and flesh tore away. He then used it to stove in the head of the Talon woman that had rolled away from him and began slipping in with a flurry of strikes. Her body fell limp before him. A volley of three arrows impaled themselves into his left shoulder blade, forcing him forward. He stepped on the Talon woman's corpse and lost his footing as her armor collapsed under the weight of his boot. He barrel rolled across the ground shattering the arrow shafts in his shoulder and grunting with the pain.

He rose to a standing position and felt his breath fleeing from his lungs, knowing that at least one of the arrows must have punctured his lung. Dunmaris was reloading another flight of arrows but was forced to abandon the effort when he noticed Egrim bellowing and charging at him with a speed that was definitely not possible for someone even half the man's size.

A flash of steel caught Kasha's eye as the last of the Talons loyal to Zunibar darted toward her, blade raised for a killing blow. She twisted away, but not quite fast enough feeling the dagger carve a burning line across her abdomen. Pain flared through her body as warm blood began seeping into the fabric of her dress.

The Talon's triumphant grin lasted only a moment. Kasha surged forward, closing the distance between them. Her fingers traced a complex pattern through the air as she gathered the last remnants of her arcane energy. Crystalline ice materialized beneath the Talon's chin. The spike punched through flesh and bone, erupting from the top of his skull in a spray of gore and frozen brain matter.

As the body crumpled, Kasha's legs gave out. She dropped to one knee, her breath coming in ragged gasps as exhaustion threatened to overwhelm her. Blood trickled between her fingers as she pressed against her dagger wound.

Across the courtyard, Beetle's haunting laughter echoed throughout the courtyard as he danced between three Lance soldiers. The first reached for his throat only to have his own hand turn black and wither before his eyes. The second managed two steps before collapsing, his skin growing translucent as necrotic energy drained the life from his body. The third backed away in horror, but threads of dark magic wrapped around his legs like hungry serpents. His scream cut off abruptly as his flesh began to rot and slough away from his bones.

Alejak scrambled backward, trying to put distance between himself and the chaos. His back hit the mansion wall as he fumbled to reload his crossbow. A Lance man charged toward him, longsword raised high. Alejak's fingers finally found purchase on the trigger mechanism. The bolt flew true, burying itself in the man's throat, but momentum carried the dying man forward.

The former information broker's triumphant cry turned into a startled "oof" as two hundred pounds of dead weight crashed into him. The impact drove him to the ground, pinning him beneath the corpse. Blood from the soldier's wound dripped onto Alejak's face and mouth. He clawed at the corpse fervently, attempting to wrestle himself free while spitting the man's blood from his mouth. "Get off me you lummox! There is no telling what whore diseases you have festering inside you!"

Egrim's charge carried the force of an avalanche, his massive frame bearing down on Dunmaris. The enemy hobgoblin's lips moved, forming an arcane word that seemed to slice through the air itself. In an instant, Dunmaris became a blur of motion, his form splitting and multiplying until five identical versions of him stood before Egrim.

With a roar of frustration, Egrim raised his arms to tackle what he hoped was the real Dunmaris. His bulk passed through the figure like smoke, the illusion dissipating around him. Dunmaris's blade found purchase in Egrim's left thigh, cutting muscle, sinew and scraping bone. Egrim felt a sharp pain like flames shoot through his leg and radiating down to his foot.

Egrim stumbled forward, his leg threatening to buckle beneath him. He caught himself, pivoting on his good leg to face the hobgoblin Talon. Blood ran freely down his thigh, but the wound wasn't arterial as Dunmaris had intended. "Tricky fucker," Egrim spat, his breath coming in ragged gasps.

His right eye suddenly flared with ethereal light, casting dull emerald shadows across his face. Dunmaris tilted his head at the display, genuine curiosity breaking through his anger. His multiple images shifted and danced, but to Egrim's enhanced sight, one held true color while the others were an odd monotone palette.

Egrim launched himself toward the leftmost Dunmaris, his movement telegraphing an obvious attack. Dunmaris's mouth curved into a slight smile, and he prepared to capitalize on the mistake. But at the last possible moment, Egrim planted his wounded leg and pivoted hard to the right.

The pain that shot through his thigh was worth it. His roundhouse kick caught the real Dunmaris square in the chest, the impact releasing a sound like thunder. The Talon Sergeant's eyes widened in shock as his feet left the ground. He sailed backward through the air, his illusory doubles vanishing like morning mist as his concentration shattered.

Dunmaris crashed into the courtyard wall several feet away, stones cracking under the force of the impact. He slumped forward, gasping for the breath that had been driven from his lungs. He could feel the shifting of broken ribs with each gasp. His hand still gripped his blade, but the arm trembled with the effort to hold it. It was then that he noticed the wrought iron protruding from his chest. Egrim's kick had driven him into the wall at just the right spot for his body to collide with one of the arcane lamp mounts on the inside of the exterior wall.

Blood pooled in his mouth, and he dropped his blade, feeling all of his strength leave him. He huffed in surprised amusement as his head lolled to the side, eyes now blank.

"Not so clever now. Prick?" Egrim growled, though he couldn't keep the pain from his voice as his leg protested the abuse. Blood continued to seep from the wound, but he forced himself to stay upright. He blinked rapidly, forcing the shimmer in his eye to fade.

Zunibar stalked toward Kasha, each footfall deliberate and menacing. He loomed over her kneeling figure, blocking out the light from the windows behind him. "Perhaps now that you've had your little outburst, you'll be more... amenable to our arrangement."

His hand shot out, fingers wrapping around her throat. She clawed at his grip as he lifted her off the ground, her feet dangling helplessly. Blood from her wound dripped onto his forearm causing him to grimace in distaste.

"We could have saved the bloodshed for later. I'm going to enjoy breaking you." His fetid breath washed over her face. "Going to make you beg for death before I'm done using that sweet little body of yours." Kasha's eyes rolled into the back of her head as she began to lose consciousness.

Behind him, Alejak crept forward through the bodies of the courtyard, a dagger gleaming in his hand. He kept his steps smooth and calculated as he closed the distance.

Across the courtyard, Egrim's head snapped up at Kasha's strangled gasp. The sight of her suspended in Zunibar's grasp sent a wave of renewed fury through his blood. His injuries shrieked in objection as he forced himself upright, crimson seeping like several small creeks from his shoulder and thigh.

"I'm sorry," he whispered, his voice barely audible over the sound of his thundering heart. "I have no choice."

Green fire erupted from his eye and silver light began to shimmer at the center of his chest. Power flooded his limbs, washing away pain and exhaustion in a tide of desperate strength. The courtyard stones cracked beneath his feet as he propelled himself forward with unnatural speed.

Zunibar's eyes widened as Egrim hurtled through the air toward him. The troll barely had time to register the sight before Egrim's emerald-wreathed fist connected with his face. There was a sound like glass shattering mixed with a thunderclap as Zunibar's arcane shield overloaded.

The resulting explosion of arcane energy hurled everyone nearby through the air. Egrim and Alejak crashed into the mansion wall with bone-jarring force before tumbling down between it and the overly large decorative hedges. Kasha was thrown backward, her body slamming against the iron gate with enough force to bend the metal, though the shock of it forced her mind to reawaken. Beetle's thin frame cartwheeled through the air before crashing into the mansion's front steps with a wet thud.

For a moment, all was silent except for the soft patter of blood dripping onto stone and the crackle of residual arcane energy in the air. Then, from somewhere in the darkness came the sound of Zunibar's laughter, wet and gurgling, but unmistakably alive.

Adenus squatted down behind Kasha on the other side of the gate. He was peering over her shoulder, enjoying the sight of Zunibar Tolgar on his knees and knuckles panting for breath. "Ms. Volstruk, I would hate for you to miss this opportunity for revenge, and the missed revenue from my tables at your establishment of course. Surely, you've got a second wind in there somewhere, right?"

She huffed and sucked a bit of blood from her swollen lip before spitting it to the cobblestone walkway. "Gauntlet Adenus,"

"Yes, my Lady?"

"Kindly shut the fuck up."

"That's the spirit."

Egrim's eyes jolted open. "Fuck." He groaned through clenched teeth. Turning over and coming to rest on all fours, he could just barely see under the bottom leaves of the hedges. Kasha was slowly rising to her feet with a wobble, Zunibar slumped over on hands and knees.

"What in the Hells?" Alejak muttered to Egrim left.

The large man shifted his head, feeling a crack in his neck as he did so. Alejak wasn't staring at the scene before them. He was looking Egrim up and down. Egrim's brow furrowed in confusion. A confusion that promptly left his mind when he noticed the green tint of his hand in the dirt. He looked down at his chest and quickly pulled a sliver of the shattered arcane shield from something hard that lay beneath his flesh.

"You're an... how is that poss-" Alejak's voice was cut off by the massive hands that almost instantly surrounded his neck. His eyes began to bulge in terror and then from extreme pressure.

"I was supposed to wait until you gave the deed back to Arialyn. She'll have to forgive me." Egrim's hands tightened.

Blood vessels ruptured in Alejak's eyes. "I-ehg-keep... secret." He choked out.

"Doubtful." Egrim gave one final pulsing squeeze, and the muffled sound of crushed vertebrae whispered into the night around them. He let loose the corpse that was Alejak and looked back out into the courtyard.

He began to hyperventilate. Zunibar looked done for, but he couldn't know that for sure. Not from this distance. He looked down at himself and cursed. "Come on damn you. Come on." He placed his hand over the middle of his chest and practically begged. The illusion pulsed out in a shimmering silver wave from his chest.

Kasha limped forward, each step sending fresh sensations of pain through her abdomen where the Talon's blade had cut her. She stopped fifteen feet from Zunibar, watching as blood and other fluids dripped from his ruined face onto the courtyard stones. Even on his hands and knees, the giant troll was nearly at eye level with her. When he looked up, she had to force herself not to recoil at the sight of his mangled features. The right side of his skull was partially caved in, a milky eye dangling from its socket, jaw hanging at an unnatural angle.

Her mind struggled to process what she had witnessed moments ago. Egrim had moved with impossible speed, his fist connecting with Zunibar's face with such force that it had shattered both the magical barrier and the troll's bones beneath. She had seen Egrim lift full kegs and move heavy furniture during the tavern's remodel with relative ease, but this was something else entirely.

Kasha's lips curled into a sneer as years of suppressed rage finally found their voice. "Do you know how many nights I laid awake, jumping at every shadow?" Her voice trembled with fury rather than fear. "I spent years looking over my shoulder, wondering if today would be the day you found me again. You and that damned contract haunted every moment of my life after I escaped."

She took another step forward, ice crystals forming in the air around her clenched fists. "But the worst part? The worst part was knowing what you did to my mother. How you broke her spirit piece by piece until death was her only escape. Until she was so afraid of living that she left me behind to fend for myself. I watched her die, you bastard. I'm going to make you pay for every moment of suffering you caused me."

Zunibar tried to laugh, but the sound came out as a wet gurgle through his shattered jaw. Blood bubbled from between his lips as he struggled to form words.

"You're not in the Helspires anymore," Kasha spat, frost spreading across the ground beneath her feet. "And I'm not that terrified little girl you used to torment. I'm the last thing you're ever going to see, you miserable cunt."

The air crackled with arcane energy as Zunibar's shield began to shimmer back into existence. Sparks of protective magic danced across the invisible barrier, threatening to deny Kasha her revenge. Her hands trembled as she gathered more power, frost and ice crystallizing in intricate patterns around her fingers, but the shield threatened to reform before she could strike.

Zunibar pushed himself up, his destroyed face twisting into what might have been a smile. His right knee buckled beneath him, but he caught himself, managing to stay somewhat upright. The sight of him still standing, still defying her, made Kasha's blood boil despite the frost gathering around her.

A blur of motion caught her eye as Egrim emerged from the shadows behind Zunibar. She hadn't even heard him, let alone seen the huge man's approach. His hands seized the troll's arms and wrenched them backward. Zunibar's screamed in agony as Egrim drove him down to his knees.

Egrim grasped the finger that wore the ring that powered Zunibar's arcane shield. With a savage twist, he tore the digit clean off, tossing it aside. The magical barrier flickered and died as the severed finger bounced across the courtyard stones.

"This is her moment. I won't allow you to deny her of it any longer." Egrim snarled, and with one fluid motion, he yanked Zunibar's arms upward. The wet pop of shoulder joints dislocating mixed with the troll's howls of torture. Egrim stepped to the side, letting go of the subdued and demoralized Zunibar, and met Kasha's eyes. His eyes, not his words, showed his pride in her.

Kasha's first frost-covered fist connected with Zunibar's jaw, sending teeth and blood spraying across the courtyard. She struck again and again, each impact releasing small explosions of crystalline ice that tore into the troll's flesh. Still, he remained upright on his knees, refusing to fall, refusing to give her the satisfaction of complete dominance.

Kasha snapped. Years of suppressed trauma, of nightmares and fear and rage, burst forth like a dam breaking. She seized Zunibar's face between her hands, fingers digging into what remained of his ruined flesh. Her scream started low and built into a feral roar of fury, pain and release.

Frost erupted from her palms, spreading across Zunibar's features with frightening speed. Ice crystals formed in his remaining eye, in his throat, in his very mind. The freezing power poured from her in an uncontrolled torrent, transforming the troll into a grotesque ice sculpture from the inside out. His final expression of defiance froze permanently on his face as the last vestiges of life left his body.

The frost coating Kasha's hands evaporated like morning dew as her rage finally burned itself out. Her shoulders began to shake, not with fury but with deep, wracking sobs that seemed to come from somewhere far beneath her years of carefully maintained control and perfection. Her legs gave out beneath her, but she fell right into Egrim's arms. He brought her closer, cradling her against his chest.

She looked up at him through tear-blurred vision, her expression a complicated tangle of emotions - love warring with exhaustion, gratitude mixing with a bone-deep weariness that threatened to pull her under. Her lips parted as if to speak, but no words came. The last remnants of her arcane energy slipped away like water through cupped hands, and consciousness followed shortly after. Her head lolled against Egrim's forearm and her eyes fluttered shut.

Egrim held her close, feeling the steady rise and fall of her chest against him. His eyes quickly swept across the courtyard, taking in the carnage their revenge had wrought. Bodies of Lance men and Talons lay scattered like broken dolls, their blood turning black in the dim moon light that peaked through the clouds above. The frozen statue that had been Zunibar still knelt in the center of it all, his final expression now a permanent monument to his defeat.

Something nagged at the edge of Egrim's awareness. He scanned the bodies again, more carefully this time. The sickly thin form of Beetle was conspicuously absent from among the dead. The last he'd seen of the disturbing orc; he'd been thrown against the mansion steps. But there was no body there now, only a dark stain that might have been blood.

"Well," Adenus murmured, just loud enough for Egrim to hear. "It seems at least one of the night soirees was a success."

Egrim's arms tightened protectively around Kasha as he and Adenus's eyes both moved to the balcony, a soft scrapping sound bringing their attention to it. The wooden and glass double doors swung open as Captain Ethan appeared with a grisly display quite literally in hand.

Adenus clapped his hands together once in a display of seeming approval and inclined his head in a barely perceptible bow before calling back after the Captain's declaration of succession as the new Lance. "So be it. You know where to find us."

Egrim's lip curled into a smirk, and he gave a light chuckle of amusement. He called back to the Adenus over his shoulder. "Your idea?"

Adenus took in a gasp of shock. "My dear friend. I am appalled at the allegation." Egrim heard the footsteps of the crafty dark elf as he headed back to his carriage. "Brutal work you did there my good man. Seems to be a little bit more to you than anyone is truly aware."

Egrim pivoted toward Adenus, still clutching Kasha's unconscious body to him. Adenus could feel his eyes on the back of his neck. "I am a vault of secrets. Please send some word when Madam Volstruk is up and about. I'll send a care package to the Tits in the morning."

Adenus closed the carriage door and gave it a quick rap for the driver to head out. The carriage pulled away from the gate, and Egrim heard Callus jogging up behind him.

"Is she okay?" The worry in his voice was thick.

Egrim turned. "Yes, I believe so. Just overexerted herself, I think. Where is Arialyn?"

"I'm right here." She said as she too, rushed forward with haste. "Kneel down, hurry."

Egrim knelt down and made Kasha as presentable to Arialyn as he could without setting her down on the ground. She produced an everlight match from her belt and flicked it to life. Holding it over her head she peered at the woman that had quickly become her best friend. Other than the busted lip, a very bruised left cheek and a cut to her abdomen that appeared to be a bleeder but nothing remotely lethal, she seemed fine. She placed her hands simultaneously over the swollen area of Kasha's face and abdomen, mumbling words that Egrim had yet to be able to understand despite seeing her do this minor medicae arcana several times.

The blueish light radiated from her hands for several seconds before it dulled and she pulled her hands away. Arialyn stumbled back a step on wobbly legs. Callus dropped to one knee and steadied her. She shook her head. "Anymore and I'll be joining the Madame here."

Egrim and Callus saw that Kasha's face, while still swollen, showed remarkable improvement over its prior appearance and her abdominal wound had stopped bleeding. Arialyn steadied herself against Callus and stood again, pulling a small sack from another pouch on her belt.

"I'll never understand how you fit so many damn pockets and pouches in that damn thing." Callus said as he grabbed Kasha's dangling hand.

Arialyn held the pouch near Kasha's nose and paused. "You fellas might want to hold your breath for the next ten beats or so."

She pinched the pouch and waved it in front of Kasha's face. With a sudden gasp she awoke and sat up in Egrim's cradled grip. Egrim's excitement would have been far more palpable had he held his breath in time. He barely had time to set Kasha down before turning and having the worst coughing fit of his life, nearly vomiting.

Kasha's head turned everyway it could in a blur, taking in the scene around her. "We, did it?" She was still gasping.

Arialyn held up a finger, telling her to wait just a moment. She threw the pouch aside and then counted her fingers down in front of Kasha to a beat of five before Callus began to laugh, no longer able to hold his amusement at Egrim's predicament any longer. This of course quickly resulted in him becoming the next victim of the smelling salts.

Arialyn looked at Kasha and shook her head. When she finally got to ten, she let out her breath. "Yes, almost without a hitch."

Kasha leaned against Arialyn, tears coming unbidden again. They embraced in the comfort of success. Over her small friend's shoulder, Kasha saw the mockery of an ice sculpture she had turned her once captor into. She grinned through her tears with sweet satisfaction.

By the time she stood Callus and Egrim had righted themselves, both clearly embarrassed at their previous states. The four of them looked at the ice Zunibar.

Egrim stepped next to Kasha and tentatively placed his hand on her lower back. She glanced up at him and her face told him what he needed to know. *I'm fine.*

"You once said fighting was an art. That art enough for you, old man?" Egrim tilted his head at Callus.

"Pfft, she did that. Not you. I imagine you did that to his skull though. I guess you sort of helped. It gives him a certain grotesque quality. So...I suppose." Callus was moving to shake Egrim's hand with mock approval when Kasha suddenly grabbed the arcabus from Arialyn's belt and fired into the frozen Zunibar. The entirety of the macabre ice sculpture shattered.

Callus quickly pulled his hand back. "Doesn't count anymore."

"Fuck you."

Kasha handed the arcabus back to Arialyn with a silent look of apology for ripping it from her belt. Arialyn shook her head and shrugged. "I'd never deny you a tool that you needed."

Reality suddenly came crashing back and Arialyn began to frantically look for Alejak. "Alejak? Beetle? Where are they?"

Egrim cleared his throat. "Beetle's gone. Last I saw him he was twisted on the doorsteps." He gestured to where he had seen the pestilent orc's body fall. "And Alejak's corpse is over there." He pointed over to the bushes where he had choked the life from the onyx tiefling.

Arialyn ran faster than Callus and reached the hedges first. There they found Alejak's corpse. His eyes were bulging from his head, blood engorged orbs that clued Callus in to exactly how his former foe met his end. He stood and peered at Egrim disapprovingly.

Egrim threw his hands up and shook his head in a wordless, *it wasn't me,* gesture.

Arialyn searched through Alejak's pockets. "Please, please, please."

"It won't be on him, love." Callus chided carefully.

Arialyn stopped and her head perked up as her fingers grasped onto a piece of rolled parchment. "Oh yeah, smartass. Then what is this?"

She unrolled it and held it up for Callus to read. He bent down and had to squint his eyes to read the small script. He laughed. "Appears to be a receipt for 'one gentle tugging with cuddling after.' Gross."

Arialyn flipped the parchment around and cursed. She grabbed the body by the collar and started punching his lifeless face. Callus had a hard time understanding all of the words that were coming out of her mouth.

"We'll find the deed, Arialyn." He stood behind her with his arms crossed. She continued to strike the dead man for several more seconds until her fists hurt and she was out of breath. "Poor little thing tuckered herself out."

She stared at the bloody face before her. "Fuck you."

"Why do people keep telling me that tonight?"

CHAPTER THIRTY-THREE

MOTHER IS ALWAYS RIGHT

Isque flicked his finger against the shimmering barrier that enclosed the forge room, the magical dome rippling like water at his touch. The sound was barely audible—a soft chime that contrasted sharply with the muffled screams it had been restraining. He smiled with satisfaction at his handiwork. No one outside would hear what transpired within these walls, no matter how loudly the half-dwarf chose to express his discomfort.

The Seeker turned his attention back to his quarry, blonde hair cascading over his shoulder and falling in his victims face as he crouched beside the broken form sprawled across the stone floor. Bornar lay in a pool of his own blood, his olive skin mottled with burns from where Isque had pressed heated metal against flesh. The stench of charred hair and skin hung heavy in the air, mixing with the acrid smell of the forge's dying embers.

"Just tell me where the pact mortal is going," Isque said conversationally, as if discussing the weather rather than torture. "Tell me, and I'll make the pain stop. Surely that's a fair trade?"

Bornar spat blood and saliva across the stones beside Isque's boots. His face was so swollen that the words came out slurred and barely intelligible. "Wouldn't... matter if I did... tell you." He struggled to focus his one good eye on the Fae. "Kovag would... tear you apart. Only sending... you to your death. Should thank me."

Isque's laugh was like chiming bells, beautiful and cold. "Kovag, is it?" He clapped his hands together in delight. "How wonderful! We didn't know the pact mortal's name until this very moment. Thank you for that delicious morsel of information. So much easier to question others when you have a name."

The color drained from what little of Bornar's face wasn't already purple with bruising. His mouth opened and closed like a fish gasping for air as he realized his mistake. "Fuck," he wheezed. "Fucking... clum sy..."

"Indeed, you were." Isque stood gracefully, brushing dirt and soot from his lunar weave. "Now then, where was dear Kovag heading? And more importantly," His voice took on a sharper edge. "—is the vulpine child still with him?"

Bornar's jaw clenched shut, his face a mask of defiance despite his broken state. He turned his head away from Isque, staring at the wall with stubborn determination.

The Seeker's playful demeanor evaporated like morning mist. His features hardened into something predatory as irritation flared in his chest. In one fluid motion, he seized Bornar by the throat and hauled him upright. The half-dwarf's a few feet from ground as Isque's grip tightened.

"I asked you a question." Isque hissed, his voice losing all pretense of civility. He turned and held Bornar over the forge, where red-hot coals still glowed like malevolent eyes in the darkness. The heat radiating from them was intense enough to make the air shimmer and Bornar's skin began to sizzle again.

Bornar kicked and flailed, but Isque's strength was far beyond that of anyone he had ever come across. Isque began to slowly lower him closer to the coals.

"Where is he going?" Isque repeated, each word precise and cutting. "Answer me, or we will visit your smelter next." He gestured with his free hand toward the corner of the forge where molten iron still bubbled and churned in its crucible, orange light dancing across the walls like liquid fire.

The heat from the coals began to set his clothes on fire. Bornar beat his fists against Isque's arm, desperately trying to break free. Sweat poured down his face, mixing with the blood from his wounds. But still, he said nothing.

Bornar's burning boot kicked at the coals. His face contorted into a warped smile even in extreme pain he was in. He drove the tip of his boot deep into the glowing coals. The impact sending a shower of red-hot embers exploding outward like angry fireflies directly into Isque's, searing his pale skin and forcing him to release his grip.

Bornar crashed down into the forge bed itself, his body landing among the burning coals with a sickening hiss. The smell of charring flesh further filled the air as he rolled out frantically. He managed to roll himself over the edge of the forge, tumbling to the stone floor in a fiery heap.

Isque staggered backward, one hand pressed to his face where angry red welts were already forming across his cheek and forehead. His perfect features were marred by the burns, and fury blazed in his eyes as he recovered his composure. "You miserable little—"

But Bornar was already moving. The half-dwarf pushed himself to his feet with trembling arms, his gaze fixed on the corner of the forge where the smelter's crucible bubbled. Orange light danced across his ruined face.

Kovag, you bastard, Bornar thought, a grim smile tugging at his split lips. *You'll owe me a drink in Thromgrid's hall for this one.*

Without hesitation, he broke into a lurching run. His burned and broken body protested every step, but stubborn determination carried him forward. Isque's shout of alarm echoed behind him, but it was too late.

Bornar dove headfirst into the smelter.

The molten metal embraced him like a lover's kiss, and his suffering ended in an instant. There was no scream, no final words, just the brief flare of superheated steam as his body was consumed by the liquid fire.

Isque stood frozen, his mouth hanging open in genuine shock. For several heartbeats, he simply stared at the bubbling surface of the smelter where Bornar had disappeared. Then, slowly, he began to clap.

"Well, that was just damned impressive," he said, his voice filled with sick admiration. "Inconvenient, but impressive nevertheless."

The sound of his applause echoed hollowly in the forge room, mixing with the gentle bubbling of molten metal. He shook his head in something approaching respect. "I do so appreciate proper commitment to one's principles."

Suddenly, the air beside him shimmered, and Amjani's voice reached out to him from the Umbra realm, urgent and excited.

"Isque! There was a massive spike in the arcane web. The pact mortal did something that sent an incredible flow of the arcane. I know exactly where Elirel is now. You need to come to me immediately."

Isque glanced once more at the smelter where Bornar's body had vanished, still wearing that expression of twisted admiration. "I got what I could here anyway," he replied to the empty air. "The pact mortal's name is Kovag. I'll join you presently, my dear Amjani."

He flicked his finger again, and the magical barrier around the forge dissolved like morning mist.

Elirel's consciousness snapped back to her body with enough force to make the obsidian walls around them shudder. She found Oakira still on her knees, chest heaving as she recovered from the agony of Kovag's assault on their connection. She wore rage like a veil as she looked down at her daughter, her expression slowly turning to a mixture of pity and frustration.

"Do you understand now?" she asked, her voice carrying the weight of her hatred for the Kovag. "Do you see how your misplaced feelings have complicated everything? That beast would tear itself apart rather than bend to our will."

Oakira pushed herself up, using the basin for support. Her legs trembled, but her voice remained steady. "You are wrong, mother. The complications began when you started dictating how I should handle him." She wiped blood from the corner of her mouth with the back of her hand. "The truth is, we were too effective at what you set out to accomplish. The power we have gathered from hunting the renegades and Forgotten, it terrifies you because it worked better than you planned. To make it worse for you, we did the majority of it without your *guidance*." Oakira's last word dripped with disdain.

"Daughter-" Elirel's tone softened, reaching out to touch Oakira's cheek. "Are you alright?"

Oakira jerked away from her mother's touch. "I need to go to him. I have to try and salvage what little trust remains after your interference."

The willow wing blossom in her chest pulsed weakly, a reminder of how close Kovag had come to destroying their connection entirely.

"Absolutely not," Elirel's voice hardened again. "I forbid it."

"You forbid it?" Oakira scowled with a twisted chuckle, the sound bitter and sharp. "I am done being the child, mother. All of this is your fault! You made me find him! You made me pull away! You made me sit back and do nothing when his mother and sister were dying! I am going to him, and I am going to fix this. The plan will continue but it will continue on my terms."

Elirel felt heat rise in her again. That damned mongrel had poisoned her own daughter against her. She was seconds away from rebuking Oakira when she felt it, the approaching presence of the Seekers, no doubt drawn by the pact mortal's tantrum. They were close now, too close. She kept her face carefully neutral, hiding the knowledge from her daughter and hoping she could not sense them too.

"Very well," she said, her voice carefully measured. "Go to your pet. Perhaps you can indeed salvage something from this disaster."

Oakira paused, studying her mother's face for any sign of deception at her sudden flexibility. She found none or perhaps she refused to see any. She gathered her power and prepared to cross the veil between worlds. "I'll return soon."

"Of course, daughter," Elirel whispered as Oakira began to fade. "Just know everything I have done was for you. They refused to see the blessing you are, and I wanted to make them then see the nightmare they made."

All she received in return was the barest smile from Oakira before she vanished. She watched the space where her daughter had been, feeling the Seekers drawing ever closer. "I am sorry," she murmured to the empty air.

The walls seemed to pulse with the remnants of Oakira's departure as Elirel gathered what precious little power remained to her. Her fingers traced complex patterns in the air, weaving a chaotic web of energy designed to mask Oakira's trail. There was no need to hide her own spell work anymore, they knew exactly where she was. The effort left her even more drained; her legs trembled with the effort to remain standing.

She had barely lowered her hands when Amjani and Isque burst into the clearing, their lunar weave armor gleaming with captured radiant moonlight against the dark stones. Their blades sang as they drew them in perfect unison, the silver metal catching the faint light that filtered through the umbral canopy above.

"Nowhere left to run, Lady Elirel," Amjani's voice held within it the confidence of the most successful Seeker the Lunar Court had known. The Master Seeker moved like water as she circled to Elirel's left, her blade held at the ready.

Isque mirrored her movement to the right, his playful demeanor replaced by a disturbing coolness. The black portions of his armor seemed to soak in the shadows around them with zeal.

Elirel's lip curled in contempt. "Does your master even tell you why you hunt us?" She spat the words like venom. "Or do you simply come to heel when Thruva snaps his fingers?"

"Where is the abomination?" Isque's question cut through her attempt at dialogue.

"My daughter," Elirel corrected, her voice sharp with an arcane edge that seemed to cut into the Seekers ears, "is beyond your reach now." Her eyes darted between them, noting how they continued to close the distance in perfect synchronization. Even in her current state, she could feel the tension crackling in the bodies of the two Seekers.

"You cling to hope that has long since abandoned you," Amjani said, her blade catching a stray beam of light. "The trail is fresh. She cannot have gone far."

A bitter laugh escaped Elirel's throat. "You simple creatures. Do you think I would let you anywhere near her?" She drew herself up to her full height, silver hair writhing with the last vestiges of her power as she levitated off the umbral stone. "You can't even see the strings your Lord has on you that puppet your every move."

The Seekers exchanged a brief glance, something unspoken passing between them. Elirel noticed Isque's hand drift to his chest, where something beneath his armor seemed to pulse with a dull golden light.

"Enough games," Amjani's voice hardened. "Tell us where she went, or we will take the information from what is left of you."

Elirel's smile was all teeth and shadow. "You can try, little Seekers. But assuming you survive me, you will be in no shap-" She was forced to cut her words short as the pair darted in for her.

The fight ended before it truly began. Elirel's attacks, once capable of devastating an entire squadron of Seekers, if need be, now barely caused their armor to shimmer as they deflected her weakened lunar fire. Her legs gave out beneath her as Isque swept at them from behind, and she found herself face-down on the cold obsidian floor, her cheek pressed against the stone as he pinned her arms behind her back.

"Well, that was disappointingly easy," Isque muttered, his knee pressing firmly between her shoulder blades. The playfulness returning to him now that they already had the upper hand.

Amjani circled them once, her blade still drawn. "Hold her steady. I need to contact Lord Thruva. Without the abomination, we need to see how he wants her handled." She turned and walked several paces away, her fingers already weaving the communication spell.

As soon as Amjani was out of earshot, Isque felt the coin beneath his armor grow warm. He reached for it with his free hand, careful to keep Elirel secured beneath him. She was frighteningly weak, especially for an ArchFae. The metal hummed with an otherworldly energy as Duke Dalmoth's voice whispered through his mind.

"Press it to her head, my faithful Isque. Let her hear my words."

Isque complied, ensuring the gesture remained hidden from Amjani's view. He watched as her body tensed at the contact.

"My beloved Elirel," Dalmoth's voice dripped with mock affection, the sound like oil sliding across stone. *"How far you've fallen, trying to hide our little secret. Did you really think you could keep her from me forever?"*

Elirel's breath caught in her throat, her entire body going rigid beneath Isque's weight. The voice she had ripped from her memory by her own mother. This was... no. It could not be.

"Allow me to restore to you what was taken by your own wretched mother." The coin flared in ultraviolet light that only Elirel could witness.

The memories crashed through Elirel's mind like shards of broken glass, each one cutting deeper than the last. She saw herself, younger and foolishly naive, wandering the twilight gardens of the Lunar Court. There stood Dalmoth, devastatingly handsome in his carefully crafted glamour, shadows dancing at the edges of his form as he beckoned her closer with honeyed words and promises of forbidden knowledge. She knew then that she loved him.

The scene shifted violently, and she found herself crouched behind a column of pure moonstone, her heart breaking in her chest as she watched Dalmoth's true form tower over Lord Thruva. Their voices echoed in her restored memory, speaking of usurping Lady Valene, and of chains that bound something ancient in the void plane, of using her, of creating something that would unleash that power and bring Dalmoth and Thruva with it as generals.

"The child will be the key," Dalmoth had rumbled, his voice like stones grinding together. "Through our offspring, we will unlock what has been bound for millennia."

Her stomach churned as the memory of them discovering her eavesdropping washed over her. The terror in her chest as shadows had wrapped around her throat, dragging her into Dalmoth's embrace. His true form had been horrifying, massive and ever-shifting, with chains that moved of their own accord and that same roguishly handsome smile that now brought fear instead of yearning.

Tears streamed down her face as she remembered running to her mother, clothes torn and spirit shattered. But Lady Valene's eyes had already held traces of void corruption, swirling darkness that spoke of Dalmoth's influence. Yet somehow, through whatever remained of her sanity, her mother had gathered enough clarity for one final act of protection.

"My sweet child," Lady Valene had whispered, her hands cupping Elirel's face as void magic crackled around them. "I cannot undo what has been done, but I can make it as though it never was. It will not be perfect... they have tainted me. Keep my grandchild safe." Her mother's life force had begun to drain away as she enacted one of the forbidden vitae spells, her shining skin turning white as snow.

The memory of her mother's sacrifice burned through Elirel's mind like wildfire. The spell had worked, not just on her, but on the entire Lunar Court. Every trace of Dalmoth's presence, every memory of his plot, every whisper of the thing bound in chains in the void plane, all of it had been wiped away. The cost had been her mother's very life. But as she had warned, it had not been perfect. Some had remembered and some later recalled their plotting.

Now, pinned beneath Isque with Dalmoth's coin pressed against her temple, Elirel understood with horrifying clarity. Oakira wasn't just her daughter, she was the key Dalmoth had spoken of. The tool he meant to use to unlock whatever horror waited in chains beyond the veil.

Her tears turned to living frustration that slid down her cheeks, leaving trails on the dark stone. She wanted to scream, to plead, but her voice failed her. All she could do was lie there, pinned beneath an unwitting pawns knee, as her worst nightmare spoke directly into her mind.

"All your bitch of a mother managed to do was delay the inevitable, and our dear daughter's increase in power will just make every part of the plan from here on out far easier. She may even live to see the ruin we bring to Yonara. Please know, that as you bleed out here soon, I will always think fondly of being inside you so long ago." His laugh felt like a needles piercing her mind.

The coin disappeared beneath Isque's armor as quickly as it had appeared. He leaned down close to Elirel's ear, his voice barely a whisper. "What did he tell you? What does Lord Dalmoth want with your daughter?"

Elirel's sensed the unease in Isque's voice. "Listen to me, you must keep them away from her." Her eyes begged with her very soul as she turned her head just enough to meet his gaze. "The void holds something in chains that they mean to-"

The rest of her warning was cut short as Amjani's boot connected with Elirel's jaw. Blood sprayed across the dark stone floor as the Master Seeker knelt beside them, her hands already alight with the arcane.

"Enough talk," Amjani snarled, pressing her palm against Elirel's forehead. "Lord Thruva wants her dead, but not until she shows me where the abomination is."

The spell tore through Elirel's mental defenses like paper, forcing a connection between their minds. Through Elirel's eyes, Amjani caught a glimpse of Oakira standing beside a campfire, her form partially obscured by the massive frame of a half-orc holding a vulpine child. Now they had his name and his face.

But Elirel wasn't finished. She had nothing left except to tap into her very essence, into the well of arcane energy that sustained her immortal life. She gathered it all, every drop, compressing it into a final, devastating burst.

"For my daughter," she whispered, and released everything.

The explosion of raw lunar energy was blinding. It ripped through Amjani and Isque's armor like it was made of linen, sending them flying backwards through the air. Their bodies slammed against the obsidian walls with bone-crushing force as the radiant energy seared their flesh and the stones of the Umbra fell upon them.

With her last breath, Elirel reached out across the realms to her daughter. *'Oakira, my love, I am sorry. Stay away from Thruva. Do not proceed with our plan. The Seekers know your mortal's face now - hide, both of you. I have bought you some time.'*

The message faded as Elirel's body crumbled to ash, stardust scattering across the Umbra floor. On opposite sides of the chamber, Amjani and Isque lay motionless under crumbled stone, their lunar weave armor smoking and their bodies broken. The coin beneath Isque's ruined breastplate pulsed once with an angry crimson light, then went dark.

Kovag sat just inside the tent's entrance, his massive frame filling the entryway. Blood still seeped from the wound in his chest, staining his tunic a deeper crimson. Saffron lay half-asleep in his arms; her small form curled protectively against him.

The rain continued to fall as Oakira materialized before the campfire, its flames hissing and sputtering against the downpour. Her sheer robes clung to her, confirming to Kovag that she was physically present rather than projecting herself across the realms. Water ran in rivulets down her face, darkening her reddish-brown hair to the color of old blood.

His heart betrayed him the moment he saw her, leaping in his chest despite everything he knew she had done, everything he suspected she was still doing. The willow wing blossom thrummed weakly, echoing the conflicting emotions that stormed through him. Part of him wanted to scream at her, to demand answers about her mother's threats, about the Seekers she had mentioned and about the lies she had told him of his family. Another part ached to tell her how much he had missed her, how the moons never seemed as bright when she was gone.

Instead, he said nothing. His Fae-touched eye reflected the firelight as he stared at her, his face an unreadable mask. Blood trickled from the corner of his mouth, a reminder of how close he had come to destroying their connection entirely.

Saffron stirred in his lap, roused by the tumult of emotions flowing through their bond. She pushed herself up, her golden eyes finding Oakira through the rain. Her fur bristled as she sensed Kovag's inner turmoil, felt the deep well of betrayal that lay beneath his surface thoughts. Her small hands gripped his tunic tighter as she fixed Oakira with a glare that carried all the protective fury her young body could muster.

Through their connection, Kovag felt Saffron's instinctive desire to protect him, even from someone who clearly held such power over him. It was almost amusing, this tiny child trying to shield him from a being who could probably unmake them both with a wave of her hand. Almost.

The silence stretched between them, broken only by the crackling of the struggling fire and the steady drumming of rain on canvas. Oakira took a step forward, her feet barely seeming to touch the mud beneath them. The movement caused Saffron to press herself more firmly against Kovag's chest, ignoring his blood that stained her fur.

His hand came up to rest protectively on Saffron's back, but his eyes never left Oakira's face. The deadened look in them a physical manifestation of the distance that had grown between them.

Oakira moved with ethereal grace. Her form shimmered and adjusted to fit as she settled beside Kovag in the tent's entrance. Her proximity made the willow wing blossom flutter, a sensation that brought equal parts comfort and pain. Saffron shifted in his lap, turning to keep her suspicious piercing eyes fixed on the Fae woman.

"I heard you," Oakira whispered, her voice carrying despite the drumming rain. "Every time you called out to me, I heard you." She reached out as if to touch his arm but stopped short, her hand hovering in the space between them. "The Seekers... they can trace the threads of power that connect us. I feared they would follow our tether back to mother and me, or worse, directly to you. I told you that before."

Kovag's jaw clenched, but he maintained his stony silence and stared into the fire. Blood continued to seep from his chest wound, though far slower now. Saffron's tail curled around his wrist, her presence anchoring him against the tide of feelings Oakira's words stirred.

"I allowed my mother to dictate how I should handle our pact," Oakira continued, finally lowering her hand to her lap. "It was perhaps the gravest mistake I have made in all my centuries." Her eyes, bright with unshed tears, searched his face for any reaction as he continued to stare into the fire. "But Kovag, I fear you have misunderstood the nature of our pact from the beginning."

Lightning split the sky, illuminating the tent in harsh white light. In that brief flash, Kovag saw in his periphery the pain etched across Oakira's features, genuine and raw. The willow wing blossom waned in response to her distress.

"What we share, what we have done together..." her voice caught slightly. "I care for you, deeply. But the love you seek, the kind of love that leads to family and futures together, I cannot give you that. You knew that. I never could have. Not just because of what I am, but because of what that love would do to you." She gestured to his bleeding chest. "Our connection already causes you such pain. A deeper bond would consume you entirely."

Saffron growled low in her throat, a sound that surprised both adults. Her small hands gripped Kovag's tunic tighter as she projected feelings of fierce warning through their bond. The message was clear, she wouldn't let anyone hurt him, not even this powerful Fae woman who made his heart ache so deeply.

"You lied to me." He said flatly, eyes coated in fresh tears. "You told me they were alive and well at a time when they were both in the ground."

Oakira reached out to him, her fingers trailing down his arm and sending a wave of regenerative energy through him that sealed his wounds faster than he could pull his arm away from her touch. She pulled her own hand back in rebuke as he shifted his arm from her.

"I promised to make your mother's tavern profitable and to make sure your sister did not die from her illness. The pact said nothing about keeping them alive, Kovag." Her eyes joined his in the campfire.

"Why lie to me, and why come to me now if you're so worried about the Seekers?"

Oakira bit her lips in frustration with both herself and her mother. "After what you just did... it let me know I had hurt you far greater than I had ever imagined possible. That's why I am here now. As for lying, you were already pulling away from me as you realized we could not be what you wanted. If I told you that your family was gone, I feared you would abandon our pact and the work we had accomplished. The work our pact had agreed to fulfill. It was a mistake. I am sorry."

Kovag huffed at her words, his muscles tensing beneath Saffron's protective grip. "I never pulled away from you until you began leaving so quickly after laying with me. We used to lay together for hours, laughing and enjoying each other." He looked down at Saffron and then back to the fire. "But you're right." His voice rough with emotion. "But being right doesn't excuse the lies. All you did was prove my suspicions correct. I was never more than a means to an end for you and that witch you call mother."

Rain continued to drum against the canvas as silence stretched between them. "I loved you. Even though I knew I was not supposed to." He finally managed, his words barely audible above the storm. "Did you ever love me?"

Oakira's ethereal features softened, a sadness crossing her face that made her seem almost mortal. "I cared for you deeply, Kovag. More than I should have." She yearned to touch him, to try and bring him some sort of comfort, but knew that it would only make her words hurt worse. "But love... that was never something we could have shared."

Though he had known what her answer would be, the words cut him deeper than any blade. Saffron pressed herself tighter against him, burying her face in his chest as his anguish washed over her through their bond. She trembled as she began to cry the tears he refused to shed.

"I told you this when we made our pact," Oakira continued, her voice gentle but firm. "I reminded you every time we shared ourselves beneath the moons. Why did you agree to the pact? Why did you continue to follow it?" she asked after a moment, genuine curiosity coloring her tone. "If you knew what we could never be?"

Kovag's bitter laugh held no humor. "A beautiful woman came to me and showed me what I thought was love for the first time in my life." His Fae-touched eye flickered with remembered passion. "You made me feel things no woman had ever even tried to give me. I had never even been gifted a kiss before you. Then you told me you could save my mother's tavern and my sister's life." He shook his head, remembering how young and naive he had been. "I was barely a man. Of course, I said yes. You might as well have asked me if I wanted to continue breathing."

The fire clung to life before them as Oakira absorbed his words, understanding dawning in her eyes. She had known he was young when she chose him, but perhaps she hadn't truly comprehended just how vulnerable that youth had made him to her manipulations. She had taken a young man and set him up to have the love and joy crushed out of his life. She might as well have stood in front of him as a child and killed his puppy in front of his very eyes while laughing in his face. She had taken innocence from him and replaced it with pain.

"I have long felt sorrow for what has transpired between us but always told myself that you knew the terms. Now I see that I have truly wronged." She brought her knees up to her chest and wept into her crossed arms.

Kovag felt a piece of him begging to reach for her, to pull Oakira to him and tell her that he forgave her for it all. He quietly suffocated that feeling as he looked to the spot in the mud where Saffron lay lifeless less than an hour ago.

They sat there for a time, the only sounds over the silence being the rain and Oakira's own suffering. She regained herself as Kovag finally spoke. "Your mother is a cunt."

The sudden and outright insult of it brought a choked laugh from her throat. "She definitely can be."

She wiped her face clean and looked at the child he held in his arms like his own daughter. "You named her Saffron? After the spice you loved in the pastry your mother used to make?" She cursed herself for bringing up his mother.

"Yes. Her eyes remind me of the color."

"I do not think keeping her with you is wise, but I will help you keep her safe as best I can." She was about to tell him that she would not stay away any longer. Coming to him like this might be too risky but she would not remain silent any longer. She bit her own lip, the urge to tell him fought with the knowledge of how close they were to their end goal. Coming to him so often again would jeopardize everything he had bled and lost for her. It didn't matter. Her very words were slammed from her own thoughts as the voice of her mother took over and the realization of what had just happened hit her.

'Oakira, my love, I am sorry. Stay away from Thruva. Do not proceed with our plan. The Seekers know your mortal's face now - hide, both of you. I have bought you some time.'

She grabbed at her temples and screamed, standing and stumbling back against the tent, nearly knocking one of the support poles over. The power of her mother's words cast through the web as she died, hit her like an arcane bolt to an exposed wound.

The words echoed even in Kovag's head and Oakira's reaction was so powerful that he felt compelled to his feet with Saffron still in his arms, the surge of adrenaline making him brace for an attack from something in the darkness of the night around them.

The pain subsided enough for Oakira to steady herself against the tent pole. Her body trembling as she processed what had just happened. Rain continued to cascade over her, creating a shimmering effect that made her appear even more otherworldly.

"They killed her," she whispered, her voice cracking. "The Seekers... she sacrificed herself." Tears fell from her eyes, evaporating into mist from the heat her anger was producing before they could reach the ground. Her body felt as though it were on fire. Her chest heaved and her clenched fists crackled and burst into Forgotten flames. She stumbled back several feet before stopping and planting her feet firmly into the mud.

Oakira drew into herself and then threw her arms out and her head to the sky with an otherworldly scream that Kovag had only ever heard from the Forgotten that he had slain. Lunar Fae light mixed with

Forgotten helfire erupted from her body, burning away her clothing. Just as quickly as it happened it was over, and she fell to her knees.

Kovag felt the willow wing blossom burn with a new sensation. He took several steps away from Oakira and turned his body to keep Saffron away from whatever was happening.

Oakira's voice was changed, no longer like a musical lyre. There was a bass in it he had never heard before. "She was manipulative and cold." Oakira rose to her feet and bagan to pace around the fire. Her feet never quite touched the ground as she moved, leaving no impressions in the mud. "But everything she did, every scheme and plot was to protect me. All of it to make them pay for turning her only daughter away and casting her out as an abomination."

Her voice rose to a scream that made Saffron burrow deeper into Kovag's embrace. "And now they will get what they asked for! I will tear the Lunar Court apart stone by stone!"

"Oakira," Kovag's deep voice cut through her rage. "You need to calm yourself. Something had changed in you."

She whirled to face him, her hair writhing like living flames. "They know your face now, Kovag. The Seekers saw you through my mother's eyes. They will hunt you down, torture you for information about me. They will use you to draw me out." Her form flickered like a candle in a storm. "Even without access to the arcane web, they can scry your location. They will find you now that they have seen you and I am not done with you. We are not done with our plan."

Kovag looked down at Saffron, who stared up at him with worried golden eyes. "I have to protect her."

Oakira looked at Saffron and then back at Kovag. A wave of regret for everything that she had done to him paled to the rage she felt now. She needed him now more than ever, but they would still need to go into hiding. Her mother was right about one thing, no, she was right about everything. They needed to vanish and regroup.

"We vanish. We bide our time and, in a year, or so, when they think we've given up, we will start to slowly acquire power again." She set her feet back to the ground near the fire.

Kovag shook his head. "I will do nothing if you do not help keep Saffron safe."

Oakira felt something terrible well up inside her as though she wanted to strike Kovag for refusing her. She shook her head, fighting that violent thought away. She quickly schemed. "I can cast a glamour on both of you. Your outward appearances will change, but your essences will remain the same. Scrying requires that the caster knows what you look like. With different faces, the Seekers won't be able to scry on you. Do not use the gifts I have given you or you will risk leaving an arcane trail for them to follow."

Kovag set Saffron down gently and squatted down, poorly trying to be at eye level with their size difference. "Do you understand what's happening, Saffy? We need to look different so the Seekers can't find us."

Saffron nodded, her eyes reflecting both understanding and trust. Kovag felt her acceptance mixed with an undercurrent of fear, not of the change itself, but of the people hunting them. He thought for the millionth time that she was not safe with him and hoped that Mother Maudrid would be able to offer some solution that would keep her safe.

Saffron felt the undercurrent of his thoughts and looked at him in a strange mixture of pleading anger. Kovag shook his head. "I won't abandon you. I swear it."

Oakira stepped forward, her new form oppressive. "Kovag, I..." she paused, struggling to find the right words. "I am truly sorry for everything. When I am done with you." She shook her own head, wondering how she could speak to him like this. "When this is done, when Thruva falls and our pact is complete, I swear I will do everything in my power to help you find the life you deserve."

His face remained impassive. He wanted nothing more than to believe her, but he held no faith in the words that felt hollow in his ears and empty on his soul. He truly felt he was a tool, even if he was favored tool, he was still just a tool and whatever just changed in her made him feel firmly in place as something less than. He said nothing, simply nodding once.

Oakira raised her hands, fingers moving in as she wove the glamour. Silver-green light danced between her fingertips, forming intricate sigils in the air. The magic swirled around Kovag and Saffron like a gentle breeze, settling over them like a second skin.

Kovag felt the spell take hold, watching as his green-tinged skin paled to a human tone. Saffron saw his tusks recede, and a scar form on the left side of his lip where his tusk had broken. His frame shrank slightly, though he remained impressively built. Beside him, Saffron's vulpine features shifted and changed, her fur melting away to reveal reddish skin, her vulpine features transforming into those of a young tiefling girl. Her ears became horns and her tail slender and pointed.

The pair turned to each other, studying their new appearances with wonder and uncertainty. They both gazed at their reflections in pools of rainwater that shimmered in the twin moon's light. Kovag ran a hand over his lips and found that he could still feel his tusks. While Saffron looked at her reflection in a pool of water that shimmered in the moons light. She reached to touch her horns and felt her ears, the mismatch between her sight and touch were jarring.

"The glamour will hold indefinitely." Oakira explained, her voice growing distant as she prepared to leave. "You only appear visually different. The glamour will cause all who come into contract with you physically to remember things differently. The magic will muddle their minds into thinking that what they see is what they feel. While some-one might touch Saffron's fur the magic will make them immediately remember it as flesh. But be careful with the blossom, Kovag. It is the key to keeping the illusion whole."

She stepped back, her form beginning to fade. "I will be away for a long while. The arcane web will be watched closely now."

"I'm used to your absence." Kovag said flatly.

A snarl came across Oakira's face at his disrespect. Again, she shook her head in confusion at her own reaction. A sad smile washed over her before turning into one of determination. She nodded sullenly and vanished in a silvery wisp.

There was no sound here now, save the dying rain and the light crackle of the campfire. Kovag knelt and pulled Saffron close, feeling her small arms wrap around his neck. They remained that way for a long moment, two changed beings holding onto the only real thing they had left, each other.

Kovag pulled back from their embrace, his newly 'human' hands gentle as they wiped the tears from Saffron's now sharper tiefling features. The glamour was unsettling. Their bond told him that what he physically felt was different than what his mind truly perceived. It was going to take some getting used to for the both of them

It was still hours before dawn, but he didn't want to waste any time moving from this spot. He quickly gathered up camp and stowed it all away on Lucky, who true her name, had gone through the whole affair unscathed. Within minutes he had dowsed the fire and had the tent and bedroll stowed away with Saffron securely in front of him in Lucky's saddle.

"I suppose we need new names." He said softly as he looked down to study Saffron's new face. "And a story to tell anyone that might need to hear it." He felt her curiosity peek through the lingering fear. "It could be like a game?"

He settled fully in the saddle and fought the urge to use his Fae-touched eye to bring the night into clarity. Saffron leaned back against him and played with one of the braids of his beard that fell over her shoulder. Thankfully that had stayed as is. Though he reluctantly figured he'd need to trim it for added camouflage.

"Egrim," His voice nearly caught on the name. "It was my true father's name. What do you think?"

She looked up at Kovag and smiled. "Egrim it is then."

Saffron gazed back up at him and he was thankful Oakira had kept the freckles on her cheeks and nose in this new tiefling image. She patted her chest, and he felt a pull of inquiry from her mind.

"I'm getting to you, calm down." he continued, "How about Gertrim?"

Her eyes narrowed and she glared at him, her lips in a pout.

"I'm only joking, Saffy. Hmm..." His throat tightened, "How about Morrigan? It was my sister's name." He smiled as he used her full name for the first time since they had been kids. "She was kind and brave, just like you."

Saffron's face lit up with a cheerful smile that should not have been possible from a child after everything they had been through. It was like sunlight breaking through storm clouds. She nodded enthusiastically, her new tiefling tail swishing over his leg with excitement.

"Morrigan it is then," he said, still surprised by the resilience she had. "On our way to Hus'rokn and the Wylds we're going to have to go around Toz Kraggos. It's a vile place. After we pass that we'll be deep into the Resurgence Wilds and well on our way. We'll find Mother Maudrid and see if she can tell us where more of your people might be in hiding. Alright?"

Morrigan grabbed his hand and squeezed it hard, digging her nails in. She shook her head strongly. He felt a wave of something that made his stomach feel empty, like he had just had a chair kicked out from under him by surprise.

"You don't want to find more of your people?" He asked, confused.

She shook her head again, looking up at him and latching on to his arm while using her finger to point up at him and then to her chest. She frantically repeated the movement several times. When he looked uncertain of her meaning she held one hand to her chest and the other above her and against his.

The realization of her intent could have knocked him off the horse. "I'm your people." He whispered.

Saffron nodded enthusiastically and squeezed his arm again and then lightly bit him.

"Ouch. What was that for?" It hadn't really hurt, but that was something she had never done before.

Saffron shrugged her shoulders innocently.

He raised an eyebrow at her as she leaned back against him again and continued to play with one of his beard braids.

'I'm her people.' He thought.

"Perhaps we just see what else we can learn about them then?"

There was a wave of warmth from her that he took as agreement.

"We'll figure out our story on the way there," he assured her. "Something simple but tragic that people won't question too much." He paused, looking down at her. "But no matter what story we tell others or how long we look like this, you're still Saffron. You're still my..."

She laid her head against his arm in response before he finished his sentence, and he felt her warmth push through his body again.

DEPTH OF DEVOTION

Thruva sat upon his stone throne, fingers absently rotating the raw void ring around his middle finger. The eternal night sky that made up the walls of the Lunar Citadel seemed darker than usual, as if responding to its master's brooding mood. The white-gold highlights of his silk robes caught what little light remained, creating an unsettling dance of shadows across his perfect features.

Battle Master Argus Thilandri stood at attention at the base of the dais, his lunar weave armor betraying no movement despite his growing discomfort with the silence. The absence of Thruva's wives felt particularly pronounced in the empty chamber. Even the air seemed stagnant, devoid of the usual gentle breeze that perpetually moved through the Court.

"My Lord," Argus ventured carefully, his voice barely disturbing the heavy quiet, "shall I summon your wives? Perhaps their presence might ease your mind?"

Thruva's only response was a grunt of negation, his attention never leaving the void ring as it circled his finger. The gesture reminded Argus of a predator toying with its prey before the kill. However, whether the predator was Thruva or the ring he could not say.

Another uncomfortable moment stretched between them, broken only by the soft whisper of Thruva's robes as he shifted on his throne. Argus weighed his next words carefully, knowing he treaded on dangerous ground.

"My Lord," he began, his tone measured and respectful, "perhaps we might consider dispatching additional Seekers to replace Amjani and Isque? The hunt for your niece and her mortal grows more pressing with each passing moment."

The change in Thruva was instant and terrifying. He surged to his feet, his perfect features contorting with rage as void energy crackled around him like black lightning. The walls of the citadel seemed to pulse with his fury, the eternal night growing darker still.

"Would you have me announce the deepest shame of our Court from the highest spire of the citadel?" Thruva's voice boomed through the chamber, each word dripping with barely contained violence. "Shall I gather every member of our realm to share the tale of my sister's betrayal? Set forth the memory back into the minds of all?"

Argus took an involuntary step backward, his martial training warring with his instinct to flee. The void ring on Thruva's finger pulsed with an unholy light as the Arch Fae descended the dais with predatory grace.

"If you ever speak of this matter outside of my direct questioning again," Thruva hissed, looming over his Battle Master, "I will personally burn your soul from within with the void itself. Do you understand?"

"Yes, my Lord," Argus managed, bowing so low his forehead nearly touched the floor. "Forgive my presumption."

The transformation was instantaneous. Like a storm dissolving into clear skies, Thruva's rage evaporated, replaced by his usual ethereal composure. He extended his hand, placing it upon Argus's bowed head with a gentleness that seemed impossible given his previous fury. The touch carried an unsettling chill that made Argus's scalp tingle beneath his Battle Master's helm.

"Rise, my faithful guardian," Thruva's voice had returned to its symphonic quality, though something discordant lurked beneath the surface. "Your concern, while misplaced, comes from a place of loyalty. This I know."

Argus straightened, his instincts screaming at him to maintain distance from the Arch Fae. Yet duty anchored him in place as his eyes were drawn to the void ring on Thruva's finger. The raw energy emanating from it felt wrong, like a wound in reality itself. In all his centuries of service, he had never known his lord to dabble in such dangerous magics. The ring seemed to pulse in response to his attention, and for a moment, Argus could have sworn he heard whispers emanating from it, speaking in a language that made his teeth ache.

Thruva glided back to his throne, his movements carrying the same deliberate grace as always, yet somehow seeming mechanical, as if he were a puppet being guided by invisible strings. The white-gold threads in his robes caught the eternal moonlight, creating patterns that reminded Argus of chains.

"We must be patient," Thruva murmured, more to himself than to Argus. His fingers began their endless rotation of the void ring once more. "The pieces are in motion, the board set." His lips barely moved as he spoke, and Argus wasn't entirely certain the words were meant for him.

The Battle Master forced himself to remain still, though every fiber of his being urged him to flee the chamber. His duty was to protect Lord Thruva, even from himself if necessary. But as he watched his lord whisper to the ring, observed the way the void energy seemed to seep into the perfect features of the Arch Fae's face, Argus wondered if he hadn't already failed in that duty.

"Soon," Thruva breathed, his voice barely audible. The ring pulsed again, and this time Argus was certain he saw something move within its depths, something that should not exist in any realm. "Soon all will be as it should be." A smile crept across Thruva's face, beautiful and terrible all at once, as he continued his quiet communion with the void.

Through the gossamer curtains that separated the infirmary beds, moonlight filtered in eternal streams across Amjani's sleeping form. Her recovery had been slower than the healers expected, despite her wounds knitting together faster than Isque's. The explosion of Elirel's final spell had nearly torn her apart, and even now, months later, the silvery scars that traced across her body seemed to pulse with remembered agony.

Isque sat beside her bed, his own bandaged form a testament to their failure. The burns that marked half his face had begun to heal, though the healers warned him they would likely never fade completely. He hardly cared about the scars - his attention remained fixed on Amjani's hand clasped in his own.

She whimpered in her sleep, her head turning fitfully on the pillow. These nightmares had become routine, her screams often echoing through the infirmary in the endless night. Isque gently stroked her hand with his thumb, careful of the newly healed flesh.

"I almost lost you," he whispered, his voice rough with emotion. "When I saw you lying there, broken and burning..." He swallowed hard, the memory making his own scars ache. "I cannot bear the thought of a realm without you in it, my dearest Amjani. Soon you'll be well enough to leave this place, and then..." He lifted her hand to his lips, pressing a gentle kiss to her knuckles and praying this failure would force her to see reason and flee the Court with him. "Then you'll finally be mine."

Amjani stirred, her eyes fluttering open. She turned her head toward him, a smile playing across her lips as she squeezed his hand weakly. For a moment, the tenderness in her gaze made his heart skip.

Then awareness returned to her features, and while the smile remained, it took on a sharper edge. "Taking liberties while I sleep, Seeker Isque?" Her voice carried both warning and warmth. "I do hope your hands haven't wandered anywhere else during my recovery."

The seductive undertone in her voice made his breath catch, even as the stern reminder of protocol beneath her words caused him to carefully release her hand. "I would never dream of such impropriety, Master Seeker. Well, that is a lie. I dreamed of it often, but I would never do so... and get caught." he replied while attempting to return her playful tone, though his eyes betrayed his longing.

She shifted in the bed, wincing slightly. "See that you don't," she murmured, her tone softening. "We both know what boundaries must remain, no matter how..." she paused, her eyes traveling over his scarred features, "tempting it might be to cross them. I must admit, however, it was more tempting when your face was not so grotesque."

Isque placed his hand over his heart in mock offense, his scarred features twisting into an exaggerated expression of hurt. "You wound me, my dearest Amjani. And here I thought my rugged new appearance might make me even more irresistible." His attempt at levity fell flat as he caught sight of the fresh scars that traced across her own flesh, visible where her healing robes had shifted.

His playful demeanor faded, replaced by something more somber. "We nearly died, Amjani. When I saw you lying there, broken and burning..." He swallowed hard, the memory making his own scars throb. "It made me realize how fragile even immortal life can be."

She watched him carefully, her expression guarded but not unkind. The eternal moonlight streaming through the gossamer curtains caught the silver in her amber hair, creating a halo effect that made his heart ache.

"I know how dedicated you are to the Lunar Court, to Lord Thruva," he continued, his voice dropping lower. "And as long as you remain here, serving them, then I shall-"

White-hot pain exploded behind his eyes, driving the words from his mouth. In his mind, he heard the rumbling voice of Duke Dalmoth, like boulders grinding against each other: *"Remember your oath, little Seeker. The only way you will ever claim her is to follow through. Remember what torments await you should you stray from our path."*

The agony lasted only seconds, but it left him gasping, sweat beading on his forehead. When his vision cleared, he found Amjani studying him with narrowed eyes, all trace of warmth gone from her expression.

"My duty will always be to Lord Thruva and the Lunar Court," she said, her voice carrying an edge sharp enough to draw blood. "As should yours be, unless..." Her eyes locked onto his, fierce and uncompromising. "Unless you are an oath breaker, Seeker Isque?"

He felt the weight of her words, heavy with unspoken threat. The pain in his head pulsed in time with his heartbeat as he forced himself to meet her gaze.

"In which case," she continued, her tone growing colder still, "I will shred your body until there is nothing left. You have toyed with your words far too many times in my presence. Allude to such frivolity of our oaths again and I will do it simply for honor's sake."

The ghost of his earlier smile played across his scarred lips, though it didn't reach his eyes. "My dearest Amjani," he said softly, "I would expect nothing less."

A sudden thrum of power rippled through the Arcane Web, making the eternal moonlight flicker. Amjani jolted upright in her bed, silver scars gleaming as her body tensed. Beside her, Isque shot to his feet, his scarred face twisting with recognition.

"Her pact mortal," Amjani breathed, her voice tight with pain and anticipation.

Isque's lips curled into a bitter smile. "The fool. To use his power now..."

Before either could say more, the twilight walls of the infirmary shimmered and parted. Battle Master Argus strode through, his lunar weave armor catching the moonlight and setting about a prismatic aura as he announced, "Lord Thruva approaches."

Isque dropped to one knee immediately, his head bowed low. Amjani forced herself from the bed with visible effort, her newly healed flesh protesting as she mirrored his pose. The eternal night beyond the gossamer curtains seemed to darken as Lord Thruva entered, his white-gold robes swirling around him like liquid starlight.

"Are you prepared to redeem yourselves?" Thruva's symphonic voice carried an undercurrent of something discordant, something... wrong.

"Yes, my Lord," Amjani answered without hesitation, her voice strong despite her weakened state.

"Of course, my Lord," Isque echoed, though his eyes remained fixed on the floor.

One of the healer rushed forward into the space, her robes billowing around her. "My Lord, please," she protested, "they need more time to recover. Their wounds-"

Thruva's hand stretched out toward her, fingers splayed, though he didn't even turn to look at her. Purple void energy erupted from the healer's pores as she screamed, her voice cutting off abruptly as she collapsed. Where a beautiful Fae woman had stood moments before, only a withered husk remained, her flesh gray and desiccated as if she had aged millennia in seconds.

Amjani didn't flinch, her face a mask of perfect devotion. But Isque felt his stomach turn, and he saw Argus's hand tighten imperceptibly on his weapon's hilt. The wrongness of the power Thruva wielded hung in the air like a physical presence, tainting the eternal moonlight with shadows within shadows that shouldn't exist.

"You leave within the hour," Thruva commanded, his perfect features betraying no reaction to the death he had just dealt. "Quickly Seeker Isque, where did the pulse originate from?"

Isque realized he was holding his breath and released it quickly. He was testing him now? He shook his head and tried to focus despite the scene he had just witnessed. He centered himself and let his mind wonder the Arcane Web and hunt the origin point. His eyes flitted about beneath their lids rapidly as he got closer.

"Somewhere in the northeastern part of the Scarred Lands, my Lord." His breathing had become rapid. It was a clear sign that he was still not nearly mended. He had to expend far too much energy to trace Oakira's pact mortal. Before Elirel nearly left him a corpse, he would have been able to find the mortal's location with the ease of a simple jog, but now his body immediately felt the weight of a days sprint.

Thruva's face twisted into a contemplative expression as he paced before the kneeling Seekers. The void ring pulsed with each graceful step, casting unsettling shadows across the infirmary's sheer curtains.

"Hus'rokn," he mused, his symphonic voice carrying that same discordant undertone. "The mongrel would seek refuge there. It's a cesspool of his kind, after all." His lip curled in disgust. "And The Wilds to the east would suit his little Vulpine pet well. It's less congested there."

Amjani's silver scars tightened as she forced herself to remain still, though Isque could see the tremor in her shoulders from maintaining the position. "My Lord," she ventured, "how do you wish us to proceed once we locate them?"

Thruva stopped his pacing, turning to face them with an ethereal grace that seemed somehow mechanical. "Bring them to me. Alive." His perfect features split into a smile that made Isque's stomach turn. "I have prepared a special chamber within our Court. There, we will... convince them to draw my dear niece out of hiding."

The way Thruva caressed the void ring as he spoke sent chills down Isque's spine. Thruva's fascination with the ring was no longer subtle. He could even see Battle Master Argus shift his left foot as though his mind was barely winning a war with his body to flee. Isque kept his eyes fixed on the floor, not daring to look up as the Arch Fae continued.

"The mongrel's connection to her through their pact will serve as a beacon," Thruva explained, his voice taking on an almost dreamy quality. "If he will not cooperate then perhaps the sound of the child's screams will stir in him an eagerness to call our abomination forth. If she refuses to come even then... well then the real fun will begin."

Argus shifted almost imperceptibly at these words, his hand tightening on his weapon. But Amjani showed no reaction, her face a mask of perfect devotion. "It shall be done, my Lord."

"Yes," Thruva breathed. "It shall. And when my wayward niece arrives to save her pets..." He trailed off, leaving the threat unspoken.

Isque felt Duke Dalmoth's presence press against his mind, a warning pressure behind his eyes. He pushed back the pain, forcing himself to maintain his composure as Thruva glided toward the infirmary's exit.

"Do not fail me again," the Arch Fae commanded, his voice carrying the weight of ages. "Or what happened to that healer will seem a mercy by comparison."

As Thruva disappeared through the shimmering walls, Isque finally dared to look up. He caught Amjani's eye, seeing in her gaze a determination that matched the steel in her voice when she spoke.

"It may take us some time to find our prey. We'll have to wait for him to use some of his power again, but now we will be close enough grab the thread and pull us to him. Our Lord commanded us to leave within the hour. We will be ready in half the time. Bring me my armor."

CHAPTER THIRTY-FIVE

NOT SO NEAT LITTLE BOW

Lemmy circled overhead, picking fights with the sparrows that were nesting in a nearby tree while cawing with seemingly high amusement. He was being a twat. At least that was Kasha's opinion. Morrigan sat on Arialyn's stormer, sitting as close as possible to the handles and pretending she was speeding through the streets.

Three days had passed since the mansion massacre and everything since then had been a blur. Arialyn, Kasha and Egrim had gone back to the Tits and Tarts as fast as they could to make sure everything was still alright.

Kasha had closed early on opening night, which was a huge faux pas that she only allowed because of the severity of the circumstances of the night. Lorisse had stayed with Morrigan in her room and Merle, along with a handful of Gauntlet members had kept watch over the place in Kasha's absence.

Callus had gone with Ethan, Herodin and the remaining Talons to some undisclosed location that Ethan refused to speak of. Callus hadn't even been allowed to leave once they got there. He sent letters to Arialyn via a courier of Shield Rosamunda explaining that those in attendance needed to be kept away from public eye until the details of what comes next were hashed out among those present.

"I'm not waiting out here much longer." Egrim huffed with annoyance.

Kasha grabbed ahold of his arm and leaned into him. "Stop it. Morrigan is having fun and this is important. Ethan has helped me out a lot over the years and I want to be here when he comes out and makes it official. I wouldn't have gotten the new location without him."

Arialyn knelt beside the stormer, her fingers nimbly adjusting a loose connection in the arcane core housing. Morrigan leaned over, watching intently as purple sparks danced between Arialyn's skilled hands.

"Want to learn how it works?" Arialyn asked, glancing up with a playful smile. Morrigan nodded eagerly, her eyes wide with fascination. "Well, first you have to promise not to tell your father I'm teaching you dangerous arcanomancer secrets."

Morrigan's tail swished with excitement as she made an exaggerated crossing motion over her heart. Behind them, Kasha stifled a laugh at Egrim's eye roll. "Could you at least pretend to make an effort at not letting me overhear you."

The peaceful moment shattered as the heavy doors of the Governor's Keep swung open. Callus emerged first, followed by Ethan, but they weren't alone. Herodin and the six familiar faces of the Talons that had joined their side in the fight stepped out into the afternoon light.

"They aren't wearing their Talons of Misery gear anymore." Arialyn muttered, rising from her crouching position. Her hand unconsciously drifted toward the arcabus at her hip.

They watched as Herodin and four of the former Talons exchanged firm handshakes with the other two members of their former gang. The separation felt deliberate, ceremonial almost. The pair turned and walked away, disappearing into the busy streets of Hus'rokn without a backward glance.

Kasha's fingers tightened on Egrim's arm as Ethan spoke briefly to Herodin and the remaining four others. Though they couldn't hear the exchange, the Captain's authoritative body language over them suggested something official had transpired. After a moment, Herodin and his companions headed off in a different direction, their bearing notably more professional than their departed fellows.

"Did we just witness what I think we did?" Kasha asked, her voice soft and somewhat disbelieving.

Egrim's eyes narrowed as he watched Callus and Ethan approach. "Looks like the Captain's already adding to his new crew."

"With Talons?" Arialyn scoffed, though her expression showed more confusion than judgment. "That's... unexpected."

Morrigan had abandoned her play, pressing close to Egrim's side as she sensed the slight tension and excitement in the adults around her. Lemmy swooped down to perch on her shoulder, his beak rubbing against her ear and making soothing clicking noises.

As they drew near it was obvious in Ethan's expression that much had changed. He held less of the look of despair he carried when he arrived back in Hus'rokn a few nights ago. Though, they could all see the hollowness Serine's death created was still behind his new mask, there was signs of the old Captain beneath it as well.

Throughout the days spent at the Governor's Keep, Ethan racked his mind with what this new position would mean. Not just for him but for the city. Almost all the time he had for himself he spent staring at the note Arialyn had hidden within the puzzle box. *She is in love with you, jackass.'*

He thought about every time he and Serine had been alone. At least the times he could remember. There was not a single moment of awkwardness, bitterness or unease. He had been a fool. A Gods damned fool. He also realized he had been wrong. She was right, he couldn't be half in and half out anymore. When he spoke with Adenus he thought he had made his choice. He realized he chose wrong. He was going to change that and make Serine proud of the man he could be, the man she would have wanted him to be.

Callus's approach on the other hand, was all smiles and he ran to Arialyn as she did the same. She leapt into his arms, and he spun her around, kissing her.

"Don't ever leave me alone that long ever again. You hear me?" Her words were harsh but her expression forgiving.

Callus side eyed the Captain. "I told you I was going to be in trouble."

Kasha released Egrim's arm and stepped forward, her eyes darting between Ethan and Callus. "I thought that was going to be a short-term alliance." She motioned down the street in the direction Herodin and the others left.

Callus gave an exaggerated shrug, though the hint of a smile played at the corner of his mouth. "What? A bunch of criminals can't be reformed into other more organized and leashed criminals? Excuse me, city officials."

Egrim shook his head. "New animal, same stripes."

Ethan nodded, straightening his guard uniform and flicking the new patch on his right shoulder. The usual city guard emblem replaced with the Lance insignia, a gray background with a red lance running diagonally. "They are no longer Talons. Herodin and those four with him are joining my personal guard. We're rebuilding the Lance from the ground up." He paused, glancing at the others who had walked away. "The other's took their share of Zunibar's coin as promised and are burying the name Talon of Misery. They are choosing a different path that takes them far away from here."

Egrim grunted. "What about the Lance members still loyal to Authern?"

"That's where Herodin and his men come in," Ethan explained, his expression hardening slightly. "They'll help track down the MIA holdouts. Those willing to fall in line under the new leadership can stay. The others..." He let the implication hang in the air.

Arialyn shifted impatiently. "Yeah, yeah. What about Beetle and the deed to my bloody shop? Have you found him?"

The new Lance placed his hands on his hips and sighed, shaking his head in disappointment. "No, but we found where he took Alejak after the brawl at the Lucky Talisman. All we found was the corpse of that Marvin fellow that was so loyal to Alejak."

Arialyn's hands began to shake with rage. Her brow furrowed and she pursed her lips.

Callus busted in quickly. "The deed was on the body. It's taken care of Squi-love. My love." He figured calling her squirt now might end with him getting an arcane bolt shot at his cock.

The sigh of relief Arialyn gave made it seem as though she had been holding her breath since she found out about the deed being stolen.

Ethan continued. "However, we will keep looking for Beetle. The idea of that monstrosity wandering around my city makes me shiver."

Callus looked perturbed. "You need to be careful looking for him. He's heavily tethered to Odhrum Voidspawn. I can feel it. I don't know if he can be killed by normal means."

Egrim nodded. "I saw him do some very interesting things in that courtyard. He's more powerful than he lets on. Or he's insane enough to be unaware of it."

"Fucking perfect." Ethan groaned as though it was just one more thing to be piled on the shit show he willingly signed up for.

"So," Arialyn said changing the subject to more desirable places, "you're all official now then?" Her eyes shifted to Callus. He looked at Ethan with a mockingly grandiose wave. "You're looking at the newly titled Lance Captain Ethan Giantfeller."

Ethan shook his head. "That last bit sounds so Godsdamn stupid."

Arialyn couldn't help herself. "That is pretty awful."

"Come up with that genius surname all on your own?" Kasha chided.

"Rosamunda's idea of a joke." Callus chuckled. "A pretty decent one too."

Ethan nodded, his face breaking into a grimaced smile. "Adenus and Rose both oathed me in. The Three remain intact, just with a slight change in management."

"Slight change?" Kasha laughed, though there was a nervous edge to it. "Shield Rosamunda didn't give you any push back at all?"

"Push back?" Ethan chuckled, shaking his head in amazement. "She was practically giddy about it. I've never seen her so pleased. Said something about *finally having someone with sense running the Lance.'* The Lance is no longer in the business of assassination and indentured service contracts. The Lance now runs the city guard. Which I am perfectly built for. Almost like it was meant to be."

Morrigan tugged at Egrim's sleeve, her eyes wide with curiosity. Egrim bent down to whisper something in her ear, causing her to nod seriously before returning to the stormer, though her attention remained fixed on the adults' conversation.

"Well," Kasha said, smoothing her dress, "I suppose this calls for a celebration. Good thing we happen to own an establishment perfect for such occasions."

He held up his hands. "Kasha, I couldn't ask you to do that."

She waved his gesture off. "Then it is a good thing I offered, isn't it?"

He bowed and spread his hands open in an accepting gesture. "Then just let me know the time and place. I'll be there."

Ethan shifted his weight and cleared his throat dramatically, drawing everyone's attention. "Now that the official business is done..." He turned to Callus and Egrim with an exaggerated formality that made Kasha scoff. "My dear gentlemen of exceptional violence..."

Callus groaned. "Here we go."

"While I already know the answer," Ethan continued, placing his hand over his heart, "I would be remiss in my duties as the newly appointed Lance Captain if I didn't formally offer you both positions within my organization." He already felt the glares coming from both Arialyn and Kasha. "Would you do me the honor of becoming my lieutenants?"

Morrigan giggled from her perch on the stormer, and Lemmy cawed what sounded suspiciously like laughter.

Egrim crossed his arms, his beard braids swaying as he shook his head. "I don't play well with others. You know that. Your uniform supplier would go bankrupt trying to outfit me repeatedly anyway."

"He's got a point," Callus added. "Could probably save some coin in the pants area though." His voice went to a whisper. "Not a lot going on in the special area I hear."

"Baby's arm holding an apple, for your information." Egrim said the words as if they were fact and let the uncomfortable silence settle around them. Kasha spared a very quick glance that Arialyn caught, causing Kasha to blush.

Ethan turned his eye on Callus. "And you, my childhood hero?"

"I'm going to pretend you didn't just say that," Callus muttered, through a broken smile of embarrassment for the man. "I'll pass on the official position, but you know where to find me if you need help. Just don't make it a habit. I have a shop to run and a lady to please."

"Callus!" Arialyn protested with a blush that Kasha now had her chance to smirk at.

"Well, can't blame a man for trying. Now, if you'll excuse me, I have a mansion to inspect." He straightened his new Lance insignia. "Apparently, I acquired Alabaster's old place in this deal."

"Burn some sage," Kasha suggested. "Lots of sage."

"I was thinking more along the lines of demolition and rebuilding," Ethan replied with a wink. He bowed to them all with flourish. "Now, if you'll excuse me, I have pretentious rich people things to attend to. I need to practice my condescending stare in the mirror."

As he walked away, Callus called after him, "Don't forget to practice your dramatic cape swish!"

Ethan responded with a rather rude hand gesture without looking back, causing Morrigan to cover her mouth in shock while Lemmy squawked his approval.

Kasha leaned against Egrim, her brow furrowed in thought. "How is he really doing?"

Callus sighed in an encouraging way. "Oddly enough, a little better. I still saw him crying a few times off on his own when he thought no one was around. Her death is going to take a long time to stop hurting him so badly. But he kept telling me he has a plan and it's because of her that things in this city will get better. I think the Captain is far craftier than we gather."

Egrim snorted. "If he isn't dealing with the indenture service contracts, then who is?"

"Seems that is between the contract holder and the servant in question, but the City Guard will take charge of investigating contract disputes."

"So, the Lance is going legitimate? Well, as legitimate as anything gets in Hus'rokn." Kasha questioned him somewhat in dismay.

"Indeed." Callus confirmed. "Pretty sure he and Adenus are working on something behind the scenes though. There was a lot of subtle eye contact between the two. Not sure what but I suppose we'll find out in time. He's diverted my questioning the few times I've hinted at it."

Kasha cleared her throat, watching as Egrim moved to help Morrigan down from the stormer. "Speaking of celebrations," she said, nearly dancing on her tiptoes, "everything for the wedding is falling into place beautifully. Though I do need you both to stop by for measurements as soon as possible."

Callus froze. "I'm sorry, what?"

Arialyn's face fell, and she let out a dramatic groan that made Morrigan peek around Egrim's shoulder with curiosity. "I told her you finally proposed, and she just started planning everything. I tried to stop her, but she already had a book of ideas and contacts!" She turned to Kasha. "And you," she pointed a finger at Kasha, "have already had me measured three fucking times. I swear if you try to stuff me into another corset-"

"Now, hold on a minute. Let's not be hasty." Callus chuckled, reaching down to pat Arialyn's head like one might soothe an irritated puppy. "Be good for Kasha. She's putting a lot of work into this."

Arialyn snapped at his hand playfully, her teeth clicking together just shy of his fingers. The display made Morrigan burst into giggles, and she bared her own teeth in mimicry of Arialyn's gesture.

"Bad puppy," Callus scolded, wagging his finger at Arialyn with mock sternness. "Both of you." He included Morrigan in his finger-wagging, which only made the young girl giggle harder.

Arialyn raised an eyebrow at Callus. "So, you went from shock to everything is fine just because I mentioned a corset?"

Callus nodded with a goofy grin. "Yes."

"Told you." Kasha said as she poked Arialyn on her cheek.

Kasha couldn't help but smile at their antics. "Oh! And I almost forgot," she said, reaching into a hidden pocket of her dress. "I received a letter from Carl this morning via the witch raven." She produced a slightly crumpled piece of parchment, holding it up triumphantly. "He's confirmed he'll be attending, and he's bringing several barrels of the Blood Ale Company's finest as a wedding gift."

"Really?" Callus's face lit up. "The cranky old goat actually wrote that?"

"Well," Kasha smirked, glancing at the letter, "his exact words were 'I suppose I have to show up since you lot won't stop pestering me about it. Four witch ravens in two days was a bit much. I'll bring some decent drink so I can be properly lubricated for forced social interaction.'"

Arialyn snorted. "That sounds more like him."

"There was also a postscript. Although in different, more elegant penmanship," Kasha continued, her eyes twinkling with mischief. "It read 'Are there going to be whores? Please say there will be whores -F-'. Do you know who the hell 'F' is?"

"Sounds like Fithra. She's their Sergeant-at-Arms. I've only met her twice. She is dangerous and horny but makes good conversation. And she flusters Carl, so she'll be entertaining."

"Great." Arialyn mused with an eye roll.

Morrigan balanced on top of the stormer's seat, dancing from one side to the other in a playful rhythm. Lemmy mirrored her movements on the handlebars, his talons gripping and releasing as he hopped back and forth with obvious delight. The adults' conversation created a comfortable backdrop of chatter about weddings and celebrations, their voices covering over her like a familiar blanket.

She was mid-hop when something made her freeze completely, one foot still raised in the air. Her ears twitched, swiveling toward a sound that seemed to come from everywhere and nowhere at once. A whisper, soft and insistent, threading through the afternoon air like one of those biting insects she hated so much on the journey here.

Her eyes followed the pull of the sound, scanning the busy street until they locked onto something that made her breath catch. There, embedded in the weathered stone of an ornate fountain across the way, was a piece of purple crystal. It glittered with an inner light that seemed to pulse in rhythm with her heartbeat, and she found it a similar pretty hue to void ore crystals she'd seen in Arialyn's arcabus and the gems that powered Callus's braces.

The whispering grew stronger, more urgent, and Morrigan shook her head as if trying to dislodge water from her ears. But the sound only intensified, wrapping around her thoughts like tendrils of shadow. The world began to tilt and spin, the familiar street blurring at the edges as dizziness washed over her in waves.

Within her mind's eye, a figure began to take shape, short and wreathed in shadows of black and purple that seemed to writhe and dance. The body of the figure was warped and seemed like it was in the middle of a physical metamorphosis. The whispers coalesced into something almost like words, and through the growing fog in her head, she heard a name spoken with reverent hunger, *'Voidtongue.'*

The name felt like an impact in her brain, and her small body swayed dangerously on the stormer. Memories of years of nightmares came flooding back in waves that threatened to overtake her mind, nightmares she always forgot when she awoke, but nevertheless brought sheer terror straight into her heart. Her vision tunneled, the purple crystal seeming to grow larger and brighter until it filled her entire field of view. The shadowy figure reached toward her with arms that weren't quite arms. Claws? The whispers became a roar that threatened to drown out everything else.

Morrigan's foot slipped, and she tumbled backward off the stormer with a whimpering cry of alarm.

Callus reacted before anyone else could and swiftly slid on his knees catching her before she could hit the ground. She found herself cradled against Callus's chest, his face playful but with concern. "Got you, little one," he murmured, his voice cutting through the lingering echoes in her head.

Egrim was beside them in an instant, taking his daughter from Callus and holding her firmly in his arms. "Morrigan? What happened? Are you hurt?"

She blinked up at them both, the memory of the whispers and the shadowy figure already fading like fog in a storm. The dizziness was receding, leaving behind only a vague sense of unease and the faint taste of something metallic on her tongue. She shook her head, trying to clear the remaining fog and managed a small smile to reassure her worried father.

Egrim kissed the top of her head. "I need you to be more careful. But only a little."

CHAPTER THIRTY-SIX

THE BREAKING POINT

Kasha had never been more thrilled or overwhelmed in her life. The new Witch's Tits and Tarts Tavern had been open for two weeks, minus the night of the assault on Zunibar and the former Lance, and each day was busier than the last. They were out of tarts every day by mid evening and had just recently started baking more to accommodate the demand. The twelve barrels of Bloody Ale Company Red that Carl had shipped to her as a gift on opening night had all been tapped and run dry by the end of the first week. Her serving girls were getting such incredible tips that she feared some of them might decide to take sudden and extended vacations and those that were renting out rooms upstairs for erotic pleasures were booked solid for the next three months.

Egrim had been a massive help. There had been no violence of any kind after the opening night dust up with the Talons of Misery. Hells, the only person to get rowdy after that night immediately apologized when Egrim appeared in his vision and politely excused himself.

But, Egrim had been of far more use to her than just being the muscle for the tavern. He had made Kasha laugh and kept her from spinning out of control during the most chaotic times. The shoulder massages he gave her when they finally closed for the night were a very welcome event and one that she couldn't help but desire. His hands completely enveloped her shoulders. She had enjoyed his touch so much that she had started lying to him when he asked if he had got all the knots out. She would insist that she was still bunched up in one shoulder blade or the other.

Three nights ago, she had celebrated a little at closing time and taken a few shots with Arialyn. When Egrim had massaged her shoulder that night she had grabbed ahold of one of his hands and kissed it. She caught herself in the middle of the act and tried to play it off as though she had nodded off to sleep and caught herself with his hand. He either believed her or didn't know how to respond to her excuse.

Morrigan was even coming out of her shell more and more. When they first opened, she wouldn't even come out of her and Egrim's room during opening hours. Something Egrim had told Kasha he was fine with. He didn't particularly want her around people who were not keen on monitoring their own ale intake, even if they were all behaving themselves. Over the last few nights, however, she had begun to come out of their room and sit with her legs hanging between the openings in the wooden rails of the mezzanine as Lemmy perched near her for her comfort. Kasha had even noticed her smiling a few times when people began to dance on the nights they had musicians play.

Kasha was zoned out for the moment, leaning against the doorframe to the kitchen just behind the bar. The Raucous Ruffians were playing their second set of the night. The musical troupe had three members to their name. Jezel, who had played for the Tits on opening night, got Kasha to hire her full band. She played the lyre in a manner that could lull you to sleep or drive you to dance on tables. Phinst, the goblin percussionist, had hands that moved so fast and smooth many of the women, and a few of the men, wondered if he was as dexterous in other situations. Their flutist was an orc that went by the name Graunch. He had wowed people with the ability to mix orcish throat singing behind Jezel's soothing voice. The Raucous Ruffians had been so well received that Kasha had asked them to play two nights a week for the next six weeks with the opportunity for an extension when that was over.

Kasha was enamored with the band to be sure, but one of the main perks of late was that Egrim and Morrigan had begun to dance up on the mezzanine. Egrim refused to take true breaks at any time throughout their opening hours, but at least twice a night when the Ruffians played, he would make it a point to go upstairs and dance with Morrigan.

Sometimes it was a slow dance where he would pick her up and hum along with the tune while Morrigan rested her head against her father's shoulder and others they would stomp around with only half the rhythm necessary to look as though they knew what they were doing. Morrigan would smile from ear to ear for the entirety of their dance, either way. These dances were one of the very rare times she saw Egrim let his guard down fully. It warmed and broke her heart at the same time. No matter what she told herself about how she wanted to live her life, seeing them like this was a reminder of what she desired and what she couldn't have at the same time.

Egrim was on the mezzanine with Morrigan right now, stomping around to Morrigan's favorite song of the Raucous Ruffians set. Thankfully, it seemed Morrigan didn't know what the song was actually about. If she understood the Grimalkin language she would have had many questions that Egrim would rather not have answer at her age.

Egrim, to Kasha's eyes, was pretending to be even less coordinated than usual and Morrigan was laughing hysterically. The song reached its peak, and he picked her up and spun her around in circles. As the song ended, he sat her feet back down on the ground and bowed as she curtsied in return.

Kasha's smile beamed enough to hide the small tear that was dripping from her cheek. She tried hard to stop her mind from spinning out of control to memories she had buried as deep as she possibly could.

She even put her mental Madame mask back on and shook her head in a failed attempt to bring her mind back to reality. She looked down at her harlequin skirt of gold and onyx and smoothed out a few wrinkles. After that she checked her breasts to make sure she didn't need to reoil any spots. She held her hand out in front of her face. Just to perk herself up a bit she moved her fingers in a few simple arcane patterns and hit herself with a small burst of frosty air.

It was beginning to work until she heard Morrigan laugh hysterically as Egrim crouched down and tickled her. Then, just like that, her mind fell down a spiral that she had avoided sliding down for a long time.

The sweet scent of jasmine and honey drifted up from the alcoholic tea in Kasha's hands as she watched the bard perform. His fingers danced across the lyre strings with elegant grace, and his voice carried an almost supernatural quality that made her heart flutter. The Summer Spark Festival had transformed the usually austere streets of Hus'rokn into a vibrant celebration of life and culture.

She adjusted her position on the stone edge of the flower bed, careful not to spill her drink. The thin leather pants she wore clung uncomfortably in the summer heat, but she knew they flattered her hips. Her exposed shoulders and low neckline had already drawn appreciative glances from several passersby, though none had dared approach the striking tiefling woman.

The dark dwarf woman who had sold her the tea wandered past, offering samples to other festival-goers. She caught Kasha's eye and gave her a knowing wink. The tea was strong, perfectly balanced between the bite of alcohol and the sweetness of honey. Kasha made a mental note to get the vendor's name before she left, such skill with beverages could be useful if she ever managed to open her own establishment.

But for now, she let herself be carried away by the bard's performance. His honey-blonde hair caught the late afternoon sun, and his smile seemed to be directed at each member of his audience individually. When his eyes met hers, Kasha felt her breath leave her entirely. There was something in that gaze that spoke of possibilities, of music and laughter.

The crowd around him had grown, but somehow, he kept finding moments to glance her way. Each time their eyes met, his smile grew warmer, more intimate. Kasha found herself smoothing her hair, though she knew the updo was still perfectly in place. She hadn't felt anything even close to this since Callus. She looked back on that fateful night still uncertain if it was her actions that caused the blunder or her inaction after her failed wooing of her longtime friend. Not long after they had all left her for the Helspires.

Her thoughts drifted briefly to Callus, wondering if he still fought in the arena, if he was even still alive. She pushed the dark thoughts away. This wasn't the time for old wounds. The festival was about new beginnings, about hope.

The bard finished his song with a flourish that drew enthusiastic applause from the crowd. As they began to disperse, he carefully set his lyre in its case and made his way toward her. Kasha's heart quickened as he approached, his confident stride and charming smile making her *feel like a young girl again. She turned her head away and took another sip of her spiced tea, fanning disinterest.*

"I couldn't help but notice you enjoying the performance," he said, his voice as melodic in conversation as it was in song. "I'm Folkvar. Might I have the pleasure of your name?"

Kasha took another sip of her tea to steady herself before responding, "I'm Kasha. Your music is... enchanting."

Folkvar's smile widened at her compliment, and he gave her an elegant half-bow. "Enchanting is easy when there's someone in the audience who has already cast their own spell over the performer." His voice carried the perfect blend of confidence and humility.

Kasha rolled her eyes playfully but couldn't completely hide her smile. "Do those lines usually work for you?" She took another sip of her tea, using the moment to compose herself. The sway of her tail betrayed her attraction despite her attempted nonchalance.

"I wouldn't know," he replied, settling beside her on the stone edge of the flower bed. "I save my best material for truly special occasions." His shoulder barely brushed against hers, the contact seemingly accidental but perfectly calculated.

"Are you from Hus'rokn?" His eyes caught the late afternoon light in a way that made them appear to sparkle. "Or did you travel here for the festival?"

Kasha shifted slightly, sitting on her tail to stop it's betrayal. "I've lived here most of my life. I work as a barmaid at a tavern in the Wylds. The Copper Kettle." She watched his reaction carefully, having learned long ago that some men's interest cooled rapidly when they learned of her profession.

Instead, Folkvar's face lit up with genuine pleasure. "Ah, then you're exactly my type of woman. I've always believed the best women know their way around spirits and come with horns." He gestured playfully toward her curved horns, careful not to actually touch them.

The tea in Kasha's cup had dwindled to barely a mouthful, and she swirled it thoughtfully. "Are you just going to flirt with me all afternoon, or are you going to ask me out like a proper gentleman?" She kept her tone light but direct, tired of the dance even as she enjoyed it.

Folkvar laughed, the sound rich and melodious. "I was getting there, I assure you."

"Better hurry," she said, lifting her cup. "My drink is almost empty, and then I'll have to get up and find another one." She took the final sip, her eyes never leaving his over the rim of the cup.

"Then allow me to prevent such a tragedy." He stood and offered her his hand with theatrical flourish. "Would you do me the honor of joining me for dinner this evening? I know a lovely place near the Trade Gate that serves the most excellent Brightborn whisky cocktails, and you seem like the type of lady that likes a strong drink."

Kasha lay in their bed, the silk sheets cool against her heated skin. The memory of her wedding day still danced behind her closed eyes. She had spent hours that morning obsessing over every detail of her appearance, a habit born from years under Zunibar's cruel scrutiny. Each imperfection had been a reason for punishment then, and even now, years later, she couldn't shake the compulsion to achieve perfection.

She remembered how her hands had trembled as she applied her makeup for the fifth time, convinced the previous attempts weren't good enough. The way she had torn through three different hairstyles before Lorisse had finally grabbed her hands and forced her to sit still. How she had made Mother Maudrid inspect every inch of her dress for even the smallest flaw, terrified that one loose thread would ruin everything.

The old witch had returned a few months back from the Helspires with terrible news about their former circus family of Sylus's Traveling Spectacles and Callus's fate. The news had shattered Kasha's heart into a thousand pieces. Her family was gone and her best friend, estranged as he may be, had given over to the dark recesses of his mind that she now knew he had always feared. Even still, Mother Maudird had been far more distraught, and Kasha had buried her own feelings to try and take Mother Maudrid's mind off the events by asking for help in planning her wedding.

"You're spiraling again, dear," Mother Maudrid had said, her wrinkled face pinched with concern. She had pulled Kasha aside just before the ceremony, her eyes carrying something heavy that Kasha had chosen to ignore. "Are you certain about this man? There's something about..." Mother Maudrid had stopped mid-sentence when she saw Kasha's eyes light up at the site of Folkvar. But Kasha had been too focused on maintaining her perfect appearance to truly hear the uncertainty in Mother Maudrid's voice.

Now, as they lay in bed, Folkvar's fingers traced lazy patterns across her bare shoulder and she felt truly happy for the first time in years.

"You were absolutely stunning today," Folkvar murmured, pressing a kiss to cheek. "I can't wait to see how beautiful our children will be."

The words hit Kasha like a bucket of ice water. She kept her body deliberately still, fighting the sudden urge to curl her tail around herself protectively. "Children?" she asked, trying to keep her voice light.

"Of course," Folkvar said, propping himself up on an elbow to look at her. His smile was warm, genuine. "I want a whole house full of little ones. Can't you just imagine it? A few strong sons to carry on my name, maybe a daughter with your grace."

Kasha's throat tightened. She had told him before that she was afraid of trying to have children. Tiefling's had a notoriously difficulty time achieving conception. How some went years, decades even, without successfully carrying a child. How many of her kind simply couldn't bear children at all, and how many died in the process. Tieflings were just born as a matter of luck or misfortune depending on who you asked. Traces of Fae or Forgotten lineage somewhere in the family. So, it was believed. She had told him specifically that she feared what the repeated losses would do to her and that was even if they were lucky enough to get pregnant in the first place. She had thought the matter settled.

Kasha's heart raced as she searched for the right words. The silk sheets suddenly felt constricting rather than cooling against her skin.

"I..." she began, her voice barely above a whisper. "I thought we discussed this already. You know tieflings, we... it's not easy for us to bear children. Many of us can't at all." She kept her eyes fixed on the ceiling, afraid to see disappointment cloud his features.

Folkvar's hand moved to cup her cheek, gently turning her face toward his. Instead of the frustration she expected, his eyes held nothing but warmth and understanding. "My love," he said softly, "that is not how it will be for us."

Her breath caught in her throat as tears threatened to spill from her eyes. "I don't want to disappoint you." Beneath the sheets she rubbed her hands together with worry.

He pulled her closer, pressing a gentle kiss on her forehead. "There are many ways to build a family, Kasha. If we try and it doesn't happen naturally, we could always adopt. There are so many children in need of loving parents in this damn city. Hells, Hus'rokn has three orphanages." His fingers traced the curve of her horn soothingly. His eyes narrowed as he squinted at something. He licked his finger and rubbed at something he must have seen on the golden seam of her horn. That was the third time he had done that tonight. "Would that be something you'd consider?"

The thought of adoption sparked something unexpected in Kasha's chest, a tiny flame of hope she hadn't dared to nurture before. The image of giving a home to a child who needed one, of being able to provide the love and security she'd once desperately yearned for herself, brought a small smile to her lips despite her reservations. She briefly found it odd that the thought of turning out like her own mother was far from her own mind.

Still, caution tempered her response. "We can try," she said carefully, her tail slowly uncurling from her thigh. "But please, don't get your hopes up too high. I don't want to break your heart if..." She couldn't finish the sentence, but Folkvar seemed to understand.

"You could never break my heart," he assured her, though something flickered behind his eyes that she couldn't quite read. "We'll take it one day at a time, and whatever happens, happens." He pulled her closer, and she nestled against his chest, allowing herself to be soothed by the steady rhythm of his heartbeat.

As she drifted toward sleep, a small voice in the back of her mind whispered that she was making a mistake, that she was setting herself up for heartbreak. But the warmth of Folkvar's embrace and the gentle way he held her made it easy to ignore that warning, to believe that maybe, just maybe, she could have the family she'd never dared to dream of.

Kasha stumbled through the darkened streets with one hand pressed against the rough stone walls of buildings for support. Each step sent fresh waves of pain through her abdomen, and the warm trickle down her thigh made her heart tremble in panic. She had already tried the midwife's door, but there had been no answer, just hollow knocking echoing through empty rooms.

Hus'rokn was too far to run. Mother Maudrid was her only hope now. Kasha had seen her work miracles with Callus's injuries, watched her deliver healthy babies to the women of the Traveling Spectacles. If anyone could help her now, it would be Mother Maudrid.

Another cramp seized her, and she doubled over, pressing her forehead against the cool stone wall. The metallic scent of blood filled her nostrils, making her stomach turn. "Please," she whispered, though she wasn't sure who she was begging the gods, the child she might be losing, or herself.

She thought of Folkvar, supposedly performing in Toz'Naluunod. His absence felt like a deep wound, deeper than the pain wracking her body. Over the past two years, she had watched him grow more distant with each failed attempt at pregnancy. His warm smiles had become forced, his touches less frequent. When he announced his touring schedule, she hadn't missed the relief in his voice.

Kasha pushed herself away from the wall, forcing herself to keep moving. Mother Maudrid's home wasn't far now. Just a few more streets. She could make it. She had to make it.

The pain struck again, stronger this time. Her knees buckled, and she caught herself against an empty merchant's cart, sending it rattling against its wheels. Her tail wrapped instinctively around her waist, as if it could somehow hold everything together.

"Should have made him stay," she muttered through clenched teeth. "Should have made him..." But she knew it wouldn't have mattered. The light had gone out of his eyes months ago, replaced by something that looked too much like resignation. Or worse, resentment.

Mother Maudrid's door came into view, a welcome sight in the darkness. Light still burned behind her windows. Kasha knew she often worked late into the night. She forced herself forward, each step an exercise in will over agony. She raised her fist to knock, then hesitated as another wave of pain washed over her.

What if this was it? What if this was her last chance at having a child? What if Folkvar never...

The door swung open before she could knock. Mother Maudrid stood there in her purple robes, her wrinkled face creased with concern. "Lemmy was acting strangely. I knew something was up." She looked Kasha over to see the sweaty sheen over her face and then the blood trickling down her ankle now.

"Get in, my girl!" Mother Maudrid pulled her inside and slammed the door shut behind her.

Mother Maudrid's eyes flashed with a mixture of fear and resolve. "Lemmy! Get to that damn midwife's house and break the windows if you have to. I don't care what it takes. Get her here now!"

Lemmy let out a harsh squawk of understanding and took flight through a small thatch opening in the ceiling, disappearing into the night.

With surprising strength for her age, Mother Maudrid swept her arm across the wooden table, sending herbs, bottles, and implements crashing to the floor with a cacophony of shattering glass. "Up you go, dear," she commanded, helping Kasha onto the now-clear surface.

Mother Maudrid shoved a pillow beneath Kasha's hips and thrust another into her arms. "Squeeze this when it hurts. Better the pillow than your tail." She rummaged through her shelves, muttering curses until she found what she sought, a small crystal vial filled with murky liquid.

"Drink," she ordered, uncorking the vial and holding it to Kasha's lips. The liquid tasted like rotten fish mixed with bitter herbs, making Kasha gag as she forced it down. "It's for the pain," Mother Maudrid explained, already moving between her legs. "Though I won't lie, it tastes like a merman's ass."

Mother Maudrid moved between her legs and lifted her nightgown. Through the haze of pain, Kasha caught the flash of concern that crossed Mother Maudrid's face as she began her work. The expression was quickly masked, but Kasha had known her far too long to not recognize when something was truly wrong.

She couldn't see exactly what Mother Maudrid was doing, but she felt the pinching and pressure as she worked frantically. Blood-soaked cloths began piling up on the floor, each one making Kasha's heart sink further. The coppery scent of blood grew stronger, mixing with the herbs and incense that perpetually perfumed Mother Maudrid's home.

Kasha felt more and more lightheaded as the seconds passed. "Is...the baby...is it-"

"Stay with me, my sweet girl," Mother Maudrid commanded, her usual gruff tone carrying an edge of worry that made Kasha's throat tighten. More cloths joined the growing pile, their deep crimson stains visible even in the dim lamplight.

The pain began to dull, whether from the potion or blood loss, Kasha wasn't sure. She squeezed the pillow tighter, her tail grasping the edge of the table, and tried to focus on the sound of Mother Maudrid's voice as the old woman worked to save what they both feared might already be lost.

The door swung open so hard it rattled the hinges. Kasha turned to see her midwife, eyes wide with horror, just before her eyes rolled back and her head fell against the table.

Through the haze of memory, Kasha heard Mother Maudrid's voice grow distant, replaced by the sounds of the Raucous Ruffians playing. She blinked away tears and forced herself to focus on the present, on the warmth and life filling her establishment.

Above her, Egrim's deep laugh echoed across the mezzanine as he twirled Morrigan one final time. The sight of them together made Kasha's chest ache in a way that was both painful and sweet. She watched as he scooped his little girl up and carried her toward their room, probably for bedtime. His massive frame moved with gentleness that still surprised her, his beard brushing the top of Morrigan's head as she nestled against his chest.

"Kasha?" Lorisse's voice cut through the haze she was feeling. The half-elf server stood nearby, concern evident in her eyes. "Are you alright? You've been standing over here for quite a while."

Kasha straightened her shoulders and smoothed her skirt nervously, slipping back into her role as easily as donning a familiar dress. "Yes. Just taking a moment to appreciate our success." She gestured to the crowded tavern, where patrons laughed and danced to the music. "Make sure the Ruffians have fresh drinks for their last song, would you?"

She smiled, though uneasiness was still plain on her face. Lorisse hurried off to fulfill her request, Kasha's eyes drifted back to the mezzanine. Egrim had disappeared into the room with Morrigan, but she could picture them clearly. He was probably tucking her in with the same care he showed in everything involving her.

She touched her abdomen briefly, she couldn't feel the scar through her skirt, but she knew it was there. Healed physically but raw as ever in her mind. She told herself that the past was the past. She had built something here, something real and vibrant and alive. Something that was hers alone.

But as she watched the door to Egrim and Morrigan's room reopen, she couldn't help but mourn what she had lost and would never have the chance to have again. It was too much. She couldn't be out here right now. It was close enough to closing time and she had faith that Lorisse could handle the hour or so that was left.

She caught Lorisse's eyes and gestured toward the stairs, mouthing "turning in" before ascending. Each step felt heavier than the last as memories continued to assault her mind. By the time she reached her door, tears were flowing freely down her cheeks, small droplets falling onto her chest and dripping to her harlequin skirt, leaving dark spots on the fabric.

Her hand trembled as she reached for the doorknob. A soft click from one door down the hall made her freeze. Egrim emerged from the neighboring room, a content smile on his face that vanished the moment he saw her state.

He crossed the distance between them in three long strides, his large hand extending toward her shoulder. "Kasha, are you alright?"

She flinched away from his touch before she could stop herself, immediately regretting the action when she saw the hurt flash across his face. His hand hung in the air between them, uncertain.

"I'm sorry," she whispered, managing a weak smile that didn't reach her eyes. "I didn't mean to..."

Egrim's looked down to the main floor below, his jaw setting in a hard line. "Who was it? Did someone-"

"No, nothing like that." She interrupted, wiping at her tears with shaking fingers. Her throat felt tight as she considered telling him everything, just so she could get it off her chest. Lorisse was the only person alive that knew. She wanted to trust him with these pieces of herself, but the fear that he would leave like all the others held her tongue.

He reached for her again, slower this time, and placed his hand on her back. The gentle pressure of his touch broke her, and she turned into his chest, burying her face against him. His arms encircled her, strong and steady, and she felt the rumble of his voice through his chest as he murmured soft words of comfort.

His warmth surrounded her, and for a moment she allowed herself to feel safe, protected. But the voice in her head whispered that she didn't deserve this tenderness, that she was broken in ways that couldn't be fixed. That eventually, even if he did have feelings for her, he would realize how damaged and imperfect she was and just leave like everyone else.

Egrim's chest felt rigid as he held her. The weight of his own secrets pressed down on him like a collapsing cliff face. Every sob that shook her frame drove daggers into his heart, and he couldn't take it anymore. He needed to tell her. Tell her everything. He was tired of running from what he wanted, from who he truly was, from the feelings that had been growing since the moment she'd hired him.

He took a heavy breath, steadying himself. "I need to tell you something."

Kasha stiffened in his arms, then pushed away from him. Her eyes, still wet with tears, held a resigned sadness that made his heart ache. She'd heard those words before, he realized. She was already preparing herself for goodbye.

"Not tonight," she said, her voice trembling slightly as she reached for her door. "Lorisse needs your help closing up."

"Kasha, please," he reached for her again, his hand seeking hers. "This is important. I need to-"

"I said not tonight!" Her voice rose sharply, drawing a concerned chirp from Lemmy somewhere down the hall. "I need..." she swallowed hard, composing herself. "I need to be alone right now. Please."

Before he could protest further, she slipped inside her room. The door closed with a soft click that somehow hurt more than if she'd slammed it.

Egrim stood there, confused and heartbroken. His hand moved toward the doorknob of its own accord, but he stopped short. The metal gleamed in the dim light of the hall, taunting him. Slowly, he pulled his hand back.

"I'm not who you think I am," he whispered to the closed door, "but I'm in love you."

The words hung in the air, too quiet for anyone but himself to hear, yet somehow, they seemed to echo in the open hallway. He touched the spot where his eye had once been, feeling the familiar texture of the Fae-touched replacement through his glamour. The truth sat heavy on his tongue - about who he and Morrigan really were, about why they could never truly settle anywhere, about the pact that bound him and betrayed him, A pact he regretted more with every passing day.

But she hadn't wanted to hear what he had to say. Perhaps she was right, tonight wasn't the time. He could still taste the salt of her tears on his chest where she'd pressed her face against him.

With a deep sigh, he turned away from her door. The sounds of the tavern below drifted up with Lorisse calling last rounds, the Ruffians packing up their instruments, the general bustle of another successful night coming to a close. He'd help close up, as she'd asked. It was the least he could do.

CHAPTER THIRTY-SEVEN

A FATED UNION

One Month Later

The ceremony was to begin soon. Callus had made an arrangement with the Wyld Trade Authority and the business owners on a section of Mother Maudrid's former street to allow them to conduct the nuptials near what had been her shop. He wanted it to feel as though Mother Maudrid had been witness to the event. In his mind, she would be watching from her porch in the same old rocking chair she used to sit in back in the Spectacles days.

He stood at an altar of gorgeously carved white oak. The wooden arch held flowers of more colors than he knew flowers could come in. Ivy was woven throughout its lattice work and then shaped into a heart around the area that the couple would stand together. He wore a vibrant green silk tunic that Kasha's personal seamstress had made special for him. Kasha had her sew designs of various weapons into the fabric, but from afar they appeared to be woven tree branches. He teared up and hugged her for a solid minute when she presented it to him.

Next to Callus stood Egrim. He was wearing a similar tunic design, but of a duller green and with no weapon adornments. He felt uncomfortable being in this position. He and Callus had become what he considered to be friends, of course, but he still didn't feel that they were on terms that he should be standing next to the hobgoblin on his wedding day. He felt that if anyone should be standing next to him it should have been Carl. But that poor bastard had been ever more unlucky and was standing in the middle of the elegant arch ready to lead the damned ceremony. Egrim reasoned that he had gotten the better end of the deal.

Carl looked out over the small crowd and met Fithra's eyes. She, unlike Carl, was still in her Blood Ale Company garb and was trying, mostly failing, to hold in a laugh. Seeing the starch assed Carl Just Carl gussied up in a black dress tunic and holding a book of marriage ceremonies was something she would never be able to fully describe to the rest of the Company in a way that would give it the full justice it deserved. Carl groaned and then traded looks with Egrim. They both regarded each other as two people who noticed just how out of place the other felt. The only difference between them was that Carl was trying his damnedest to hold a smile. It honestly looked more like a caged animal bearing it's teeth.

He had originally refused Callus's request, but then the damn hobgoblin did what he had never done before and told Carl he owed him for what the Bloody Ale Company had done to his tribe when he was a baby. It was a low tactic, but Callus was not above using it to get the big man to relent and agree.

Kasha stood in a position to be right behind Arialyn when she finally made her entrance and took the bride's place. Egrim could not help but stare at her. Her light pink dress was plain, so as to not take away from the bride, but it still made her look like a goddess to him. She blushed and looked away, noting the half ass attempt at a smile Carl was holding.

She beamed at Carl, her sharper tiefling canines suddenly more prominent, and whispered to him between clenched teeth. "You are smiling like a rabid dog you old goat."

The term 'old goat' pulled Carl back to his fondest memory of that orcish girl that stole his heart so long ago. He couldn't help the genuine smile that lit up his face now. It lit up his face so much that Callus, even in his nervously distracted state, saw it and turned to him. "No. Are you drunk?"

Arialyn's entrance music kicked up as Carl responded to the jab. "You should be looking at her not me, fool."

The Raucous Ruffians had shown great versatility in their repertoire. They exchanged their usual bawdy ballads for the sweet and smooth tunes of the day. Kasha had questioned Callus's decision to hire them for the occasion and had been forced to admit now that she was wrong.

Those in attendance all knew the couple for various reasons. Some were frequent customers of the Amethyst Artificer or the Witch's Tits and Tarts, or the Tits staff. Ethan stood vigil with several of his newer Lance Guard at various posts around the gathered wedding party. Kasha noted Herodin, who unbelievably to her, had been appointed Ethan's right hand after the sudden conquest, no, promotion to the Three. The grimalkin whispered something to the Captain who nodded at his words with a confidence she had not seen in the man in a while. Neither the bride nor the groom had any blood relation in attendance. Found family was what they had and neither of them had the tiniest bit of an issue with it.

Egrim's look of discomfort changed abruptly at the sight of Morrigan walking down the aisle. She was the cutest she had ever been in his eyes. She had been starring at Kasha's dress for the occasion for two weeks. Kasha had even caught her trying it on, desperately working to hold it up as she shuffled across the room with her head held high like a queen.

Kasha immediately put a work order in for her to have one just like it, but of an appropriate size for the young girl's frame.

Egrim had feared she'd be too nervous, but she walked confidently, and it was only now that he gleamed the probable cause. The little monster had a shiny silver butterknife tucked into the ribbon belt at her waist. He recognized it as one Callus had been using earlier and eyeballed the hobgoblin with narrow eyes.

Callus kept his eyes on the advancing Morrigan while smirking at Egrim. "You should just get her a special one made and be done with it."

Step after step the flowers flew in the air. She was meant to throw them into the aisle of course, but she had her head held so high and eyes shut with such regality that she threw the flowers directly into the faces of those in the inner seats as she past them.

Kasha held her bouquet over her mouth to hide her smile. Egrim shook his head with the widest grin Kasha had ever seen and Callus squatted down as she finally made it to the altar. Morrigan grabbed the second to last flower from the basket and then unceremoniously tossed it to the side. Several people in the first few rows could no longer hold back and snickered at the sight. She placed the last flower, a blue and white petaled exotic flower that Callus had never seen before, over Callus's left ear and then held her hand out.

Callus gently took her hand and kissed it as she curtsied. He whispered to her with a tease. "Careful Morrigan, or all eyes will be on you and not the bride."

Morrigan smiled and then rushed to Kasha's side. With her part in the ceremony over she no longer knew what to do and clung to Kasha's dress nervously. Kasha placed her hand calmly on Morrigan's shoulder and held her close.

Callus stood and spoke over his shoulder. "I envy you, Egrim."

The big man knew that Callus meant he envied him having a child. Something Callus and Arialyn would never get to have naturally. 'Mongrels' and the pure races couldn't produce children together. Another fact the Empire used as an excuse to drive them out or enslave them during the Mongrel War. Orcs and tieflings were the only races considered mongrels that were capable of producing offspring with those of the pure races. It is said that orcs were once humans, humans that had been corrupted by Zorog a millennia before the fall of Varl's Wall and the emergence of the Voidscar. As for tieflings, they carried a random drop of ancient Fae of Forgotten blood that could pop up in any of the peoples of Yonara.

Kasha heard Callus's words and felt a wound in her heart reopen for the hundredth time. She couldn't lie to herself anymore either. She wanted a family. She wanted to have someone to hold her every night. She wanted to get woken up because someone had a nightmare and needed their mother. To look across the room and see someone she loved holding her child and smiling at her. She knew she would never have that. She placed a hand by her side and onto Morrigan's shoulders with a gentle squeeze. Had it not been for the attendees rising to their feet as the bride entered, she may very well have fallen to tears of sadness. Thankfully Arialyn's entrance changed those to tears of joy at the sight of her friend. She looked even more beautiful than when Kasha helped her try the dress on.

Arialyn posed in front of Kasha's full mirror in her wedding dress. It was a silvery white strapless gown that Kasha had personally embroidered several of the tools of Arialyn's trade upon in gold and purple thread.

Arialyn felt beyond silly in the posh thing. She wasn't a girlie girl and never had been. She had grease under her fingernails right now for Triumvirate's sake. "Kasha, I am grateful. Truly, I am. But I feel absurd."

Kasha stood behind Arialyn and smoothed out a few wrinkles over her rear. She squatted down and moved her hands under Arialyn's arms and grabbed her bust. She boosted her breasts and the bodice, driving her cleavage up further.

Arialyn raised an eyebrow and smirked at her in the mirror. "Really?"

Kasha pinched her lips together. "Yes, really. I have a special oil we'll put on those girls the day of as well."

Arialyn groaned in irritation. "Kasha, I love you. Dearly even. I just...this isn't me."

Kasha smiled in the mirror and spoke with an even and heartfelt tone. "Sweetheart, this isn't for you. This is for him. I let you talk me out of getting you a dress for my opening night, but I will be damned if the woman marrying my best friend shows up in overalls." Her eyes began to water. "When he sees you in this gown...you'll know why it was worth it to be uncomfortable for a few hours."

She looked at herself in the mirror again and considered Kasha's words. She sighed lightly. "Fine."

Kasha hugged her from behind. "You look stunning dear."

Arialyn met her eyes in the mirror again and hugged Kasha's arms. "Thank you."

Kasha let go of her and spun her sideways in the mirror. "And have you seen your ass in this thing?" She accentuated the statement with a spank that made Arialyn rise to her tiptoes.

She smacked Kasha's arm "For fucks sake, Kasha."

Arialyn slowly walked to the altar, keeping her eyes down. When she finally got the courage to look up at Callus, she knew Kasha had been right. It was worth it. Her man, her hard ass, stubborn, bruiser of a man was nearly weeping at the sight of her. His reaction made her own eyes water, and she had to blink her eyes rapidly to control the flood. Once she made it to the altar Kasha frantically stopped her. "Wait, just a second."

She motioned for Lorisse to come forward. Arialyn immediately glared at them both as Lorisse hastily brought over a step stool, set it down and then bowed low as she walked backward. Everyone broke into laughter, even Arialyn. "Bitch."

Once she stood atop the three steps, she was at chest height with Callus. She had to admit it was at least a gorgeously crafted piece that matched the white oak arch. She tossed her bouquet over her shoulder at Kasha who was not expecting it and almost fumbled the flowers. Arialyn looked over her shoulder and stuck her tongue out at her playfully. Morrigan giggled, abruptly remembered people were watching and moved even further behind Kasha. Callus smiled as Kasha narrowed her eyes with amusement and blew her bangs out of her face.

Carl smiled at the couple, clearly forgetting his queue to speak. Callus shifted his foot and tapped the grizzled man's boot. Carl's face showed the slightest hint of embarrassment as he cleared his throat and looked over the small crowd of people, purposefully avoiding Fithra's eyes.

The Company man held it together and only stumbled over his words a handful of times until Callus and Arialyn spoke their vows. It was then that he had to bite the inside of his lip so hard it drew blood, just so he wouldn't tear up. He'd be damned if he would let Fithra see that and bring that tale back to the Company.

At the ceremony's conclusion Callus pulled Arialyn off of the step stool and then deeply, and somewhat inappropriately in front of company, kissed her with the sincerest of smiles.

Kasha was still crying from the vows they had spoken to each other. Callus told Arialyn that she finally gave him the home his soul needed, and she elegantly voiced how he had enchanted her for seeing who she truly was and not just accepting it but embracing it wholeheartedly.

The newlyweds exited the gathered crowd and mounted Arialyn's stormer. She allowed Callus to drive this time. It didn't matter how many times Kasha saw the two of them on the contraption, she always got a giggle out of Callus being able to reach all of the controls even though he sat behind Arialyn. They headed off to the Amethyst Artificer to get changed into more comfortable attire and most certainly sully every surface in the place with intense love making, while everyone that was invited to the reception headed to the Witch's Tits and Tarts.

CHAPTER THIRTY-EIGHT

LIE TO ME

Callus and Arialyn showed up a little later than they had intended to. Kasha had actually sent Egrim to go and check on them. Instead, he had winked at her, poking her in the ribs and told her they were probably still celebrating and there was no way in the hells he was going to walk in on that. Judging by Arialyn's disheveled hair and the almost childlike grin on Callus's face when they snuck in through the backroom, she guessed they had celebrated multiple times at home and probably once behind the tavern.

She grinned at Callus, and he simply shrugged his shoulders with a chuckle. Kasha ran over to Arialyn and dropped low to embrace her. "I told you that you wouldn't regret the dress. You were absolutely stunning."

Arialyn blushed, the smell of orcish grog from her mouth evident. "I kept it on for the first round at home." She snickered.

Kasha's eyes briefly flared in surprise, not from the talk of sexual celebration, but that the words came directly from Arialyn's mouth. She had always been pretty conservative in talking about her and Callus's activities, not prudish, but reserved. Kasha was about to kiss her cheek when Arialyn poked her in the tits and then the nose. "Boop and boop."

Kasha couldn't hold her laughter now and looked up at Callus. "You drove the stormer here, right?"

Callus swayed and repeated Arialyn's gestures, tit and nose in order. "What stormer? A wizard flew us here...he looked rather like a donkey come to think of it. Hells, did we ride here on an ass?"

Arialyn laughed so hard she fell over. Callus straightened up, clearly having been messing with Kasha. As sober as a nun, he put his arm around Kasha's shoulder and turned her to look at his wife, laughing hysterically on the floor. "She had a single solitary bottle... I married this."

He was trying to mockingly appear irritated for comedic value, but his smile was far too wide for anyone in their right mind to believe he was anything but utterly lost within the gnome that rolled around on the floor. Kasha felt a battle of emotions inside her very soul. She was thrilled for her friend. Absolutely grateful that he had found what he had needed all those years ago when she came to him in the middle of the night and was denied. The other emotion was a darker one, despair. She had briefly thought she knew what love was like. That portion of her life had ended with her being worse than alone. Loneliness seemed to be the underlying theme in her life. If a bard sang her tale, there would be few moments that would cause the tavern patrons to cheer.

Kasha felt selfish again, but she wasn't about to let her own feelings of emptiness ruin the night. Tonight was for her best friends. She threw her arms around Callus's neck and squeezed him tight. Callus was somewhat surprised by the sudden embrace. Something told him to hold her tighter than usual.

She spoke into his ear as they held each other. "I love you, Callus. You found your home." She kissed his cheek. "The way I can tell when one of you is thinking about the other when you're not together... that is what true love is. That is what people are lucky to find."

Callus squeezed her even tighter. That was what he had been noticing about her. What a fool he had been. All this time and he had only seen his friend, not the woman that yearned for someone to love her the way he and Arialyn do. "I love you too. Always will." He didn't know what else to say.

Kasha pulled back and kissed him quickly on the lips before kneeling to Arialyn and pulling her up to stand again. She wobbled and steadied herself on Kasha, first on her tits and then with a blush moved her hands to her shoulders. "Sorry, Kasha." She giggled.

Kasha giggled herself and then grabbed Arialyn by the cheeks. "You were a beautiful bride, and you bring Callus the happiness he has always deserved. I love you for it." She pulled her in and kissed her as well.

Arialyn's face changed from one of jovial intoxication to confusion and shock. She stared at Kasha for a second and then giggled so hard that she fell to the floor again.

"I'll just let you tend to the giggle box here." Kasha said to Callus as she stood again. She looked in one of the many mirrors that she had placed all over the Tits and Tarts. The girls always needed to be able to make sure they looked pristine. She pushed her hair out of her eyes and cupped her breasts up. "Ass out, tits up. The girls looking well?" She asked Callus.

He raised an eyebrow. "They are never anything but stunning Kasha."

She turned and walked out into the main room quickly. Callus held his hand out to Arialyn. "Come on squirt."

The hated nickname sobered her up enough that she was able to kick his left foot and pull him down onto her on the floor of the backroom. She kissed him deeply, giving him a look of deep yearning.

"Bloody hells woman, right now? You're going to make it fall off."

Kasha walked back into the main room, the sounds of celebration washing over her like a warm tide. The scent of fresh tarts mingled with ale and the perfumed oils of her serving girls, creating an atmosphere that was uniquely hers.

Her eyes swept across the crowd, taking in the sight of friends and customers mingling freely. Lorisse moved gracefully between tables, her perkiness drawing appreciative glances as she served drinks with her characteristic warm smile. Near the bar, she spotted Carl and Fithra deep in conversation with Captain Ethan, the three of them looking surprisingly comfortable together and seemingly discussing battle stories based on their gestures.

A movement on the mezzanine caught her attention. Mufz was emerging from one of the upstairs rooms, her green skin glistening with a light sheen of sweat. The goblin woman was adjusting her thin skirt as a young human man stepped out behind her, his face flushed with satisfaction and wearing a giddy grin that made Kasha wonder if that had been his first time with a woman.

Mufz stood on her tip toes and kissed the man's cheek playfully. "Thank you for the lovely evening, darling." She purred in her characteristically crude but playful tone. "Come back soon, and maybe next time we can explore the area to the rear of that forest you were so fascinated with."

The man's grin widened impossibly as he practically skipped down the stairs, nearly stumbling in his eagerness. Kasha shook her head with amusement, Mufz certainly knew how to keep her clients happy.

For the first time since the reception had begun, Mufz looked down into the crowd below. Her large, expressive eyes suddenly went wide, and her mouth fell open in obvious recognition. Following her gaze, Kasha saw she was staring directly at Carl, who was gesturing animatedly while telling some story to his companions.

Mufz frantically waved her hands, trying to catch Kasha's attention. When their eyes met, she motioned urgently for Kasha to come upstairs. Curious, Kasha made her way through the crowd and climbed the stairs to the mezzanine.

"Kasha, love," Mufz said breathlessly, her voice a little hoarse from her... activities, "I had no bloody idea you knew Carl Just Carl."

Kasha raised an eyebrow, glancing back down Carl who apparently had someone in a headlock in the story he was telling. "We're longtime friends. How do you know him? And how in the hells did you not see him earlier? He's been here since the ceremony started."

Mufz let out a bark of laughter, running her hands through her wild hair. "Darling, I've been so busy today I fear my cunny is swollen from more than just excitement, if you catch my meaning." She gestured toward her room with a wicked grin. "That was my seventh client since this afternoon. I haven't had time to peek over the railing once."

Kasha couldn't help but laugh at the Mufz's characteristic bluntness. "Seven? Mufz, you're going to kill yourself at this rate."

"Better way to go than most," Mufz replied with a shrug, then her expression grew more serious. "But Carl... that's a name from my past, love. Do you know how he got the nickname, Bloody Knuckle Carl?"

Kasha crossed her arms beneath her breasts and turned to look down at Carl. "He said it was from a fighting tournament at a large tavern in Kol'Theron. My old employer, Sylus, was there."

Mufz snorted out a laugh. "I'm sure that is what he prefers to tell people but that is not even remotely the truth. I mean there was a tournament, I was there too."

Kasha side eyed Mufz. "Well, spill it."

Mufz set her chin on the railing. "Like I said, there was a tournament, and he did win it. Afterward however, he was drunk and in the mood to celebrate. I wasn't yet in this line of work. I was just doing some modeling for sculptures and paintings. I flirted. He reciprocated. All the rooms were full, so we ducked into a supply closet and well…"

Kasha's grin grew extra wide. "Oh, really? But why the bloody knuckle name then?"

Mufz snorted again. "He pounded me so hard, he kick started my moon cycle."

Kasha's mouth fell open, and she stared down at Mufz to make sure she heard her correctly.

"It was nearly pitch black in that closet and the last thing he did was…" Mufz made a rapid motion with her middle and ring finger. "We walked out, and his hand was a dark crimson."

Kasha laughed so hard that Carl and his current company looked up to see what the fuss was about. His face went ghost white before turning into a scowl. "Shit."

Fithra caught sight of Mufz and then looked at Carl, covering her mouth with the look of a kid that just saw their sibling get caught doing something incredibly stupid.

"Hi Carl!" Mufz called down.

Carl looked at Fithra and spoke through gritted teeth. "Don't." He then turned to face Mufz with the most unauthentic smile he could muster. "Mufalina, good to see you."

"Why don't you come on up and say hi." She bit her lip playfully.

"Maybe later. You talk to your sister recently?" His fist clenched with anticipation and relaxed once he heard her response.

"Which one, Cutter?"

"Aye."

"Not in a few years."

"Good." Carl grabbed a new bottle off the counter and quickly went for a walk with Fithra giggling in tow and Ethan wondering what the fuck he was missing out on.

The Raucous Ruffians had resumed their usual sound for the majority of the reception. Fast and upbeat tunes resonated off the walls of the Tits and Tarts Tavern. Lorisse was dancing to the dwarven jig on the center table. Fithra had shared more than a few bottles with Carl after the sudden reunion with Mufz. The drinking had turned into a contest. It was evident Carl had lost, as he was face down on the bar top. Fithra may have won that contest, but she was losing the one against her own inhibitions. She pulled off her own soft leather top and set it and her Bloody Ale Company pauldron down next to Carl's drooling head.

The room was spinning in her head, but no one would have been able to tell due to the dexterous prance she made over to the table with Lorisse. She leapt upon it and started to mimic the dwarven creek dance that the half elven woman was performing. Lorisse slowed down her movements to teach Fithra the dance. Despite the high amount of ale that swam through her vessels, Fithra picked up on it within seconds. They danced back-to-back for the next two songs before the spinning room caught up with the company woman and she nearly fell off the table. A laughing Lorisse escorted her to one of the side rooms. The pair shared blushing glances of interest before disappearing behind a closed door.

If Carl had been aware of the event he would have been kicking himself for not being sober. Fithra had been the Company member to take interest in making sure he saw the most action way back when he was a waster. He had always harbored a bit of a crush on her. Nothing serious, just a manly desire to taste something he was not supposed to touch.

Egrim stood at the base of the stairs, both watching the crowd and making sure no one went to the second floor that wasn't supposed to be there. Kasha saddled up to him and hugged his right arm. The sudden touch caused him to shut his eyes and calm his mind.

"You haven't seen Adenus, have you? He said he'd make an appearance."

Egrim shook his head. "No one from the Gauntlet, other than Merle and the two dealers."

Kasha gave him a perplexed look before shrugging. "Morrigan in bed?" She asked as she too began to watched the main room.

He nodded. "Well, I put her to bed. I doubt she is actually sleeping. Probably playing with Lemmy."

Kasha smiled warmly. "He's good for her, I think. Occupies her thoughts when you're not able to be near."

"She enjoys your company as well. Surely you know that by now, don't you?" His head snapped to the door. A drunken pair of orcs stumbled in. Callus and Arialyn didn't have many people on their guest list for the reception. In truth, much like the wedding earlier in the day, most of the people they had allowed were just regulars of the Tits and Tarts or the Amethyst Artificer. Not people that the bride and groom were necessarily close to. But it had been established that no one else was allowed in.

Egrim's voice was deep and bellowing. "Can't you fucking read? Sign on the door said, 'Closed for private event.' Fuck off before you get fucked." The two orcs were nearly stunned sober. They turned to the voice in a manner that suggested they were ready to silence whoever dared to speak to them with such distaste. It took half a second for them to immediately size up Egrim and simply turn around and leave the way they came.

The newlyweds came out of the backroom moments later. Arialyn sat upon Callus's left shoulder. He had his left arm wrapped up and over her thighs to keep his inebriated wife secure. Her hair was even more tussled than before. Callus was smoothing his mutton chops out with his right hand. Kasha noted a shine to his facial hair that was not there when they arrived, and she blushed. *"He's mopping that mess up."* She thought.

Merle hummed along with the Raucous Ruffians tune and sat a mug of freshly poured ale down on the bar top and slid it over to Lance Captain Ethan. Callus deftly intercepted it mid-slide and raised it to his lips.

Ethan scowled mildly. "That was the last of the Bloody Ale Blonde, you jackass."

"I'll consider it a wedding gift." Callus voiced over the music and chatter of the attendees.

Kasha nudged Egrim's side. The one damn spot that he was ticklish and she had found it a few weeks ago and made sure that he knew she was fully aware of it nearly every day.

"Dammit Kasha. What?" He said with a restrained chuckle.

"They're here. Officially." She pointed toward the bar at Callus and his bride perched on his shoulder. "Would you do the honors of collecting everyone's attention for me please?"

"As the lady commands." Egrim clapped his hands together loudly three times. "Oi! Listen up ladies and what passes for gentlemen tonight!"

Kasha climbed to a point where she was slightly taller than Egrim. "The bride and groom have arrived!"

She held her hands out, gesturing towards the couple at the bar. Callus raised his ale mug and Arialyn straightened her back and threw her hand up as if she was modeling.

Callus shook his head with a chuckle. "We're really going to have to work on your tolerance, squirt."

Kasha continued. "Thank you all for coming to this most lovely occasion! We honor the love and commitment of Callus Kordec and Arialyn Foghand, two of my dearest friends."

Carl suddenly shot up on his stool. "Friends!"

All eyes turned to him for a moment. Callus nearly spit out his ale, laughing. Arialyn was hit with another fit of laughter and would have fallen from Callus's shoulder and landed poorly on the floor if he hadn't tightened his grip around her thighs.

Carl would have looked embarrassed if that was something he had been sober enough to do. Callus handed him his ale mug. He clapped him on the shoulder. Carl grumbled and sat back down on the stool with his new drink and a smile.

Time froze briefly for Kasha. She realized everyone that she cared about in life was right here, right now. Everyone together and happy. It warmed her soul. She wanted this. She had never wanted anything more than this. "Enjoy the food and drink! Celebrate the happy couple and rejoice in these rare times of joy!"

The main room erupted with laughter and cheers. Egrim glanced at her over his shoulder with a whisper. "Rare times of joy? That was depressing in a very stealthy way."

She smacked the back of his head lightly. "Shut it you big ox."

The hour had grown very late. Only a few handfuls of the attendees remained and several of them were asleep, their heads on tables or shoulders and one somehow on the floor despite the person's body still mostly in their chair. Carl had managed to sober up enough to realize Fithra was no longer about. In Carl's life, history had proven that no Company man or woman should travel alone, so he began looking around for her. He knocked on a few doors and saw some things that, had he been fully sober, would have made him vomit. Eventually, he stumbled onto the side room that Fithra and Lorisse had been taking up for the last few hours.

When he knocked and called out for Fithra he picked up barely audible whispers. Fithra answered very shortly after wearing nothing but a mischievous grin. His stunned eyes had flashed over her lean body and then past her to Lorisse who lay on the bed in a similar state of undress. He hadn't been remotely prepared for the sight his eyes took in. He had been far less prepared when Fithra pulled him into the room by his belt. Callus had remarked to Arialyn, Kasha and Egrim that perhaps the event would loosen the old man up a bit.

The Lance Captain had bid them all a good night and offered to have three Lance men guard the front and rear entrance as a further gift so that they could all fully relax at the end of the night. Kasha accepted on behalf of the newlyweds and soon after it was just the four of them sitting around the bar top trading stories with only a handful of straggling regulars playing cards at the Gauntlet table.

Callus and Kasha told several stories about their youth and the mischief they got up to together, including a particularly interesting tale of the theft of what turned out to be a fake sapphire from a wealthy merchant in the Wylds. They had been caught but in the process the Trade Authority had discovered that the merchant was selling fakes. The pair were given leniency for incidentally aiding in the apprehension of a forger. Sylus didn't even have them punished. He had just laughed and told them to be more careful.

Arialyn ran through the tale of her family and the Fold of the Silver Cedar, the druidic order she had grown up in, traveling to Timberhold and her finding out about the art of arcanomancy. She went into details of some of her first forays into the art, but her mood had started to turn sour when she got to the spots where she drew the ire of her father and some of their community for practicing the new taboo arcane form.

Kasha kicked at Egrim's boot to spur him to change the subject quickly. Egrim had a moment of panic. He didn't know what to say. He had nothing that wouldn't give away secrets of himself. Thankfully Morrigan came to mind, and he hurriedly told them all about a time she was riding a tamed dire rat at a fair back in the Brightborn kingdom. She had eaten so much candy that she puked all over the handler. The dire rat had apparently not been fed that day and tried to take a chunk out of the vomit covered handler. The story was true, except it had truly been him when he was a kid and not Morrigan.

After that the four grew quiet. Thankfully Jezel, the Raucous Ruffians' lyre player had chosen now to announce that she was about to play her closing solo, something she did every night they played. Usually, it was to help calm down the rowdy drunks, but tonight it was meant for Callus and Arialyn. She played a soft and sweet elvish wedding song that seemed to almost summon Callus and Arialyn to the dance floor.

Kasha turned and leaned back against the bar with her elbows. Egrim stood behind the bar but at just the right angle to see Kasha's full profile. He had seen her topless in her 'working' clothes nearly every day for the last few months and yet each time he stopped to look at her it was as if he was seeing her form for the first time. She was the most beautiful creature he had ever been blessed to witness. Even more captivating than *her*. He shook his head to get *her* out of his mind. He didn't want to think about any of that right now. His mind cleared and he admired Kasha as she watched their newlywed friends dance.

For the first few moments Arialyn leaned against Callus, her head against his waist. Finally, she looked up at him and rolled her eyes. "Just do it already."

Callus smiled at her with tears in his eyes. "If that is what my wife wants." He lifted her and held her to him.

Arialyn wrapped her legs around him and stared into his eyes. There was a time when she would have probably felt a little humiliated, being held up like this, almost like she was a child. But he was hers and she was his. Damn what anyone else had to say. She kissed the tears from his eyes. "I'm your home, Callus. Don't you ever forget it."

They leaned their foreheads against one another and continued their dance.

Egrim caught a change in Kasha's expression as she watched their friends dance. She had been smiling with her entire face for a time.

But something now caused her eyes to lose their brightness. It was like she was only smiling with her lips now, forcing it. It was nearly imperceptible, but he saw her lips move wordlessly. His eyes homed in on them and he was able to read her silent words. *'Do I not deserve what they have?'* He reached over the bar to her arm and placed his hand gently upon it. "Kasha, would you like to dance?"

Her head turned to him quickly and with a slightly frightened look, as though her mind was somewhere else entirely. She gathered herself quickly and her face lit up for just a split second before it faded again. She wanted to tell him yes, but it would just be a reminder to her of what she couldn't have and apparently what the world didn't feel she deserved. She shook her head. "No...thank you. I am feeling quite exhausted."

She pushed herself off the bar. "I already told Ethan's men to get everyone out that isn't scheduled to stay the night after the last song. I'm going to head to bed. Good night, Egrim. I hope you sleep well. Give Morrigan a kiss for me."

She spoke the words swiftly and with a stiffness that made Egrim feel as though any argument wouldn't be well received. He let his hand drop to the bar top and watched her walk away. He wasn't sure how much longer he could take this. He had been feeling more and more hollow with each passing day since he arrived here. Keeping Kasha in the dark about his past was supposed to keep her safe, but now more than ever he felt like the only thing it was doing was hurting her and destroying what hope he had of ever being happy.

The charade had taken too much out of him. It had taken too much from him. He decided right then and there that he no longer cared. So much had happened to him in the last few years. His family, that was supposed to have been protected, now lay in the ground. He still couldn't reconcile not being able to see them one last time. *She* had been absent for so long and *she* had been the only thing that had made him feel the love a man needs, as misguided and twisted as it was. He was used to being a nomad. His duties to *her* had demanded it, but hiding was another situation all together.

As chaotic and scary as the last year had been, he realized this was the happiest he had been in a very long time. They made him happy, these two ladies that suddenly came into his life, Kasha and his daughter... Saffron.

Kovag buried Egrim in his mind at that very moment. Kasha would at least know who he truly was and why he had lied to her. He hoped she would understand and that she would still feel for him what he knew in his core she did right now.

Kovag'dresh, pact mortal of Oakira, looked around the main room of the Tits and Tarts Tavern. If Oakira could play loose with their pact rules, then he would too. He made sure no one looked his way. The glamour over his eye shimmered as the solid green orb shined through for just a moment. Kasha had just stepped inside her suite, about to close the door behind her. He willed himself to be there and with a blink of his eye he was. He grabbed her arm gently from behind her. "Kasha."

She flinched, not at his touch but at the unexpectedness of it. She hadn't heard him climb the stairs behind her. She was crying. "Please, Egrim. I want to be alone."

"No," He turned her around to face him. He wiped the tears away from one of her cheeks with his thumb.

She looked away from his face. She couldn't handle seeing his eyes right now. "I'm fine. Really. It's just too much stress is all. I just ne-"

He pulled her against his chest and held her tight, his massive arms making her seem so small and frail. "No."

Kovag closed the door behind him and picked her up. Her emotions were raw, and this simple act broke the cracking wall that had held them at bay. She threw her arms around his neck and began to shake. He walked toward her bed and kicked off his boots as he went. He laid her down and delicately removed her own knee-high boots. As he peeled back the covers of her bed, he climbed in and pulled her to him. Her tears turned to sobbing now. She let it all out. Every bit of emotion she had held back for so long. Abandonment. Betrayal. Loneliness. This damn desire, no, fear of imperfection. All of it.

She buried her face and pulled her arms to her chest and curled into this man that had stolen her heart without even trying. She wondered if he truly knew what she longed for. That's when she felt a wet drop against her temple. She pulled away from him and saw that he too was crying. Her spirit felt it then. They both desired something they thought they couldn't have and neither of them truly knew why the other wouldn't allow it for themselves.

Her hands cupped his face, and a thumb caressed the scar on his lip. "Just for tonight...lie to me. Tell me we belong together."

He felt incredibly selfish now. He was in hiding from Fae Seekers and possibly even agents of the Empire still. He wanted to be with her. But even after he tells her the truth, at some point he and Saffron would have to leave this place, right? He may never be able to come back. He could promise her he would return, and something could happen that makes that impossible. Or worse he could die before he made it back. She didn't even know what he really looked like and that felt incredibly wrong. "Kasha, you need to kn-"

She placed her hand over his lips. Her eyes were searching his and he felt exposed in a way he never had before. "Whatever it is, I don't care. Please, lie to me."

He chose not to lie to her and instead said what he felt were the truest words he had ever spoken. "We belong to one another."

Their lips came together and took the breath from each of them. There was peace in the kiss, even with the hint of sadness. As if they both thought that some hidden force would stop them from doing it again. Nothing did. They came together once again. Their lips danced in passionate elegance. Lust was there to be sure, but unlike the first kiss two share, it was in the background of a longing to reside in this moment for as long as possible.

She grabbed his hand and brought it to her breast. It nearly disappeared in Kovag's large hand. He squeezed her firmly and in a way that made her feel something she had never felt before when touched for pleasure, safe. Her body shuddered as she exhaled.

Her nails dung into his shoulder. "This was my favorite shirt of yours."

He didn't have time to ask why she said 'was.' She set her finger to each button and a spark burned away the thread that held them all in place. He felt a slight tingle with each zap. She pushed him to his back and pulled his shirt to the sides. She climbed onto his waist and leaned down to kiss him before trailing down his neck and chest. Her fingers wove through his chest hair like she was scratching a large cat. Kovag shivered beneath her touch.

Kasha eyed the button at his pants and held her finger up. She giggled as his eyes went wide. He deftly moved his hands to the button before he allowed her to risk missing and shocking something that didn't need any further encouragement to come to attention. She raised up just enough for him to move his pants off and then sat back down. He felt her warmth part over him and realized she hadn't been wearing anything under her skirt all night. She moved her hips back and forth, sliding across his length but not yet taking him in.

He reached down and grabbed at the waistband of her skirt. "Favorite skirt." He ripped it apart with one smooth motion.

Kasha bit her lip at the aggressive maneuver and grinned down at him. Her back arched and he grabbed her thighs as she glided across him. His hand ran up her stomach and across her chest to her neck and shoulder. His hands were rough but tender in their touch. He rolled her over and remained between her legs.

His hands ran up and down her outer thighs. He pressed against her slowly. Kasha reached for his beard and lightly pulled him down on top of her with it. As she did so she felt him become fully enveloped inside her. They halted for a moment and savored the feeling of the other before their hips heaved together. He thrust his arms beneath her, cradling her and locked his lips to hers. They remained like this, their moans muffled by each other's mouths, until they had no choice but to pull away at the peak of their pleasure.

Kovag elevated himself over her. He studied her face as she did the same to his. Again, she pulled him down on to her and he nuzzled against her neck with a nibble at the smooth skin there.

Eventually he rolled over, scooping her up and held her next to him. Kasha could feel the tension in him. He wanted to say something but was struggling with it. She didn't want to hear him recite the words she feared the most. Unspoken words that she played in her head from him over and over again already. She knew he would have to leave at some point, he'd said as much in the past. He never let her forget it. But, just this time, just for tonight, she wanted to pretend it wasn't true.

"Don't. You can say whatever it is in the morning. For the rest of the night, we lie." She said as she ducked under the covers and took Kovag's breath away again.

Lemmy settled on the windowsill, methodically working his beak through the last stubborn streaks of rouge that clung to his pristine white feathers. The little one had been particularly enthusiastic with her "beautification" efforts today, and while he cherished these moments of innocent play, the cosmetics were becoming increasingly difficult to remove without proper assistance. The innocence of the young girl reminded him of when Kasha had been nearly as young. He had played with her in much the same way when she would have her longer visits with Mother Maudrid long ago. He missed the old woman dearly.

His ruby eyes swept across the small room, taking in the peaceful scene. Morrigan lay curled beneath her blankets, her breathing steady but not quite deep enough for true rest. Something nagged at the edges of Lemmy's consciousness—a familiar wrongness that he'd learned to recognize over the months since her arrival.

A glance toward the mirror on the far wall confirmed what his enhanced senses already knew. The reflection showed a small tiefling girl with light red skin and budding horns, exactly as everyone else saw her. But when Lemmy turned his gaze directly to the bed, his familiar sight pierced through the glamour to reveal the truth: light orange fur, pointed vulpine ears that twitched even in sleep, and a bushy tail wrapped protectively around her own waist.

The deception didn't trouble him. He'd known from the moment Egrim, or whatever the large man's true name might be, had arrived with her in the tavern that chaotic night. Lemmy had lived long enough to recognize the scent of concealment magic, the subtle wrongness that clung to those hiding their true nature. The man reeked of it, though his own disguise was far more sophisticated than the child's.

A rhythmic thumping from the adjacent room drew his attention, accompanied by muffled sounds that made his head cock curiously to one side. Kasha's voice carried through the walls in a pattern he'd never heard before, breathless gasps and soft cries that seemed to alternate between distress and... something else entirely. The bed frame creaked in a steady rhythm, as if she and Egrim were engaged in some sort of vigorous game.

Strange, Lemmy mused, his corvid mind struggling to categorize the unfamiliar sounds. *Kasha has never played such energetic games before. Perhaps it's a human game?*

His contemplation was interrupted by a soft whimper from the bed. Morrigan's peaceful expression had twisted into one of fear, her small hands clutching at the blankets as her breathing quickened. The familiar wrongness intensified, and Lemmy felt the pull of her distress like a leash.

Without hesitation, he launched himself from the windowsill and perched on the ornate bedpost. His eyes rolled back until only stark white showed, matching the pristine color of his feathers. The world around him dissolved as his consciousness dove into the churning darkness of the child's nightmare.

There. The twisted presence that haunted her dreams materialized in the void, a figure wreathed in shadows and crackling with void energy that made Lemmy's spiritual form recoil. The entity's body remained frustratingly indistinct, shifting and writhing like smoke given malevolent purpose. But one detail stood out with terrifying clarity: a hand that was no longer quite humanoid, elongated fingers morphed into a crustacean-like claw that gleamed with malice.

The claw reached out, grasping not for Morrigan as Lemmy had expected, but toward a familiar figure with amethyst hair and purple eyes. Arialyn stood frozen in the nightmare landscape, unaware of the approaching danger.

Lemmy did as he had every time since he had noticed her trouble with these nightmares. He fluttered over her face to wake her, his white wings creating gentle currents of air that stirred the auburn strands of hair and fur clinging to her damp forehead. His talons barely grazed her cheek as he landed softly beside her on the pillow.

Morrigan shot up with a sharp intake of breath, her true golden eyes wide and unfocused as that familiar dread washed over her like a cold tide. The nightmare's tendrils still clung to the edges of her consciousness, shadow and claw and the terrible wrongness that always accompanied the dark figure. But just as quickly as the terror had seized her, it began to fade into the frustrating nothingness where all her nightmares seemed to disappear, leaving only the hollow ache of something important lost.

She blinked several times, her breathing gradually slowing as the present reasserted itself. The soft glow of full moonlight through her window, the familiar scents of the tavern below, the comforting weight of her blankets, all of it anchored her back to safety.

Lemmy rolled over on his back in her lap, his freshly cleaned white belly exposed as he made a series of soft, soothing warbles. The sound was like liquid comfort, a gentle melody that seemed to chase away the last wisps of whatever darkness had plagued her sleep. His ruby eyes gazed up at her with an intelligence that went far beyond what most expected from a corvid, and she felt the familiar wash of comfort in his presence.

Morrigan's face transformed, the lingering traces of fear melting away as a genuine smile spread across her features. She scooped Lemmy up with both hands, cradling him against her chest as she pulled the soft blanket over them both. The familiar weight of him, the way his feathers tickled against her chin, the steady rhythm of his tiny heartbeat, it all combined to create a cocoon of safety that no nightmare could penetrate.

She didn't speak the words, couldn't speak them even if she'd wanted to. The ability to voice her thoughts hadn't been granted to her yet. But Lemmy felt the warmth of love radiating from her like heat from a hearth, a pure emotion that needed no words to convey its depth.

The albino raven nestled against her chin, his beak gently preening a strand of her hair as his own breathing began to slow. The rhythmic sounds from the adjacent room had finally quieted, leaving only the peaceful silence of the late night. Whatever games Kasha and Egrim had been playing seemed to have concluded, and the tavern settled into the deep quiet that it had every night.

Within moments, both child and familiar had drifted back into sleep, this time untroubled by the lingering echoes of things best left forgotten.

CHAPTER THIRTY-NINE

FEAR NO MORE

The warm water was a soothing massage to her aching muscles. Kasha hadn't gotten much sleep, but what little she received had felt the most rejuvenating of any sleep in the last several years. Even now she could still smell his scent on her skin. A musky mixture of sweat and wood. She had always wondered why he smelled like wood. Oak? Pine? She didn't know the scent of trees very well. All the woodwork and carpentry she had paid for in the renovations of this building had given her that knowledge.

She had always assumed that was why he smelled that way. He moved much of the wood and performed some of the less intricate work himself. Yet, all of that had been completed a month ago. Why did he still smell like a forest after rain?

She felt a curl of the towel on her head come loose and caught it quickly, tucking it back into place. Excess dye from the towel collected on her finger.

"Shit." She hurriedly washed it off in the tub before it could stain her finger.

She was smiling, thinking about last night. Her time with him had made her reconsider much. She had spent her entire life blaming herself for nearly everything that had gone wrong in it. Her time in the Helspires, her mother, the death of the goblin that smuggled her out of the Helspires. She could never remember his name. He had been killed by raiders on their way to Toz'Naluunod. Those same raiders sold her on the slave market there. She spent two weeks cleaning the home of the grimalkin family that bought her. They were cruel.

The mother would whip her for the smallest offense. The daughter would make Kasha think she wanted to play with her and then when Kasha would let her guard down, she would yell that Kasha had broken something, and the mother would beat her again. The father had eyed her the way she had seen Zunibar eye her mother sometimes and it had made her very uncomfortable. Had it not been for the kindhearted boy in the family, she would probably still be there.

He told his mother he was taking her to the market with him to get candies for him and his sister. Once they were near the edge of the city, he unshackled her and told her to run. As badly as she wanted to leave, she feared being in this world alone or worse being recaptured and brought back to be punished. She had heard stories of slaves that had had their legs maimed just enough that they could no longer run. The boy finally had to yell at her and pushed her like someone does to a dog they were trying to get rid of. She shrunk back from him, and he had tripped and fallen in the street right into the pounding feet of a horse.

She blamed herself for Callus feeling alone when he started fighting in the arenas. She hadn't been enough to help him. Not enough to make him happy and it had hurt her. Their friendship changed a little that night. It didn't matter that he later told her it was something missing inside him and that it had nothing to do with her. She still felt guilty.

She hadn't left with the Traveling Spectacles when they had gone to the Helspires for Callus's championship win and reign thereafter. They had all died. All except Callus and Mother Maudrid. She always wondered if she could have changed the course of any of that by being a better friend to him and mustering the courage to tell them fully about her past. Then maybe they could have helped her. Maybe he and the rest of the Traveling Spectacles would have stayed.

What caused her the most overwhelming feeling of guilt though, was for the loss of her son. The loss became all the more real when she finally awoke to see his impossibly small, bruised body. It was something she couldn't control, she knew that, but it still made her soul ache. She needed to tell Egrim. Tell him why she was holding herself back from him. His reasons for holding back from her didn't matter to her right now. She had been staring into the mirror in her washroom for half an hour telling herself she was done with guilt. That frightened little girl she had been, the one that hid her true feelings from nearly everyone and always tried to make others happy, she would be buried in this bath. Buried along with the constant need for perfection that trauma had given her.

She unraveled the towel from her head and tossed it to the floor. With a deep breath she submerged in the tub and ran her fingers through her hair, washing out the excess black dye. She stood in the tub and faced the mirror. Her vision poured over her reflection with intense scrutiny. Only this time, instead of focusing on every detail that didn't meet the standards of excellence she had sought after all these years; she saw all the things that made her uniquely her. Kasha Volstruk.

Her left horn had been broken and reattached with a gold seam. A small scar on the right side of her neck from a scrape her and Callus had as kids with some street rat children. Her left breast was slightly smaller than her right. Neither of them was the size she had always wanted. Her hips were a bit wide, and relative to her upper body she thought they made her look oddly put together. Her inner labia protruded from her outer. She had once been teased that it looked like a cat that fell asleep with its tongue out. Then there was the surgical scar at the base of her belly, a scar she had always made sure rested below the waistband of her skirts. The scar of the loss she would never get back and from which nothing else would ever grow.

Her eyes caught something in the mirror then. She thought it a bruise. Technically it was, although these were lovingly given by the mouth of a man that she had fallen in love with, despite her best efforts. She saw similar spots that he had gifted her. Nearly all of them were on or next to the places on her body that she had always tried to hide. She had hated those imperfections. Yet, he had seemingly sought them out and paid special attention to love each one. Kasha closed her eyes, remembering the feeling of his hands and lips on each of those areas as she studied them. She felt nearly weightless, years of regrets and insecurities gone.

Finally, she met her own eyes in the glass and smiled through tears. The dye trailed from her hair and down her body in muted and thin streaks of black. As the water found curves and creases to make its rivers back to the tub, she accepted and acknowledged two new loves. Her love for him and her love for herself.

"One last thing to complete my statement." She stepped out of the tub and moved to the mirror, grabbing the pair of shears that rested next to the wash basin.

Kovag had been awake for nearly half an hour. He woke up facing the wall opposite Kasha's side of the bed. At first, he was immensely disappointed to not have her in his arms. That feeling remained but was held in the back of his mind, behind the voices battling in his head. One said to get up and leave before she wakes up and the other screamed for him to roll over and grab her, tell her you love her. Tell her everything and pray to any of the gods that would listen that she understood. He couldn't conclude what would cause her the least pain, so he laid there paralyzed with indecision and second guessing his actions last night.

He had been so steadfast in his resolve to tell her everything last night, then she forced him to wait. Now he felt himself waver.

Finally, one voice screamed louder than the other and he turned to face her in the bed and found it empty. He sighed but noticed the light of flickering candles dancing under the door to Kasha's washroom. He relaxed and laid his head back onto the pillow. The intensity of the moonlight that shone through the window slats reminded him of the pact. Was it really tonight? He was both surprised and unbothered that he had let the time of the month slip from his mind. With a reluctant and irritated groan, he got out of bed and stood at the spot on the floor that received the most light from the twin full moons of silver. He stood with his feet shoulder width apart and arms outstretched. He focused the spot in the middle of his chest where the willow wing blossom lay hidden.

"Oakira." He whispered.

He waited several minutes and repeated the process. She didn't come nor did she call to him. Nothing. How many months had it been since she had told him to take Saffron and go into hiding. How many months had she not so much as sent him a thrum in his chest to let him know she was still there. Two years and seven months since she had last lay with him, and even that last time had been... telling. He was positive now that even if she had not fully abandoned him, she had at least cast him aside without much care. He felt hollow again.

He trudged over to the bed and sat down. The sound of a light splash of water came from the washroom and a smile came unbidden. It was the smell of her pillow that pulled him back down onto the bed. That alone banished the hollow feeling inside him. He grabbed it and brought it to his face. Her scent filled him to his core. Then he heard her washroom door. The hollow space inside him that had just been filled, flooded and exploded inside him.

Kasha stepped into the room and halted when she found him awake, his hands holding her pillow to his face. Those hands. Those hands that were so calloused and yet held her so secure and gentle last night. His body alone took up two thirds of her bed. This colossal man that could crush people's bones at will, made the sweetest gentle yet passionate love to her last night. His moans were like purrs and his growls had vibrated every inch of her body and soul. The way he looked at her now, she felt like he thought he was looking at the Bright One herself.

"Does he truly love me?" She dared to hope. She stood in a light blue robe of sheer silk.

Kovag was speechless. In the pale light of the twin full moons, she indeed was a goddess to him. His Goddess. He knew then that if she would have him, he would worship at her alter even beyond death.

Her robe hugged her body as though it was a mortal begging to be as close to the Goddess of the Soul as it could. If she had truly been a goddess, he would have burned a nation to build her a temple right then and there if all she did was ask.

She had changed her hair. Deep black waves fell atop her shoulders like the hanging branches and leaves of a willow. It accented her sharper features and the gold seam on her horn. She came to bed and sat on the edge. He tried to speak but couldn't, so astonished was he by the aura about her. He reached up and ran his fingers through her damp hair and smiled.

Kasha turned halfway toward him on the bed. "I have decided on something, and I need you to let me finish before you say anything."

He wanted to protest. It was HE that needed to say something. He wanted beg her to be still and let him confess who he truly was. But he just nodded, mouth half open in awe. Still, somewhere in the back of his mind, he prayed she wasn't about to say it was all a mistake and he needed to leave. Afraid that she would say lying to each other, even for one night, caused more pain then she was willing to hold. He shook his head and looked away with worry. He saw his false reflection. It felt like he ripped his own heart out. He made love to her as this false man. She didn't share herself with him, Kovag. She gave herself to the man, Egrim. He felt so overwhelmed with guilt that he opened his mouth again to blurt everything out to her. And he would have, but she spoke first.

"I have not told anyone what I am about to tell you. Not even Callus or Arialyn. Lorisse knows. She was there for most of it." She stopped for a moment to gather her strength.

"I was in love with someone several years back. After Callus, Sylus and the rest of the Traveling Spectacles left for the Helspires, but before I opened the Tits and Tarts. His name was Folkvar. A bard. A very talented one if I'm truthful. That was part of what attracted me to him. He had a warm smile and made me laugh, even when I didn't want to. He charmed everyone. There wasn't a soul that he couldn't convince to like him. That probably should have set alarms off in my head. Looking back, I know now that Mother Maudrid had tried to warn me." She looked out the window and rubbed her hands together. She felt her courage begin to fade.

Kovag placed his hand reassuringly on her thigh. His simple touch renewed her confidence, and she continued, though with a wavering in her voice.

"He pursued me. I didn't make it hard. Everything between us was fast. It... he, had felt so natural. We married. He wanted children. I assume you know that it is not common for tieflings to bear children." She looked at him and saw his confirmation with a nod.

"I was afraid to even try. In fact, I had told him before we married that I didn't want to attempt it. I absolutely wanted children. But I resigned myself to a life without them, like most of my people do. I didn't want to get my hopes up, despite my longing to have a child. However, I did become pregnant...for a time."

Her eyes welled with tears and Kovag moved closer to her.

"I lost our... my son. A sweet little baby boy midway through my pregnancy. Mother Maudrid and my midwife had to cut him out. I was losing too much blood. I still remember when my head hit the table as I passed out. Afterward the midwife said with what they had to do to stop the bleeding I would never be able to have children." She traced the scar near her waist and then felt his hand over hers.

"Afterward, Folkvar returned home from a 'tour,' He had already grown distant. This set him over the edge. He blamed me. Said I should have been more careful. Said we had been blessed with this opportunity and I squandered it. He went crazy. He..." She swallowed hard and cleared her throat. "No man will ever lay hands on me like that again. One day I awoke to find him gone. He left me. So, I thought." She felt a weird smile cross her face. A smile of gratitude but regret as well.

"They found his body washed up on the riverbank a week later. A Trade Authority's detective said he was poisoned. They found a small sachet of herbs and rat bones in his vest. Mother Maudrid denied it, but I know she had a hand in it. There was a short time that I was angry with her. But it didn't take me long to feel gratitude for what she had done. She found a small measure of retribution for me and made sure he didn't harm anyone else ever again. Still, I couldn't provide what he desired. It has been a common theme in my life, not being what someone needs me to be. That and tragedy." She locked eyes with him now, the man SHE desired. The person she hoped would finally provide her with what she needed; to be allowed to be selfish in her personal life for once.

"My mother gave up and left me to fend for myself in the most wretched of places I can imagine. Amos, the goblin that saved me," A small laugh came as she finally remembered the goblin man's name.

"He died getting me away from the Helspires. Slavers found us and killed him when he refused to sell me to them. Then they sold me to a family in Toz'Naluunod. The son of that family set me free and died in doing so. I made it here, to Hus'rokn, as a child. You can imagine the things that happened to get me here from there. I've blocked most of them out of my mind I think, which is for the best I think. I found a home with the Traveling Spectacles. I will forever be thankful for that. For Sylus, Mother Maudrid, Callus and the others. Still, they left me. I know, in truth, that I refused to go with them, so I don't blame them for it. I was too afraid to go anywhere near there for fear of Zunibar finding me. Had I told them, that situation probably would have resolved itself, but I didn't want Callus and Sylus to get into trouble there. But I didn't say anything, and they all wanted to walk a different path than I did, but it hurt still. Then Folkvar. I have never trusted anyone new or let anyone in at all in since then." She paused for a moment as she readied herself to give him her final admission.

"Then you and Morrigan came. I felt something in you. I tried so gods damn hard to deny it. Fear of being driven further into myself by your refusal or you leaving when things got complicated. My soul grows weary of the game we play with each other and even more so of the mask I put on. A mask I wear not just for you, but for everyone." She shifted on the bed and turned fully toward him now. "I don't know what you are running from Egrim. I don't know what that means for the safety of your daughter. I don't know what kind of woman her mother was or what you lost in her as your wife. What I do know is that it is breaking me to not let you know how I feel. I tell you with restrained actions and glances that I desire you, but keeping distant with my words. I see the way you look at Morrigan and the children that play about in the street. You want more. I cannot keep you here, I know that, and I cannot provide you with more children. I can't even tell you that I am not so irreparably damaged that I can make you happy or be a haven for you on your most tiresome of days." She trailed off and looked at the floor.

Kovag scooted closer to her and touched her face, bringing her eyes back to his.

Kasha cleared her throat, her eyes moist. "Choose me. Stay with me. I don't care if you are running from the gods themselves. I will fight whatever the odds are. I'm used to playing against loaded dice. I love you and I love Morrigan. She is the sweetest bright-eyed and inquisitive girl I have ever met. Let me make you both happy. Be mine and make me happy."

He felt himself being ripped in half by her words. He didn't care that she couldn't have children. In his eyes he already had a daughter. Morrigan, no, Saffron was the best thing that had ever come into his life. He needed no other children. None could ever measure up to half of what she was. All he wanted, needed, was Kasha. He looked at her hand in his. She would understand the truth of it all. She bared her soul to him, raw. He needed to tell her everything, but he couldn't tell her what she wanted to hear until she knew him. The real him.

It took every bit of his will to look back into her eyes again and hope he wasn't about to break her heart. "Nothing would complete me more, but you need to know who we really are and exactly what we're running from."

He opened his mouth, and his words were cut off by the sounds of an explosive force downstairs.

CHAPTER FORTY

CUNT PUNCH

Kovag jumped to his feet, grabbed Kasha's hand and pulled her toward the door. The sounds coming from below were so violent and destructive that they made the entire building shudder. As they rushed to the door of the madame's suite, Kovag felt a wave of energy that was like Oakira's but more savage in nature. *"They found us."* That was what went through his head as he ripped the door off the hinges and came to a stop at the railing of the mezzanine with Kasha right behind him. The sight below froze the blood in Kovag's veins.

Bodies lay scattered across the tavern floor like discarded dolls, their limbs twisted at unnatural angles. Dark pools spread beneath them, reflecting the flickering light of the few remaining sconces. The metallic scent of blood hung thick in the air, mixing with something else, something that made Kovag's senses recoil. Lunar magic meant for one thing and one thing only, pain and death.

Two beings unlike anything Kasha had ever seen dominated the center of the room. They appeared almost elven at first glance, but wrong in ways that made her mind struggle to process what she was seeing. Their ears stretched impossibly long, curling backward in a crescent shape and nearly reaching their shoulders. Their features held an otherworldly sharpness that seemed to cut through reality itself. The female's amber hair cascaded past her knees like liquid gold, while silver armor adorned a tall frame that seemed built to be nothing but a predator.

The male beside her wore similar armor, though his was partially black, and his blonde hair matched his companion's impossible length. Both moved with a fluid grace that suggested they weren't entirely bound by the same physical laws of this realm.

"Lorisse!" Kasha's scream tore from her throat as she spotted her dearest friend.

The female creature, for Kasha could think of no other word, held Lorisse by her dark blonde hair, lifting her partially off the ground with her nakedness displayed. Lorisse's face was streaked with tears, her mouth open in silent agony as she struggled against the iron grip. Her feet barely touched the floor, and her hands clawed desperately at the fingers tangled in her hair.

"Please," Lorisse sobbed, her voice carrying up to the mezzanine. "Please, I don't know anything. I don't know who you're looking for!"

Kovag's eyes swept the scene below, cataloging threats and searching for any sign of movement among the fallen. Near the male creature's feet, two familiar forms lay motionless. Carl and Fithra's naked bodies remained motionless. Carl's face was a mask of crimson and Fithra's dark skin seemed ashen in the dim lighting. Neither moved, but Kovag's Fae touched eye honed in on them both and saw the slightest movement of breathing. Unconscious, not dead. Yet. The same could not be said for the Lance men that Lance Captain Ethan had left to safeguard the tavern. They lay in several pieces across the floor.

The female's head tilted upward at Kasha's scream, and when their eyes met, Kasha felt something cold and alien probe at the edges of her mind. The woman's lips curved into wicked smile.

"Ah," she said, her voice musical. Somehow that made the words more terrifying. "The proprietress joins us at last. How...efficient."

Kovag felt his glamour wavering under the stress, the magic that disguised his true appearance flickering like a candle in the wind. His hand found Kasha's arm, pulling her back from the railing.

"You need to-" he began, but the male craned his head forward and took notice of the glamour around Kovag.

Isque clapped his hands together as he finally solved the puzzle. "It's him. She put a glamour on you. Puzzle solved my sweet."

Amjani raised an eyebrow and nodded. "We did not think your master had such power yet. That explains why you were so hard to find. I do not suppose you would be willing to come quietly? We can reunite you with some friends."

She nodded to Isque, and he reached into a small bag at his side whose opening enlarged as he pulled an object from it. He held it by what hair remained. "It was a little difficult to keep the malformed dwarf preserved but I assume you can make him out." Isque saw no look of recognition on Kovag's features. "Well, he did most of these burns to himself, believe it or not. He had a decent forge, for a mortal."

A wildness glazed over Kovag's eyes. *Bornar.*

Isque dropped Bornar's head and pulled another from the unnatural bag. "This one is a more recent find."

Kasha's hands shot to cover her mouth and hold back the bile that rose in her throat. She recognized in the creature's hands the head of Adenus.

"Submit, and we will only add," Amjani looked around them, counting. "Three more heads to the collection."

Kovag's eyes darted involuntarily to the door beside them, the room where Saffron slept. The glance lasted barely half a heartbeat, but it was enough.

Amjani's raptor like gaze followed his line of sight, and her smile widened with cruel understanding. "Ah, yes. The vulpine girl." Her voice was like chimes in the wind. "Seeker Isque, he is not going to cooperate. Let us make the pact mortal more compliant. Retrieve the child."

"No!" Kovag roared, feeling his throat tear with the sheer force he placed in the cry.

Isque blurred, reality bending around him as he teleported in a shimmer of silver light. One moment he stood among the carnage below, the next he materialized directly in front of Saffron's door, his hand already reaching for the handle.

The desperate fury that flooded Kovag's system shattered the careful glamour Oakira had woven around him. The magic unraveled like smoke in a hurricane, revealing his true form in an explosive transformation that made the air itself crackle with released energy.

Where the tall, broad-shouldered human had stood moments before, a massive half-orc towered over Kasha in its place. Light green skin replaced the tanned flesh she had known. Tusks protruded from his lower lip, a broken one where she had previously seen a scarred lip on the man she knew as Egrim. His brown eyes had become one brown, one blazing Fae-touched green that seemed to burn with inner fire. The black hair she had run her fingers through remained, but now it framed features that were unmistakably orcish in their brutal beauty.

Kasha's mind reeled, but there was no time to process the revelation. Her hands ignited with crackling frost as she turned to face Amjani, arcane energy coursing through her veins like liquid ice. Lorisse kicked frantically.

Kasha screamed. "Get away from her!"

The temperature in the room plummeted as Kasha's power manifested, her breath misting in the suddenly frigid air. Frost began spreading across the wooden railing beneath her hands.

Just as Amjani opened her mouth to respond, one of the downstairs doors exploded outward in a shower of splinters. Callus burst through the wreckage, the Hangman's Spear materializing in his grip as he charged across the blood-slicked floor. He gave no war cry. His mouth sat slightly open and his vision focused as he drove the weapon toward Amjani's back.

The Master Seeker was forced to release Lorisse, who crumpled to the floor gasping, as she spun to meet Callus's assault. Her silver armor rang like a bell as the spear's point scraped across it, leaving a thin line of scratched metal.

From the doorway Callus had emerged, the sharp crack of Arialyn's arcabus split the air. The void ore-powered projectile sizzled past Amjani's head, close enough to singe her hair, and embedded itself in the wall behind her with a shower of splinters.

"Kasha, we've got her! Help-" Arialyn shouted, her voice halting as she noticed the strangely familiar and yet entirely new figure battling the other Lunar Fae outside of Morrigan's door.

Kovag's body moved with desperation as Isque's scimitars whistled through the air where his head had been a heartbeat before. The Lunar Fae's blade sang with arcane energy, leaving trails of silver light as it carved deadly arcs through the space between them. Kovag ducked low, feeling the wind of another strike slice through a tuft of his black hair, then rolled sideways as the point drove into the wooden floor where it would have pinned his foot to the ground.

Isque pressed his attack with viciously accurate strikes that kept Kovag from attempting to do anything but dodge. A scimitar came down in a vicious overhead strike that would have cleaved Kovag from shoulder to hip. Without conscious thought, Kovag threw his left arm up and roared a word in the Fae tongue.

A shimmering disc of silver energy materialized just above his forearm, catching the scimitar's edge with a sound like shattering crystal.

The force of the impact drove Kovag to one knee, but the arcane shield held. Sparks of conflicting magic cascaded around them as Lunar steel met summoned Fae protection.

Isque twirled around and faked what would have been a glancing blow to Kovag's knee but then twisted the blade at an angle Kovag couldn't have predicated and plunged it into his gut. Kovag's reply was only a silent gasp as all his breath left him in an instant. Isque's smug smile, looking down on Kovag, made him recollect himself. The arrogance of the Fae pushing him onward. He grabbed a hold of the hand Isque had on the embedded scimitar and then slammed his forehead into the Lunar Fae's nose.

Isque's eyes shut in pain and blood poured forth from his shattered nose. Kovag surged upward from his crouch, his right fist already glowing with the same familiar emerald arcane force. The hook connected with Isque's midsection just below his armor's edge, and the arcane enhancement sent the Lunar Fae flying backward. However, Kovag still had a hold of his arm and yanked him back toward him, burying another arcane bow into Isque's sternum. Isque's shock at the crack Kovag had made in his armor was abruptly replaced by the pain of his body crashing into a solid wood wall.

His momentum carried him further, and for a brief moment he teetered on the edge of the mezzanine railing, but his grace was such that he simply leapt backward in a flip and landed with ease on the railing. He smiled at Oakira's pact mortal in approval.

"Kasha!" Kovag bellowed, not taking his eyes off the recovering Fae. "Save her! Please!"

Kasha burst through Morrigan's door with frost still crackling around her fingers, ready to shield the child from whatever threat awaited. But she stopped dead in her tracks, her mind struggling to process what she saw.

The small tiefling girl she knew as Morrigan was gone. In her place huddled a terrified vulpine child with light orange fur that seemed to glow in fading firelight from the hearth in the room. Golden eyes that had once appeared as dark brown now shimmered with an inner light and pointed fox ears twitched nervously atop her head. A bushy tail, previously rough and ridged as a tiefling's should be, curled around her waist as she hugged her knees to her chest. Still the child held a butter knife, though now it shook with fear.

Saffron caught Kasha's confused expression and looked down at herself. The shimmering field of the glamour that hid her and Kovag was entirely gone. Tears steamed even harder now and she looked at Kasha, pleading.

Lemmy squawked indignantly from his perch on Saffron's shoulder, his white feathers ruffled with agitation. The raven's red eyes darted between the chaos outside the door and the frightened child beneath him.

Kasha shook herself from her stupor. Whatever Morrigan truly was didn't matter, she was still the sweet, silent child who needed protection. "Come on, sweetness," Kasha said, extending her hand.

Saffron's golden eyes met hers, and without hesitation, she grasped Kasha's outstretched fingers. Together they rushed to the window as the sounds of battle raged behind them.

Kasha reached for the latch and grasped the wooden frame, but the moment her fingers touched the latch, the world around her shifted. The sounds of battle faded to a distant echo as memory crashed over her like a tide of ice water. Her hand jerked away from the window.

She was six years old again, standing in her and her mother's quarters inside Zunibar's opulent mansion. She could hear his heavy footsteps thundering down the hallway. Her mother's lifeless eyes stared at nothing from the floor and the empty pouch of spice still by the bed. Her fingers trembled as she climbed the windowsill and jumped.

The flashback hit with such force that Kasha's knees nearly buckled. She could smell the heavy scent of spice, feel the silk curtains against her trembling hands as she'd climbed onto the windowsill three stories above the cobblestones. The terror of that leap, the certainty that she would die, the desperate hope that death would be better than what awaited her if she stayed.

"No," she whispered, shaking her head violently to dispel the memory.

Saffron's small hand tugged at Kasha's robe, her eyes wide with fear and pleading in the same way her previously known brown eyes had. The child's touch anchored Kasha back to the present, to the immediate danger that surrounded them. She scooped Saffron into her arms and lunged for the window latch.

It wouldn't budge.

Panic clawed at her throat as she threw her weight against the frame, her fingers scrabbling desperately at the mechanism. The wood groaned under her assault but remained stubbornly sealed. She tried again, harder this time, her panicked attempts to open the window leaving bits of arcane frost behind.

She hissed through gritted teeth. "Come on, come on you damned thing!"

Then she looked through the glass and her mouth dropped open in disbelief. Where the narrow alley should have been, where the buildings across the way should have stood illuminated by moonlight, there was nothing. Absolute, consuming blackness pressed against the window like a living thing. No stars, no moons, no distant glow from the city beyond. Just an endless blackness that seemed to swallow light itself.

Magic. It had to be magic. She'd never seen anything this powerful. *"What are those people?"*

Kasha set Saffron down behind her and stepped back from the window, her hands humming with the arcane. Lemmy launched himself from Saffron's shoulder to perch on Kasha's, his talons digging into the silk of her robe.

"Stay back, sweetness." She commanded, then unleashed her fury.

Spears of ice erupted from her palms, slamming into the window with enough force to shatter stone. The glass blew into thousands of pieces but the black wall of nothingness remained solid. She tried again, this time with a concentrated beam of frost that could freeze a body part in mere seconds. Still, the darkness remained.

Desperation clawed at her as she switched tactics. She called forth bursts of arcane flame that should have melted the frame to slag. The fire washed harmlessly over the surface like water over stone.

"Hells!" She pounded her fists against the unyielding barrier.

She had no choice. "Morrigan." Was that even her name? "Come here."

Saffron leapt into her outstretched arms as Kasha bolted through the bedroom door. She turned to see Kovag bleeding from his stomach wound, still pressing his attack against Isque, who moved about the mezzanine railing like it was dance floor. The Lunar Fae's scimitars flicked out in playful cuts, opening shallow wounds across Kovag's arms and shoulders with casual cruelty. She felt a sickening feeling, watching the person she had known as Egrim being picked apart.

Below, Callus and Arialyn fought valiantly against Amjani, but the Master Seeker moved like liquid mercury, always one step ahead of their attacks.

And there, by the front door, Lorisse frantically pulled and pushed at the handle, her naked form trembling as she met the same magical resistance that had trapped Kasha and Saffron upstairs. With no options for escape, Kasha positioned herself in the furthest corner from the fighting and placed Saffron behind her.

They were caged.

Callus pressed his advantage as Amjani's attention flickered between him and Arialyn's position inside the bedroom doorway. The Master Seeker's silver armor bore fresh scratches from their exchange, but she moved with the same predatory ease that made her seem untouchable. He needed to change that.

The Reaver feinted left with the Hangman's Spear, drawing her guard in that direction, then whirled the spear overhead and switched it to his other hand. Amjani's pale eyes widened in confusion for just a heartbeat, long enough for Callus to raise his right hand and pull on an invisible rope.

The air around Amjani's throat shimmered, and a spectral noose materialized from nothing, its ethereal rope glowing with the cold touch of the grave. The divine magic of the Hanged One pulsed through the construct as it snapped tight around the Lunar Fae's neck with an audible *crack*.

Amjani dropped her blades and her hands flew to her throat, clawing at the ghostly rope that felt as solid as iron against her flesh. Her eyes went wide with surprise and something that might have been the briefest hint of fear.

Callus yanked hard on the spectral tether, his muscles straining as he hauled the Master Seeker toward him like a fish on a line. Amjani's feet left the ground as she was jerked forward, her perfect composure vanished.

"Now!" Callus roared.

Arialyn didn't hesitate. She bolted from the room in a full sprint across the tavern's main floor. The arcabus cracked three times in rapid succession, void ore projectiles screaming through the air where Callus had positioned her target. The first shot took Amjani in the left hip, tearing through silver armor and flesh with a wet *thunk*. The second grazed her thigh, opening a line of crimson across pale skin. The third punched clean through her side, sending droplets of Fae blood spattering across the tavern floor.

Amjani's scream was like breaking crystal, a sound that made the remaining sconces waver. She twisted in the noose's grip, her face contorting with pain and rage.

The Master Seeker raised her hand, silver light gathering around her fingers as she prepared to teleport herself to Arialyn's position for revenge. The magic built, reality beginning to bend around her.

Then it simply... stopped.

The teleportation magic collapsed like a house of cards, the gathered energy dissipating harmlessly into the air. Amjani's eyes went wide with genuine shock as she felt the spectral noose pulse with divine power. The Hanged One's influence flowed through the construct, severing her connection to the arcane forces she commanded.

"Impossible." She choked her voice hoarse from the pressure around her throat.

Amjani unsheathed a hidden dagger and whirled the lunar forged blade in her hand, its edge whistling through the air. The blade bit into the spectral noose and then forced it to break.

Free from the divine binding, she extended one hand toward Arialyn. A flick of her wrist sending an invisible force slamming into the Arialyn like a giant's fist. Her feet left the ground as she was hurled upward, her small form crashing into the ceiling with bone-jarring impact before gravity reclaimed her. She plummeted down onto one of the main room tables, the heavy wood splintering beneath her as she hit with a nauseating sound.

"Arialyn!" Callus spun around to place himself between the two women, but Amjani was already moving.

The Master Seeker flipped in place, arcane wind whipping around her like a miniature hurricane. Her kick caught Callus in the temple with the force of a war hammer, the impact lifting him off his feet and sending him crashing to the blood-slicked floor. Stars exploded across his vision as he now fought a battle to remain conscious.

Kasha pressed herself as far back into the corner of the mezzanine as she could, while still leaving Saffron room to breathe. She could feel the girl trembling, her small hands clutching at Kasha's silk robe. There was nowhere left to run, nowhere left to hide. The magical barrier had trapped them all like rats in a cage.

Frost crackled around Kasha's fingers as she watched Kovag struggle against Isque's relentless assault. The half-orc's movements were growing sluggish, blood loss from his stomach wound taking its toll. Isque danced around him with cruel grace, his scimitars opening fresh cuts with each pass. Kovag willed Isque to be slowed, made feeble and even blind. None of the spells took effect.

Kasha raised her hand and focused her remaining strength. Three razor-sharp ice shards materialized in the air before her, each one gleaming like crystalline daggers that spiraled around each other. With a sharp gesture, she sent them screaming through the air toward Isque's back.

Isque detected the attack at the last second. He twisted away from the projectiles, but one of them caught his ankle and the sudden movement threw off his perfect balance. His left foot slipped on the bloody railing, and for just a heartbeat, his guard dropped.

Kovag seized the opening. His right hand shot out, fingers splayed, then yanked back toward his chest as if grasping an invisible rope. Life faded from Isque's eyes as he felt his own strength drain away, pulled from his body by some unseen force. His knees buckled as the stolen vitality flowed into Kovag's wounds, sealing some of them completely.

He surged forward with renewed vigor, his massive frame colliding with Isque like a battering ram. They crashed through the railing of the mezzanine and to the floor together, the wooden planks groaning under their combined weight. Isque's scimitars clattered away across the tavern as Kovag pinned him down.

Kovag raised his fist, green energy crackling around his knuckles as he prepared to end this. But Isque suddenly dissolved into wisps of gray mist, flowing like smoke between Kovag's fingers.

The mist reformed behind him in an instant. Isque materialized with his arm wrapped around Kovag's throat, a curved dagger appearing in his free hand. The blade punched through muscle and sinew as he drove it deep into Kovag's shoulder, then dragged it downward in a vicious slice.

"I have tired of this game." Isque hissed into Kovag's ear, his voice cold and confident.

The dagger flicked out again, this time slashing across the back of Kovag's thighs. Hamstrings parted like cut rope, and Kovag's legs gave out beneath him with a roar of agony.

Isque raised his free hand toward the ceiling, and lunar light materialized on the ceiling above them. Not the gentle silver glow that had streamed through the windows, but something harsh and burning. The concentrated beam lanced down like a spear of molten silver, searing into Kovag's exposed back.

His scream tore through the tavern, a sound of pure anguish that made even the walls seemingly shudder. His body convulsed once, then went terrifyingly still.

"No!" Kasha stumbled forward, her legs weak from arcane exhaustion.

Behind her, Saffron darted out from their hiding spot, her fur bristling with fury as she, to Kasha's complete dismay, ran and leapt off the mezzanine. She came down on Isque's back and plunged the butterknife into an opening in the armor at the Lunar Fae's neck.

Isque cursed, his grip on Kovag loosening as he reached backward to try and rip the knife free. Instead he grabbed Saffron by the throat and held her high.

Kovag's eyes fluttered open at the sound of her voice. He tried to push himself up, his arms trembling with the effort, but his strength failed him. He collapsed back to the floor with a grunt of pain.

Kasha used what arcane energy she had left aimed at the butterknife in the back of Isque's neck, sending a shock through the metal. The jolt caused the Seeker to shudder and lose his grip on Saffron. She landed unsteadily on her feet and immediately ran to Kovag's side. She placed her hands on his back, willing the healing power she once gave him to somehow come forth again. She squinted hard and held her breath. It was useless.

Down on the main floor, Callus dragged himself to his feet, his vision still swimming from Amjani's devastating kick. Blood trickled from his temple as he shook his head, trying to clear the stars that danced across his sight. Across the room, Arialyn was struggling to rise, her left arm hanging at an unnatural angle and crimson streaming from a gash on her forehead where she'd struck the ceiling.

Callus raised his right hand, the Ring of Anguish pulsing with light as three orange beams of necrotic energy screamed toward the Master Seeker. Amjani's scimitars moved in a blur, deflecting each beam with contemptuous ease. The redirected energy scorched the walls behind her, leaving smoking craters in the wood.

Callus roared and launched himself through the air, the Hangman's Spear thrust forward while his right leg cocked back for a devastating kick. For a heartbeat, he thought he had her, the spear point aimed true for her heart, his boot ready to crush her ribs.

Then Amjani simply wasn't there.

She shimmered like heat waves rising from summer stone, her form becoming translucent as she moved faster than mortal eyes could follow. Callus's vision couldn't track her movements. One moment she stood before him, the next she was everywhere and nowhere at once.

The cuts came from impossible angles. Her scimitar opened a line across his ribs from the left while simultaneously slashing his shoulder from the right. Another strike carved through his thigh as a fourth needled through his arm brace. The wounds appeared faster than pain could register, silver steel moving with supernatural speed.

Callus crashed to his knees, blood pooling beneath him as his strength fled through a dozen wounds. The Hangman's Spear clattered to the floor and vanished from nerveless fingers as he swayed, fighting to remain upright.

Amjani solidified before him, her pale features arranged in an expression of mock pity. "How disappointing," she said, her musical voice dripping with false sympathy. "I had not expected to find one of the gods chosen in this dump. Perhaps the Hanged One should have selected a worthier champion."

She raised her scimitar, moonlight streaming from its edge as she prepared to deliver the killing blow. "Still, there is honor in claiming the life of a divine servant, even one so-"

Bright lights suddenly danced directly in her eyes, blinding her. Callus turned to see Arialyn's working arm outstretched. She had apparently been practicing one of the spells from that old tome the Captain had procured for her.

"What a delightful parlor trick. Mortal arcanomancer playing with a children's spel-" Amjani's words cut off in a strangled gasp as she doubled over, her face contorting in agony. A stream of vomit splashed onto the floor as she clutched between her thighs.

Just to the side of her and avoiding most of the vomit, Carl Just Carl knelt still half unconscious, his meaty fist still extended from the devastating uppercut he'd just delivered between the Master Seeker's legs and into the most sensitive part of her anatomy.

"Cunt punch," he declared with a satisfied smirk, then promptly collapsed back to the floor, unconscious once more.

Arialyn fired her arcabus. The arcane projectile struck Amjani's wrist, shattering the bones, sending her dagger spinning away into the darkness.

Callus forced himself back to his feet and swung the Hangman's Spear in a twirl over his head before bringing the edge of the spear top against and through Amjani's throat

Callus brought the spear back around and plunged in through the heart of her armor. Then, with a sneer, he wrenched the weapon free and brought it around in a perfect arc that separated her head from her shoulders.

Isque's scimitars hung poised above Kasha and Saffron as he prepared to end their lives. The Seeker's face was a mask of sinister satisfaction.

Then he felt more than heard the last grunt of life leave Amjani.

He felt a tearing, ripping agony that had nothing to do with the pain of his wounds. His connection to Amjani, forged through centuries of partnership and something deeper than duty, was now simply gone. The bond that had linked them snapped like an overstretched rope, leaving a gaping wound in his consciousness.

"No," he whispered, his weapons trembling in suddenly numb fingers. "No, no, no..."

The scimitars clattered to the floor as his hands flew to his chest, clawing at the phantom pain that bloomed there. His perfect composure cracked like ice in spring, revealing raw desperation beneath.

A scream tore from his throat, a keening wail of a soul being flayed alive. He tore himself away from his prey and ran to the fallen body of the woman he had done all of this for in the first place. His knees crashed to the wet wooden floor next to the headless body of Amjani.

"Amjani," he sobbed, gathering her severed head into his arms with infinite tenderness. Her hair spilled through his fingers like liquid gold, still impossibly beautiful even in its death. "Mine, you were supposed to be mine..."

He cradled her head against his chest, his tears falling onto her pale cheeks as he rocked back and forth. His other hand found her body, pressing against the wound where Callus had driven the Hangman's Spear through her heart. The silver armor was already growing cold beneath his touch.

"This wasn't... we were," he whispered, his voice breaking. "I was promised."

Callus rose slowly from where he knelt, his movements careful and deliberate as he backed toward the collapsed and broken table where Arialyn struggled to sit upright. His eyes never left the grieving Fae, but his peripheral vision caught movement on the floor where the half orc that had been the human Egrim lay. Callus could see the vulpine girl there as well, laying over the man and crying.

Egrim. The man who had shared drinks with him, who had helped move furniture and listened to his stories of the arena. The quiet, careful and often irritating stranger who had protected Kasha and raised a daughter with such gentle devotion. He had been hiding behind a glamour this entire time.

That's what he couldn't tell me. Callus realized, pieces of conversations clicking into place. *That's why he always seemed like he was holding something back.*

Kasha made her way down the stairs and started to move slowly toward Carl and Fithra, but Isque's eyes blazed in her direction, and she stopped. She pressed herself to the wall and began to shift around to Kovag and Saffron. Kasha sat on her knees beside Kovag's motionless form, her silk robe stained with his blood. Saffron, no longer the tiefling child they had known, pressed against her side, small shoulders shaking with silent sobs.

Kasha rocked her back and forth, her own hazel eyes wide with confusion and shock as she stared down at the man she thought she knew. The face was familiar yet foreign, the features she had memorized transformed by his true nature. Her mind struggled to reconcile the gentle human she had fallen in love with the bleeding half-orc who lay dying before her.

"This is what you were keeping her from," she whispered to no one, her voice barely audible above Isque's continued weeping. "This is why you were trying to be distant."

The air in the tavern suddenly crackled with otherworldly energy as reality tore open like fabric. A portal materialized in the space between the main floor and mezzanine, its edges shimmering with lunar light that pulsed like a heartbeat. Purple arcane discharges sparked along its rim, each one carrying the unmistakable taint of void energy that made the very air taste of copper and despair.

All eyes except Isque's, turned toward the phenomenon. The grieving Seeker remained hunched over Amjani's corpse, lost in his anguish.

Arialyn's mouth fell open with dread. "Callus... the void."

A silhouette emerged from the portal's depths, moving with deliberate slowness as though the figure desired a dramatic flair. The figure's outline wavered like shimmering heat, growing more distinct with each step forward. When he spoke, his voice carried the remnants of what had once been beautiful, a symphony now corrupted into discord, notes that should have been harmonious now grinding against each other like broken glass.

"How curious," the figure mused, his words echoing strangely in the confined space. "The company that Oakira's pact mortal keeps is interesting."

Kasha felt a stillness in her veins as the voice seemed to probe at her very mind and soul. Beside Kovag's motionless form, she instinctively pulled Saffron closer.

"A tiefling with an unusually high concentration of Forgotten blood in her lineage," the voice continued, and Kasha could feel unseen eyes dissecting her heritage like a scholar examining a specimen. "How deliciously ironic that she should find herself caring for one bound to the Lunar Court."

The figure's attention shifted, and Saffron whimpered as that terrible gaze fell upon her. "And a vulpine child. How rare her people have become in this mortal age. So few left in all of Yonara. She may even be the last. I don't feel others in existence right now. Such a precious little thing. It would be a shame to let her go to waste."

Finally, the figure reached the portal's edge, and they could see him clearly. What had once been a magnificent Lunar Arch Fae now stood corrupted beyond recognition. Lord Thruva's statuesque form was marred by strange protrusions that jutted from his shoulders and spine like crystalline growths. Purple void fissures snaked across his face and arms, pulsing with malevolent energy that made the air around him shimmer with wrongness.

His gaze fell upon Arialyn, who struggled to remain upright against the broken table. "Ah, the blasphemer," he said, his voice dripping with contempt. "They speak of you in the Void, you who makes the blood of Lady Zorog inert of its most precious gifts. How dare you rob her gifts of divine corruption. There is one among my new kin that seeks to claim you."

Then his eyes bore into Callus, and Thruva tilted his head with peaked predatory curiosity. "And you... I can smell the void that once coursed through your veins. All but burnt out now, but the scent lingers."

Callus felt something invasive probe at his memories, flashes of his past playing out like scenes from a nightmare. The fight with Xapos and the tainted blades the maniacal halfling had used them against him. The battle with Raseg and Lindri and the subsequent arcane void arc that was made when he redirected Raseg's attack through him and into Lindri.

"Yes," Thruva whispered with satisfaction. "I see it all."

The corrupt form raised a gnarled hand with curiosity and traced tethers in the air that were visible only to him. He followed one from Callus to Kovag and smirked as he gestured to Kovag. "This one was present at what would have been your baptism into Lady Zorog's embrace. He got in the way of the completion of the divine blades of the mad halfling. They were only half forged when they were used against you. Shame. Yet another prize this mongrel denied my Lady. Now the corpse god claims you. Unfortunate. You would have been a great tool on our side of the coming war."

He snapped his fingers with casual indifference.

The void ore in Arialyn's arcabus suddenly went dark, its purple glow extinguished as the purified energy was drawn away like water through a drain. Callus's braces sparked once, then died completely as their power source was ripped from them.

Without the arcane support that had kept him mobile, Callus's right leg and left arm failed him instantly. He crashed to the floor with a grunt of pain, his body betraying him as surely as if the limbs had been severed.

"Much better," Thruva said with dark satisfaction.

Isque's shoulders shook as he finally lifted his head from Amjani's lifeless form, bloody tears streaming down his face. His perfect features were twisted with grief and something else, a dawning realization that cut deeper than any blade.

"You," he whispered, his voice cracking as he stared up at his corrupted Lord. "I tried to warn her. I told her you were being consumed by the void, that the corruption was spreading through the Court like poison." His hands trembled as he clutched Amjani's head closer to his chest. "But she would not listen. Her blind loyalty to the damned Lunar court and you took her from me. She said you were strong enough to wield that power. I wish she had been right."

Thruva's laugh was like breaking crystal mixed with grinding stone. "How touching. The little spy finally shows his true colors."

"If only she had listened," Isque continued, his voice rising with desperate anguish. "If only she had seen what you were becoming, what you were planning!"

"Pathetic," Thruva spat, his void-cracked features contorting with disgust. "Stop your sniveling, you may still be of use to us."

With a casual flick of his fingers an invisible force seized Isque like a giant's fist. The grieving Seeker's scream was cut short as he was ripped away from Amjani's corpse and hurled through the portal with bone-breaking violence. His body tumbled across cold stone on the other side, rolling until he crashed against what sounded like a wall.

From beyond the portal came the scrape of desperate movement, then Isque's voice, hoarse and broken as he spoke into his true master's coin, "Duke, please, I've served faithfully."

But then Lord Thruva's words hit him. He called him *little spy.'* He knew, and then he said, *'you may still be of use to us.'* To us? The sound of the coin hitting stone echoed through the dimensional rift, followed by Duke Dalmoth's rumbling laughter. "Did you truly think either side valued you, little Seeker? You were a tool, nothing more. I must admit for the master sleuth that you are this was quite daft of you."

Isque's anguished cry of realization drifted back through the portal, the sound of a man finally understanding how completely it had been used.

Kovag's eyes fluttered open at the commotion. With tremendous effort, he pushed himself up on trembling arms, blood streaming from his wounds as he hauled himself to his knees. His legs refused to support him, but he managed to grip the bar top and pull himself upright.

"Thruva," he called out, his voice barely above a whisper but carrying clearly in the unnatural silence. "I'll give you what you want, but only me."

The corrupted Arch Fae turned those terrible void-touched eyes toward him, amusement dancing in their depths. "How noble. The half-breed mongrel tries to play hero." His smile was a thing of nightmares. "I could have lived with that. That was before I came to know the company you keep. Now, I will simply start with you... and the girl."

Kovag's blood raged. "No!"

Thruva's fingers flicked again with a dismissive summoning gesture as a noble might give a the lowest of servants.

As though he had been caught in a great storm, Kovag was ripped away from the bar, crashing through several chairs and a table before he went careening through the portal. The magic grabbed Saffron as well. However, her small hands were locked around Kasha's with desperate strength. The vulpine child's grip was like iron, born of terror and absolute trust.

Kasha felt the pull, reality blurring around her as she was dragged along with the child she'd grown so attached to. Her last glimpse from inside the tavern was Callus reaching toward them with his only viable arm, Arialyn's horrified face, Lorisse trembling over Carl and Fithra, and the spreading pool of blood where everything had gone so terribly wrong.

ENDING THE MASQUERADE

There was a terrible ringing bell in her head with a mind jarring and unending toll. Kasha felt the cool stone floor against her cheek as her eyes slowly began to part and some semblance of focus came back to them. She got to her hands and knees and saw the small puddle of blood beneath her before she felt the drops falling from a gash on her forehead.

Kasha's vision sharpened as the bell-like ringing in her skull began to fade, replaced by a growing awareness of her surroundings. The memory came crashing back. The portal's violent pull, her desperate decision to wrap herself around whoever Morrigan really was as they tumbled through the portal's opening, using her own body as a shield against whatever awaited them on the other side.

How long have I been unconscious? The question formed as she pushed herself up from the cold stone, wiping blood from her forehead with the back of her hand. But as her eyes found the shimmering portal behind her, she realized it couldn't have been more than a minute. Maybe less.

Through the dimensional rift, she could see into her beloved tavern, now a scene of devastation that made her heart clench. Callus had dragged himself across the life-soaked floor using only his two working limbs, the Hangman's Spear clutched in his fist as he pressed against the portal's edge. His scarred face was contorted with desperation as he tried to force his way through the barrier, but the magical threshold held firm against his assault.

She witnessed Arialyn cast aside her useless arcabus, the weapon now nothing more than a desk weight without its void ore power source. She knelt beside the broken table, her injured arm cradled against her chest as she watched the portal with wide, terrified eyes.

In the background, Lorisse was dragging the unconscious forms of Fithra and Carl as far from the portal as her strength would allow, her body trembling with effort and fear. Her mouth moved frantically, shouting something, screaming Kasha's name, but no sound reached across the dimensional divide.

The silence was absolute and unnerving.

Then Thruva's voice cut through the silence like a scythe, shrill and terrible. "Ah, the sorceress stirs. How delightful."

Kasha spun toward the sound, her heart hammering as she took in the corrupted Arch Fae's presence. He stood over Kovag's battered form with one clawed hand wrapped around his throat as he hauled him upright. Kovag's legs couldn't support him, the damage from Isque's attacks had been too severe. But somehow, he managed to remain on his knees through sheer stubborn will.

Saffron darted forward with a fierce hiss, her small butter knife raised like a sword as she aimed for Thruva's leg. The corrupted Fae barely glanced down before subtly backhanding her like an annoying fly. The child flew through the air, crashing against the stone wall with a dreadful thud before sliding to the floor in a motionless heap.

"Morrigan!" Kasha started toward the fallen child, but Kovag's movement caught her attention.

Despite his wounds, despite the blood loss that should have rendered him unconscious, Kovag somehow found the strength to drive his fist toward Thruva's midsection. The punch was pathetically weak. Barely more than a tap against the Arch Fae's corrupted body, but emerald-green light pulsed around his knuckles as the blow connected.

Thruva's face didn't even register the pain, if there was any. He simply shook his head and extended his finger at Kovag, a lance of void energy pierced his shoulder, and he fell back on his knees again. The wail of pain that came from him was something Kasha hadn't imagined he could have ever voiced. Not him. Not the man she had come to know. Then again, did she truly know this man?

Kasha rose on unsteady legs and ran to Saffron's crumpled body, her silk robe billowing behind her as she crossed the cold stone floor. "Morrigan!" The name felt strange on her tongue now that she wasn't sure if it was real, but it was the only name she had for the child who had become so precious to her.

She dropped to her knees beside the girl, her hands trembling as she gently lifted Saffron into her arms. Relief flooded through her as she felt the steady rise and fall of her chest, she was breathing. A trickle of blood ran from Saffron's nose and lip where she'd struck the wall, but her pulse was strong beneath Kasha's fingers.

Cradling the girl protectively against herself, Kasha began backing toward the shimmering portal. If she could just reach it, just get through—

Her outstretched hand met resistance that sent electric shocks racing up her arm. The portal's edge felt like a wall of buzzing energy, crackling with power that made her teeth ache and her vision blur. She pressed harder, desperation driving her to ignore the pain. She could feel the warmth of Callus's hand on the other side of the barrier, but the magic held firm. Whatever magic Thruva commanded, it had sealed their escape route as surely as iron bars. Between this new prison and the black walls the Seekers had erected around the Tits and Tarts, Kasha would have fallen into a complete panicked meltdown if she had the option. Even still, she had to fight to remain in control.

Across the chamber, Isque struggled to his knees, his perfect features marred by grief and growing horror as he took in the changes in Lord Thruva. His pale eyes found the corpses sprawled near the far wall. Argus Thilandri, Thruva's own Battle Master and bodyguard was draped over the arm of the Lunar Throne. The once-proud Lunar Fae was nothing more than a burned-out husk now, his body twisted and blackened as if void energy had been forced through him until it hollowed him out entirely. The bodies of the Arch Fae's wives were in scattered pieces. Each one showing signs of their own void corruption. *Did Argus kill them? Did he see the writing on the walls and act, only to be slain for betraying his master?*

Duke Dalmoth's laughter still echoed in his mind, a mocking reminder of how thoroughly he'd been played by them both the Fae and Forgotten. With a snarl of disgust, Isque hurled the Forgotten Duke's coin away from him. It clattered across the stone floor, the sound sharp in the oppressive silence.

"Damn you," he spat at Thruva, his voice cracking with rage and betrayal. "Damn your hubris and your—"

Thruva's fingers snapped with nothing more than an afterthought.

Isque's mouth clamped shut as if invisible hands had seized his jaw. He clawed at his throat, his eyes wide with panic as he found himself unable to speak, unable to even part his lips. The Lunar Arch Fae hadn't even spared a glance in his direction.

"Oakira," Thruva called out, his voice seemed to penetrate the very stones around them. "I know you are near, little abomination. I tracked you to this quaint pocket of *my* Lunar realm, and now it is sealed. There is no escape for you or your precious mortal."

Silence answered him, broken only by Kovag's labored breathing and the distant sound of Kasha's desperate attempts to breach the portal.

Thruva's void-fractured features arranged themselves in a patient smile. "The sooner you show yourself, the less torment your pact mortal will endure."

Still nothing.

"Very well," Thruva said with a theatrical sigh. "I have all the time in the realms, but he does not."

Lightning quick, he tapped Kovag's Fae touched eye with his finger. Kovag groaned in pain but again refused to fall. He felt a growing ache beginning to take root in his eye. A thrum of pain radiated in his head, and he finally doubled over, nearly biting his tongue from the sudden shock. The aches ceased, but a second later he could feel it building again.

Thruva smiled down at him, his facial features seemingly shifting across his face. "Do not despair now, my dear mongrel. It will get much worse each time. I assure you. Save your whimpering for later."

Thruva walked to his throne with all the cavalier depth of a monarch without a care. What was once an ornate and beautiful construct of lunar vision was now a mass of twisted dark-silver and void-touched crystal. A gust of wind came from his mouth with just enough force to turn the hollowed-out husk of Argus to dust, removing him from the corrupt throne. He settled onto the throne with regal composure, positioning himself roughly thirty paces from where Kovag sat on his haunches bleeding on the cold stone.

Kasha shifted carefully across the cold stone floor; Saffron's unconscious form cradled protectively in her arms. Each step brought her closer to Kovag and she could see the way his shoulders trembled with the effort of remaining upright. Blood continued to seep from his wounds as it began to form small pools beneath him in dark crimson puddles.

For just a heartbeat, less than a breath, a thought flashed through her mind like lightning. Then just as quickly, the fantasy left her.

Thruva's laughter filled the chamber. "Oh, my dear," he said, his voice dripping with amusement. "You are absolutely correct to abandon that foolish notion. Such an attack would accomplish nothing more than ensuring all three of you die in the most excruciating manner possible and at this moment I am content to torture him alone."

Kasha froze mid-step, her blood turning to ice in her veins. She hadn't spoken. She hadn't even fully formed the thought before dismissing it herself. Yet somehow...

"Mortified, are we?" Thruva tapped his temple with one clawed finger, the void fissures in his face rearranging themselves in a predatory smile. "How deliciously transparent minds have become now that I carry the best of Lady Zorog's gifts. Every stray thought, every desperate plan, every flicker of hope or despair. I can hear it all as clearly as if you were shouting."

His terrible gaze shifted toward where Isque knelt in silence, his jaw still magically sealed. "Which is precisely why I know our dear Seeker is about to make the final mistake that will cost him his miserable life."

Isque's pale eyes widened with something that might have been fear or defiance. His hand had been creeping slowly toward his boot, where a small knife was concealed. A backup weapon he'd never once had to use. But now, under Thruva's knowing stare, his fingers trembled and released their grip. The blade clattered to the stone floor with a metallic ring that echoed through the chamber.

"Wise choice," Thruva said with mock approval. "Though it matters little. Your usefulness has reached its end and your loyalty was...lacking."

Kasha finally reached Kovag's side, sinking to her knees beside him while keeping Saffron clutched against her chest. Up close, she could see the full extent of his injuries. The deep gashes across his back, the puncture wounds in his shoulder and thigh, the way his breathing came in short, pained gasps. His right eye, now a solid green orb, was beginning to cloud over with an unnatural darkness that pulsed in rhythm with his heartbeat.

It took great effort but his face shifted to hers. "I'm...sorry. I..."

"No. No. No. Not yet. No admissions and words previously unspoken to be suddenly voiced just yet," Thruva continued, settling more comfortably on his twisted throne, "First, we must have formal introductions. It is only fitting as many of us here do not know the others by name. At least, not our true names." His eyes flashed to Kovag with amusement. "I am Lord Thruva, Arch Fae of the Lunar Court and Blessed of our Lady of Madness, Zorog." He twirled his hand in a grandiose gesture and inclined his head.

Thruva's gaze swept across the chamber with immense pleasure, savoring each moment of his captive audience's terror. He gestured grandly toward the dust pile that now rested not too far from the throne.

"Allow me to present the late Argus Thilandri," he announced with mock reverence, his voice carrying the twisted remnants of courtly protocol. "Battle Master of the Lunar Court, my most loyal bodyguard, and unfortunately for him, the first to witness my glorious transformation after he dared to suggest I had gone too far." The corrupted Arch Fae's smile widened, revealing teeth that seemed to shift between silver and shadow. "Poor Argus simply could not appreciate the gifts I had bestowed upon my wives. Gifts that Lady Zorog blessed me with for my immense loyalty. When he attempted to *save* them from the void's embrace, well..." He sighed indifferently. "The resulting demonstration of my new capabilities left him rather... empty. Although, to his credit, he was able to slaughter my sweet creations before I could rend his soul from his wretched body."

His attention shifted to Isque, who knelt in enforced silence, his mouth still magically sealed. Thruva's laughter bubbled up like poison from a well, delighted and cruel.

"And here we have Seeker Isque of the Lunar Court," he continued, his tone dripping with malicious amusement. "Three-quarter moon rank, and worth every bit of it. Though a bit of a disgrace now." Thruva leaned forward on his twisted throne, savoring the moment. "You see, dear Isque here has been playing a most dangerous game. A double agent, feeding information to Duke Dalmoth of the Forgotten while feigning loyalty to me. What our clever little spy failed to realize is that the Duke and I have been working together for quite some time now and our little pawn played his part with perfection."

Isque's pale eyes shut with shame as the full confirmation of what he had only recently come to suspect washed over him. His hands clenched into fists, but the magical binding held his voice captive.

"Oh yes, every secret you passed along, every betrayal you thought you were committing. All of it served our purposes perfectly. You were never a double agent, my dear Seeker. You were simply a piece on a gaming board with rules far too complex for even your brilliant mind to grasp, and now that piece has outlived its usefulness. Master Seeker Amjani's death was an unfortunate loss in this venture, however."

Thruva's vision moved to Callus and the others on the other side of the portal into the Tits and Tarts. His vision momentarily shifted from pleasure in his current games to anger. "Neither the Duke nor I knew we'd run into the chosen of the Hanged One or the blasphemous arcanomancer. I dare say Seeker Isque, now that I think of it, you should thank me. With Master Seeker Amjani dead there was no way you would have walked out of that tavern alive." He chuckled. "I saved your life. Ironic."

Callus leaned against the barrier, pressing the tip of the Hangman's Spear into the portal's edge. To Thruva's slight surprise the tip of the weapon was slowly boring a hole in the arcane wall. The look of rage on the hobgoblin's face brought his vast joy.

"KASHA!" Callus's voice was hoarse from overuse.

Arialyn had moved behind the bar, working frantically with one hand to remove the power source from the arcane cooling box she had made for Kasha. She had already managed to pop the expended void ore from her arcabus, ready to replace it with the cooling box's charged one.

His eyes then fell upon Kasha, and his expression shifted to one of exaggerated courtesy. "Lady Kasha Volstruk," he said with a sweeping bow of his head, "my apologies. Madame Volstruk, proprietress of the delightfully named 'Witch's Tits and Tarts Tavern.' A tiefling of considerable untapped arcane talent and, carrying a rather impressive concentration of Forgotten blood in her veins. How fitting that one touched by my allies' essence should find herself caring for..." His eyes flicked meaningfully toward Kovag. "This mongrel," Thruva continued, his voice hardening with contempt as he indicated the bleeding half-orc. "Kovag'Dresh, pact mortal to my dear half-breed abomination of a niece, Oakira. A creature so thoroughly corrupted by her Forgotten father's influence that she barely qualifies as Fae at all. Although, he is my partner, so perhaps I should not speak too harshly of his impact on her."

Finally, he stared at Saffron, unconscious in Kasha's arms. "And lastly, this precious little morsel." His voice sounded hungry now. "A vulpine child. How deliciously rare. The blood of the Torvox runs strong in this one, I can smell it from here. She will make a fine addition to my collection of thralls once I've properly... educated her."

"Fuck you." Kovag managed to mumble, blood spilling from his mouth. Pain rocked him again as his eye felt like it was trying to rip itself from his skull.

"I will not be interrupted by a mongrel." Thruva's face twisted and rearranged again. As it did, his voice took on a higher pitch, as though he gave himself over to something else. "I find myself in a mood for greater entertainment. The wait for my dear selfish Oakira grows tiresome already, and I do so hate boredom."

His smile widened, revealing teeth that seemed to shift between silver and the deep purple of the void. "I propose a story to pass the time. A tale of false love and greedy betrayal. And afterward..." He leaned forward, his eyes gleaming with malicious delight. "We shall see whose heart aches more once the tale is finished." Thruva leaned forward with eager anticipation in his eyes.

Kasha felt Saffron stir slightly in her arms, the child's breathing becoming more regular as consciousness slowly returned. She pressed her lips to the girl's forehead, trying to offer what comfort she could while her mind raced with desperate possibilities, anything she could possibly think of to escape or buy more time for some kind of opening.

Thruva's voice took on the lilting cadence of a court minstrel, his tone theatrical and mocking as he began his tale. The corrupted Arch Fae gestured grandly from his twisted throne, his movements far too exaggerated and performative.

"Once upon a time," he began, his words sounded like a parent telling a bedtime story to a sickly child, "there lived a pathetic half-breed mongrel, so desperate for love that he would have sold his very soul for a kind word and a gentle touch."

Kovag's jaw clenched, fresh blood seeping between his teeth as Thruva's words entered his ears like a poison.

"This poor, simple creature had watched his beloved sister waste away in sickness, her life ebbing like sand through an hourglass. His dear mother's tavern, the only home he had ever truly known, crumbled around them. Debts were mounting like storm clouds on the horizon." Thruva's smile widened to an impossible degree as he watched Kovag's face contort with pain that had nothing to do with his physical wounds. He was tearing wide open the scars at the core of the pact mortal and dragging them through the coals of a forge.

"Enter my clever niece," his voice took on a tone of mock admiration. "Beautiful Oakira, wise beyond her years if I am woefully honest, who saw opportunity where others might see tragedy. What better mark than a mongrel whose heart was already broken? Whose need for affection ran so deep it had carved caverns in his soul?"

Kasha felt Kovag trembling beside her, his breathing becoming more ragged as each word struck him like a punch in the gut. She saw tears mingle with blood. Where she once saw a towering man, she now saw a chastised and terrified boy.

"The bargain was deliciously simple," Thruva went on, his fingers dancing through the air as if conducting an orchestra. "The sister would live, the tavern would prosper, and all it would cost our desperate hero was his freedom. His will. His very sense of self." The Arch Fae leaned forward, his edges of his eyes seeping with void in cruel delight. "And to keep him properly motivated, all my dear niece had to do was spread her legs from time to time. A small price for such devoted service, wouldn't you agree?"

"Stop," Kasha whispered, her voice barely audible.

But Thruva was just getting started. "Oh, but the most delicious part," he continued, his voice rising with theatrical excitement, "was how eagerly our mongrel lapped up every scrap of false affection she threw his way. Like a starving dog grateful for table scraps, he convinced himself it was love. True love!"

Thruva's laughter filled the chamber, echoing off the stone walls. "Tell me, mongrel, did you truly believe she cared for you? Did you think those moans of pleasure were real? Or did some small part of you always know you were nothing more than a tool, kept sharp with just enough kindness to ensure your continued obedience?"

Kovag's good eye glistened wet with tears. The pain in his Fae-touched eye intensified, sending a wave of agony through his skull that left him gasping at the unbearable truth. In that small moment he wasn't sure which pain hurt worse.

"Such wasted potential," Thruva mused, shaking his head in mock disappointment. "All that muscle, all that strength, and yet you never once took what you truly wanted. You could have claimed any woman who caught your fancy, could have seized affection by force rather than begging for it like a whipped cur. But no, you chose to remain a pathetic, lovesick fool, dancing to the tune of a manipulative little half-breed who saw you as nothing more than a convenient puppet."

Saffron's golden eyes fluttered open, unfocused and glassy as consciousness slowly returned. For a moment she seemed confused, her small vulpine ears twitching as she tried to orient herself in Kasha's arms. Then her gaze found Kovag's kneeling form just a foot away, and her expression transformed into something that broke Kasha's heart.

The child's face crumpled as she took in the blood collecting beneath him, the way his body trembled with each labored breath, the darkness spreading through the green orb like spilled ink. A sob tore from her throat. It was the loudest sound Kasha had ever heard her make as Saffron reached out desperately toward the man who had been her protector, her father in all but blood.

Kovag tried to lift his arm toward her, his fingers stretching across what felt like an impossible distance between them. But his strength failed him, and his hand fell back to the stone with a wet slap that left crimson fingerprints on the cold floor.

Saffron's sobs intensified, her body shaking as she buried her face against Kasha's chest. The sound echoed through the chamber—raw, primal grief that seemed to pierce even the corrupted stones around them.

"Stop it," Kasha said again, her voice stronger now, edged with fury as she held the weeping child closer. "Stop it!"

"Oh, but there is so much more to tell," Thruva interrupted, his voice taking on renewed enthusiasm as if Saffron's anguish had only whetted his appetite for cruelty. "You see, our mongrel here is quite the accomplished hunter. Fae and Forgotten alike fell before his might, their power siphoned away to feed my dear niece's growing strength."

Thruva gestured grandly, his movements becoming even more animated as he warmed to his tale. "He was remarkably efficient, I must admit. Oakira chose her tool well. Strong enough to face supernatural threats, desperate enough to never question his orders, and just intelligent enough to adapt his tactics when needed."

Kovag's shoulders sagged further as Thruva's story both enhanced the truth and warped it at the same time. The pain in his eye began to ache with every pulse now, but currently it was nothing compared to the agony of having his deepest shames laid bare before the woman he loved.

"But here comes the truly delicious irony," Thruva continued, his smile horrendously and truly splitting his face in two. "While our faithful mongrel was busy fulfilling his end of the bargain, hunting down threats and feeding power to his beloved mistress, what do you think happened to those precious lives he thought he was protecting by making the deal with my niece?"

The Arch Fae paused for dramatic effect, savoring the moment like fine wine before swiftly clapping his hands together for emphasis.

"His mother died of a wasting sickness. The same one his sister had been inflicted with and one so easily cured by Fae magic, yet Oakira was mysteriously absent when the end came. The tavern failed within months, debts overwhelmed his sister, and within months it was all ripped away from her, despite his faithful service." Thruva's laughter was like breaking glass. "And his dear sister? She died screaming in childbirth, her life leaking away on stained sheets while her devoted brother was off playing hero for a creature who could not be bothered to lift a finger to save her."

Kovag's head shook slowly, denial warring with the terrible truth in Thruva's words.

"All things Oakira could have prevented with a thought," Lord Thruva mused, shaking his head in artificial disappointment. "Such spectacular failure on her part. I blame my sister for raising the girl so poorly. Too much sentiment, not enough pragmatism."

The words cut deep because they carried just enough truth to wound, even as Kovag knew the full story was more complex than Thruva's cruel telling.

"Shall I go on?" Thruva asked, though he had no intent of stopping.

Kasha's only response was to hold Saffron closer and attempt to shield her ears. A quick glance back at the portal and the shocked and pained looks on the faces of her friends, and Kasha got the suspicion that they were able to hear everything on their side.

The void fissures of Thruva's face throbbed and rearranged themselves again. This time into an expression of pure ecstasy as he felt an intoxicating rush of power coursing through his changed form. The blessing of Zorog had elevated him beyond anything he had ever imagined possible. Where once he had been merely an Arch Fae, powerful but still bound by the limitations of his nature, now he stood on the precipice of true divinity.

"Do you feel it?" he whispered, his voice trembling with rapture as he addressed the chamber at large. "The exquisite sensation of absolute knowledge? Every secret, every hidden shame, every carefully buried truth, all of it laid bare before me like an open book thanks to my Lady's gifts."

His fingers twitched with anticipation as he turned his terrible gaze toward Kovag's broken body. "I had always been likened to a demi-god among my people, but now... now I am but one step below our Lady of Madness herself. A minor deity in my own right, with all the delicious privileges that entails."

Thruva made a delicate plucking motion with his fingers, as if drawing an invisible string from the air. Kovag's body convulsed as something vital was torn from within him. Not flesh or blood, but something far more precious. Memories, experiences, the very fabric of his past unraveled like thread from a tapestry and flowed toward the Lord Thruva's waiting grasp.

"Oh, how delightfully sordid," Thruva purred as the stolen recollections played out before his mind's eye. "Such elaborate deceptions, such carefully constructed lies. Speak truthfully, sweet sorceress, did you truly believe any of it was real?"

Kasha's rocked back and forth with Saffron as dread settled in her stomach like a stone. "What are you talking about?"

"All of it," Thruva said with exaggerated delight. "Every single word that fell from his lips was a fabrication designed to manipulate your tender heart. The grieving widower, the devoted father, the gentle soul seeking refuge from his tragic past, all of it nothing more than an elaborate performance."

He began to salivate as he savored the growing doubt in Kasha's eyes. "His entire persona was made to drag you into his web of lies," he continued with mocking emphasis on the false identity and sniffed the air. His twisted face settled Kasha on fully. "By the smell coming from between your thighs, it worked splendidly for him."

Kovag jerked forward as if struck, his strength finally failing him completely. He crashed face-first onto the cold stone, tears and blood mixing into a puddle beneath his cheek. The impact sent fresh waves of anguish through his battered body, adding to the torment of watching Kasha's face crumble as Thruva's words sank in.

"The child isn't his daughter," Thruva went on relentlessly. "Of course, you probably know that part now. He was never married, never loved anyone but himself and his precious Oakira. You were nothing more than convenient camouflage. A lonely, desperate woman so starved for affection that she would accept any scrap of attention thrown her way. Sounds familiar does it not?"

"No," Kovag choked out, his voice barely audible as he struggled to lift his head from the stone. A bloody frothed collected at his lips as he fought to form words through his pain. "I had to... keep her safe. But, you... us... real." His body rocked as he sobbed. "Always... real."

But even as the words began to leave his lips, Kovag knew how hollow they must sound in the wake of Thruva's revelations. How could she believe anything he said now?

Thruva's amusement erupted like a volcanic explosion, echoing off the stone walls with such force that dust rained down from the ceiling above. The sound was pure madness given voice, a symphony of cruelty that seemed to shake the very foundations of the pocket realm.

"Magnificent!" he roared, wiping tears of mirth from his warped features. "Oh, how deliciously wretched! Even now, bleeding out on my floor like a butchered animal, he still tries to convince you his feelings are real!"

The corrupt Arch Fae rose from his twisted throne, his movements fluid and predatory as he began to pace around his captives. "Oakira!" His voice penetrating every shadow and crevice of the chamber. "My dear, stubborn niece! Surely you can see that your precious mongrel's mind is about to shatter like glass beneath a hammer!"

He gestured grandly toward Kovag. "The pain I'm about to inflict will break what little sanity he has left. There is no escape from this pocket of my realm. I've sealed every possible exit, every dimensional fold, every whisper of arcane energy that might carry you away. You might as well show yourself and spare him the worst of what's to come. If you every had any real feelings for him."

Thruva paused in his pacing, tilting his head as if listening for a response that never came. "I must admit, I am genuinely impressed by your ability to remain hidden from me here. The amount of power you've accumulated must be truly staggering for you to cloak yourself so thoroughly in my own domain. Your mongrel has been remarkably efficient in his harvesting. How many Fae and Forgotten fell to feed your growing strength? Dozens? Hundreds?"

Saffron's silent sobs continued to wrack her small frame as she pressed her face deeper into Kasha's chest, her tiny hands clutching at the silk of Kasha's robe with desperate strength. Each shuddering breath seemed to tear something vital from her, leaving her smaller and more fragile with every passing moment.

Kasha's hand trembled as she reached toward Kovag's bloodied form, her fingers stretching across the space between them. But doubt crashed over her like a tide, Thruva's revelations warring with months of shared moments, gentle touches, quiet conversations in the darkness of her room. Had any of it been real? Had she been nothing more than a convenient fool, so desperate for love that she'd accepted lies as truth?

Her hand began to pull away, tears streaming down her cheeks as she struggled with the weight of her uncertainty.

"Please," Kovag whispered, the word barely audible as blood pooled on the ground by his mouth. His true eye found hers, and in its depths she saw something that cut through all of Thruva's poison. Raw, desperate honesty.

"Should have... left," he managed, each word a monumental effort that sent fresh waves of agony through his broken body. "Only stayed... because of you. You are perfect... a goddess among us."

His breathing hitched, shallow and ragged. "Last night... you said...y ou were never what anyone needed. But you're... exactly what I needed. What we needed. Just as... you are."

Kovag's body shuddered violently, his strength spent. "Came looking for... Maudrid. Told she might know... where to find more vulpine... for Saffron." Blood now began to pour from his nose. "Her name is Saffron." His eyes moved to his chosen daughter in Kasha's arms. "Found Maudrid's home... found you, Callus, Arialyn instead. Followed you... wanted to see if you... might know."

His voice cracked completely. "Tried to... tell you everything. Last night. You stopped me. You told me... to lie to you. But I didn't. I meant it all." A sound that might have been his soul shattering left his throat, wet and broken. "Sorry I... didn't flee. Soon as I... fell in love with you. My selfish... desire. Getting you and... my daughter killed."

Kasha's hand trembled back toward Kovag's broken body, her heart warring between desperate hope and crushing doubt. Thruva's revelations had shattered something fundamental inside her, but the raw honesty in Kovag's voice, the way he'd spoken her name like a prayer—it cut through the poison of the Arch Fae's words like sunlight through storm clouds. No one had ever called her perfect before. No one had ever said she was exactly what they needed, just as she was. If it was a lie, it was the sweetest one ever told.

Her hand was inches away when Kovag's body suddenly arched off the ground, his spine bowing impossibly as a scream tore from his throat that seemed to come from the very depths of his mind. His Fae-touched eye blazed with void purple and smoky gray, the colors swirling and pulsing like a miniature storm contained within the green orb. His entire body convulsed in rhythmic spasms, each one more violent than the last, as if something was trying to claw its way out from inside him.

Kasha recoiled instinctively, her hand jerking back as if burned. "Stop it!" she sobbed, her voice breaking as she watched Kovag writhe in agony. "Please, stop it!"

But Thruva only smiled wider, his corrupt features arranging themselves in an expression of pure ecstasy as he fed on Kovag's suffering.

Kasha frantically looked around the chamber, anger welling up inside her. "You Fae bitch! Get out here and stop this!"

Across the chamber, Isque had seen enough. He was going to die today but he wouldn't do it as a trembling thrall. The Seeker's jaw was still magically sealed, but his hands were free, and fury burned in his pale eyes like cold fire. He snatched up the knife he'd dropped earlier, the blade catching what little light filtered through the dimensional space as he launched himself at Lord Thruva.

Even as he moved, Isque tried to weave lunar flame between his fingers, a spell that should have lanced across Thruva's hand and possibly destroyed the ring of raw void that hummed with malevolent energy on his finger. But the magic unraveled before it could form, the threads of power dissolving like smoke in his grasp.

Still, his speed was impossible, his movements fluid as water as he closed the distance between them. The knife flashed in a silver arc, catching Thruva across the cheek and opening a gash that wept purplish-black ichor instead of blood.

Thruva's head snapped to the side from the impact, surprise flickering across his features for just an instant before rage replaced it. With a wave of his hand, an arcane force seized Isque by the throat and slammed him against the far stone wall. The Seeker's feet dangled several feet off the ground as magical pressure crushed his windpipe, his hands clawing desperately at his neck.

The commotion, the screaming, the sight of her father convulsing in agony was too much for Saffron. She tore herself free from Kasha's protective embrace, her golden eyes blazing with a fury that seemed far too large for her young body.

She turned toward Thruva and opened her mouth, and what emerged was not the voice of a frightened child but something primal and devastating. A reverberating arcane force of piercing sound erupted from her throat, carrying with it years of pain, all her pent-up terror, all her desperate love for the man who had become her father in every way that mattered and the woman that warmed the parts of his heart that she could not. Her pack.

The sound hit Thruva like a tidal wave, sending him skidding backward across the stone floor. His hands flew to his ears as the sonic assault penetrated his defenses, and for the first time since his transformation, genuine pain flickered across his features. His concentration shattered like glass, the magical bonds holding both Kovag and Isque faltering under the assault.

Isque dropped to the floor, gasping and clutching at his bruised throat as blessed air filled his lungs once more. Kovag's convulsions ceased abruptly, his body going limp against the cold stone as the void energy retreated from his eye.

Turning his head with tremendous effort, his gaze found Saffron. Despite everything—the pain, the blood loss, the certainty of approaching death—a weak smile spread across his battered face. His daughter had found her voice at last. Matron Vadrida had told him that she would speak when she had found her pack. She was no longer the silent, broken child he'd rescued from that Forgotten bitch's dungeon of horrors. However, he breathed a heavy sigh, knowing with crystal clarity that she had found it too late.

Saffron's devastating scream finally reached its limit, the primal force that had erupted from her small throat cutting off abruptly as her strength gave out. She collapsed forward onto her hands and knees beside her father, her body shaking with exhaustion and the aftershocks of unleashing power she didn't understand. Golden tears streamed down her face as she crawled closer to her true father, her small hands reaching desperately toward his bloodied face as he somehow managed to smile at her.

Kasha stared at the pair through her own tears, shock warring with maternal instinct as she witnessed what the child had just accomplished. The raw power that had emerged from Saffron's throat defied everything she thought she knew about magic, about the quiet little girl who had never spoken a word in all the months she'd known her. Yet even as wonder filled her mind, her heart ached for both of them—the broken man bleeding out on cold stone and the child who had found her voice only to watch her world crumble around her.

A shimmer of lunar light began to coalesce in the air beside Kovag's prone form, silver radiance gathering like morning mist touched by starlight. The luminescence grew brighter, more substantial, until it took on the rough outline of a humanoid figure. Then, as if stepping through a doorway between worlds, Oakira emerged from the light.

She was recognizable yet transformed, no longer the conflicted half-breed who had struggled with her dual nature, but something far more magnificent and terrible. Her reddish-brown hair now cascaded in waves that seemed to move with their own ethereal wind, and her bright green eyes blazed with power that spoke of divinity touched by madness. Her thin but supple build had gained an otherworldly elegance, every movement flowing with the grace of someone who had transcended Fae and Forgotten limitations.

Most striking of all were the wisps of energy that danced around her form, threads of pure lunar light intertwined with the darker flames of Forgotten power. They created an aura that was both beautiful and deeply unsettling. She appeared more mature now, as if the weight of accumulated power had aged her beyond her years, lending her features a regal bearing that commanded attention and respect.

All eyes in the chamber turned toward her except for Thruva, who remained hunched over with his hands pressed firmly against his ears, still reeling from Saffron's sonic assault. Even Isque, gasping on the floor where he'd fallen, stared in amazement at the transformation that had overtaken the abomination he'd once hunted.

Oakira's lips parted, and words flowed forth in a language that predated the current age, not the melodic tongue of the Fae courts, nor the harsh syllables of Forgotten speech, but something older and more fundamental. Even Isque, with all his knowledge of ancient dialects and courtly languages, found himself unable to comprehend the meaning behind the flowing syllables that seemed to reshape reality with each carefully pronounced word.

All within the chamber felt briefly as though they moved through a pool of thick honey, and then ceased in their movement entirely. One by one, each of them found themselves unable to move, their bodies held in perfect stasis while their minds remained fully conscious and aware.

Chapter Forty-Two

VOID RISING

O akira moved through the chamber without a sound, her feet seemingly hovering just above the ground as she moved. Her gown appeared to be endless as it waved against a nonexistent wind. The wisps of lunar light and Forgotten flame that danced around her cast shifting shadows on the stone walls, creating an otherworldly atmosphere that seemed to bend reality itself to her will.

Her gaze fell upon Thruva first, and her expression transformed into something terrible to behold. Pure, undiluted hatred blazed in her green eyes as she looked upon her corrupted uncle, the being who had orchestrated so much of her suffering and pain. She could see him struggling against her temporal binding. His void-etched features contorted with shock and rage that his own niece, the half-breed abomination he'd dismissed, possessed power enough to hold him immobile. The surprise in his eyes was almost as satisfying as the fury.

Her attention shifted to Isque, and moonlight flared within her irises like cold fire. Here was one of the Seekers who had hunted her mother, who had participated in Elirel's capture and ultimate demise. The pale-eyed Fae's face was frozen in an expression of awe and terror, his body held rigid where he'd fallen after Thruva's assault. Oakira's lips curved in a smile that held no warmth, only the promise of justice long delayed.

When her gaze moved to Kasha, the hatred melted away, replaced by something far more complex. Sadness pooled in her eyes, mixed with guilt that sat heavy on her evolved features. This woman had shown kindness to Kovag. Something she had never been able to give him, and if she was honest, never fully attempted. Kasha had given him genuine affection without manipulation, love without strings attached. The tiefling's tear-streaked face was frozen in desperate concern, her hand still reaching toward the man she'd come to care for. Even though he had hidden himself from her, she still reached for him and Oakira found herself wondering what that kind of love and devotion must feel like.

Finally, Oakira's looked upon Kovag, and tears began to fall down her own cheeks like liquid starlight. Her pact mortal, her faithful hunter, her... what had he become to her? The sight of him broken and bleeding on the cold stone sent a lance of pain through her heart that she hadn't expected. His body was held motionless by her spell, but his eyes—those beautiful brown eyes that had looked at her with such devotion for so long—were fixed on Kasha with desperate love and regret plain to see by anyone.

As if sensing her presence, his eyes shifted to meet hers and even frozen in time she could see the pain that flickered there. Not just physical agony from his wounds, but something far deeper. The ache of seeing her again after over two years of her neglectful separation. Then add to it the reality of having his new carefully constructed life torn apart by those that hunted the very person he'd served so faithfully.

It was then that she noticed something very peculiar. Her spell, which had frozen every other being in the chamber, seemed to have no effect on the vulpine child clinging to Kovag's side. Saffron continued to sob, now audibly, her golden tears falling freely as she pressed herself against her father's motionless form.

Oakira's head tilted with curiosity at this unexpected development, but she pushed the questions aside, knowing that the answers would not matter shortly.

She moved closer and rather than kneeling down, she decreased in size, her transformed presence casting both light and shadow across their forms as she became the petite creature Kovag had first met. Saffron's eyes widened with fear and protective fury as she saw this strange and powerful being that had caused her father the nightmares that she herself had witnessed over the last several months. She placed herself between them and tried to push Oakira away.

But Oakira didn't budge under the child's desperate assault. Instead, she looked at Saffron with gentle eyes that held recently gained but ancient wisdom and terrible power in equal measure.

"Do not worry, Saffron Kovagsdottir," her voice carrying harmonics that seemed to resonate with the very fabric of reality. "We are about to fix it all." Her head turned to regard Callus and the Hangman's Spear on the other side of the portal for a split second.

Callus noted her words and brief glance with confusion. He then noticed his spear had made a small amount of progress in breaking through the portal and he began to push against it with more vigor.

Arialyn finally managed to remove the void core from the arcane cooling box and was about to install it into her arcabus when Callus called something out to her that they were unable to hear on this side of the portal.

She rushed to Callus's side as he shouted more. She looked at the small cracks beginning to form under the spear's tip and then abruptly dropped to Callus's leg brace and began plucking the spent void crystals from the sockets.

Saffron stopped her futile efforts to push the immovable woman and plopped down beside Kovag again, her body trembling with exhaustion and fear. She threw herself protectively over his motionless body, her eyes never leaving Oakira's face as distrust radiated from every part of her being. Her vulpine ears lay flat against her head, and her bushy tail wrapped around Kovag's arm like a living shield.

As she pressed herself against her father's bloodied chest, a subtle warmth began to emanate from her. At first it was barely perceptible, just a gentle heat that seemed to pulse in rhythm with her heartbeat. But gradually, the warmth grew stronger, taking on a golden luminescence that made her fur shimmer like spun sunlight.

Saffron sat up abruptly, staring down at her own hands in shock as the golden glow intensified around her fingers. The light seemed to flow from her pores, casting faint dancing shadows across the stone floor as it pulsed with increasing brightness. She held her hands up before her face, watching in wonder as the radiance played across her palms like captured starfire.

Impossibly small flowers began to erupt from the cold stone around her and Kovag. Tiny white blossoms pushed through hairline cracks in the floor, their petals unfurling with impossible speed as they reached toward the golden light emanating from her. The flowers spread in a perfect circle around the pair, creating a garden of hope in the midst of despair.

Memory crashed over Saffron like a tide, the morning they had awakened beneath the ancient oak tree, Kovag's fever broken and his crossbow wound mysteriously healed. She remembered his gentle questions about whether she had somehow helped him, her own confusion at his recovery. She had tried to replicate it right after his questioning but had failed to feel anything. She had dismissed it then, with no understanding of how he had healed but thankful for it. Again, she tried after the attack at the temple in Ferrum Plains. But now, seeing the flowers bloom and feeling the power flowing through her, understanding dawned with crystal clarity. Something inside her had changed. She knew how to do it now.

Without hesitation, she threw herself back over Kovag's broken body, pressing her glowing hands against his worst wounds. The effect wasn't miraculous, she wasn't even sure it was enough to save his life, but gradually, the worst of his injuries began to respond. The steady flow of blood that had gone on so long it had become a weeping trickle now stopped entirely and some of the smaller wounds sealed themselves entirely under her touch.

Oakira watched this display with a smile that held both wonder and profound sadness. "The wonders of the vulpine people were a gift taken from the world of Yonara too cruelly," she said softly, her voice carrying weighty with grief. "Your people were the healers of the wild places, the bridge between nature and civilization. When the Shale Plague claimed the Torvox people so many millennia ago, your people lost their teachers and protectors. The Vulpine were all that was left to keep the void truly at bay."

She reached out slowly, telegraphing her movements so as not to startle the child, and placed a single finger against Saffron's temple. The moment their skin made contact, the little girl's eyes dilated as knowledge flooded her mind. Understanding of her heritage, her gifts, and the terrible truth of her uniqueness forced its way into her mind.

She was the last of her arcanely gifted people. She had never cared about finding more of her own people. She had found her people, but the thought of being the last of her kind was a far worse feeling than she could imagine. Kovag and Kasha *had* to live. They all had to live. They needed each other.

The golden light emanating from Saffron's small form began to flicker like a candle in a dying wind. Her breathing became labored as she poured every ounce of her newfound power into healing her father's wounds, her tiny hands began to tremble against his bloodied chest. The flowers that had bloomed around them started to wilt at their edges, their petals curling inward as if reflecting the child's diminishing strength.

"Easy, child," Oakira whispered, her voice gentle with concern as she watched Saffron's golden glow fade to barely perceptible wisps. "You've done all that you can."

But Saffron refused to stop, her ears pinned back with determination as sweat began to drip down her back and she pressed harder against his wounds. A soft whimper escaped her throat, not of pain, but of desperate frustration as she felt her power slipping away like sand through her fingers. The healing warmth that had flowed so freely moments before now came in stuttering pulses, each one weaker than the last.

Her golden eyes rolled back, showing only the whites as exhaustion finally claimed her. She collapsed forward onto Kovag's chest, her body going completely limp as unconsciousness claimed her. The last of the flowers around them withered and crumbled to dust, leaving only the faintest trace of their miraculous bloom.

Oakira peered into Kovag's wide eyes. "She has much to learn of what she is capable. I have no doubt that you will guide her..." Her breath caught in her throat.

Her fingers traced the rigid line of Kovag's jaw, her touch feather-light against skin that couldn't respond to her caress. Fresh tears spilled down her cheeks as she leaned closer, her voice breaking with each word.

"I am so sorry, Kovag'Dresh." Her thumb brushed across his cheekbone, following one of the many paths of dried blood. "I took a wonderful, trusting man and nearly destroyed him with my selfishness. You deserved so much better than what I gave you."

She pressed her lips gently to his forehead, the kiss lingering as starlight danced around them. When she pulled back, her green eyes were pools of regret.

"In the end, I did come to love you," she whispered, her voice barely audible and only for him. "But it was a selfish love, born of necessity and shaped by my own fears. It never could have been what you needed. Never what you deserved." Her hand cupped his face tenderly. "You needed someone who could give you a home, a family, a life free from the shadows of my world. Someone who could love you without conditions or ulterior motives."

Her gaze shifted briefly to Kasha, tears still glistening on the tiefling's cheeks.

"Someone who could love you simply for being you."

Oakira's voice wavered, ringing the weightiness of her final confession. "There is one more secret you must know, one last omission of truth that I must confess." Her fingers trembled against his face as she struggled with the words. "The powers I gave you through our pact... you never needed to honor our bond to keep them."

Fresh tears carved new paths of lunar silver down her cheeks as she continued. "Every ability I bestowed upon you became yours the moment it was given. I could not have taken them back without immense effort and considerable risk to us both." Her laugh was bitter and broken. "But I let you believe otherwise because I needed you and you knew you needed to protect her. Your... daughter."

She pressed her forehead against his, their faces only inches apart. "Each enhancement, every gift of strength or sight or arcane ability. They were yours to keep regardless of whether you served me faithfully. I could have released you from our pact years ago and you would have retained everything."

Her voice cracked with shame. "I am sorry for that deception as well, my faithful hunter. You stayed bound to me not because you had to, but because I made you believe you had no choice."

Across the chamber, Isque remained frozen in place by Oakira's temporal binding, his pale eyes wide with shock at what he had just witnessed. The vulpine child's display of power defied everything he thought he knew of the arcane, about the lost peoples of Yonara, about the very nature of healing itself. Such raw, untrained ability should have been impossible, yet he had seen it with his own eyes.

Had his pupils not been so dilated by the shock, he wouldn't have caught the most subtle of movements in his peripheral vision. His eyes strained against the magical paralysis, muscles burning with effort as he fought to turn his gaze as far left as possible. The spell held his body rigid, but his eyes could still move within their sockets, and what he saw sent rime through his veins.

Thruva's thumb was rotating the raw void ring back and forth on his index finger.

The movement was barely perceptible, just the slightest twisting motion that could have been dismissed as a slight shimmer of the arcane field that held him in place. But Isque knew better. He had studied the Thruva's mannerisms during their time together, had catalogued every gesture and habit in the way only a trained observer could. This was deliberate. Calculated.

Thruva was not affected by the spell. His paralysis was false. This was a trap.

Dread crashed over Isque like a tide as the implications became clear. Whatever void-filled plan Lord Thruva was working, whatever trap he was preparing to spring, Oakira had walked directly into it. The half-breed's attention was focused entirely on the unconscious child and her wounded pact mortal, leaving her completely vulnerable to whatever Thruva had in store.

Isque threw every ounce of his will against the temporal binding, his muscles screaming in protest as he fought to break free. He had to warn her, had to do something, anything, to prevent whatever horror was about to unfold. Whatever punishment Oakira might inflict upon him for the death of Elirel would be nothing compared to the devastation Thruva would unleash if his deception succeeded.

Oakira rose gracefully from beside Kovag and Saffron, her presence expanding as she moved toward the statuesque Kasha. The wisps of lunar light and Forgotten flame that danced around her grew brighter as she returned to her transcended size. Her ethereal gown resumed its unending flow behind her like liquid starlight, and the very air seemed to shimmer with power in her wake.

She stopped before Kasha, studying her face. Even frozen in time, Kasha's expression spoke volumes. The desperate conflict between love and betrayal, the anguish of discovering that the man she'd fallen for might never have existed at all. Her hand was still reaching for Kovag, suspended in that moment of strength within terrible uncertainty.

"Oh, sweet Kasha," Oakira whispered. "You think you have lost him? You think Egrim was nothing but smoke and mirrors, a cruel deception designed to manipulate your tender broken heart."

A sad smile curved Oakira's lips as she reached out, her fingers hovering just above Kasha's temple. "But you saw the real Kovag the entire time. My spell simply... adjusted your perception, masked what your eyes beheld but never touched what your heart knew to be true."

Her fingertip made contact with Kasha's skin, and a cool warmth flowed between them like a soothing hot spring.

The memories came flooding back in a rush of sensations and emotions, each one rewriting itself as the glamour fell away like mist. Kasha relived every precious moment, but now she saw them as they truly were.

She remembered that first afternoon when she'd offered to brush Saffron's hair, the child sitting so still and trusting on the bar top. But now she saw herself working carefully around delicate vulpine ears instead of budding tiefling horns, her fingers gentle as they untangled the soft orange fur that caught the tavern's blue flame light.

The memory of noticing Egrim's lip scar for the first time shifted and reformed. She'd been teasing him about his beard, reaching up to trace the mark on his lip, but now she saw her fingers following the line where his broken tusk had left its permanent reminder. The scar was the same, but the face around it was green-skinned and tusked, unmistakably orcish in his strong features.

Laughter bubbled up through the memory as she watched Saffron playing dress-up in her bridesmaid's dress, the child's delight infectious as she spun in circles. But now Kasha could see the bushy tail that had poked out from beneath the trailing fabric, wagging with pure joy as the little girl pretended to be a princess.

Several nights at the Tits and Tarts came back to her. Kovag's hands working the tension from her shoulders after particularly difficult and busy nights, his touch gentle despite his massive size. She remembered how those green fingers had known exactly where to press, how his strength had been tempered with such careful tenderness.

And then came the most intimate memories, the ones that made her heart race even in her frozen state. She saw herself beneath him, his true form revealed in the moons light that shown through the shutters of her suite's windows. Green skin gleaming with sweat. His eyes, one brown and the other solid green, dark with desire as he worshiped every inch of her body. She remembered how he'd kissed her scar of loss, the one she always hid from the world, murmuring against her skin that she was perfect. How his tusks had grazed her throat as he whispered her name like a prayer.

Every touch, every kiss, every whispered endearment, all of it had been real. The man, not the mask. It was like rubbing sleep from her eyes in the morning and seeing everything with crystal clarity. How could she have ever doubted.

Oakira's stare lingered on Kasha's face, but now her attention shifted to what she saw deeper within, something hidden beneath the surface. Her eyes began to glow with an inner light as she peered beyond the physical realm, studying the very essence of the woman before her. What she saw there made her tilt her head in puzzlement.

"Fascinating," she murmured with wonder. "You have no idea, do you?"

The wisps of energy around Oakira pulsed brighter as she leaned closer, her ethereal presence casting dancing shadows across Kasha's frozen features. "There is a heavy amount of Forgotten blood in your veins, Kasha Volstruk. Tieflings all carry the blood of Fae and Forgotten since your people were made by one such as me long long ago. But you, perhaps a great-grandmother or great-great-grandmother who caught the eye of one of the lesser Forgotten. I can see it, dormant and un-tapped, waiting for the right catalyst to awaken."

Oakira's head shifted again as she studied Kasha more intently, her expression growing thoughtful. "With enough control and willingness to open yourself to what lies within, you could rival some of the lesser Mana Wardens of the Arcanum Centralis. The power sleeps in your blood like embers waiting for breath to become flame." She smiles thoughtfully. "A frosty flame, but a flame nevertheless."

But even as she spoke of such potential, Oakira's expression changed to one of gentle understanding. She could see deeper than bloodlines and magical heritage, she could see into the very heart of what Kasha truly desired. And what she found there was not ambition or hunger for power, but something far more precious and infinitely more fragile.

"But you have no interest in such things, do you?" Her voice softened with something that might have been envy. "You never wanted to command arcane forces or bend reality to your will. You wanted a quiet life, a warm hearth, children's laughter echoing through your home. You wanted someone to love you not for what you could become, but for who you are."

A wistful smile crossed Oakira's transformed features, and for a moment the terrible power that surrounded her seemed to dim. "I understand that desire more than you know. I wish... I wish I had been given that choice in life. To simply be loved, to love in return, to build something small and beautiful instead of accumulating power like a miser hoards gold. All of this mess started for me because I simply wanted to be accepted."

She straightened then, her presence expanding once more as she gave Kasha a slight, respectful bow. "I know you will take far better care of him than I did," she said with regret. A weak, shameful expression played at her lips. "Though you will not have to try hard, considering how thoroughly I failed him."

Kasha's eyes were drawn inexorably toward the still forms of Kovag and Saffron. Kovag's eye was fixed on her with desperate intensity, and in that gaze, she saw everything she needed to know. Love. Real, honest, unguarded love that had nothing to do with glamours or deception. Her heart swelled with fierce protectiveness as she looked at them. Her family, broken and bleeding but still hers.

If we survive this, she thought, *I will never let them go. I will hold onto them with everything I have and never doubt again.*

Oakira moved away from them then, gliding across the stone floor toward where Isque remained frozen. She paused beside the Seeker, looking down at him with cold satisfaction.

"Soon you will be less than a memory," she said softly, her voice carrying the promise of absolute finality.

Isque's eyes expanded with desperate urgency, straining against the magical paralysis as he fought to communicate the danger. There was terror in his, not for himself, but for all the realms. He could feel Thruva's presence swelling with anticipation, could sense the trap closing around them all, but Oakira interpreted his pleading look as nothing more than a coward's final plea for mercy.

She moved on without another glance, her attention turning toward her uncle. Her hatred for the being that turned her life upside down for no other reason than what she was, something she had no control over. If he had just accepted her, then all of the Lunar realm would have been compelled to allow her to live in peace. Her mother would still be alive and would never have become so bitter.

As Oakira approached Thruva, her hatred for him began to manifest physically in her ascended state. The wisps of lunar light that had danced around her darkened to smoky gray, while the Forgotten flames grew brighter and more violent, licking at the air like hungry tongues. Her wraithlike beauty twisted into something terrible, still magnificent, but now dripping with absolute malice.

Her features sharpened, becoming more angular and predatory. The reddish-brown waves of her hair writhed like living serpents, and her bright green eyes blazed with the inner fire of vengeance long denied. The very air around her seemed to thicken with malevolent energy, and shadows gathered at her feet like loyal hounds awaiting their master's command.

When she spoke, there was a resonance of an ancient well of power and bottomless fury:

"Behold, Uncle mine, architect of anguish,

Your niece stands before you, no longer the frightened child

Who cowered beneath your contempt and scorn.

You who deemed my very existence an abomination,

Who poisoned my mother's heart with your hatred,

Who sent your Seekers to hunt us like beasts

Through realms both mortal and divine.

Did you think your cruelty would break me?

Did you believe your rejection would unmake

What the union of light and shadow had wrought?

You feared what I might become,

And in your fear, you ensured I became

Something far worse than your nightmares dared conjure.

Every tear my mother shed in exile,

Every night we fled from your Seekers,

Every moment of loneliness and despair—

All of it carved into my soul like sacred scripture,

Teaching me the true meaning of hatred,

Showing me the depths of my own darkness.

You wanted an abomination, dear Uncle?

You shall have one beyond your wildest terror."

As she reached the crescendo of her speech, Oakira's form darkened further still. The last vestiges of her Fae beauty twisted into something that belonged more to nightmare than dream, her presence becoming a vortex that seemed to devour light itself.

She leaned in close to Thruva's ear, her voice dropping to a whisper of finality. "Elirel, *my mother* whom you took from me, taught me all the Forbidden Vitae Spells before her death. In mere moments, the Lunar Court will be no more."

With that declaration, Oakira did exactly what the Lunar Court had feared since her birth. "Io renunzia della vita mia e dono a l'arcano del fin." Arcane force erupted from her soul as she formally renounced her Fae heritage, the words of rejection tearing through reality itself like a blade through silk.

But as the power reached its peak, Thruva's voice cut through the chaos with calm satisfaction.

"Well done, my little abomination."

Oakira's body went still with shock as she realized the truth, he had not held by her spell.

Lord Thruva chided her. "Did you really think your paltry pact mortal could siphon enough of the arcane for you to conjure any spells that could hold me?"

She tried to pull away, but Thruva's hand shot out like a striking serpent, his fingers closing around her throat with crushing force as tendrils of the void burst from his chest and held her wrists and ankles.

"Your father was right," he said with dark amusement. "You were too blinded by hatred to see all the warning signs."

The balanced power within Oakira shifted violently as she expelled the Fae portion of her soul. She felt hollow yet swelling with terrible new strength, her very essence rewriting itself in ways that would have realm ending consequences.

The shock that had frozen Oakira's features melted away like ice before flame, replaced by a smile of terrible confidence. Even with Thruva's hand crushing her throat and void tendrils binding her limbs, she looked upon her uncle with something approaching pity.

"You think you've won?" Her voice came out as a rasp. "It is too late, Uncle. The ritual is already complete. In moments, my half-empty soul will erupt, and all of the Lunar realm—the entire court, every Lunar Fae within it, will cease to exist."

Thruva's response was not the rage or desperation she expected. Instead, he threw back his head and cackled—a sound so filled with manic glee that it echoed in the chamber like the cries of the damned. His void-touched features shifted further, becoming more grotesque as his triumph consumed him. Strange protrusions crested his flesh, new mouths, eyes, limbs and countless other atrocities became a part of his new body.

"Oh, my dear little abomination," he wheezed between fits of laughter, "even now you can't see it. That was the plan all along. Did you truly believe this was about preserving the Lunar Court? About maintaining some semblance of order? I have outgrown the Court. I am above the Fae now."

Oakira's confident expression faltered as understanding began to dawn.

"You are the key, child. The key to breaking the barrier that has kept the Void at bay for millennia." His grip tightened around her throat as his voice contorted with pure hatred. "Through your sacrifice, through the destruction of the Lunar realm itself, Lady Zorog—Queen of Madness, Goddess of Destruction—will finally bring her wrath upon Yonara once more."

Her life, her pain, her entire existence. All of it orchestrated for her to be a tool. The irony of the parallels between her and Kovag played like a macabre joke in her mind. She played her part flawlessly for an audience she didn't even know existed.

On the other side of the portal Callus was on steady feet again thanks for Arialyn's quick and masterful work. His braces were reenergized thanks to the void core Arialyn had extracted from the arcane colling box.

Callus was pressing the Hangman's Spear into the barrier with all the strength he could summon to him. The small cracks began to expand rapidly around the spear tip as the divine weapon showed its power in the hands of The Hanged One's champion.

Thruva glared at Oakira. "Yes, I will perish in your coming devastation," Thruva continued with sacrilegious fervor. "But only briefly. My glorious Queen will pluck my soul from the very hands of The Hanged One and reinstate me as her Herald. I will be reborn in a world that we shall remake in her image."

Oakira's temporal binding that had held the chamber in stasis suddenly shattered like glass. She could no longer maintain the stasis spell. Her concentration, obliterated by revelation and horror.

"OAKIRA, FLEE!" Isque's voice rang out as he launched himself through the air. The Seeker moved with all the grace and speed his training had given him, silver armor gleaming as he threw himself between Oakira and whatever final horror Thruva had planned.

The newly crowned Void Lord Thruva didn't even bother to look at the pitiful incoming attack. Without a thought, he lashed out with a tendril of pure void energy. The dark force struck Isque mid-leap, and the effect was instantaneous and horrifying. The life drained from his body in a second, his flesh withering and crumbling as he collapsed to the stone floor. Nothing remained but a desiccated husk in tarnished armor.

Across the chamber, Kovag fought against his wounds and exhaustion, forcing his battered body to respond. With tremendous effort, he pushed himself to his feet and gathered a still unconscious Saffron in his arms. Kasha moved to his side, and together they held the child between them, their eyes meeting in a moment of perfect understanding. Love and regret passed between them—love for what they had found, regret that they were about to lose it all before it had truly begun.

Thruva raised his hand, the raw void ring vibrating with malicious energy. "And now, dear niece, you fulfill your destiny."

He plunged his hand deep into Oakira's chest. Purple arcane fissures immediately began eating through her flesh like acid, spreading outward from the point of contact as void energy consumed her from within.

Oakira's scream of suffering tore through the chamber, a sound that seemed to crack the very foundations of reality.

"OAKIRA!" Kovag's voice broke as he cried out to her, even now his heart breaking as he watched the woman that held his heart for a time being destroyed before his eyes.

Through the agony of void energy consuming her flesh, Oakira's eyes found Kovag, Kasha, and Saffron huddled together across the chamber. Even as purple fissures spread like poison through her body, she managed to raise her free hand, arcane power flowing from her fingertips despite Thruva's grip on her throat.

The barrier of the portal shattered under the power of the Hangman's Spear and Callus nearly fell through and into the dimensional space. "Run! Hurry!"

Oakira extended her hand toward the trio. "Good-bye my sweet beast."

"No!" Kovag began, reaching toward Oakira.

With a gesture that cost her dearly, Oakira unleashed a wave of force that sent Kovag, Kasha, and Saffron hurtling backward through the portal. They tumbled into the safety of the tavern just as the dimensional gateway slammed shut as Oakira closed her fist. A sound like thunder shook the chamber as stone began to fall around the two immense sources of power.

The chamber erupted in chaotic pulses of arcane energy. Fae silver, Forgotten crimson, and void purple, clashed against each other like warring storms. Lightning crackled through the air in brilliant displays of power that tore through flesh, while waves of concussive force rippled outward from Oakira's failing shell of a body.

Thruva's voice cut through the maelstrom, filled with dark satisfaction. "You have only prolonged the inevitable, child. When Lady Zorog restores me to life, I will personally see to the corruption of your precious pact mortal and his ilk. Their souls will burn in service to Zorog for all eternity."

Through the agony consuming her, Oakira managed to gather enough saliva to spit directly into Thruva's twisted face. Her voice came out as a rasp, but her words were absolute defiance.

"I may not be able to stop what you've started, Uncle," she gasped, purple fissures spreading across her cheeks like poisonous veins. "But I can ensure that Zorog cannot bring back what she doesn't remember ever existed."

Confusion flickered across Thruva's grotesque features. "What are you—"

""Io libero dono vita mia ad colpire te da memoria di tutti."" The words of the Forbidden Vitae Spell tore from Oakira's throat with the speed of a wildfire, each syllable costing her precious life force as she spoke the incantation that would wipe Thruva from all memory—past, present, and future.

Understanding dawned in Thruva's mind just as the spell took hold. "You cannot—"

"I told you. She taught me *all* the Forbidden Vitae Spells," Oakira whispered with satisfaction in her final breath.

Thruva's rage exploded outward as void tendrils lashed into Oakira, tearing through her flesh with renewed fury. But even as the pain threatened to shatter her consciousness, Oakira laughed—a sound of pure, vindictive joy that echoed around them.

She smiled up at the writhing mass of corruption above her, her mind already beginning to fragment as the memory spell took hold. Her last coherent thought was a moment of perfect confusion, *Who am I laughing at?*

The explosion that consumed Oakira's fractured soul tore through dimensions like a scythe through wheat. The Lunar Court—every tower, every gleaming spire, every ancient hall where Fae had walked for millennia simply ceased to exist. Not destroyed, not conquered, but *unmade,* as if it had never been at all.

The invisible tapestry of magic, the Arcane Web, that connected all things, convulsed. Threads of power that had been woven through countless ages snapped and reformed, struggling to compensate for the sudden absence of an entire realm. Where the Lunar Court's influence had once stabilized vast portions of the Web, gaping holes now yawned like wounds in reality itself.

Across Yonara, mages and sorcerers gasped as they felt the rupture pass through them like a hammer blow. In the Arcanum Centralis, ancient artifacts cracked, their stored energies dissipating into nothingness. The Mana Wardens scrambled to their scrying pools, watching in horror as sections of the Web grew threadbare, then transparent, then disappeared entirely.

But worse was what seeped through those gaps. Void energy, the same corruption that had once powered Varl's Wall, began to bleed into the wounded Web like poison into an open wound. The barrier that had protected Yonara since the end of the Age of Suffering flickered and failed in hundreds of places, allowing tendrils of nothingness to snake through reality's foundation.

In distant corners of the world, Void Tears began opening with increasing frequency. The carefully maintained balance between order and chaos, between existence and oblivion, tilted toward darkness.

The Web strained to heal itself, new connections forming frantically to bridge the devastation. But for every thread that reformed, another withered under the void's touch. The magical foundation of Yonara itself was beginning to unravel, thread by thread, spell by spell.

And somewhere in the writhing chaos of competing energies, something vast and terrible stirred, drawn by the scent of a universe laid bare. Deep in her vast realm of nothingness, The Lady of Madness grinned.

The trio tumbled through the portal's closing maw like broken dolls, their bodies rolling across the tavern floor in a tangle of limbs and desperate embraces. Kovag twisted his mass at the last second, using his bulk to shield Saffron and Kasha from the worst of the impact as they crashed into a cluster of tables and chairs. Wood splintered and metal screeched against the still blood-soaked wooden floor as furniture scattered like leaves in a storm.

Despite his efforts, the force of their landing and his weakened state forced him to lose grip on Kasha and she was sent sprawling away from him. Kovag's wounds, barely held together by Saffron's healing light, tore open anew as he slammed into the tavern wall. Dark blood seeped through his torn flesh, providing a fresh coat of blood to the already stained floor.

Arialyn bolted for Saffron and Kovag with panic as she rushed across the debris-strewn floor and came to a kneeling halt beside them. Kovag relaxed his grip on Saffron and Arialyn placed the girl on the floor beside him as she rapidly assessed her wounds and began to heal what she could.

Behind her, Callus and Lorisse ran to help Kasha, as she held her head in both hands and groaned in pain. Callus gripped his best friend tight, kissing her forehead with tears in his eyes. "Are you alright?"

She shook her head slowly as the spinning room began to slow and then desperately looked around for Kovag and Saffron, making the room return to whirling. "Callus! Where are they? I need them." As she finished slurring the words out, she saw them half the tavern away. Kovag lay nearly motionless with his wounds beginning to bleed again and Saffron limp as Arialyn's glowing blue hands moved about her. She tried to rise to her feet, but they were wobbly and gave out before she could even put enough strength in them to move. She cried out, "Kovag! Saffron!"

Callus quickly lifted her in his arms, "I've got you." He motioned for Lorisse to grab one of the few unbroken chairs and set it by Kovag. He moved to gently place Kasha in the chair near them but she protested.

"No, next to him. Please." She was starting to choke on her words as she sobbed, almost uncontrollably.

Kovag groaned and forced himself into a sitting position against the remains of a shattered table, his breathing labored and wet. Each exhale sent fresh rivulets of crimson down his chest, and his skin had taken on an alarming pallor. When he looked up, Callus was setting Kasha into the open crook of his arm. He gave his new friend a weak nod of gratitude at the gesture.

Kasha laid her head against his chest and peered up into his eyes. His own looked at his daughter and then back to his love. "Kasha…"

Kasha shook her head. "Don't. I believe you. Kovag, I love you."

He opened his mouth to tell her the same, but she held a finger to his lips. "I know. Save your strength, please. We need you."

She shifted her attention to Lorisse. "Check if the barrier is still around the tavern."

Lorisse ran to the front door and opened it. It was just after dawn and there were already a few tavern regulars standing at the door waiting to order fresh tarts. Several of them immediately perked up from their early morning daze and gawked at Lorisse's naked form before seeing past her to the carnage within.

"Fetch every healer you know. Now!" She ripped a coat off the hanger near the door that a patron had drunkenly left behind and threw it around her before returning to the unconscious bodies of Carl and Fithra.

"How are they Lorisse?" Callus asked as he ran to grab a bottle of water from the arcane colling box. Thankfully it was insulated, and the bottle was still cold. He started to rush back but then immediately grabbed a bottle of Mommy Milkers Breakfast Stout.

"They're both breathing. Pulses are steady but Fithra is wheezing pretty bad." Lorisse was in an absolute panic. There was so much destruction and loss of life around her. She had never been witness to even a portion of this sort of trauma in her life. Her entire body was trembling.

Callus rushed over to them and knelt down between them. He upended the bottle of water on Carl's face and the old man shot up, gasping and spitting. "Cunt punch!" He sat up, leaning on his hand and looking around the tavern. He found Callus cradling Fithra and tipping a bottle of stout into her mouth. "I get a rude awakening, and she gets fucking ale?!" He looked around at the state of the tavern and his mouth fell open.

"You're not an alcoholic. Hells, old man, read the room." He was smirking at Carl as Fithra began to suck at the stout bottle and open her eyes.

"Are you... trying to flirt with me, boy?" Fithra's attempt at seducing Callus made him shake his head. She looked ridiculous with her face half swollen while trying to reach for his crotch.

"For fuck's sake, woman." Carl slapped her hand away from Callus.

Saffron began to shift in Arialyn's arms as her arcane medicae worked to mend the trauma she had received from several blows to the head. Even half-asleep Saffron could feel the warmth of Arialyn's healing repair her throat that she had nearly torn apart with the scream she sent at that horrifying creature. Her eyes fluttered but did not yet open to consciousness.

Kovag watched with hope, but his eyelids began to grow heavy, and he caught his own head lobbing to the side.

"Surely you have more fight in you than that, green boy." Callus's voice was filled with relief but a mocking tone that he hoped would force the man to bolster his strength out of a masculine need to rise to Callus's prodding.

Kovag's voice came out as a gasp. "Fuck you."

"Knew you were the same man." Callus chuckled.

Kovag attempted to rise, his muscles trembling with the effort, but he couldn't summon enough strength to move. He collapsed back against the broken wood with a grunt of pain and frustration and coughed again, wincing in pain. "Saffron?"

Kasha steadied the man as best she could and sat up, looking at the girl. *Their girl.*

"Saffron, wake up, sweetness." Arialyn's voice was gentle but urgent as she tapped the child's face with careful fingers. Golden eyes fluttered open and immediately filled with tears as the trauma of what she had witnessed came flooding back. She hugged Arialyn briefly, seeking comfort in familiar arms, but her gaze quickly found her father.

Despite his pain, he managed a weak smile just for her, the same expression of unconditional love he'd worn since the day he'd found her broken and afraid.

Saffron scrambled to her feet and ran to him, throwing herself against his wounded chest with complete trust that he would catch her. His arms closed around her protectively. He ignored the impact as it sent fresh waves of pain through his battered body.

Kasha leaned on her hands and smiled with immense gratitude at Arialyn as a wave of fresh vertigo hit her. Callus rushed to steady her. She shook her head as restored memories and the horror of what they'd barely escaped slammed back into her mind. The tavern felt surreal after the nightmare of that starlit chamber, too warm and bright and *safe* to be real.

Saffron looked up from Kovag's shoulder and into Kasha's eyes, then extended her hand out while still keeping her head against her father. Desperate urgency shown on her face. There was something in Saffron's expression, a need that went beyond comfort, beyond fear. She needed them both.

Kasha leaned in with easy decisiveness against Kovag's chest and placed her arm around Saffron, completing their small circle.

Saffron immediately shifted her position and placed herself between the two, her small body forming a bridge between the people who had become her world. Her pack.

For a moment, she simply breathed in their presence, feeling truly secure for the first time since the portal had torn them from their peaceful evening. Then, with her face buried against Kovag's chest and Kasha's hand stroking her hair, she spoke her first true words in the sweetest voice any in the room had ever heard.

"Papa."

Kovag looked at Kasha and began to cry.

"Mama."

Kasha's mouth fell open as she cried with pure joy for the first time that she could remember.

EPILOGUE

One Year Later

(Takes place concurrently with the Lavender & Ginger epilogue, at first told from another perspective)

Kasha set to oiling her breasts right as Arialyn turned and exited the Tits and Tarts. Finding that much scornfruit for the tarts she wanted made for Callus had been a challenge in itself, let alone the baking of the delicate fruit. She was glad she wasn't going to be around for the aftermath it did on his stomach. She remembered the time he first had the damned fruit way back in their Traveling Spectacles days. That training session of his has been less than pleasant to observe.

They had all come together and celebrated the two year anniversary of the Amethyst Artificer last evening and into the early night. Her and Arialyn had talked a fair bit of that evening in her madame's suite while the boys continued the celebration down in the main room. Carl and Fithra had come to the celebration rather by accident as they were already in Hus'rokn for some trade deals on Bloody Ale Company ales for multiple establishments, Kasha's include. They had brought another Bloody Ale Company member with them that had been blooded in recently but had said they told him to stay at the Trade Gate to keep an eye out for a particular fool that was trying to avoid paying their invoice.

Kasha stopped oiling herself and held her hand to her lips with a smile. She was beyond thrilled for her friend. Arialyn was pregnant. Or at least, she was pretty sure she was. Kasha had squealed so loudly at the news the Saffron had fallen out of her chair and Lemmy with her.

"Does Callus know?" she asked.

"I haven't told him yet. It's not supposed to be possible, Kasha. You know that. How did this happen?" Arialyn's face held both hope and fear in equal measure.

Kasha shook her head at that. "I don't know, but this is good news, right?"

Arialyn shrugged her shoulders. "If it's real? Then, yes. I can't think of anything that would make me happier. Which is something I am somewhat shocked to say. I had never really given much thought to having a child. Now though... now that it might be a possibility, I am floored by how exciting it could be. And I know Callus will be beside himself with pride. I just need to know it is truly happening before I tell him."

Kasha leaned forward and grabbed Arialyn's hands with the kindest smile of reassurance. "Lorisse knows an old witch that lives in the forge district. I'll arrange a meeting for you if you'd like. She an orcish woman and a priestess of Bjomda. Lorisse's mother even used to see the woman for various, less than traditional things. Perhaps she can shed some light on what's going on. Lorisse has said on more than one occasion that the old woman sees things no one else can. She's seen some issues the healers in town have failed to notice. If there is anything that isn't in the medicae realm going on, perhaps she'll see it."

Arialyn nodded and bit her lip. "Thank you, twat-tart."

"Aunt Arialyn, you're not supposed to say words like that around children." Saffron wagged a finger at her with mocking disapproval.

Arialyn rolled her eyes playfully. "I'm sure you have never heard anything worse in this place, have you?"

Saffron stuck her tongue out and summoned Lemmy to her shoulder. "Nope."

She came over to Arialyn and hugged her around the belly. "I hope it's a boy."

Arialyn felt a tear beginning to form and leaned down, kissing Saffron on the head. "Sweetness, you have to keep this a secret for now, okay?"

"Yes, Aunt Arialyn. But Uncle Callus is going to be very happy. Can I be there when you tell him?" Her vulpine ears flopped to the sides, clearing indicating that she was begging.

"We'll see, sweetness."

Kasha heard the stormer hum to life outside the tavern and the sound of it speeding away down the street. She set the oil back under the counter and saw the note Lorisse had given her with the time and place for Arialyn to meet the old witch. "Shit."

Kovag came from the kitchen with a guilty look on his face. "You made her pickle infused cocoa cookies?"

Kasha kept her eyes on the front door. "Yes, why?"

He chuckled. "Sounds like pregnancy craving food."

Kasha snapped around with surprise. "Were you eavesdropping yesterday?!"

"What? No, why in the Hells would I-" He stopped once he realized Kasha's reaction. "Wait, is she pregnant? She can't be pregnant. Not with Callus's-"

"Are you suggesting that Arialyn, someone who has worn a dress exactly once in her life and blushes when she hears the word 'pussy' would dare to sleep with anyone else?" Kasha cocked her hip to side and glared at Kovag, daring him to say that was what he was thinking.

He waved his hands in a negative gesture. "Gods no! She's far too in love with him. But, how? Pure and-" He nearly said mongrel. "She can't have a child with a hobgoblin."

"She's pregnant?!"

Kasha's eyes slammed shut as the familiar voice of Carl boomed from the doorway of one of the lower rooms behind her. She sighed heavily. "She's going to kill me."

Above on the mezzanine Saffron giggled and called down. "Mama, you're in trouble."

Carl Just Carl exited the Witch's Tits and Tarts Tavern with a grumble and a foul mood as he adjusted his Bloody Ale Company pauldron on his left shoulder. The foul mood wasn't because of the errand Kasha had asked him for but because Fithra, his lovely superior and Sergeant-at-Arms, had decided to stay behind and keep Lorisse company. He had shared a bed with them both again last night, but that didn't mean he was any less irritated that Fithra got to stay behind in that warm bed with Lorisse. He may have been in his sixties, but everything still operated as well as it did in his twenties. At least, that is what he thought based on the noises they made with him.

He was jealous. Plain and simple. Which is exactly why he was keen to take that frustration out on the next person he came across.

"Oi! Carl." The voice of the newest Bloody Ale Company member called out to him far too early in the morning for Carl's liking.

"You think just because you're blooded in now that I won't knock you in the dirt for that cheery ass attitude in the morning? Do I look cheery to you, Drogdan?" Carl stared at the man that looked so much like the dead Bogdan it was uncanny. Cousins, he had been told.

Drogdan stopped several feet from the Trade Gate guardhouse and tied a leather cord around his thick dreadlocks, feeling as uneasy as he had when he was still a Waster just a month ago. "Sorry, sir."

"Stupidity runs in the family I guess." Carl huffed as he kicked out his boot and swept at the younger man's feet.

Drogdan sidestepped and smirked. "Not this ti-" His bravado abruptly ceased when Carl buried his fist in his gut. Drogdan doubled over and heaved.

"Ah, mood improved. Good job, kid." Carl dusted his hands off and continued toward the Trade Gate guardhouse. "Keep up."

"Fucker." Drogdan spat.

"That's the spirit."

Carl saw Ethan come out of the guardhouse in his full set of scale mail and uniform. He had yet to see the man out of full armor and uniform in the two times he'd been back to Hus'rokn over the last year. Much had changed in the power structure of the city.

Ethan finished tying on his sword belt. "Carl, how's the ale treating you this morning?"

"Far better now that I worked out that aching muscle." Carl smirked over his shoulder at Drogdan who was giving him a rude hand gesture. "Don't tell the kid, but I like him. One of our better recruits in the last few years." He whispered. "So, Lance Captain, what kept you from the celebration yesterday?"

Ethan shook his head. "Lance General now, Carl."

"I'd say it's an old habit and to forgive me, but you know I don't really care." Carl shrugged. He never really cared for titles and wasn't about to start now.

"With the rumors of void tears in the city and ambitious upstarts trying to take Adenus's place, I've been too busy to appreciate the perks of my role, like delegating tasks so I can enjoy some damned downtime. The Lucky Talisman finally has new ownership, but people still think they can be one of the Three by taking it over." He shook his head. ""They can't understand that there is no more 'The Three'. After Governor Rosamunda and I transformed this place into a formal governorship, tensions ran high for several months. Fortunately, the city has adjusted well to Rosamunda as the long-term sitting Governor. By transitioning the City Guard into a City Militia, and with me as it's General, it has become much easier to prevent new threats like Authern, Zunibar, or Alabaster from emerging. However, I still have to contend with wannabe criminals who think they'll be the next big name in Hus'rokn." He didn't say it, but he took pride in knowing that Serine would have been happy with the changes he had helped put into place in the city.

This had been his plan as soon as he accepted Adenus's offer. Of course, the former head of the Gauntlet wasn't aware of that. The way the transition occurred had obviously not gone the way Ethan had planned when he took the lead of the Lance over a year ago. However, this actually worked out more smoothly and required less finesse and politicking than he would have been required to do with his original plan. He hated politicking anyway. How could he have possibly conceived of Fae getting involved at the lead of some figure that no one in the tavern that night had been able to recall. He had hated to lose Adenus the way they did, but it meant the his plans came to fruition much faster.

"We're off to check into a supposed void tear in the sewers. Another bullshit cry of worg I'm sure. I know they have to be happening out there with all the reports we've gotten from around Yonara, but we haven't had a confirmed sighting here yet. I hope it stays that way too." Lance General Ethan sighed and tightened a strap on his shoulder.

"Well, have fun in the muck and shit." Carl slapped the man on the shoulder and moved through the Trade Gate unimpeded, thanks to a nonchalant wave of Ethan's hand to one of the guards. Drogdan jogged up to the old man as they moved into the Wylds.

"What're we doing, Carl?" Drogdan asked while twirling the ring that once belonged to his cousin, Bogdan. Carl had been surprised to find the ring untouched by the pyre he had laid Bogdan to rest on and brought it home to Kol'Theron, unsure of what to do with it. But once Drogdan showed up and signed on as a waster he felt he had no choice but to give it to the man once he was blooded into the Company and given his pauldron.

"I have a note to deliver to a friend." Carl reached into his belt pouch to make sure the note was still there. There was no reason to believe it wouldn't be, but the importance of the message made him worry about losing it. *How could she possibly be pregnant?*

As they traveled through the Wylds Carl remained silent. He simply walked and breathed deep the scents of salt and fresh water that wafted in from the torrential rivers that encircled the city. They passed by one of the Wyld Mages on her raised pillar. She was keeping her portion of the river tumultuous with very little interest. No one had tried to sail into the rivers and raid the Wylds for over three centuries. The position of River Warden was shared by many but no longer viewed as a prestigious one. Those days were long gone. Now it was considered where mages went to retire.

Drogdan had been talking endlessly for the first half hour of the trip but had soon grown silent when he realized Carl hadn't heard a single thing he'd said. He had spent the rest of the trek summoning spectral blue daggers from the ring and then making them vanish in the air.

They were nearing the last turn to the street of the Amethyst Artificer when several people came running and screaming from that very corner.

After they ran passed Carl and Drogdan, they could hear the strange otherworldly shrieks and groans coming from that direction.

"Drogdan, ready yourself." Carl unhooked his Warhammer from his belt and kicked himself for leaving his Company shield behind at the tavern.

They rounded the corner and both stopped dead in their tracks at the sight of a rolling mass of limbs, eyes and mouths that leaked purple mist of the void. Then came the naked hobgoblin holding a spear and jumping into the air thrusting forward and piercing the monstrosity.

The sight of Callus Kordec fully nude but wearing the most serious battle-hardened expression was an unsettling sight. It was one that was hard to look away from. Like a runaway caravan accident. You wanted to look away but found the entire event intriguing.

"Carl, if you're dragging me to some strange sex thing, I don't think I want to participate. Maybe just watch the first time?" Drogdan said after he managed to close his mouth.

Carl heard the unmistakable ear-piercing shot of Arialyn's arcabus before he was able to see the gnomish woman. He found her now staring at some small monstrosity that was stepping from one of the void tears they had been hearing about. She seemed rooted in place by shock.

"Drogdan, kill every one of these fucking things you can. Go!" Carl yelled as he sprinted toward Arialyn.

Drogdan nodded and began spinning, dancing, and performing acrobatic marvels while unleashing a hail of ghostly blue daggers into the void creatures. Many fell at the first wound, but several continued their onslaught.

Carl rushed in from the side and bore down on the warped figure at the portals opening. Its clawed hand was raised and aimed at Arialyn. He hurled his Warhammer as a red flare erupted from it like brimstone.

It smashed into the face of the creature, tearing and searing a portion of its cheek away.

Before the figure even turned back to assess the new threat, his face had reformed. Even with the few structural changes Carl saw a resemblance to Arialyn but the terror on her face told him there was no love lost between her and whatever or whoever this creature was.

"Your pathetic mortal weaponry is a child's toy compared to the gifts Lady Zorog has bestowed upon the Voidtongue, Fogjeck." He resumed his threatening posture and again pointed his clawed hand at his daughter and launched a void bolt for her stomach.

"This one isn't mortal made you son-of-a-bitch!" The Hangman's Spear tore through the air like a ballista and impaled the man once known as Wenjeck Foghand, sending him back through the portal and forcing it to collapse.

The impact of the spear forced the void bolt off course just enough so it would have missed Arialyn's abdomen, but Carl was already mid-air in a leap to protect mother and child. The bolt of pure void clipped the old man in the side. He hit the ground and rolled, coming to a rest on his back and panting.

Around them every voidling that had remained living turned to ash and shattered in the light breeze.

"Donkey tits, it's in my mouth!" Drogdan protested from down the street as he coughed and wiped at his tongue to remove the strange bitter taste.

Arialyn stood motionless and in shock as Callus came to her side. "Are you hurt?"

She said nothing until he shook her. "I'm fine. That was... my father."

"Your what?" Callus looked back to where the portal had been with confusion evident in his expression.

Carl's groan brought them both back to reality and they moved to him quickly. Arialyn knelt beside him and looked at the wound. The void bolt had torn away the ringmail at his side, but his skin appeared to be nothing more than bruised.

Callus squatted down near Carl's head. "Thank you again, old man. You can stop lying around now."

Carl's eyes had been closed with pain and when he finally opened them, he wished he hadn't. "Get your fucking cock out of my face!"

Callus stood quickly, somewhat embarrassed. *Should have put on pants.* He said to himself again. "I didn't have time to put on pants when this bullshit kicked off. And let's not act like you didn't wander out drunk and swinging dick last night with Fithra and Lorisse. What was it you were breathlessly begging? Oh, that's right, 'I need a breather.' Amateur."

"Is now really the time?" Arialyn shook her head. "Carl, we need to get you into the shop. I need to look at your wound closer. I see nothing but you look like you're in a good bit of pain."

"It's not from whatever the Hells that was, my dear. My back is finally catching up with me." Carl groaned as Callus pulled him up to his feet. For the briefest of moments, he felt a wave of wooziness crash over him and the sound of a disturbing and far-off whisper rang in his ears. He shook his head and blinked his eyes several times. "Kasha forgot to give you this." He retrieved the note from his belt pouch and handed it to her.

Arialyn knew immediately what must be in the note and quickly tucked it away in her own pouch.

Callus raised an eyebrow. "What was that?"

Drogdan interrupted as he came jogging over. "You must be Callus. And that means you're Arialyn. Pleased to meet you." He waved somewhat awkwardly and swiped a strange piece of decayed flesh from his leather pants.

"Who's the new guy?" Callus asked while extending his hand to the man.

Carl chuckled. "You're not going to fucking believe this."

BONUS CHAPTER FROM UNTITLED BOOK 3

RETURN OF THE OLD BLOOD

Arialyn guided her stormer through the winding streets toward Hus'rokn's forge district, the familiar hum of the arcane engine doing little to calm her nerves. Percival sat perched in the small basket she'd attached to the front, his mismatched eyes looking in opposite directions as usual, one focused on the road ahead, the other seemingly watching a bird that had caught his attention three blocks back.

The increased presence of the new City Militia was a testament to Lance General Ethan's new power and command. The void tear attacks had only just happened yesterday and yet the patrols were out in number with eyes everywhere.

The weight of the note in her pouch felt heavier than it should have. *Bjomwyn Uzmira, forge district, third house past Ironmonger's Row. She's expecting you at midday. - Lorisse*

Guilt gnawed at her stomach as she thought about Callus back at the shop, probably charming customers with all the grace of a war hammer to the face. She'd told him she was going to source some specialty metals for a new project—not entirely a lie, but not the truth either. The deception sat poorly with her, but she needed to know for certain before she got his hopes up.

How is this even possible? The question had been circling her mind for nearly a week like a persistent fly. Gnomes and hobgoblins simply d idn't... couldn't... The biological incompatibility was well-documented. Yet here she was, with all the signs pointing to something that should be impossible.

She turned onto a street lined with modest brick houses, a stark contrast to the industrial clanging and smoke-belching forges just a few blocks away. The address Lorisse had given her led to what appeared to be the most ordinary house imaginable. Red brick, blue shutters, a small garden with herbs growing in neat rows. Hardly what she had envisioned in her mind.

Arialyn brought the stormer to a stop and stared at the unremarkable dwelling. "This seems like an odd place for a witch to live," she murmured to Percival as she dismounted.

Percival hopped down from his basket and rubbed against her calf, letting out a small meow that felt reassuring. Callus had no idea how much she valued what he had done for her by constructing Percival. This wasn't her old cat, Percy, but he was as damn close as was possible without her being the one to reconstruct him.

She approached the front door, her hand hesitating just before knocking. What if this was all in her head? What if she was just letting hope cloud her judgment?Before her knuckles could make contact with the wood, a voice called out from within. "Come in, child! The door's open!"

Arialyn exchanged a glance with Percival, whose eyes were split again. One now looking up at the door, and the other one down at a beetle crawling across the threshold. She pushed the door open and stepped inside.

The interior was shockingly normal. Comfortable furniture, family portraits on the walls, the warm scent of baking bread wafting from somewhere deeper in the house. If not for the voice that had called to her, she might have thought she'd entered the wrong home entirely.

"Kitchen's this way, dear!" the voice called again. "Just finished making tea. Perfect timing!"

Arialyn made her way toward the sound, Percival padding silently beside her on his mechanical paws. "Did you... sense us coming?" she asked as she entered the kitchen.

Rich laughter filled the air. "Oh, child, no. Lorisse told me exactly when you'd be arriving."

Arialyn felt heat rise to her cheeks, embarrassed by her foolish question. Of course, Lorisse had simply told the woman when to expect her. There was nothing mystical about it. She moved to the small wooden table and sat down carefully, placing her hands in her lap and fidgeting with one of the seams of her coveralls.

The woman who turned to greet her defied every expectation Arialyn had formed. Bjomwyn stood just over six feet tall, her gray-green skin bearing the deep mottled patches that spoke of advanced age, yet she moved with surprising ease as she gathered a tea set. Deep lines mapped her weathered face. Crow's feet hinted at countless visions, while laugh lines suggested humor found in the darkest of prophecies.

But it was her eyes that truly caught Arialyn's attention. One was completely black, a solid orb that reflected no light, the unmistakable mark of the orcish goddess Bjomda's favor. The other shifted between vibrant green and stormy gray, bright and alert despite the ancient face that housed it. Her iron-gray hair hung in long braids threaded with bone charms and small obsidian beads that clicked softly as she moved.

"Don't mind the staring, little lamb," Bjomwyn said with gentle amusement. "Most folks take a moment to adjust to these old eyes of mine."

Arialyn's gaze swept the kitchen, taking in details that confirmed what she'd already suspected. A collection of unblinking black eyes—carved from obsidian, painted on pottery, etched into wooden spoons watching from every surface. Bjomda's symbol was everywhere, woven into the very fabric of the space. Bundles of herbs hung from the rafters, some she recognized, others very alien to her. A mortar and pestle sat on the counter, stained dark with whatever had been ground within it most recently.

Percival, apparently deciding the table looked like the perfect perch, leaped up with a small mechanical whir and settled himself directly in the center, his tail twitching as it occasionally sparked.

"Percival, no!" Arialyn reached for him immediately. "That's terribly rude. Get down."

"Oh, nonsense!" Bjomwyn waved away her concern with a flour-dusted hand, setting down a steaming teapot. "A table's just wood, child. Nothing that can't be wiped clean." She paused mid-pour, her eyes fixing on Percival with sudden intensity. "Though I must say, I've never seen a cat quite like..."

The old orc leaned closer, her weathered features creasing with fascination as she took in Percival's metallic form. One of his eyes tracked her movement while the other remained fixed on a dust mote floating in a shaft of sunlight.

"Is this arcanomancy?" Bjomwyn asked, her voice filled with wonder.

Arialyn's nervous fidgeting stopped instantly, replaced by the familiar spark that always ignited when someone showed genuine interest in her craft. "Yes! It's a fusion of mechanical engineering and arcane theory. You see, the framework requires precise arcane core calibration to achieve the neural mimicry patterns, and then there's the behavioral matrix encoding—though that's incredibly complex because you have to account for—"

She caught herself gesturing wildly with her hands, words tumbling out faster than she could think them. "I actually taught some basic principles to my husband, Callus, and he constructed Percival himself. Well, he tried to, anyway. The optical alignment is obviously flawed, but the core functions work beautifully, and really it was such a thoughtful gesture because my original mechanical cat, Percy, was destroyed when a gang Callus used to run with, the Talons of Misery, they killed Percy during a raid on my old shop. Callus felt terrible about it even though it wasn't directly his fault, so he spent a year learning from me just so he could—"

Arialyn stopped abruptly, realizing she'd been speaking without breathing. Bjomwyn sat across from her with slightly widened eyes, looking like someone who'd just been caught in a sudden rainstorm of information.

Then the old woman smiled, and a warm, genuine expression reached her mismatched eyes. "My, you do have passion for your work."

The blush returned to Arialyn's cheeks with a vengeance. "I'm sorry. I get carried away when I'm nervous, and I'm very nervous right now." She reached out to stroke Percival's head, finding comfort in his purring. "I don't usually ramble like that to strangers."

"Nothing to apologize for, little lamb. No, lamb doesn't work for you. Little squirrel. That is a better fit," Bjomwyn said gently, pouring tea into two cups. "Passion is a beautiful thing. Now, what brings you to this old witch's table? Lorisse was rather mum about the why."

Arialyn bit her lip knowing that once she spoke her concern she would probably find out it was a false hope and something else was wrong. She couldn't believe how attached she had already become to the idea of being a mother.

Arialyn opened her mouth to speak when a sleek black cat with just a speck of gray under its left eye leaped gracefully onto the table. Percival immediately stood and arched his back, his mechanical joints whirring softly as his defensive programming engaged.

The black cat paid no mind to Percival's threatening posture and simply meowed a soft, welcoming sound before rubbing along his metallic side. Almost instantly, Percival's back relaxed, his tail settling into a gentle sway.

Bjomwyn chuckled, the sound warm as honey. "That's Marigold. Sweet to all creatures, something I rather wish wasn't always the case. She's brought home more wounded birds and stray mice than I care to count."

Marigold began attempting to groom Percival's head with her rough tongue, but immediately pulled back with a disgusted expression, shaking her head at the metallic taste. She was about to leap down from the table when Percival surprised everyone by lowering his head and beginning to groom her fur with his mechanical tongue.

Marigold settled down with a contented purr, stretching out along the table as if she'd found the perfect spot for an afternoon nap.

Bjomwyn coughed gently, drawing Arialyn's attention back to the matter at hand. "Now then, little squirrel, what brings you to my table?"

Arialyn straightened in her chair, her hands clasping together tightly. "I... I believe I'm pregnant."

The old witch's expression didn't change, but her mismatched eyes studied Arialyn's face carefully. "And why does this concern you, child? Are you here seeking to rid yourself of it?"

"No!" Arialyn sat up straight, her voice sharp with refusal. The very suggestion sent a protective surge through her that surprised her with its intensity. She settled back into her chair, her voice softening. "No, that's not... it's just that my husband, Callus, he's a hobgoblin."

Understanding dawned in Bjomwyn's ancient features. "Ah." She nodded slowly, the bone charms in her hair clicking together. "I see the issue now."

The old witch stood with surprising vigor, moving to a cabinet filled with jars and bundles of dried herbs. "Drink your tea, dear. It's chamomile and lavender, I smell one of those on you by the way, calming on the nerves. You'll need steady hands and a clear mind for what comes next."

Arialyn lifted the cup with trembling fingers, inhaling the soothing steam before taking a tentative sip. The warm liquid did help settle some of the anxiety churning in her stomach.

Bjomwyn gathered several small jars, selecting pinches of various herbs. She retrieved the dark mortar and pestle from the counter, then reached for something that made Arialyn's head tilt. It was a badger skull, polished smooth with age and use.

"The spirits don't coddle, little squirrel," Bjomwyn said without looking back, her voice gentle but firm. "Neither do I. But they do reveal truth to those brave enough to seek it."

Bjomwyn returned to the table, but this time she settled beside Arialyn rather than across from her. The proximity made Arialyn aware of the faint scent of a deep earthiness, like grave dirt, that seemed to emanate from her very being.

The implements were arranged with haste. Four candles emerged from the collection Bjomwyn had gathered, each placed at a corner of the table. Red for fire, green for earth, white for air, and blue for water. Arialyn recognized the elemental arrangement from her studies of arcane theory, though she'd never seen it used in quite this context.

Bjomwyn paused, her weathered face turning toward Arialyn with an intensity that made her shift uncomfortably. The old witch's nose twitched, not with distaste but with something that looked almost like concern. She seemed to be scenting the air around Arialyn, her black eye reflecting nothing while the other narrowed with focus.

"Interesting," Bjomwyn murmured, though she didn't elaborate on what she'd detected.

The witch retrieved one final candle. This one was a deep purple that seemed to absorb light rather than reflect it and placed it in the center of the table. With gentle but firm hands, she scooped up both cats and set them on the floor. Marigold mewed in protest while Percival's tail sparked once in what might have been mechanical indignation.

Bjomwyn raised her hand, fingers splayed toward the ceiling. The light seemed to drain from the room like water down a drain, leaving them in absolute darkness for a heartbeat that felt eternal. Then, as if summoned by some ancient command, all five candles burst into flame simultaneously, their combined glow casting dancing shadows across the kitchen walls. Literal dancing shadows that Arialyn could swear she saw faces in.

"That was..." she began, but Bjomwyn had already begun to chant.

The words were guttural, rolling from the old orc's throat in tones that seemed to resonate in Arialyn's bones. She couldn't understand the language, ancient orcish, perhaps, or something even older. The cadence was hypnotic, almost musical in its harsh beauty.

From one of her jars, Bjomwyn poured a clear liquid into large wooden bowl. The sharp scent of vinegar filled the air, making Arialyn's nose wrinkle. The contents of the mortar followed, creating a mixture that bubbled and hissed softly.

The chanting continued as Bjomwyn extended her hand toward Arialyn, palm up, expectant. Slowly, uncertainly, Arialyn reached out and placed her hand in the witch's weathered grasp. Bjomwyn's skin was surprisingly warm, calloused from years of work but gentle in its touch.

Lightning-quick, a curved knife appeared in Bjomwyn's other hand. The blade drew across Arialyn's palm before she could even register the motion, and her hand was plunged into the bowl before the pain could fully register.

Arialyn winced, her free hand instinctively moving toward the arcabus at her hip. For a split second, every defensive instinct screamed at her to draw the weapon, to protect herself from this strange ritual. But then the concoction in the bowl began to send a soothing warmth that spread from the wound up through her arm and to her belly. She forced herself to relax.

The candle flames flickered higher, and Bjomwyn's chanting grew more intense.

The chanting ceased as abruptly as it had begun, leaving an echoing silence that seemed to press against Arialyn's eardrums. Bjomwyn's weathered hands lifted Arialyn's dripping palm from the bowl and guiding it toward the badger skull's gaping maw.

The mixture of blood, herbs, and that sharp-scented liquid poured into the skull's mouth with a wet, organic sound that made Arialyn's stomach lurch. She watched in fascination and growing unease as the liquid disappeared into the bone cavity, seemingly absorbed rather than simply pooling within.

Then the empty eye sockets began to glow.

Two small red orbs materialized where once there had been nothing but hollow darkness, pulsing with an inner light that cast crimson shadows across the kitchen walls. They joined in the dance of the shadowy faces she had already seen from the light of the candles. The skull itself seemed to shudder, as if something had awakened within its weathered confines.

Bjomwyn leaned forward, her own mismatched eyes reflecting the skull's eerie glow. She began speaking in orcish, her voice taking on a conversational tone that was somehow more unsettling than her earlier chanting. Arialyn caught fragments of words like "child," "blood," and "truth" but the rest flowed past her limited understanding of the language.

The red orbs pulsed brighter, and Bjomwyn nodded as if receiving answers to unspoken questions. Finally, she turned to Arialyn with a smile that transformed her weathered features into something almost maternal.

"You are indeed pregnant with Callus's child, little squirrel. A son." she said, her voice warm with certainty.

Relief flooded through Arialyn so intensely that she nearly sobbed. Her free hand moved instinctively to her stomach, a protective gesture that felt more natural than breathing. "But how is that possible?"

"Patience, little squirrel." Bjomwyn held up a finger, her attention drawn back to the skull. The red orbs were swirling now, spinning within their sockets like tiny maelstroms. She paused, listening to some-thing only she could hear, occasionally murmuring responses in orcish.

After several long moments, she straightened, her expression growing more serious. "The tear in the arcane web that occurred about a year ago. I'm sure one as skilled in arcanomancy as yourself felt it at some point. It did more than simply break the barrier keeping the void at bay." Her voice almost seemed to belong to someone else. "The magic and bloodlines of the Torvox people, long held from this world since the fall of Varl's ancient wall, have begun to seep back into Yonara along with the taint of the void. That is perhaps the only balm we can hope for in this great tragedy."

Arialyn's mind raced, connecting fragments of historical knowledge. The Torvox, the nature-bound people who had died out after Varl's Wall fell, their arcane blood proving fatal when the magical barriers collapsed.

"Either you or Callus carries a spark of that ancient blood," Bjomwyn continued, her gaze intense. "Dormant for generations, awakened now by the breaking of the barrier. It is this heritage, combined with the current state of the arcane web, that has made your union fertile."

The red orbs pulsed once more before slowly fading, leaving the skull empty and lifeless once again. Bjomwyn gently bandaged Arialyn's palm with strips of clean linen, her touch surprisingly tender as the candles faded out and light returned to the kitchen.

"Your child will be unique, little squirrel," she murmured. "I suspect more will be coming to me over the coming months with similar concerns as yours."

Arialyn sat in stunned silence, her hands pressed protectively against her stomach as if she could somehow feel the impossible life growing within. The weight of Bjomwyn's words settled over her like a heavy blanket—her child would be unique, part of something larger than she could comprehend. The ancient bloodline of the Torvox, awakened by the very forces that threatened their world.

A son. The thought sent a warm flutter through her chest, followed immediately by a surge of fierce protectiveness she'd never experienced before.

Bjomwyn returned to her seat across the table, settling with the careful grace of someone whose bones suddenly remembered just how old they were. Her mismatched eyes remained fixed on Arialyn with an intensity that made her shift uncomfortably.

"There's something else, little squirrel," Bjomwyn said, her voice losing its earlier warmth. "I smell the void on you."

Arialyn straightened in her chair, her defensive instincts flaring. "I work with void ore," she said carefully. "I've developed techniques to render its corruption inert while maintaining its arcane properties as a power source. It's perfectly safe when properly done."

"Impressive," Bjomwyn interrupted, genuine admiration creeping into her tone. "I do not know if the Brightborn engineers have even managed such a feat without losing themselves to the taint. Your mind must be remarkably disciplined."

The praise should have felt good, but something in the old witch's expression suggested there was more to come. Arialyn waited, her hands still pressed against her belly.

Bjomwyn's black eye seemed to draw in Arialyn's full attention as she leaned forward. "But that's not the void scent I'm detecting, child. The skull showed me something else. You're being hunted by something dangerous from the void realm."

A chill ran down Arialyn's spine as yesterday's terror came flooding back. The portal tearing open outside their shop, the writhing mass of limbs and eyes, the corrupt beings that flooded into the street and most horrifying of all, her father.

"One of the void tears from yesterday opened right outside my shop," she said, her voice barely above a whisper. "Someone... someone from my past came through it. He tried to take me."

Bjomwyn's weathered features darkened. "Who?"

"My father." The words tasted bitter on her tongue. "Wenjeck Foghand. But he wasn't... he wasn't himself anymore. He called himself the Voidtongue, said he served Zorog now." She shuddered at the memory of those familiar features twisted by void corruption. "He aimed for my stomach specifically. If my husband and a friend hadn't intervened..."

The old witch's expression grew grim, her fingers unconsciously moving to trace one of the bone charms in her hair. "The void realm remembers bloodlines, little squirrel. If your father has been claimed by it, he may not be done hunting you or what you carry." She shook her head, the regret in her weathered features was unmistakable, and Arialyn felt her stomach drop even further.

"I'm sorry, little squirrel," the old witch said, her voice apologetic of unwelcome prophecy. "The spirits rarely speak of threats without reason. You must be careful moving forward in your studies of the void ore. What you've accomplished is remarkable, but the void remembers those who touch its essence, even safely."

Arialyn's hands pressed over her belly even harder, her bandaged palm throbbing with a dull ache that seemed to echo her rising panic. Tears began to form in her eyes.

"Remain close to your husband," Bjomwyn continued, her mismatched eyes intense with urgency. "Bjomda and The Hanged One are kindred spirits. Death and fate intertwined like lovers' fingers. Callus carries the mark of The Hanged One's favor; this I was shown. He will be vital to your survival in the days to come."

Arialyn began to nod slowly, her mind reeling as the implications crashed over her like a tide. How could that ritual have shown the witch so much? The depth of knowledge that had emerged from blood and bone was staggering, terrifying in its completeness.

Fear crept up her throat like bile. Her child, her impossible, precious son, was already in danger before he'd even had a chance to truly begin growing within her. The protective instincts that had flared when Bjomwyn mentioned ending the pregnancy now roared to life with the intensity of a forge fire. Her breathing quickened, and she felt the familiar tightness in her chest that preceded a panic attack.

Bjomwyn's weathered features softened immediately, recognizing the signs of panic building in the young woman. She shifted the conversation with gentle expertise.

"Have you considered a name for your son?" she asked, her voice deliberately warm and conversational.

The question cut through Arialyn's spiraling thoughts like a blade through silk. She blinked, her breathing slowly steadying as her mind latched onto something hopeful, something beautiful instead of terrifying.

"A name?" she repeated, her voice still shaky but gaining strength. "I... no, I haven't even told Callus yet. I wanted to be certain first."

Bjomwyn smiled, the expression transforming her ancient features into something almost grandmotherly. "Names have power, little squirrel. Especially for children born of impossible unions under extraordinary circumstances. The right name can be protection, guidance, a blessing woven into the very fabric of a soul."

Arialyn found herself unconsciously stroking her stomach, her panic receding as wonder took its place. A son. She was carrying Callus's son, against all odds and natural law. Whatever dangers lay ahead, this miracle existed within her.

"Syndrin," she said softly, "after the only man that has ever truly seen me, the man who saved me. Callus's true birth name, Syndrin."

APPENDICES

LORE/NATIONS/ETC

<u>A BRIEF HISTORY OF THE WORLD OF YONARA</u>
Yes, the following pages are brief...you try making your own fantasy
world and see how much there is to explain :P

The world of Yonara has seen three Ages. The first was The Platinum Age spanning roughly three thousand years and took place from recorded time until the rise of Varl's Wall. The Age of Suffering spanned roughly two and a half thousand years and took place from the rise of Varl's Wall until its demise and the creation of the Great Scar. The current Age, the Scarred Age, has spanned roughly six thousand years and encompasses the time from the fall of Varl's Wall and the creation of the Great Scar to present.

Varl's Wall, an obsidian shimmering and titanic magical surface that cut into Yonara from deep within its core to the highest points in the skies, began forming with the rise of the Cult of the Void Heart. These cultists fanatically followed the teachings of Zorog, the Goddess of Madness, Destruction and Transformation. Under the leadership of High Sorcerer Varl Marzadal, a corrupt high elf Noble, the Cult of the

Void Heart harnessed the power of its namesake, believed to be the very heart of Zorog herself, to begin the slow but inevitable demise of the world of Yonara. Varl's Wall began its slow expansion in the far east of the main continent of Rusvaro. The expanse was slow at first, believed to only have been moving at about two feet per year. Repeated attempts were made by the various kingdoms and agencies on the west side of Varl's Wall to determine the origin and power of it but to no avail.

Magical and physical attempts to destroy the wall failed. Attempts to fell the wall continued but, with no solution in sight, the people of Yonara kept wide-eyed vigil that eventually waned to disinterest. It wasn't for another one thousand five-hundred years that the origins of the wall were discovered. Varl himself stepped out from behind the wall to lead his now corrupted dark elves and their abominations in a war on the remainder of Yonara in the name of Zorog. The people of Rusvaro learned over the years that all manner of evil creatures emerged from the wall and raided the untainted land. Any beings that entered the black void of the wall either never returned, returned mentally devastated or as something entirely different than when they entered. All of them chained to the will of Zorog and her Cult.

Another eight hundred years passed before the peoples of Yonara were able to unite and began to fight back with any significant impact. Raiding from the wall began to slow for a time. But with renewed vigor the wall began to expand at an alarming rate. It began to consume one to two miles per year. It was the fabled Meritocracy of Spearfall that found a way to stop the wall for good. Under the leadership of the sons of Terestai Hunter, the former Spearfall Warden of War, they sought out a broad alliance of all that would hear the call. First to answer, were the dwarven kingdoms, of which there were three. Shortly after, the wild tribes of the Torvox, people who were reportedly closer to nature than most beasts, joined the cause. This led eventually to the elven people of both the Woodland and the High kingdoms near the sea joining the fray. Last to pledge to the cause were the two human kingdoms to the Northwest whose land they had believed lay safely across the Dividing Sea. Together they laid siege to the final temple dedicated to Zorog which hid within its depths, the Void Heart. Immediately upon the relic's destruction the wall vanished, revealing the now desolate wastes that had laid hidden behind its dark curtain.

A great weight had been lifted from the people of Rusvaro. However, in destroying this relic, a ripple of corruption ran through the arcane web of Yonara causing a complete collapse of arcane power. The reverberation was felt throughout the world. The magical barrier that had protected Spearfall fell, the floating cities of the Arcane Watch and the Mana Wardens plummeted to the ground, the Fae were displaced into a dimension that was only lightly tethered to Yonara and the magic that flowed throughout the world all but faded away. Perhaps the greatest loss was the sudden illness, The Shale Plague, that spread among the wild tribes of the torvox. This plague only targeted those with the arcane blood of nature that they carried in their veins. All of those of pureblood died within moments to days and only a fraction of those with partial torvox blood lived through the plague. At present none live who have a detectable hint of those lost people. A Great Scar was left in the stead of the final mile of the wall. In the current age the scar varies from half to two miles across and plummets to a recorded depth of three thousand feet.

Over the next thousand years Spearfall faded into myth, the Arcane Watch dissolved to time, and the people of Yonara fell to despair. It was in the year 2386 of the Scarred Age that mana began to seep back into the realm. The year 2452 held the first documented interaction with the Fae since the Scarring. In 3483 the studies of the arcane had finally taken enough of a hold that schools of magic began to emerge with the magocracy of The Arcanum Centralis being the first to create a college of learning.

At present, in 6004 of the Scarred Age, the realm of Yonara is as healed as it has ever been. The northern continent, once held by two human kingdoms, now falls under the banner of the unified Oskon Empire. On the main continent of Rusvaro, the west side, known as the Emeraldom is controlled by the three Wolf Lords, fabled to be descendants of the sons of Terestai Hunter of Spearfall. Between the Emeraldom and the Great Scar is the united Dwarven Kingdom of Havrarlug Brightborn. East of the Great Scar is a near lawless land that still shows signs of the desolation caused by Varl's Wall. The land is largely controlled by warring bands of marauders, though over the last four hundred years cities and territories within its corruption have begun to take hold, areas such as the Helspires in the south and Hus'rokn in the northeast.

To the far west of Rusvaro is an island that one thousand two-hundred years ago was established as a penal colony but is currently divided by two independent nations, collectively known as the Exiled States. The elven controlled area to the north named Nemsera, and a dragonscale area to the south called the Scaled Isles. A large city, Kol'Theron, sits dead center between the elven and dragonscale states. It serves as a natural divide between the two as it is bordered by tall mountain peaks on either side. It is controlled by a self-made half dwarf-half orc Prince. Kol'Theron occasionally acts as a mediator between the two states. It is also home to the sanctioned Mercenary Companies of Kol'Theron, whose services are sought after worldwide for their strict codes that uphold the contracts they sign with their employers. At present The Oskon Empire is in negotiations with Nemsera to be annexed into the Empire's territory. The Scaled Isles have reluctantly reached out to the Wolf Lords and Havrarlug Brightborn for possible aid should this turn to probable conflict

However, the cause of most conflict between the nations of Yonara over the last forty odd years has been the Emperor's Decree of Purity.

What started out long-term discrimination against the 'mongrel' races of Yonara rapidly turned to banishment and then, with the Decree of Purity, the outright hunting of those of non-human, elf, dwarf, halfling, or gnomish blood. This decree initially caused a brief war between the Empire and the combined strength of the Emeraldom and the Brightborn Kingdom. The Arcanum Centralis brokered a tentative peace, however. A peace that has lasted thirty-seven years. This has not stopped the Empire's genocide into the other nations, however, as the discrimination and murder of those of the 'mongrel' races has seeped into various pockets of the other nations; as well as resistance forces who seek retribution against the 'pure' races as a whole with the same vitriolic hate.

Rumors of spacial void tears popping up at random across the realm have been heard. These tears in the fabric of reality bear a striking resemblance to historical accounts of Varl's Wall. When these Void Tears appear, the reports show they disappear in moments or after several days. All verified accounts say that the land under the tear is tainted and that beings that have come to be called Netherlings have emerged. These Netherlings either attack the people of Rusvaro or flee into the distance.

GODS OF YONARA

PROGENITOR PANTHEON

The Progenitor: A cosmic being believed to have found the realm of Yonara, a barren land with a slumbering goddess within. Seeing the beauty beneath her surface he seeded her and left. The Progenitor breathed life back into Yonara and from his seed she bore their children. It is said he returns every thousand years, to see the world he helped to create. His symbol is a jade phallus.

Yonara: Goddess of Wilderness and the Sea. She is the mother of Kordok, Zorog, The Hanged One and the Bright One. Her followers believe in the natural way of life. Any metal weapons wielded by her followers must be made of the Druids and Clerics of her circles to ensure the minerals were extracted from her properly. These weapons are stamped with her symbol, a green spiral.

Kordok the Stormsmith: God of Storms, Strength and Law. Many view him as the protector of the mortal races. He is the god of the warriors, smiths and seekers of justice. His symbol is a brown Oak with a yellow Lightning Bolt.

The Hanged One: God of Death and Sacrifice. Twin brother of The Bright One. Their sister Zorog attempted to slay them in jealousy of their bond of mind and soul. Kordok intervened but could not stop the maiming that took from them their bond of mind and destroyed their true names. Worshiped by assassins, gamblers, soldiers and priests of the natural order of death. His symbol is a black noose.

The Bright One: Goddess of Life and twin sister of The Hanged One. She is worshiped by mothers and women, entertainers, artists and those with a lust for life. Her symbol is white petaled flower.

Zorog the Betrayer: Goddess of Madness and Destruction. She seeks to destroy the world her mother and siblings hold dear. She is the Goddess of dark sorcerers, murders, and those of a dark nature. Her symbol is a red laughing skull with long pale hair.

PANTHEON OF THE FORGE

The Forge Father: He is the father of the dwarves, God of the mountains and all they hold. Believed to have forged the Dwarven race. He gave an eye and hand to forge the other gods of this pantheon. He replaced his eye with a bright red ruby and his hand with a golden hammer. His symbol is a fiery golden anvil.

Thromgrid: Goddess of joy, friendship, love and alcohol. She was crafted from the Forge Father's eye. Her symbol is two clasped hands in the shape of a heart stamped on a keg.

Volfmir: God of vengeance and grudges. He was crafted from the Forge Father's severed hand. His symbol is a severed bloody hand.

GODS OF THE ORCS

Grujok: Great Father of Orc Kind. During the first two ages of Yonara, he bid his followers to make war on all who opposed him and bring about a Green Flood to Yonara, a green-skinned world crafted by his desire. Mid-second age his followers began to fade and Grujok in desperation made a deal with Zorog to aid her in return for greater power and glory. The failure of Zorog to hold her end of the deal ultimately led to many orcs turning their backs on him, earning him the name "The Spurned." His symbol is a clinched orcish fist with a broken manacle.

Ehrmus "The Glorious": Redeemer of orc kind. He pushes his followers to bring glory and redemption to orc kind through honorable combat, war and tribal diplomacy. He is the half-brother of Grujok the Spurned. Ehrums seeks to turn the fate of orc kind after the subjugation and void corruption he believes Grujok brought about by allying with Zorog. His symbol is an open orcish hand pierced by a dagger.

Bjomda "Black Eye": She is the shaman goddess of orcs. When seen in visions she is presented, simultaneously, as both a beautiful young green skinned orc maiden and as a hunched back gray skinned orc crone. She helps weave the fates of Ehrums's chosen. Orcs born with solid eyes are revered for their innate shamanic abilities. Her symbol is an unblinking black eye.

Odhrum Voidspawn: Odhrum is the bastard son of Grujok and Zorog. He was part of the negotiation between Grujok and Zorog's alliance. However, Zorog wished nothing to do with his misshapen form and he failed to meet Grujok's expectations for the union. Odhrum is seen as very malnourished, frail and covered in various skin diseases. He attracts those who relish the suffering of others and seek their own base pleasures. He has no symbol.

INDEPENDENT GODS OF YONARA

The Triumvirate: The Sun, and twin Moons in the sky. Worshiped mostly by the Woodland races of Yonara. Those that follow the Triumvirate also follow an animistic approach to spirits in nature and the elements.

Uzul: The Supreme Hunter. A primal demigod of nature that stalks the forests of Yonara. He is worshiped by various peoples.

The Great Dragons: Elder dragons that are said to have ruled the world of Yonara before her seeding by the Progenitor. They are mostly worshiped by dragonscale, although those of the other races of Yonara are welcomed by some of the Great Dragons and their cults.

The Forgotten: Said to be spawned from the spilled blood of the Twin Gods. These are beings considered by most to be the Archfiends, demons and devils of the Underrealm and beings similar in nature. They work their chaotic will on the weak minded and those that seek out evil or to forge a deal, quite literally, with the devil.

The Fae: The Fae were made by the spilled pleasure of the union of the Progenitor and Yonara. That energy fed on the innate arcane web of power that radiated across the land. After the emergence of the Great Scar, they were not seen for ages. In recent centuries, however, they have begun to seep back into the mortal realm. They are arcane creatures capable of wondrous and terrible things with some of the oldest approaching near godhood.

It is said that all of the gods/goddesses not of the Progenitor Pantheon are born of those Forgotten and Fae that found ways to elevate themselves.

RULING NATIONS OF YONARA

Emeraldom: The land in the west of the main continent of Rusvaro. Its lands hold bountiful forests and glades with sprawling hills and mountains to the eastern edge of their borders. All races can be found within the Emeraldom in some capacity. The bulk of the cultural make-up is human, elf and orc. Dark elves had a rough period of adjustment throughout history since the fall of Varl's Wall but are now relatively welcomed. It is an Oligarchy ruled by the three Wolf Lords, rumored to be descendants of the mythical three sons of Terestai of Spearfall. While the people of the fabled Spearfall were known to ride dire wolves into battle the Wolf Lords and their people bring wolves to battle but none are large enough to be ridden. It is said that the dire wolves were one of the casualties of the Great Scar. Wolves are abundant in the Emeraldom, but few are larger than standard forest wolves. There are still some claims that larger dire wolves have been spotted over the last fifty years, but these are largely unsubstantiated. There are three main cities and several towns within the Emeraldom. Their relations with the Oskon Empire, once peaceful, have become tense after Emperor Victarius Oskon's Decree of Purity and the three-year Mongrel War that declared the 'mongrel' races unclean and worthy of extermination. The Kingdom of Havrarlug Brightborn and the Emeraldom have good relations with trade routes and a treaty of mutual aid. The Emeraldom has recently begun diplomatic talks with the Scaled Isles as tensions rise between them and the neighboring country of Nemsera. Pop. 225,000

Oskon Empire: The Oskon Empire is ruled by Emperor Victarius Oskon, known now as Victarius the Unyielding. The Oskon Empire is an Autocracy. They are a very rich nation due to an overabundance of natural resources. After the Great Scar the two human kingdoms began to form a union. In the early stages of the Sacred Age high elves fell under extreme prejudice as Varl and his army were mostly fallen high elves. The newly formed Oskon Empire signed a treaty and welcomed the high elf lords into their Empire. The high elves brought with them arcane knowledge, which unfortunately for them slowly faded over the years until the Arcane Reemergence. Within recent memory Emperor

Victarius Oskon with the aid of his advisors enacted the Decree of Purity. This piece of legislature outlawed those of half-blood. All people of the Empire may only be of the pure blood of one of the pure races of Yonara. They defined the pure races as human, elf, dwarf, gnome and halfling. This resulted in the three yearlong Mongrel War with the Emeraldom and the Brightborn Kingdom. After a peace was brokered by the Arcanum Centralis the Oskon Empire's discrimination of the mongrel races was tempered down from extermination to strict exile, at least in the public eye. Anyone who is found to have sired an infant of impure blood or to be harboring any of the mongrel races are immediately stripped of all property and exiled. There are four sprawling cities and many towns within its borders. The Oskron Empire has tense relations with the Emeraldom at present due to the current treaty and both being unprepared for a return to open war. Their relations with the Kingdom of Havrarlug Brightborn are better, but this is largely due to their strict resource trade agreements that were brokered into the treaty. They have recently reached out to Nemsera in the Exiled States to come to an agreement for trade and possible induction into the Empire. Pop. 550,000

<u>The Brightborn Kingdom:</u> It is a monarchy ruled by King Havrarlug Brightborn, Keeper of the Voidbreaker. If legend speaks true, the Voidbreaker was once wielded by Ragnus Keghammer who was present at the destruction of Varl's Wall. Havrarlug wields the most power but keeps a council of three Huscarls. They each preside over their own specialty, war, commerce and religion. The cultural makeup of the Brightborn Kingdom is roughly seventy percent dwarven. The other thirty percent is made up of the other various races of Yonara although the orcish people are viewed with mistrust. The Brightborn Kingdom borders the Great Scar and as such uses a great deal of resources keeping the border with the Scarred Lands safe from the marauders and chaos of the Void Wastes to the east. The kingdom has one stronghold with three castles housed by Havrarlug Brightborn's family members. They have good relations with the Emeraldom and share several trade routes. Each has emissaries within each other's capitals. They keep a strong tie to the Oskon Empire, but this is due mainly to an ironclad trade agreement written into the Mongrel War treaty. They have no solid relationship with the Exiled States. Pop. 210,000

The Scarred Lands Region: A mostly barren wasteland that lies east of the Great Scar on the main continent of Rusvaro. Once covered in rolling plains and forests both tropical and temperate, the landscape is now harsh desert and rocky crags of desolate wasteland with only a few areas in the northern Resurgence Wilds beginning to make an ecological comeback. This transformation occurred nearly three millennia ago when the betrayer goddess Zorog used her disciple, Varl, to lead a crusade of corruption across the continents. Though their combined efforts were eventually thwarted, the repercussions were vast, and many are still present to this day. The result of their failure brought about an arcane explosion that irreparably changed the realm forever. The land is largely controlled by warring bands of marauders, though over the centuries cities and territories within the desolate expanse have begun to take hold, areas such as the Helspires in the south and Hus'rokn in the northeast. The 'mongrel' races have long been the primary residents of the area, but their number surged even higher as many fled here during and after the Emperor's Decree of Purity to escape persecution from the Mongrel War. While civilization is present, it remains a very dangerous place where survival often depends on strength, cunning, or the protection of one of the established settlements. The proximity to the Great Scar means that strange phenomena and void-touched creatures are not uncommon, making travel treacherous for the unprepared. Pop. ~175,000

Arcanum Centralis: The floating city known as the Mana Spire floats over the river at the triple border of the three large nations mentioned above and is controlled by the Mana Wardens. They serve as a training ground for many sorcerers and wizards and those that harbor arcane talents. They are responsible for a lot of the reeducation in the uses of arcane power and continue to aid in research that is bringing forgotten schools of magic back into the world. They frequently host the rulers of nations and their representatives for diplomatic discussions. The Arcanum Centralis is ruled by a council of Arch Mages. They remain effectively neutral in their dealings with the nations of Yonara. Pop 250

Scaled Isles: This is the Dragonborn controlled portion of the Exiled States. The cultural make-up of the Isles is about fifty percent dragonscale, with the majority of the rest being of human, orcish, and goblin heritage. The Immortal Khan Zidkan the Red rules over the Scaled Isles. There is one major port city in the south with an orc stronghold in the east and a small human city in the west. A few towns and villages scatter the landscape. Of the five surviving Elder Dragons two are rumored to live here in hibernation. Pop 55,000

Nemsera: This is the elven controlled portion of the Exiled States in the north. The territory is almost purely elven and is one of the only territories where dark elves are fully accepted. Siveifa Sageburn rules as Duchess. A small number of half-elves, humans and halflings have residences in the seaside cities. Pop. 62,000

Kol'Theron: The central city in the Exiled States is bordered by mountains on both the east and west and by Nemsera in the north and the Scaled Isles in the south. A half-dwarf/half-orc named Xalandar the Pretty is the self-proclaimed Prince of Kol'Theron. Rumors say he is the bastard nephew of King Havrarlug Brightborn. Kol'Theron is known for its fine forges, taverns, and gambling dens as well as other vices. It exports weapons, spice and mercenaries through the realm. Their strict code has made their services famous and sought after by all who can afford them. Their contracts shall not be completed until the objective is reached, the mercenary band has no remaining living members, or the client violates the terms of the contract. No mercenary band may hold against another what was done to them while serving out a contract and no violence may be perpetrated by one Company to another within the city limits, regardless of reason. Pop. 14,000

The Calendar according to the Arcanum Centralis

Yonara's solar and lunar cycles match best with a year containing two hundred and fifty solar days. These are broken into five months with five weeks containing five days each. Why the fascination with fives? This can be traced back to the long-deceased Arch Mage Ambrose Peculiaris who simply had a strange fetish that required everything to come in sets of five. He actually petitioned the Arcanum Centralis for a five-month year but was subsequently denied and then banished from the Arcanum Centralis. The banishment was unrelated to the five months a year petition. His banishment was instead imposed after revelations of his unnatural proclivities with summoned familiars. This also led to the abandonment of a ludicrous system of hours in the day that fluctuated per week and the adoption of the standard twenty-four-hour day.

The 5 Days of the week

Handra

Yondra

Kordra

Bridra

Progendra (typically viewed as a rest day)

The 10 Months of the year

Geranis (Spring)

Affliction

Ravenwood (Summer)

Ashspire

Plasmafire

Sanguine (Fall)

Crystal Moon

Snows Hunger (Winter)

Starfall

Nightshadow